"[A] RIVETING,
PROVOCATIVE STORY . . .

The criminal mind, racial bias, journalistic ego and the flawed fabric of the American criminal justice system are potent raw materials for psychological suspense master Katzenbach. . . . The story generally proceeds at a breakneck pace, enhanced by ear-perfect dialogue and complex characterizations."

—*Publishers Weekly*

"A classic cat-and-mouse story . . . Katzenbach's triumph is that he remains in absolute control of his story, carefully reeling out facts like a fly fisherman. And in Tanny Brown, he has created a strong, memorable character who deserves to live on in the pages of other books besides the excellent JUST CAUSE."

—*The Orlando Sentinel*

"Put on your seat belt. . . . [JUST CAUSE] really moves. It will grab you even if you think you know what's going to happen. Maybe you do. Maybe you don't."

—*Palm Beach Post*

"Simmering intensity . . . JUST CAUSE won't disappoint."

—*Booklist*

JUST CAUSE

John Katzenbach

BALLANTINE BOOKS • NEW YORK

This book is for my mother, and to the memory of three men: V. A. Eagle, Wm. A. Nixon, and H. Simons.

Library of Congress Catalog Card Number: 91-15135

ISBN 0-345-38019-3

This edition published by arrangement with G. P. Putnam's Sons

Manufactured in the United States of America

First Ballantine Books Edition: April 1993

10 9 8 7 6 5 4

I am especially grateful for the assistance of my friends Joe Oglesby, of *The Miami Herald*, and Athelia Knight, of *The Washington Post*. Their wise suggestions immeasurably aided the preparation of this manuscript. It, of course, would have been impossible to accomplish without the help and tolerance of my wife, Madeleine Blais, and children, as well.

Whoever fights monsters should see to it that in the process he does not become a monster. And when you look long into an abyss, the abyss also looks into you.

FRIEDRICH WILHELM NIETZSCHE
Beyond Good and Evil

Hell is paved with good intentions, not with bad ones.

GEORGE BERNARD SHAW
Maxims for Revolutionists

ONE

PRISONERS

When you win the prize they tell you a joke: Now you know the first line of your own obituary.

ONE
═A MAN OF OPINIONS

ON the morning that he received the letter, Matthew Cowart awakened alone to a false winter.

A steady north wind had picked up after midnight and seemed to push the nighttime black away, smearing the morning sky with a dirty gray that made a lie of the city's image. As he walked from his apartment to the street outside, he could hear the breeze rattle and push at a palm tree, making the fronds clash together like so many swords.

He hunched his shoulders together tightly and wished that he'd worn a sweater beneath his suit coat. Every year there were a few mornings like this one, filled with the promise of bleak skies and blustery winds. Nature making a small joke, causing the tourists on Miami Beach to grumble and walk the sandy stretches in their sweaters. In Little Havana, the older Cuban women would wear heavy woolen overcoats and curse the wind, forgetting that in the summer they carried parasols and cursed the heat. In Liberty City, the rat holes in the crack houses would whistle with cold. The junkies would shiver and struggle with their pipes. But soon enough the city would return to sweaty, sticky normalcy.

One day, he thought as he walked briskly, perhaps two. Then the warm air will freshen out of the South and we will all quickly forget the cold.

Matthew Cowart was a man moving light through life.

Circumstances and bad luck had cut away many of the accoutrements of impending middle age; a simple divorce had sliced away his wife and child, messy death his parents; his friends had slid into separate existences defined by rising careers, squads of young children, car payments, and mortgages. For a time there had been attempts by some to include him in outings and parties, but, as his solitude had grown, accompanied by his apparent comfort in it, these invitations had fallen off and finally stopped. His social life was defined by an occasional office party and shop talk. He had no lover and felt a vague confusion as to why he didn't. His own apartment was modest, in a sturdy high rise overlooking the bay, built in the 1950s. He had filled it with old furniture, bookcases stuffed with mystery novels and true crime nonfiction, chipped but utilitarian dinnerware, a few forgettable framed prints hanging on the walls.

Sometimes he thought that when his wife had taken their daughter, all the color had fled from his life. His own needs were satisfied by exercise—an obligatory six miles a day, running through a downtown park, an occasional game of pickup basketball at the YMCA—and his job at the newspaper. He felt possessed of a remarkable freedom yet somehow worried that he had so few recognizable debts.

The wind was still gusting hard, pulling and tugging at a trio of flags outside the main entrance to *The Miami Journal*. He paused momentarily, looking up at the stolid yellow square building. The paper's name was emblazoned in huge red, electric letters against one wall. It was a famous place, well known for its aggressiveness and power. On the other side, the paper looked over the bay. He could see wild waters splashing up against the dock where huge rolls of newsprint were unloaded. Once, while sitting alone in the cafeteria eating a sandwich, he'd spotted a family of manatees cavorting about in the pale blue water, no more than ten yards from the loading dock. Their brown backs burst through the surface, then fell back beneath the waves. He'd looked about for someone to tell but had found no one, and had spent the next few days, at lunch, staring constantly out at the shifting blue-green surface for another glimpse of the animals. It was what he liked about Florida; the state seemed cut from some jungle, which was always threatening to overtake all the development and return it to something primeval. The paper was forever doing stories about twelve-foot alligators getting trapped on entrance ramps to the interstate and stopping traffic. He loved those stories: an ancient beast confronting a modern one.

Cowart moved quickly through the double doors that led to the *Journal*'s newsroom, waving at the receptionist who sat partially hidden behind a telephone console. Next to the entrance was a wall devoted to plaques, citations, and awards: a parade of Pulitzers, Kennedys, Cabots, Pyles, and others with more mundane names. He paused at a bank of mailboxes to pick up his morning mail, flipping rapidly through the usual handouts and dozens of press releases, political statements, and proposals that arrived every day from the congressional delegation, the mayor's office, the county manager's office, and various police agencies, all alerting him to some development that they thought worthy of editorial attention. He sighed, wondering how much money was wasted on all these hopeless efforts. One envelope, however, caught his eye. He separated it from the pile.

It was a thin, white envelope with his name and address written in sturdy block print. There was a return address in the corner, giving a post office box number in Starke, Florida, in the northern portion of the state. The state prison, he thought instantly.

He put it on top of the other letters and headed toward his office, maneuvering amidst the room of desks, nodding at the few reporters who were in early and already working the telephones. He waved at the city editor, who had his feet up on his desk in the center of the room and was reading the last edition. Then he moved through a set of doors in the rear of the newsroom marked EDITORIAL. He was halfway into his cubicle when he heard a voice from nearby.

"Ahh, the young Turk arrives early. What could bring you in before the hordes? Unsettled by the troubles in Beirut? Sleepless over the president's economic recovery program?"

Cowart stuck his head around a partition. "Morning, Will. Actually, I just wanted to use the WATS line to call my daughter. I'll leave the truly deep and useless worrying to you."

Will Martin laughed and brushed a forelock of white hair out of his eyes, a motion that belonged more to a child than an old man. "Go. Abuse the abundant financial generosity of our beloved newspaper. When you get finished, take a look at the story on the Local page. It seems that one of our black-robed dispensers of justice cut something of a deal for an old buddy caught driving under the influence. It could be time for one of your ever-popular crime-and-punishment crusades."

"I'll look at it," Cowart said.

"Damn cold this morning," said Martin. "What's the point

of living down here if you still have to shiver on the way to work? Might as well be Alaska.''

"Why don't we editorialize against the weather? We're always trying to influence the heavens, anyway. Maybe they'll listen to us this time.''

"You've got a point.'' Martin smiled.

"And you're just the man for the job,'' Cowart said.

"True,'' Martin replied. "Not steeped in sin, like you, I have a much better connection to the Almighty. It helps in this job.''

"That's because you're so much closer to joining him than I.''

His neighbor roared. "You're an ageist,'' he protested, waggling a finger. "Probably a sexist, a racist, a pacifist—all the other *ists*, too.''

Cowart laughed and headed to his desk, dumping the pile of mail in the middle and leaving the single envelope on top. He reached out for it, while with the other hand he started dialing his ex-wife's number. With any luck, he thought, they should be at breakfast.

He crooked the receiver beneath his shoulder and ear, freeing his hand while the connection was being made. As the telephone began ringing he opened the envelope and took out a single sheet of yellow legal-ruled paper.

Dear Mr. Cowart:
I am currently awaiting execution on Death Row for a crime that I DID NOT COMMIT.

"Hello?''

He put the letter down. "Hello, Sandy. It's Matt. I just wanted to talk to Becky for a minute. I hope I didn't disturb anything.''

"Hello, Matt.'' He heard a hesitation in her voice. "No, it's just we're getting ready to go. Tom has to be in court early, so he's taking her to school, and . . .'' She paused, then continued. "No, it's okay. I have a few things I need to talk over with you anyway. But they've got to go, so can you make it quick?''

He closed his eyes and thought how painful it was not to be involved in the routine of his daughter's life. He imagined spilling milk at breakfast, reading books at night, holding her hand when she got sick, admiring the pictures she drew in school. He bit back his disappointment. "Sure. I just wanted to say hi.''

"I'll get her.''

The phone clunked on the table and in the silence that followed, Matthew Cowart looked at the words: I DID NOT COMMIT.

He remembered his wife on the day they'd met, in the newspaper office at the University of Michigan. She'd been small, but her intensity had seemed to contradict her size. She'd been a graphic design student, who worked part-time doing layouts and headlines, poring over page proofs, pushing her dark wavy hair away from her face, concentrating so hard she rarely heard the phone ring or reacted to any of the dirty jokes that flew about in the unbridled newsroom air. She'd been a person of precision and order, with a draftsman's approach to life. The daughter of a Midwestern-city fire captain who'd died in the line of duty, and a grade-school teacher, she craved possessions, longed for comforts. He'd thought her beautiful, was intimidated by her desire, and was surprised when she'd agreed to go on a date with him; surprised further when, after a dozen dates, she'd slept with him.

He'd been the sports editor, which she had thought was a silly waste of time. Overmuscled men in bizarre outfits fighting over variously shaped balls, she would say. He had tried to educate her to the romance of the events, but she had been intransigent. After a while, he had switched to covering real news, throwing himself tenaciously after stories, as their relationship had solidified. He'd loved the endless hours, the pursuit of the story, the seduction of writing. She'd thought he would be famous or, if not famous, important. She'd followed him when he got his first job offer on a small Midwestern paper. A half dozen years later, they'd still been together. On the same day that she announced she was pregnant, he got his offer from the *Journal*. He was to cover criminal courts. She was to have Becky.

"Daddy?"

"Hi, honey."

"Hi, Daddy. Mommy says I can only talk for a minute. Got to get to school."

"Is it cold there, too, honey? You should wear a coat."

"I will. Tom got me a coat with a pirate on it that's all orange for the Bucs. I'm going to wear that. I got to meet some of the players, too. They were at a picnic where we were helping get money for charity."

"That's great," Matthew replied. Damn, he thought.

"Are football players important, Daddy?"

He laughed. "Sort of."

"Daddy, is something wrong?"

"No, honey, why?"

"Well, you don't usually call in the morning."

"I just woke up missing you and wanted to hear your voice."

"I miss you, too, Daddy. Will you take me back to Disney World?"

"This spring. I promise."

"Daddy, I've got to go. Tom is waving for me. Oh, Daddy, guess what? We have a special club in second grade called the hundred-book club. You get a prize when you read one hundred books. I just made it!"

"Fantastic! What do you get?"

"A special plaque and a party at the end of the year."

"That's great. What was your favorite book?"

"Oh, that's easy. The one you sent me: *The Reluctant Dragon.*" She laughed. "It reminds me of you."

He laughed with her.

"I've got to go," she said again.

"Okay. I love you and I really miss you."

"Me too. Bye-bye."

"Bye," he said, but she had already left the telephone.

There was another blank moment until his ex-wife picked up the line. He spoke first.

"A charity picnic with football players?"

He had always wanted to hate the man who'd replaced him, wanted to hate him for what he did, which was corporate law, how he looked, which was stocky and chesty, with the build of a man who spent lunchtimes lifting weights at an expensive health club, wanted to imagine that he was cruel, a thoughtless lover, a poor stepfather, an inadequate provider, but he was none of those things. Shortly after his ex-wife had announced her impending marriage, Tom had flown to Miami (without telling her) to meet with him. They had had drinks and dinner. The purpose had been murky, but, after the second bottle of wine, the lawyer had told him with direct honesty that he wasn't trying to replace him in his daughter's eyes, but because he was going to be there, he was going to do his damnedest to help her love him, too. Cowart had believed him, had felt an odd sort of satisfaction and relief, ordered another bottle of wine and decided he sort of liked his successor.

"It's the law firm. They help sponsor some of the United Way stuff in Tampa. That's how the football players get involved. Becky was pretty impressed, but of course Tom didn't tell her how many games the Bucs won last year."

"That makes sense."

"I suppose so. They certainly are the biggest men I've ever seen." Sandy laughed.

There was a momentary pause before she continued. "How are you? How's Miami?"

He laughed. "Miami's cold, which makes everyone crazy. You know how it is, nobody owns a winter coat, nobody has any heat in their homes. Everyone shivers and gets a little insane until it heats up again. I'm okay. I fit right in."

"Still having the nightmares?"

"Not too much. Every so often. It's under control."

It was a mild falsehood, one he knew she would disbelieve but would accept without further questioning. He shrugged hard, thinking how much he hated the night.

"You could get some help. The paper would pay."

"Waste of time. I haven't had one in months," he lied more flagrantly.

He heard her take a breath.

"What's wrong?" he asked.

"Well," she said, "I suppose I should just tell you."

"So just tell me."

"Tom and I are going to have a baby. Becky's no longer going to be alone."

He felt a bit dizzy, and a dozen different thoughts and feelings ricocheted within him. "Well, well, well. Congratulations."

"Thank you," his ex-wife said. "But you don't understand."

"What?"

"Becky's going to be part of a family. Even more than before."

"Yes?"

"You don't see, do you? What will happen. That you'll be the one squeezed out. At least, that's what I'm afraid of. It's already hard for her, with you being in the other part of the state."

He felt as if someone had slapped him across the face. "I'm not the one in the other part of the state. You are. You're the one that moved out."

"That's old business," Sandy replied. After a moment, she continued. "Anyway, things are going to change."

"I don't see why . . ." he stammered.

"Trust me," she said. Her tone displayed that she had considered her words carefully, far in advance. "Less time for you. I'm sure of it. I've been thinking about it a lot."

"But that's not the agreement."

"The agreement can change. We knew that."

"I don't think so," he replied, the first edge of anger sliding into his voice.

"Well," she said abruptly. "I'm not going to allow myself to get upset talking about it. We'll see."

"But . . ."

"Matt, I have to go. I just wanted you to know."

"Great," he said. "Thanks a bunch."

"We can discuss this later, if there's anything to discuss."

Sure, he thought, after you've talked to attorneys and social workers and edited me out completely. He knew the thought was untrue, but it refused to be dislodged.

"It's not your life we're talking about," she added. "Not anymore. It's mine."

And then she hung up.

You're wrong, he thought. He looked about his work cubicle. Through a small window he could see the sky stretching slate gray over the downtown. Then he looked down at the words in front of him: I DID NOT COMMIT.

We are all innocent, he thought. It is proving it that is so hard.

Then, trying to banish the conversation from his mind, he picked up the letter and continued reading:

On May 4th, 1987, I had just returned home to my grand-mother's house in the town of Pachoula, Escambia County. At the time I was a college student at Rutgers University in New Brunswick, New Jersey, just completing my junior year. I had been visiting her for several days, when I was picked up by the sheriff's office for questioning in a rape-murder that took place a few miles from my grandmother's place. The victim was white. I am black. An eyewitness had seen a green Ford sedan similar to one I owned leaving the scene where the girl disappeared. I was held without food or water or sleep and without a chance to talk to counsel for thirty-six hours straight. I was beaten several times by deputies. They used folded telephone books to pound on me, because those don't make any marks. They told me they would kill me and one held a revolver to my head and kept pulling the trigger. Each time the hammer clicked down on an empty cylinder. At the end of this they told me that if I confessed, everything would be okay. I was scared and exhausted, so I did. Not knowing any details, but letting them lead me through the crime, I confessed. After what they put me through, I would have confessed to anything.

BUT I DID NOT DO IT!

I tried to recant my confession within hours, but I was unsuccessful. My public defender attorney only visited me three times before my trial. He also did no investigation, called no witnesses who would have placed me elsewhere at the time of the crime, failed to get the illegally obtained confession suppressed. An all-white jury heard the evidence and convicted me after an hour's deliberation. It took them another hour to recommend the death penalty. The white judge passed this sentence on. He called me an animal that ought to be taken outside and shot.

I have now been on Death Row for three years. I have every hope that the courts will overturn my conviction, but that may take many more years. Can you help me? I have learned from other prisoners that you have written editorials condemning the death penalty. I am an innocent man, facing the supreme punishment because of a racist system that was stacked against me. Prejudice, ignorance and evil have put me into this situation. Please help me.

I have written the names of my new lawyer and witnesses below. I have put your name on my approved visiting list, if you decide to come talk with me.

There is one other thing. Not only am I innocent of the charges against me, but I can tell you the name of the man who did commit the crime.

Hoping you will help,
Robert Earl Ferguson
#212009
The Florida State Prison
Starke, Fla.

It took Cowart several moments to digest the letter. He read it through several times, trying to sort through his impressions. The man was clearly articulate, educated, and sophisticated, but prisoners who claimed innocence, especially Death Row prisoners, were the norm rather than the exception. He had always wondered why the majority of men, even confronting their own demise, stuck to an image of innocence. It was true of the hardest psychopaths, the mass killers who cared so little for human life that they would as soon kill someone as talk with them—but who, when confronted, would maintain that aura unless persuaded that confession might somehow help them. It was as if the word meant something different to them, as if the compilation of horrors they had suffered somehow wiped the slate clean.

The thought made him remember the boy's eyes. The eyes had been prominent in a number of his nightmares.

It had been late, crawling through the thick heat of Miami summertime night toward morning, when he'd gotten the call, rousing him from sleep, directing him to a house only ten or twelve blocks from his own. A city editor, gruff with the hour, jaded with the job, sending him to a horror show.

It was when he'd still been cityside, working general assignment, which meant mostly murder stories. He had arrived at the address and spent an hour pacing around outside the police line, waiting for something to happen, staring across the dark at a trim, single-story ranch house with a well-manicured lawn and a new BMW parked in the driveway. It was the middle-class home of a junior executive and his wife. He could see crime-scene technicians and various detectives and medical examiner's office personnel moving about within the house, but he could not see what had happened. The entire area was lit by pulsating police lights, throwing quick snatches of red or blue across the area. The lights seemed to thicken in the humid air. The few neighbors who'd ventured out had been uniform in their description of the couple who lived in the house: nice, friendly, but kept to themselves. This was a litany known to all reporters. People who have been murdered were always said to have kept to themselves, whether they had or not. It was as if neighbors needed to rapidly disassociate themselves from whatever terror had fallen out of the sky.

Finally, he'd spotted Vernon Hawkins leaving the house through a side door. The old detective had ducked away from the police strobes and the television cameras and had pushed himself up against a tree, as if in great exhaustion.

He had known Hawkins for years, through dozens of stories. The veteran detective had always had a special liking for Cowart, had tipped him off frequently, shown him things that were confidential, explained things that were secret, let the reporter in on the inexorably ugly life of the homicide detective. Cowart had surreptitiously slid beneath the yellow police line and approached the detective. The man had frowned, then shrugged and gestured for him to sit.

The detective lit a cigarette. Then he stared for an instant at the glowing end. "These things are murder," he said with a rueful laugh. "They're killing me. Used to be slowly, but I'm getting older, so it's speeding up."

"So why don't you quit?" Cowart asked.

"Because they're the only things I've ever found that get the smell of death out of my nostrils."

The detective took a long drag and the red glow illuminated the lines in the man's face.

After a moment of silence, the detective turned toward Cowart. "So, Matty, what brings you out on a night like this? Ought to be home with that pretty wife of yours."

"C'mon, Vernon."

The detective smiled quietly and put his head back gently against the tree. "You're gonna end up like me, with nothing better to do at night except go to crime scenes."

"Give me a break, Vernon. What can you tell me about the inside?"

The detective laughed briefly. "Guy naked and dead. Throat cut while he was in bed. Woman naked and dead. Throat cut while she was in bed. Blood all over the fucking place."

"And?"

"Suspect in custody."

"Who?"

"A teenager. A runaway kid from Des Moines they picked up earlier this evening. Drove all the way to the Fort Lauderdale strip to find him. They were into kinky threesomes. The only trouble was, after having their fun with the lad, he decided that their hundred bucks wasn't quite all there was to be had. You know, he saw the car, saw the nice neighborhood and everything. They argued. He pulled out an old-style straight razor. Those things are still a helluva weapon. First shot got the guy right across the jugular. . . ."

The detective demonstrated in the night air, abruptly slashing the darkness with a swift chopping motion.

". . . The man goes down like he's been shot. Gurgles a couple of times and that's it. He's alive just long enough to realize he's dying. A tough way to go. The wife starts screaming, of course, tries to run. So the kid grabs her by the hair, pulls her head back, and bingo. Real fast, she only got off one more scream. Tough luck, though. It was enough to alert a neighbor who called us. Some guy with insomnia walking his dog. We got the kid as he came out the front door. He was loading up the car with the stereo, television, clothes, anything he could get his hands on. Covered in blood.''

He looked out across the yard and said vacantly, "Matty, what's Hawkins' First Law of the Street?"

Cowart smiled through the darkness. Hawkins liked to speak in maxims. "The first law, Vernon, is never look for your trouble, because trouble will always find you when it wants to."

The detective nodded. "Real sweet kid. Real sweet psychopathic kid. Says he had nothing to do with it."

"Christ."

"Not that strange," the detective continued. "I mean, the kid probably blames Mr. Junior Exec and his wife there for what happened. If they hadn't tried to stiff him, you know what I mean."

"But . . ."

"No remorse. Not a shred of sympathy or anything human. Just a kid. Tells me everything that happened. Then he says to me, 'I didn't do nothing. I'm innocent. I want a lawyer.' We're standing there and there's blood all over and he says he didn't do nothing. I guess that's because it didn't mean anything to him. I guess. Christ . . ."

He leaned back in defeat and exhaustion. "You know how old this kid is? Fifteen. Just fifteen a month ago. Ought to be home worrying about pimples, dates, and homework. He'll do juvie time for sure. Bet the house on it."

The detective closed his eyes and sighed. "I didn't do nothing. I didn't do nothing. Jesus."

He held out his hand. "Look at that. I'm fifty-fucking-nine years old and gonna retire and I thought I'd seen and heard it all."

The hand was quivering. Cowart could see it move in the light thrown from the pulsating police lights.

"You know," Hawkins said as he stared at his hand, "I'm getting so I don't want to hear any more. I'd almost rather shoot it out with some crazy fuck than I would hear one more guy talk about doing something terrible as if it means no more than nothing. Like it wasn't some life that he snuffed out, it was just a candy wrapper he crumpled up and tossed away. Like littering instead of first-degree murder.''

He turned to Cowart. "You want to see?"

"Of course. Let's go," he replied, too quickly.

Hawkins looked at him closely. "Don't be so sure. You always want to see so damn quick. It ain't nice. Take my word for it this time."

"No," Cowart said. "It's my job, too."

The detective shrugged. "I take you in, you gotta promise something."

"What's that?"

"You see what he did, then I show him to you—no questions, you just get a look at him, he's in the kitchen—but you make sure you get into the paper that he's no boy next door. Got it? That he's not some poor, disadvantaged little kid. That's what his lawyer's gonna start saying just as soon as he gets here. I want it different. You tell them that he's a stone-cold killer, got it? Stone-cold. I don't wanna have anybody pick up the paper and see a picture of him and think, How could a nice kid like that have done this?"

"I can do that," Cowart said.

"Okay." The detective shrugged, rose, and they started to walk toward the front door. As they were about to pass inside, he turned to Cowart and said, "You sure? These are folks just like you and me. You won't forget this one. Not ever."

"Let's go."

"Matty, let an old guy look out for you for once."

"Come on, Vernon."

"It's your nightmare, then," the detective said. He'd been absolutely right about that.

Cowart remembered staring at the executive and his wife. There was so much blood it was almost as if they were dressed. Every time the police photographer's flash exploded, the bodies glistened for an instant.

Wordlessly, he had followed the detective into the kitchen. The boy sat there wearing sneakers and jeans, his slight torso naked, one arm handcuffed to a chair. Streaks of blood marked his body, but he ignored them and casually smoked a cigarette with his free hand. It made him look even younger, like a child trying to act older, cooler, to impress the policemen in the room but really only appearing slightly silly. Cowart noted a smear of blood in the boy's blond hair, matting the curls together, another tinge of dried brown blood on the boy's cheek. The kid didn't even need to shave yet.

The boy looked up when Cowart and the detective entered the room. "Who's that?" he asked, nodding toward Cowart.

For an instant Matthew locked his eyes with the boy's. They

were an ancient blue, endlessly evil, like staring at the iron edge of an executioner's sword.

"He's a reporter, with the *Journal*," Hawkins said.

"Hey, reporter!" the kid said, suddenly smiling.

"What?"

"You tell everybody I didn't do nothing," he said. Then he laughed in a high-pitched, wheezing way that echoed after Cowart and forever froze in his memory, as Hawkins steered him out of the room, back out into the hurrying dawn.

He had gone to his office and written the story of the junior executive, his wife, and the teenager. He'd described the white sheets crumpled and brown with blood, the red spatter marks marking the walls with Daliesque horror. He'd written about the neighborhood and the trim house and a framed testimonial on the wall attesting to the victim's membership in an advanced sales club. He'd written about suburban dreams and the lure of forbidden sex. He'd described the Fort Lauderdale strip where children cruised nightly, aging far beyond their years every minute. And he'd described the boy's eyes, burning them into the story, just the way his friend had asked him to.

He'd ended the story with the boy's words.

When he'd gone home that night, carrying a copy of the first edition under his arm, his story jamming the front page, he had felt an exhaustion that had gone far beyond lack of sleep. He had crawled into his bed, pulling himself up against his wife, even knowing that she planned to leave him, shivering, flu-like, unable to find any warmth in the world.

Cowart shook his head to dispel the morning and looked around his work cubicle.

Hawkins was dead now. Retired with a little ceremony, given a pension, and released to cough his life away with emphysema. Cowart had gone to the ceremony and clapped when the chief of police had cited the detective's contributions. He'd gone to see him in the detective's small Miami Beach apartment every time he could. It had been a barren place, decorated with some old clippings of stories Cowart and others had written. "Remember the rules," Hawkins had told him at the end of each visit, "and if you can't remember what I told you about the street, then make up your own rules and live by them." They had laughed. Then he'd gone to the hospital as frequently as possible, taking off early and surreptitiously from his office to go and trade stories with the detective, until the last time, when he'd arrived and found Hawkins unconscious beneath an oxygen

tent, and Cowart hadn't known whether the detective heard him
when he whispered his name, or felt him when he picked up his
hand. He had sat beside the bed for one long night, not even
knowing when it was that the detective's life had slipped away
in the darkness. Then he'd gone to the funeral, along with a few
other old policemen. There'd been a flag, a coffin, a few words
from a priest. No wife. No children. Dry eyes. Just a nightmare's worth of memories being lowered slowly into the ground.
He wondered if it would be the same when he died.

I wonder what happened to the kid, he thought. Probably out
of juvenile hall and out on the street. Or on Death Row beside
the letter writer. Or dead.

He looked at the letter.

This really should be a news story, he thought, not an editorial. He ought to hand it to someone on the city desk and let
them check it out. I don't do that anymore. I am a man of
opinions. I write from a distance, a member of a board which
votes and decides and adopts positions, not passions. I have
given up my name.

He half rose from his chair to do exactly that, then stopped.

An innocent man.

In all the crimes and trials he'd covered, he tried to remember
ever seeing a genuinely innocent man. He'd seen plenty of not-
guilty verdicts, charges dismissed for lack of evidence, cases
lost by sheer defensive eloquence or stumbling prosecution. But
he could not recall someone genuinely innocent. He'd asked
Hawkins once if he'd ever arrested someone like that, and he'd
laughed. "A man who really didn't do it? Ah, you screw up a
bunch, that's for sure. A lot of guys walk who shouldn't. But
bust somebody who's really innocent? That's the worst possible
case. I don't know if I could live with that. No, sir. That's the
only one I'd ever really lose sleep over."

He held the letter in his hand. I DID NOT COMMIT. He
wondered, Is someone losing sleep over Robert Earl Ferguson?

He felt a hot flush of excitement. If it's true, he thought . . .
He did not complete the idea in his head but swallowed swiftly,
curbing a sudden flash of ambition.

Cowart remembered an interview he'd read years before about
a graceful, aging basketball player who was finally hanging up
his sneakers after a long career. The man had talked about his
achievements and disappointments in the same breath, as if
treating them each with a sort of restrained and equal dignity.
He had been asked why he was finally quitting, and he started

to talk about his family and children, his need to put the game of his childhood away finally and get on with his life. Then he'd talked about his legs, not as if they were a part of his body, but as if they were old and good friends. He'd said that he could no longer jump the way he'd once been able to, that now when he gathered himself to soar toward the hoop, the leg muscles that once had seemed to launch him so easily screamed with age and pain, insisting he quit. And he had said that without his legs' cooperation, continuing was useless. Then he had gone out to his final game and scored thirty-eight points effortlessly—shifting, twisting, and leaping above the rim as he had years earlier. It was as if the man's body had given him one last opportunity to force an indelible memory on people. Cowart had thought the same was true of reporting; that it took a certain youth that knew no exhaustion, a drive that would shunt aside sleep, hunger, love, all in the singular pursuit of a story. The best reporters had legs that carried them higher and farther when others were falling back to rest.

He flexed his leg muscles involuntarily.

I had those once, he thought. Before I retired back here to get away from the nightmares, to wear suits and act responsible and age gracefully. Now I'm divorced and my ex-wife is going to steal the only thing I ever really loved without restriction, and I sit back here, hiding from reality, issuing opinions about events that influence no one.

He clutched the letter in his hand.

Innocent, he thought. Let's see.

The library at the *Journal* was an odd combination of the old and the new. It was located just past the newsroom, beyond the desks where the soft-news feature writers sat. In the rear of the library were rows of long metal filing cabinets that housed clippings that dated back decades. In the past, every day the paper had been dissected by person, subject, location, and event, each cutting filed away appropriately. Now this was all done on state-of-the-art computers, huge terminals with large screens. The librarians simply went through each story, highlighting the key people and words, then transmitting them into so many electronic files. Cowart preferred the old way. He liked being able to arrange a bunch of inky clips about, picking and choosing what he needed. It was like being able to hold some history in his hand. Now, it was efficient, quick, and soulless. He never neglected to tease the librarians about this when he used the library.

When he walked through the doors, he was spotted by a young woman. She was blonde, with a striking sheet of hair, tall and trim. She wore wire-rimmed glasses, sometimes peering over the top.

"Don't say it, Matt."

"Don't say what?"

"Just don't say what you always say. That you liked it more the old way."

"I won't say it."

"Good."

"Because you just said it."

"Doesn't count," the young woman laughed. She rose and went to where he was standing at a counter. "So how can I help you?"

"Laura the librarian. Has anyone told you that you'll wreck your eyes staring at that computer screen all day?"

"Everyone."

"Suppose I give you a name . . ."

". . . And I'll do the old computer magic."

"Robert Earl Ferguson."

"What else?"

"Death Row. Sentenced about three years ago in Escambia County."

"All right. Let's see . . ." She sat primly at a computer and typed in the name and punched a button. Cowart could see the screen go blank, save for a single word, which flashed continuously in a corner: *Searching*. Then the machine seemed to hiccup and some words formed.

"What's it say?" he asked.

"A couple of entries. Let me check." The librarian hit some more characters and another set of words appeared on the screen. She read off the headlines: "Former college student convicted in girl's murder, sentenced to death penalty; Appeal rejected in rural murder case; Florida Supreme Court to hear Death Row cases. That's all. Three stories. All from the Gulf Coast edition. Nothing ran in the main run, except the last, which is probably a roundup story."

"Not much for a murder and death sentence," Cowart said. "You know, in the old days, it seemed we covered every murder trial . . ."

"No more."

"Life meant more then."

The librarian shrugged. "Violent death used to be more sensational than it is now, and you're much too young to be talking about the old days. You probably mean the seventies. . . ." She smiled and Cowart laughed with her. "Anyway, death sentences are getting to be old hat in Florida these days. We've got . . ." She hesitated, pushing her head back and examining the ceiling for an instant. ". . . More than two hundred men on Death Row now. The governor signs a couple of death warrants every month. Doesn't mean they get it, but . . ." She looked at him and smiled. "But Matt, you know all that. You wrote those editorials last year. About being a civilized nation. Right?" She nodded her head toward him.

"Right. I remember the main thrust was: We shouldn't sanction state murder. Three editorials, a total of maybe ninety column inches. In reply, we ran more than fifty letters that were, how shall I put it? Contrary to my position. We ran fifty, but we got maybe five quadrillion. The nicest ones merely suggested that I ought to be beheaded in a public square. The nasty ones were more inventive."

The librarian smiled. "Popularity is not our job, right? Would you like me to print these for you?"

"Please. But I'd rather be loved. . . ."

She grinned at him and then turned to her computer. She played her fingers across the keyboard again and a high-speed printer in the corner of the room began whirring and shaking as it printed the news stories. "There you go. On to something?"

"Maybe," Cowart replied. He took the sheaf of paper out of the computer. "Man says he didn't do it."

The young woman laughed. "Now that would be interesting. And unique." She turned back to the computer screen and Cowart headed back to his office.

The events that had landed Robert Earl Ferguson on Death Row began to take on form and shape as Cowart read through the news stories. The library's offering had been minimal, but enough to create a portrait in his imagination. He learned that the victim in the case was an eleven-year-old girl, and that her body had been discovered concealed in scrub brush at the edge of a swamp.

It was easy for him to envision the murky green and brown foliage concealing the body. It would have had a sucking, oozing quality of sickness, an appropriate place to find death.

He read on. The victim was the child of a local city-council member, and she had last been seen walking home from school. Cowart saw a wide, single-story cinder-block building standing alone in a rural, dusty field. It would be painted a faded pink or institutional green, colors that could barely be brightened by children's excited voices greeting the end of the school day. That was when one of the teachers in the elementary grades had seen her getting into a green Ford with out-of-state plates. Why? What would make her get into a stranger's car? The thought made him shiver and feel an instant flush of fear for his own daughter. She wouldn't do that, he told himself abruptly. When the little girl failed to arrive home, an alarm had gone out. Cowart knew that the local television stations would have shown a picture on the evening news that night. It would have been of a ponytailed youngster, smiling, showing braces on her teeth. A family photo, taken in hope and promise, used obscenely to fill the airwaves with despair.

More than twenty-four hours later, deputies searching the area had uncovered her remains. The news story had been filled with euphemisms: "brutal assault," "savage attack," "torn and ripped body," which Cowart recognized as the shorthand of journalism; unwilling to describe in great detail the actual horror that the child had faced, the writer had resorted to a comfortable series of clichés.

It must have been a terrible death, he thought. People wanted to know what happened, but not really, because if they did they would not sleep either.

He read on. As best he could tell, Ferguson had been the first and only suspect. Police had picked him up shortly after the victim's body had been discovered, because of the similarity with his car. He'd been questioned—there was nothing in any of the stories about being held incommunicado or beaten—and confessed. The confession, followed by a blood-type matchup and the vehicle identification, appeared to have been the only evidence against him, but Cowart was circumspect. Trials took on a certain momentum of their own, like great theater. A detail which seemed small or questionable when mentioned in a news story could become immense in a juror's eyes.

Ferguson had been correct about the judge's sentencing. The quote ". . . an animal that ought to be taken outside and shot" appeared prominently in the story. The judge had probably been up for reelection that year, he thought.

The other library entries had provided some additional information: primarily that Ferguson's initial appeal, based upon the sufficiency of evidence against him, had been rejected by the first district court of appeals. That was to be expected. It was still pending before the Florida Supreme Court. It was clear to Cowart that Ferguson had not yet really begun to gnaw away at the courts. He had numerous avenues of appeal and had yet to travel them.

Cowart sat back at his desk and tried to picture what had happened.

He saw a rural county in the backwoods of Florida. He knew this was a part of the state that had absolutely nothing in common with the popular images of Florida, not the well-scrubbed, smiling faces of the middle class that flocked to Orlando and Disney World, nor the beered-up frat boys who headed to the beaches during their spring breaks, nor the tourists who drove their mobile homes to Cape Canaveral for space shots. Certainly, this Florida had nothing to do with the cosmopolitan, loose-fitting image of Miami, which styled itself as some sort of American Casablanca.

But in Pachoula, he thought, even in the eighties, when a little white girl is raped and murdered and the man that did it is black, a more primal America takes over. An America that people would prefer not to remember.

Is that what happened to Ferguson? It was certainly possible.

Cowart picked up the telephone to call the attorney handling Ferguson's appeal.

It took most of the remainder of the morning to get through to the lawyer. When Cowart finally did connect with the man, he was immediately struck by the lawyer's licorice-sweet southern accent.

"Mr. Cowart, this is Roy Black. What's got a Miami newspaper man interested in things up here in Escambia County?" He pronounced the word "here" *he-yah*.

"Thanks for calling back, Mr. Black. I'm curious about one of your clients. A Robert Earl Ferguson."

The lawyer laughed briefly. "Well, I sorta figured it would be Mr. Ferguson's case that you were calling about when my gal here handed me your phone message. Whatcha wanna know?"

"First tell me about his case."

"Well, State Supreme Court has the package right now. We contend that the evidence against Mr. Ferguson was hardly sufficient to convict him. And we're saying right out that the trial judge shoulda suppressed that confession of his'n. You oughta read it. Probably the most convenient document of its sort I ever saw. Just like the police wrote it up in the sheriff's department up here. And, without that confession, they got no case at all. If Robert Earl doesn't say what they want him to say, they don't even get two minutes in court. Not even in the worst, redneck, racist court in the world.''

"What about the blood evidence?"

"Crime lab in Escambia County is pretty primitive, not like what y'all are used to down there in Miami. They only typed it down to its major group. Type O positive. That's what the semen they found in the deceased was, that's what Robert Earl is. Of course, the same is true of maybe a couple thousand men in that county. But his trial attorney failed to cross-examine the medical folks on that score.''

"And the car?''

"Green Ford with out-of-state plates. Nobody identified Robert Earl, and nobody said for sure that it was his car that little gal got into. This wasn't what you call circumstantial evidence, hell, it was coincidental. Shoulda been laughed out of the trial.''

"You weren't his trial attorney, were you?''

"No, sir. That honor went to another.''

"Have you attacked the competency of the representation?''

"Not yet. But we will. A third-year fella at the University of Florida law school coulda done better. A *high school* senior coulda done better. Makes me angry. I can hardly wait until I write that brief up. But I don't want to shoot off all the cannons right at the start.''

"What do you mean?''

"Mr. Cowart,'' the attorney said slowly, "do y'all understand the nature of appellate work in death cases? The idea is to keep taking little old bites at the apple. That way you can drag that sucker out for years and years. Make people forget. Give time a bit of a chance to do some good. You don't take your best shot first, because that'll put your boy right in the old hot seat, if you catch my drift.''

"I understand that,'' Cowart said. "But suppose you've got an innocent man sitting up there?''

"That what Robert Earl told you?''

"Yes.''

"Told me that, too.''

"Well, Mr. Black, do you believe him?''

"Hmmm, maybe. Maybe more'n most of the times I hear that from someone enjoying the hospitality of the state of Florida. But you understand, Mr. Cowart, I don't really indulge in the luxury of allowing myself to subscribe to the guilt or innocence of my clients. I have to concern myself with the simple fact that they been convicted in a court of law and I got to undo that in a court of law. If I can undo a wrong, well, then when I die and go to heaven I trust they will welcome me with angels playing trumpets. Of course, I also maybe sometimes undo some rights and replace them with wrongs, so there's the very real possibility that I may be met at that other place with folks carrying pitchforks and wearing little pointy tails. That's the nature of the law, sir. But you work for a newspaper. Newspapers are a helluva lot more concerned with the public's impression of right and wrong, truth and justice, than I am. Newspaper also has a helluva lot more influence with the trial judge who could order up a new trial, or the governor and the state Board of Pardons, if you catch my drift, sir. Perhaps you could do a little something for Robert Earl?''

"I might.''

"Why don't you go see the man? He's real smart and well-spoken.'' Black laughed. "Speaks a sight better'n I do. Probably smart enough to be a lawyer. Sure a helluva lot smarter than that attorney he had at his trial, who must have been asleep most of the time they were putting his client in the electric chair.''

"Tell me about his trial attorney.''

"Old guy. Been handling cases up there for maybe a hundred, two hundred years. It's a small area, up in Pachoula. Everybody knows each other. They come on down to the Escambia County courthouse and it's like everyone's having a party. A murder-case party. They don't like me too much.''

"No, I wouldn't think so.''

"Of course, they didn't like Robert Earl too much, either. Going off to college and all and coming home in a big car. People probably felt pretty good when he was arrested. Not exactly what they're used to. Of course, they ain't used to sex murders neither.''

"What's the place like?'' Cowart asked.

"Just like what you'd expect, city boy. It's sort of what the papers and the chamber of commerce likes to call the New South. That means they got some new ideas and some old ideas. But then, it ain't that bad, either. Lots of development dollars going in up there.''

''I think I know what you mean.''

''You go up and take a look for yourself,'' the attorney said. ''But let me give you a piece of advice: Just because someone talks like I do and sounds like some character outa William Faulkner or Flannery O'Connor, don't you naturally assume they are dumb. 'Cause they aren't.''

''So noted.''

The lawyer laughed. ''I bet you didn't think I'd read those authors.''

''It hadn't crossed my mind.''

''It will before you get finished with Robert Earl. And try to remember another thing. People there are probably pretty satisfied with what happened to Robert Earl. So don't go up expecting to make a lot of friends. Sources, as you folks in the papers like to call 'em.''

''One other thing bothers me,'' Cowart said. ''He says he knows the name of the real killer.''

''Now, I don't know nothing about that. He might. Hell, he probably does. It's a small place is Pachoula. But this I do know . . .'' The attorney's voice changed, growing less jocular and taking on a directness that surprised Cowart. ''. . . I do know that man was unfairly convicted and I mean to have him off Death Row, whether he did it or not. Maybe not this year, in this court, but some year in some court. I have grown up and spent my life with all those good ole boys, rednecks, and crackers, and I ain't gonna lose this one. I don't care whether he did it or not.''

''But if he didn't . . .''

''Well, somebody kilt that little gal. I suspect somebody's gonna have to pay.''

''I've got a lot of questions,'' Cowart said.

''I suspect so. This is a case with a lot of questions. Sometimes that just happens, you know. Trial's supposed to clear everything up, actually makes it more confused. Seems that happened here to old Robert Earl.''

''So, you think I ought to take a look at it?''

''Sure,'' said the lawyer. Cowart could feel his smile across the telephone line. ''I do. I don't know what you'll find, excepting a lot of prejudice and dirt-poor thinking. Maybe you can help set an innocent man free.''

"So you do think he's innocent?"

"Did I say that? Nah, I mean only that he shoulda been found not guilty in a court of law. There's a big difference, you know."

TWO
ONE MAN ON DEATH
————————————————*ROW*

Cowart stopped the rental car on the access road to the Florida State Prison and stared across the fields at the stolid dark buildings that held the majority of the state's maximum-security prisoners. There were two prisons, actually, separated by a small river, the Union Correctional Institution on one side, Raiford Prison on the other. He could see cattle grazing in distant green fields, and dust rising in small clouds where inmate work crews labored amidst growing areas. There were watchtowers at the corners and he thought he could make out the glint of weapons held by the watchers. He did not know which building housed Death Row and the room where the state's electric chair was kept, but he'd been told that it split off from the main prison. He could see twelve-foot-high double rows of chain link fence topped with curled strands of barbed wire. The wire gleamed in the morning sun. He got out and stood by the car. A stand of pine trees rose up straight and green on the edge of the roadway, as if pointing in accusation at the crystal blue sky. A cool breeze rustled through the branches, then slid over Cowart's forehead amidst the building humidity.

He had had no difficulty persuading Will Martin and the other members of the editorial board to cut him loose to pursue the circumstances surrounding the conviction of Robert Earl Ferguson, though Martin had expressed some snorting skepticism which Cowart had ignored.

''Don't you remember Pitts and Lee?'' Cowart had replied.

27

Freddie Pitts and Wilbert Lee had been sentenced to die for the murder of a gas-station attendant in North Florida. Both men had confessed to a crime they hadn't done. It had taken years of reporting by one of the *Journal*'s most famous reporters to set them free. He'd won a Pulitzer. In the *Journal* newsroom, it was the first story any new reporter was told.

"That was different."

"Why?"

"That was in 1963. Might as well have been 1863. Things have changed."

"Really? How about that guy in Texas, the one the documentary filmmaker got off Death Row there?"

"That was different."

"How much?"

Martin had laughed. "That's a good question. Go. With my blessing. Answer that question. And remember, when you're all finished playing reporter again, you can always come home to the ivory tower." He'd shooed Cowart on his way.

The city desk had been informed and promised assistance should he need any. He had detected a note of jealousy that the story had landed in his lap. He recognized the advantage that he had over the cityside staff. First, he was going to be able to work alone; the city desk would have assigned a team to the story. The *Journal*, like so many newspapers and television stations, had a full-time investigative squad with a snappy title like "The Spotlight Team" or "The I-team." They would have approached the story with the subtlety of an invading force. And, Cowart realized, unlike the regular reporters on the staff, he would have no deadline, no assistant city editor breathing down his neck, wondering every day where the story was. He could find out what he could, structure as he saw fit, write it as he wanted. Or discard it if it wasn't true.

He tried to hold on to this last thought, to armor himself against disappointment, but as he headed down the road and pulled into the prison, he sensed his pulse quickening. A series of warning signs was posted on the access road, informing passersby that by entering the area they were consenting to a search, that any firearms and narcotics violations would be punished by a term in prison. He passed through a gate where a gray-jacketed guard checked his identification against a list and sullenly waved him through, then parked in an area designated VISITORS and entered the administration building.

There was some confusion when he checked with a secretary.

She had apparently lost his entrance request. He waited patiently by her desk while she shuffled through papers, apologizing rapidly, until she found it. He was then asked to wait in an adjacent office until an officer could escort him to where he was to meet Robert Earl Ferguson.

After a few minutes, an older man with a gray-tinged Marine Corps haircut and bearing entered the room. The man had a huge, gnarled hand, which he shot forward at Cowart. "Sergeant Rogers. I'm day officer on the Row today."

"Glad to meet you."

"There are a few formalities, Mr. Cowart, sir, if you don't mind."

"Like?"

"I need to frisk you and search your tape recorder and briefcase. I have a statement you need to sign about being taken hostage . . ."

"What's that?"

"It's just a statement saying you're entering the Florida State Prison of your own wish and that, if taken hostage during your stay here, you will not sue the state of Florida, nor will you expect extraordinary efforts to secure your freedom."

"Extraordinary efforts?"

The man laughed and rubbed his hand through his brush of hair. "What it means is that you don't expect us to risk our asses to save yours."

Cowart smiled and made a face. "Sounds like a bad deal for me."

Sergeant Rogers grinned. "That it is. Of course, prison is a bad deal for just about everybody, except those of us who get to head home at night."

Cowart took the paper from the sergeant and signed it with a mock flourish. "Well," he said, still smiling, "can't say you guys give me a lot of confidence right here at the start."

"Oh, you ain't got nothing to worry about, not visiting Robert Earl. He's a gentleman and he ain't crazy." As he spoke, the sergeant methodically searched through Cowart's briefcase. He also opened up the tape recorder to inspect the insides and popped the battery compartment to ascertain that there were batteries in the space. "Now, it's not like you were coming in to visit Willie Arthur or Specs Wilson—they were those two bikers from Fort Lauderdale that let a little fun with that girl they picked up hitchhiking get out of hand—or Jose Salazar—you know, he killed two cops. Undercover guys in a drug deal.

You know what he made them do before he killed 'em? To each other? You oughta find out. It'll open your mind to how bad folks can be when they set their minds right to it. Or some of the other lovely guys we got in here. Most of the worst come from downstate, from your hometown. What y'all doing down there anyway, that makes folks kill each other so bad?''

"Sergeant, if I could answer that question . . .''

They both grinned. Sergeant Rogers put down Cowart's briefcase and gestured for him to hold his hands up in the air. "Sure helps to have a sense of humor around here," the sergeant said as his hands flitted across Cowart's body. The sergeant patted him down rapidly.

"Okay," the sergeant said. "Let me brief you on the drill. It's gonna be just you and him. I'm just there for security. Be right outside the door. You need help, you just yell. But that ain't gonna happen, because we're talking about one of the non-crazy men on the Row. Hell, we're gonna use the executive suite . . .''

"The what?''

"The executive suite. That's what we call the interview room for the best behaved. Now, it's just a table and chairs, so it ain't no big deal. We've got other facilities that are more secure. And Robert Earl won't have no restraints. Not even leg irons. But no hand contact. I mean you can give him a smoke . . .''

"I don't.''

"Good. Smart man. You can take papers from him, if he hands you documents. But if you wanted to hand him anything, it would have to go through me.''

"Like hand him what?''

"Oh, maybe a file and hacksaw and some road maps.''

Cowart looked surprised.

"Hey, just kidding," the sergeant said. "Of course, in here, that's the one joke we never much make. Escape. Not funny, you know. But there's lots of different ways to escape a prison. Even Death Row. A lot of the inmates think talking to reporters is one way.''

"Help them escape?''

"Help them get out. Everyone always wants the press to get excited about their case. Inmates never think they got a fair shake. They think that maybe if they make enough of a stink, they'll get a new trial. Happens. That's why prison people like me always hate to see reporters. Hate to see those little pads of paper, those camera crews and lights. Just gets everyone riled up, excited about nothing much. People think it's the loss of freedoms that makes for trouble in prisons. They're wrong. Worse thing by far is expectations getting raised and then smashed. It's just another story for you guys. But for the guys inside, it's their lives you're talking about. They think one story, the right story, and they'll just walk on out of here. You and I know that ain't necessarily true. Disappointment. Big, angry, frustrating disappointment. Causes more trouble than you'd like to know. What we like is routine. No wild hopes, no dreams. Just one day exactly like the last. Don't sound exciting, but of course, you don't want to be around a prison when things get exciting.''

"Well, I'm sorry. But I'm just here checking a few facts.''

"In my experience, Mr. Cowart, there ain't no such thing as a fact, except two maybe, one being born and one being dying. But, no problem. I ain't as hard-core as some around here. I kinda like a little change of pace, as long as it's within reason. Just don't hand him nothing. It'll only make it worse for him.''

"Worse than Death Row?''

"You got to understand, even on the Row there's lots of ways of doing your time. We can make it real hard, or not so tough. Right now, Robert Earl, he's got it pretty good. Oh, he still gets his cell tossed every day, and he still gets a strip search after a little meeting like this one here today, but he's got yard privileges now and books and such. You wouldn't think it, but even in prison there's all sorts of little things we can take away that will make his life a lot worse.''

"I've got nothing for him. But he may have some papers or something . . .''

"Well, that's okay. We ain't so concerned with stuff being smuggled out of the prison. . . .''

The sergeant laughed again. He had a booming laugh to match his forthright speech. Rogers was obviously the sort of man who could tell you much or make your life miserable, depending on his inclination. "You're also supposed to tell me how long you're gonna be.''

"I don't know.''

"Well, hell, I got all morning, so take your time. Afterwards I'll give you a little tour of the place. You ever seen Old Sparky?''

"No.''

"It's an education.''

The sergeant rose. He was a wide, powerful man, with the

sort of bearing that implied he'd seen much trouble in his life and always managed to deal with it successfully.

"Kinda puts things in perspective, if you know what I mean."

Cowart followed him through the doorway, feeling dwarfed by the man's broad back.

He was led through a series of locked doors and a metal detector manned by an officer who grinned at the sergeant as they passed through. They came to a terminal center where several wings of the immense wheel-like prison building came together. In that moment, Cowart was aware of the noise of prison, a constant cacophony of raised voices and metallic clangs and crashes as doors swung open, only to be slammed shut and locked again. A radio somewhere was playing country music. A television set was tuned to a soap opera; he could hear the voices, then the ubiquitous music of commercials. He felt a sensation of motion about him, as if caught in a strong river current, but, save for the sergeant and a pair of other officers manning a small booth in the center of the room, there were few people about. He could see inside the booth and noted an electronic board that showed which doors were open and which were shut. Cameras mounted in the corners by the ceiling and television monitors showed flickering gray images from each cell tier as well. Cowart noticed that the floor was a spotless yellow linoleum, worn bright by the flood of people and the never-ending efforts of prison trustees. He saw one man, wearing a blue jumpsuit, diligently swabbing a corner area with a dirty gray mop, endlessly going over and over a spot that was already clean.

"That's Q, R, and S wings," said the sergeant. "Death Row. Actually, I guess you'd have to say Death Rows. Hell, we've even got an overcrowding problem on Death Row. Says something, don't it? The chair's down there. Looks like the other areas, but it ain't the same. No, sir."

Cowart stared down the narrow, high corridors. The cell tiers were on the left, rising up three stories, with stairs at either end. The wall facing the cells contained three rows of dirty windows that swung open to let in the air. There was an empty space between the catwalk outside the bank of cells and the windows. He realized the men could lie locked in each small cell and stare out across and through to the sky, a distance of perhaps thirty feet that might as well have been a million miles. It made him shudder.

"There's Robert Earl over there," the sergeant said.

Cowart spun about and saw the sergeant pointing toward a small barred cage in a far corner of the terminal area. There were four men inside, sitting on an iron bench, staring out at him. Three men wore blue jumpsuits, like the trustee. One man wore bright orange. He was partially obscured by the bodies of the other men.

"You don't want to wear the orange," the sergeant said quietly. "That means the clock's ticking down on your life."

Cowart started toward the cage but was stopped by the sergeant's sudden grip on his shoulder. He could feel the strength in the man's fingertips.

"Wrong way. Interview room's over here. When someone comes to visit, we search the men and make a list of everything. they have—papers, law books, whatever. Then they go into isolation, over there. We bring him to you. Then, when it's all said and done, we reverse the process. Takes goddamn forever, but security, you know. We do like to have our security."

Cowart nodded and was steered into an interview room. It was a plain white office with a single steel table in the center and a pair of old, scarred brown chairs. A mirror was on one wall. An ashtray in the center. Nothing else.

He pointed at the mirror. "Two-way?" he asked.

"Sure is," replied the sergeant. "That a problem?"

"Nope. Hey, you sure this is the executive suite?" He turned toward the sergeant and smiled. "Us city boys are accustomed to a bit more in the way of creature comforts."

Sergeant Rogers laughed. "Why, that's what I would have guessed. Sorry, this is it."

"It'll do," Cowart said. "Thanks."

He took a seat and waited for Ferguson.

His first impression of the prisoner was of a young man in his mid-twenties, just shorter than six feet, with a boyish slight build, but possessing a deceptive, wiry strength that passed through his handshake. Robert Earl Ferguson had rolled his sleeves up, displaying knotted arm muscles. He was thin, with narrow hips and shoulders like a distance runner, with an athlete's easy grace in the manner he walked. His hair was short, his skin dark. His eyes were alert, quick, penetrating; Matthew Cowart had the sensation that he was measured by the prisoner in a moment's time, assessed, read, and stored away.

"Thank you for coming," the prisoner said.

"It wasn't a big deal."

"It will be," Ferguson replied confidently. He was carrying a stack of legal papers, which he arranged on the table in front of him. Cowart saw the prisoner glance over at Sergeant Rogers, who nodded, turned, and exited through the door, slamming it shut with a crash.

Cowart sat, took out a notepad and pen, and arranged a tape recorder in the center of the table. "You mind?" he asked.

"No," Ferguson responded. "It makes sense."

"Why did you write me?" Cowart asked. "Just curious, you know. Like, how did you get my name?"

The prisoner smiled and rocked back in his seat. He seemed oddly relaxed for what should have been a critical moment.

"Last year you won a Florida Bar Association award for a series of editorials about the death penalty. Your name was in the Tallahassee paper. It was passed on to me by another man on the Row. It didn't hurt that you work for the biggest and most influential paper in the state."

"Why did you wait to contact me?"

"Well, to be honest, I thought the appeals court was going to throw out my conviction. When they didn't, I hired a new lawyer—well, hired isn't quite right—I got a new lawyer and started being more aggressive about my situation. You see, Mr. Cowart, even when I got convicted and sentenced to die, I still really didn't think it was happening to me. I felt like it was all a dream or something. I was going to wake up any moment and be back at school. Or maybe like someone was just going to come along and say, 'Hey, hold everything. There's been a terrible mistake made here . . .' and so I wasn't really thinking right. I didn't realize that you have to fight hard to save your life. You can't trust the system to do it for you."

There's the first quote of my story, Cowart thought.

The prisoner leaned forward, placing his hands on the table, then, just as rapidly, leaned back, so that he could use his hands to gesture in short, precise movements, using motion to underscore his words. He had a soft yet sturdy voice, one that seemed to carry the weight of words easily. He hunched his shoulders forward as he spoke, as if being pushed by the force of his beliefs. The effect was immediate, it narrowed the small room down to the simple space between the reporter and the prisoner, filling the arena with a sort of superheated strength.

"I thought just being innocent was going to be enough, you see. I thought that's the way it all worked. I thought I didn't have to do anything. Then, when I got here, I got some education. Real education.''

"What do you mean?"

"Well, the men on Death Row have a kind of informal way of passing information about lawyers, appeals, clemency, you name it. You see, over there . . .," he gestured toward the main prison buildings, "the convicts think of what they're gonna do when they get out. Or maybe they think about escaping. They think about how they're going to do their time, and they think about making a life inside. They have the luxury to dream about something, a future, even if it's a future behind bars. They can always dream about freedom. And they have the greatest gift of all, the gift of uncertainty. They don't know what life will hold for them.

"Not us. We know how we're gonna end up. We know that there will come a day when the state will send two thousand five hundred electric volts into your brain. We know we've got five, maybe ten years. It's like having a terrible weight around your neck all the time, that you're struggling to hold up. Every minute goes by, you think, Did I waste that time? Every night comes, you think, There's another day gone. Every day arrives, you realize another night lost. That weight around your neck is the accumulation of all those moments that just passed. All those hopes just fading away. So, our concerns aren't the same."

They were both quiet for an instant. Cowart could hear his own breath easing in and out, almost as if he'd just run up a flight of stairs. "You sound like a philosopher."

"All the men on Death Row are. Even the crazy ones who scream and howl all the time. Or the retards who barely know what is happening to them. But they know the weight. Those of us with a little formal education just sound better. But we're all the same."

"You've changed here?"

"Who wouldn't?"

Cowart nodded.

"When my initial appeal failed, some of the others, some of the men who've been on the Row five, eight, maybe ten years, started to talk to me about making a future for myself. I'm a young man, Mr. Cowart, and I don't want it to end here. So I got a better lawyer, and I wrote you a letter. I need your help."

"We'll get to that in a minute." Cowart was uncertain precisely what role to play in the interview. He knew he wanted to maintain some sort of professional distance, but he didn't know how great. He had spent some time trying to think of how he would act in front of the prisoner, but had been unsuccessful. He felt a little foolish, sitting across from a man convicted of murder, in the midst of a prison holding men who'd committed the most unthinkable acts, and trying to act tough.

"Why don't you start by telling me a little bit about yourself? Like, how come a person from Pachoula doesn't have an accent?"

Ferguson laughed again. "I can, if you want to hear it. I mean, if'n I'z wan'ta, I'z kin speechify lak da tiredest ol' backwoods black you done ever heard. . . ." Ferguson sat back, sort of slumping into his chair, mimicking a man rocking in a rocking chair. The slow drawl of his words seemed to sweeten the still air of the small room. Then he pitched forward abruptly and the accent shifted. "Yo, mutha, I ken also talk like a homeboy from da streets, 'cause I know dat sheeit jes' as well. Right on." Just as quickly, that disappeared too, replaced by the wiry earnest man sitting with elbows on the table and speaking in a regular, even voice. "And I can also sound precisely as I have, like a person who has attended college and was heading to a degree and perhaps a future in business. Because that's what I was as well."

Cowart was taken aback by the quick changes. They seemed to be more than simple alterations in accent and tone. The changes in inflection were mimicked by subtle alterations of body English and bearing, so that Robert Earl Ferguson became the image he was projecting with his voice. "Impressive," Cowart said. "You must have a good ear."

Ferguson nodded. "You see, the three accents reflect my three parts. I was born in Newark, New Jersey. My momma was a maid. She used to ride the bus out to all the white suburbs every day at six A.M., then back at night, day in, day out, cleaning white folks' homes. My daddy was in the army, and he disappeared when I was three or four. They weren't ever really married, anyway. Then, when I was seven, my momma died. Heart trouble, they told us, but I never really knew. Just one day she was having trouble breathing and she walked herself down to the clinic and that was all we ever saw of her. I was sent down to Pachoula to live with my grandmother. You have no idea what that was like for a little kid. Getting out of that ghetto to where there were trees and rivers and clean air. I thought I was in paradise, even if we didn't have indoor plumbing. They were the best years of my life. I would walk to the school. Read at night by candlelight. We ate the fish I caught in the streams. It was like being in some other century. I thought I'd never leave, until my grandmother got sick. She was scared she couldn't watch over me, and so it was arranged I would be sent back to Newark to live with my aunt and her new husband. That's where I finished high school, got into college. But I used to love coming down to visit my grandmother. Vacations, I would take the all-night bus from Newark down to Atlanta, change there for Mobile, get the local to Pachoula. I had no use for the city. I thought of myself as a country boy, I guess. I didn't like Newark much.''

Ferguson shook his head and a small smile creased his face. "Those damn bus rides," he said softly. "They were the start of all my troubles."

"What do you mean?"

Ferguson continued shaking his head but answered, "By the time I got finished riding, it was nearly thirty hours. Humming along the freeway, then right through every country town and back road. Bouncing along, a little carsick, needing to use the can, filled up with folks that needed to bathe. Poor folks who couldn't afford the plane fare. I didn't like it much. That's why I bought the car, you see. A secondhand Ford Granada. Dark green. Cost me twelve hundred bucks from another student. Only had sixty-six thousand miles on it. Cherry. Sheeit! I loved cruising in that car. . . ."

Ferguson's voice was smooth and distant.

"But . . ."

"But if I hadn't had the car, I never would have been picked up by the sheriff's men investigating the crime."

"Tell me about that."

"There's really not that much to tell. The afternoon of the killing, I was at home with my grandmother. She would have testified to that, if anybody'd had the sense to ask her. . . ."

"Anybody else see you? Like, not a relative?"

"Oh, uh, oh, I don't recall anyone. Just her and me. If you go see her, you'll see why. Her place is an old shack about a half mile past any of the other old shacks. Dirt-road poor."

"Go on."

"Well, not long after they found the little girl's body, two detectives come out to the house to see me. I was in the front, washing the car. Boy, I did like to see that sucker shine! There I was, middle of the day, they come out and ask me what was I doing a couple of days before. They start looking at the car and at me, not really listening to what I say.''

''Which detectives?''

''Brown and Wilcox. I knew both those bastards. Knew they hated my guts. I should have known not to trust them.''

''How'd you know that? How come they hated you?''

''Pachoula's a small place. Some folks like to see it just keep on keepin' on, as they say. I mean, they knew I had a future. They knew I was going to be somebody. They didn't like it. Didn't like my attitude, I guess.''

''Go on.''

''After I tell them, they say they need to take a statement from me in town, so off I go, not a complaint in the world. Christ! If I knew then what I know now . . . But you see, Mr. Cowart, I didn't think I had anything to fear. Hell, I barely knew what they were taking a statement about. They said it was a missing persons case. Not murder.''

''And.''

''Like I said in my letter, it was the last daylight I saw for thirty-six hours. They brought me into a little room like this one, sat me down and asked me if I wanted an attorney. I still didn't know what was going on, so I said no. Handed me a constitutional-rights form and told me to sign it. Damn, was I dumb! I should have known that when they sit a nigger in that chair in one of those rooms, the only way he's ever going to get to stand up again is when he tells them what they want to hear, whether he did it or not.''

All jocularity had disappeared from Ferguson's voice, replaced with a metallic edge of anger constrained by great pressure. Cowart felt swept along by the story he was hearing, as if caught in a tidal wave of words.

''Brown was the good cop. Wilcox, the bad cop. Oldest routine in the world.'' Ferguson almost spat in disgust.

''And?''

''I sit down, they start in asking me this, asking me that, asking me about this little girl that disappeared. I keep telling them I don't know nothing. They keep at it. All day. Right into the night. Hammering away. Same questions over and over, just like when I said 'No,' it didn't mean a damn thing. They keep going. No trips to the bathroom. No food. No drink. Just questions, over and over. Finally, after I don't know how many hours, they lose it. They're screaming at me something fierce and the next thing I know, Wilcox slaps me across the face. Wham!

Then he shoves his face down about six inches from mine and says, 'Have I got your attention now, boy?' ''

Ferguson looked at Cowart as if to measure the impact that his words were having, and continued in an even voice, filled with bitterness.

"He did, indeed. He kept screaming at me then. I remember thinking that he was going to have a heart attack or a stroke or something, he was so red in the face. It was like he was possessed or something. 'I want to know what you did to that little girl!' he screams. 'Tell me what you did to her!' He's shouting all the time and Brown walks out of the room so I'm alone with this madman. 'Tell me, did you fuck her and then kill her, or was it the other way around?' Man, he kept that up for hours. I kept saying no, no, no, what do you mean, what are you talking about. He showed me the pictures of the little girl and kept asking, 'Was it good? Did you like it when she fought? Did you like it when she screamed? Did you like it when you cut her the first time? How about when you cut her the twentieth time, was that good?' Over and over, over and over, hour after hour.''

Ferguson took a deep breath. "Every so often he would take a break, just leave me in that little room alone, cuffed to the chair. Maybe he went out, took a nap, got something to eat. He'd be out five minutes once, then a half hour or more. Left me sitting there a couple of hours one time. I just sat there, you know, too scared and too stupid to do a damn thing for myself.

"I guess he got frustrated, finally, with my refusing to confess, because eventually he started to whale on me. Started by just slapping me about the head and shoulders a bit more frequently. Stood me up once and punched me in the stomach. I was shaking. They wouldn't even take me to the can, and I wet myself. I didn't know what he was doing when he took the telephone book and rolled it up. Man, it was like being hit with a baseball bat. Knocked me right to the floor.''

Cowart nodded. He had heard of the technique. Hawkins had explained it to him one night. The telephone book had the impact of a leather sap, but the paper wouldn't cut the skin or really leave a bruise.

"I still wouldn't say anything, so finally he left. Brown comes in. I haven't seen him in hours. I'm just shaking and moaning and figuring I'm gonna die in that room. Brown looks at me. Picks me up off the floor. All sugar and spice. Man, he says he's sorry for everything that Wilcox has done. Man, he knows it hurts. He'll help me. He'll get me something to eat. He'll get me a Coke. He'll get me some fresh clothes and he'll let me go to the bathroom. Man, all I got to do is trust him. Trust him and tell him what I did to that little girl. I tell him nothing, but he keeps at it. He says, 'Bobby Earl, I think you're hurt bad. I think you're gonna be pissing blood. I think you need a doctor real bad. Just tell me what you did, and we'll take you right over to the infirmary.' I tell him I didn't do nothing and he loses it. He screams at me, 'We know what you did, you just got to tell us!' Then he takes out his weapon. It wasn't his regular gun, the one he wears on his hip, but a little snub-nosed thirty-eight he had hidden in an ankle holster. Wilcox comes in right then and cuffs me with my hands behind my back, grabs my head and holds it so I'm looking right down the barrel of that little gun. Brown says, 'Start in talking now.' I says, 'I didn't do anything!' and he pulls the trigger. Man! I can still see that finger curling around the trigger and tugging back so slow. I thought my heart stopped. It clicks down on an empty chamber. I'm crying now, just like a baby, blubbering away. He says, 'Bobby Earl, you got real lucky with that one. You think you're real lucky today? How many empty chambers I got in here?' He pulls the trigger again and it clicks again. 'Damn!' he says. 'I think it misfired.' And then he cracks open that little gun, swings the cylinder right out and pulls out a bullet. He looks at it real careful like and says, 'Man, how about that? A dud. Maybe it'll work this time.' And I watch him put it back into the gun. He points the gun right at me and says, 'Last chance, nigger.' And I believe him this time and I say, 'I did it, I did it, whatever you want, I did.' And that was the confession.''

Matthew Cowart took a deep breath and tried to digest the story. He suddenly felt that there was no air in the small inter-view room, as if the walls had grown hot and stifling, and he were baking in the abrupt heat. ''And?'' he asked.

''And now I'm here,'' Ferguson replied.

''You told this to your attorney?''

''Of course. He pointed out the obvious: There were two police detectives and just one of me. And there was a beautiful little dead white girl. Who do you think was going to get be-lieved?''

Cowart nodded. ''Why should I believe you now?''

''I don't know,'' Ferguson replied angrily. He glared at Cowart for an instant. ''Maybe because I'm telling the truth.''

''Would you take a polygraph test?''

''I took one for my attorney. Got the results right here. Damn thing came back 'Inconclusive.' I think I was too jumpy when they strapped all those wires onto me. Didn't do me no good at all. I'd take another one, if you want. Don't know if it'd do any good. Can't use it in court.''

"Of course. But I need some corroboration.''

"Right. I know that. But hell, that's what happened.''

"How can I prove that story, so I can put it in the paper?''

Ferguson thought for a moment, his eyes still burrowing into Cowart's. After a few seconds, a small smile tore through some of the intensity in the convicted man's face.

"The gun,'' he said. "That might do it.''

"How so?''

"Well, I remember before they took me into that little room, they made a big deal of checking their sidearms at the desk. I remember he had that little sucker hidden under his pants. I bet he'll lie to you about that gun, if you can figure out a way of tripping him up.''

Cowart nodded. "Maybe.''

The two men grew quiet again. Cowart looked down at the tape recorder and watched the tape spinning on its capstan. "Why did they pick you?'' he asked.

"I was convenient. I was right there. I was black. They made the green car. My blood type was the same—of course, they figured that out later. But I was there and the community was about to go crazy—I mean, the white community. They wanted somebody and they had me in their hand. Who better?''

"That seems like mighty convenient reasoning.''

Ferguson's eyes flashed, an instant moment of anger, and Cowart saw him ball his hand into a fist. He watched the prisoner fight and regain control.

"They always hated me there. Because I wasn't a dumb backwoods shuffling nigger like they were used to. They hated that I went to college. They hated that I knew all the big-city things I did. They knew me and they hated me. For what I was and for what I was going to be.''

Cowart started to ask a question, but Ferguson thrust both hands straight out, gripping the edge of the table to steady himself. His voice was barely contained, and Cowart felt the man's rage pour over him. He could see the sinews on the prisoner's neck stand out. His face was flushed, his voice had lost its steadiness and quavered with emotion. Cowart saw Ferguson struggling hard with himself, as if he were about to break under the stress of remembering. In that moment,

Cowart wondered what it would be like to stand in the way
of all that fury.

"You go there. You take a look at Pachoula. Escambia
County. It's right south from Alabama, not more than twenty,
thirty miles. Fifty years ago, they just would have hung me from
the nearest tree. They would have been wearing white suits with
little pointy hats and burning crosses. Times have changed," he
spoke bitterly, "but not that goddamn much. Now they've hung
up with all the benefits and trappings of civilization. I got a trial,
yes sir. I got an attorney, yes sir. A jury of my peers, yes sir. I
got to enjoy all my constitutional rights, yes sir. Why, this damn
lynching was nice and legal." Ferguson's voice shook with emotion. "You go there, Mr. White Reporter, and start asking some
questions and you'll see. You think this is the nineteen nineties?
You're gonna find out that things haven't moved along quite as
quickly. You'll see."

He sat back in the chair, glaring at Cowart.

The prison sounds seemed distant, as if they were separated
by miles from the walls, corridors, and cells. Cowart was suddenly aware how small the room was. This is a story about small
rooms, he thought. He could feel hatred flooding from the prisoner in great waves, an endless flow of frustration and despair,
and felt swept along with it.

Ferguson continued to stare across the table at Cowart, as if
considering his next words. "Come on, Mr. Cowart. Do you
think things work the same in Pachoula as they do in Miami?"

"No."

"Damn right they don't. Hell, you know the funniest thing?
If I had done this crime—which I didn't—but if I had, and it
was down in Miami? Well, you know what would have happened with the shabby evidence they had against me? I'd have
been offered a deal to second degree and sentenced to five to
life. Maybe do four years. And that's only if my public defender didn't get the whole thing thrown out. Which he would
have. I had no record. I was a college student. I had a future.
They had no evidence. What do you think, Mr. Cowart. In
Miami?"

"In Miami, you're probably right. A deal. No doubt."

"In Pachoula, death. No doubt."

"That's the system."

"Damn the system. Damn it to hell. And one more
thing: I didn't do it. I didn't damn do the crime. Hey, I
may not be perfect. Hell, up in Newark, I got into a couple

of scrapes as a teenager. Same thing down in Pachoula. You can check those out. But dammit, I didn't kill that little girl.''

Ferguson paused. ''But I know who did.''

They were both silent for an instant.

''Let's get to that,'' Cowart said. ''Who and how?''

Ferguson rocked back in his seat. Cowart saw a single smile, not a grin, not something that preceded a laugh, but a cruel scar on the man's face. He was aware that something had slipped from the room, some of the intensity of anger. Ferguson changed in those few seconds, just as effectively as he had earlier when he had changed accents.

''I can't tell you that yet,'' the prisoner replied.

''Bullshit,'' Cowart said, letting a touch of displeasure slip into his own voice. ''Don't be coy.''

Ferguson shook his head. ''I'll tell you,'' he said, ''but only when you believe.''

''What sort of game is this?''

Ferguson leaned forward, narrowing the space between the two men. He fixed Cowart with a steady, frightening glare. ''This is no fucking game,'' he said quietly. ''This is my fucking life. They want to take it and this is the best card I've got. Don't ask me to play it before I'm ready.''

Cowart did not reply.

''You go check out what I've told you. And then, when you believe I'm innocent, when you see those fuckers have railroaded me, then I'll tell you.''

When a desperate man asks you to play a game, Hawkins had once said, it's best to play by his rules.

Cowart nodded.

Both men were quiet. Ferguson locked his eyes onto Cowart's, watching for a response. Neither man moved, as if they were fastened together. Cowart realized that he no longer had any choice, that this was the reporter's dilemma: He had heard a man tell him a story of evil and wrongs. He was compelled to discover the truth. He could no more walk away from the story than he could fly.

''So, Mr. Cowart,'' Ferguson said, ''that's the story. Will you help me?''

Cowart thought of the thousands of words he'd written about death and dying, about all the stories of pain and agony that had flowed through him, leaving just the tiniest bit of scar tissue behind that had built up into so many sleeping nightmare visions. In all the stories he'd written, he'd never saved anyone from even a pinprick of despair. Certainly never saved a life.

"I'll do what I can," he replied.

THREE
════════════════PACHOULA

Escambia County is tucked away in the far northwest corner of Florida, touched on two borders by the state of Alabama. It shares its cultural kinship with the states to its immediate north. It was once primarily a rural area, with many small farms that rolled green over hillsides, separated by dense thickets of scrubby pine and the looped and tied tendrils of great willows and vines. But in recent years, as with much of the South, it has seen a burst of construction, a suburbanizing of its once country lands, as its major city, the port town of Pensacola, has expanded, growing shopping malls and housing developments where there was once open space. But, at the same time, it has retained a marshy commonality with Mobile, which is not far by interstate highway, and with the salt water tidal regions of the Gulf shore. Like many areas of the deep South, it has the contradictory air of remembered poverty and new pride, a sense of rigid place fueled by generations who have found the living there, if not necessarily easy, then better than elsewhere.

The evening commuter flight into the small airport was a frightening series of stomach-churning bumps and dips, passing along the edges of huge gray storm clouds that seemed to resent the intrusion of the twin-engine plane. The passenger compartment alternately filled with streaks of light and sudden dark as the plane cut in and out of the thick clouds and red swords of sunshine fading fast over the Gulf of Mexico. Cowart listened to the engines laboring against the winds, their pitch rising and falling like a racer's breath. He rocked in the cocoon of the plane, thinking about the man on Death Row and what awaited him in Pachoula.

Ferguson had stirred a war within him. He had come away from his meeting with the prisoner insisting to himself that he maintain objectivity, that he listen to everything and weigh every word equally. But at the same time, staring through the beads of water that marched across the plane's window, he knew that he would not be heading toward Pachoula if he expected to be dissuaded from the story. He clenched his fists in his lap as the small plane skidded across the sky, remembering Ferguson's voice, still feeling the man's ice-cold anger. Then he thought about the girl. Eleven years old. Not a time to die. Remember that, too.

The plane landed in a driving thunderstorm, careening down the runway. Through the window, Cowart saw a line of green trees on the airport edge, standing dark and black against the sky.

He drove his rental car through the enveloping darkness to the Admiral Benbow Inn just off the interstate, on the outskirts of Pachoula. After inspecting the modest, oppressively neat room, he went down to the bar in the motel, slid between two salesmen, and ordered a beer from the young woman. She had mousy brown hair that flounced around her face, drawing all the features in tight so that when she frowned, her whole face seemed to scowl along with her lips, an edgy toughness that spoke of handing too many drinks to too many salesmen and refusing too many offers of companionship issued over shaky hands clutching scotch and ginger ale. She drew the beer from a tap, eyeing Cowart the entire time, sensing when the froth from the beer was about to slide over the lip of the glass. "Y'all ain't from around here, are you?"

He shook his head.

"Don't tell me," she said. "I like to guess. Just say, the rain in Spain falls mainly in the plain."

He laughed and repeated the phrase.

She smiled at him, just losing a small edge from her distance. "Not from Mobile or Montgomery, that's for sure. Not even Tallahassee or New Orleans. Got to be two places: either Miami or Atlanta; but if it's Atlanta, then you ain't originally from there but from somewhere else, like New York, and you'd just be calling Atlanta home temporary-like."

"Not bad," he replied. "Miami."

She eyed him carefully, pleased with herself. "Let's see," she said. "I see a pretty nice suit, but real conservative, like a lawyer might wear. . . ." She leaned across the bar and rubbed her thumb and forefinger against the lapel of his jacket. "Nice. Not like the polyester princes selling livestock vitamin supplement that we get in here mainly. But the hair's a bit shaggy over the ears and I can see a couple of gray streaks just getting started. So you're a bit too old—what, about thirty-five?—to be running errands. If you were a lawyer that old, you'd damn well have to have some fresh-cheeked just-outa-school assistant you'd send here on business instead of coming yourself. Now, I don't figure you for a cop, 'cause you ain't got that look, and not real estate or business either. You don't have the look of a salesman, like these guys do. So now, what would bring a guy like you all the way up here from Miami? Only one thing left I can think of, so I'd guess you're a reporter here for some story."

He laughed. "Bingo. And thirty-seven."

She turned to draw another glass of beer, which she set in front of another man, then returned to Cowart. "You just passing through? Can't imagine what kinda story would bring you up here. There ain't much happening around here, in case you hadn't already noticed."

Cowart hesitated, wondering whether he should keep his mouth shut or not. Then he shrugged and thought, If she figured out who I was in the first two minutes, it isn't going to be much of a secret around here when I start talking to the cops and lawyers.

"A murder story," he said.

She nodded. "Had to be. Now you've got me interested. What sort of story? Hell, I can't remember the last killing we had around here. Now, can't say the same for Mobile or Pensacola. You looking at those drug dealers? Jesus, they say that there's cocaine coming in all up and down the Gulf, tons of it, every night. Sometimes we get some Spanish-speaking folks in here. Last week three guys came in, all wearing sharp suits and those little beeper things on their belts. They sat down like they owned the place and ordered a bottle of champagne before dinner. I had to send the boy out to the liquor store for it. Wasn't hard to figure out what they were celebrating."

"No, not drugs," Cowart said. "How long have you been here?"

"A couple of years. Came to Pensacola with my husband,

who was a flier. Now he still flies and he ain't my husband and I'm stuck here on the ground.''

"Do you remember a case, about three years old, a little girl named Joanie Shriver? Allegedly killed by a fellow named Robert Earl Ferguson?''

"Little girl they found by Miller's Swamp?''

"That's it.''

"I remember that one. It happened right when me and my old man, damn his eyes, got here. Just about my first week tending this bar.'' She laughed briefly. "Hell, I thought this damn job was always gonna be that exciting. Folks were real interested in that little girl. There were newspapermen from Tallahassee and television all the way from Atlanta. That's how I got to recognize your type. They all pretty much hung out here. Of course, there's no place else, really. It was quite a set-to for a couple of days, until they announced they caught the boy that killed her. But that was all back then. Ain't you a little late coming around?''

"I just heard about it.''

"But that boy's in prison. On Death Row.''

"There are some questions about how he got put there. Some inconsistencies.''

The woman put her head back and laughed. "Man,'' she said, "I don't bet that's gonna make a lot of difference. Good luck, Miami.''

Then she turned to help another customer, leaving Cowart alone with his beer. She did not return.

The morning broke clear and fast. The early sun seemed determined to erase every residual street puddle remaining from the rain the day before. The day's heat built steadily, mixing with an insistent humidity. Cowart could feel his shirt sticking to his back as he walked from the motel to his rental car, then drove through Pachoula.

The town seemed to have established itself with tenacity, situated on a flat stretch of land not far from the interstate, surrounded by farmland, serving as a sort of link between the two. It was a bit far north for successful orange groves, but he passed a few farms with well-ordered rows of trees, others with cattle grazing in the fields. He figured he was coming in on the prosperous side of the town; the houses were single-story cinder block or red-brick construction, the ubiquitous ranch houses that stand for a certain sort of status. They all had large television antennas. Some even had satellite dishes in their yards. As he closed on Pachoula, the roadside gave way to convenience stores and gas stations. He passed a small shopping center with a large grocery store, a card shop, a pizza parlor, and a restaurant clinging to the edges. He noticed that there were more houses stretched in the areas off the main street into town, more single-family, trim, well-kept homes that spoke of solidity and meager success.

The center of town was only a three-block square area, with a movie theater, some offices, some more stores, and a couple of stoplights. The streets were clean, and he wondered whether they had been swept by the storm the night before or by community diligence.

He drove through, heading away from the hardware stores, auto parts outlets, and fast-food restaurants, on a small, two-lane road. It seemed to him that there was a slight change in the land around him, a fallow brown streakiness that contradicted the lush green he'd seen moments earlier. The roadway grew bumpy and the houses he saw by the road were now wooden-frame houses, swaybacked with age, all painted a fading whitewashed pale color. The highway slid into a stand of trees, swallowing him with darkness. The variegated light pouring through the branches of the willows and pines made seeing his way difficult. He almost missed the dirt road cutting off to his left. The tires spun briefly in the mud before gaining some purchase, and he started bouncing down the road. It ran along a long hedgerow. Occasionally, over the top, he could see small farms. He slowed and passed three wooden shacks jumbled together at the edge of the dirt. An old black man stared at him as he slowly rolled past. He checked his odometer and drove another half mile, to another shack perched by the road. He pulled in front and got out of the car.

The shack had a front porch with a single rocker. There was a small chicken coop around the side, and chickens pecked away in the dirt. The road ended in the front yard. An old Chevy station wagon, with its hood up, was parked around the side.

A steady, solid heat washed over him. He heard a dog bark in the distance. The rich brown dirt that served as a front yard was packed hard underfoot, solid enough to have survived the previous evening's rainstorm. He turned and saw that the house stared out across a wide field, lined by dark forest.

Cowart hesitated, then approached the front porch.

When he put his foot on the first step, he heard a voice call out from inside, "I see you. Now what y'all want?"

He stopped and replied, "I'm looking for Mrs. Emma Mae Ferguson."

"Whatcha need her for?"

"I want to talk to her."

"You ain't tellin' me nothin'. Whatcha need her for?"

"I want to talk to her about her grandson."

The front door, half of it screen that was peeling away from the cracked wood, opened slightly. An old black woman with gray hair pulled severely behind her head stepped out. She was slight of frame, but sinewy, and moved slowly, but with a firmness of carriage that seemed to imply that age and brittle bones didn't really mean much more than inconvenience.

"You police?"

"No. I'm Matthew Cowart. From *The Miami Journal.* I'm a reporter."

"Who sent you?"

"Nobody sent me. I just came. Are you Mrs. Ferguson?"

"Mebbe."

"Please, Mrs. Ferguson, I want to talk about Robert Earl."

"He's a good boy and they took him away from me."

"Yes, I know. I'm trying to help."

"How can you help? You a lawyer? Lawyers done enough wrong for that boy already."

"No, ma'am. Please, could we just sit and talk for a few minutes? I don't mean to do anything except try to help your grandson. He told me to come and see you."

"You saw my boy?"

"Yes."

"How they treating him?"

"He seemed fine. Frustrated, but fine."

"Bobby Earl was a good boy. A real good boy."

"I know. Please."

"All right, Mr. Reporter. I'll sit and listen. Tell me what you want to know."

The old woman nodded her head at the rocker and moved gingerly toward it. She motioned toward the top step on the porch, and Matthew Cowart sat down, almost at her feet.

"Well, ma'am, what I need to know about are three days almost three years ago. I need to know what Robert Earl was doing on the day the little girl disappeared, on the next day, and the day after that, when he was arrested. Do you remember those times?''

She snorted. "Mr. Reporter, I may be old, but I ain't dumb. My eyesight may not be as good as it once was, but my memory is fine. And how in the Lord's name would I ever forget those days, after all that's come and passed since?''

"Well, that's why I'm here.''

She squinted down at him through the porch shade. "You sure you're here to help Bobby Earl?''

"Yes, ma'am. As best as I can.''

"How're you gonna help him? What can you do that that sharp-talking lawyer cain't do?''

"Write a story for the paper.''

"Papers already written a whole lot of stories about Bobby Earl. They mostly helped put him in the Death Row there, best as I can figure it.''

"I don't think this would be the same.''

"Why not?''

He didn't have a ready answer for that question. After a moment, he replied, "Look, Mrs. Ferguson, ma'am, I can hardly make things worse. And I still need some answers if I'm going to help.''

The old woman smiled at him again. "That's true. All right, Mr. Reporter. Ask your questions.''

"On the day of the little girl's murder . . .''

"He was right here with me. All day. Didn't go out, except in the morning to catch some fish. Bass. I remember because we fried them for dinner that night.''

"Are you sure?''

"Of course I'm sure. Where was he to go?''

"Well, he had his car.''

"And I'da heard it if he started it up and drove off. I ain't deaf. He didn't go nowheres that day.''

"Did you tell this to the police?''

"Sure did.''

"And?''

"They didn't believe me. They said, 'Emma Mae, you sure he didn't slip away in the afternoon? You sure he didn't leave your sight? Mebbe you took a nap or somethin'.' But I didn't, and I tole them so. Then they tole me I was just plain wrong and they got angry and they went off. I never saw them much again.''

"What about Robert Earl's attorney?''

"Asked the same damn questions. Same damn answers. Didn't believe me none, either. Said I had too much reason to lie, to cover up for that boy. That was true. He was my darlin' gal's boy and I loved him plenty. Even when he went off'n to New Jersey and then came back all street tough and talking trash and actin' so hard, I still loved him fine. And he was doing good, too, mind you. He was my college boy. Can you imagine that, Mr. White Reporter? You look around you. You think a lot of us get to go to college? Make somethin' of ourselves? How many you figure?"

She snorted again and waited for an answer, which he didn't offer. After a moment, she continued. "That was true. My boy. My best boy. My pride. Sure I'da lied for him. But I didn't. I'm a believer in Jesus, but to save my boy I'da hopped up to the devil hisself and spat in his eye. I just never got the chance, 'cause they didn't believe in me, no sir."

"But the truth is?"

"He was here with me."

"And the next day?"

"Here with me."

"And when the police came?"

"He was right outside, polishing that old car of his. Didn't give them no lip. No trouble. Just yes sir, no sir and went right along. See what it did for him?"

"You sound angry."

The small woman pitched forward in the chair, her entire body rigid with emotion. She slapped her palms down hard on the arms of the rocker, making two pistol shots that echoed in the clear morning air.

"Angry? Y'all asking me if I'm angry? They done tore my boy from me and sent him away so they's can kill him. I ain't got the words in me to tell you about no anger. I ain't got the evil in me that I could say what I really and truly feel."

She got up out of the chair and started to walk back inside. "I ain't got nothing but hate and bitter empty left, Mr. Reporter. You write that down good."

Then she disappeared into the shack's shadows, clacking the door shut hard behind her, leaving Matthew Cowart scribbling her words into his notepad.

It was noontime when he arrived at the school. It was very much the way he had pictured it, a solid, unimaginative cinder-block building with an American flag hanging limply in the

humid air outside. There were yellow school buses parked
around the side and a playground with swings and basketball
hoops and a fine covering of dust in back. He parked and approached the school, slowly feeling the wave of children's voices
rise up and carry him forward. It was the lunch hour and there
was a certain contained mayhem within the double doors. Children quickstepped about, clutching paper bags or lunch boxes,
buzzing with conversation. The walls of the school were decorated with their artwork, splashes of color and shape arranged
in displays, with small signs explaining what the artwork represented. He stared at the pictures for an instant, reminded of
all the drawings and colored paper and glue montages he was
forever receiving in the mail from his own daughter and which
now decorated his office. He pushed past, heading through a
vestibule toward a door marked ADMINISTRATION. It swung open
as he approached and he saw two girls exit, giggling together in
great secret animation. One was black, the other white. He
watched them disappear down a corridor. His eyes caught a
small framed picture hanging on a wall, and he went over to
look at it.

It was a little girl's picture. She had blond hair, freckles, and
a wide smile, displaying a mouth filled with braces. She wore a
clean white shirt with a gold chain around her neck. He could
read the name "Joanie" stamped in thin letters in the center of
the chain. There was a small plaque beneath the picture. It read:

Joanie Shriver
1976–1987
Our Friend and Beloved Classmate
She will be missed by all

He added the picture on the wall to all the mental observations
he was accumulating. Then he turned away and walked inside
the school's office.

A middle-aged woman with a slightly harried air looked up
from behind a counter. "Can I help you?"

"Yes. I'm looking for Amy Kaplan."

"She was just here. Is she expecting you?"

"I spoke with her on the phone the other day. My name is
Cowart. I'm from Miami."

"You're the reporter?"

He nodded.

"She said you were going to be here. Let me see if I can find her." There was a note of bitterness in the woman's voice. She did not smile at Cowart.

The woman stood up and walked across the office, disappearing for an instant into the faculty lounge, then reemerging with a young woman. Cowart saw she was pretty, with a sweep of auburn hair pushed back from an open, smiling face.

"I'm Amy Kaplan, Mr. Cowart."

They shook hands.

"I'm sorry to interrupt your lunch."

She shrugged. "Probably the best time. Still, like I said on the telephone, I'm not sure what I can do for you."

"The car," he said. "And what you saw."

"You know, it's probably best if I show you where I was standing. I can explain it there."

They walked outside without saying anything. The young teacher stood by the front of the school and turned, pointing down a roadway. "See," she said, "we always have a teacher out here, checking on the kids after school. It used to be mostly to make sure the boys don't get into fights and the girls head straight home, instead of hanging around and gossiping. Kids do that, you know, more'n anybody it seems. Now, of course, there's another reason to be out here."

She looked over at him, eyeing him for an instant. Then she went on. ". . . Anyway, on the afternoon Joanie disappeared, just about everyone had cleared off and I was about to go back inside, when I spotted her, down by the big willow over there. . . ." She pointed perhaps fifty yards down the road. Then she put her hand to her mouth and hesitated.

"Oh, God," she said.

"I'm sorry," Cowart said.

He watched the young woman fixing her eyes on the spot down the road as if she could see it all again, in her memory, in that moment. He saw her lip quiver just the slightest bit, but she shook her head to tell him she was all right.

"It's okay. I was young. It was my first year. I remember, she saw me and turned and waved, that's how I knew it was her." Some of the firmness of her voice had slid away in the heat.

"And?"

"She walked just under the shadows there, right past the green car. I saw her turn, I guess because somebody'd said something to her, and then the door opened, and she got inside. The car pulled away.''

The young woman took a deep breath. ''She just got right in. Damn.'' She whispered the swearword under her breath. ''Just right in, Mr. Cowart, as if she hadn't a care in the world. Sometimes I still see her, in my dreams. Waving at me. I hate it.''

Cowart thought of his own nightmares and wanted to turn to the young woman and tell her that he, too, didn't sleep at night. But he didn't.

''That's what's always bothered me,'' Amy Kaplan continued. ''I mean, in a way, if she'd been grabbed and struggled or called for help or something . . .'' The woman's voice was broken with remembered emotion, ''. . . I might have done something. I'd have screamed and maybe run after her. Maybe I could have fought or done something. I don't know. Something. But it was just a regular May afternoon. And it was so hot, I wanted to get back inside, so I didn't really look.''

Cowart stared down the street, measuring distances. ''It was in the shadows?''

''Yes.''

''But you're sure it was green. Dark green?''

''Yes.''

''Not black?''

''You sound like the detectives and the attorneys. Sure, it could have been black. But my heart and my memory say dark green.''

''You didn't see a hand, pushing open the door from inside?''

She hesitated. ''That's a good question. They didn't ask that. They asked me if I saw the driver. He would have had to lean across to open the door. I couldn't see him. . . .'' She strained with recall. ''No. No hand. Just the door swinging open.''

''And the license plates?''

''Well, you know, Florida plates have that orange outline of the state on a white background. All I really noticed was that these were darker and from somewhere else.''

''When did they show you Robert Earl Ferguson's car?''

''They just showed me a picture, a couple of days later.''

''You never saw the car itself?''

''Not that I recall. Except on the day she disappeared.''

''Tell me about the picture.''

''There were a couple, like taken by an instant camera.''

''What view?''

''I beg your pardon?''

"What angle did they take the pictures from?"

"Oh, I see. Well, they were from the side."

"But you saw the car from the back."

"That's right. But the color was right. And the shape was the same. And . . ."

"And what?"

"Nothing."

"You would have seen the brake lights when the car took off. When the driver put it into gear, the brake lights would have flashed. Would you remember what shape they were?"

"I don't know. They didn't ask me that."

"What did they ask?"

"There wasn't a lot. Not by the police. Not at the trial. I was so nervous, getting up there to testify, but it was all over in a few seconds."

"What about the cross-examination?"

"He just asked me whether I was sure about the color, like you did. And I said I could be wrong, but I didn't think so. That seemed to please him real well, and that was it."

Cowart looked down the roadway again, then at the young woman. She seemed resolved to the memories, her eyes staring off away from him.

"Do you think he did it?"

She breathed in and thought for an instant. "He was convicted."

"But what do you think?"

She took a deep breath. "The thing that always bothered me was that she just got into the car. Didn't seem to hesitate for an instant. If she didn't know him, why, I can't see why she'd do that. We try to teach the kids to be safe kids and smart kids, Mr. Cowart. We have classes in safety. In never trusting a stranger. Even here in Pachoula, though you might not believe it. We aren't so backwoods backwards as you probably think. A lot of people come here from the city, like I did. There's people here, too, professional people who commute down to Pensacola or over to Mobile, because this is a safe, friendly place. But the kids are taught to be safe. They learn. So I never understood that. It never made sense to me that she just got into that car."

He nodded. "That's a question I have, too," he said.

She turned angrily toward him. "Well, the first damn person I'd ask is Robert Earl Ferguson."

He didn't reply, and in a moment she softened. "I'm sorry for snapping at you. We all blame ourselves. Everyone at the school. You don't know what it was like, with the other children. Kids were afraid to come to school. When they got here, they were too afraid to listen. At home they couldn't sleep. And when they did sleep, they had nightmares. Tantrums. Bed-wettings. Sudden bursts of anger or tears. The kids with discipline problems got worse. The kids who were withdrawn and moody got worse. The normal, everyday, ordinary kids had trouble. We had school meetings. Psychologists from the university came down to help the kids. It was awful. It will always be awful.''

She looked around her. ''I don't know, but it was like something broke here that day, and no one really knows if it can ever be fixed.''

They remained silent for an instant. Finally, she asked, ''Have I helped?''

''Sure. Do you mind just one more question?'' he replied. ''And I might have to get back to you after I talk with some of the other people involved. Like the cops.''

''That'd be okay,'' she said. ''You know where to find me. Shoot.''

He smiled. ''Just tell me what it was that went through your mind a couple of minutes ago, when we were talking about the pictures of the car, and you cut it off.''

She stopped and frowned. ''Nothing,'' she replied.

He looked at her.

''Oh, well, there was something.''

''Yes?''

''When the police showed me the pictures, they told me that they had the killer. That he'd confessed and everything. My identifying the car was just a formality, they said. I didn't realize that it was so important until months later, just before the trial. That always bugged me, you know. They showed me pictures, said, 'Here's the killer's car, right?' And I looked at them and said, 'Sure.' I don't know, it always bothered me they did it that way.''

Cowart didn't say anything but thought, It bothers me, too.

A newspaper story is a compilation of moments, accumulated in quotations, in the shift of a person's eyes, in the cut of their clothes. It adds in words the tiny observations of the reporter, what he sees, how he hears. It is buttressed by the past, by a sturdy foundation of detail. Cowart knew that he needed to acquire more substance, and he spent the afternoon reading newspaper clippings in the library of *The Pensacola News*. It helped

him to understand the unique frenzy that had overtaken the town
when the little girl's mother had called the police to say that her
daughter hadn't come home from school. There had been a
small-town explosion of concern. In Miami, the police would
have told the mother that they couldn't do anything for twenty-
four hours. And they would have assumed that the girl was a
runaway, fleeing from a beating, from a stepfather's sexual ad-
vances, or into the arms of some boyfriend, hanging out by the
high school in a new black Pontiac Firebird.

Not in Pachoula. The local police started cruising the streets
immediately, searching for the girl. They had ridden with bull-
horns, calling her name, up the back roads surrounding the town.
The fire department had assisted, sirens starting up and wailing
throughout the quiet May evening. Telephones started ringing
in all the residential neighborhoods. Word had spread with
alarming swiftness up and down each side street. Small groups
of parents had gathered and started walking the backyards, all
searching for little Joanie Shriver. Scouts were mobilized. People left their businesses early to join in the search. As the long
early-summer night started to slide down, it must have seemed
as if the whole town was outside, hunting for the child.

Of course, she was already dead then, he thought. She was
dead the moment she stepped off the curb into that car.

The search had continued with spotlights and a helicopter
brought in that night from the state police barracks near Pensacola. It had buzzed, its rotors throbbing, its spotlight probing
the darkness, past midnight. In the first morning light, tracker
dogs were brought in and the hunt had widened. By noontime
the town had gathered itself like an army camp preparing itself
for a long march, all documented by the arrival of television
cameras and newspaper reporters.

The little girl's body had been discovered in the late afternoon
by two firemen diligently searching the edge of the swamp,
walking through the sucking ooze in hip waders, swatting at
mosquitoes and calling the little girl's name. One of the men
had spotted a flash of blond hair at the edge of the water, just
caught by the dying light.

He imagined the news must have savaged the town, just as
surely as the girl's body had been savaged. He realized two
things: To be picked up for questioning in the death of Joanie
Shriver was to have stepped into the center of a whirlwind; and
the pressure on the two police detectives to catch the killer had

to have been immense. Perhaps, he thought, unbearably immense.

Hamilton Burns was a small, florid, gray-haired man. His voice, like so many others in Pachoula, tinged with the rhythmic locutions of the South. It was late in the day, and as he motioned to Matthew Cowart to sit in an overstuffed red leather chair, he mentioned something about the "sun being over the yardarm," and fixed himself a tumbler of bourbon after magically producing a bottle from a bottom desk drawer. Cowart shook his head when the bottle was proffered in his direction. "Need a bit of ice," Burns said, and he went to a corner of the small office, where a half-sized refrigerator stacked high with legal documents occupied some precious floor space. Cowart noticed that he limped as he walked. He looked around the office. It was paneled in wood, with legal books filling one wall. There were several framed diplomas and a testimonial from the local Knights of Columbus. There were a few pictures of a grinning Hamilton Burns arm in arm with the governor and other politicians.

The lawyer took a long pull at his glass, sat back, swiveling in his seat behind the desk opposite Cowart and said, "So y'all want to know about Robert Earl Ferguson. What can I tell you? I think he's got a shot on appeal for a new trial, especially with that old sonuvabitch Roy Black handling his case."

"On what issue?"

"Why, that damn confession, what else? Judge shoulda suppressed the shit out of it."

"We'll get to that. Can you start by telling me how you came into the case?"

"Oh, court appointment. Judge calls me up, asks me if I'll handle it. Regular public defenders were overburdened, like always. I guess a little too hot for 'em, anyway. Folks was screaming for that boy's neck. I don't think they wanted any part of Ferguson. No sir, no way."

"And you took it?"

"When the judge calls, you answer. Hell, most of my cases are court appointed. I couldn't rightly turn this one down."

"You billed the court twenty thousand dollars afterwards."

"It takes a lot of time to defend a killer."

"At a hundred bucks an hour?"

"Hell, I lost money on the deal. Hell's bells, it was weeks before anybody'd even talk to me again in this town. People acted like I was some kind of pariah. A Judas. All for representing that boy. Walk down the street, no more 'Good morning, Mr. Burns.' 'Nice day, Mr. Burns.' People'd cross the street to avoid talking to me. This is a small town. You figure out how much I lost in cases that went to other attorneys because I'd represented Bobby Earl. You figure that out before you go criticizing me for what I got.''

The attorney looked discomfited. Cowart wondered whether he thought it was he that had gotten convicted, instead of Ferguson.

"Had you ever handled a murder case before?"

"A couple."

"Chair cases?"

"No. Mostly like domestic disputes. You know, husband and wife get to arguing and one of them decides to underscore their point with a handgun. . . ." He laughed. "That'd be manslaughter, murder two at worse. I handle a lot of vehicular homicides and the like. Councilman's boy gets drunk and smashes up a car. But hell, defending somebody from a jaywalking charge and defending someone from murder's the same in the long run. You got to do what you got to do."

"I see," Cowart said, writing quickly in his notepad and for the instant avoiding the eyes of the lawyer. "Tell me about the defense."

"There ain't that much to tell. I moved for a change of venue. Denied. I moved to suppress the confession. Denied. I went to Bobby Earl and said, 'Boy, we got to plead guilty. First-degree murder. Go on down, take the twenty-five years, no parole. Save your life.' That way, he'd still have some living left to do when he gets out. 'No way,' the boy says. Stubborn-like. Got that fuck-you kind of attitude. Keeps right on saying, 'I didn't do it.' So what's left for me? I tried to pick a jury that warn't prejudiced. Good luck. Case went on. I argued reasonable doubt till I was fair blue in the face. We lost. What's to tell?"

"How come you didn't call his grandmother with an alibi?"

"Nobody'd believe her. You met that little old battle-ax? All she knows is her darling grandson is well-nigh perfect and wouldn't hurt a flea. 'Course, she's the only one that believes that. She gets on the stand and starts lying, things gonna be worse. Mighty worse."

"I don't see how they could be worse than what happened."

"Well, that's hindsight, Mr. Cowart, and you know it."

"Suppose she was telling the truth?"

"She might be. It was a judgment call."

"The car?"

"That damn teacher even admitted it could have been a different color. Sheeit. Said it right on the stand. I can't understand why the jury didn't buy it."

"Did you know that the police showed her a picture of Ferguson's car after telling her he'd confessed?"

"Say what? No. She didn't say that when I deposed her."

"She said it to me."

"Well, I'll be damned."

The lawyer poured himself another drink and gulped at it. No, you won't be, Cowart thought. But Ferguson will.

"What about the blood evidence?"

"Type O positive. Fits half the males in the county, I'd wager. I cross-examined the technicians on that, and why they didn't type it down to its enzyme base better, or do genetic screening or some other fancy shit. Of course, I knew the answer: They had a match and they didn't want to do something special that might screw it up. So, hell, it just seemed to fit. And there was Robert Earl, sitting there in the trial, squirming away, looking hangdog and guilty as sin. It just didn't do no good."

"The confession?"

"Shoulda been suppressed. I think they beat it out of that boy. I do, sir. That I do. But hell, once it was in, that was the whole ball of wax, if you know what I mean. Ain't no juror gonna disagree with that boy's own words. Every time they asked him, 'Did ya'll do this, or did y'all do that,' and he answered, 'Yes, sir.' 'Yes, sir.' 'Yes, sir.' All those yes, sirs. Couldn't do much about them. That was all she wrote. I tried, sir, I tried my best. I argued reasonable doubt. I argued lack of conclusive evidence. I asked those jurors, Where is the murder weapon? Something that positively points at Bobby Earl. I told them you can't just kill someone and not have some sort of mark on you. But he didn't. I argued upside and downside, rightside and leftside, over, under, around, and through. I promise you, sir, I did. It just didn't do any damn good. I kept looking over at those folks sitting in the box and I knew right away that it didn't make no damn difference what I said. All they could hear was that damn confession. His own words just staring at him off the page. Yes, sir. Yes, sir. Yes, sir. Put himself right in that electric chair, he did, just like he was pulling up a seat at the dinner table. People here was mighty upset with what happened to that little girl and they wanted to like get it finished, get it over, get it all done with right fast, so they could go on living the way they was used to. And you couldn't find two folks in this town who'd a got up and said a nice thing about that boy. Something about him, you know, attitude and all. No sir, no one liked him. Not even the black folks. Now I'm not saying there weren't no prejudice involved . . ."

"All-white jury. You couldn't find one black qualified?"

"I tried, sir. I tried. Prosecution just used their peremptory challenges to whack each and every one right off the panel."

"Didn't you object?"

"Objection overruled. Noted for the record. Maybe that'll work on appeal."

"Doesn't it bother you?"

"How so?"

"Well, what you're saying is that Ferguson didn't get a fair trial and that he may be innocent. And he's sitting right now on Death Row."

The lawyer shrugged. "I don't know," he said slowly. "Yeah, the trial, well, that's right. But innocent. Hell, his own words. That damn confession."

"But you said you believed they beat it out of him."

"I do, sir. But . . ."

"But what?"

"I'm old-fashioned. I like to believe that if'n you didn't do something, there's nothing in the world'll make you say you did. That bothers me."

"Of course," Cowart responded coldly, "the law is filled with examples of coerced and manipulated confessions, right?"

"That's correct."

"Hundreds. Thousands."

"That's correct."

The lawyer looked away, his face flushed red. "I guess. Of course, now what with Roy Black on the case, and now you're here, maybe gonna write a little something that'll wake up that trial judge or maybe something that the governor can't miss, well, things have a way of working their ways right out."

"It'll work out?"

"Things do. Even justice. Takes time."

"Well, it sounds like he didn't have much of a chance the first time."

"You asking me for my opinion?"

"Yes."

"No, sir. No chance."

Especially with you arguing his case, Cowart thought. More

worried about your standing in Pachoula than putting someone on the Row.

The lawyer leaned back in his chair and swished his drink nervously around in his hand so that the bourbon and ice tinkled.

Night like impenetrable black water covered the town. Cowart moved slowly through the streets, stepping through the odd lights tossed from streetlamps or from storefront displays that remained lit. But these moments of dull brightness were small; it was as if with the sun falling, Pachoula gave itself over completely to the darkness. There was a country freshness in the air, a palpable quiet. He could hear his own footsteps as they slapped at the pavement.

He had difficulty falling asleep that night. Motel sounds—a loud, drunken voice, a creaking bed in the next room, a door slamming, the ice and soda machines being used—all intruded on his imagination, interrupting his sorting through of what he'd learned and what he'd seen. It was well past midnight when sleep finally buried him, but it was an awful rest.

In his dreams, he was driving a car slowly through the riot-lit streets of midnight Miami. Light from burning buildings caressed the car, tossing shadows across the front. He had driven slowly, maneuvering carefully to avoid broken glass and debris in the roadway, all the time aware he was closing in on the center of the riot but knowing that it was his job to see it and record it. As he had pulled the car around a corner, he spotted the dream mob, dancing, looting, racing through the flickering fire lights toward him. He could see the people shouting, and it seemed to him they were calling his name. Suddenly, in the car next to him, a piercing voice screamed, panic-stricken. He turned and saw that it was the little murdered girl. Before he could ask what was she doing there, the car was surrounded. He saw Robert Earl Ferguson's face and suddenly felt dozens of hands pulling him from behind the wheel as the car was rocked, pitching back and forth as if it were a ship lost at sea in a hurricane. He saw the girl being pulled from the car, but as she slipped from his wild, grasping hands, her face changed terribly and he heard the words "Daddy, save me!"

He awakened, gasping for breath. He staggered from the bed, got himself a glass of water, and stared into the bathroom mirror as if looking for some visible wound, but seeing only a ridge of sweat plastering his hair by his forehead. Then he went back and sat by the window, remembering.

Some half-dozen years earlier, he had watched the frenzy as a mob pulled two teenage boys from a van. The boys had been white, the attackers black. The teenagers had unwittingly wandered into the riot area, gotten lost, tried to escape, only to drive themselves farther into the melee. *I wish it were a dream,* he thought. *I wish I hadn't been there.* The crowd had surged about the screaming youths, pushing and pulling them, tossing them about until finally they had both disappeared beneath a siege of kicking feet and pummeling fists, crushed down by rocks, shot by pistols. He had been a block distant, not close enough to be a helpful eyewitness for the police, just close enough to never forget what he saw. He had been hiding in the lee of a burning building beside a photographer who kept clicking pictures and cursing that he didn't have a long lens. They waited through the deaths, finally seeing the two mangled bodies abandoned in the street. He had run then, when the mob had finished and had poured in another direction, back to his car, trying to escape the same fate, knowing he would never escape the vision. Many people had died that night.

He remembered writing his story in the newsroom, as helpless as the two young men he'd seen die, trapped by the images that slid from him onto the page.

But at least I didn't die, he thought.

Just a tiny part of me.

He shuddered again, turned it into a shrug, and rose, stretching and flexing his muscles as if to reinvigorate himself. He needed to be alert, he admonished himself. Today he would interview the two detectives. He wondered what they would say. And whether he could believe any of it.

Then he went to the shower, as if by letting the water flow steadily over him, he could cleanse his memory as well.

FOUR
―――――*THE DETECTIVES*

A SECRETARY in the major-crimes offices of the Escambia County Sheriff's Department pointed Matthew Cowart toward a lumpy fake-leather couch, and told him to wait while she contacted the two detectives. She was a young woman, probably pretty but with a face marred by a frowning boredom, her hair pulled back severely and a rigid set to her shoulders beneath the dull brown of her policewoman's uniform. He thanked her and took a seat. The woman dialed a number and spoke quietly, so that he was unable to make out what she was saying. "Someone'll be here in a couple," the woman said to him as she hung up the phone. Then she turned away, examining some paperwork on her desk, studiously ignoring him. So, he thought, everyone knows why I'm here.

The homicide division was in a new building adjacent to the county lockup. It had a modern quiet to it, the noise disappearing in the thick brown carpet and baffled by stark white wall partitions that separated the detectives' desks from the waiting area where Cowart cooled his heels. He tried to concentrate on his upcoming interview but found his mind wandering. The quiet was disconcerting.

He found himself thinking of his home. His father had been the managing editor of a small daily paper in a midsize New England city, a mill town that had grown up into something more important, thanks to some lucky investments by large corporations that brought in money and new blood and a certain undeniable quaintness in the local architecture. He was a distant man who worked hard, leaving before light, coming home after dark. He wore simple blue or gray suits that seemed to hang from an ascetic's lean body; an angular sharp man, not quick to smile, fingertips stained with nicotine and newsprint.

His father had been possessed, mostly with the never-ending ins and outs, details and dramatics, of the daily paper. What had electrified his father had been the gathering of news, a story, particularly one that burst on the front page, crying for attention. An aberration, an evil, some wrongdoing—then his father's rigidity relaxed, and he would spin with a sort of jumpy, exhausting delight, like a dancer hearing music for the first time after years of silence. In those moments, his father was like a terrier, ready to latch on to something and bite tightly, worrying it to oblivion.

Am I that different? he wondered. Not really. His ex-wife used to call him a romantic, as if it were an insult. A knight-errant—he looked up and saw a man enter the waiting area—but, he thought, with the heart of a bulldog.

"You Cowart?" the man asked, not unfriendly.

Cowart rose. "That's right."

"I'm Bruce Wilcox." The man held out his hand. "Come on, it'll be a few minutes before Lieutenant Brown gets back in. We can talk back here."

The detective led Cowart through a warren of desks to a glass-walled office in a corner, overseeing the work area. There was a title on the door: LT. T.A. BROWN, HOMICIDE DIVISION. Wilcox closed the door and settled behind a large gray desk, motioning to Cowart to take a seat in front of him. "We had a small plane crash this morning," he said as he began arranging some documents on the desk. "Little Piper Cub on a training run. Tanny had to go to the site and supervise the recovery of the student and the pilot. Guys went down at the edge of a swamp. Messy business. First you've got to wade through all that muck to get to the plane. Then you've got to haul the guys out. I heard there was a fire. Ever have to try to handle a burned body? God, it's a mess. A righteous mess."

The detective shook his head, clearly pleased that he'd managed to avoid this particular assignment.

Cowart looked at the detective. He was a compact, short man, with long but slicked-back hair and an easygoing manner, probably in his late twenties. Wilcox had taken off his sportcoat—a loud, red-checked design—and slung it over the back of the chair. He rocked in his seat like a man wanting to put his feet up on the desk. Cowart saw a set of wide shoulders and powerful arms more suited to a man considerably bigger.

". . . Anyway," the detective continued, "hauling bodies is one of the drawbacks to the job. Usually it's me that gets the duty . . ." He held up his arm and made a muscle. "I wrestled in high school, and I ain't big, so I can squeeze into some space half the size of most of the other guys. I expect down in Miami they got technicians and rescue people and the like who get to fiddly-fuck about with dead folks. Up here, it kinda falls to us. Everybody dead is our business. First, we figure out if there was or wasn't a murder. Of course, that's not so hard when you've got a crashed plane smoldering on the ground in front of you. Then we ship them off to the morgue."

"So, how's business?" Cowart asked.

"Death is always steady work," the detective replied. He laughed briefly. "No layoffs. No furloughs. No slack time. Just good, steady work. Hell, they ought to have a union just for homicide detectives. There's always someone up and dying."

"What about murders? Up here . . ."

"Well, you're probably aware that we've got a drug problem up and down the Gulf Coast. Isn't that a great way of putting it? A drug problem. Makes it sound kinda cute. More like a drug hurricane, if you ask me. Anyway, it does create a bit of extra business, no doubt."

"That's something new."

"That's right. Just the last couple of years."

"But before the drug trade?"

"Domestic disputes. Vehicular homicides. Occasionally, a couple of good old boys will get to shooting or stabbing over cards or women or dog fights. That's pretty much the norm for the county. We get some big-city troubles in Pensacola a bit. Especially with the servicemen. Bar fights, you know. There's a good deal of prostitution about the base, and that leads to some cutting and shooting as well. Butterfly knives and little pearl-handled thirty-two-caliber handguns. Pretty much what you'd expect, like I said. Nothing too unusual."

"But Joanie Shriver?"

The detective paused, thinking before answering. "She was different."

"Why?"

"She was just different. She was just . . ." He hesitated, suddenly forcing his hand into a clenched fist and waving it in the air in front of him. "Everybody felt it. She was . . ." He interrupted himself again, taking a deep breath. "We ought to wait for Tanny. It was his case, really."

"I thought his name was Theodore."

"It is. Tanny's his nickname. It was his dad's before him. His dad used to run a little leather tanning business on the side. Always had that red dye color to his hands and arms. Tanny worked with him, right through high school, summers home from college. Picked up the nickname, just the same. I don't think anyone, except his momma, ever called him Theodore." He pronounced the name *See-oh-door*.

"Both of you guys are local? I mean . . ."

"I know what you mean. Sure, but Tanny's ten years older than me. He grew up in Pachoula. Went to the high school. He was quite an athlete in those days. Went off to Florida State to play football but ended up slogging about in the jungle with the First Air Cavalry. Came back with some medals and finished school and got a job on the force. Me, I was a navy brat. My dad was the shore patrol superintendent at the base for years. I just hung on after high school. Did a bit of junior college. Took the police academy exam and stayed. It was my dad steered me into police work."

"How long have you been working homicide?"

"Me? About three years. Tanny's been at it longer."

"Like it?"

"It's different. A lot more interesting than driving a patrol car. You get to use your head." He tapped himself on the forehead.

"And Joanie Shriver?"

The detective hunched his shoulders together as if drawing inward. "She was my first real case. I mean, most murders, you know, they're subject murders, that's what we call them. You arrive on the scene and there's the murderer standing right next to the victim. . . ."

That was true. Cowart remembered Vernon Hawkins saying when he went to the scene of a murder he always looked first for the person who wasn't crying but was standing wide-eyed, in shock, confused. That was the killer.

". . . Or else, now, these drug things. But that's just collecting the bodies for the most part. You know what they call them down at the state attorney's office? Felony littering. You don't ever really expect to make a murder case on a body found out in the water, that's been floating about for three days, that doesn't have any ID and not much of a face after the fish get finished. Single gunshot wound to the back of the head. Designer jeans and gold chains. No, those you just tag and bag, yes sir. But little Joanie, man, she had a face. She wasn't some anonymous Colombian drug runner. She was different.''

He paused, thinking. Then he added, ''She was like everybody's little sister.''

Detective Wilcox appeared about ready to say something else when the telephone on the desk rang. He picked it up, grunted a few words in greeting, listened, then handed it over to Cowart. ''It's the boss. Wants to speak to you.''

''Yes?''

''Mr. Cowart?'' He heard a slow, distant, even, deep voice, one that didn't betray any of the Southernisms with which he was becoming so familiar. ''This is Lieutenant Brown. I'm going to be delayed here at this crash site.''

''Is there some sort of problem?''

The man laughed, a small bitter burst. ''I suppose that depends on how you look at it. None that one wouldn't expect with a burned plane, a dead pilot and student, all sunk in ten feet of swamp, a hysterical pair of wives, an angry flight-school owner, and a couple of park rangers pissed off because this particular landing came down in the midst of a bird sanctuary.''

''Well, I'll be happy to wait . . .''

The detective interrupted. ''What I think would be wise is if Detective Wilcox took you out and showed you where Joanie Shriver's body was found. There are a few other sights of interest as well, which we believe will help you in writing your story. By the time you two get finished, I will have cleared this location, and we can discuss Mr. Robert Earl Ferguson and his crime at our leisure.''

Cowart listened to the clipped, orderly voice. The lieutenant sounded like the sort of man who could make a suggestion into a demand merely by lowering his tone.

''That'd be fine.'' Cowart handed the phone back to Detective Wilcox, who listened to the earpiece momentarily and replied, ''You sure they're expecting him? I wouldn't want to . . . ,'' then started dipping his head in agreement, as if the other man could see him. He hung up.

''All right,'' he said. ''Time for the grand tour. You got any boots and jeans back at your hotel room? It ain't too nice where I'm taking you.''

Cowart nodded and followed after the short detective, who bounced down the hallway with a sort of impish enthusiasm.

They drove through the bright morning sun in the detective's unmarked squad car. Wilcox rolled down his window, letting the warm air flood the interior. He hummed to himself snatches of country-and-western songs. Occasionally he would half-sing some plaintive lyric, "Mommas don't let your babies grow up to be homicide detectives . . .," and grin at Cowart. The journalist stared out across the countryside, feeling unsettled. He had expected rage from the detective, an explosion of animosity and frustration. They knew why he was there. They knew what he intended to do. His presence could be nothing but trouble for them—especially when he wrote that they had tortured Ferguson to obtain his confession. Instead, he got humming.

"So tell me," Wilcox finally asked as he steered the car down a shaded street. "What did you think of Bobby Earl? You went up to Starke, right?"

"He tells an interesting story."

"I bet he does. But what'd'ya think of him?"

"I don't know. Not yet." It was a lie, Cowart realized, but he wasn't sure precisely how much of one.

"Well, I pegged him in the first five seconds. Soon as I saw him."

"That's pretty much what he says."

The detective burst out with a single crack of laughter. "Of course, I bet he didn't say I was right, though, huh?"

"Nope."

"Didn't think so. Anyway, how's he doing?"

"He seems okay. He's bitter," Cowart replied.

"I'd expect that. How's he look?"

"He's not crazy, if that's what you mean."

The detective laughed. "No, I wouldn't figure Bobby Earl would get crazy. Not even on the Row. He was always a cold-hearted son of a bitch. Stayed frosty right to the end when that judge told him where he was gonna end up."

Wilcox seemed to think for an instant, then he shook his head at a sudden memory. "You know, Mr. Cowart, he was like that from the first minute we picked him up. Never blinked, never let on nothing right up until he finally told us what happened. And when he did confess, it was steady-like. Just the facts, Christ. It wasn't like he was talking about anything more difficult than stamping on a bug. I went home that night and I got so damn drunk, Tanny had to come by and pour me into bed. He scared me.''

"I'm very interested in that confession," Cowart said.

"I expect you are. Ain't that the whole ball of wax?" He laughed. "Well, you're gonna have to wait for Tanny. Then we'll tell you about the whole thing.''

I bet you will, Cowart thought. Aloud, he asked, "But he scared you?''

"It wasn't him so much as what I felt he could do.''

The detective didn't elaborate. Wilcox pulled the car around a corner, and Cowart saw that they'd approached the school where the abduction took place. "We're gonna start here," Wilcox said. He stopped the car under a dark willow tree. "Here's where she gets in. Now watch carefully.''

He drove forward swiftly, took a fast right turn, then another quick left, heading down a long street with single-story homes set back amidst shrubbery and pines.

"See, we're still heading toward Joanie's house, so there's nothing yet for her to get scared about. But we're already out of sight of anyone at the school. Now watch this.''

He pulled the car to a stop sign at a Y intersection. Down one street there were more homes, spaced wider apart. Down the other fork in the road there were a few decrepit shacks before a yellow-green, neglected hayfield and swaybacked brown barn at the edge of a dark tunnel-like overgrowth of forest and twisted swamp. "She'd want to go that way," the detective said, pointing toward the houses. "He went the other way. I think this is where he popped her first. . . ." The detective clenched his fist and made a mock punching motion toward Cowart. "He's strong, strong as a goddamn horse. He may not look big, but he's plenty big enough to handle a little eleven-year-old girl. It must have surprised the hell out of her. Forces her down, floors it . . .''

In that instant, all the easygoing jocularity that had marked the detective's behavior vanished. In a single, murderous gesture, Wilcox suddenly reached over and grabbed Cowart's arm up by the shoulder. In the same motion, he punched the accelerator and the car shot forward, fishtailing briefly in loose gravel and dirt. His fingers pinching into Cowart's muscles, tugging him sideways off balance in the seat, Wilcox steered the car down the left fork in the road. Cowart shouted out, a grunting mixture of surprise and fear as he fought to hang on to the armrest in the wildly pitching vehicle. The car swerved, skid-

ding around a corner, and Cowart was tossed against the door.
The detective's grip tightened. He, too, was shouting, roaring
words that made no sense, his face red with exertion. Within
seconds they were past the shacks, bouncing on a washboard
highway, disappearing into cool shadows thrown by the enveloping forest. The dark trees seemed to leap out at them as the
car raced ahead. The speed was dizzying. The engine surged
and howled and Cowart froze, expecting to be slammed into
death.

"Scream!" the detective demanded sharply.

"What?"

"Go ahead, scream!" he shouted. "Yell for help, damn you!"

Cowart stared at the detective's red face and mad eyes. Both
men's voices were raised over the noise of the hurtling engine
and the scraping and scrabbling of the tires against the road.

"Let go!" Cowart yelled. "What the hell are you doing?"
Shadows and branches whipped past him, leaping from the sides
of the road at them like so many attacking beasts.

"Stop, goddammit, stop!"

Abruptly, Wilcox released him, grabbed the steering wheel
with both hands and simultaneously slammed on the brakes.
Cowart thrust out his arm to try to prevent himself from pitching
into the windshield as the car screeched and shimmied to a stop.

"There," the detective said. He exhaled rapidly. His hands
were shaking.

"What the hell?" Cowart shouted. "You trying to get us both
killed?"

The detective didn't answer. He just leaned his head back and
inhaled rapidly, as if trying to gain back the control that had fled
with the wild ride; then he turned to Cowart, fixing him with
small, narrowed eyes. "Relax, Mr. Reporter-man," he said
steadily. "Take a look around you."

"Jesus, what was that little show for?"

"Just showing you a little reality."

Cowart took a deep breath. "By driving crazy and trying to
kill us?"

"No," the detective replied slowly. He grinned, his even
white teeth glistening. "Just showing you how easy it was for
Ferguson to take that child from civilization into the fucking
jungle. Take a look around you. You think there's anybody can
hear you if you scream for help? Who's gonna come along and
help you out? Look at where you are, Cowart. What do you
see?"

Cowart stared out the window and saw dark swamp and forest stretching around him, covering him like a shroud.

"Who do you see who's gonna help you?"

"Nobody."

"Who do you see who's gonna help a little eleven-year-old girl?"

"Nobody."

"You see where you are? You're in hell. It takes five minutes. That's all. And civilization is gone. This is the fucking jungle. Get the point?"

"I get the point."

"I just wanted you to see it with Joanie Shriver's eyes."

"I get the point."

"All right," the detective said, smiling again. "That's how fast it happened. Then he took her farther in. Let's go."

Wilcox got out of the car and went to the trunk. He got out two pairs of bulky brown rubber wading pants and tossed one pair to Cowart. "That'll have to do."

Cowart started to struggle into the waders. As he was doing so, he looked down. He bent down suddenly and felt the ground. Then he walked to the rear of the police cruiser and stood next to the detective. He took a deep breath, smiling to himself. All right, he thought, two can play.

"Tire tracks," he said abruptly, pointing down at the ground with his finger.

"Say what?"

"Fucking tire tracks. Look at this dirt. If he drove her in here, there would be tire tracks. You could have matched them up with his tires. Or don't you cowboys know about such things?"

Wilcox grinned, refusing to rise to the bait. "It was May. Dirt turns to dust."

"Not under this cover."

The detective paused, staring at the reporter. Then he laughed, a wry smile creasing his face. "You ain't dumb, are you?"

Cowart didn't reply.

"Local reporters wouldn't be that sharp. No, sir."

"Don't flatter me. Why didn't you make any tire prints?"

"Because this area was drove all over by rescue personnel and search fucking parties. That was one of the big problems we had at the start. As soon as the word hit that she'd been found, everybody tore ass out here. I mean everybody. And they trampled the shit out of the crime scene. It was a fucking mess before Tanny and I got there. Firemen, ambulance drivers, Boy Scouts, Christ, you name it. There was no control whatsoever. Nobody preserved a damn thing. So suppose we made a tire track. A footprint. A piece of ripped cloth on a bramble, something. No way to match it up. By the time we got here, and damn, we were moving as fast as we could, this place was crawling with folks. Hell, they'd even moved her body out of the location, pulled her up on the shore.''

The detective thought for a minute. "Can't really blame 'em," he went on. "People were crazy for that little girl. It wouldn't have been Christian to leave her in the muck getting gnawed on by snapping turtles.''

Christianity had nothing to do with this case, Cowart thought. It is all evil. But he said, "So, they fucked up?''

"Yeah." The detective looked at him. "I don't want to see that in the paper. I mean, you can point out the scene was a mess. But I don't want to see 'Detective Wilcox said the crime scene was fucked up . . .' but yeah, that's right, it was.''

Cowart watched the detective slip into the waders. He remembered another Hawkins maxim: If you look close enough, the scene will tell you everything. But Wilcox and Brown had had no scene. They had had no evidence that wasn't contaminated. So they'd had to get the other thing that would get them into a court of law: a confession.

The detective tightened his straps and waved to Cowart. "Come on, city boy. Let me show you a real good dying place.''

He stepped off into the woods, his waders rustling against the shrub brush as he walked.

The place where Joanie Shriver had died was dark and enclosed by tangled vines and weeds, with overhanging branches that blocked out the sun like a cave made by nature. It was a small rise, perhaps ten feet above the edge of the swamp, which lurked with black water and mud, stretching away from the forest. Cowart's hands and face were scratched from pushing thorns out of his path. They had traveled a bare fifty yards from the car, but it had been a difficult trip. He was sweating hard, perspiration dripping into his eyes and stinging them. As he stood in the small clearing, he thought it seemed diseased somehow. For a terrible instant, he pictured his own daughter there, and he caught his breath. Find a tough question, he insisted to himself looking at the detective. Something to break the clammy hold his imagination had thrust on him.

"How could he haul some kid kicking and screaming through that?" Cowart said slowly.

"We figure she was unconscious. Deadweight."

"How come?"

"No defensive wounds on the hands or arms . . ." He held up his arms, crossing them in front of his face, demonstrating. "Like she was fighting against that knife. No sign that she fought back at all, like skin under her fingernails. There was a pretty large contusion on the side of her head. Pathologist figured she was knocked out pretty early. I suppose that was some comfort. At least she didn't know much about what was happening to her."

Wilcox walked over to a tree trunk and pointed down. "This is where we found her clothes. Crazy thing was, they were all folded up nice and polite."

He walked a few steps away, back into the center of the clearing. He looked up as if trying to see through the overhang to the sky, shook his head, then motioned to Cowart. "This is where we found the major blood residue. Killed her right here."

"How come no murder weapon was ever discovered?"

The detective shrugged. "Look around you. We went all over the area. Used a metal detector. Nothing. Either he threw it away someplace else, or I don't know. Look, you could walk down to the edge of the swamp, take a knife and just stick it straight down in the mud ten, twelve inches and we'd never find it. Not unless you stepped on the damn thing."

The detective continued to walk through the clearing. "There was a little blood trail leading right along here. The autopsy showed that the rape was premortem. About half the cuts were, too. But a bunch were afterwards. Kinda like he went crazy when she was dead, just cutting and slashing. Anyway, after he was finished, he dragged her down here and dumped her in the water."

He pointed to the swamp edge. "He pushed her down, got her under those roots there. You couldn't see her unless you were right on top of her. He'd tossed some loose brush on top. We were lucky to find her as quick as we did. Hell, we were lucky to find her at all. The guys would have gone right past her, 'cept one of them had his hat knocked off by a low branch. When he reached out to grab the hat, he spotted her down there. Just damn-fool blind luck, really."

"But what about his clothing, wouldn't there be some sign? Like blood or hair or something?"

"We tossed his house pretty good after the confession. But we didn't come up with nothing."

"Same for the car. There had to be something."

"When we picked the son of a bitch up, he was just finishing cleaning out that car. Scrubbed it down real fine. There was a section cut out of the rug on the passenger's side, too. That was long gone. Anyway, the damn car was shining like it was brand-new. We didn't find anything." The detective rubbed his forehead, then looked at the sweat on his fingers. "We don't have the same kind of forensic capability that your big-city guys have, anyway. I mean, we aren't in the dark ages or anything, but lab work up here is slow and not altogether reliable. There may have been something that a real pro could have found with one of those FBI spectrographs. We didn't. We tried hard, but we come up with nothing."

He paused. "Well, actually, we found one thing, but it didn't help none."

"What was that?"

"A single pubic hair. Trouble was, it didn't match up with Joanie Shriver's. But it wasn't Ferguson's neither."

Cowart shook his head. He could feel the heat, the closeness of the air suffocating him. "If he confessed, why didn't he tell you where the clothes were? Why didn't he tell you where he hid the knife? What's the point of a confession unless you get all the details straight?"

Wilcox glared at Cowart, reddening. He started to say something, but then chewed back his words, leaving the questions hanging in the still, hot air of the clearing. "Let's go," he said. He turned and started to make his way out of the location, not looking back to see if Cowart was following. "We got someplace we gotta be."

Cowart took one last lingering look at the murder site. He wanted to sear it into his memory. Feeling a mixture of excitement and disgust, he trailed after the detective.

The detective pulled the unmarked car to a stop in front of a small house more or less like all the other houses in that block. It was single-story, white, cinder block, with a well-cropped lawn and an attached garage. A red-brick walkway led down to the sidewalk. Cowart could see a patio area stretching around the back, a black kettle grill on one side. A tall pine tree shaded half the house from the day's heat, throwing a large shadow across the front. He did not know where they were or why they had stopped, so he turned away from the house and looked at the detective.

"Your next interview," Wilcox said. He had been quiet since they'd left the crime scene and now a tinge of harshness had crept into his voice. "If you're up for it."

"Whose house is it?" Cowart asked uneasily.

"Joanie Shriver's."

Cowart took a deep breath. "That's . . ."

"That's where she was heading. Never got there." He glanced down at his watch. "Tanny told them we'd be here by eleven and we're a bit late, so we'd better get a move on. Unless . . ."

"Unless what?"

"Unless this is an interview you don't want to do."

Cowart looked at the detective, up at the house, then back to the detective. "I get it," he said. "You want to see how sympathetic I am to them, right? You already figured out I'm going to be real easy on Robert Earl Ferguson, so this is part of some test, right?"

The detective turned away.

"Right?"

Wilcox spun in the seat and stared at him. "What you haven't figured out yet, Mr. Cowart, is that son of a bitch killed that little girl. Now, you want to see what that really means, or not?"

"I generally schedule my own interviews," Cowart replied, more pompously than he wanted.

"So, you want to go? Come back maybe when it's more convenient?"

He sensed that was what the detective wanted. Wilcox wanted immensely to have every reason in the world to hate him, and this would be a good one to start with.

"No," Cowart said, opening the car door. "Let's talk to the people."

He slammed the car door behind him and walked quickly up the pathway, then rang the doorbell as Wilcox chased after him. For an instant he heard shuffling noises from behind the door, then it swung open. He found himself staring into the face of a middle-aged woman who had an unmistakable housewife's look. She wore little makeup but had spent time fixing her light brown hair that morning. It haloed her face. She wore a simple tan housedress and sandals. Her eyes were bright blue and for a moment, Cowart saw the little girl's chin, cheeks, and nose in the mother's face, looking at him expectantly. He swallowed the vision and said, "Mrs. Shriver? I'm Matthew Cowart, from *The Miami Journal*. I believe Lieutenant Brown told you . . ."

She nodded and interrupted him. "Yes, yes, please come in, Mr. Cowart. Please, call me Betty. Tanny said Detective Wilcox would be bringing you around this morning. You're doing a story about Ferguson, we know. My husband's here, please, we would like to talk with you."

Her voice had an easygoing pleasantness to it that failed to conceal her anxiety. She clipped off her words carefully, he thought, because she doesn't want to lose them to emotion quite yet. He followed the woman into the house, thinking, But she will.

The murdered girl's mother led Cowart down a small hallway and into the living room. He was aware that Wilcox was trailing behind, but he ignored him. A bulky, large-bellied, balding man rose from a reclining chair when he entered the room. The man struggled for a moment to push himself out of the seat, then stepped forward to shake Cowart's hand. "I'm George Shriver," he said. "I'm glad we had this opportunity."

Cowart nodded and quickly glanced around, trying to lock details to his memory. The room, like the exterior, was trim and modern. The furniture was simple, colorful prints were hung on the walls. It had a cozy haphazardness to it, as if each item in the room had been purchased independently from the others, solely because it was admired, not necessarily because it could match up with anything else. The overall impression was slightly disjointed but exceptionally comfortable. One wall was devoted to family photos, and Cowart's eyes fell on them. The same photograph of Joanie he'd seen at school hung in the center of the wall, surrounded by other shots. He noted an older brother and sister, and the usual family portraits.

George Shriver followed his eyes. "The two older kids, George Junior and Anne, are away at school. They're both at the University of Florida. They probably would have wanted to be here," he said.

"Joanie was the baby," said Betty Shriver. "She'd have been getting ready for high school." The woman caught her breath suddenly, her lip quivering. Cowart saw her struggle and turn away from the photographs. Her husband reached out a huge, chunky hand and gently steered her over to the couch, where she sat down. She immediately rose, asking, "Mr. Cowart, please, where are my manners? Can I get you something to drink?"

"Ice water would be nice," Cowart replied, turning away from the photographs and standing next to an armchair. The woman disappeared for a moment. Cowart asked George Shriver an innocuous question, something to dispel the pall that had fallen over the room.

"You're a city councilman?"

"Ex," he replied. "Now I just spend my time down at the store. I own a couple of hardware stores, one here in Pachoula, another down on the way to Pensacola. Keeps me busy. Especially right now, waiting on the spring."

He paused, then continued. "Ex-councilman. Used to be I was interested in all that, but I kinda fell out of it when Joanie was taken from us, and we spent so much time with the trial and all, and it just sort of slipped away, and I never got back into it again. That happened a lot. If 'n we hadn't had the others, George Junior and Anne, I suspect we would have just stopped. I don't know what might have happened to us."

Mrs. Shriver returned and handed Cowart a glass of ice water. He saw that she had taken a moment to compose herself.

"I'm sorry if this is difficult for you," he said.

"No. Rather speak our feelings than hide them," replied George Shriver. He sat down on the couch next to his wife, throwing his arm around her. "You don't never lose the pain," he said. "It maybe gets a bit duller, you know, like it's not so sharp so it's pricking at you all the time. But little things bring it back. I'll just be sitting in the chair, and I'll hear some neighbor's child's voice, way outside, and for just an instant, I'll think it's her. And that hurts, Mr. Cowart. That's real pain. Or maybe I'll come down here in the morning to fix myself coffee, and I'll sit here staring at those pictures, just like you did. And all I can think of is that it didn't happen, no sir, that she's gonna come bouncing out of her room, just like she always did, all morning sunshine and happiness and ready to jump right into the day, sir, because that's the sort of child she was. Just all golden."

The big man's eyes had filled with tears as he spoke, but his voice had remained steady.

"I go to church a bit more than I used to; it's a comfort. And the damnedest things, Mr. Cowart, will just make me hurt. I saw a special on television a year ago about the children starving in Ethiopia. Man, that's all the way on the other side of the world and, hell, I ain't ever been anywhere except North Florida, save for the army. But now, I been sending the relief organizations

money every month. A hundred here, a hundred there. I couldn't
stand it, you know, thinking that some babies were gonna die
just because they couldn't eat. I hated it. I thought how much I
loved my baby, and she was stolen from me. So, I guess I did
it for her. I must be crazy. I'll be in the store, working on the
receipts, and it'll start to get late, and I'll remember some time
that I stayed to work late and missed dinner with the kids and
got home late so they were all asleep, especially my baby, and
I'd go in and see her laying there. And I would hate that memory
because I missed one of her laughs, or one of her smiles, and
there were so few of them, they were precious, sir. Like little
diamonds.''

George Shriver leaned his head back, staring into the ceiling.
He was breathing hard, sweating profusely, his white shirt rising
and falling as he fought for breath and struggled with memories.

His wife had grown quiet, but her eyes had reddened and her
hands shook in her lap. ''We ain't special people, Mr. Cowart,''
she said slowly. ''George's worked hard and made something of
hisself, so that the kids would have it easier. George Junior is
going to be an engineer. Anne is a whizbang at chemistry and
the sciences. She's got a chance to go on to medical school.''
The woman's eyes glistened with a sudden pride. ''Can you
imagine that? A doctor from our family. We've just worked hard
so that they could be something better, you know.''

''Tell me,'' Cowart said carefully, ''what you think about
Robert Earl Ferguson.''

There was a solid loud quiet while they collected their
thoughts. He saw Betty Shriver take a deep breath before answering.

''It's a hate that goes way beyond hate,'' she said. ''It's an
awful, unchristian anger, Mr. Cowart. It's just a terrible black
rage inside that never goes away.''

George Shriver shook his head. ''There was a time when I
would have killed him myself, just so easy, I wouldn't of thought
about it no more than you would if you slapped a mosquito off'n
your arm. I don't know if that's true for me anymore. You know,
Mr. Cowart, this is a conservative community here. People go
to church. Salute the flag. Say grace before they eat and vote
Republican now that the Democrats have forgotten what they're
all about. I think if you were to grab ten folks off the street,
they'd say, No, don't give that boy the electric chair; send him
back here and let us take care of him. Fifty years ago, he'd a
been lynched. Hell, less than fifty. Things have changed, I think.

But the longer it all goes on, the longer I think that it was us that got sentenced, not just him. Months pass. Years pass. He's got all these lawyers working for him, and we find out about another appeal, another hearing, another something, and it brings it all back. We don't ever get the chance to put it all behind us. Not that you can, mind you. But at least you ought to get the chance to put it someplace and get on with what's left of your life, even if it is all sick and wrong now.''

He sighed and shook his head. ''It's like we're living in a kinda prison right alongside him.''

After a few seconds, Cowart asked, ''But you know what I'm doing?''

''Yes, sir,'' both husband and wife replied in unison.

''Tell me what you know,'' he asked.

Betty Shriver leaned forward. ''We know that you're looking at the case. See if there wasn't some unfairness connected to it. Right?''

''That's about as close as you could guess.''

''What do you think was unfair?'' George Shriver asked. This was spoken mildly, curiously, not angrily.

''Well, that was my question for you. What do you think about what happened in the trial?''

''I think the sonuvabitch got convicted, that's what. . . .'' he responded, his voice rising quickly. But his wife put her hand on his leg and he seemed visibly to slow himself.

''We sat through it all, Mr. Cowart,'' Betty Shriver said. ''Every minute. We saw him sitting there. You could see a sort of fear in his eyes, sir, a sort of desperate anger at everyone as it all happened. I'm told he hated Pachoula, and that he hated all the folks here, black and white, just the same. You could see that hatred every time he squirmed about in his seat. I guess the jury saw it, too.''

''And the evidence?''

''They asked him if he did it and he said yes. Now who would say that if'n it warn't true? He said he did it. His own words. Damn his eyes. His own words.''

There was another quiet then, before George Shriver added, ''Well, of course, I was bothered that they didn't have more on him. We talked to Tanny and Detective Wilcox for hours about all that. Tanny sat right where you're sitting, night after night. They explained what happened. They explained that the case was shaky to begin with. So many lucky things happened to bring him to trial. Hell, they might never even have found Joanie,

that was luck, too. I wished they'd had more evidence, yes sir.
I did. But they had enough. They had the boy's own words and
that was good enough for me.''

And there it is, Cowart thought.

After a moment, Betty Shriver asked quietly, ''Are you gonna
write a story?''

Cowart nodded and replied, ''I'm still unsure exactly what
kind of story.''

''What'll happen?''

''I don't know.''

She frowned and persisted. ''It'll help him, won't it?''

''I can't tell that,'' he said.

''But it could hardly hurt him, right?''

He nodded again. ''That's true. After all, he's on Death Row.
What's he got to lose?''

''I'd like to see him stay there,'' she said. She rose and gestured to him to follow her. They walked through a corridor,
down a wing of the house. She paused in front of a door, putting
her hand on the knob but not opening it. ''I'd hoped he'd stay
there until he goes to meet his maker. That's when he'll truly
have to answer for all that hate that robbed us of our little girl.
I wouldn't want to have his life, no sir, not at all. But even more,
I wouldn't want to have his death. But you do what you have to
do, Mr. Cowart. Just remember this.''

She swung the door open.

He looked inside and saw a girl's bedroom. The wallpaper
was pink and white and there was a fluffy ruffle around the bed.
There were plush toys with large sad eyes, and two bright mo-
biles hanging from the ceiling. There were pictures of ballerinas
and a large poster of Mary Lou Retton, the gymnast, on the
walls. There was a bookcase stuffed with books. He saw some
titles: *Misty of Chincoteague*, *Black Beauty*, and *Little Women*.
There was a funny picture of Joanie Shriver wearing outlandish
makeup and dressed like a roaring-twenties flapper on the bureau top. Next to that was a box filled to overflowing with brightly
colored costume jewelry. In the corner of the room was a large
dollhouse filled with small figures and a fluffy pink boa hanging
over the edge of the bed.

''That's the way it was the morning she left us forever. It'll
always be that way,'' she said. Then the murdered girl's mother
turned abruptly, her eyes filling, sobs summoned from her heart.
For an instant she faced the wall, her shoulders heaving. Then
she walked away unsteadily, disappearing through another door,

which closed behind her, but not tight enough to obscure the painful weeping which filled the house. Cowart looked back toward the living room and saw the murdered girl's father sitting, staring blankly ahead, tears flooding down his own cheeks, incapable of moving. He wanted to shut his own eyes, but instead found himself looking with terrified fascination at the little girl's room. All the little-girl items, knickknacks, and decorations leapt out at him, and for an instant he thought he couldn't breathe. Each sob from the mother seemed to press on his own chest. He thought he might pass out, but instead he turned away from the room, knowing he would never forget it, and jerked his head toward Detective Wilcox. For an instant, he tried to apologize and to thank George Shriver, but he realized his words were as empty as their agony. So, instead, tiptoeing like some burglar of the soul, he quietly showed himself out the door.

Cowart sat wordlessly in Lieutenant Brown's office. Detective Wilcox was seated behind the desk, pawing through a large file marked "SHRIVER," ignoring the reporter. They had not spoken since leaving the house. Cowart looked out the window and saw a large oak tree bend with a sudden breeze, its leafy branches tossing about as if unsettled, then slowly returning to position.

His reverie was interrupted when Wilcox found what he was searching for, and tossed a yellow manila envelope on the desk in front of him.

"Here. I saw you take a nice long look at that pretty picture of Joanie Shriver on the wall at her house. Thought maybe you'd like to see what she looked like after Ferguson got finished with her."

There no longer was any pretense to the detective's tones. Every word seemed tied down with barely adequate restraints.

He picked up the packet without replying and slid the photographs out. The worst was the first: Joanie Shriver was stretched out on a slab in the medical examiner's office before the start of the autopsy. Dirt and blood still marred her features. She was naked, her little girl's body just starting to show the signs of adulthood. He could see slash marks and stab wounds across her chest, slicing down at the budding breasts. Her stomach and crotch, too, were punctured in a dozen spots by the knife. He stared on, wondering whether he would get sick, staring instead at the girl's face. It seemed puffy, the skin almost sagging, the result of hours spent submerged in the swamp. He thought for an instant about many bodies he'd seen at dozens of

crime sites, and of hundreds of autopsy photos from trials he
had covered. He looked back at the remains of Joanie Shriver
and saw that despite all the evil done to her, she had retained
her little girl's identity. Even in death it was locked into her face.
That seemed to pain him even more.

He started to flip through the others, mostly scene pictures
that showed how she appeared after being pulled from the
swamp. He saw as well the truth to what Bruce Wilcox had said.
There were dozens of muddy footprints around the body. He
continued looking through the pictures, finding more signs of
the contamination of the murder location, only looking up when
the door opened behind him, and he heard Wilcox say, "Christ,
Tanny, what took you so long?"

He stood up, turning, and his eyes met Lieutenant Theodore
Brown's.

"Pleased to meet you, Mr. Cowart," the policeman said,
extending his hand.

Cowart grasped it, at a loss for words. He took in the policeman's appearance in a second: Tanny Brown was immense,
linebacker-size, well over six feet, broad-shouldered, with
long, powerful arms. His hair was cropped close, and he wore
glasses. But mostly what he was was black, a resonating, deep,
dark onyx.

"Something wrong?" Tanny Brown asked.

"No," Cowart replied, recovering. "I didn't know you were
black."

"What, you city boys think we're all crackers like Wilcox up
here in the panhandle?"

"No. Just surprised. Sorry."

"No problem. Actually," the policeman continued in his
steady, unaccented voice, "I'm used to the surprise factor. But
if you were to go to Mobile, Montgomery, or Atlanta, you'd find
many more black faces wearing policeman's uniforms than you
would expect. Things change. Even the police, though I doubt
you'd believe that."

"Why?"

"Because," Brown continued, speaking simply and clearly,
"the only reason you're here is if you believe the crap that murdering bastard and his attorneys have told you."

Cowart didn't reply. He merely took his seat and watched as
the lieutenant took over the chair that Wilcox had occupied. The
detective grabbed a folding chair and sat down next to the lieutenant.

"Do you believe it?" Brown asked abruptly.

"Why? Is it important for you to know what I believe?"

"Well, could make things simpler. You could tell me yes, you believe that we beat the confession out of that kid, and then we wouldn't really have much to talk about. I'd say, No, we didn't, that's absurd, and you could write that down in your little notebook and that would be the end of it. You'd write your story and whatever happens happens."

"Let's not make it simple," Cowart replied.

"I didn't think so," Brown answered. "So what do you want to know?"

"I want to know everything. From the beginning. And especially I want to know what made you pick up Ferguson and then I want to know about that confession. And don't leave anything out. Isn't that what you'd say to someone whose statement you were about to take?"

Tanny Brown settled his large body into the chair and smiled, but not because he was pleased. "Yes, that's what I would say," he answered. He spun about in the chair, thinking, but all the time eyeing Cowart steadily.

"Robert Earl Ferguson was at the top of the short list of prime suspects from the first minute the girl was discovered."

"Why?"

"He had been a suspect in other assaults."

"What? I've never heard that before. What other assaults?"

"A half-dozen rapes in Santa Rosa County, and over the 'Bama border near Atmore and Bay Minette."

"What evidence do you have that he was involved in other assaults?"

Brown shook his head. "No evidence. He physically fit the best description we could piece together, working with detectives in those communities. And the rapes all corresponded to times when he was out of school, on vacation, visiting that old grandmother of his."

"Yes, and?"

"And that's it."

Cowart was silent for an instant. "That's it? No forensic evidence to tie him to those assaults? I presume you did show his picture to the women."

"Yes. Nobody could make him."

"And the hair you found in his car—the one that didn't match Joanie Shriver's—you ran comparisons with the victims in those other cases?"

"Yes."

"And?"

"No matchups."

"The modus operandi in the other attacks was the same as in the Shriver abduction?"

"No. Each of the other cases had some similarities, but aspects that were different as well. A gun was used to threaten the victims in a couple of cases, a knife in others. A couple of women were followed home. One was out jogging. No consistent pattern that we could determine."

"Were the victims white?" Cowart asked.

"Yes."

"Were they young, like Joanie Shriver?"

"No. They were all adults."

Cowart paused, considering, before continuing his questions.

"You know, Lieutenant, what the FBI statistics on black-on-white rape are?"

"I know you're going to tell me."

Cowart surged on. "Less than four percent of the cases reported nationwide. It's a rarity, despite all the stereotyping and paranoia. How many black-on-white cases have you had in Pachoula before Robert Earl Ferguson?"

"None that I can recall. And don't lecture me about stereotypes." Brown eyed Cowart. Wilcox shifted about in his seat angrily.

"Statistics don't mean anything," he added quietly.

"No?" Cowart asked. "Okay. But he was home on vacation."

"Right."

"And nobody liked him much. That I've learned."

"That's correct. He was a snide rat bastard. Looked down at folks."

Cowart stared at the policeman. "You know how silly that sounds? An unpopular person comes to visit his grandmother and you want to make him on rape charges. No wonder he didn't like it around here."

Tanny Brown started to say something angry in reply, but then stopped. For a few seconds he simply watched Cowart, as if trying to burrow into him with his eyes. Finally he replied, slowly, "Yes. I know how silly it sounds. We must be silly people." His eyes had narrowed sharply.

Cowart leaned forward in his chair, speaking in his own, steady, unaffected voice. You've got no edge on me, he thought.

"But that's why you went to his grandmother's house first, looking for him?"

"That's right."

Brown started to say something else, then closed his mouth abruptly. Cowart could feel the tension between the two of them and knew, in that moment, what the lieutenant had been prepared to say. So he said it for him. "Because you had a feeling, right? That old policeman's sixth sense. A suspicion that you had to act on. That's what you were about to say, right?"

Brown glared at him.

"Right. Yes. Exactly." He stopped and looked over at Wilcox, then back at Cowart. "Bruce said you were slick," he spoke quietly, "but I guess I had to see it for myself."

Cowart eyed the lieutenant with the same cold glance that he was receiving. "I'm not slick. I'm just doing what you would do."

"No, that's incorrect," Brown said acidly. "I wouldn't be trying to help that murdering bastard off of Death Row."

The reporter and the policeman were both silent.

After a few moments, Brown said, "This isn't going right."

"That's correct, if what you want is to persuade me that Ferguson's a liar."

Brown stood up and started pacing the floor, obviously thinking hard. He moved with a rugged intensity, like a sprinter coiled at the starting line, waiting for the starter's gun to sound, the muscles in his body shifting about easily, letting Cowart know all the time that he was not a person who enjoyed the sensation of being confined, either in the small room or by details.

"He was wrong," the policeman said. "I knew it from the first time I saw him, long before Joanie was killed. I know that's not evidence, but I knew it."

"When was that?"

"A year before the murder. I rousted him from the front of the high school. He was just sitting in that car, watching the kids leave."

"What were you doing there?"

"Picking up my daughter. That's when I spotted him. Saw him a few times after that. Every time, he was doing something that made me uncomfortable. Hanging in the wrong spot at the wrong time. Or driving slowly down the street, following some young woman. I wasn't the only one that noticed it. A couple of the Pachoula patrolmen came to me saying the same. He got busted once, around midnight, right behind a small apartment building, just standing around. Tried to hide when the squad car rolled past. Charges got dropped right away. But still . . .''

"I still don't hear anything like evidence."

"Goddammit!" the lieutenant's voice soared for the first time. "Don't you hear? We didn't have any. All we had was impressions. Like the impression you get when you get to Ferguson's house and he's scrubbing out that car—and he's already deep-sixed a slice of rug. Like when the first thing out of his mouth is, 'I didn't do that girl,' before he's heard a question. And how he sits in an interview room, laughing because he knows you haven't got anything. But all those impressions add up to something more than instinct, because he finally talks. And, yes sir, all those impressions turn out to be absolutely right because he confesses to killing that girl.''

"So, where's the knife? Where's his clothes covered with blood and mud?''

"He wouldn't tell us.''

"Did he tell you how he staked out the school? How he got her to get into the car? What he said to her? Whether she fought? What did he tell you?''

"Here, goddammit, read for yourself!''

Lieutenant Brown seized a sheaf of papers from the file on his desk and tossed them toward Cowart. He looked down and saw that it was the transcript of the confession, taken by a court stenographer. It was short, only three pages long. The two detectives had gone through all of his rights with him, especially the right to an attorney. The rights colloquy occupied more than an entire page of the confession. They'd asked him whether he understood this and he'd replied he had. Their first question was phrased in traditional cop-ese: "Now, on or about three P.M. on May 4, 1987, did you have occasion to be in a location at the corner of Grand and Spring streets, which is next to King Elementary School?" And Ferguson had replied monosyllabically, "Yes." The detectives had then asked him whether he had seen the young woman later known to him as Joanie Shriver, and again, his reply had been the single affirmative. They had then painstakingly brought him through the entire scenario, each time phrasing their narrative as a question and receiving a positive answer, but not one of them elaborated with even the meagerest detail. When they had asked him about the weapon and the other crucial aspects of the crime, he'd replied that he couldn't remember. The final question was designed to establish premeditation. It was the one that had put Ferguson on Death Row:

"Did you go to that location intending to kidnap and kill a young woman on that day?" and he'd replied again with a simple, awful "Yes."

Cowart shook his head. Ferguson had volunteered nothing except a single word, "Yes," over and over. He turned toward Brown and Wilcox. "Not exactly a model confession, is it?"

Wilcox, who had been sitting unsteadily, shifting about with an obvious, growing frustration, finally jumped up, his face red with anger, shaking his fist at the reporter. "What the hell do you want? Dammit, he did that little girl just as sure as I'm standing here now. You just don't want to hear the truth, damn you!"

"Truth?" Cowart shook his head and Wilcox seemed to explode. He sprang from behind the desk and grabbed hold of Cowart's jacket, pulling the reporter to his feet. "You're gonna get me really angry, asshole! You don't want to do that!"

Tanny Brown jackknifed his bulk across the desk, seizing the detective with one hand and jerking him backward, controlling the smaller, wiry man easily. He did not say anything, especially when Wilcox turned toward his superior officer, still sputtering with barely controlled anger. The detective tried to say something to Brown, then turned toward Cowart. Finally, choking, fists clenched, he stormed from the office.

Cowart straightened his jacket and sat back down heavily. He breathed in and out, feeling the adrenaline pumping in his ears. After a few minutes of silence, he looked over at Brown.

"You're going to tell me now that he didn't hit Ferguson, right? That he never lost it during thirty-six hours of interrogation?"

The lieutenant paused for an instant, thinking, as if trying to assess the damage done by the outburst before replying. Then he shook his head.

"No, truth is, he did. Early on, once or twice, before I stopped him. Just slapped Ferguson across the face."

"No punch to the stomach?"

"Not that I saw."

"How about telephone books?"

"An old technique," Brown said sadly, his voice growing quieter. "No. Despite what Mr. Ferguson says."

The lieutenant turned away for the first time, looking out the window. After a moment or two, he said, "Mr. Cowart, I don't think I can make you understand. That little girl's death just got under all our skins and it's still there. And it was the worst for us. We had to make some sort of case out of that emotional mess. It bent us all. We weren't evil or bad. But we wanted that killer caught. I didn't sleep for three days. None of us did. But we had him, and there he was, smiling back at us just like nothing was wrong. I don't blame Bruce Wilcox for losing it a bit. I think we were all at the edge. And even then, with the confession—you're right, it's not a textbook confession, but it was the best we could get out of that closemouthed son of a bitch—even then it was all so fragile. This conviction is held together by the thinnest of threads. We all know that. And so, you come along, asking questions, and each one of those questions just shreds a little bit of those threads and we get a little crazy. There. That's my apology for my partner. And for sending you to the Shrivers. I don't want this conviction to shatter. More than anything else, I don't want to lose this one. I couldn't face those folks. I couldn't face my own family. I couldn't face myself. I want that man to die for what he did.''

The lieutenant finished his confession and waited for Cowart's reply. The reporter felt a sudden rush of success and decided to press his advantage. ''What's the policy with your department on taking weapons into interrogation rooms?''

''Simple: You don't. Check them with the sergeant on duty. Every cop knows that. Why?''

''Would you mind standing up for a moment.''

Brown shrugged and stood.

''Now, let me see your ankles.''

He looked surprised and hesitated. ''I don't get it.''

''Indulge me, Lieutenant.''

Brown stared angrily at him. ''Is this what you want to see?'' He lifted his leg, putting his shoe up on the desk, raising his trouser leg at the same time. There was a small, brown-leather ankle holster holding a snub-nosed .38-caliber pistol strapped to his calf.

The lieutenant lowered his leg.

''Now, you didn't point that weapon at Ferguson and tell him you were going to kill him if he didn't confess, did you?''

''No, absolutely not.'' Cold indignation rode the detective's voice.

''And you never pulled the trigger on an empty chamber?''

''No.''

''So, how would he know about that gun if you hadn't shown it to him?''

Brown stared across the desk at Cowart, an ice-like anger

behind his eyes. "This interview is finished," he said. He pointed at the door.

"You're wrong," Cowart said, rising. "It's just beginning."

FIVE
——DEATH ROW AGAIN

THERE is a zone reporters find, a space like the marksman's narrowing of vision down the barrel, past the sight and directly to the center of the target, where other considerations of life fade away, and they begin to see their story take shape within their imaginations. The gaps in the narrative, the prose holes that need information start to become obvious; like a gravedigger swinging shovels of soil on top of a coffin, the reporter fills the breaches in his story.

Matthew Cowart had reached that place.

He drummed his fingers impatiently on the linoleum-topped table, waiting for Sergeant Rogers to escort Ferguson into the interview room. His trip to Pachoula had left him energized with questions, suffused with answers. The story was half-settled in his mind, had been from the moment that Tanny Brown had angrily conceded that Ferguson had been slapped by Wilcox. That small admission had opened an entire vista of lies. Matthew Cowart did not know what precisely had happened between the detectives and their quarry, but he knew that there were enough questions to warrant his story, and probably to reopen the case. What he hungered for now was the second element. If Ferguson hadn't killed the little girl, then who had? When Ferguson appeared in the doorway, an unlit cigarette hanging from his lip, arms filled with legal folders, Cowart wanted to jump to his feet.

The two men shook hands and Cowart watched Ferguson

settle into the chair opposite him. "I'm gonna be outside," the sergeant said, closing the reporter and the convict in the small room. There was the audible click of a dead bolt lock. The prisoner was smiling, not with pleasure but with smugness, and for just a moment, as he measured the grin in front of him against the cold anger he had seen in Tanny Brown's eyes, Cowart felt a swaying within him. Then the feeling fled and Ferguson dropped his papers onto the tabletop, making a muffled thudding sound with their weight.

"I knew you'd be back," Ferguson said. "I knew what you'd find there."

"And what do you think that was?"

"That I was telling the truth."

Cowart hesitated, then sought to knock a bit of the prisoner's confidence astray. "I found out you were telling some truths."

Ferguson bristled instantly. "What the hell do you mean? Didn't you talk to those cops? Didn't you see that cracker red-neck town? Couldn't you see what sort of place it is?"

"One of those cracker cops was black. You didn't tell me that."

"What, you think that just because he's the same color as me that automatically makes him okay? You think he's my brother? That he ain't as much a racist as that little worm partner of his? Where you been, Mr. Reporter? Tanny Brown's worse than the worst redneck sheriff you ever imagined. He makes all the Bulls and Bubbas and all those other Deep South cops look like a bunch of bleeding hearts from the ACLU. He's white right to his heart and soul and the only thing he hates worse than himself is folks his own color. You go ask around. Find out who the big head-banger in Pachoula is. People'd tell you it was that pig. I promise."

Ferguson had snapped to his feet. He was pacing about the cell, pounding one fist into an open palm, the sharp slapping noise punctuating his words. "Didn't you talk to that old alky lawyer who sold me out?"

"I talked to him."

"Did you talk to my grandmother?"

"Yes."

"Didn't you go over the case?"

"I saw they didn't have much."

"Didn't you see why they had to have that confession?"

"Yes."

"Didn't you see the gun?"

"I saw it."

"Didn't you read that confession?"

"I read it."

"They beat me, those bastards."

"They admitted hitting you once or twice . . ."

"Once or twice! Christ! That's nice. They probably said it was like some little love taps or something, huh? More like a little mistake than an actual beating, right?"

"That's pretty much what they implied."

"Bastards!"

"Take it easy . . ."

"Take it easy! You tell me, how am I to take it easy? Those lying sons of bitches can just sit out there and say any damn thing they want. Me, all I've got are the walls and the chair waiting."

Ferguson's voice had risen and his mouth opened again, but instead he grew silent and stopped abruptly in the middle of the room. He looked over at Cowart, as if trying to regain some of the cool that had dissipated so swiftly. He seemed to think hard about what he was going to say before continuing.

"Were you aware, Mr. Cowart, we were in a lockdown until this morning? You know what that means, don't you?" Ferguson spoke with obvious restraint clipped to his voice.

"Tell me."

"Governor signed a death warrant. We all get locked down into the cells twenty-four hours a day until the warrant expires or the execution takes place."

"What happened?"

"Man got a stay from the fifth circuit." Ferguson shook his head. "But he's running close to the edge. You know how it works. First you take all the appeals that stem from the case. Then you start in on the big issues, like the constitutionality of the death penalty. Or maybe the racial makeup of the jury. That's a real favorite around here. Keep arguing away at those. Try to come up with something new. Something all those legal minds haven't thought of yet. All the time, ticktock, ticktock. Time's running out."

Ferguson walked back to his seat and sat carefully, folding his hands on the table in front of him. "You know what a lockdown does to your soul? It makes it grow all frozen cold inside. You're trapped, feeling every tick of that damn clock like it was tapping at your heart. You feel as if it's you that's gonna die, because you know that someday they're gonna come and lock down the Row because that warrant's been signed with your name on it. It's like they're killing you there, slowly, just letting the blood drip out drop by drop, bleeding you to death. That's when the Row goes crazy. You can ask Sergeant Rogers, he'll tell you. First there's a lot of angry shouting and yelling, but that only lasts for a few minutes. Then a quiet comes over the Row. It's almost like you can hear the men sweating nightmares. Then something happens, some little noise will break it and pretty soon the silence gets lost because some of the men start yelling again, and others start screaming. One man, he screamed for twelve straight hours before he passed out. A lockdown squeezes all the sanity out of you, just leaves all the hate and madness. That's all that's left. Then they take you away.''

Ferguson spoke the last very softly, then he got up and started pacing again. ''You know what I hated about Pachoula? Its complacency. How nice it is. Just damn nice and quiet.''

Ferguson clenched his fist. ''I hated the way everything had a place and worked just right. Everyone knew each other and knew exactly how life was going to work. Get up in the morning. Go to work. Yes sir, no sir. Drive home. Have a drink. Eat dinner. Turn on the television. Go to bed. Do it again the next day. Friday night, go to the high-school game. Saturday, go on a picnic. Sunday, go to church. Didn't make any difference if you were white or black—'cept the whites ran things and the blacks lifted and carried, same as everywhere in the South. And what I hated was that everyone liked it. Christ, how they loved that routine. Shuffling in and out of each day, just the same as the day before, same as the day after. Year after year.''

''And you?''

''You're right. I didn't fit. Because I wanted something different. I was going to make something of myself. My granny, she was the same. The black folks down there used to say she was a hard old woman who put on airs about how fine she was, even though she lived in a little shack with no indoor plumbing and a chicken coop in the back. The ones that made it out—like your goddamn Tanny Brown—couldn't stand that she had pride. Couldn't stand that she wouldn't bow her head to no one. You met her. She strike you as the type likely to step aside on the sidewalk and let someone else pass?''

''No, she didn't.''

''She's been a fighter all her life. And when I came along, and I wasn't a get-along type like they wanted, well, they just came after me.''

He looked ready to go on, but Cowart stopped him. "Okay, Ferguson, fine. Let's say that's all true. And let's say that I write the story: Flimsy evidence. Questionable identification. Bad lawyer. Beaten confession. That's only half of what you promised." He had Ferguson's full attention now. "I want the name. The real killer, you said. No more screwing around."

"What promises do I have . . ."

"None. My story, to tell as I report it."

"Yeah, but it's my life. Maybe my death."

"No promises."

Ferguson sat down and looked over at Cowart. "What do you really know about me?" he asked.

The question set Cowart back. What did he know? "What you've told me. What others have told me."

"Do you think you know me?"

"Maybe a bit."

Ferguson snorted. "You're wrong." He seemed to hesitate, as if rethinking what he had just said. "What you see is what I am. I may not be perfect, and maybe I said and did things I shouldn't have. Maybe I shouldn't have pissed off that whole town so much so that when trouble came driving down the roadway, they only thought to look for me, and they let their trouble just drive on past, without even knowing it."

"I don't get it."

"You will." Ferguson closed his eyes. "I know I may come on a bit strong sometimes, but you got to be the way you are, right?"

"I suppose."

"That's what happened in Pachoula, you see. Trouble came to town. Stopped a couple of minutes and then left me behind to get swept up with all the other broken little pieces of life there." He laughed at Cowart's expression. "Let me try again. Imagine a man—a very bad man—driving a car heading south, pulling off the roadway into Pachoula. He stops, maybe to eat a burger and some fries, beneath a tree, just outside a school yard. Spots a young girl. Talks her into his car because he looks nice enough. You've seen that place. It ain't hard to find yourself out in the swamp in a couple of minutes, all alone and quiet. He does her right there and drives on. Leaves that place forever, never thinking about what he did for more'n one or two minutes, and that's only to remember how good it felt to him to take that little girl's life."

"Keep going."

"Man zigzags down the state. A little trouble in Bay City. A bit in Tallahassee. Orlando. Lakeland. Tampa. All the way to Miami. Schoolgirl. Tourist couple. Waitress in a bar. Problem is, when he gets to the big city, he's not quite as careful, and he's busted. Busted bad, busted big time. Murder one. Sound familiar?"

"Starting to. Keep going."

"After a couple of years in court, man ends up right here on the Row. And what does he discover when he gets here? A big joke. Biggest joke he could ever imagine. Man in the cell next to him is waiting a date for the crime he committed and nearly goddamn forgot about because there were so many crimes, they all sort of got rolled together in his mind. Laughs so hard he'd like to split a gut. Only it isn't so funny for the man in the next cell, is it?"

"You're telling me that . . ."

"That's right, Mr. Cowart. The man who killed Joanie Shriver is right here on Death Row. Do you know a man named Blair Sullivan?"

Cowart breathed in sharply. The name exploded like shrapnel in his head. "I do."

"Everyone knows Blair Sullivan, right, Mr. Reporter?"

"That's right."

"Well, he's the one that did her."

Cowart felt his face flush. He wanted to loosen his tie, stick his head out some window, stand in a breeze somewhere, anything to give himself some air. "How do you know?"

"The man told me! Thought it was the funniest damn thing."

"Tell me exactly what he said."

"Not too long after he got sent up here, he was moved into the cell next to mine. He's not all there, you know. Laughs when nobody's made a joke. Cries for no reason. Talks to himself. Talks to God. Shit, man's got this awful soft voice, kinda makes a hissing sound, like a snake or something. He's the craziest motherfucker I've ever met. But crazy same as a damn fox, you know.

"Anyway, after a week or two, we get to talking and of course he asks me what I'm doing there. So I tell him the truth: I'm waiting on the death man for a crime I didn't do. This makes him grin and chuckle and he asks me what crime. So I tell him: Little girl in Pachoula. Little blond girl, he says, with braces? Yeah, I say. And then he starts to laugh and laugh. Beginning of May? he asks. Right, I says. Little girl all cut up with a knife, body tossed in a swamp? he asks. Right again, I say, but how come you know so much about this? And he keeps giggling and laughing and snorting and just rolling about, wheezing, he thinks it's so funny. Hell, he says, I know you didn't do that girl, 'cause I did. And she was mighty fine, too. Man, he says, you are the sorriest fuck on this row, and he keeps laughing and laughing. I was ready to kill him right there, you see, right there, and I start screaming and yelling and trying to get through the bars. Goon squad comes down the row, flak jackets and truncheons and those helmets with the plastic shit in front of their eyes. They pound my ass for a bit and haul me off to isolation. You know isolation? It's just a little room with no window and a bucket and a cement cot. They toss you in there naked until you get your act together sufficiently.

"By the time I got out, they had shifted him off to another tier. We don't get exercise the same time, so I don't see him. Word has it, he's really off the deep end. I can hear him sometimes at night, yelling for me. Bobby Earl, he calls out, kinda high-pitched and nasty. Bobbbbby Earrrrll! Why won't you talk to meeeeee? Then he laughs when I don't call back. Just laughs and laughs and laughs.''

Cowart shivered. He wanted to have a moment to stand back and assess the story he'd heard, but there was no time. He was locked in, fastened by the words that had flowed from Robert Earl Ferguson.

"How can I prove this?''

"I don't know, man! It ain't my job to prove things!''

"How can I confirm it?''

"Damn! The sergeant'll tell you they had to move Sullivan away from me. But he don't know why. No one knows why, except you and me and him.''

"But I can't . . .''

"I don't want to hear what you can and can't do, Mr. Reporter. People all my life have been telling me lots of can'ts. You can't be this, you can't do that, you can't have this, you can't even want that. That's my whole life, man, in one word. I don't want to hear it no more.''

Cowart was silent. "Well,'' he said, "I'll check . . .''

Ferguson turned swiftly, pushing his face toward him, his eyes electric with fury. "That's right. You go *check*,'' the prisoner said. "Go ask that bastard. You'll see, damn you, you'll see.''

Then Ferguson rose abruptly, pushing himself away from the

table. "Now you know. What you gonna do? What can you do? Go ask some more damn questions, but make damn sure I ain't dead before you finish asking 'em."

The prisoner walked over to the door and started pounding on it. The noise was like gunshots reverberating in the small room. "We're finished in here!" he called. "Sergeant Rogers! Damn!" The door staggered under the violence of his assault. When the prison guard swung the door open, Ferguson tossed a single look back at Cowart, then said, "I want to go back to my cell. I want to be alone. I don't need to make any more talk. No, sir." He held out his hands and they were cuffed. As the manacles were clicked shut around his wrists, he looked once more at the reporter. His eyes were piercing, harsh, filled with challenge and demand. Then he turned and disappeared through the doorway, leaving Cowart sitting quietly, feeling for all the world as if his legs were dangling over the edge of a whirlpool, threatening to suck him in.

As he was being shown the way out of the prison, Cowart asked the sergeant, "Where's Blair Sullivan?"

Sergeant Rogers snorted. "Sully? He's in Q wing. Stays in his cell all day, reading the Bible and writing letters. He writes to a bunch of psychiatrists and to the families of his victims. He writes them obscene descriptions of what he did to their loved ones. We don't mail those. We don't tell him that, but I think he suspects." The sergeant shook his head. "He's not playing with a full deck, that one. He's also got a real thing about Robert Earl. Calls his name out, kinda taunting-like, sometimes in the middle of the night. Did Bobby Earl tell you he tried to kill Sullivan when they were in adjacent cells? It was kinda odd, really. They got along fine at first, talking away through the bars. Then Robert Earl just goes crazy, screaming and thrashing about, trying to get at Sullivan. It's just about the only real trouble he's ever given us. Landed in the hole for a brief vacation. Now they're on the separation list."

"What's that?"

"Just what it sounds like. No contact whatsoever, under any circumstances. It's a list we keep to try to prevent some of the boys from killing one another before the state has the opportunity to juice them all legal-like."

"Suppose I wanted to talk to Sullivan?"

The sergeant shook his head. "The man's genuinely evil, Mr.

Cowart. Hell, he even scares me, and I've seen just about every kind of head case killer this world's got to offer.''

"Why?"

"Well, you know, we got some men here who'd kill you and not even think about it, means nothing to them to take a life. We've got madmen and sex killers and psychopaths and thrill seekers and contract boys and hit men, you name it. But Sullivan, well, he's twisted a little different. Can't exactly say why. It's like he would fit into any of the categories we've got, just like one of those damn lizards that changes color . . .''

"A chameleon?"

"Yeah. Right. It's almost like he's every sort, rolled up into one, so he's no specific type at all." Sergeant Rogers paused. "Man just scares me. I can't say I'm ever happy to see anyone go to the chair, but I won't think twice about strapping that sucker in. Gonna be soon, too.''

"How so? He's only been on the Row a year or so, right?"

"That's right. But he's fired all his lawyers, like that guy did up in Utah a few years back. He's got just his automatic appeal to the state Supreme Court pending, and he says when that's finished, that's the end of the line. Says he can't wait to get to hell because they'll roll out the red carpet for him.''

"You think he'll stick to that?"

"I told you. He ain't like other folks. Not even like other killers. I think he'll stick hard. Living, dying, seems all the same to him. My guess is he'll just laugh, like he laughs at everything, and plop himself down in the chair like it ain't no big deal.''

"I need to talk to him.''

"No one needs to talk to that man.''

"I do. Can you arrange it?"

Rogers stopped and stared at him. "This got something to do with Bobby Earl?''

"Maybe.''

He shrugged. "Well, best I can do is ask the man. He says yes, I'll set it up. He says no, and that's all she wrote.''

"Fair enough.''

"Won't be like talking to Bobby Earl in the executive suite. We'll have to use the cage.''

"Whatever. Just try for me.''

"All right, Mr. Cowart. You call me in the morning, and I'll try to get some sort of answer for you.''

They both walked silently through the sally-port entrance to the prison. For an instant they stood in the vestibule, before the doors. Then Rogers walked beside Cowart out into the sunlight. The reporter saw the prison guard shade his eyes and stare up through the pale blue sky toward the glaring sun. The sergeant stood, breathing in clear air, his eyes closed for an instant as if trying to force some of the clamminess of confinement away with fresh air. Then he shook his head and, without saying anything further, walked back inside the prison.

Ferguson was right, Cowart thought. Everyone knew Blair Sullivan.

Florida has an odd way of spawning killers of unique proportions, almost as if, like the gnarled mangroves that flourish in the salt water-tinged sandy dirt near the ocean, evil takes root in the state and fights its way into the ground. And those not born there seem to gravitate toward the state with alarming frequency, as if following some unusual gravitational swing of the earth, driven by tides and the awful desires of men. It gives the state a sort of routine familiarity with evil; a shrugging acceptance of the paranoic who opens fire with an automatic weapon in a fast-food outlet, or the bloated bodies of drug couriers gathering maggots in the Everglades. Drifters, crazies, contract murderers, killers willed with madness, passion, or devoid of reason or emotion, all find their way, it seems, to Florida.

Blair Sullivan, heading south, had killed a dozen people that he owned up to before arriving in Miami. The killings had been murders of convenience, really; just folks who happened to brush up against the man and wind up dead. The night manager of a small roadside motel, a waitress in a coffee shop, the clerk at a small store, an old tourist couple changing a tire by the road. What had made this particular killing spree so frightening was its utter random application. Some victims were robbed. Some raped. Some were simply killed, for no apparent reason or unfathomable reasons, like the gas-station attendant shot right through his protective cage, not because he was being robbed, but because he wasn't quick enough to make change of a twenty-dollar bill. Sullivan had been arrested in Miami minutes after he'd finished dealing with a young couple he'd found necking on a deserted road. He had taken his time with the pair, tying the teenage boy up and letting him watch as he raped the girl, then letting the girl watch as he slit the boy's throat. He had been slashing away at the young woman's body when a state trooper patrolling the area had spotted him. "Just bad luck," Sullivan had told the judge, arrogant, unrepentant, at his sentencing. "If I'd been just a little bit quicker, I would have got the trooper, too."

Cowart dialed the telephone in his room and within a few minutes was connected with the city desk at *The Miami Journal.* He asked for Edna McGee, the courthouse reporter who'd covered Sullivan's conviction and sentencing. The telephone played Muzak momentarily before she came on the line.

"Hey, Edna?"

"Matty? Where are you?"

"Stuck in a twenty-buck-a-night motel in Starke, trying to get it all figured out."

"You'll let me know if you do, huh? So, how's the story going? Rumors all over the newsroom that you're on to something real good."

"It's going along."

"That guy really kill that girl or what?"

"I don't know. There's some real questions. Cops even admitted hitting him before getting the confession. Not as bad as he says they did, of course, but still, you know."

"No kidding? Sounds good. You know, even the smallest little bit of coercion should cause a judge to throw out the man's confession. And if the cops admitted lying, even a little, well, watch out."

"That kinda bothers me, Edna. Why would they admit hitting the guy? It can't help them."

"Matty, you know as well as I that cops are the world's worst liars. They try and it just screws them up. They get all turned around. It's just not in their natures. So, finally, they end up telling the truth. You just got to hang in there long enough, keep asking the questions. Eventually, they'll always come around. Now, how can I help you?"

"Blair Sullivan."

"Sully? Whew, now that's interesting. What's he got to do with all this?"

"Well, his name came up in a kind of unusual context. I can't really talk about it."

"C'mon. Tell me."

"Give me a break, Edna. As soon as I'm certain, you'll be the first."

"Promise?"

"Sure."

"Double-promise?"

"Edna. C'mon."

"Okay. Okay. Blair Sullivan. Sully. Jesus. You know, I'm a liberal, but that guy, I don't know. You know what he made that girl do, before killing her? I never put it into a story. I couldn't. When the jurors heard it, one of them got sick, right in the jury box. They had to take a recess to clean up the mess. After she'd watched her boyfriend bleed to death, Sully made her bend down and . . ."

"I don't want to know," Cowart interrupted.

The woman on the phone fell abruptly into silence. After a moment, she asked, "So, what do you want to know?"

"Can you tell me about his route south?"

"Sure. The tabloids called it 'The Death Trip.' Well, it was pretty well documented. He started out by killing his landlady in Louisiana, outside of New Orleans, then a prostitute in Mobile, Alabama. He claims he knifed a sailor in Pensacola, some guy he picked up in a gay bar and left in a trash heap, then . . ."

"When was that?"

"It's in my notes. Hang on, they're in my bottom drawer." Matthew Cowart heard the telephone being put down on the desktop and could just make out the sounds of drawers being opened and then slammed shut. "I found it. Hang on. Here it is. Should have been late April, early May at the latest, right when he crossed over into the Sunshine State."

"Then what?"

"Still heading downstate slowly. Incredible, really. APBs in three states, BOLOs, FBI flyers with his picture, NCIC computer bulletins. And nobody spots him. At least, not nobody who lived. It was end of June before he reached Miami. Must have taken him a long time to wash all the blood off his clothes."

"What about cars?"

"Well, he used three, all stolen. A Chevy, a Mercury, and an Olds. Just abandoned them and hot-wired something new. Kept stealing plates, you know, that sort of thing. Always picked nondescript cars, real dull, not-the-type-to-get-attention cars. Said he always drove the speed limit, too."

"When he first came to Florida, what was he driving?"

"Wait. I'm checking my notebook. You know, there's a guy at the Tampa *Tribune* trying to write a book about him? Tried to go see him, but Sully just kicked him out. Wouldn't talk to him, I heard from the prosecutors. I'm still checking. He's fired all his lawyers, you know that? I think he'll check out before the end of the year. The governor's got to be getting writer's cramp he must be so anxious to sign a death warrant for Sully. Here it is: brown Mercury Monarch.''

"No Ford?"

"No. But you know, the Mercury's just about the same car. Same body, same design. Easy to get them mixed up.''

"Light brown?"

"No, dark."

Cowart breathed in hard. It fits, he thought.

"So, Matty, gonna tell me what this is all about?''

"Let me just check a few things, then I'll let you know.''

"Come on, Matty. I hate not knowing.''

"I'll get back to you.''

"Promise?''

"Sure.''

"You know the rumors are just gonna get worse around here?''

"I know.''

She hung up the phone, leaving Matthew Cowart alone. The room about him filled quickly with fearsome thoughts and terrifying explanations: Ford into Mercury. Green into brown. Black into white. One man into another.

"I don't properly understand it, but you're in luck, boy,'' Sergeant Rogers said jovially, his voice betraying no sign of the early hour.

"How so?''

"Mr. Sullivan says he'll see you. Sure would piss off that guy from Tampa who was here the other week. Wouldn't see him. Sure would piss off all the damn lawyers who've been trying to get in to see Sully, too. He won't see them, neither. Hell, the only folks he sees are a couple of shrinks that the FBI sent down from the Behavioral Sciences Unit. You know, the boys that study mass murderers. And I think the only reason he sees them is so that none of the damn lawyers can file papers claiming he's incompetent and get a court order to handle his appeals. Did I tell you Mr. Sullivan is one unique fellow?''

"I'll be damned,'' Cowart said.

"No, he will, to be sure. But that's not our concern, now, is it?''

"I'll be right over.''

"Take your time. We don't move Mr. Sullivan without a bit of caution, mind you. Not since nine months ago when he jumped one of the Row guards outside the shower and chewed the man's ear clean off. Said it tasted good. Said he'd of eaten the man's whole head if we hadn't pulled him off the top. That's Sully for you.''

''Why'd he do that?''

''The man called him crazy. You know, nothing special. Just like you'd say to your old lady, Hey, you're crazy to want to buy that new dress. Or you'd say to yourself, I'm crazy to want to pay my taxes on time. Like no big deal, huh? But it sure was the wrong damn word to use with Sullivan, all right. Just, bam! And he was on top of that man, chewing away like some sort of mongrel dog. The guy he took after, too, had to be twice his size. Didn't make no difference. And there they were rolling about, blood flying all over and the man screaming all the time, get offa me, you crazy sonuvabitch. 'Course it didn't make Sully do anything except fight harder. We had to pry him off with nightsticks, cool him down in the hole for a couple of months. I imagine it was that word, though, got it all started, kept it all going. It was just like pulling the man's trigger, he exploded so quick. Taught me something. Taught everyone on the Row something. To be a bit more cautious about the words we use. Sully, well, I gather he's very concerned about vocabulary.''

Rogers paused, letting a momentary silence slip into the air. Then he added, ''So's the other guy, now.''

Cowart was escorted by a young, gray-suited guard who said nothing and acted as if he were accompanying some disease-bearing organism down a whitewashed corridor filled with glare from sunlight pouring through a bank of high windows, placed beyond anyone's reach. The light made the world seem fuzzy and indistinct. The reporter tried to clear his mind as they walked. He listened to the tapping of their soles on the polished floor. There was a technique he used, a blanking-out where he tried not to think of anything, not to envision the upcoming interview, not to remember other stories he'd written or people he knew, anything at all; he wanted to exclude every detail and become a blotter, absorbing every sound and sight of the event that was about to happen.

He counted the clicking footsteps of the corrections officer as they passed down the corridor and through a locked set of double doors. As the count neared one hundred, they came into an open area, overseen by a pair of guards in a cubicle with catwalks and stairs leading up to housing tiers. In the junction of the space made by all the paths converging was a wire cage. In the center of the cage was a single steel-gray table and two benches. These were bolted to the floor. On one side of the table was a large metal ring welded into the side. Cowart was shown through the cage's single opening and motioned to take a seat opposite the side with the ring.

"The son of a bitch'll be here in a minute. You wait," the guard said. Then he turned and walked swiftly out of the cage, disappearing up one of the stairwells and down a catwalk.

Within a moment or so came a pounding on one of the doors that opened onto the area. Then a voice shouted over the intercom, "Security Detail! Five men coming through!"

There was a harsh blare from an electronic lock being opened and Cowart looked up to see Sergeant Rogers, wearing a flak jacket and a helmet, leading a squad into the area. The orange jumpsuit of the prisoner was obscured by men on either side of him, and a third behind. The group moved in quickstep right into the cage.

Blair Sullivan was hobbled by shackles connecting his hands and feet. The men that surrounded him marched with military precision, each boot hitting the floor in unison while he half-skipped in their midst, like a child trying desperately to keep up with a Fourth of July parade.

He was a cadaverously thin man, not tall, with purple-red tattoos crawling up the bleached white skin of each forearm and a shock of black hair streaked with gray. He had dark eyes that flickered about rapidly, taking in the cage, the guards, and Matthew Cowart. One eyelid seemed to twitch mildly as if each eye worked independently of the other. There was a flush looseness about his grin, about the languid way he stood while the sergeant cautiously undid the handcuff chain from where it was connected to his feet, almost as if he was able to disconnect the manacles from his mind. The corrections officers that flanked him stood at port arms with riot batons. The prisoner smiled at them, mock-friendly. The sergeant then ran the chain through the metal ring on the table and refastened it to a large leather belt that encircled the man's waist.

"All right. Sit down," Rogers ordered brusquely.

The three guards stood back quickly from the prisoner, who eased himself into the steel seat. He had locked his eyes onto Cowart's. The light grin still wandered about the prisoner's lips, but his eyes were narrowed and probing.

"All right," the sergeant said again. "Have at it."

He led the corrections officers from the cage, pausing to lock it securely.

"They don't like me," Blair Sullivan said with a sigh.

"Why not?"

"Dietary reasons," he replied, laughing abruptly. The laugh degenerated within seconds into a wheeze, followed by a hacking cough. Sullivan produced a pack of cigarettes from his shirt pocket, along with a box of wooden matches. He had to stoop toward the table to manage this, half-bending in his seat as he lit the cigarette, the range of his arms limited by the chain that fastened his wrists to the table.

"Of course, they don't have to like me to kill me. You mind if I smoke?" he asked Cowart.

"No, go ahead."

"It's sort of funny, don't you think?"

"What?"

"The condemned man smoking a cigarette. While everybody in the world is trying so damn hard to quit smoking, folks here living on the Row just naturally chain-smoke. Hell, we're probably R. J. Reynolds' best customers. I suspect we'd engage in every bad or dangerous vice we could if they'd let us. As it is, we just smoke. It's not like any of us are terribly worried about contracting lung cancer, although I suspect that if you managed to get damn sick enough, I mean really sick like unto death, then the state would be reluctant to drop your tail into the chair. The state gets squeamish about such things, Cowart. They don't want to execute somebody who's sick of mind or body. No, sir. They want the men they juice to be physically fit and mentally sound. There was a big uproar in Texas a couple of years back when that state tried to kill some poor sucker who had suffered a heart attack when his warrant was signed. It postponed the execution until the man was well enough to walk to his death. Didn't want to wheel him into the chamber on some hospital gurney, no way. That would offend the sensibilities of the do-gooders and the bleeding hearts. And there's a great story, back from the thirties, about some gangster in New York. Man, soon as he got to the Row, he started eating and eating. He was a big man getting bigger, you see. Got fatter and fatter and fatter and fatter and fatter. Ate bread and potatoes and spaghetti until it was coming out his ears. Starches, you see. You know what he figured? He figured he could beat the chair by getting so big that they couldn't fit him into it! I love it. Trouble was, he didn't quite make it. It was a tight squeeze, but damn, he still fit. Joke was on him, then, wasn't it? He must have looked like a pig roast by the time they got through with him. You tell me where's the logic in all that? Huh?''

He laughed again. ''There's no place like Death Row for letting you see all the little ironies of life.'' He stared over at Cowart, his one eyelid twitching quickly.

''Tell me, Cowart, you a killer, too?''

''What?''

''I mean, you ever take a life? In the army, maybe? You're old enough for Vietnam, you go there? No, probably not. You ain't got that faraway look that vets get when they start in to remembering. But maybe you smashed a car up as a teenager or something. Kill your best buddy or your main squeeze on a Saturday night? Or maybe you told the doctors at some damn hospital to pull the plug on your old mom or dad when they got so decrepit a respirator had to keep them alive. Did you do that, Cowart? You ever tell your wife or girlfriend to get an abortion? Didn't want any little ones crawling in the way of success? Maybe you're a bit more upscale, Cowart, huh? Take a little toot or two of cocaine at some party down in Miami, maybe? Know how many lives were lost over that shipment? Just guessing, mind you. Come on, Cowart, tell me, you a killer, too?''

''No, I don't think so.''

Blair Sullivan snorted. ''You're wrong. Everybody's a killer. You just got to look hard enough. Take a broad enough definition of the word. Haven't you ever been in a shopping mall and seen some ragged mean momma just light into her kid, wallop 'em good right there in front of everybody? What you think's going on there? Look at that child's eyes, you'll see them go icy cold, sir. A killer in the making. So, why don't you look inside yourself as well. You got those icy eyes, too, Cowart. You got it in you. I know. I can tell just by looking at you.''

''That's quite a trick.''

''Not a trick. A special ability, I guess. You know, takes one to know one, that sort of thing. You get thick enough with death and dying, Cowart, and you can spot the signs.''

''Well, you're mistaken this time.''

''Am I? We'll see. We'll see about that.''

Sullivan lounged about in the hard metal chair, striking a relaxed pose but all the time letting his eyes burrow deeper into Cowart's heart. ''It gets easy, you know.''

''What does?''

''Killing.''

"How?"

"Familiarity. You learn real quick how people die. Some die hard, some die soft. Some fight like the devil, others just go along quietly. Some plead for their lives, some spit in your eye. Some cry, some laugh. Some call out for their mommas, others tell you they'll see you in hell. Some folks'll hang on to life real strong, others just give it up easy. But in the end, everybody's just the same. Getting stiff and cold. You. Me. Everybody's the same at the end."

"Maybe at the end. But people get there in a lot of different ways."

Sullivan laughed. "That's true enough. That's a real Death Row observation, Cowart. That's exactly what some fellow on the Row would say, after about eight years and a hundred appeals and time running out quick. A lot of different ways."

He drew hard on the cigarette and blew smoke up into the still prison air. For a moment Blair Sullivan's eyes followed the trail of smoke as it slowly dissipated. "We're all smoke, aren't we? When it comes right down to it. That's what I told those shrinks, but I don't think they wanted to hear that too much."

"What shrinks?"

"From the FBI. They got this special Behavioral Sciences section that's trying like crazy to figure out what makes mass murderers, so they can do something about this particular American pastime. . . ." He grinned. "Of course, they ain't having a whole helluva lot of success, 'cause each and every one of us has our own little reasons. Couple of real nice guys, though. They like to come down here, give me Minnesota Multiphasic Personality tests and Thematic Apperception tests and Rorschach tests and I.Q. tests and, Christ knows, they'll probably want to give me the fucking college board exams next time. They like it when I talk about my momma a lot, and when I tell them how much I hated that old bat and especially my stepdaddy. He beat me, you know. Beat me real bad every time I opened my mouth. Used his fists, used his belt, used his prick. Beat me and fucked me, fucked me and beat me. Day in, day out, regular as Sundays. Man, I hated them. Sure do. Still do, yes sir. They're in their seventies now, still living in a little cinder-block bungalow in the Upper Keys with a crucifix on the wall and a full-color picture of Jesus, still thinking that their savior's gonna come right through the door and lift them up into heaven. They cross themselves when they hear my name and say things like, 'Well, the boy was always in the devil's thrall,' and stuff like that. Those boys from the FBI are sure interested in all that. You interested in that stuff, too, Cowart? Or do you just want to know why I killed all those folks, including some I hardly even knew?''

"Yes."

He laughed harshly. "Well, it's an easy enough question to answer: I was just on my way back home and sort of got sidetracked. Distracted, you might say. Never did make it all the way. That make sense to you?''

"Not exactly."

Sullivan grinned and rolled his eyes. "Life's a mystery, ain't it?''

"If you say so."

"That's right. If I say so. Of course you're a bit more interested in another little mystery, aren't you, Cowart? You don't really care about some other folks, do you? That ain't why you're here."

"No."

"Tell me why you want to talk to a bad old guy like myself?''

"Robert Earl Ferguson and Pachoula, Florida."

As best he could, Blair Sullivan threw back his head and bellowed a single sharp laugh that echoed off the prison walls. Cowart saw a number of the corrections officers swing their heads, watch momentarily, then turn back to their tasks.

"Well now, those are interesting subjects, Cowart. Mighty interesting. But we'll have to get to them in a minute."

"Okay. Why?"

Blair Sullivan pitched forward across the table, bringing his face as close as possible to Cowart's. The chain that linked him to the table rattled and strained with the sudden pressure. A vein stood out on the prisoner's neck and his face flushed suddenly. "Because you don't know me well enough yet."

Then he sat back abruptly, reaching for another cigarette, which he lit off the stub of the first. "Tell me something about yourself, Cowart, then maybe we can talk. I like to know who I'm dealing with."

"What do you need to know?"

"Got a wife?"

"Ex-wife."

The prisoner hooted. "Kids?"

Matthew Cowart hesitated, then replied, "None."

"Liar. Live alone or you got a girlfriend?"

"Alone."

"Apartment or a house?"

"Little apartment."

"Got any close friends?"

Again, he hesitated. "Sure."

"Liar. That's twice and I'm counting. What do you do at night?"

"Sit around. Read. Watch a ball game."

"Keep to yourself mostly, huh?"

"That's right."

The eyelid twitched again. "Have trouble sleeping?"

"No."

"Liar. That's three times. You ought to be ashamed, lying to a condemned man. Same as Matthew did to Jesus before the cock crowed. Now, do you dream at night?"

"What the hell . . ."

Blair Sullivan whispered sharply, "Play the game, Cowart, or else I'll walk out of here without answering any of your frigging questions."

"Sure. I dream. Everyone dreams."

"What about?"

"People like you," Cowart said angrily.

Sullivan laughed again. "Got me on that one." He leaned back in his seat and watched Cowart. "Nightmares, huh? Because that's what we are, aren't we? Nightmares."

"That's right," Cowart replied.

"That's what I tried to tell those boys from the FBI, but they weren't listening. That's all we are, smoke and nightmares. We just walk and talk and bring a little bit of darkness and fear to this earth. Gospel according to John: 'Ye are of your father the devil, and the lusts of your father ye will do. He was a murderer from the beginning, and abode not in the truth, because there is no truth in him.' Got that? Eighth verse. Now, there might be a bunch of fancy shrink words to describe it all, but, hell, that's just a bunch of medical gobbledygook, right?"

"Right, I guess."

"You know what? You've got to be a free man to be a good killer. Free, Cowart. Not hung up on all the silly shit that bogs down ordinary lives. A free man."

Cowart didn't reply.

"Let me tell you something else: It ain't hard to kill folks.

That's what I told them. And you don't really think about it much after, neither. I mean, you got too many things to think about, like disposing of bodies and weapons and getting bloodstains off'n your hands and such. Hell, after a murder, you're downright busy, you know. Just figuring out what to do next and how to get the hell outa there.''

"Well, if killing is easy, what was hard?"

Sullivan smiled. "That's a good question. They never asked that one." He thought for a moment, turning his face upward toward the ceiling. "I think that what was hardest was getting here to the Row and figuring that I never did kill the folks I wanted to kill the most, you know.''

"What do you mean?"

"Ain't that always the hardest thing in life, Cowart? Lost opportunities. They're what we regret the most. What keeps us up at night.''

"I still don't get it.''

Sullivan shifted about in his seat, leaning forward again toward Cowart, whispering in a conspiratorial voice, "You got to get it. If not now, you will someday. You got to remember it, too, because it'll be important someday. Someday when you least expect it, you'll remember: Who is it that Blair Sullivan hates most? Who does it bother him every day to know they're alive and well and living out their days? It's real important for you to remember that, Cowart.''

"You're not going to tell me?"

"No, sir.''

"Jesus Christ . . .''

"Don't use that name in vain! I'm sensitive to those things.''

"I just meant . . .''

Blair Sullivan pitched forward again. "Do you think these chains could really hold me if I wanted to rip your face off? Do you think these puny little bars could contain me? Do you think I could not rise up and burst free and tear your body apart and drink your blood like it was the water of life in a second's time?''

Cowart recoiled sharply.

"I can. So don't anger me, Cowart.''

He stared across the table.

"I am not crazy and I believe in Jesus, though he'll most likely see my ass kicked straight to hell. But it don't bother me none, no sir, because my life's been hell, and so should my death be.''

Blair Sullivan was silent. Then he leaned back in the metal seat and readopted his lazy, almost insulting tone. ''You see, Cowart, what separates me from you ain't bars and chains and all that shit. It's one simple little detail. I am not afraid of dying. Death, where is your sting, I fear it not. Put me in the chair, shoot me up with a lethal injection, plop me down in front of a firing squad, or stretch me by the neck. Hell, you can throw me to the lions and I'll go along saying my prayers and looking forward to the next world, where I suspect I'll raise as much hell as I have in this one. You know what's strange, Cowart?''

''What?''

''I'm more afraid of living here like some damn beast than dying. I don't want to be poked and prodded by shrinks, argued and discussed by lawyers. Hell, I don't want to be written about by you guys. I just want to move on, you know. Move right on.''

''That's why you fired the attorneys? That's why you're not contesting your conviction?''

He barked a laugh. ''Sure. Hell, Cowart, look at me. What do you see?''

''A killer.''

''Right.'' Sullivan smiled. ''That's right. I killed those folks. I'd of killed more if I hadn't been caught. I'd of killed that trooper—man, he was one lucky sonuvabitch. All I had was my knife, which I was busy using on that little gal to have some fun. I left my damn gun with my pants, and he got a clean drop on me. Still don't know why he didn't shoot me then and save everybody so damn much trouble. But, hell, he got me fair and square. I can't complain about that. I had my chances. He even read me my rights after he got me cuffed. His voice was cracking and his hands were twitching, and he was more excited than I was, by a long shot. And, anyway, I hear that arresting me gave his career a real boost, and I take some pride in that, yes sir. So, what I got to argue about? Just give some more fucking lawyers more fucking work. Screw 'em. It ain't like life is so great I got a real need to hang around, you know.''

Both men were silent, considering the words which hung in the air inside the cage.

''So, Cowart, you got a question?''

"Yes. Pachoula."

"Nice town. Been there. Real friendly. But that ain't a question."

"What happened in Pachoula?"

"You been talking to Robert Earl Ferguson. You gonna do a story about him? My old tier mate?"

"What happened between you two?"

"We got to talking. That's all."

Blair Sullivan, faint smile flitting about his face, relaxed, toyed with his answers. Cowart wanted to shake the man, rattle the truth out of him. But instead, he kept asking questions. "What did you talk about?"

"His unfair conviction. You know those cops beat that boy to obtain his confession? Hell, all they had to do for me was buy me a Coca-Cola and I was talking their ears off."

"What else?"

"We talked about cars. Seems we were partial to similar vehicles."

"And?"

"Coincidence. We talked a bit about being in the same place at about the same time. A remarkability, that, don't you think?"

"Yes."

"We talked about that little town and what happened to make it lose its virginity, like." Again Sullivan grinned. "I like that. Lose its virginity. Ain't that what happened? To that little girl and to that town."

"Did you kill that girl? Joanie Shriver. Did you kill her?"

"Did I?" Blair Sullivan rolled his eyes and smiled. "Now, let me see if I can recollect. You know, Cowart, they all start to bunch together in my memory. . . ."

"Did you?"

"Hell, Cowart. You're starting to sound all frantic and excited the way Bobby Earl did. He got so damn frustrated with my natural recollection process he like to kill me. Now, that's an unusual thing, even for Death Row, don't you think?"

"Did you?"

Blair Sullivan pitched forward in his seat again, dropping the jocular, teasing tones, whispering hoarsely, "You'd like to know, huh?'' He rocked back in the seat, eyeing the reporter. ''Tell me something, Cowart, will you?''

''What?''

''You ever felt the power of life and death in your hands? Did you ever know the sweet feeling of strength, know you control someone else's life or death? Completely. Utterly. All of it. Right there in your hand. You ever felt that, Cowart?''

''No.''

''It's the best drug there is. It's just like shooting electricity into your soul with a needle. There ain't nothing like knowing that someone's life is yours. . . .''

He held up his fist, as if he was holding a fruit. He squeezed the air. The handcuff chain rattled in the metal bracket. ''Let me tell you a few things, Cowart.'' He paused, staring at the reporter. ''One: I am filled with power. You may think I am an impotent prisoner, handcuffed and shackled and locked in an eight-by-seven cell each night and day, but I am filled with strength that reaches way beyond those bars, sir. Far beyond. I can touch any soul I want to, just as easy as dialing a telephone. No one is beyond my reach, Cowart. No one.''

He stopped, then asked, ''Got that?''

Cowart nodded.

''Two: I ain't going to tell you if I killed that little girl or not. Hell, if I told you the truth, it would make everything too easy. And how could you believe me, anyway? Especially after all the things the papers have written about me. What sort of credibility do I have? If killing somebody's easy for me, how easy you think is lying?''

Cowart started to speak, but a single glance from Sullivan made him halt, his mouth open.

''You want to know something, Cowart? I quit school in tenth grade, but I never quit learning. I'll bet I'm better read and better educated than you. What do you read? *Time* and *Newsweek*. Maybe *The New York Times Book Review?* Probably *Sports Illustrated* when you're on the can. But I've read Freud and Jung and kinda prefer the disciple to the master. I've read Shakespeare, Elizabethan poetry and American history, with an emphasis on the Civil War. I like novelists, too, especially ones that are filled with the politics of irony like James Joyce, Faulkner, Conrad, and Orwell. I like to read classics. Little bit of Dickens and Proust. I enjoy Thucydides and reading about the arrogance of the Athenians, and Sophocles because he talks about each and every one of us. Prison's a great place for reading, Cowart. Ain't nobody gonna tell you what to read or not. And you got all the time in the world. I suspect it's a damn sight better than most graduate schools. Of course, this time I don't exactly have all that time, after all, so now I just occupy myself with the Good Book.''

"Hasn't it taught you anything about truth and charity?"

Blair Sullivan screeched a laugh that echoed about the cage. "I like you, Cowart. You're a funny man. You know what the Bible's all about? It's about cheating and killing and lying and murder and robbery and idolatry and all sorts of things that are right up my alley, so to speak."

The prisoner stared over at Cowart. He smiled wickedly. "Okay, Cowart. Let's have some fun."

"Fun?"

"Yeah." He giggled and wheezed. "About seven miles from the spot where little Joanie Shriver was killed, there is an intersection where County Route Fifty intersects with State Route One-Twenty. A hundred yards before that intersection there is a small culvert that runs under the roadway, right near a big old stand of willow trees that kinda droop down and toss a bit of shade on the road on a summer day. If you were to pull over your car at that spot and go down to the right-hand side of that culvert and reach your hand down under the lip where the culvert pipe protrudes out, stick your hand right under whatever greasy old water is flowing through there, you might find something. Something important. Something real interesting."

"What?"

"Come on, Cowart. You don't expect me to spoil the surprise, do you?"

"Suppose I go and find this something, what then?"

"Then you'll have a real intriguing question to pose to your readers in your articles, Cowart."

"What question is that?"

"How does Blair Sullivan know how this item got to that location?"

"I . . ."

"That's the question, isn't it, always? How does he know something? You'll have to figure it out for yourself, Cowart, because you and I ain't gonna talk again. Not at least until I can feel the breath of Mr. Death right behind my neck.''

Blair Sullivan stood up then and suddenly bellowed, ''Sergeant! I'm finished with this pig! Get him outa my sight before I eat his head right off!''

He grinned at Cowart, rattling his chains while the air reverberated with the echo of the murderer's voice and the impatient sound of footsteps hurrying toward the cage.

SIX

THE CULVERT

A LIGHT breeze out of the south played with the increasing morning heat, sending great gray-white clouds sliding across the rich blue of the Gulf sky and swirling the moist air about him as he crossed the motel's parking lot. Cowart carried a bag with a pair of gardening gloves and a large lantern-flashlight purchased the evening before at a convenience store. He quickstepped toward his car, preoccupied with what he'd heard from the two men on Death Row, confident that he was heading toward a puzzle piece that would complete the picture in his mind. He did not see the detective until he was almost upon him.

Tanny Brown was leaning up against the reporter's car, shading his eyes with his hand, watching him approach.

"In a hurry to get somewhere?" the detective asked.

Cowart stopped in his tracks. "You've got good sources. I only got in last night."

Tanny Brown nodded. "I'll take that as a compliment. Not too much gets by us in a little place like Pachoula."

"You sure about that?"

The detective refused to rise to the bait. "Perhaps I'd better not take it as a compliment," he said slowly. Then he continued. "How long you planning on staying?"

Cowart hesitated before replying. "This sounds like a conversation out of some B movie."

The detective frowned. "Let me try again. I heard last night that you'd checked into the motel here. Obviously you still have some unanswered questions, otherwise you wouldn't be here."

"Right."

"What sort of questions?"

Cowart didn't reply. Instead he watched as the detective shifted about. He had an odd thought: Even though it was bright daylight, the policeman had a way of narrowing the world down, compressing it the way the night does. He could sense a nervousness within him and a small, unsettling vulnerability.

"I thought you'd already made up your mind about Mr. Ferguson and us."

"You thought wrong."

The detective smiled, shaking his head slowly, letting Cowart know he recognized this for a lie. "You're a hard case, aren't you, Mr. Cowart?"

He did not say this angrily or aggressively, but mildly, as if prompted by a bemused curiosity.

"I don't know what you mean, Lieutenant."

"I mean, you got an idea in your head and you aren't gonna let go of it, are you?"

"If you mean have I got some serious doubts about the guilt of Robert Earl Ferguson, well, yes, that's true."

"Can I ask you a question, Mr. Cowart?"

"Go ahead."

The detective took a deep breath, then leaned forward, speaking barely above a whisper. "You've seen him. You've talked to him. You've stood right next to the man and smelled him. Felt him. What do you think he is?"

"I don't know."

"You can't tell me that your skin didn't shrivel up a bit and you didn't feel a little sweat under the arms when you were talking with Mr. Ferguson, can you? That what you'd expect talking to an innocent man?"

"You're talking about impressions, not evidence."

"That's right. Don't tell me that you don't deal in impressions. Now what do you think he is?"

"I don't know."

"Hell you don't."

In that moment, Cowart remembered the tattoos on the pale flesh of Blair Sullivan's arms. Some painstaking artist had constructed a pair of ornate Oriental dragons, one on each forearm, which seemed to slither down across the skin, undulating with each small flex of the man's tendons. The dragons were a faded red and blue ornamented with green scales. Their claws were extended and their jaws gaped open in menace so that when Sullivan reached out his arms to seize something or someone, so did the pair of dragons. He thought, right then, of blurting out Sullivan's name and watching its impact on the detective, but it was too important a clue to waste like that.

The detective stared at the reporter, shifting his weight forward and speaking softly. "You ever watched a pair of old, mean dogs, Mr. Cowart? You know the way they sort of snuffle about, circling around, measuring each other up? The thing that always made me wonder was how it was those old dogs decided to fight. Sometimes, you know, they get the scent and then just back on down, maybe wag their old tails a bit, and then go on about their business of being a dog, whatever it is. But sometimes, just quick as you know, one dog'll growl and bare those teeth and they all of a sudden start to rip into each other as if their damn lives depended on tearing the other's throat out." He paused. "You tell me, Mr. Cowart. Why do those dogs walk away sometimes? And why sometimes do they fight?"

"I don't know."

"Suppose they can smell something?"

"I guess so."

Tanny Brown leaned back against the car, lifting his head up into the sunlight, staring up at the clouds that slid past. He directed his words toward the expanse of pale blue. "You know, when I was a little boy, I thought all white folks were special somehow. It was real easy to think that way. All I had to see was that they always had the good jobs and the big cars and the nice houses. I hated white folks for a long time. Then I got older. Got to go to high school with whites. Went to the army, fought alongside whites. Came back, got my degree in a college with whites. Became a policeman, one of the first black cops on an all-white force. Now we're twenty percent black and rising. Put white folks in jail right alongside black folks. And I learned a little bit more every step of the way. And you know what I learned? That evil is color-blind. It don't make no difference what color you are. If you're a wrong one, you're wrong, black, white, green, yellow, red."

He looked down out of the sky. "Now, that's simple, isn't it, Mr. Cowart?"

"Too simple."

"That must be because I'm a country fellow at heart," Tanny Brown replied. "I'm an old dog. And I got the scent."

The two men stood next to the car, silently staring at each other. Brown seemed to sigh, and he rubbed a large hand through his closely cropped hair. "I ought to be laughing at all this, you know."

"What do you mean?"

"You'll figure it out. So where are you going?"

"On a treasure hunt."

The detective smiled. "Can I come along? You make it sound like a game, and I could certainly use some childish pleasure, don't you think? Not much easy laughter in being a policeman, just lots of gallows humor. Or do I have to follow you?"

Cowart realized that as much as he wanted to, he would not be able to hide from the policeman. He made the easy decision. "Jump in," he said, gesturing toward the passenger seat.

The two men drove in silence for a few miles. Cowart watched the highway wash through the windshield, while the detective stared out at the passing countryside. The quiet seemed uncomfortable, and Cowart shifted about in his seat, trying to stretch his arms out stiffly toward the steering wheel. He was used to rapid assessments about personality and character, and so far Tanny Brown had eluded him. He glanced over at the detective, who seemed to be lost in thought himself. Cowart tried to appraise the man, like an auctioneer before the start of bidding. Despite his musculature and imposing size, Brown's modest tan suit hung loosely about his arms and shoulders, as if he'd purposefully had it cut two sizes too large to diminish his physique. Although the day was warming, he wore his red tie tight to the neck of a pale blue button-down shirt. As Cowart stole glances away from the roadway, he watched the detective clean a pair of gold wire-rimmed glasses and put them on, giving him a bookish appearance that again contradicted his bulk. Then Brown took out a small pen and notepad and made some notations swiftly, a motion not unlike a reporter's. After finishing his writing, the detective put away pad, pen, and glasses and continued to stare through the window. He lifted his hand slightly, as if pushing an idea up into the air, and gestured at the passing countryside. "It was all different ten years ago. And twenty years ago, it was different again."

"How so?"

"See that gas station? The drive-in, serve-yourself Exxon Mini-Mart with the grocery store and the computer-driven, digital-read-out automatic pumps?"

They swept past the station.

"Sure. What about it?"

"Five years ago, it was a little Dixie Gas, owned by a guy who probably'd been in the Klan in the fifties. A couple of old pumps, a stars-and-bars hanging in the window and a sign that said BAIT 'N AMMO. Hell, the guy was lucky he could spell that much, and he still had to abbreviate one of three words. But he had prime location. Sold it. Made a bundle. Retired to one of these little houses you see growing up around here in developments named Fox Run or Bass Creek or Elysian Fields, I guess." The detective laughed to himself. "I like that. When I retire, it's got to be to some place called the Elysian Fields. Or maybe Valhalla, that's probably more appropriate for a cop, huh? The warriors of modern society. Of course, I'd have to die with my weapon in my hand, right?"

"That's right," Cowart replied. He was tense. The detective seemed to fill the small interior of the car, as if there were more to him than Cowart could see. "Lots has changed?"

"Look around. The road is good, that means tax dollars. No more mom-and-pops. Now it's all 7-Eleven and Winn-Dixie and Southland Corporation. You want your car lubed, you go to a corporation. You want to see a dentist, you go to a professional association. You want to buy something, you go to a mall. Hell, the quarterback on the high-school football team is a teacher's son and black, and the best wide receiver is a mechanic's boy and white. How about that?"

"Things didn't seem to have changed much where Ferguson's grandmother lives."

"No, that's right. Old South. Dirt poor. Hot in the summer. Cold in the winter. Wood stove and outdoor plumbing and bare feet kicking at the dust. Not everything has changed, and that's the sort of place that exists to remind us how much more changing we've got to do."

"Gas stations are one thing," Cowart said, "what about attitudes?"

Brown laughed. "Those change more slowly, don't they? Everybody cheers when that teacher's boy throws the ball and that mechanic's boy catches it for a touchdown. But either of those kids wanted to date the other's sister, well, I think the cheering would stop damn fast. But then, you must know all about that in your business, don't you?"

The reporter nodded, unsure whether he was being teased, insulted, or complimented. They swept past some tract housing being built on a wide field. A yellow bulldozer was uprooting a swath through a green field, turning over a scar of reddish dirt. It made a grinding and digging noise, momentarily filling the car with the sound of machinery working hard. Nearby, a work crew in hard hats and sweat-drenched shirts was stacking lumber and cinder block. In the car, the two men were silent until they cruised past the construction site. Then Cowart asked, "So, where's Wilcox today?"

"Bruce? Oh, we had a couple of traffic fatalities late last night. I sent him down to officially witness the autopsies. It teaches you a new respect for seat belts and driving around drunk and what happens when you've got construction workers like the ones we just passed getting paid on Thursdays."

"He needs lessons like that?"

"We all do. Part of growing into the job."

"Like his temper?"

"That's something he will learn to control. Despite his manner, he is a very cautious observer, and astute. You'd be surprised how good he is with evidence and with people. It's not often his temper boils over like that."

"He should have controlled it with Ferguson."

"I think you do not yet understand how strung out we all were over what happened to that little girl."

"That's beside the point and you know it."

"No, that is precisely the point. You just don't want to hear it."

Cowart was quieted by the detective's admonition. After a moment, however, he started in again. "You know what will happen when I write that he struck Ferguson?"

"I know what you think will happen."

"He'll get a new trial."

"Maybe. I guess, probably."

"You sound like someone who knows something, who's not talking."

"No, Mr. Cowart, I sound like someone who understands the system."

"Well, the system says you can't beat a confession out of a defendant."

"Is that what we did? I think I told you only that Wilcox slapped Ferguson once or twice. Slapped. Open hand. Hardly more than an attention-getting device. You think getting a confession from a murderer is a tea party, all nice and proper every time? Christ. And anyway, it was almost twenty-four hours later before he confessed. Where's the cause and effect?''

"That's not what Ferguson says."

"I suppose he says we tortured him all that time."

"Yes.''

"No food. No drink. No sleep. Constant physical abuse coupled with deprivation and fear. Old tactics, remarkably successful. Been around since the Stone Age. That's what he says?''

"Pretty much. Do you deny it?''

Tanny Brown smiled and nodded. "Of course. It didn't happen that way. If it had, we'd have damn well gotten a better confession out of that closemouthed son of a bitch. We'd have found out how he sweet-talked Joanie into that car and where he stashed his clothes and that piece of rug and all the rest of the shit he wouldn't tell us.''

Cowart felt a surge of indecision again. What the policeman said was true.

Brown paused, thinking. Then he added, "There you go, that'll help your story, won't it? An official denial.''

"Yes.''

"But it won't stop your story?''

"No.''

"Ah, well, I suppose it's much more convenient for you to believe him.''

"I didn't say that.''

"No? What makes his version more plausible than what I told you?''

"I'm not making that judgment.''

"The hell you aren't.'' Brown pivoted in his seat and glared at Cowart. "That's the standard reporter's excuse, isn't it? The 'Hey, I just put all the versions out there and let the readers decide whom to believe . . .' speech, right?''

Cowart, unsettled, nodded.

The detective nodded back and returned his gaze to the window.

Cowart fell into a hole of quiet as he steered the car slowly down the roadway. He saw that he was driving past the intersection described by Blair Sullivan. He peered down the roadway, looking for the stand of willow trees.

"What are you looking for?'' Brown asked.

"Willow trees and a culvert that runs beneath the road.''

The detective frowned and took a second before replying. "Right down the road. Slow down, I'll show you.''

He pointed ahead and Matthew Cowart saw the trees and a small dirt space where he could pull over. He parked the car and got out.

"Okay," said the detective, "we found the willows. Now what are we looking for?"

"I'm not sure."

"Mr. Cowart, perhaps if you were a bit more forthcoming . . ."

"Under the culvert. I was told to look under the culvert."

"Who told you to look under the culvert, for what?"

The reporter shook his head. "Not yet. Let's just take a look first."

The detective snorted, but followed after him.

Matthew Cowart walked to the side of the road and stared down at the edge of the slate-gray, rusted pipe that protruded into a tangle of scrub brush, rock, and moss. It was surrounded by the inevitable array of litter: beer cans, plastic soda bottles, unrecognizable paper wrappings, an old dirty white hightop sneaker, and a rank, half-eaten bucket of fried chicken. A trickle of black dirty water dripped from the end of the metal cylinder. He hesitated, then scrambled down into the damp, thorny undergrowth. The bushes tugged at his clothing and he could feel ooze beneath his feet. The detective followed him without hesitation, instantly ripping and muddying his suit. He paid it no mind.

"Tell me," the reporter asked, "is this thing always like this, or . . ."

"No. When it rains hard, this whole area will fill up, all muck swamp and mud. Takes a day or so to dry out again. Over and over."

Cowart slid on the gloves. "Hold the flashlight," he said.

Gingerly, he got down on his knees and, with the detective balancing next to him, flashing the light beneath the edge of the culvert, the reporter started scraping away built-up dirt and rock.

"Mr. Cowart, do you know what you're doing?"

He didn't answer but continued pulling the debris away, pitching it behind him.

"Perhaps if you told me . . ."

He caught a glimpse of something in the light beam. He started to dig harder. The detective saw that he'd seen something and tried to peer down, under the lip, at what it was. Matthew Cowart scratched away some wet leaves and mud. He saw a handle and grasped it. He pulled hard. For an instant there was resistance, as if the earth would not give it up without a struggle, then it came free. He stood up abruptly, turning toward the detective, holding out his hand.

A wild, self-satisfied excitement filled him. "One knife," he said slowly.

The detective stared at it.

"One murder weapon, I suspect."

The four-inch blade and handle of the knife were crusted with rust and dirt. It was black with age and the elements, and for an instant Cowart feared the weapon would disintegrate in his hand.

Tanny Brown looked hard at Matthew Cowart, pulled a clean cloth from a pocket and took the knife by the tip, wrapping it gently. "I'll take that," he said firmly.

The detective placed the knife in his suit pocket. "Not much left of it," he said slowly, with disappointment. "We'll run it through the lab, but I wouldn't count on much." He stared down at the culvert, then up into the sky. "Step back," he continued softly. "Don't touch anything else. There may be something of forensic value, and I don't want it further disturbed." He fixed Cowart with a long, hard stare. "If this location relates to a crime, then I want it properly preserved."

"You know what it relates to," Cowart replied.

Brown stepped away for an instant, shaking his head. "You son of a bitch," he said softly, turning abruptly and scrambling back up the incline toward the reporter's car. He stood for an instant on the roadway, hand clenched, face set. Then, suddenly, with a swiftness that seemed to break the still morning, he kicked at the open car door. The noise of his foot slamming into the metal reverberated amidst the heat and sunlight, fading slowly like a distant shot.

Cowart sat alone in the policeman's office, waiting. He watched through the window as night slid over the town, a sudden surge of darkness that seemed to fight its way out of shadowy corners and from beneath shade trees to take over the atmosphere. It was a wintertime swiftness, with none of the slow lingering daylight of summer.

The day had been spent on edge. He had watched as a team of crime-scene technicians had carefully processed the culvert for other evidence. He had watched as they had bagged and tagged all the debris, dirt samples, and some pieces of unrecognizable trash. He knew they would find nothing, but had waited patiently through the search.

By late afternoon, Tanny Brown and he had driven back to the police headquarters, where the detective had put him in the office to await the results of the laboratory examination of the knife. The two men had shared little but silence.

Cowart turned to the wall of the office and gazed at a framed photograph of the detective and his family, standing outside a whitewashed church. A wife and two daughters, one all pigtails and braces with an insouciance that penetrated even the austerity of her Sunday clothes; the other a teenage vixen-in-the-making with smooth skin and a figure pushing hard at the starched white of her blouse. The detective and his wife were smiling calmly at the camera, trying to look comfortable.

He was hit with a sudden twinge. He had thrown out all the pictures of himself with his wife and child after the divorce. Now he wondered why.

He let his eyes wander over the other wall decorations. There was a series of marksmanship plaques for winning the annual county handgun contest. A framed citation from the mayor and city council attesting to his bravery on an obscure occasion. A framed medal, a Bronze Star, along with another citation. Next to it was a picture of a younger, far leaner Tanny Brown in fatigues in Southeast Asia.

The door opened behind him, and Cowart turned. The detective was impassive, his face set.

"Hey," Cowart said, "what did you get the medal for?"

"What?"

Cowart gestured at the wall.

"Oh. That. I was a medic. Platoon got caught in an ambush and four guys got dropped out in a paddy. I went out and brought them in, one after the other. It was no big deal except we had a reporter from *The Washington Post* along with us that day. My lieutenant figured he'd fucked up so bad walking us into the ambush that he better do something, so he made sure I got cited for a medal. Kinda deflected the bad impression the newspaper guy was going to come away with after spending four hours having his ass shot at and his face pushed down in a swamp crawling with leeches. Did you go?"

"No," Cowart said. "My lottery number was three-twenty. It never came up."

The detective nodded, gesturing toward a chair. He plumped himself down behind the desk.

"Nothing," the detective said.

"Fingerprints? Blood? Anything?"

"Not yet. We're going to send it off to the FBI lab and see what they can do. They've got fancier equipment than we do."

"But nothing?"

"Well, the medical examiner says the blade is the right size to have caused the stab wounds. The deepest wound measured the same distance as the blade of the knife. That's something."

Cowart pulled out his notepad and started taking notes. "Can you trace the knife?"

"It's a cheap, typical nineteen-ninety-five, buy-it-in-any-sporting-goods-store-type knife. We'll try, but there's no identifying serial number or manufacturer's mark." He hesitated and looked hard at Cowart. "But what's the point?"

"What?"

"You heard me. It's time to stop playing games. Who told you about the knife? Is it the one that killed Joanie Shriver? Talk to me."

Cowart hesitated.

"You gonna make me read all about it? Or what?" Harsh insistence crawled over the fatigue in his voice.

"I'll tell you one thing: Robert Earl Ferguson didn't tell me where to look for that knife."

"You're telling me that someone else told you where to find the weapon that may have been used to kill Joanie Shriver?"

"That's right."

"You care to share this information?"

Matthew Cowart looked up from his scribblings. "Tell me one thing first, Lieutenant. If I say who told me about that knife, are you going to reopen the murder investigation? Are you willing to go to the state attorney? To get up in front of the trial judge and say that the case needs to be reopened?"

The detective scowled. "I can't make a promise like that before I know anything. Come on, Cowart. Tell me."

Cowart shook his head. "I just don't know if I can trust you, Lieutenant. It's as simple as that."

In that moment, Tanny Brown looked like a man primed to explode. "I thought you understood one thing," the detective said, almost whispering.

"What?"

"That in this town until that man pays, the murder of Joanie Shriver will never be closed."

"That's the question, isn't it? Who pays?"

"We're all paying. All of us. All the time." He slammed his

fist down hard on the table. The sound echoed in the small room. "You got something to say, say it!"

Matthew Cowart thought hard about what he knew and what he didn't know and finally replied, "Blair Sullivan told me where to find that knife."

The name had the expected impact on the policeman. He looked surprised, then shocked, like a batter expecting a fastball watching a curve dip over the corner of the plate.

"Sullivan? What has he got to do with this?"

"You ought to know. He passed right by Pachoula in May 1987, busy killing all sorts of folks."

"I know that, but . . ."

"And he knew where that knife was."

Brown stared at him. A few stretched seconds of silence filled the room. "Did Sullivan say he killed Joanie Shriver?"

"No, he didn't."

"Did he say Ferguson *didn't* kill that girl?"

"Not exactly, but . . ."

"Did he say anything *exactly* to contradict the original trial?"

"He knew about the knife."

"He knew about *a* knife. We don't know it is *the* knife, and without any forensics, it's nothing more than a piece of rusted metal. Come on, Cowart, you know Sullivan's stone crazy. Did he give you anything that could even remotely be called evidence?"

Brown's eyes had narrowed. Cowart could see him processing information rapidly, speculating, absorbing, discarding. He thought right then, It's too hard for him. He won't want to consider any possibilities of mistake. He has his killer and he's satisfied.

"Nothing else."

"Then that's not enough to reopen an investigation that resulted in a conviction."

"No? Okay. Get ready to read it in the paper. Then we'll see if it's enough."

The policeman glared at Cowart and pointed at the door. "Leave, Mr. Cowart. Leave right now. Get in your rental car and go back to the motel. Pack your bags. Drive to the airport. Get on a plane and go back to your city. Don't come back. Understand?"

Cowart bristled. He could feel a surge of his own frustrated anger pushing through him. "Are you threatening me?"

The detective shook his head. "No. I'm giving advice."

"And?"

"Take it."

Matthew Cowart picked himself out of the chair and gave the detective a long stare. The two men's eyes locked, a visual game of arm wrestling. When the detective finally swerved away, turning his back, Cowart spun about and walked through the door, closed it sharply behind him, and paced briskly through the bright fluorescent lights of the police headquarters, as if pushing a wave in front of him, watching uniformed officers and other detectives step aside. He could sense the pressure of their eyes on his back as he stepped through the corridors, quieting a dozen conversations in his wake. He heard a few words muttered behind him, heard his name spoken several times with distaste. He didn't glance around, didn't alter his step. He rode the elevator alone and walked out through the wide glass doors onto the street. There he turned and looked back up toward the detective's office. For an instant he could see Tanny Brown standing in his window, staring out at him. Again their eyes locked. Matthew Cowart shook his head slightly, just the barest motion from side to side.

He saw the detective wheel aside, disappearing from the window.

Cowart stood rigid for an instant, letting the night envelop him. Then he strode away, walking slowly at first but rapidly gaining momentum and pace until he was marching briskly across the town, the words that would become his story beginning to gather deep within him, parading in military array across his imagination.

SEVEN
WORDS

RETURNING home, however, a spreading exhaustion forced the living to fade into his notebooks and let the dead take over his imagination.

It was late, well past midnight on a clear Miami night and the sky seemed an endless black painted with great brushstrokes into an infinity of blinking starlight. He wanted someone to share his impending triumph but realized there was no one. All were gone, stolen by age, divorce, and too many dyings. Especially he wanted his parents, but they were long gone.

His mother had died when he was still a young man. She'd been mousy and quiet, with an athletic, bony thinness that made her embrace hard-edged and brittle, which she'd compensated for with a soft, almost lush voice used to great advantage in storytelling. A product of times that had created her as a housewife and kept her mired there, she'd raised him and his brothers and sisters in an endless cycle of diapers, formula, and teething that had given way to scraped knees and imaginary hurts, homework, basketball practices, and the occasional, inevitable heartbreaks of adolescence.

She'd died swiftly but undramatically at the beginning of her old age. Inoperable colonic cancer. Five weeks, a magical, steady progression from health to death, marked daily by the yellowing of her skin and growing weakness in her voice and walk. His father had died right along with her, which was odd. As Cowart had grown older, he had come to know of his father's boisterous infidelities. They had always been short-lived and poorly concealed. In retrospect they had seemed far less evil than the affair with the newspaper, which had robbed him of time and sapped his enthusiasm for being with his family. So, when his father had followed her funeral with six months of obsessive, endless weeks devoted to work, only to announce at the end that he was taking early retirement, it had surprised all the children.

They had had long conversations on the telephone, questioning his act, wondering what he would do, all alone in a big and now insistently empty, echoing suburban home, surrounded by young families who would find his presence unusual and probably unsettling. Matthew Cowart had been the last of a half-dozen children, grown into teachers, a lawyer, a doctor, an artist, and himself and spread across the states, none close enough to help their father, suddenly old. They had all failed to see the obvious. He'd shot himself on his wedding anniversary.

I should have known, he thought. I should have seen what was coming. His father had called him two nights earlier. They'd talked gingerly, distantly, about news stories and reporting. His father had said, "Remember: It's not the facts that they want. It's the truth." He had rarely said that sort of thing to his son before, and when Cowart had tried to get him to continue, he'd gruffly signed off.

The police had found him sitting at his desk, a small revolver in one hand, a bullet wound in his forehead, and her picture in his lap. Cowart had spoken with the detectives afterward, forever a reporter, forcing them to describe the scene with all the small details that, once heard, could never be forgotten, and stripped the dying of all its drama: that his father'd worn old red slippers and a blue business suit and a flowered tie that she'd purchased for him some forgettable Father's Day in the past; that a copy of that day's edition of the paper, red-penciled with notes, had been spread before him on the desk next to a diet soda and a half-eaten cheese sandwich. He'd remembered to write a check to the cleaning lady and left it taped to his antique green-shaded banker's lamp. There had been a half-dozen crumpled papers strewn about his chair, tossed haphazardly aside, all notes started and abandoned, to his children.

The stars blinked above him.

I was the youngest, he thought. The only one to try his profession. I thought it would make us closer. I thought I could do it better. I thought he would be proud. Or jealous.

Instead, he was more remote.

He thought of his mother's smile. His daughter's reminded him of her. And I let my wife take her with hardly a whimper. He felt a sudden dark emptiness at that thought, which was instantly replaced with the nightmare memory of the crime-scene photographs of little Joanie Shriver.

He lowered his head and peered down the street. In the distance, he could see the boulevard glistening with yellow streetlamps and the sweeping headlights of passing cars. He turned away, hearing a siren wailing some ways away, and entered his apartment building. He rose in the elevator, stepped across the corridor, and opened the door to his apartment. For an instant, he hesitated in the entranceway, flipping on the lights and peering about himself. He saw a bachelor's disarray, books stuffed into shelves, framed posters on the walls, a desk littered with papers, magazines, and clipped articles. He looked about for something familiar that would tell him he was home. Then he sighed, locked the door behind himself, and went about the business of unpacking and going to bed.

Cowart spent a long week working the telephone, filling in the background for the story. There were brusque calls to the prosecutors who'd convicted Ferguson and didn't want to talk with any reporters. There were longer calls to the men who'd worked the cases against Blair Sullivan. A detective in Pensacola had confirmed Sullivan's presence in Escambia County at the time of Joanie Shriver's murder; a gasoline credit-card receipt from a station near Pachoula was dated the day before the girl was murdered. The prosecutors in Miami showed Cowart the knife that Sullivan had been using when he was arrested; it was a cheap, nondescript four-inch blade, similar but not identical to the one he'd found beneath the culvert.

He had held the knife in his hand and thought, It fits.

Other pieces fell into line.

He spoke at length with officials at Rutgers, obtaining Ferguson's modest grade record. He'd been a steady, insistently indifferent student, one who seemed to possess only meager interest in anything other than completing his courses, which he'd done steadily, if not spectacularly. A proctor in a dorm remembered him as a quiet, unfriendly underclassman, not given to partying or socializing in any distinguishable fashion. A loner, the man had said, who kept primarily to himself and had moved into an apartment shortly after his first year at the university.

Cowart spoke to Ferguson's high-school guidance counselor, who said much the same, though pointed out that in Newark, Ferguson's grades were much higher. Neither man had been able to give him the name of a single real friend of the convicted man.

He began to see Ferguson as a man floating on the fringe of life, unsure of himself, unsure of who he was or where he had been going, a man waiting for something to happen to him, when the worst possible thing had swept him up. He did not see him as much innocent as a victim of his own passivity. A man to be taken advantage of. It helped him to understand what had happened in Pachoula. He thought of the contrast between the two black men at the core of his story: One didn't like pitching and reeling in the back of a bus, the other ran out under fire to help others. One drifted through college, the other became a policeman. Ferguson hadn't had a chance, he thought, when confronted by the force of Tanny Brown's personality.

By the end of the week, a photographer dispatched by the *Journal* to North Florida had returned. He spread his pictures out on a layout desk before Cowart. There was a full-color shot of Ferguson in his cell, peering out at the camera between the bars. There was a shot of the culvert, other shots of Pachoula, the Shriver house, the school. There was the same picture that Cowart had seen hanging in the elementary school. There was a shot of Tanny Brown and Bruce Wilcox, striding out of the Escambia County homicide offices.

"How'd you get that?" Cowart asked.

"Spent the day staked out, waiting for them. Can't say they were real pleased, either."

Cowart nodded, glad that he hadn't been there. "What about Sully?"

"He wouldn't let me shoot him," the photographer replied. "But I've got a good shot of him from his trial. Here." He handed the picture to Cowart.

It was Blair Sullivan marching down a courtroom corridor, shackled hand and foot, braced by two huge detectives. He was sneering at the camera, half-laughing, half-threatening.

"One thing I can't figure," the photographer said.

"What's that?"

"Well, if you saw that man coming at you out on the street, you sure as hell would run fast the other way. You sure wouldn't get into the car with him. But Ferguson, hell, you know, even when he's staring out at you angry, he still don't look that damn bad, you know. I mean, I could see letting him talk me into a car.''

"You don't know," Cowart replied. He picked up the picture of Sullivan. "The man's a psychopathic killer. He could talk you into anything. It's not just that little girl. Think about all the other folks he killed. How about that old couple, after he helped change their tire? They probably thanked him before he killed them. Or the waitress. She went with him, remember? Just looking to have a little good time. Thought she was going to have a party. She didn't make him for a killer. The kid in the convenience store? He had one of those emergency alarm buttons right under the register. But he didn't hit it.''

"Didn't have the chance, I think."

Cowart shrugged.

"Well," the photographer said, "I sure as hell wouldn't get into a car with him.''

"That's right. You'd be dead.''

He commandeered his old desk in a back corner of the newsroom, spreading all his notes out around himself, staring into a computer screen. There was a single moment, when the screen was empty before him, that he felt a quick nervousness. It had been some time since he'd written a news story, and he wondered if the skill had left him. Then he thought, It's all there, and let excitement overcome any doubts. He found himself describing the two men in their cells, the way they had appeared, the way they'd talked. He sketched out what he'd seen of Pachoula, and he outlined the hulking intensity of the one detective and the abrupt anger of the other. The words came easily, steadily. He thought of nothing else.

It took him three days to write the first story, two days to construct the follow. He spent a day polishing, another day writing sidebars. Two days were spent going over it line by line with the city editor. Another day with lawyers, a frustrating word-by-word analysis. He hovered over the layout desk as it was budgeted for the front of the Sunday paper. The main headline was: A CASE OF QUESTIONS. He liked that. The subhead was: TWO MEN, ONE CRIME AND A MURDER THAT NO ONE CAN FORGET. He liked that as well.

He lay sleepless in bed at night, thinking, There it is. I've done it. I've really done it.

On the Saturday before the story was to run, he called Tanny Brown. The detective was home, and the homicide offices wouldn't give Cowart his unlisted telephone number. He told a secretary to have the detective call him back, which the man did an hour later.

"Cowart? Tanny Brown here. I thought we'd finished talking for now."

"I just wanted to give you a chance to respond to what's going to be in the story."

"Like your damn photographer gave us a chance?"

"I'm sorry about that."

"Ambushed us."

"Sorry."

Brown paused. "Well, at least tell me the picture doesn't look too damn bad. We've always got our vanity, you know."

Cowart could not tell if the detective was joking or not.

"It's not bad," he said. "Like something out of *Dragnet*."

"Good enough. Now, what do you want?"

"Do you want to respond to the story we're running tomorrow?"

"Tomorrow? I'll be damned. Guess I'll have to get up early and go down to the paper store. Gonna be a big deal?"

"That's right."

"Front page, huh? Gonna make you a star, right, Cowart? Make you famous?"

"I don't know about that."

The detective laughed mockingly. "This is Robert Earl's big shot, right? You think it'll do the trick for him? You think you can walk him off the Row?"

"I don't know. It's a pretty interesting story."

"I bet."

"I just wanted to give you the opportunity to respond."

"You'll tell me what it says now?"

"Yes. That's correct. Now it's written."

Tanny Brown's voice paused over the telephone line. "I suppose you got all that stuff about beating him up and that crap? The bit with the gun, right?"

"It says what he contends. It also says what you said."

"Just not quite as strong, though, huh?"

"No, they have equal weight."

Brown laughed. "I bet," he said.

"So, would you like to comment directly?"

"I like that word, 'comment.' Says a bunch, doesn't it? Nice and safe. You want me to *comment* on what it says?" A sharp sarcasm tinged his voice.

"Right. I wanted you to have the opportunity."

"I got it. An opportunity to dig a bigger grave for myself," the detective said. "Get myself in more trouble than I'm already going to be in, just because I didn't bullshit you. Sure." He took a breath and continued, almost sadly. "I could have stonewalled the whole thing, but I didn't. Is that in your story?"

"Of course."

Tanny Brown laughed briefly, wryly. "You know, I know you got an idea what's gonna happen because of all this. But I'll tell you one thing. You're wrong. You're dead wrong."

"Is that what you want to say?"

"Things never work out as smoothly or as simply as people think. There's always a mess. Always questions. Always doubts."

"Is *that* what you want to say?"

"You're wrong. Just wrong."

"Okay. If that's what you want to say."

"No, that's what I want you to understand." The detective laughed abruptly. "Still the hard case, ain't you, Cowart? You don't have to answer that. I already know the answer." He let a beat slip by, then another.

Cowart listened to the deep, angry breathing on the line before Tanny Brown finally spoke, rumbling his words like a distant storm. "Okay, here's a comment: Go fuck yourself."

And then he hung up.

EIGHT

ANOTHER LETTER
——*FROM DEATH ROW*

HE did not see or speak with Ferguson until the hearing. The same was true for the detectives, who refused to return any of his phone calls in the weeks after the stories ran. His requests for information were handled summarily by prosecutors up in Escambia County, who were scrambling for a strategy. On the other hand, Ferguson's defense attorneys were effusive, calling him almost daily to inform him of developments, filing a barrage of motions in front of the judge who'd presided over Ferguson's murder trial.

When his story had appeared, Cowart had been caught up in a natural momentum created by the allegations he'd printed, like being driven down a street by sweeping sheets of rain. The television and newspaper press inundated the case, crawling with rapacity over all the people, events, and locations that had constituted his tale, retelling it, reforming it in dozens of different yet fundamentally similar ways. To all involved, it had been a story of several fascinations: the tainted confession, the disquieted town still restless from the child's murder, the iron-hard detectives, and ultimately, the awful irony that the one killer could see the other go to the electric chair simply by keeping his mouth shut. This, of course, Blair Sullivan did, summarily refusing all interviews, refusing to speak with reporters, lawyers, police, even a crew from *60 Minutes*. He made one call, to Matthew Cowart, perhaps ten days after the articles appeared. The call was collect. Cowart was at his desk, back in the editorial department, reading *The New York Times* version of the story (QUESTIONS RAISED IN FLORIDA PANHANDLE MURDER CASE) when the phone rang and the clipped voice of the long-distance operator asked him if he would accept a call from a Mr. Sullivan in Starke, Florida. He was momentarily confused, then electrified. He leaned forward in his seat and heard the familiar soft twang of Sergeant Rogers at the prison.

"Cowart? You there, fella?"

"Hello, Sergeant. Yes?"

"We're bringing in Sully. He wants to talk to y'all."

"How're things up there?"

The sergeant laughed. "Hell, I shoulda known better than to let you in here. This place been buzzing like a damn bee's nest since your stories. All of a sudden, everybody on Death Row's calling up every damn reporter in the state, for sure. And every damn reporter is showing up here demanding interviews and tours and every damn thing." The sergeant's laugh continued to barrel over the telephone line. "Got this place more excited than the time both the main and the backup generators went out, and all the inmates thought it was the hand of Fate opening the doors for them."

"I'm sorry if I caused you some trouble . . ."

"Oh, hell, I don't mind. Takes the edge off the sameness, you know. Of course, likely to be a mite difficult around here when things do settle down. Which they will, sooner or later."

"How about Ferguson?"

"Bobby Earl? He's so busy giving interviews I think they ought to give him his'n own talk show on late-night TV, like Johnny Carson or that Letterman guy."

Cowart smiled. "And Sully?"

There was a pause, then the sergeant spoke softly. "Won't talk to no one about nothing, no sir. Not just reporters or shrinks. Bobby Earl's attorney been 'round maybe five, six times. Those two detectives from Pachoula came by, but he just laughed at them and spat in their eyes. Subpoenas, threats, promises, whatever, you name it, don't do no good. He don't want to talk, especially about that little gal in Pachoula. He sings some hymns to himself and writes more letters and studies the Bible hard. Keeps asking me what's happening, so I fill him in as best as possible, bring him the papers and the magazines and such. He watches the television each night, so he can see those two detectives call you every name in the book. And then he just laughs it all off."

"What do you think?"

"I think he's having fun. His own kind of fun."

"That's scary."

"I told you about that man."

"So why does he want to talk to me?"

"I don't know. He just up and asks me this morning if'n I'll put the call through."

"So put him on."

The sergeant coughed with concern. "Ain't that easy. You remember, we like a few precautions moving Mr. Sullivan."

"Of course. How's he look?"

"He don't look no different from when you saw him, save maybe a bit of excitement about him. Got a little bit of a glow to him, like he's been putting on weight, which he ain't, cause he don't eat much at all. Like I said, I think he's having fun. He's right lively."

"Uh-huh. Hey, Sergeant, you didn't say what you thought of the story."

"No? Well, I thought it real interesting."

"And?"

"Well, Mr. Cowart, I got to say, you hang around prisons long enough, especially Death Row, and you're likely to hear every damn strange story there is."

Before Cowart could ask another question, he heard loud voices in the background and shuffling sounds by the telephone. The sergeant said, "He's coming in now."

"This a private conversation?" Cowart asked.

"You mean, is this phone bugged? Hell if I know. It's the line we use mainly for lawyers, so I doubt it, 'cause they'd make a helluva stink. Anyway, here he is, just one second, we got to cuff his hands."

There was a momentary silence. Cowart could hear the sergeant speaking in the background. "That too tight, Sully?" And he heard the prisoner reply, "Nah, it's okay." Then there were some indistinct noises and the sound of a door closing, and finally Blair Sullivan's voice.

"Well, well, well, Mr. Cowart. The world-famous reporter, how yah doing?"

"Fine, Mr. Sullivan."

"Good. Good. So what d'you think, Cowart? Our boy Bobby Earl gonna walk in the air of freedom? Do you think that god of good fortune's gonna pluck him out from behind these bars, from out of the shadow of death, huh? You think the gears of justice gonna start grinding away on him now?'' Sullivan laughed hoarsely.

''I don't know. His attorney has filed a motion for a new trial back in the court that convicted him . . .''

''You think that's gonna do the trick?''

''We'll see.''

Sullivan coughed. ''That's right, you're right.''

Both men were silent.

After a moment, Cowart asked, ''So, why have you called me?''

''Hang on,'' Sullivan replied. ''I'm trying to get this damn smoke lit. It's hard. I got to put the phone down.'' There was a clunking sound before Cowart heard his voice again. ''Ahh, there we go. You asked?''

''Why'd you call?''

''I just wanted to hear how famous you're getting.''

''What?''

''Why, hell, Cowart, I see your story all over the news. Sure got everybody's attention, didn't you? Just by sticking your hand under a greasy old culvert, right?''

''I guess.''

''Pretty easy way to get famous, huh?''

''That wasn't all there was to it.''

Sullivan spat out another laugh. ''I suppose not. But you sure looked fine answering all those questions on *Nightline*. Real confident and sure of yourself.''

''You wouldn't talk to them.''

''Nah. I thought I'd let you and Bobby Earl do the talking.'' Sullivan hesitated and then whistled. ''Of course, now I noticed that those policemen from Pachoula didn't want to do much talking neither. I think they don't believe Bobby Earl. And they don't believe you. And they sure as hell don't believe in me.''

Sullivan burst out with a mocking bray. ''Now, ain't that some pigheadedness! Just goes to show some folks be blind to anything, huh?''

Cowart didn't reply.

''Ain't that a question, Cowart? Didn't I ask you something?'' Blair Sullivan whispered harshly.

''Yes,'' Cowart replied quickly. ''Some folks are blind to anything.''

The prisoner paused. ''Well, we ought to help the shingles to drop from their eyes, oughtn't we, Mr. Famous Reporter Man? Lead them to the path of enlightenment, what you say?''

"How?" Cowart pitched forward at his desk. He could feel sweat streaking down under his arms, tickling his ribs.

"Now suppose I were to tell you something else. Something real interesting."

Cowart's hand seized a pencil and he grabbed a stack of blank paper to take notes. "Like what?"

"I'm thinking. Don't push me."

"Okay. Take your time." Here it comes, he thought.

"It would be interesting to know, wouldn't it, how that little girl got into that car, huh? That would pique your interest, wouldn't it, Cowart?"

"Yes. How?"

"Not so fast. I'm still thinking. You got to be cautious with your words these days. Don't want anything misunderstood, if you follow my meaning. Say, do you know it was a lovely day that that poor gal died, wasn't it, Cowart? Did you find out that it was hot but sort of dry at the same time, with a little breeze blowing that cooled things off a bit and with like a great wide big blue sky up above and lots of flowers blooming all about. A real pretty day to die. And imagine how cool and comfortable it must have felt back there in that swamp under all that shade. You think that maybe the man who killed little Joanie—ain't that a sweet name—just lay back afterwards and enjoyed what a fine day it was for just a few minutes? And let the cool shade bring a nice calm to him?"

"How cool was it?"

Blair Sullivan laughed sharply. "Now how would I know that, Cowart? Really?"

He wheezed in air, whistling on the phone line. "Think of all the things those two pig cops would like to know. Like clothes and bloodstains and why there warn't no fingerprints and hair and dirt samples and all that stuff."

"Why?"

"Well," Sullivan replied breezily, "I suspect that the killer of little Joanie knew enough to have two sets of clothes with him. So he could take the one set off—that one set that's all covered with blood and shit—and ditch them somewhere. He probably had the sense to keep a couple of extra-big old plastic garbage bags in his car as well, so he could wrap up that bloody clothing so's no one would notice it."

Cowart's stomach clenched. He remembered a Miami detective telling him of finding spare clothes and a roll of garbage bags in the trunk of Blair Sullivan's car the night he was arrested.

He closed his eyes for an instant and asked, "Where would the killer dump the stuff?"

"Oh, someplace like a Salvation Army depository. You know, there's one at the shopping mall right outside Pensacola. But that's only if it weren't too messy, you know. Or if he really wanted to be careful, he'd maybe toss it in a big old Dempsey Dumpster, like the types they have at the rest areas on the interstate. Like at the Willow Creek exchange. That big one. Gets picked up every week and all that stuff just chucked right in a landfill. Nobody ever looks at what they're throwing out. Buried away under tons of garbage, yes sir. Never find that stuff again."

"Is that what happened?"

He didn't reply. Instead, Sullivan continued, saying, "I bet those cops, and you, too, Cowart, and maybe that little girl's grieving momma and poppa, would especially like to know why at all that little girl gets into that car, huh? Isn't that something, after all? Why does it happen, right?"

"Tell me why."

He hissed over the line. "God's will, Cowart."

There was a moment's silence.

"Or maybe the Devil's. You think of that, Cowart? Maybe God was just having a bad day that day, so he let his former number-one executive officer make a bit of mischief, huh?"

Cowart didn't reply. He listened to the whispered words that slid across the phone line, landing heavily in his ear.

"Well, Cowart, I bet that *whoever* it was talked that little girl into his car, said something like, 'Honey, can you give me some directions, please? I'm lost and need to find my way.' Now ain't that the Lord's own truth, Cowart? That man there in that car, why I can see him as clear as the hand in front of me. Why he was lost, Cowart. Lost in so many ways. But he found himself that day, didn't he?"

Sullivan inhaled sharply before continuing. "And when he's got that little gal's attention, what's he gonna say? Maybe he said, 'Honey, I'll just give you a lift down to the corner, huh?' Just as easy and natural as you like."

Sullivan hesitated again. "Easy and natural, yes sir. Just exactly like a nightmare. No different than exactly what those good folks try to tell those children to look out for and stay clear from."

He paused, then added breezily, "Except she didn't, did she?"

"Is that what you said to her?" Cowart asked unsteadily.

"Did I say that's what I said to her? Did I now? No, I only

said that's probably what somebody said to her. Somebody who was feeling kind of mean and murderous on that day and was just lucky enough to spot that little gal."

He laughed again. Then he sneezed.

"Why'd you do it?" Cowart asked abruptly.

"Did I say I did?" Sullivan replied, giggling.

"No. You just tease me with . . ."

"Well, forgive me for having my fun."

"Why don't you just tell me the truth? Why don't you just come forward and tell the truth?"

"What, and wreck all my enjoyment? Cowart, you don't know how a man gets his pleasures on Death Row."

"Will allowing an innocent man to fry . . ."

"Am I doing that? Why, don't we have a mighty system of criminal justice to take care of those things? Make damn certain no innocent man gets a hot squat?"

"You know what I'm saying."

"Yes I do," Sullivan replied softly, menacingly. "And I don't give a damn."

"So why have you called me?"

Sullivan paused on the phone line. When his voice returned, it was quiet and deadly. "Because I wanted you to know how interested I have become in your career, Cowart."

"That's . . ."

"Don't interrupt me!" Sullivan bit off his words. "I have told you that before! When I speak, you damn listen, Mr. Reporter Man. Got that?"

"Yes."

"Because I wanted to tell you something."

"What's that?"

"I wanted to tell you it isn't over. It's just beginning."

"What do you mean?"

"You figure it out."

Cowart waited. After a moment, Sullivan said, "I think we'll talk again someday. I do enjoy our little chats. So much seems to happen after we talk. Oh, one thing."

"What's that?"

"Did you hear, Florida high court's got my automatic appeal set for their fall term. They sure do like to keep a man waiting. I guess they're thinking maybe I'll change my mind or something. Decide to start playing out my appeals and all. Maybe hire some hotshot like Bobby Earl did and start questioning whether it's *constitutional* to fry my old sorry tail. I like that. I like their concern for old Sully.''

He paused. "But we do know one thing, don't we, Mr. Reporter?''

"What's that?''

"That they're damn wrong. I wouldn't change my mind about things if Jesus Hisself came down and asked me nice and personal to.''

Then he hung the telephone up abruptly.

Cowart rose then from his seat. He decided to go to the men's room, where he spent several minutes running cold water over his wrists, trying to control the sudden heat that had overtaken him, and to slow his racing heart.

His ex-wife called him, too, one evening as he was getting ready to leave work, the day after he had appeared on *Nightline*.

"Matty?'' Sandy said. "We saw you on the tube.''

Her voice had a sort of girlish excitement about it, which reminded him of the better times, when they'd been young, and their relationship hadn't been burdened. He was surprised to hear from her and pleased at the same time. He felt a sort of false modest delight.

"Hello, Sandy. How're you doing?''

"Oh, fine. Getting fat. Tired all the time. You remember how it was.''

Not really, he thought. He remembered he'd spent most of her pregnancy working fourteen-hour days on the city desk.

"What did you think?''

"It must have been exciting for you. It was a hell of a story.''

"Still is.''

"What's going to happen to those two men?''

"I don't know. I think Ferguson will get a new trial. The other . . .''

She interrupted. "He scared me.''

"He's a pretty twisted man.''

"What will happen to him?''

"If he doesn't start filing appeals, the governor will sign a death warrant for him as soon as the state Supreme Court upholds his conviction. There's not much doubt they'll do that.''

"When will that happen?''

"I don't know. The court usually announces its decisions at several times, right up to the New Year. There'll be just a single little line in the sheaf of decisions: In Re: The State of Florida versus Blair Sullivan. The judgment and sentence of the trial court is affirmed. It's all pretty bloodless until the governor's order arrives at the prison. You know, lots of papers and signatures and official seals and that sort of stuff, until it falls on somebody actually to have to juice the guy. The guards there call it doing the deathwork.''

"I don't think the world will be a lesser place when he's gone," Sandy said with a small shudder in her voice.

Cowart didn't reply.

"But if he never owns up to what he did, what will happen to Ferguson?''

"I don't know. The state could try him again. He could get pardoned. He could sit on Death Row. All sorts of strange things can happen.''

"If they execute Sullivan, will anyone ever really know the truth?''

"Know the truth? Hell, I think we *know* the truth now. The truth is that Ferguson shouldn't be on Death Row. But *prove* the truth? That's a whole other thing. Real hard.''

"And what will happen to you now?''

"Same old stuff. I'll follow this story to the end. Then write some more editorials until I get old and my teeth fall out and they decide to turn me into glue. That's what they do to old racehorses and editorial writers, you know.''

She laughed. "Come on. You're going to win a Pulitzer.''

He smiled. "I doubt it," he lied.

"Yeah, you will. I can feel it. Then they'll probably put you out to stud.''

"I should be so lucky.''

"You will be. You're going to win one. You deserve to. It was a hell of a story. Just like Pitts and Lee.''

She, too, remembered that story, he realized. "Yeah. You know what happened to those guys after they got the judge to order up a new trial? They got convicted again, by a racist jury just as damn stupid as the first. It wasn't until the governor pardoned them that they got off Death Row. People forget that. Twelve years it took them.''

"But they got off and that guy won the Pulitzer.''

He laughed. "Well, that's right.''

"You will, too. Won't take twelve years, either.''

"Well, we'll see.''

"Will you stay with the *Journal?*''

"No reason to leave.''

"Oh, come on. What if the *Times* or the *Post* calls?"

"We'll see."

They both laughed. After a momentary pause, she said, "I always knew someday you'd find the right story. I always knew someday you'd do it."

"What am I supposed to say?"

"Nothing. I just knew you'd do it."

"What about Becky? Did she stay up to watch me on *Nightline?*"

Sandy hesitated. "Well, no. It's much too much past her bedtime . . ."

"You could have taped it."

"And what would she have heard her daddy talk about? About somebody who murdered a little girl? A little girl who got raped and then stabbed, what was it, thirty-six times? And then tossed into a swamp? I didn't think that was too swift an idea."

She was right, he realized, though he hated the thought. "Still, I wish she'd seen."

"It's safe here," Sandy said.

"What?"

"It's safe here. Tampa isn't a big city. I mean, it's big, but not big. It seems to move a little slower. And it's not at all like Miami. It's not all drugs and riots and weird, the way Miami is. She doesn't have to know about little girls that get kidnapped and raped and stabbed to death. Not yet, at least. She can grow up a bit, and be a kid, and not have to worry all the time."

"You mean you don't have to worry all the time."

"Well, is that wrong?"

"No."

"You know what I can never understand? It's why everyone who works at the paper always thinks everything bad just happens to other people."

"We don't think that."

"It seems that way."

He didn't want to argue. "Well, maybe."

She forced a laugh. "I'm sorry if I've rained on your parade. Really, I wanted to call to congratulate you and tell you that I really was proud."

"Proud but divorced."

She hesitated. "Yes. But amicably, I thought."

"I'm sorry. That was unfair."

"Okay."

There was another pause.

"When can we talk about Becky's next visit?"

"I don't know. I'll be hung up on this story until there's some sort of resolution. But when, I don't know."

"I'll call you then."

"Okay."

"And congratulations again."

"Thanks."

He hung up the telephone and realized that he was sometimes a fool, incapable of saying what he wanted, articulating what he needed. He pounded the desk in frustration. Then he went to the window of his cubicle and looked out over the city. Afternoon traffic was flowing toward the expressway, like so many body nerves pulsating with the desire to head home to family. He felt his solitude surround him. The city seemed baked beneath the hot blue sky, the light-colored buildings reflected the sun's strength. He watched a tangle of cars in an intersection maneuvering like so many aggressive bugs on the earth. It is dangerous, he thought.

It is not safe.

Two motorists had shot it out two days earlier following a fender bender, blazing away in the midst of rush-hour traffic, each armed with nearly identical, expensive nine-millimeter semiautomatics. Neither man had been hurt, but a teenager driving past had taken a ricochet in the lung and remained in critical condition at a local hospital. This was a routine Miami story, a by-product of the heat and conflicting cultures and a populace that seemed to consider handguns an integral part of their couture. He remembered writing almost the same story a half-dozen years earlier. Remembered a dozen more times the story had been written, so frequently that what had been once a front-page story was now six paragraphs on an inside page.

He thought of his daughter and wondered, Why does she need to know? Why does she need to know anything about evil and the awful desires of some men?

He did not know the answer to that question.

There were thick black television cables snaking out the entranceway to the courtroom. Several cameramen were setting up video tape recorders in the hallway, taking their feeds from the single camera allowed in the courtroom. A mix of print and television reporters milled about in the corridor; the television personnel all slightly sharper dressed, better coiffed, and seemingly cleaner than their newspaper competitors, who affected a slightly disheveled appearance to set themselves apart self-righteously.

"Out in force," said the photographer who walked beside him, fiddling with the lens on his Leica. "No one wants to miss this dance."

It was some ten weeks since the stories had appeared. Filings and maneuverings had postponed the hearing twice. Outside the Escambia County courthouse the thick Florida sun was energetically baking the earth. It was cool inside the modern building. Voices carried and echoed off high ceilings so that people spoke mainly in whispers, even when they didn't have to. There was a small sign in gold paint next to the wide brown courtroom doors: CIRCUIT COURT JUDGE HARLEY TRENCH.

"That the guy that called him a wild animal?" the photographer asked.

"You got it."

"I don't imagine he's going to be too pleased to see all this." The photographer gestured with his camera toward the crowd of reporters and camera technicians.

"No, wrong. It's an election year. He's gonna love the publicity."

"But only if he does the right thing."

"The popular thing."

"I doubt they're gonna be the same."

Cowart nodded. "I don't think so, either. But you can't tell. I bet he's back in chambers right now calling every local politician between here and the Alabama border, trying to figure out what to do."

The photographer laughed. "And they're probably calling every district worker, trying to figure out what to tell him. What d'you think, Matty? You think he'll cut him loose or not?"

"No idea."

He looked down the corridor and saw a group of jeans-clad young people surrounding an older, short black man, who was wearing a suit. "Get a shot of them," he told the photographer. "They're from the anti-death-penalty group here to make some noise."

"Where's the Klan?"

"Probably somewhere. They're not so organized anymore. They're probably going to be late. Or maybe they went to the wrong place."

"Got the wrong day, maybe. They were probably here yesterday, got bored and confused, and left."

The two men laughed.

"It's going to be a zoo," Cowart said.

The photographer paused in his step. "Yeah. And there's the tigers, waiting for your tail."

He gestured and Cowart saw Tanny Brown and Bruce Wilcox slumped up against a wall, trying to stay out of the way of the cameramen.

He hesitated, then said, "Well, might as well see what's in the tiger's den." And he walked briskly toward the two men.

Bruce Wilcox pivoted, presenting Cowart with the back of his sportcoat. But Tanny Brown moved away from the wall and nodded in meager greeting. "Well, Mr. Cowart. You sure have caused some commotion."

"It happens, Lieutenant."

"You pleased?"

"I'm just doing my job. Just like you. Just like Wilcox."

Brown looked past Cowart at the photographer. "Hey, you! Next time try to get my right profile. Makes me look ten years younger and makes my kids a lot happier to see it. They think I'm getting too old for all this. Like, who needs the aggravation, hey?"

Brown smiled, turned slightly to demonstrate for the photographer, and put his finger on his cheek, pointing.

"See?" he said. "Much better than that old scowling sneak shot you took."

"Sorry about that."

The policeman shrugged. "Goes with the territory, I guess."

"How come you wouldn't return my phone calls?" Cowart asked.

"We didn't have nothing more to talk about."

Cowart shook his head. "What about Blair Sullivan?"

"He didn't do it," Brown replied.

"How can you be so sure?"

"I can't be. Not yet. But it doesn't feel right. That's all."

"You're wrong," Cowart said quietly. "Motive. Opportunity. A well-known predilection. You know the man. You can't see him doing that crime? What about the knife in the culvert?"

The lieutenant shrugged again. "I can *see* him doing it. Sure. But that doesn't mean jack shit."

"Instincts again, Lieutenant?"

Tanny Brown laughed before continuing. "I am not going to talk to you anymore about the substantive issues of the case," he said, slipping into the practiced tones of a man who'd testified hundreds of times before hundreds of judges. "We'll see what goes on in there." He pointed at the courtroom. "Afterwards, maybe we'll talk."

Detective Wilcox stepped around then, staring at Tanny Brown. "Then you'll talk! Then! I can't believe you're willing to give this bastard the time of day after he hung us out to dry. Made us look like . . ."

The lieutenant held up his hand. "Don't say what he made us look like. I'm tired of that." He turned toward Cowart. "When this dog and pony show is all over, you get in touch. We'll talk again. But one thing."

"What's that?"

"You remember the last thing I told you?"

"Sure," Cowart said. "You told me to go fuck myself."

Tanny Brown smiled. "Well," he said quietly, "keep at it." The big detective paused, then added, "Walked right into that one, Mr. Cowart."

Wilcox snorted a laugh and clapped the bigger man on the back. He made a pistol figure with his forefinger and fist and pointed it at Cowart, firing it slowly, dramatically. "Zap!" he said. The two detectives then wandered toward the courtroom, leaving Cowart and the photographer hanging in the corridor.

Robert Earl Ferguson strode into the courtroom, flanked by a pair of gray-suited jail guards, wearing a new blue pinstripe suit and carrying a yellow legal pad. Cowart heard another reporter murmur, "Looks like he's ready for law school," and watched as Ferguson shook hands with Roy Black and his young assistant, glared once in the direction of Brown and Wilcox, nodded toward Cowart, and then turned and waited for the judge to arrive.

Within moments, the courtroom was summoned to its feet.

Judge Harley Trench was a short, rotund man with silver-gray hair and a monklike bald spot on the crown of his head. He had an instant officiousness to him, a clipped orderliness as he arranged papers swiftly on the bench before him, then looked up at the attorneys, slowly removing a set of wire-rimmed glasses from inside his robes and adjusting them on his nose, giving him the appearance of a fat crow on a high wire.

"All right. Y'all want to get this going?" he said swiftly, gesturing at Roy Black.

The defense attorney rose. He was tall and thin, with hair that curled long over the collar of his shirt. He moved slowly, with exaggerated, theatrical style, gesturing with his arms as he made his points. Cowart thought he would not be likely to get much slack from the short man on the bench, whose frown deepened with each word.

"We're here, your honor, on a motion for a new trial. This motion takes several forms: We contend that there is new exculpatory evidence in the case; we contend that if this new evidence were presented to a jury, they would have no alternative but to return a verdict of not guilty, finding reasonable doubt that Mr. Ferguson killed Joanie Shriver. We also contend that the court erred in its prior ruling on the admissibility of the confession Mr. Ferguson allegedly made.''

The attorney pivoted toward the detectives when he spoke the word "allegedly," drawing it out, labeling it with sarcasm.

"Isn't that an issue for the court of appeals?" the judge asked briskly.

"No, sir. Under Rivkind, 320 Florida twelve, 1978, and State of Florida versus Stark, 211 Florida thirteen, 1982, and others, sir, we respectfully submit that it was your honor who was prevented from having all the evidence when you made your ruling . . ."

"Objection!"

Cowart saw that the assistant state attorney had jumped up. He was a young man, in his late twenties, probably no more than a few years out of law school. He was wearing a three-piece tan suit and spoke in choppy, abrupt sentences. There had been considerable speculation about the fact that he'd been assigned to the case. Given the widespread publicity and interest, it had been assumed that the Escambia County state attorney would argue the matter himself, to give weight to the state's position through prestige. When the young attorney had shown up alone, the veteran reporters had nodded their heads in understanding. His name was Boylan, and he had refused to give Cowart even the time the hearing was supposed to begin.

"Mr. Black implies that the state withheld information. That is categorically untrue. Your honor, this is a matter for the appellate courts to decide.''

"Your honor, if I may finish?''

"Go ahead, Mr. Black. The objection is overruled.''

Boylan sat and Black continued.

"We contend, sir, that the outcome of that hearing would have been different, and that the state, without Mr. Ferguson's alleged confession, would not have been able to continue with their prosecution of the case. At worst, your honor, if the truth had been presented to the jury, Mr. Ferguson's trial attorney would have been able to make a powerful argument to those folks.''

"I understand," the judge replied, holding up a hand to cut off any further talk by the defense lawyer. "Mr. Boylan?"

"Your honor, the state contends this is a matter for the appellate courts. As far as new evidence is concerned, sir, statements in a newspaper do not constitute bona fide evidence that a court of law should consider.''

"Why not?" asked the judge abruptly, scowling at the prosecutor. "What makes those statements any less relevant, if the defense can prove they took place? I don't know how they are going to do that, of course, but why shouldn't they have the opportunity?''

"We contend they are hearsay, your honor, and should be excluded.''

The judge shook his head. "There are all sorts of exceptions to the hearsay rules, Mr. Boylan. You know that. You were in this court a week ago arguing the opposite." The judge looked out at the audience. "I'll hear the matter," he said abruptly. "Call your first witness.''

"That's it," Cowart whispered to the photographer.

"What?"

"If he hears it, he's made up his mind."

The photographer shrugged his shoulders. The court bailiff rose and intoned, "Detective Bruce Wilcox."

As Wilcox was being sworn in, the assistant state attorney rose and said, "Your honor, I see several witnesses present in the courtroom. I believe the witness rule should be invoked.''

The judge nodded and said, "All witnesses to wait outside."

Cowart saw Tanny Brown rise and exit the courtroom. His eyes followed the slow path the detective made as he paced down the aisle. He was followed by a smaller man Cowart recognized as an assistant medical examiner. He spotted, to his surprise, an official from the state prison as well, a man he'd seen on visits to Death Row. When he turned back, he saw the prosecutor pointing at him.

"Isn't Mr. Cowart a witness?"

"Not at this time," Roy Black replied with a slight smile.

The prosecutor started to say something, then stopped.

The judge leaned forward, his tone brisk and slightly disbelieving. "You don't intend to call Mr. Cowart to the stand?"

"Not at this time, your honor. Nor do we intend to call Mr. and Mrs. Shriver."

He gestured toward the front row where the murdered girl's parents sat stoically, trying to look straight ahead, trying to ignore the television cameras that swept in their direction, along with the eyes of each spectator.

The judge shrugged. "Proceed," he said.

The defense lawyer walked to a speaking podium and paused before addressing Detective Wilcox, who had settled into the witness chair, pitching forward slightly, hands on the railing, like a man waiting for the start of a stakes race.

For the first few moments, the lawyer merely set the scene. He made the detective describe the circumstances surrounding the arrest of Ferguson. He made the detective concede that Ferguson had gone along without a whimper. He made the detective acknowledge that the only link, initially, to Ferguson was the similarity of the automobile. Then, he finally asked, "So, he was arrested because of the car?"

"No, sir. He wasn't actually placed under arrest until he confessed to the crime."

"But that was some time after he was taken into custody? More than twenty-four hours, right?"

"Right."

"And do you think he thought he could leave at any time during that interrogation?"

"He never asked to leave."

"Do you think he thought he could?"

"I don't know what he was thinking."

"Let's talk about that interrogation. Do you remember testifying in this courtroom in a hearing such as this three years ago?"

"I do."

"Do you remember being asked by Mr. Burns: Question: 'Did you strike Mr. Ferguson at the time of the confession?' and your reply, 'I did not.' Now, is that a truthful statement, sir?"

"It is."

"Are you familiar with a series of articles which appeared in *The Miami Journal* some weeks back pertaining to this case?"

"I am."

"Let me read you a paragraph. Quote: 'Detectives denied that Ferguson was beaten in order to obtain a confession. But they did concede that he was "slapped" by Detective Wilcox at the beginning of the questioning.' Are you familiar with that statement, sir, in the newspaper?''

"I am."

"And is it truthful?"

"It is."

Roy Black paced about the podium in sudden exasperation. "Well, which is true?"

Detective Wilcox leaned back, allowing the smallest of grins to penetrate his lips. "Both statements are true, sir. It is true that at the outset of the interview, I slapped Mr. Ferguson twice. With an open hand. Not hard. It was after he called me a name, and I couldn't control my temper for that one moment, sir. But hours passed before he confessed, sir. Almost an entire day. During that time we made jokes and spoke in a friendly fashion. He was given food and rest. He never requested an attorney, nor did he ask to go home. It was my impression, sir, that when he confessed it made him feel much better about what he'd done."

Detective Wilcox shot a glance at Ferguson, who was scowling, shaking his head, and scribbling on his legal pad. His eyes caught Cowart's for an instant, and he smiled.

Roy Black let fury ride the edges of his questions. "Now, after you slapped him, Detective, what do you think he thought? Do you think he thought he wasn't under arrest? That he was free to go? Or do you think he thought you were going to beat on him some more?"

"I don't know."

"Well, how did he act after you slapped him?"

"He grew more respectful. It didn't seem like Ferguson thought it was any big deal."

"And?"

"And I apologized at the request of my superior officer."

"Well, I'm sure that looking back from Death Row, that apology made all the difference in the world," the lawyer said sarcastically.

"Objection!" Boylan stood slowly.

"I'll withdraw the remark," Black replied.

"Right," said the judge. "Precisely." He glared at the defense attorney.

"No more questions."

"The state?"

"Yes, your honor. Just one or two. Detective Wilcox, have you had occasion to take other statements from people confessing to crimes?"

"Yes. Many times."

"How many have been suppressed?"

"None."

"Objection! Irrelevant!"

"Objection sustained and stricken. Continue, please."

"Now, just so I can be certain, you say Mr. Ferguson finally confessed some twenty-four hours after being asked to give a statement?"

"Correct."

"And the alleged slapping, that took place in . . . ."

"Maybe the first five minutes."

"And were there any other physical threats directed toward Mr. Ferguson?"

"None."

"Verbal threats?"

"None."

"Any type of threats?"

"No."

"Thank you." The prosecutor sat down. Wilcox rose and walked across the courtroom, adopting a fierce look until he maneuvered past the camera, when he broke into a grin.

Tanny Brown was next to the stand. He sat in the seat quietly, relaxed, with the calm exterior of someone who'd been in the position he occupied many times. Cowart listened carefully as the lieutenant explained the difficulty surrounding the case, and told the judge that the car was the first, and really the only, piece of evidence they had to go on. He described Ferguson as nervous, anxious, evasive when they arrived at his grandmother's shack. He said that Ferguson's movements had been abrupt, furtive, and that he had refused to explain why he was so busy washing out his car, or to explain satisfactorily where the missing section of car rug was. He said that this physical nervousness led him to suspect that Ferguson was concealing information. He then conceded that Ferguson was slapped twice. Nothing more.

His words echoed his partner's. "Detective Wilcox struck the subject twice, with an open hand. Not hard. He was more respectful afterwards. But I personally apologized to the suspect, and I insisted that Detective Wilcox do the same."

"And what was the effect of those apologies?"

"He seemed to relax. It did not seem that Mr. Ferguson thought being slapped was much of a big deal."

"I'm sure. It's a bigger deal now, right, Lieutenant?"

Tanny Brown paused before answering the exasperated question. "That is correct, Counselor. It is a much bigger deal now."

"And of course, you never pulled a handgun during that interrogation and pointed it at my client?"

"No, sir."

"You never pulled the trigger on an empty cylinder and told him to confess?"

"No, sir."

"You never threatened him with his life?"

"No, sir."

"As far as you're concerned, the statement he gave was entirely voluntary?"

"Correct."

"Stand up, please, Lieutenant."

"Sir?"

"Stand up and step down."

Tanny Brown did what was requested. The defense attorney walked over and seized a chair from behind his table.

The prosecutor rose. "Your honor, I fail to see the point of this demonstration."

The judge leaned over. "Mr. Black?"

"If your honor will indulge me just this once . . ."

The judge glanced toward the television camera, which had pivoted, following the detective. "All right. But get on with it."

"Stand there, Lieutenant."

Tanny Brown stood easily in the center of the room, his hands clasped behind him, waiting.

Black turned toward Ferguson and nodded.

The prisoner then stood up and swiftly walked out from behind the defense table. For an instant, he stood next to the lieutenant, just long enough to allow the difference in the sizes between the two men to be seen. Then he sat in the chair. The effect was immediate; it seemed that Tanny Brown dwarfed the smaller man.

"Now, when he sat there like that, handcuffed and alone, you don't think he feared for his life?"

"No."

"No? Thank you. Please return to your seat."

Cowart smiled. A bit of theater just for the press, he thought. That was the footage that would make all the evening newscasts, the hulking detective perched over the slight, smaller man. It wouldn't have any impact on the judge's decision, but he recognized that Roy Black was playing to more audiences than the one.

"Let's move on to something else, Lieutenant."

"Fine."

"Do you recall an occasion where you were presented with a knife that was discovered beneath a rain culvert some three or four miles from the scene of the crime?"

"Yes."

"How did you get that knife?"

"Mr. Cowart of *The Miami Journal* found it."

"And what did an examination of that knife reveal?"

"The blade length matched some of the deep cuts in the deceased."

"Anything else?"

"Yes. A microscopic analysis of the blade and handle showed small particles of blood residue."

Cowart sat up straight. This was something new.

"And what were the results of those examinations?"

"The blood grouping matched that of the deceased."

"Who performed these tests?"

"The FBI labs."

"And what conclusion did you reach?"

"That the knife may have been the murder weapon."

Cowart scribbled frantically. The other reporters did the same.

"Whose knife was it, Lieutenant?"

"We cannot tell. There were no fingerprints on it, nor were there any identifying marks."

"Well, how did the reporter know where to locate it?"

"I have no idea."

"Do you know a man named Blair Sullivan?"

"Yes. He's a mass murderer."

"Was he ever a suspect in this case?"

"No."

"Is he now?"

"No."

"But was he in Escambia County at the time of Joanie Shriver's murder?"

Tanny Brown hesitated, then replied, "Yes."

"Do you know that Mr. Sullivan told Mr. Cowart where to find that knife?"

"I read that in a newspaper article. But I don't *know* that. I have no control over what appears in the press."

"Absolutely. Have you attempted to interview Mr. Sullivan, in connection with this case?"

"Yes. He refuses to cooperate."

"Just exactly how did he refuse to cooperate?"

"He laughed at us and wouldn't give a statement."

"Well, precisely what did he say when he wouldn't give you a statement? And how did it happen?"

Tanny Brown gritted his teeth and glared at the attorney.

"I believe there's a question pending, Lieutenant."

"We confronted him in his cell at the state prison in Starke. We, that's Detective Wilcox and myself, told him why we were there and we informed him of his rights. He exposed his backside to us, and then he said, 'I refuse to answer your questions on the grounds that my replies might tend to incriminate me.' "

"The Fifth Amendment to the Constitution."

"Yes, sir."

"How many times did he repeat it?"

"I don't know. At least a dozen."

"And did he say these words in a normal tone of voice?"

Tanny Brown shifted in the witness seat, displaying discomfort for the first time. Matthew Cowart watched him closely. He could see the detective struggling inwardly.

"No, sir. Not in a normal tone of voice."

"Then how, please, Lieutenant?"

Tanny Brown scowled. "He was singing. First in a singsong, nursery rhyme kind of tone. Then blasting it out at the top of his lungs as we left the prison."

"Singing?"

"That's right," Brown replied slowly, angrily. "And laughing."

"Thank you, Lieutenant."

When the large man stepped down from the stand, his hands were clenched and all in the courtroom could see the ridges in his neck muscles made by anger. But the image that remained in the tight air of the hearing was of the killer in his cell, singing his refusal like a caged mockingbird.

The assistant medical examiner testified swiftly, buttressing the details about the knife that Brown had already outlined. Then it was Ferguson's turn. Cowart noted the confident way the convicted man walked across the courtroom, taking his seat, hunching over slightly, as if leaning toward the questions from his attorney. Ferguson used a small voice, answering briskly but quietly, as if trying to diminish his presence on the stand. He was unhurried and articulate.

Well coached, Cowart thought.

He remembered the description of Ferguson at his trial, eyes shifting about as if searching for a place to hide from the facts that tumbled from the witnesses' mouths.

Not this time, Cowart realized. He scribbled a note in his pad to remind himself later to draw the distinction.

He listened as Black efficiently led Ferguson through the now-familiar tale of the coerced confession. Ferguson told again of being hit, of being threatened with the gun. Then he described being placed in his cell on Death Row, and of the eventual arrival of Blair Sullivan in the cell next to him.

"And what did Mr. Sullivan tell you?"

"Objection. Hearsay." The prosecutor's voice was firm and smug. "He can only say what he said or what he did."

"Sustained."

"All right," Black answered smoothly. "Did you have a conversation with Mr. Sullivan?"

"Yes."

"And what was the result of that conversation?"

"I grew enraged and tried to attack him. We were moved to different sections of the prison."

"And what action did you take because of that conversation?"

"I wrote to Mr. Cowart of *The Miami Journal.*"

"And what did you ultimately tell him?"

"I told him that Blair Sullivan killed Joanie Shriver."

"Objection!"

"On what grounds?"

The judge held up his hand. "I'll hear this. It's why we're here." He nodded toward the defense attorney.

Black paused, slightly open-mouthed for an instant, as if assessing the wind currents in the courtroom, almost as if he could sense or smell the way things were going for him.

"I have no further questions at this time."

The young prosecutor jumped to the podium, clearly enraged. "What proof have you that this story took place?"

"None. I only know that Mr. Cowart talked to Mr. Sullivan and then went and discovered the knife."

"Do you expect this court to believe that a man would confess murder to you in a prison cell?"

"It's happened many times before."

"That's not responsive."

"I don't expect anything."

"When you confessed to the murder of Joanie Shriver, you were telling the truth then, right?"

"No."

"But you were under oath, correct?"

"Yes."

"And you're facing the death penalty for that crime, right?"

"Yes."

"And you would lie to save your skin, wouldn't you?"

When this question quivered in the air, Cowart saw Ferguson glance quickly toward Black. He could just see the defense attorney's face crease into a slight, knowing smile, and see him nod his head imperceptibly toward the man on the stand.

They knew this was coming, he thought.

Ferguson took a deep breath on the stand.

"You would lie, to save your life, wouldn't you, Mr. Ferguson?" the prosecutor asked sharply, once again.

"Yes," Ferguson replied slowly. "I would."

"Thank you," Boylan said, picking up a sheaf of papers.

"But I'm not," Ferguson added just as the prosecutor started to turn toward his seat, forcing the man to arrest his motion awkwardly.

"You're not lying now?"

"That's correct."

"Even though your life depends upon it?"

"My life depends upon the truth, Mr. Boylan," Ferguson replied. The prosecutor started angrily, as if to launch himself at the prisoner, only to catch himself at the last moment. "Sure it does," he said sarcastically. "No more questions."

There was a momentary pause while Ferguson resumed his seat at the defense table.

"Anything else, Mr. Black?" the judge asked.

"Yes, sir. One last witness. We would call Mr. Norman Sims to the stand."

Within a few moments, a smallish, sandy-haired man, wearing glasses and an ill-fitting brown suit, walked through the court and took the witness stand. Black almost jumped to the podium.

"Mr. Sims, will you identify yourself for the court, please?"

"My name is Norman Sims. I'm an assistant superintendent at the state prison at Starke."

"And what are your duties there?"

The man hesitated. He had a slow, mildly accented voice. "You want me to say everything I got to do?"

Black shook his head. "I'm sorry, Mr. Sims. Let me put it to you this way: Does your job include reviewing and censoring the mail that comes to and from Death Row inmates?"

"I don't like that word . . ."

"Censor?"

"Right. I inspect the mail, sir. Occasionally, we have reason to intercept something. Usually it's contraband. I don't stop nobody from writing whatever they want to."

"But in the case of Mr. Blair Sullivan . . ."

"That's a special case, sir."

"What is it he does?"

"He writes obscene letters to the families of his victims."

"What do you do with these letters?"

"Well, in each case, sir, I have tried to contact the family members they are addressed to. Then I inform them of the letters and ask whether they want to see it or not. I try to let them know what's in it. Most don't want to see 'em."

"Very good. Admirable, even. Does Mr. Sullivan know you intercept his mail?"

"I don't know. Probably. He seems to know just about every damn thing going on in the prison. Sorry, your honor."

The judge nodded, and Black continued. "Now, did you have occasion to intercept a letter within the past three weeks?"

"I did, sir."

"To whom was that letter addressed?"

"To a Mr. and Mrs. George Shriver here in Pachoula."

Black bounced across the court and shoved a sheet of paper toward the witness. "Is this the letter?"

The prison superintendent stared at it for a moment. "Yes, sir. It has my initials at the top, and a stamp. I wrote a note on it, too, that reflects the conversation I had with the Shrivers. They didn't want to hear none of it, sir, after I told them, general-like, what the letter said."

Black took the letter, handed it to the court clerk, who marked it as an exhibit, then handed it back to the witness. Black started to ask a question, then cut himself off. He turned from the judge and witness and walked over to the bar, to where the Shrivers were sitting. Cowart heard him whisper, "Folks, I'm going to have him read the letter. It might be rough. I'm sorry. But if y'all want to leave, then now's the time to do it. I'll see you get your seats back when you want 'em."

The folksiness of his tone, so alien to the clipped words of his questions, surprised Cowart. He saw Mr. and Mrs. Shriver nod and lean their heads together.

He saw the large man rise then and take his wife by the hand. The courtroom was silent as they walked out. Their footsteps echoed slightly, and the doors creaked shut behind them. Black paused, watching them, then delayed another second or so as the doors swung closed. He nodded his head slightly.

"Mr. Sims, please read the letter."

The witness coughed and turned toward the judge. "It's a bit filthy, your honor. I don't know that . . ."

The judge interrupted. "Read the letter."

The witness bent his head slightly and peered down through his glasses. He read in a quick, hurried voice filled with embarrassment, stumbling on the obscenities.

". . . Dear Mr. and Mrs. Shriver: I have been wrong not to write you before this, but I have been real busy getting ready to die. I just wanted you to know what a sweet little piece of fuck your little baby was. Dipping a prick in and out of her snatch was like picking cherries on a summer morning. It was just the tastiest bit of fresh new pussy imaginable. The only thing better than fucking her was killing her. Sticking a knife into her ripe skin was kinda like carving up a melon. That's what she was, all right. Like a bit of fruit. Too bad she's all rotten and used up now. She'd be an awful cold and dirty fuck now, right? All green and maggoty from being underground. Too bad. But she sure was tasty while she lasted . . ." He looked up at the defense attorney. "It was signed: Your good friend, Blair Sullivan."

Black looked up at the ceiling, letting the impact of the letter filter through the air. Then he asked, "He's written to other victims' families?"

"Yes, sir. To just about all the folks of all the people he confessed killing."

"Does he write regularly?"

"No, sir. Just when he seems to get the urge. Most of the letters are even worse'n this one. He gets even more specific, sometimes."

"I imagine."

"Yes, sir."

"No further questions."

The prosecutor rose slowly. Boylan was shaking his head. "Now, Mr. Sims, he doesn't say specifically in that letter that he killed Joanie Shriver?"

"No, sir. He says what I read. He says she was tasty, sir. But he doesn't say he killed her, no sir, but it sure seems like that's what he was saying."

The prosecutor seemed deflated. He started to ask another question, then stopped. "Nothing further," he said.

Mr. Sims picked himself up from the witness stand and walked quickly out of the courtroom. There was a minute or two before the Shrivers returned. Cowart saw their eyes were red with tears.

"I'll hear arguments now," Judge Trench said.

The two attorneys were blissfully brief, which surprised Cowart. They were predictable as well. He tried to take notes, but stared instead at the man and woman fighting tears in the front row. He saw they would not turn and look at Ferguson. Instead, their eyes were locked forward, up on the judge, their backs rigid, their shoulders set, leaning slightly toward him, as if they were fighting the strong winds of a gale.

When the lawyers finished, the judge spoke sharply. "I'll want to see citations for each position. I'll rule after I review the law. Set this down for a week from now."

Then he stood abruptly and disappeared through a door toward his chambers.

There was a moment of confusion as the crowd rose. Cowart saw Ferguson shake hands with the attorney and follow the guards through a door in the back of the courtroom leading to a holding cell. Cowart turned and saw the Shrivers surrounded by reporters, struggling to extricate themselves from the narrow aisle of the courtroom, and exit. In the same instant, he saw Roy Black motion to the prosecutor, gesturing at the trouble the couple were having. Mrs. Shriver was holding up her arm, as if she could fend off the questions raining down on her like so many droplets from the sky. He saw George Shriver drape an arm around his wife, his face reddening as he struggled to get past. Boylan reached them after a moment and managed to get them steered around, like a ship changing direction in the high seas, and he led them the other way, heading through the door to the judge's chambers. Cowart heard the photographer at his elbow say, "I got a shot, don't worry." Black caught his eye then and surreptitiously made a thumbs-up sign. But Cowart felt first an odd emptiness, followed by a nervousness that contradicted the excitement of the moment.

He heard voices around him: Black was being interviewed by one camera crew, the lawyer bathed in the glare of the minicam. He was saying, ". . . Of course we thought we made our point there. You can't help but see there's all sorts of questions still floating about this case. I don't know why the state won't understand that . . .''

At the same moment, a few feet away, Boylan was replying to another camera, glowing with the same intensity in the same light. "It's our position that the right man is sitting on Death Row for a terrible crime. We intend to adhere to that position. Even if the judge were to grant Mr. Ferguson a new trial, we believe there's more than sufficient evidence to convict him once again.''

A reporter's voice called out, "Even without a confession?''

"Absolutely,'' the lawyer replied. Someone laughed, but as Boylan pivoted, glaring, they stopped.

"How come your boss didn't come down and argue this motion? How come they sent you? You weren't on the original prosecuting team. How come you?''

"It just fell to me,'' he explained without explaining.

Roy Black answered the same question ten feet away. "Because elected officials don't like coming into courtrooms and getting their heads beat in. They could smell it was a loser right from the start. And, boys, you can quote me.''

Suddenly a camera with its unyielding light swung at Cowart, and he heard a question thrust his way. "Cowart? This was your story. What did you think of the hearing? How about that letter?''

He stumbled for something clever or glib to say, finally shaking his head. "Come on, Matt,'' someone shouted. "Give us a break.'' But he pushed past. "Touchy,'' someone said.

Cowart paced down the corridor and rode an escalator to the vestibule. He hurried through the doors to the courthouse and stopped on the steps. He could feel the heat surrounding him. There was a solid breeze and above him the wind tugged at a triptych of flags: county, state, and national. They made a snapping sound, cracking like gunshots with each renewed blow from the air. He saw Tanny Brown standing across the street staring at him. The detective simply frowned, then slid behind the wheel of a car. Cowart watched him pull slowly into traffic and disappear.

One week later, the judge issued a written statement ordering a new trial for Robert Earl Ferguson. There was nothing in it describing him as "a wild animal." Nor did it acknowledge the dozens of newspaper editorials that had suggested Ferguson be granted a new trial—including those papers circulating in Escambia County. The judge also ordered that the statement that Ferguson had made to detectives be suppressed. In an in-chambers motion, Roy Black requested Ferguson be released on bail. This was granted. A coalition of anti-death-penalty groups provided the money. Cowart learned later that it was fronted to them by a movie producer who'd purchased the dramatic rights to Robert Earl Ferguson's life story.

NINE
═══DEATH WARRANT

RESTLESS time flooded him.

He felt as if his life had become compartmentalized into a series of moments awaiting a signal to return to its normal continuity. He felt an annoying sense of anticipation, a nervous sort of expectation, but of precisely what he could not tell. He went to the prison on the day that Robert Earl Ferguson was released from Death Row in advance of his new trial, postponed by the judge until December. It was the first week in July, and the road to the prison sported makeshift stands selling fireworks, sparklers, flags, and red, white, and blue bunting, which hung limply from the whitewashed board walls. The Florida spring had fiercely fused into summer, the heat pounding on the earth with an endlessly patient fury, drying the dirt into a hard, cracked cement beneath his feet. Sheets of warmth wavered above the ground like hallucinations, surrounding him with a presence as strong as a New England blizzard in winter, and just as hard to maneuver in; the heat seemed to sap energy, ambition, and desire. It was almost as if the soaring temperatures slowed the entire rotation of the world.

A fitful crowd of sweating press waited for Ferguson outside the prison doors. The numbers of people gathered were thickened by members of anti-death-penalty groups, some of whom carried placards welcoming his release, and who had been chanting, "One, two, three, End the Death Pen-al-ty. Seven, eight, nine, End It for All Time" before the prisoner emerged from the prison. They broke into cheers and a smattering of applause when he came through the doors. Ferguson looked up briefly into the pale blue sky before stopping. He stood, flanked by his lanky attorney and his brittle, gray-haired grandmother. She glared at the reporters and cameramen who surged toward them, clinging with both arms to her grandson's elbow. Ferguson made a short speech, perched on the steps of the prison, so that he looked down at the crowd, saying that he believed his case showed both how the system didn't work and how it did. He said he was glad to be free. He said he was going to get a real meal first, fried chicken and greens with an ice-cream sundae with extra chocolate for dessert. He said he had no bitterness, which no one believed. He ended his speech by saying, "I just want to thank the Lord for helping to show me the way, thank my attorney, and thank *The Miami Journal* and Mr. Cowart, because he listened when it seemed no one else would. I wouldn't be standing here before you today if it weren't for him."

Cowart doubted that this final bit of speechmaking would make any of the nightly newscasts or show up in any of the other newspapers' stories. He smiled.

Reporters started to shoot questions through the heat.

"Are you going back to Pachoula?"

"Yes. That's my only real home."

"What are your plans?"

"I want to finish school. Maybe go to law school or study criminology. I've got a real good understanding now of criminal law."

There was laughter.

"What about the trial?"

"What can I say? They say they want to try me again, but I don't know how they can. I think I'll be acquitted. I just want to get on with my life, to get out of the public eye, you know. Get sort of anonymous again. It's not that I don't like you folks, but . . ."

There was more laughter. The crowd of reporters seemed to swallow up the slight man, whose head pivoted with each question, so that he was facing directly at the person who asked it. Cowart noted how comfortable Ferguson appeared, handling the questions at the impromptu news conference with humor and ease, obviously enjoying himself.

"Why do you think they're going to prosecute you again?"

"To save face. I think it's the only way they can keep from

acknowledging that they tried to execute an innocent man. An innocent black man. They would rather stick to a lie than face the truth.''

"Right on, Brother!" someone called from the group of demonstrators. "Tell it!"

Another reporter had told Cowart that these same people showed up for every execution, holding candlelight vigils and singing "We Shall Overcome" and "I Shall Be Released" right up to the time the warden emerged to announce that the verdict and judgment of the court had been carried out. There was usually a corresponding group of flag-waving fry-'em-all types in jeans, white T-shirts, and pointy-toed cowboy boots, who hooted and hollered and engaged in occasional shoving matches with the anti-death-penalty bunch. They were not present on this day.

Both groups were generally ignored by the press as much as possible.

"What about Blair Sullivan?" a television reporter shouted, thrusting a microphone at Ferguson.

"What about him? I think he's a dangerous, twisted individual."

"Do you hate him?"

"No. The good Lord instructs me to turn the other cheek. But I got to admit, sometimes it's hard."

"Do you think he'll confess and save you from the trial?"

"No. The only confessing I think he's planning on doing is when he goes to meet his Maker."

"Have you talked with him about the murder?"

"He won't talk to anybody. Especially about what he did in Pachoula."

"What do you think about those detectives?"

He hesitated. "No comment," he said. Ferguson grinned. "My attorney told me that if I couldn't say something nice, or something neutral, to say 'no comment.' There you go."

There was more laughter from the reporters.

He smiled nicely. There was a final blurring as cameramen maneuvered for a final shot and soundmen struggled with boom microphones and portable tape machines. The newspaper photographers bounced and weaved about Ferguson, the motordrives on their cameras making a sound like bugs on a still evening. The press surged toward Ferguson a last time, and he raised his hand, making a V-for-victory sign. He was steered into the backseat of a car, waving one last time through the

closed window at the last photographers shooting their final
pictures. Then the car pulled out, heading down the long access
road, the tires kicking up little puffs of dust that hovered above
the sticky black macadam highway. It soared past an inmate
work crew, marching single file slowly in the heat, sweat glistening off the dark skin of their arms. Sunlight reflected off the
shovels and pickaxes they carried on their shoulders as they
headed toward their noontime break. The men were singing a
work song. Cowart could not make out the words, but the steady
rhythms filled him.

He took his daughter to Disney World the following month.
They stayed in a room high in the Contemporary Hotel, overlooking the amusement park. Becky had developed a child's
expertise about the place, mapping out each day's assault on the
rides with the excitement of a successful general anxious to engage a beaten enemy. He was content to let her create the flow
to the day. If she wanted to ride Space Mountain or Mr. Toad's
Wild Ride four or five times in a row, that was fine. When she
wanted to eat, he made no adult pretense of nutrition, allowing
her to select a dizzying variety of hot dogs, french fries, and
cotton candy.

It was too warm to wait in line for rides during the afternoon,
so the two of them spent hours in the pool at the hotel, ducking
and cavorting about. He would toss her endlessly in the opaque
waters, let her ride on his shoulders, swim between his legs.
Then, with the meager cooling that slid into the air as the sun
dropped, they would get dressed and head back to the park for
the fireworks and light shows.

Each night he ended up carrying her, exhausted and fast
asleep, back on the monorail to the hotel, up to the room, where
he would gently slip her under the covers of her bed and listen
to her regular, easy breathing, the child sound blocking all
thoughts from his head and giving him a sort of peace.

He had but one nightmare during the time there: A sudden
dream-vision of Ferguson and Sullivan forcing him onto a roller
coaster ride and seizing his daughter away from him.

He awoke gasping and heard Becky say, "Daddy?"

"I'm all right, honey. Everything's all right."

She sighed and rolled over once in bed before tumbling back
into sleep.

He remained in the bed, feeling the clammy sheets surround
him.

The week had passed with a child's urgency, all rolled together into nonstop activity. When it came time to take her home, he did it slowly, stopping at Water World for a ride on the slide, then pulling off the thruway for hamburgers. He stopped again for ice cream and finally, a fourth time, to find a toy store and buy yet another gift. By the time they reached the expensive Tampa suburb where his ex-wife and her new husband lived, he was barely pushing the car down the streets, his reluctance to part with her lost in the rapid-fire, boundless excitement of his daughter, who pointed out all her friends' houses en route.

There was a long, circular drive in front of his daughter's home. An elderly black man was pushing a lawn mower across the expanse of vivid green lawn. His old truck, a red faded to a rusty brown, was parked to the side. He saw the words NED'S LAWN SERVICE COMPLETE handwritten on the side in white paint. The old man paused just for a moment to wipe his forehead and wave at Becky, who waved eagerly in return. Cowart saw the old man hunch over, bending to the task of trimming the grass to a uniform height. His shirt collar was stained a darker color than his skin.

Cowart looked up at the front door. It was a double width, carved wood. The house itself was a single-story ranch design that seemed to spread out over a small rise. He could see the black screen of an enclosed pool just above the roof line. There was a row of plants in front, trimmed meticulously like makeup carefully applied to a face. Becky bounded from the car and raced through the front door.

He stood for a moment, waiting until Sandy appeared.

She was swollen with pregnancy, moving carefully against the heat and discomfort. She had her arm wrapped around her daughter. "So, was it a success?"

"We did it all."

"I expect so. Are you exhausted?"

"A bit."

"How are things otherwise?"

"Okay."

"You know, I still worry about you."

"Well, thanks, but I'm okay. You don't have to."

"I wish we could talk. Can you come in? Have a cup of coffee? A cold drink?" She smiled. "I'd like to hear about everything. There's a lot to talk about."

"Becky can fill you in."

"That's not what I mean," she said.

He shook his head. "Got to get back. I'm late as it is."

"Tom'll be home in a half hour or so. He'd like to see you. He thought you did a helluva job on those stories."

He continued to shake his head. "Tell him thanks. But I've really got to get on the road. It'll be nearly midnight by the time I get back to Miami."

"I wish—" she started. Then she stopped and said, "Okay. I'll speak with you soon."

He nodded. "Give me a hug, honey." He got down on his knees and gave his daughter a squeeze. He could feel her energy flow through him for just an instant, all endless enthusiasm. Then she pulled away. "Bye-bye, Daddy," she said. Her voice had a small crease in it. He reached out, stroked her cheek once and said, "Now, don't tell your mother what you've been eating . . ." He lowered his voice into a stage whisper. ". . . And don't tell her about all the presents you got. She might be jealous." Becky smiled and nodded her head up and down vigorously.

Before sliding behind the wheel, he turned and waved in false gaiety at the two of them. He told himself, You play the divorced father well. You've got all the moves down pat.

His fury with himself did not subside for hours.

At the paper, Will Martin tried to get him interested in several editorial crusades, with little success. He found himself daydreaming, anticipating Ferguson's upcoming trial, although he did not expect it ever to occur. As the Florida summer dragged relentlessly into fall with no change in atmosphere or temperature, he decided to go back up to Pachoula and write some sort of story about how the town was reacting to Ferguson's release.

The first call he made from his motel room was to Tanny Brown.

"Lieutenant? Matthew Cowart here. I just wanted to save you the trouble of having to rely on your spies and sources. I'm in town for a couple of days."

"Can I ask what for?"

"Just to do an update on the Ferguson case. Are you still planning to prosecute?"

The detective laughed. "That's a decision for the state attorney, not me."

"Yeah, but he makes the decision with the information you provide him. Has anything new come up?"

"You expect me to tell you if it has?"

"I'm asking."

"Well, seeing as how Roy Black would tell you anyway, no, nothing new."

"What about Ferguson. What's he been doing?"

"Why don't you ask him?"

"I'm going to."

"Well, why don't you go out to his place, then give me a call back."

Cowart hung up the phone, vaguely impressed with the thought the detective was mocking him. He drove through the pine trees and shadows down the dirt road to Ferguson's grandmother's house, pulling in amidst the few chickens and standing on the packed dirt for a moment. He saw no signs of activity, so he mounted the steps and knocked hard on the wood frame of the door. After a moment, he heard shuffling feet, and the door pitched open a few inches.

"Mrs. Ferguson? It's me, Matthew Cowart, from the *Journal*."

The door opened a little wider.

"Whatcha want now?"

"Where's Bobby Earl? I'd like to talk to him."

"He went back north."

"What?"

"He went back up to that school in New Jersey."

"When did he leave?"

"Last week. There warn't nothing here for him, white boy. You know that as well as I do."

"But what about his trial?"

"He didn't seem too concerned."

"How can I get in touch with him?"

"He said he'd write when he got settled. That ain't happened yet."

"Did anything happen here, in Pachoula? Before he left?"

"Not that he talked about. You got any more questions, Mr. Reporter?"

"No."

Cowart stepped down from the porch and stared up at the house.

That afternoon, he called Roy Black.

"Where's Ferguson?" he demanded.

"In New Jersey. I got an address and phone, if y'all want it."

"But how can he leave the state? What about the trial, his bail?"

"Judge gave him permission. No big deal. I told him it was better to get back on with his life, and he wanted to go on up and finish school. What's so strange about that? The state has to provide us with any new discovery material, and so far they haven't sent over anything. I don't know what they're gonna do, but I'm not expecting big things from them."

"You think it's just going to slide?"

"Maybe. Go ask the detectives."

"I will."

"You got to understand, Mr. Cowart, how little those prosecutors want to get up and have their heads bashed in at trial. Public humiliation ain't high on the list for elected officials, you know. I suspect they'd find it a lot easier just to let a little bit of time flow by, so's people's memories get a bit hazy about the whole thing. Then get up and drop the charges at some cozy, little old conference back in the judge's chambers. Blame the whole failure on him for suppressing that statement. He'll turn right around and say it was the state's fault. And mostly the whole thing will dump on those two cops. Simple as that. End of story. That ain't so surprising now, is it? You've seen things just float on out of the criminal justice system before with nary a whimper?"

"From Death Row to zero?"

"You got it. Happens. Not too frequent, of course, but happens. Nothing here that I haven't seen or heard before."

"Just pick up life, after a three-year hiatus?"

"Right again. Everything back to nice and quiet normal. Excepting of course one thing."

"What's that?"

"That little girl is still dead."

He called Tanny Brown.

"Ferguson's gone back to New Jersey. Did you know that?"

"It wasn't too much of a secret. The local paper did a story on his leaving. Said he wanted to continue his education. Told the paper he didn't think he could get a job here in Pachoula because of the way people looked at him. I don't know about that. I don't know if he even tried. Anyway, he left. I think he just wanted to get out of town before somebody did something to him."

"Like who?"

"I don't really know. Some people were upset when he was

released. Of course, some others weren't. Small town, you know. People divided. Most folks were pretty confused.''

"Who was upset?"

Tanny Brown paused before replying. "I was upset. That's enough."

"So, what happens now?"

"What do you expect to happen?"

Cowart didn't have an answer for that.

He did not write the story he intended. Instead, he went back to the editorial board and worked hard on upcoming local elections. He spent hours interviewing candidates, reading position papers, and debating with the other members of the board what the newspaper's positions should be. The atmosphere was heady, collegial. The wonderful perversities of local South Florida politics, where issues like making English the official county language, or democracy in Cuba, or firearms control, provided infinite distractions. After the elections, he launched another series of editorials on water management throughout the Florida Keys. This required him to occupy his time with budget projections and ecological statements. His desk grew cluttered with sheets of paper, all covered with endless tables and charts. He had an odd thought, a pun: There's safety in numbers.

The first week in December, at a hearing before Judge Trench, the state dropped first-degree-murder charges against Robert Earl Ferguson. They complained to a small gathering of reporters that without the confession, there was little hard evidence to go on. There was a lot of posturing by both prosecutors and the defense team about how important the system was, and how no single case was more important than the rules of law that governed them all.

Tanny Brown and Bruce Wilcox were absent from the hearing.

"I don't really want to talk about it right now," Brown said when Cowart went to see him. Wilcox said, "Jesus, I barely touched the man. Jesus. If I'd really hit him, you think he'd have no marks? You think he'd still be standing? Hell, I'd a ripped his head off. Damn."

He drove through a humid evening, past the school, past the willow where Joanie Shriver had stepped out of the world. He stopped at the fork in the road, staring for an instant down the route the killer had taken before turning toward the Shriver house. He pulled in front and spotted George Shriver cutting a hedge with a gas-powered trimmer. The big man's body was wreathed in sweat when Cowart approached. He stopped, shutting down the motor, breathing in harsh gasps of air as the reporter stood by, notepad and pen poised.

"We heard," he said softly. "Tanny Brown called us, said it was official now. Of course, it didn't come as no surprise or anything. Yes sir, we knew it was going to happen. Tanny Brown once told us that it was all so fragile. That's the word I can't forget. I guess it just couldn't hold together no more, not after you started to look at it."

Cowart stood before the red-faced man uncomfortably. "Do you still think Ferguson killed your daughter? What about Sullivan? What about that letter he sent?"

"I don't know nothing anymore about it. I suspect it's as confused for the missus and me as it is for everyone else. But in my heart, you know, I still think he did it. I can't ever erase the way he looked at his trial, you know. I just can't forget that."

Mrs. Shriver brought out a glass of ice water for her husband. She looked up at Cowart with a sort of curiosity in her eyes that was ridged with anger.

"What I can't understand," she said, "is why we had to go through all this again. First you, then the other television and print folks. It was like she got killed all over again. And again and again. It got so's I couldn't turn on the television for fear that I might see her picture there again and again. It wasn't like people wouldn't let us forget. We didn't want to forget. But it got all caught up in something that I didn't understand. Like what became important was what that man Ferguson said and what that man Sullivan said and what they did and all that. Not that what was really important was that my little girl was stolen. And that was a hurt, you know, Mr. Cowart? That hurt and kept hurting so much."

The woman was crying as she spoke, but the tears didn't mar the clarity of her voice.

George Shriver took a deep breath and a long pull from his water. "Of course, we don't blame you, Mr. Cowart." He paused. "Well, hell, maybe we do a bit. Can't help but think something wrong has happened somewhere. Not your fault, I guess. Not your fault at all. Fragile, like I said. Fragile, and it all fell apart."

The big man took his wife's hand and, together, leaving the

lawn mower and Matthew Cowart standing in the front yard, they retreated into the darkness of their home.

When he spoke with Ferguson, he was overwhelmed by the elation in the man's voice. It made it seem to the reporter that he was standing close by, not talking over some distance on a telephone.

"I can't thank you enough, Mr. Cowart. It wouldn't of happened without your help."

"Yes, it would have, sooner or later."

"No, sir. You were the person who got it all moving. I'd still be on the Row if not for you."

"What are you going to do now?"

"I have plans, Mr. Cowart. Plans to make something of my life. Finish school. Make a career. Yes sir." Ferguson paused, then added, "I feel like I'm free to do anything now."

Cowart remembered the phrase from somewhere but could not place it. Instead, he asked, "How're your classes going?"

"I've learned a lot," Ferguson said. He laughed briefly. "I feel like I know a whole lot more than I did before. Yes sir. Everything's different now. It's been some education."

"Are you going to stay up in Newark?"

"I'm not sure about that. This place is colder even than I remember it, Mr. Cowart. I think I should head back south."

"Pachoula?"

Ferguson hesitated before replying. "Well, I doubt it. That place didn't make me feel altogether welcome after I got off the Row. People'd stare. I could hear talk behind my back. Lot of pointing. Couldn't go to the local convenience store without finding a patrol car waiting for me when I came out. It was like they were watching me, knowing I'd do something. Took my granny to services on Sunday, folks' heads would turn when we walked through the door. Went down looking for a job, but every place I went it seemed like the job had just been filled a couple minutes before I got there, made no difference if the boss was black or white. They all just looked at me like I was some sort of evil thing walking about in their midst that they couldn't do nothing about. That was wrong, sir. Real wrong. And there wasn't a damn thing I could do about it. But Florida's a big place, Mr. Cowart. Why, just the other day a church in Ocala asked me to come give a talk on my experiences. And they weren't the first. So there's plenty of places that don't think I'm some sort of mad dog. Just Pachoula, maybe. And that won't change as long as that Tanny Brown's there.''

''Will you stay in touch?''

''Why, of course,'' Ferguson replied.

In late January, almost a year after he'd received the letter from Robert Earl Ferguson, Matthew Cowart won a Florida Press Association award for his stories. This prize was swiftly followed by awards from the Penney-Missouri School of Journalism and an Ernie Pyle Award from Scripps-Howard.

At the same time, the Florida Supreme Court affirmed the conviction and sentence of Blair Sullivan. He got another collect phone call.

''Cowart? You there?''

''I'm here, Mr. Sullivan.''

''You hear about that court decision?''

''Yes. What are you going to do? All you got to do is talk to one attorney. Why not call Roy Black, huh?''

''Mr. Cowart, d'you think I'm a man with no convictions?'' he laughed. ''That's a pun. A man of no conscience? That's another joke. What makes you think I ain't going to stick to what I said?''

''I don't know. Maybe I think life is worth living.''

''You ain't had my life.''

''That's true.''

''And you ain't got my future. You probably think I ain't got much future. But you're gonna be surprised.''

''I'm waiting.''

''You want to know something, Mr. Cowart? The really funny thing is, I'm having a good time.''

''I'm glad to hear it.''

''You know another thing, Mr. Cowart? We're gonna talk again. When it gets close.''

''Have you been told anything about when?''

''No. Can't imagine what's taking the governor so long.''

''Do you really want to die, Mr. Sullivan?''

''I got plans, Mr. Cowart. Big plans. Death is just a little part of them. I'll call you again.''

He hung up and Matthew Cowart stifled a shiver. He thought it was like speaking with a corpse.

On the first of April, Matthew Cowart was awarded the Pulitzer Prize for distinguished local news reporting.

In the old days of wire machines that clattered and clanged out news stories in an endless flow of words, there was a sort of ritual gathering on the day the awards were to be announced, waiting for the winners' names to move on the wires. The Associated Press and United Press International usually competed to see which organization could process the awards announcement quickest and move the story fastest. The old wire machines were equipped with bells that would sound when a big story came over the wires, so there was an almost religious pealing when the winners' names were produced. There was a sort of romanticism involved in watching the Teletype crunch out the names as the assembled editors and reporters groaned or cheered. All that had been replaced by instantaneous transmission over computer lines. Now the names appeared on the ubiquitous green screens that dotted the modern newsroom. The cheers and groans were the same, however.

He had been out at a water-management conference that afternoon. When he walked into the newsroom, the entire staff rose up applauding.

A photographer snapped his picture as he was handed a glass of champagne and was pushed toward a computer screen to read the words himself. There were high fives from the managing editor and the city editor, and Will Martin said, "I knew it all along."

He was swamped with congratulatory calls. Roy Black telephoned, as did Robert Earl Ferguson, who spoke for only a few moments. Tanny Brown called and said cryptically, "Well, I'm glad to see somebody got something out of all this."

His ex-wife called, crying. "I knew you could do it," she said. He could hear a baby bawling in the background. His daughter squealed with pleasure when she spoke with him, not fully understanding what had happened but delighted nonetheless. He was interviewed on three local television stations and got a call from a literary agent, wondering whether he was interested in writing a book. The producer who'd purchased the rights to Robert Earl Ferguson's life story called, intimating that he should make a deal as well. The man was insistent, talking his way past the telephone receptionist screening the incoming calls, finally getting Matthew Cowart on the line.

"Mr. Cowart? Jeffrey Maynard here. I'm with Instacom Productions. We're very anxious to do a movie based on all the work you've done."

The producer had a breathless, agitated voice, as if each passing second was filled with lost opportunity and wasted money.

Cowart replied slowly, "I'm sorry, Mr. Maynard, but . . ."

"Don't turn me down, Mr. Cowart. How about I fly out to Miami and talk with you? Better yet, you fly here, our nickel, of course."

"I don't think so . . ."

"Let me say this, Mr. Cowart. We've spoken to almost all the principals here, and we're real interested in obtaining rights and releases from everyone. We're talking some substantial money here, and maybe the opportunity for you to get out of newspaper work."

"I don't want to get out of newspaper work."

"I thought all reporters wanted to do something else."

"You're mistaken."

"Still, I'd like to meet. We've met with the others, and we've got all sorts of cooperation on this, and . . ."

"I'll think about it, Mr. Maynard."

"Will you get back to me?"

"Sure."

Cowart hung up the telephone with absolutely no intention of doing this. He returned to the excitement that flooded the newsroom, guzzling champagne from a plastic cup, basking in the attention, all confusions and questions crushed under the weight of backslapping and congratulations.

But when he went home that night, he was still alone.

He walked into his apartment and thought of Vernon Hawkins living out solitary days with his memories and his cough. The dead detective seemed everywhere in his imagination. He kept trying to force the vision of his friend into some congratulatory pose, insisting to himself that Hawkins would have been the first to call, the first to crack an expensive bottle of champagne. But the image wouldn't stick. He could only remember the old detective lying in bed in his hospital room, muttering through the fog of drugs and oxygen, "What's the Tenth Rule of the streets, Matty?"

And his reply, "Christ, Vernon, I don't know. Get some rest."

"The Tenth Rule is: Things are never what they seem."

"Vernon, what the hell does that mean?"

"It means I'm losing my head. Get the fucking nurse, not the old one, the young one with the knockers. Tell her I need a shot. Any old shot, doesn't make any difference, as long as she rubs my rear end with an alcohol swab for a couple of minutes before shooting me up.''

He remembered summoning the nurse and watching the old man get a shot, grin wildly, and slip off into a mist of sleep.

But I won, Vernon. I did it, he said to himself. He looked down at the copy of the first edition that he carried under his arm. The picture and story were above the fold: JOURNAL WRITER TAKES PULITZER IN DEATH ROW STORY.

He spent most of the night staring out into the wide black sky, letting euphoria play with doubt, until the excitement of the award simply overcame all anxieties and he drifted off, drugged with his own shot of success.

Two weeks later, while Matthew Cowart was still riding a crest of elation, a second story moved over the electronic wires.

The story said that the governor had signed a death warrant for Blair Sullivan. It set his execution in the electric chair for midnight, seven days from the moment of signing. There was speculation that Sullivan could avoid the chair at any point by opting to file an appeal. The governor acknowledged this fact when he signed the warrant. But there was no immediate response from the prisoner.

One day passed. Then a second, third, and fourth. On the morning of the fifth day of the death warrant, as he sat at his desk, the telephone rang. He seized the receiver eagerly.

It was Sergeant Rogers from the prison.

"Cowart? You there, buddy?"

"Yeah, Sergeant. I was expecting to hear from you."

"Well, things are getting close, ain't they?"

This was a question that really demanded no answer. "What's with Sullivan?"

"Man, you ever go to the reptile house at the zoo? Watch those snakes behind those glass windows? They don't move much, except their eyes dart about, watching everything. That's what Sully's like. We're supposed to be watching him, but he's eyeing us like he expects something. This ain't like any Death Watch I ever saw before."

"What usually happens?"

"Generally speaking, this place starts crawling with lawyers, priests, and demonstrators. Everybody's wired up, racing about to different judges and courts, meeting this, talking about that. Next thing you know, it's time. One thing I'll say about when the state juices you: You don't have to face it alone. There's

family and well-wishers and people talking about God and justice and all sorts, until your ears like to fall off. That's normal.
But this ain't normal. There ain't nobody inside or outside for
Sully. He's just alone. I keep expecting him to explode, he's
wrapped so tight.''

''Will he appeal?''

''Says no.''

''What do you think?''

''He's a man of his word.''

''What about everybody else?''

''Well, the consensus here is that he'll break down, maybe
on the last day, and ask somebody to file something and get his
stay and enjoy his ten years of appeals. Latest odds are ten will
get you fifty if he actually goes to the chair. I got some money
down on that myself. That's what the governor's man thinks,
anyway. Said they just wanted to call the man's bluff. But he's
cutting it close, you know. Real fine.''

''Jesus.''

''Yeah. Hearing a lot about Him lately, too.''

''What about the preparations?''

''Well, the chair works fine, we tested it this morning. It'll
kill you right quick, no doubt about that. Anyway, he'll get
moved into an isolation cell twenty-four hours ahead. He gets
to order himself a meal, that's tradition. We don't cut his hair or
do any of the other prep work until there's just a couple of hours
left. Until then, things stay as normal as we can make them.
The other folks on the Row are mighty restless. They don't like
to see somebody not fight, you know. When Ferguson walked,
it inspired everyone, gave them all like a shot of hope. Now
Sully's got them all pretty pissed off and anxious-like. I don't
know what'll happen.''

''Sounds like it's tough on you.''

''Sure. But in the end it ain't nothing more than part of the
job.''

''Has Sully talked to anyone?''

''No. But that's the reason I'm calling.''

''What?''

''He wants to see you. In person. ASAP.''

''Me?''

''You got it. Wants you to share the nightmare, I'm guessing.
He's put you on his witness list.''

''What's that?''

"What d'you think? The invited guests of the state and Blair Sullivan for his own little going-away party."

"Jesus. He wants me to watch the execution?"

"Yup."

"Christ! I don't know if . . ."

"Why don't you ask him yourself? You got to understand, Mr. Cowart, there ain't a lot of time involved here. We're having a nice chat here on the phone, but I think you'd best be calling the airlines for a flight. Get here by this afternoon."

"Right. Right. I'll get right there. Jesus."

"It was your story, Mr. Cowart. I guess old Sully just wants to see you write the last chapter, huh? Can't say it surprises me."

Matthew Cowart didn't reply. He hung up the telephone. He stuck his head into Will Martin's office and swiftly explained the unusual summons. "Go," the older man said. "Go, right now. It's a helluva story. Just go." There was a hurried conversation with the managing editor, and a rushed trip back to his apartment to grab a toothbrush and change of clothes.

He made a noon commuter flight.

It was late afternoon when he reached the prison, driving the rental car hard through a gray, rain-streaked day. The beating noise of the windshield wipers had added urgency to his pace. Sergeant Rogers met him in the administration offices. They shook hands like old teammates at a reunion.

"You made good time," the sergeant said.

"You know, I can feel the craziness. I'm driving along, thinking about every minute, Jesus, every second, and what it means all of a sudden."

"That's right," the sergeant nodded. "There ain't nothing like having a time and date for dying to make little moments right important."

"Scary."

"That it is. Like I told you, Mr. Cowart, Death Row gives one an entirely different perspective on living."

"No demonstrators outside?"

"Not yet. You really got to hate the death penalty to want to walk in the rain for old Sully. I expect they'll show up in a day or so. Weather's supposed to clear tonight."

"Anyone else here to see him?"

"There's lawyers with papers all ready to file on call—but he ain't called for anyone, excepting you. There's been some detectives here. That pair from Pachoula came down yesterday. He wouldn't talk to them. Couple of FBI men and some guys from Orlando and Gainesville. They all want to know about a bunch of murders they still got floating on their books. He won't talk to them, neither. Just wants to talk to you. Maybe he'll tell you. Sure would help some folks if'n he would. That's what old Ted Bundy did, before he went to the chair. Cleared up a whole lot of mysteries plaguing some folks. I don't know if it counted for much when he got to the other side, but, hell, who knows?''

"Let's go.''

"That's right.''

Sergeant Rogers made a perfunctory check of Matthew Cowart's notepad and briefcase and then led him through the sally ports and metal detectors into the bowels of the prison.

Sullivan was waiting in his cell. The sergeant pulled a chair up outside and gestured for Cowart to sit.

"I need privacy,'' Sullivan coughed.

Cowart thought he had paled some. His slicked-back hair glistened in the light from a single, wire-covered bulb. Sullivan moved nervously about from wall to wall in the cell, twisting his hands together, his shoulders hunched over.

"I need my privacy,'' he repeated.

"Sully, you know there ain't nobody in either cell on right or left. You can talk here,'' the sergeant said patiently.

The prisoner allowed a smile to race across his face.

"They make it like a grave,'' he said to Matthew Cowart as the sergeant moved away. "They make it quiet and still, just so's you start to get used to the idea of living in a coffin.''

He walked to the bars and shook them once. "Just like a coffin,'' he said. "Nailed shut.''

Blair Sullivan laughed hard, until the sound disintegrated into a wheeze. "So, Cowart, you're looking mighty prosperous.''

"I'm okay. How can I help you?''

"I'll get to that, get to that. Give me a moment of pleasure or so. Hey, you heard from our boy, Bobby Earl?''

"When I won the prize, he called with congratulations. But I didn't really talk to him. I gather he's back in college.''

"That right? Somehow, I didn't make him for a real studious type. But hey, maybe college has got some special attractions for old Bobby Earl. Real special attractions.''

"What are you saying?''

"Nothing. Nothing. Nothing that you won't need to remember some time later.''

Blair Sullivan tossed back his head and let his body shiver. "You think it's cold in here, Cowart?"

Cowart could feel sweat running down his ribs. "No. It's hot."

Sullivan grinned and coughed out another laugh. "Ain't that a joke, Cowart? It's getting so I can't tell no more. Can't tell if it's hot or cold. Day or night. Just like a little child, I'm thinking. I guess that's a part of it, the dying. You just naturally head backwards in time."

He rose and walked to a small sink in the corner of the cell. He ran the single tap for a moment, leaning down and drinking with great gulps. "And thirsty, too. Keep getting dry in the mouth. Just like something keeps sucking all the moisture right out of me."

Cowart didn't say anything.

"Of course, I expect when they jolt you the first time with those twenty-five hundred volts, that's thirsty work for all involved."

Matthew Cowart felt his own throat tighten. "Are you going to file?"

Sullivan scowled. "What do you think?"

"I don't."

He stared at Cowart. "You got to understand, Cowart, right now I'm feeling more alive than ever."

"Why do you want to see me?"

"Last will and testament. Dying declaration. Famous last words. How's that sound?"

"Up to you."

Sullivan made a fist and punched the still air of the cell. "Do you remember me telling you how far I could reach? Do you remember me saying how puny these walls and bars really are, Cowart? Do you remember me saying that I don't fear death, I welcome it? I think there's gonna be a special place in hell for me, Cowart. I do. And you're gonna help me get there."

"How?"

"You're gonna do some things for me."

"What if I don't agree?"

"You will. You can't help it, Cowart. You're in this all the way, ain't you?"

Cowart nodded, wondering what he was agreeing to.

"All right, Cowart. Mr. Famous Reporter Man. I want you to go someplace for me and do some of your special-type reporting. It's a little house. I want you to knock on the door. If there ain't no answer, I want you to go right on in. Don't you mind if the door's locked. Don't you let anything keep you from walking into that house. Got that? I don't care how, but you get inside that house. You keep your eyes open. You take down all the details inside, hear? You *interview* everybody there. . . ."

Blair Sullivan ladled sarcasm onto the word. He laughed. "Then you come back and tell me what you found, and I'll tell you a story worth hearing. Blair Sullivan's legacy."

The killer put his head into his hands and then raised them up over his forehead, pushing back his hair, grinning wildly. "And that'll be a story worth the knowing, I promise."

Cowart hesitated. He felt swept up in a sudden darkness.

"Okay, Mr. Cowart," Sullivan said. "Ready? I want you to go to number thirteen—nice number, that—Tarpon Drive in Islamorada."

"That's the Keys. I just came from . . ."

"Just go there! And then come back and tell me what you find. And don't leave nothing out."

Cowart looked at the prisoner, unsure for an instant. Then the doubt fled and he rose.

"Run, Cowart. Run hard. Run fast. There's not much time."

Sullivan sat back on his bed. He turned his face away from Cowart but at the same time bellowed out, "Sergeant Rogers! Get this man out of my sight!"

His eyes twitched once toward Cowart. "Until tomorrow. That'd be day six."

Cowart nodded and paced swiftly away.

Cowart managed to catch the last flight back to Miami. It was after midnight when he dragged himself into his apartment and threw himself down, still dressed, on his bed. He felt unsettled, filled with an odd stage fright. He thought himself an actor thrust onto a stage in front of an audience but not having been told his lines, his character, or what the name of the play was. He thrust away as much thought as he could and seized a few hours of fitful sleep.

But by eight in the morning, he was driving south toward the Upper Keys, through the clear, rising heat of the morning. There were a few lazy white clouds lost in the sky, gleaming with the early sun. He maneuvered past the commuter traffic clogging South Dixie Highway heading for downtown Miami, racing the opposite way. Miami spread out, changing from a city into strips of low-slung shopping centers with garish signs and empty parking lots. The number of cars diminished as he passed through the suburbs, finally racing past rows of auto dealerships decorated with hundreds of American flags and huge banners announcing cut-rate sales, their polished fleets of vehicles gleaming with reflected light, lined up in anticipation. He could see a pair of silver jet fighters swinging wide through the crystal air, jockeying for a landing at Homestead Air Force Base, the two planes roaring, filling the air with noise but performing like ballet dancers as they swept into their approach only a few feet apart, in tandem.

A few miles farther, he crossed Card Sound Bridge, driving hard toward the Keys. The road sliced through hummocks of mangroves and marshy swamp. He saw a stork's nest on a telephone pole, and as he swept by, a single white bird rose and beat its way across the sky. A wide flat green world surrounded him for the first few miles. Then the land on his left gave way to inlets and finally to miles of Florida bay. A light chop curled the surface of the ripe blue water. He drove on.

The road to the Keys meanders through wetlands and water, occasionally rising up a few feet so that civilization can grasp hold. The rough coral-ridged earth houses marinas and condo developments whenever it gains enough solidity to support construction. It sometimes seems as if the square cinder-block buildings have spawned; a gas station spreads into a convenience store. A T-shirt shop painted bright pink takes root and flowers into a fast-food outlet. A dock gives rise to a restaurant, which hatches a motel across the roadway. Where there is enough land, there are schools and hospitals and trailer parks clinging tightly to the crushed gravel, dirt, and pieces of white shells, bleached by the sun. The ocean is never far, blinking with reflected sunlight, its wide expanse laughing at the puny, tacky efforts of civilization. He pushed past Marathon and the entrance to Pennekamp State Park. At the Whale Harbor marina he saw a huge plastic blue marlin, bigger than any fish that ever cruised the Gulf Stream, which marked the entrance to the sports fishing dock. He drove on past a strip of shops and a supermarket, the white paint on the walls fading in the inexorable hot sun of the Keys.

It was midmorning when he found Tarpon Drive.

The street was at the southern tip of the Key, a mile or so before the ocean encroached tightly and made construction impossible. The road spun off to the left, a single lane of crunching shells cutting between some trailers and small single-story houses. There was a haphazardness to the road, as if the lots were simply carved by convenience. A rusted Volkswagen bus painted in faded ancient-hippie psychedelic style sat on blocks in one front yard. Two children in diapers played in a makeshift sandbox next to it. A single woman wearing tight blue cut-off jeans and a tank top and smoking a cigarette sat on an overturned bait bucket, watching over them. She eyed Matthew Cowart with a practiced toughness. In front of another house there was a boat, with a ragged hole beneath the gunnels, up on saw-horses. Outside a trailer, an elderly couple sat in cheap green-and-white beach chairs underneath a pink umbrella. They didn't move as he rolled past. He put his window down and heard a radio turned up to some talk show. Disembodied voices filled the air with angry tones debating meaningless issues. Bent and twisted television antennas littered the sky. Cowart felt he was entering a sun-baked world of lost hopes and found poverty.

Midway down the street was a single white clapboard church behind a rusty wire fence. There was a large handwritten sign out in the front yard: FIRST KEYS BAPTIST CHURCH. ALL WEL-COME TO ENTER AND BE SAVED. He saw that the gate at the street was off its hinge and that the wooden steps leading to the front door were splintered and broken. The doors were padlocked.

He drove on, looking for number thirteen.

The house was set back thirty yards from the road beneath a gnarled mangrove tree, which cast a variegated shade across the front. It was cinder block, with old jalousie windows, their smoked glass open to catch whatever breezes filtered through the tangle of trees and brush. The shutters on the outside of the house were peeling black paint and a large crucifix was attached to the door. It was a small house, with a pair of propane fuel tanks leaning up against one wall. The yard was dirt and gravel, and dust kicked up about his feet as he walked to the front door. Scratched in the wood of the door were the words JESUS LIVES INSIDE ALL OF US.

He could hear a dog barking in the distance. The mangrove tree moved slightly, finding some small bit of wind chased by the heat. But he felt nothing.

He knocked hard. Once, twice, and a third time.

There was no answer.

He stepped back and called out, "Hello! Anyone there?"

He waited for a reply and was met with silence.

He knocked again. Shit! he swore to himself.

Cowart stepped back from the door, peering about. He could

see no car, no sign of any life. He tried calling out again. "Hello? Anyone home?"

But again there was no reply.

He had no plan, no idea what to do.

He walked back to the street and then turned and looked back at the house. What the hell am I doing here? he wondered to himself. What is this all about?

He heard a mild crunching sound up the street and saw that a mailman was getting out of a white jeep. He watched as the man stuck some circulars and letters in first one, then another mailbox. Cowart kept an eye on him as he made his way down the street toward number thirteen.

"How ya doing?" Cowart asked as the man approached.

He was a middle-aged man, wearing the blue-gray shorts and pale blue shirt of the postal service. He sported a long ponytail, which was clipped tightly in back, and a hangdog droopy mustache. He wore dark sunglasses, which hid his eyes.

"Seen better. Seen worse." He started to paw through his mailbag.

"Who lives here?" Cowart asked.

"Who wants to know?"

"I'm a reporter for *The Miami Journal*. My name is Cowart."

"I read your paper," the postman replied. "Mostly the sports section, though."

"Can you help me? I'm trying to find the folks who live here. But there's no answer at the door."

"No answer, huh? I've never seen them go anywhere."

"Who?"

"Mr. and Mrs. Calhoun. Old Dot and Fred. Usually sitting around reading the Bible and waiting for either the final day of judgment or the Sears catalogue to arrive. Generally speaking, Sears seems more dependable."

"Have they been here long?"

"Maybe six, seven years. Maybe longer. I only been down here that long."

Cowart remained confused but had another quick question. "Do they ever get any mail from Starke? From the state prison?"

The mailman dropped his bag down, sighing. "Sure do. Maybe once a month."

"Do you know who Blair Sullivan is?"

"Sure," said the mailman. "He's gonna take the hot squat. I read it in your paper the other day. This got something to do with him?"

"Maybe. I don't know," Cowart replied. He stared back at the house as the postman took out a sheaf of circulars and opened the mailbox.

"Uh-oh," he said.

"What?"

"Mail ain't been picked up."

The mailman stared across the dusty yard at the house. "I always hate that. Old folks always get their mail, always, unless something ain't right. I used to deliver on Miami Beach, you know, when I was younger. You always knew what you were going to find when the mail hadn't been picked up."

"How many days?"

"Looks like a couple. Oh shit. I hate this," said the postman.

Cowart started to approach the house again. He walked up to a window and peered in. All he could see was cheap furniture arranged in a small sitting area. There was a colored portrait of Jesus on the wall, with light radiating out of his head. "Can you see anything over there?" he asked the postman, who had joined him at the front of the house and was staring through another window, shading his eyes against the glare.

"Just an empty bedroom."

Both men stepped back and Cowart called out, "Mr. and Mrs. Calhoun! Hello!"

There was still no reply. He went to the front door and put his hand on the doorknob. It turned. He looked over at the postman, who nodded. He opened the door and stepped inside.

The smell hit him immediately.

The postman groaned and put his hand on Cowart's shoulder.

"I know what that is," he said. "First smelled it in Vietnam. Never forget it." He paused, then added, "Listen."

The smell clogged Cowart's throat and he wanted to choke, as if he was standing in smoke. Then he heard a buzzing noise coming from the back of the house.

The postman stepped back, retreating. "I'm gonna go call the cops."

"I'm gonna check," Cowart said.

"Don't," the postman said. "There's no need."

Cowart shook his head. He stepped forward, the smell and the buzzing noise seeming to gather him in, drawing him toward it. He was aware that the postman had left and he glanced back over his shoulder and saw the man hurrying toward a neighbor's house. Cowart took several more steps into the home. His eyes searched about, grasping at detail, gathering sights that could later be described, taking in the threadbare furnishings, the religious artifacts, and the thick sense that this was the last place on earth. The heat built about him inexorably, joining with the smell, which permeated his clothes, his nostrils, slid into his pores, and tugged firmly at the edges of nausea within him. He moved ahead into the kitchen.

The old man and woman were there.

They had each been tied to a chair, at either end of a linoleum-topped breakfast table. Their arms were pulled back sharply. The woman was naked, the man clothed. They were sitting across from each other, just as if they were sitting down to a meal.

Their throats had been cut.

Black blood was pooled about the base of each chair. Flies covered each face, beneath tangles of gray hair. Their heads were bent back, so that lifeless eyes stared at the ceiling.

In the center of the table, a Bible had been opened.

Cowart choked, battling unconsciousness, fear, and fighting to keep his stomach from heaving.

The heat in the room seemed to increase, washing over him in waves of thick, cloying warmth. The sound from the flies filled his ears. He took a single step and craned forward to read the words on the open page. A blood smear marked a single passage.

There be of them, that have left a name behind them, that their praises might be reported. And some there bē, which have no memorial; who are perished, as though they had never been; and are become as though they had never been born; and their children after them.

He stepped back, eyes wildly searching the room.

He saw a corner door, leading to the outside backyard, with a single chain lock that had been forced. The lock hung uselessly from splintered old wood. His eyes swept back to the old couple in front of him. The woman's flaccid breasts were streaked with brown-black blood. He stepped back fast, first one step, then another, and finally turned and rushed out the front door. He caught his breath, hands on knees, and saw the postman returning from across the street. Cowart felt a dizziness that threatened to drop him to the ground, so he sat abruptly on the front stoop.

The postman called out as he hurried toward Cowart, "Are they?"

He nodded.

"Jesus," the man said. "Is it bad?"

Cowart nodded again.

"Police are on their way."

"They were killed," Cowart said quietly.

"Murdered? No shit?"

He bent his head again.

"Jesus," the postman repeated. "Why?"

He didn't reply, only shook his head. But inwardly, his mind reeled.

I know, Cowart thought. I know.

I know who they are and I know why they died.

They were the people Blair Sullivan had told him he always wanted to kill. Always. And he'd finally done it, reaching out from behind the bars, past the gates and fences, past the prison walls and barbed wire, just as he promised he could.

Matthew Cowart just did not know how.

TEN

AN ARRANGEMENT REACHED UPON THE ——————ROAD TO HELL

It was late in the morning on the seventh day before Cowart was able to get back to the prison. Time had been trapped by the murder investigation.

He and the postman had waited quietly on the front stoop of the house for a patrol car to arrive. "This is a helluva thing," the postman had said. "And, dammit, I wanted to catch the afternoon tide, pick up some snapper for dinner. Won't get out on the boat now." He shook his head.

After a few moments, they heard a car come crunching down Tarpon Drive and they looked up to see a single policeman. He parked in front, slowly got out of his green-and-white cruiser, and approached the pair.

"Who called?" He was a young man, with a weight lifter's muscles and dark aviator shades hiding his eyes.

"I did," the postman said. "But he went inside." The man jerked a finger toward Cowart.

"Who are you?"

"A reporter for *The Miami Journal*," Cowart replied sadly.

"Uh-huh. So what've we got?"

"Two dead people. Murdered."

The policeman's voice quickened. "How do you know that?"

"Go look for yourself."

"Neither of you two move." The policeman maneuvered past them.

"Where do you think we'd go?" the postman asked quietly.

"Hell, I've been through this a whole lot more times than he has. Hey!" he called after the cop. "It's just like in the damn movies. Don't touch anything."

"I know that," the young policeman said. "Christ."

They watched him as he walked carefully into the house.

"I think he's in for the shock of his young career," Cowart said.

The postman grinned. "He probably thinks that all there is to this job is chasing speeders heading toward Key West."

Before Cowart could reply, they heard the cop say, "Holy shit!" The exclamation had a sudden high pitch to it, like the sound of a surprised gull, cartwheeling into the sky.

There was a momentary pause, then the young policeman came pounding fast through the house. He made it past Cowart and the postman, into the front yard, before he threw up.

"Hey," the postman said quietly, "I'll be damned." He tugged at his ponytail and smiled. "You said it was bad. Guess you know what the hell you're talking about."

"Must have been the smell," Cowart said, watching the young policeman heave.

After a moment, the policeman straightened. His hair was slightly out of place, his face pale. Cowart tossed him a handkerchief. The policeman nodded. "But, who, why, Jesus . . ."

"Who, is Blair Sullivan's mother and stepfather," Cowart said. "Why, is a whole different question. Now, don't you think you better call this in?"

"No shit?" said the postman. "Are you kidding me? But isn't he supposed to fry?"

"You got it."

"Christ. But how come you're here?"

That's a good question, Cowart thought but out loud replied, "I'm just looking for a story."

"Guess you got one," the postman said under his breath.

Cowart stood to the side while the crime scene was being processed, watching as technicians worked the entire area, aware that time was sliding out from beneath him. He had managed to call the city desk and inform the city editor of what had taken place. Even for a man accustomed to South Florida's inherent strangeness, the city editor had been surprised.

"What d'you think the governor will do?" he asked. "Do you think he'll stay the execution?"

"I don't know. Would you?"

"Christ, who knows? When can you get back up there and ask that crazed sonuvabitch what's happening?"

"As soon as I can get out of here."

But he was forced to wait.

Patience is needed in the processing of a murder location. Little details become magnified. The slightest thing can have importance. It is an exacting task when done by professionals who take pleasure in the painstaking application of science to violence.

Cowart steamed and fretted, thinking of Blair Sullivan waiting in the cell for him. He kept staring at his watch. It wasn't until late in the afternoon that he was finally approached by two Monroe County detectives. The first was a middle-aged man wearing a tan suit streaked with sweat. His partner was a much younger woman with dirty-blond hair combed back sharply from her face. She wore a mannish, loose-fitting cotton jacket and slacks, which hung from a lean figure. Cowart caught a glimpse of a semiautomatic pistol worn in a shoulder harness beneath the coat. Both wore dark glasses, but the woman took hers off when she stepped up to Cowart, revealing gray eyes that fixed him before she spoke.

"Mr. Cowart? My name is Andrea Shaeffer. I'm a homicide detective. This is my partner, Michael Weiss. We're in charge of the investigation. We'd like to take your statement." She produced a small notepad and a pen.

Cowart nodded. He pulled out his own notebook, and the woman smiled. "Yours is bigger than mine," she said.

"What can you tell me about the crime scene?" he asked.

"Are you asking as a reporter?"

"Of course."

"Well, how about answering our questions first? Then we'll answer some of yours."

"Mr. Cowart," Detective Weiss said, "this is a murder investigation. We're not used to having members of the press tell us about crimes before we find out about them. Usually it's the other way around. So why don't you let us know right now why and how you got here in time to discover a pair of bodies."

"Dead a couple of days," Cowart said.

Detective Shaeffer nodded. "Apparently so. But you show up this morning. How come?"

"Blair Sullivan told me to. Yesterday. From his cell on Death Row."

She wrote it down, but shook her head. "I don't get it. Did he know . . . ?"

"I don't know what he knew. He merely insisted I come here."

"How did he put it?"

"He told me to come down and interview the people in the house. I figured out afterwards who they were. I'm supposed to go back up to the prison right away." He felt flush with the heat of lost minutes.

"Do you know who killed those people?" she asked.

He hesitated. "No."

Not yet, he thought.

"Well, do you think Blair Sullivan knows who killed those people?"

"He might."

She sighed. "Mr. Cowart, you're aware how unusual this all is? It would help us if you were a bit more forthcoming."

Cowart felt Detective Shaeffer's eyes burrowing into him, as if simply by the force of her gaze she could start to probe his memory for answers. He shifted about uncomfortably.

"I have to get back to Starke," he said. "Maybe then I can help you."

She nodded. "I think one of us should go along. Maybe both of us."

"He won't talk to you," Cowart said.

"Really? Why not?"

"He doesn't like policemen." But Cowart knew that was only an excuse.

By the time he got to the prison, the day had risen hard about him and was creeping toward afternoon. He'd been held up at the house on Tarpon Drive until evening, when the detectives had finally cleared the scene. He'd driven fast back to the *Journal* newsroom, feeling the grip of time squeeze him as he threw a selection of details into a newspaper story, a hasty compilation of details painted with sensationalism, while the two detectives waited for him in the managing editor's office. They had not wanted to leave him, but they had been unable to make the last flight that night. They'd holed up in a motel not far from his apartment, meeting him shortly after daybreak. In silence they'd ridden the morning commuter flight north. Now, the two Monroe County detectives were in a rental car of their own, following close behind him.

The front of the prison had been transformed in the prior twenty-four hours. There were easily two dozen television mini-vans in the parking lot, their call letters emblazoned on the sides, lots of LIVE EYES and ACTION NEWS TEAMS. Most were equipped with portable satellite transmission capabilities for live, remote shots. Camera crews lounged around, talking, sharing stories, or working over their equipment like soldiers getting ready for a battle. An equal number of reporters and still photographers milled about as well. As promised, the roadway was marked by demonstrators from both camps, who honked and hooted and shouted imprecations at each other.

Cowart parked and tried to slide inconspicuously toward the front of the prison. He was spotted almost immediately and instantly surrounded by cameras. The two detectives worked their way toward the prison, moving on the fringe of the crowd that gathered about him.

He held up his hand. "Not right now. Just not yet, please."

"Matt," cried a television reporter he recognized from Miami. "Will Sullivan see you? Is he going to tell you what the heck is going on?"

The camera lights blended with fierce sunlight. He tried to shade his eyes. "I don't know yet, Tom. Let me find out."

"Are there any suspects?" the television man persisted.

"I don't know."

"Is Sullivan going to go through with it now?"

"I don't know. I don't know."

"What have you been told?"

"Nothing. Not yet. Nothing."

"Will you tell us when you talk to him?" another voice shouted.

"Sure," he lied, saying anything to extricate himself. He was struggling through the crowd toward the front doors. He could see Sergeant Rogers waiting for him.

"Hey, Matty," the television reporter called. "Did you hear about the governor?"

"What, Tom? No, I haven't."

"He just had a press conference, saying no stay unless Sullivan files an appeal."

Cowart nodded and stepped toward the prison door, sweeping under the broad arm of Sergeant Rogers. The two detectives had slid in before him and were striding away from the probing lights of the cameramen.

Rogers whispered in his ear, singing, as he passed, "You got to know when to hold 'em, know when to fold 'em, know when to walk away . . .''

"Thanks," said Cowart sarcastically.

"Things sure are getting interesting," the sergeant said.

"Maybe for you," Cowart said under his breath. "For me, it's getting a little difficult."

The sergeant laughed. Then he turned to the two detectives. "You must be Weiss and Shaeffer." They shook hands. "Y'all can wait in that office, right in there."

"Wait?" Weiss said sharply. "We're here to see Sullivan. Right now."

The sergeant moved slowly, grasping Cowart by the elbow and steering him toward a sally port. All the time, however, he was shaking his head. "He don't want to see you."

"But, Sergeant," Andrea Shaeffer spoke softly. "This is a murder investigation."

"I know that," the sergeant replied.

"Look, dammit, we want to see Sullivan, right now," Weiss said.

"It don't work that way, Detective. The man's got an official . . . ,'' he glanced up at a wall clock, shaking his head, "uh, nine hours and forty-two minutes of life. If'n he don't want to see somebody, hell, I ain't gonna force him. Got that?''

"But . . .''

"No buts."

"But he's going to talk to Cowart?" Shaeffer asked.

"That's right. Excuse me, miss, but I don't pretend to understand what Mr. Sullivan's got in mind by all this. But if'n you got a complaint or you think maybe he's gonna change his mind, well, you got to talk to the governor's office. Maybe they'll give you some more time. As for us, we got to work with what we got. That means Mr. Cowart and his notebook and tape recorder. Alone."

The woman nodded. She turned to her partner. "Get on the horn with the governor's office. See what the hell they say about all this." She turned to Cowart. "Mr. Cowart, you've got to do your job, I know, but please, will you ask him if he'll talk with us?''

"I can do that," Cowart replied.

"And," the detective continued, "you probably have a pretty good idea what I'd be asking him. Try to get it down on tape." She opened a briefcase and thrust a half dozen extra cassettes at him. "I'm not going anywhere. Not until we can talk again."

The reporter nodded. "I understand."

The detective looked over toward the sergeant. "It always get this weird?" she asked, smiling.

Rogers paused and returned her smile. "No, ma'am."

The sergeant looked up at the clock again. "There's a lot of talking here, but time's wasting."

Cowart gestured toward the sally port and followed the sergeant into the prison. The two men walked quickly down a long corridor, their feet slapping against the polished linoleum surface. The sergeant was shaking his head.

"What?"

"It's just I don't like all this confusion," the sergeant replied. "Things should be put in order before dying. Don't like loose ends, no sir."

"I think that's how he's always meant it to play."

"I think you're damn right there, Mr. Cowart."

"Where we going?"

The reporter was being led onto a different wing than he'd been to before.

"Sully's in the isolation cell. It's right close by the chair. Right close to an office with phones and everything, so's if there's a stay, we'll know right fast."

"How's he doing?"

"See for yourself." He pointed Cowart toward a solitary holding cell. There was a single chair set outside the bars. He approached alone and found Sullivan lying on a steel bunk, staring at a television screen. His hair had been shaved, so that he looked like a death's head mask. He was surrounded by small cartons overflowing with clothing, books, and papers—his possessions moved from his former cell. The prisoner turned abruptly in the bed, gestured widely toward the single chair, and rolled his feet off the bunk, stretching as if tired. In his hand he clutched a Bible.

"Well, well, Cowart. Took your own sweet time getting back for my party, I see."

He lit a cigarette and coughed.

"There are two detectives from Monroe County, Mr. Sullivan. They want to see you."

"Fuck 'em."

"They want to ask you about the deaths of your mother and stepfather."

"They do? Fuck 'em."

"They want me to ask you to see them."

He laughed. "Well, that makes all the difference in the world, don't it? Fuck 'em again."

Sullivan got up abruptly. He stared about for an instant, then went to the bars and grasped hold of them, pushing his face against them hard.

"Hey!" he called out. "What the hell time is it? I need to know, what time is it? Hey, somebody! Hey!"

"There's time," Cowart said slowly.

Sullivan stepped back, staring angrily toward him. "Sure. Sure."

The man shuddered, closed his eyes and took a deep breath. "You know something, Cowart? You get so you can actually feel all the muscles around and about your heart just getting a little tighter with each second."

"You could call an attorney."

"Fuck 'em. You got to play the hand you're dealt."

"You're not going to . . ."

"No. Let's get that settled. I may be a bit scared and a bit twitchy, but shit. I know about dying. Yes, sir, it's one thing I know a lot about."

Blair Sullivan shifted about in the cell, finally sitting on the edge of the bunk and leaning forward. He seemed to relax suddenly, smiling conspiratorially, rubbing his hands together eagerly.

"Tell me about your interviews," he said, laughing. "I want to know everything." Sullivan gestured at the television. "The damn television and newspapers don't have any real details. It's just a lot of general garbage. I want you to tell me."

Cowart felt cold. "Details?"

"That's right. Leave nothing out. Use all those words you're so damn clever with and paint me a real portrait, huh?"

Cowart took a deep breath, thinking, I'm as mad as he is, but he continued. "They were in the kitchen. They'd been tied up . . ."

"Good. Good. Tied tight, like hog-tied, or what?"

"No. Just their arms pulled back like this . . ." He demonstrated.

Sullivan nodded. "Good. Keep going."

"Throats cut."

Sullivan nodded.

"There was blood all over. Your mother was naked. Their heads were back like this . . ."

"Keep going. Raped?"

"I couldn't tell. There were a lot of flies."

"I like that. Buzzing around, real noisy?"

"That's right." Cowart heard the words falling from his mouth, echoing slightly. He thought some other part of him that he'd never known existed had taken over.

"Had they been in pain?" the condemned man asked.

"How would I know?"

"C'mon, Cowart. Did it look like they'd had some time to contemplate their deaths?"

"Yes. They were tied in their chairs. They must have been looking at each other, right up to the time they were killed. One got to watch the other die, I guess, unless there was more than one killer."

"No, just one," Sullivan said quietly. He rubbed his arms. "They were in the chairs?"

"Right. Tied down."

"Like me."

"What?"

"Tied in a chair. And then executed." He laughed.

Cowart felt the cold abruptly turn to heat. "There was a Bible."

". . . And some there be, which have no memorial; who are perished, as though they had never been . . ."

"That's right."

"Perfect. Just like it was supposed to be."

Sullivan stood up abruptly, wrapping his arms around himself, hugging himself as if to contain all the feelings that reverberated within him. The muscles on his arms bulged. A vein on his forehead throbbed. His pale face flushed red. He let out a great breath of air.

"I can see it," the condemned man said. "I can see it."

Sullivan raised his arms up in the cell, stretching out. Then he brought them down sharply.

"All right!" he said. "It's done." He breathed hard for a few moments, like a runner winded at the end of a race, then looked down at his hands, staring at them as he twisted them into claws. The dragon tattoos on his forearms wrenched with life. He laughed to himself, then turned back to Cowart. "But now for the little bit extra. The addition that really makes this all worthwhile."

"What are you talking about?"

Sullivan shook his head. "Get out that notepad. Get out that tape recorder. It's time to learn about death. I told you. Legacy. Old Sully's last will and testament."

As Cowart got ready, Sullivan resumed his seat on the edge of the bunk. He smoked slowly, savoring each long drag.

"You ready, Cowart?"

Cowart nodded.

"All right. All right. Where to start? Well, I'll just start in with the obvious first. Cowart, how many deaths they pinned on me?"

"Twelve. Officially."

"That's right. But we gotta be technical. I been convicted and sentenced to die for those nice folks in Miami, that cute little gal and her boyfriend. That's official-like. And then I confessed to those ten other folks, just to be hospitable, I guess. Those detectives got those stories, all right, so I ain't going into those details right now. And then there's that little gal in Pachoula—number thirteen, right?"

"Right."

"Well, we're gonna leave her aside for the moment. Let's just go back to twelve as the starting place, okay?"

"Okay. Twelve."

He let out a long, slow laugh. "Well, that ain't hardly right. No, sir. Not hardly right at all."

"How many?"

He grinned. "I been sitting here, trying to add that total up, Cowart. Adding and adding, trying to come up with a total that's accurate. Don't want to leave any room for discussion, you know."

"How many?"

"How about thirty-nine folks, Cowart?"

The condemned man leaned back on his seat, rocking slightly. He picked up his legs and wrapped his arms around his knees, continuing to rock.

"Of course, I may have missed one or two. It happens, you know. Sometimes killings just seem the same, don't have that little spark to 'em that makes 'em stand out in your mind."

Cowart didn't reply.

"Let's start with a little old lady who lived outside New Orleans. Lived alone in an apartment complex for the elderly in a little town called Jefferson. I saw her one afternoon, just walking home alone, just as nice and easy and taking in the day, like it belonged to her. So I followed her. She lived on a street called Lowell Place. I think her name was Eugenia Mae Phillips. I'm trying hard to remember these details, Cowart, because when you go to checking them all out, you'll need something to go on. This'd be about five years ago, in September. After night fell, I jimmied open a sliding door in the back. She had one of those garden-type apartments. Didn't even have a dead bolt on the back. Not a light outside, no nothing. Now why would any damn fool live in one of those? Just likely to get yourself killed, yes sir. There ain't a self-respecting rapist, robber, or killer about who don't see one of those apartments and just give a little jump for joy, 'cause they ain't no trouble at all. She should at least have had some big old vicious black dog. But she didn't. She had a parakeet. A yellow one in a cage. I killed it, too. And that's what happened. Of course, I had me a little fun with her first. She was so scared, hardly made no noise when I stuffed that pillow over her head. I did her, and five others right around there. Just rape and robbery, mainly. She was the only one I killed. Then I moved on. You know, you keep moving, ain't nothing bad gonna happen to you.''

Sullivan paused. ''You should keep that in mind, Cowart. Keep moving. Never sink in and let any roots dig in. You keep going, police don't get a fair shot at you. Hell, I got picked up for vagrancy, trespassing, suspicion of burglary, all sorts of shit. But each time, nobody ever made me. I'd spend a couple of nights in jail. Spent a month in a county lockup in Dothan, Alabama, once. That was a helluva place, Cowart. Cockroaches and rats, and smelled of shit something awful. But nobody ever made me for what I was. How could they? I wasn't nobody important. . . .''

He smiled. ''Or so they thought.''

He hesitated, looking through the iron bars. ''Of course, that ain't the situation now, is it? Right now, Blair Sullivan's a bit more important, ain't he?''

He looked up sharply toward the reporter. ''Ain't he, dammit!''

''Yes.''

''Then say it!''

''A lot more important.''

Sullivan seemed to relax, his voice slowed.

''That's right. That's right.'' He shut his eyes for a moment, but when they blinked open, there was a chilling insouciance flickering within them.

''Why, I'm probably the most damn important fellow in the state of Florida right about now, don't ya think, Cowart?''

"Maybe."

"Why, everyone wants to know what old Sully knows, ain't that true?"

"That's true."

"You getting the picture now, Cowart?"

"I think so."

"Damn right. I daresay there's a whole lot of folks gonna be right intrigued . . .," he stretched the word out, letting it roll around on his tongue like a piece of hard candy, ". . . by what old Sully has to say."

Cowart nodded.

"Good. Real good. Now, when I moved over to Mobile, I killed a kid in a 7-Eleven. Just a holdup, no big deal. You got any idea how hard it is for the cops to make you on one of those? If nobody sees you go in, nobody sees you come out, why it's just like this little touch of evil lands right there and bingo! Somebody dies. He was a nice kid, too. Begged once or twice. Said, 'Take the money. Take the money.' Said, 'Don't kill me. I'm just working my way through school. Please don't kill me.' Of course, I did. Shot him once in the back of the head with a handgun, nice and quick and easy. Got a couple of hundred bucks. Then I took a couple of Twinkies and a soda or two and some chips and left him back behind the counter. . . ."

He paused. Cowart saw a line of sweat on the man's forehead. His voice was quavering with intensity. "You got any questions, don't hesitate to let me know."

Cowart choked out, "Do you have a time, a date, a location?"

"Right, right. I'll work on that. Got to have details."

Sullivan relaxed, considering, then burst out with a short laugh. "Hell, I shoulda had a notebook, just like you. I got to rely on what I remember."

Sullivan leaned back again, setting forth details, places, and names, slowly yet steadily, ransacking his history.

Cowart listened hard, occasionally interjecting a question, trying to gain some further edge to the stories he was hearing. After the first few, the shock wore off. They took on a sort of regular terror, where all the horrors that had once happened to real people were reduced to the memoirs of a condemned man. He sought details from the killer, the accumulation of words draining each event of its passion. They had no substance, almost no connection to the world. That the events he spoke of had actually filled the last moments of once real, breathing humans was somewhere lost, as Blair Sullivan spoke with an ever-increasing, steady, sturdy, unimaginative, and utterly routine evil.

Hours slid by horribly.

Sergeant Rogers brought food. Sullivan waved him away. The traditional last meal—a pan-fried steak with whipped potatoes and apple pie—remained on a tray, congealing. Cowart simply listened.

It was a few minutes after 11 P.M. when Blair Sullivan finished, a pale smile flitting on his face.

"That's all thirty-nine," he said. "Some story, huh? It may not set a damn record, but it's gonna come damn close, right?"

He sighed deeply. "I'd a liked that, you know. The record. What the hell is the record for a fellow like me, Cowart? You got that little fact at your fingertips? Am I number one, or does that honor go to another?"

He laughed dryly. "Of course, even if I ain't number one in terms of numbers, why I sure as hell got it over most those other suckers for, what you wanna call it, Cowart? Originality?"

"Mr. Sullivan, there's not much time. If you want to . . ."

Sullivan stood, suddenly wild-eyed. "Haven't you paid any attention, boy?"

Cowart raised his hand. "I just wanted . . ."

"What you wanted isn't important! What I want, is!"

"Okay."

Sullivan looked out from between the bars. He breathed deeply and lowered his voice. "Now it's time for one more story, Cowart. Before I step out of this world. Take that nice fast ride on the state's rocket."

Cowart felt a terrible dryness within him, as if the heat from the man's words had sucked all the moisture from his body.

"Now, I will tell you the truth about little Joanie Shriver. A dying declaration is what they call it in a court of law. The last words before death. They figure no one would go to the great beyond with a lie staining their lips."

He laughed out loud. "That means it's got to be the truth . . ." He paused, then added, ". . . If you can believe it."

He stared at Cowart. "Beautiful little Joanie Shriver. Perfect little Joanie."

"Number forty," Cowart said.

Blair Sullivan shook his head. "No."

He smiled. "I didn't kill her."

Cowart's stomach clenched, and he felt a clamminess come over his forehead.

"What?"

"I didn't kill her. I killed all those others. But I didn't kill her. Sure, I was in Escambia County. And sure, if I'd a spotted her, I would have been right tempted to do so. There's no question in my mind, if I had been parked outside her school yard, I would have done exactly what was done to her. I'd have rolled down my window and said, 'Come here, little schoolgirl . . .' That I can promise. But I didn't. No, sir. I am innocent of that crime."

He paused, then repeated, "Innocent."

"But the letter . . ."

"Anyone can write a letter."

"And the knife . . ."

"Well, you're right about that. That was the knife that killed that poor little girl."

"But I don't understand . . ."

Blair Sullivan grasped his sides. His laughter turned into a solid, hacking cough, echoing in the prison corridor. "I have been waiting for this," he said. "I have been so eagerly awaiting the look on your face."

"I . . ."

"It is unique, Cowart. You look a bit sick and twisted yourself. Like it's you that's sitting in the chair. Not me. What's going on in there?" Sullivan tapped his forehead.

Cowart closed his mouth and stared at the killer.

"You thought you knew so much, didn't you, Cowart? You thought you were pretty damn smart. And now, Mr. Pulitzer Prize Reporter, let me tell you something: You ain't so smart."

He continued to laugh and cough.

"Tell me," Cowart said.

Sullivan looked up. "Is there time?"

"There's time," Cowart said between clenched teeth. He watched the man in the cell rise and start to pace about.

"I feel cold," the prisoner said.

"Who killed Joanie Shriver?"

Blair Sullivan stopped and smiled. "You know," he said.

Cowart felt the floor falling away from beneath his feet. He grasped the chair, his notebook, his pen, trying to steady himself. He watched the capstan on his tape recorder turn, recording the sudden silence.

"Tell me," he whispered.

Sullivan laughed again. "You really want to know?"

"Tell me!"

"Okay, Cowart. Imagine two men in adjacent cells on Death Row. One man wants to get out because he took a fall on the shabbiest case any detective ever put together, convicted by a cracker jury that probably believed he was the craziest murdering nigger they'd ever seen. Of course, they were right to convict him. But for all the wrong reasons. This man is filled with impatience and anger. Now the other man knows he's never gonna get out of that date with the electric chair. He may put it off some, but he knows the day's gonna come for him. Ain't no doubt about it. And the thing that bothers him the most is a bit of unfinished hatred. There is something he still wants to get done. Even if he's got to reach out from the very grasp of death to do it. Something real important to him. Something so evil and wrong that there's only one person on this earth he could ask to do it."

"Who's that?"

"Someone just like him." Sullivan stared at Cowart, freezing him into the seat. "Someone just exactly like him."

Cowart said nothing.

"And so they discover a few coincidences. Like they were in the same place at the same time, driving the same type car. And they get an idea, huh? A real fine idea. The sort of plan that not even the devil's own assistant could think up, I'd wager. The one man who'll never get off the Row will take the other's crime. And then that man, when he gets out, will do that certain something just for his partner. You beginning to see?"

Cowart didn't move.

"You see, you dumb son of a bitch! You'd a never believed it if it weren't the way it is. The poor, innocent, unjustly convicted black man. The big victim of racism and prejudice. And the real awful, bad, white guy. Would never have worked the other way around, neither. It weren't so hard to figure out. The main thing was, all I had to do was tell you about that knife and write that letter right at the right moment so's it could be read at that hearing. And the best part was, I got to keep denying the crime. Keep saying I didn't have nothing to do with it. Which was the truth. Best way to make a lie work, Cowart. Just put a little bit of truth into it. You see, I knew if I just confessed, you'd of found some way to prove I didn't do it. But all I had to do was make it look for you and all your buddies on television and in the other papers like I did it. Just make it *look* that way. Then let nature take over. All I had to do was open the door a little bit . . .''

He laughed again. "And Bobby Earl just walked right through that crack. Just as soon as you pulled it wide enough."

"How can I believe this . . ."

"Because there's two folks sitting dead in Monroe County. They're numbers forty and forty-one."

"But why tell me?"

"Well." Sullivan smiled a final time. "This isn't exactly part of the bargain I made with Bobby Earl. He thinks the bargain ended when he went down to Tarpon Drive the other day and did my business for me. I gave him life. He gives me death. Nice and simple. Shake hands and walk away. That's what he thinks. But I told you, old Sully's got a long reach. . . ." He laughed harshly. The light from the overhead bulb in the cell glistened off his shaved skull. "And, you know, Cowart, I ain't the most trustworthy man around."

Sullivan stood up, stretching his hands wide. "And this way, maybe I can take him right along with me on the road to hell. Number forty-two. Big joke on him. He'd make a fine traveling companion, so to speak. Traveling right down to hell, all quick-step and double-time."

Sullivan stopped laughing abruptly. "You see, ain't that a last little joke? He never thought I'd add this little wrinkle."

"Suppose I don't believe you?"

Sullivan cackled. "Someone just like me, Cowart. That's right." He looked over at the reporter. "Y'all want proof, huh? What you think old Bobby Earl's been doing all this time, since you set him free?"

"He's been in school, studying. He gives some speeches to church groups . . ."

"Cowart," Sullivan burst in, "you know how silly that sounds? Don't you think Bobby Earl didn't learn nothing in his little experience in our great criminal justice system? You think that boy got no sense at all?"

"I don't know . . ."

"That's right. You don't know. But you better find out. 'Cause I wager there's been a lot of tears shed over what old Bobby Earl's been up to. You just gotta go find out."

Cowart reeled beneath the assault of words. He struggled, wrestling with unnameable horrors. "I need proof," he repeated lamely.

Sullivan whistled and let his eyes roll up toward the roof of the cell. "You know, Cowart, you're like one of those old, crazy medieval monks, sitting around all day working out proofs for the existence of God. Can't you tell the truth when you hear it, boy?"

Cowart shook his head.

Sullivan smiled. "I didn't think so."

He paused a moment, savoring, before continuing. "Well, you see, I ain't dumb, so when we were working out this little arrangement, me and Bobby Earl, I found out a bit more than I used already. I had to have a little extra, just to guarantee that Bobby Earl'd do his part of the bargain. And also just so's I could help you along the path to understanding."

"What?"

"Well, let's make it an adventure, Cowart. You listen carefully. It weren't only that knife that got hid. Some other things got hid, too. . . ."

He thought for a moment before grinning at the reporter. "Well, suppose those things are in a real nasty place, yes sir. But you can see them, Cowart. If you got eyes in your ass." He burst out in a raucous laugh.

"I don't understand."

"You just remember my words exactly when you go back to Pachoula. The route to understanding can be a pretty dirty one." The harsh sound of the prisoner's voice echoed around Matthew Cowart. He remained frozen, speechless.

"How about it, Cowart? Have I managed to kill Bobby Earl, too?" He leaned forward. "And what about you, Cowart? Have I killed you?"

Blair Sullivan leaned back sharply. "That's it," he said. "End of story. End of talk. Goodbye, Cowart. It's dying time, and I'll see you in hell."

The condemned man rose and slowly turned his back on the reporter, folding his arms and staring at the back of the cell, his shoulders shaking with an awful mingling of mirth and terror. Matthew Cowart remained rooted for a few moments, unable to will his limbs to move. He felt suddenly like an old man, as if the weight of what he'd heard was pressing down on his shoulders. His mind was throbbing. His throat was dry. He saw his hand shake slightly as he reached out to pick up his notepad and tape recorder. When he rose, he was unsteady. He took one step, then another, finally stumbling away from the lone man gazing at the wall. At the end of the corridor, he stopped and tried to catch his breath. He felt fevered, nauseous, and fought to contain himself, lifting his head when he heard footsteps. He saw a grim-faced Sergeant Rogers and a squad of strong men at the end of the corridor. They were forming into a tight group. There was a white-collared priest with a line of sweat on his forehead and several prison officials nervously glancing at wristwatches. He looked up and noticed a large electric clock high on the wall. He watched the sweep hand circle inexorably. It read ten minutes before midnight.

ELEVEN

PANIC

He felt himself falling. Tumbling down, head over heels, out of control, into a black hole.

"Mr. Cowart?"

He breathed in hard.

"Mr. Cowart, you okay, boy?"

He crashed and felt his body shatter into pieces.

"Hey, Mr. Cowart, you all there?"

Cowart opened his eyes and saw the sturdy, pale visage of Sergeant Rogers.

"You got to take your place now, Mr. Cowart. We ain't waiting on anybody, and all the official witnesses got to be seated before midnight."

The sergeant paused, running his big hand through the short brush of his crew cut, a gesture of exhaustion and tension. "It ain't like some movie show you can come in late on. You okay now?"

Cowart nodded his head.

"It's a tough night for everyone," the sergeant said. "You go on in. Right through that door. You'll see a seat in front, right next to a detective from Escambia County. That's where Sully said to put you. He was real specific about that. Can you move? You sure you're okay?"

"I'll make it," Cowart croaked.

"It ain't as bad as you think," the hulking prison guard said. Then he shook his head. "Nah, that's not true. It's as bad as can be. If it don't sorta turn your stomach, then you ain't a person. But you'll get through it okay. Right?''

Cowart swallowed. "I'm okay."

The prison guard eyed him carefully. "Sully musta bent your ear something fierce. What'd he tell you all those hours? You look like a man who's seen a ghost."

I have, thought Cowart. But he replied, "About death."

The sergeant snorted. "He's the one who knows. Gonna see for himself, firsthand, now. You got to move right ahead, Mr. Cowart. Dying time don't wait for no man."

Cowart knew what he was talking about and shook his head. "Oh yes, it does," he said. "It bides its time."

Sergeant Rogers looked at the reporter closely. "Well, you ain't the one about to take the final walk. You sure you're okay? I don't want nobody passing out in there or making a scene. We got to have our decorum when we juice someone."

The prison guard tried to smile with his irony.

Cowart took a single, unsteady step toward the execution chamber, then turned and said, "I'll be okay."

He wanted to burst into laughter at the depth of the lie he'd just spoken. Okay, he said to himself. I'll be okay. It was as if some foreign voice were speaking inside of him. Sure, no problem. No big deal.

All I've done is set a killer free.

He had a sudden, awful vision of Robert Earl Ferguson standing outside the small house in the Keys, laughing at him, before entering to fulfill his part of the bargain. The sound of the murderer's voice echoed in his head. Then he remembered the eight-by-ten glossy photographs taken of Joanie Shriver at the swamp where her body had been discovered. He remembered how slick they had felt in his sweaty grasp, as if coated with blood.

I'm dead, he thought again.

But he forced his feet to drag forward. He went through the door at two minutes to twelve.

The first eyes he saw belonged to Bruce Wilcox. The bantam detective was seated in the front row wearing a brightly checked sportcoat that seemed a sick, hilarious contradiction to the dirty business at hand. He smiled grudgingly and nodded his head toward an empty seat beside him. Cowart spun his eyes about rapidly, glancing over the other two dozen or so witnesses sitting on folding chairs in two rows, gazing straight ahead as if trying to fix every detail of the event in their memories. They all seemed waxen, like figurines. No one moved.

A glass partition separated them from the execution chamber, so that it seemed as if they were watching the action on a stage or some oddly three-dimensional television set. Four men were in the chamber: two corrections officers in uniform; a third man, the doctor, carrying a small black medical bag; another man in a suit—someone whispered "from the state attorney general's office"—waiting beneath a large electric clock.

He looked at the second hand as it scythed through time.

"Siddown, Cowart," the detective hissed. "The show's about to start."

Cowart saw two other reporters from *The Tampa Tribune* and *The St. Petersburg Times*. They looked grim but mimicked the detective by motioning him toward his seat, before continuing to scribble details in small notepads. Behind them was a woman from a Miami television station. Her eyes were staring straight ahead at the still-empty chair in the execution chamber. He saw her wind a simple white handkerchief tightly around her fist.

He half-stumbled into the seat waiting for him. The unyielding metal of the chair burned into his back.

"Tough night, huh, Cowart?" the detective whispered.

He didn't answer.

The detective grunted. "Not as tough as some have it, though."

"Don't be so sure about that," Cowart replied under his breath. "How did you get here?"

"Tanny's got friends. He wanted to see if old Sully would really go through with it. Still don't believe that bullshit you wrote about him being the killer of little Joanie. Tanny said he didn't much know what it would mean if Sullivan doesn't back out. But he thought if he didn't, and I got to see it, well, it might help teach me respect for the system of justice. Tanny is always trying to teach me things. Says it makes a man a better policeman to know what can happen in the end."

The detective's eyes glistened with a hellish humor.

"Has it?" Cowart asked.

Wilcox shook his head. "It ain't happened yet. Class is still in session." He grinned at Cowart. "You're looking a bit pale. Something on your mind?"

Before Cowart could reply, Wilcox whispered, "Got any last words? It's midnight."

They waited a heartbeat or two.

A side door opened and the prison warden stepped through. Blair Sullivan was next, flanked by two guards and trailed by a third. His face was rigid and pale, a corpselike appearance. His whole wiry body seemed smaller and sickly. He wore a simple white shirt buttoned tight to the neck and dark blue trousers. A priest wearing a collar, carrying a Bible and an expression of frustrated dismay, trailed the group. The priest shuffled off to the side of the chamber, pausing only to shrug in the direction of the warden, and cracked open the Good Book. He started reading quietly to himself. Cowart saw Sullivan's eyes widen when he spotted the chair. They swung abruptly to a telephone on the wall, and for the briefest moment his knees seemed to lose some strength, and he tottered. But he regained control almost instantly and the moment of hesitation was lost. It was the first time he'd seen Sullivan act in any way vaguely human, Cowart thought. Then things started to happen swiftly, with the herky-jerkiness of a silent movie.

Sullivan was steered into the seat and two guards dropped to their knees and started fastening leg and arm braces. Brown leather straps were tightened around Sullivan's chest, bunching up his white shirt. One guard attached an electrode to the prisoner's leg. Another swooped behind the chair and seized a cap, ready to bring it down over Sullivan's head.

The warden stepped forward and started reading from the black-bordered death warrant signed by the governor of Florida. Each syllable pricked Cowart's fear, as if they were being read for him. The warden hurried his words, then took a deep breath and tried to slow his pace down. His voice seemed oddly tinny and distant. There were speakers built into the walls and microphones hidden in the death chamber.

The warden finished reading. For an instant, he stared at the sheet of paper as if searching for something else to read. Then he looked up and peered at Sullivan. "Any last words?" he asked quietly.

"Fuck you. Let 'er rip," Sullivan said. His voice quavered uncharacteristically.

The warden gestured with his right hand, the one that held the curled-up warrant, toward the guard standing behind the chair, who abruptly brought the black leather shroud cap and face mask down over the prisoner's head. The guard then attached a large electrical conductor to the cap. Sullivan squirmed then, an abrupt thrust against the bonds that held him. Cowart saw the dragon tattoos on the man's arms spring to life as the muscles beneath the skin twitched and strained. The tendons on his neck tightened like ropes pulled taut by a sudden great wind.

Sullivan was shouting something but the words were muffled by a leather chin strap and tongue pad that had been forced between his teeth. The words became inarticulate grunts and moans, rising and falling in panic pitch. In the witness room there was no noise except for the slow in and out of tortured breathing.

Cowart saw the warden nod almost imperceptibly toward a partition in the rear of the death chamber. There was a small slit there, and for an instant, he saw a pair of eyes.

The executioner's eyes.

They stared out at the man in the chair, then they disappeared.

There was a thunking sound.

Someone gasped. Another person coughed hard. There were a few whispered expletives. The lights dimmed momentarily. Then silence regained the room.

Cowart thought he could not breathe. It was as if some hand had encircled his chest and squeezed all the air from within him. He watched motionless as the color of Sullivan's fists changed from pink to white to gray.

The warden nodded again toward the rear partition.

A distant generator whine buzzed and shook the small space. A faint odor of burnt flesh crept into his nostrils and filled his stomach with renewed nausea.

There was another fracture in time as the physician waited for the 2,500 volts to slide from the dead man's body. Then he stepped forward, removing a stethoscope from his black bag.

And it was done. Cowart watched the people in the execution chamber as they circled around Sullivan's body, slumped in the polished oaken chair. It was as if they were stage players readying to break down a set after the final performance of some failed show. He and the other official witnesses stared, trying to catch a glimpse of the dead man's face as he was shifted from the killing seat into a black rubber body bag. But Sullivan was zipped away too quickly for anyone to see if his eyeballs had exploded or his skin had been scorched red and black. The body was hustled back through the side door on a gurney. It should be terrible, he thought, but it was simply routine. Perhaps that was the most terrifying aspect of it. He had witnessed the factorylike processing of evil. Death canned and bottled and delivered with all the drama of the morning milk.

"Scratch one bad guy," Wilcox said. All the jocularity had fled from his voice, replaced with a barren satisfaction. "It's all over . . ." The detective glanced at Cowart. ". . . Except for the shouting."

* * *

He walked through the prison corridors with the rest of the official witnesses toward where the other members of the press contingent and the demonstrators had crowded. He could see the artificial light of the television cameras flooding the vestibule, giving it a forced otherworldly glow. The polished floor glistened; the whitewashed walls seemed to vibrate with light. A bank of microphones was arranged behind a makeshift podium. He tried to sidle to the side of the room, edging toward the door, as the warden approached the gathering, holding up his hand to cut off questions, but there were no shadows to hide in.

"I'll read a short statement," the warden said. His voice creaked with the strain of the events. "Then I'll answer your questions. Then the pool reporters will brief you."

He gave the official time of death as 12:08 A.M. The warden droned that a representative from the state attorney general's office had been present when Sullivan had been prepared for execution and during the procedure, to make certain that there was no controversy over the events—that no one would come forward later and claim that Sullivan had been denied his rights, had been taunted or beaten—as they had more than a dozen years earlier when the state had renewed the death penalty by executing a somewhat pathetic drifter named John Spenkelink. He said that Sullivan had refused a final plea to file an appeal, right outside the execution chamber door. He quoted the dead man's final words as, "Obscenity you. Let 'er rip."

The still photographers' cameras made a whirring, clicking noise like some flight of mechanical birds taking wing en masse.

The warden then gave way to the three pool reporters. Each in turn started reading from their notepads, coolly relating the minute details of the execution. They were all pale, but their voices were steady. The woman from Miami told the crowd that Sullivan's fingers had stiffened, then curled into fists when the first jolt hit him and that his back seemed to arc away from the chair. The reporter from St. Petersburg had noticed the momentary hesitation that had stymied Sullivan for just an instant when he spotted the chair. The reporter from the Tampa *Tribune* said that Sullivan had glared at the witnesses without compassion, and that he seemed mostly angry as he was strapped in. He had noticed, too, that one of the guards had fumbled with one of the straps around the condemned man's right leg, causing him to have to redo the binding rapidly. The leather had frayed under the shock of the execution, the reporter said, and afterward was almost severed by the force of Sullivan's struggle against the electric current. Twenty-five hundred volts, the reporter reminded the gathering.

Cowart heard another voice at his shoulder. He pivoted and saw the two detectives from Monroe County.

Andrea Shaeffer's voice whispered soothingly, "What did he tell you, Mr. Cowart? Who killed those people?"

Her gray eyes were fastened onto his, a whole different sort of heat.

"He did," Cowart replied.

She reached out and grasped his arm. But before the detective could follow up, there was another clamor from the assembly.

"Where's Cowart?"

"Cowart, your turn! What happened?"

Cowart pulled away from the detective and walked unsteadily toward the podium, trying desperately to sort through everything he'd heard. He felt his hand quiver, knew his face was flushed and that sweat ringed his forehead. He pulled a white handkerchief from his pocket and slowly wiped his brow, as if he could wipe away the panic that filled him.

He thought, I have done nothing wrong. I am not the guilty person here. But he didn't believe it. He wanted a moment to think, to figure out what to say, but there was no time. Instead, he grabbed on to the first question he heard.

"Why didn't he file an appeal?" someone yelled.

Cowart took a deep breath and answered, "He didn't want to sit in prison waiting for the state to come get him. So he went and got the state. It's not that unusual. Others have done it— Texas, North Carolina, Gilmore out in Utah. It's sorta like suicide, only officially sanctioned."

He saw pens scraping across paper, his words falling onto so many blank pages.

"What did he tell you when you went back there and talked with him?"

Cowart felt pinioned by despair. And then he remembered something Sullivan had told him earlier: If you want someone to believe a lie, mix a bit of truth in with it. So he did. The killer's formula: Mix lies and truths.

"He wanted to confess," Cowart said. "It was pretty much like Ted Bundy a few years back, when he told investigators about all the crimes he'd committed before going to the chair. That's what Sullivan did."

"Why?"

"How many?"

"Who?"

He held up his hands. "Guys, give me a break. There's no confirmation on any of this. I don't know for certain if he was telling me the truth or not. He could have been lying . . ."

"Before going to the chair? C'mon!" someone shouted from the back.

Cowart bristled. "Hey! I don't know. I'll tell you one thing he told me: He said if killing people wasn't so hard for him, how hard did I think lying would be?"

There was a lull as people scribbled his words.

"Look," Cowart said, "if I tell you that Blair Sullivan confessed to the murder of Joe Blow and there was no such murder, or someone else got charged with the crime, or maybe Joe Blow's body's never been found, then, hell, we've got a mess. I'll tell you this. He confessed to multiple homicides . . ."

"How many?"

"As many as forty."

The number electrified the crowd. There were more shouted questions, the lights seemed to redouble in intensity.

"Where?"

"In Florida, Lousiana, and Alabama. There were some other crimes as well, rapes, robberies."

"How long?"

"He'd been doing them for months. Maybe years."

"What about the murders in Monroe County? His mother and stepfather? What did he tell you about them?"

Cowart breathed slowly. "He hired someone to do those crimes. At least, that's what he said."

Cowart's eyes swept over to where Shaeffer stood. He saw her stiffen and lean her head toward her partner. Weiss was red-faced. Cowart turned away swiftly.

"Hired who?"

"I don't know," Cowart said. "He wouldn't tell me."

The first lie.

"Come on! He must have told you something or somebody."

"He wouldn't get that specific."

The first lie bred another.

"You mean he tells you he's the person who arranged a double homicide and you didn't ask him how he managed it?"

"I did. He wouldn't say."

"Well, how did he contact the killer? His phone privileges

were monitored. His mail was censored. He's been in isolation on Death Row. How did he do it?'' This question was greeted with some buttressing cheers. It came from one of the pool reporters, who was shaking his head as he asked it.

''He implied he set it up through some sort of informal prison grapevine.''

Not exactly a lie, Cowart thought. An oblique truth.

''You're holding back!'' someone shouted.

He shook his head.

''Details!'' someone called out.

He held up his arms.

''You're gonna put it all in the *Journal* tomorrow, right?''

Resentment, jealousy, like the lights, flowed over him. He realized that any of the others would have sold their souls to be in his position. They all knew something had happened and hated not knowing precisely what. Information is the currency of journalism, and he was foreclosing on their estate. He knew no one in that room would ever forgive him—if the truth ever came out.

''I don't know what I'm going to do,'' he pleaded. ''I haven't had a chance to sort through anything. I've got hours of tape to go through. Give me a break.''

''Was he crazy?''

''He was a psychopath. He had his own agenda.''

That was certainly the truth. And then the question he dreaded.

''What did he tell you about Joanie Shriver? Did he finally confess to her murder?''

Cowart realized that he could simply say yes and be done with it. Destroy the tapes. Live with his memory. Instead, he stumbled and landed somewhere between truth and fiction.

''She was part of the confession,'' he said.

''He killed her?''

''He told me exactly how it was done. He knew all the details that only the killer would know.''

''Why won't you say yes or no?''

Cowart tried not to squirm. ''Guys. Sullivan was a special case. He didn't put things in yes-and-no terms. Didn't deal in absolutes, not even during his confession.''

''What did he say about Ferguson?''

Cowart took a deep breath. ''He had nothing but hatred for Ferguson.''

''Is he connected to all this?''

"It was my impression that Sullivan would have killed Ferguson, too, if he'd had the chance. If he could have made the arrangements, I think he would have put Ferguson on his list."

He exhaled slowly. He could see the interest in the room shifting back to Sullivan. By assigning Ferguson to the list of potential victims, he'd managed to give him a different status than he deserved.

"Will you provide us with a transcript of what he did say?"

He shook his head. "I'm not a pool reporter."

The questions increased in anger.

"What are you going to do now? Gonna write a book?"

"Why won't you share it?"

"What, you think you're gonna win another Pulitzer?"

He shook his head.

Not that, he thought. He doubted he would have the one he had won much longer. A prize? I'll be lucky if my prize is to live through all this.

He raised his hand. "I wish I could say that the execution tonight put an end to Blair Sullivan's story, guys. But it didn't. There's a bunch of loose ends that have to be tied up. There are detectives waiting to talk to me. I've got my own damn deadlines to meet. I'm sorry, but that's it. No more."

He walked away from the podium, followed by cameras, shouted questions, and growing dread. He felt hands grasping at him, but he pushed through the crowd, reached the prison doors, and passed through into the deep black of the hours after midnight. An anti-death-penalty group, holding candles and placards and singing hymns, was gathered by the road. The pitch of their voices washed around him, tugging him like a blustery wind, away from the prison. "What a friend we have in Jesus . . ." One of the group, a college coed wearing a hooded sweatshirt that made her seem like some odd Inquisition priest, screamed at him, her words cutting bladelike across the gentle rhythms of the hymn, "Ghoul! Killer!" But he sidestepped past her words, heading toward his car.

He was fumbling for his keys when Andrea Shaeffer caught up with him. "I need to talk to you," she said.

"I can't talk. Not now."

She grabbed him by the shirt, suddenly pulling him toward her. "Why the hell not? What's going on, Cowart? Yesterday was no good. Today was no good. Tonight's no good. When are you going to level with us?"

"Look," he cried. "They're dead, dammit! They were old

and he hated them and they got killed and there's not a damn thing anyone can do about that now! You don't have to have an answer right now. It can wait until the morning. No one else is dying tonight!''

The detective started to say something, then paused. She fixed him with a single, long, fierce glance, shut her mouth and set her jaw. Then she poked him three times in the chest with her index finger, hard, before stepping aside so that he could get into the car.

''In the morning,'' she said.

''Yes.''

''Where?''

''Miami. My office.''

''I'll be there. You be sure you're there as well.''

She stepped back from the car, menace creeping into her tone.

''Yes, dammit, yes. Miami.''

Shaeffer made a small sweeping motion with her hand, as if reluctantly granting permission for him to depart. But her eyes were filled with suspicion, narrowed to pinpoints.

He jumped behind the wheel and thrust the keys into the ignition, slamming the door. The engine fired and he snatched at the gearshift, put the car in gear, and pulled back.

But as he retreated, the headlights swept over the mocking red check of Detective Wilcox's sportcoat. He stood in the road-way, his arms crossed, watching Cowart closely, blocking the reporter's path. He shook his head with exaggerated slowness, made his fist into a pistol and fired it at him. Then he stepped aside to let him pass.

The reporter looked away. He no longer cared where he headed, as long as it was someplace else. He punched hard on the gas, swinging the wheel toward the exit gate, and drove hard into the dark. The night chased after him.

TWO

THE
═CHURCHGOER

There may come a day I will dance on your grave,
If unable to dance I will crawl across it,
Unable to dance I will crawl.

THE GRATEFUL DEAD
"Hell in a Bucket"

TWELVE

THE POLICE LIEUTENANT'S ———*SLEEPLESSNESS*

AT ten minutes to twelve on the night Blair Sullivan was scheduled to die, Lieutenant Tanny Brown glanced quickly at his watch, his pulse accelerating as he thought of the man on Death Row. Across from him, sitting on a threadbare couch, a woman wailed uncontrollably.

"Oh, Jesus, sweet Jesus, why, Lord, why?" she cried. Her voice rose and rattled the walls of the small trailer, shaking the knickknacks and bric-a-brac that decorated the fake wood-paneled walls, penetrating the thick heat that lingered in the darkness outside, oblivious of the midnight hour. Every few seconds, the red-and-blue strobe lights of the police cruisers parked in a semicircle outside struck the back wall of the cramped room and illuminated a carved crucifix that hung next to a framed blessing cut from a newspaper. The flashing lights seemed to mark the steady progression of seconds.

"Why, Lord?" the woman sobbed again.

That's a question He never seems eager to answer, Tanny Brown thought cynically. Especially in trailer parks.

He put his hand to his head for just an instant, trying to will some quiet into the world around him. Remarkably, after cutting loose with one last howl, the woman's voice drained away.

He turned toward her. She had curled up in a corner, lifting her feet from the floor, childlike, and tucking them beneath her. She seemed a preposterous killer, with stringy, unkempt brown hair, and a lean, skeletal figure. One eye was blackened and her thin wrist was wrapped in an elastic bandage. She was wearing a tattered pink housecoat, and the pushed-up sleeves revealed new purple-blue bruises on her arms. He made a mental note of these. He saw nicotine stains on her fingers as she lifted her hands to her face and gently patted the tears that flowed freely down her cheeks. When she looked at the moisture on her fingers, the look on her face made him think she expected to find blood.

Tanny Brown stared at the woman, letting the sudden quiet calm the air. *She's old*, he thought, and almost instantly corrected himself: *She's younger than I am.* Years had been beaten into her, aging her far more swiftly than the passing of time.

He motioned toward one of the uniformed officers hanging in the rear of the trailer, behind a kitchen partition.

"Fred," he said quietly, "got a cigarette for Missus Collins?"

The officer stepped forward, offering the woman his pack. She reached out while mumbling, "I'm trying to quit."

Brown leaned across and lit the cigarette for her. "Now, Missus Collins, take it slowly and tell me what happened when Buck came here after the late shift."

There came a popping sound from outside and a small explosion of light. Dammit, he thought, as he saw the woman's eyes go panicky.

"It's just a police photographer, ma'am. Now, how about a glass of water?"

"I could use something stronger," she replied, hands shaking as she lifted the cigarette to her lips and took a long drag, which ended in a brief spasm of coughing.

"A glass of water, Fred." As the man brought the drink, Brown heard voices outside. He rose abruptly. "Ma'am, you just get ahold of yourself. I'll be right back."

"You ain't gonna leave me?" She seemed abruptly terrified.

"No, just got to check on the work outside. Fred, you stay here."

He wished Wilcox were with him as he looked down at the woman's eyes fluttering about the room, on the verge of breaking down and wailing again. His partner would know instinctively how to reassure her. Bruce had a way with the poor fringe folks that they were forever dealing with, especially the white ones. They were his people. He had grown up in a world not too far removed from this one. He knew beatings, cruelty, and the acid taste of trailer-park hopes. He could sit across from a woman like this and hold her hand and have her spilling the entire incident out within seconds. Tanny Brown sighed, feeling awkward and out of place. He did not want to be there, trapped amidst the silver bullet-like shapes of the Airstreams.

He stepped from the trailer and watched as the police photographer angled about, looking for another shot of a dark shape sprawled on the thin grass and packed dirt outside the trailer. Several other policemen were measuring the location. A few others were holding back the other inhabitants of the trailer park, who craned forward with curiosity, trying to catch a glimpse of the woman's late and estranged husband. Brown walked over and stared down at the face of the man on the ground. His eyes were open, fixed in a grotesque mask that mingled surprise and death, staring at the night sky. A huge splotch of blood remained where his chest should have been. The blood had settled in a halo about his head and shoulders. On the ground, where the impact from the shotgun blast had tossed them, were a half-empty bottle of scotch and a cheap handgun. A couple of crime-scene men laughed, and he turned toward them.

"A joke?"

"Quickie divorce proceedings," said one man, bending over and bagging the bottle of scotch. "Better than Tijuana or Vegas."

"Guess old Buck here figured he could wallop his woman whether they were married or not. Turns out he was wrong," another technician whispered. There was another small burst of laughter.

"Hey," Brown said brusquely. "You guys got opinions, keep 'em down. At least until we clear the location."

"Sure," said the photographer as he popped another picture. "Wouldn't want to hurt the guy's feelings."

Brown bit back a smile of his own, a look which the other policemen caught. He waved at the men working the body in mock disgust, and that made them grin, as they continued to move about the scene.

He'd seen plenty of death: car wrecks, murder victims, men shot in war, heart attacks, and hunting accidents.

Tanny Brown remembered his aged grandmother laid out in an open casket, her dark skin stretched brittle, like the crust of an overdone bird, her hands folded neatly on her chest as if in prayer. The church had seemed a great, hollow place filled with weeping. He recalled the tightness in his throat caused by the starched white collar of his new and only dress shirt. He had been no more than six and what he remembered most was the sturdy sensation of his father's hand on his shoulder, part direction, part reassurance, guiding him past the casket. Whispered words: "Say goodbye to Granmaw, quick now, child, she's on her way to a better place and movin' fast now, so say it fast while she can still hear you."

He smiled. For years he had thought the dead could hear you, as if they were only napping. He wondered at how powerful a father's words can be. He remembered being overseas and zipping the bodies of men he'd known equally briefly and intimately into black rubber bags. At first he would always try to say something, some words of comfort, as if to steady their trip to death. But as the numbers grew and his frustration and exhaustion spiraled, he took to simply thinking a few phrases and finally, when his own tour dwindled to weeks and days, he gave up even that, performing his job with bitter silence.

He looked down at his watch. Midnight. They're walking into the room. He pictured the nervous sweat on the lip of the warden, the ashen faces of the official witnesses, a slight hesitation, then the hurried motions of the escort party as they pulled the straps tight around Sullivan's wrists and ankles.

He waited one minute.

First jolt now, he thought.

One more minute.

Second jolt.

He imagined the doctor approaching the body. He would bend down with his stethoscope, listening for the heart. Then he would raise his head and say, "The man is dead," and glance down at his own watch. The warden would step forward and face the official observers and he, too, would speak by ritual. "The judgment and sentence of the Circuit Court of the Eleventh Judicial Circuit of the State of Florida has been carried out according to law. Now God rest his soul."

He shook his head. No rest for that soul, he thought.

And none for mine, either.

He walked back into the trailer. The woman had quieted completely.

"Now, Missus Collins, you want to tell me what happened? You want to wait for your attorney? Or you want to talk now, get this straightened out?"

The woman's voice was barely more than a whimper. "He called me, you know, from that damn Sportsman's Club, where he went after getting off work at the plant. Said he weren't gonna let me do this to him. Said he was gonna take care of me without no judge and divorce lawyers, no sir.''

"Did he tell you he had a weapon?''

"Yes, sir, Mr. Brown, he did. Said he had his brother's gun and he was damn straight gonna use it this time on me.''

"This time?''

"He came over on Sunday, not so drunk that he was falling down, but plenty liquored up, and shot out the lights outside. Laughing and calling me names. Then he started to whale on me, yessir. My biggest, he's only eleven, got his arm busted trying to pull him off. I thought he'd kill us all. I was so scared; that's why I sent the kids off'n to their cuzzin's. Put all three of 'em on the bus this morning.''

The woman picked up a small fake-leather photo album from a side table. She opened it up and thrust it across at Tanny Brown. He saw three well-scrubbed faces, school pictures.

"They're good kids,'' she said. "I'm glad they weren't here for this.''

He nodded. "Why didn't you call the police on Sunday?''

"Wouldn't do no good. I even had a judge's order telling him to stay away, but it didn't do no good. Nothing did no good when he'd been drinking. Except maybe that shotgun.''

Her upper lip started to quiver and tears began to well up again in the corners of her eyes.

"Oh, Jesus, sweet Jesus,'' she whimpered.

"The shotgun? Where'd you get the shotgun?''

"I went over to Pensacola, to the Sears there, after they fixed me up at the clinic. I still got Buck's Sears card, so I charged it. I was so scared, Mr. Brown. And when I heard that old pickup of his pull up, I knew he meant to do me, I knew it.''

The woman started to cry again.

"Did you see the gun in his hand before you shot?''

"I don't know. It was dark and I was so scared. . . .''

Tanny Brown spoke quietly but firmly. He kept the photo album with the children's pictures in his hands. "Now think hard, Missus Collins. What did you see . . . ?'' The police lieutenant looked over at the uniformed officer, who nodded his head in comprehension. "Now, you wouldn't have shot unless you saw him raise that gun right at you, right?''

The woman stared at him quizzically.

"You wouldn't have shot unless you were in fear for your life, right?''

"Right,'' she replied slowly.

"Not unless you knew deadly force was the only available recourse left to you, right?"

A slow understanding seemed to fall on the woman's face, even though Brown knew she hadn't understood half the words he'd used in his question.

"Well," she said softly, "I could see he raised something right at me . . ."

"And you knew he had the gun and he had threatened you and shot at you before . . ."

"That's right, Mr. Brown. I was in fear."

"And there was no place for you to run and hide?"

The woman gestured widely. "Where you gonna hide in here? Got no recourse at all."

Brown nodded his head and looked again at the children's pictures.

"Three kids? All his?"

"No, sir. Buck weren't their daddy, and he never liked 'em much. Guess they reminded him of my other husband. But they're fine kids, Mr. Brown. Fine kids."

"Where's their real daddy?"

The woman shrugged, a movement that spoke volumes about trailer parks and bruises.

"Said he was going to Louisiana, try and get work on the oil rigs. But that's nearly seven years ago. Now, he's just gone. We weren't husband and wife official, nohow."

Tanny Brown was about to ask another question when he heard a bellow of rage from outside. Sudden voices were raised and he heard policemen shouting to each other. The woman on the couch gasped, shrinking down to the floor. "That's his brother. I know it. He'll kill me, Lord, I know."

"No, he won't," Brown said quietly. He handed the woman back the portraits of her children. She clutched the leather photo album tightly. Then he motioned for the uniformed officer to stand by the door as he returned outside.

From the doorway, he saw two other uniforms trying to restrain a large, enraged man who struggled hard against their hold. The crime-scene technicians had scattered. The man roared, tugging and jerking, pulling the officers toward the body.

"Buck, Buck! Jesus, Buck, I can't believe it! Jesus, lemme go! Lemme go! I'll kill the bitch, kill her!"

He surged forward dragging the officers. Two more policemen jumped in his path to try and slow his progress. One cop fell to the ground, cursing. The crowd of people started to cat-call and yell, their voices adding to the man's fury.

"I'll kill the bitch, dammit!"

He screamed with red-streaked rage. His contorted face was caught in the flashing strobe lights of the police cruisers, illuminating his anger. He kicked at one of the policemen struggling to hold him, his foot landing on the officer's shin. The man yelped and fell aside, grabbing at his leg.

Tanny Brown stepped from the trailer's front stoop and walked toward the dead man's brother. He put himself directly in the man's vision.

"Shut up!" he shouted.

The wild man stared at him, hesitating momentarily in his push forward. Then he lurched again. "I'll kill the bitch," he screamed.

"That your brother?" Brown shouted.

The man twisted in the grasp of the policemen. "She killed Buck, now I mean to do her. Bitch! You're dead!" he cried, directing his yell past Brown.

"Is that your brother?" Brown asked again, slightly quieter.

"You're dead, bitch! Dead!" the man snarled. "Who's asking? Who're you, nigger?"

The racial epithet stung him, but he didn't move. He considered stepping up and feeding the man his fist, but then decided against it. The man had to be stupid to call him a name, but probably wasn't so stupid he wouldn't file a complaint. A brief vision of a stack of paperwork jumped into his sight like a mirage.

One of the officers trying to hold the man back freed his nightstick. Brown shook his head and stepped up so that his face was only a few inches away from the dead man's brother.

"I'm police Lieutenant Theodore Brown, asshole, and I'm gonna get pissed in one more second, and you don't want to have me on your case, asshole."

The man hesitated. "She killed him, the bitch."

"You already said that."

"What you gonna do about it?"

Tanny Brown ignored the question. "That your gun?" he asked.

"Yeah, mine. He got it from me earlier."

"Your gun? Your brother?"

"Yeah. You gonna arrest the bitch, or am I gonna have to kill her?"

The man's struggles had slowed, but his voice had gathered an angry, challenging edge.

"You knew he was gonna come over here?"

"He told everyone at the bar."

"What was the gun for?"

"He was just gonna scare her a little, like he did the other night."

Brown turned and saw the uniformed officer standing in the light thrown from the trailer door, and the woman cowering behind the policeman. He turned back to the enraged man, who was standing still now, waiting, his arms still clasped by two officers.

The police lieutenant walked over to the dead man's body and looked down at it. Under his voice, he whispered, "Can you hear me? You ain't worth the trouble." Then he looked back at the brother.

"You gonna do something, or what?" the man demanded.

Tanny Brown smiled. "Sure," he said.

He turned to one of the crime-scene technicians. "Tom, go get Missus Collins' shotgun." The man went over to a cruiser and returned with the gun. Brown took the shotgun and jacked the pump action a single time, chambering a fresh round.

He looked over at the dead man's brother and smiled again. "Give the shotgun back to Missus Collins," he said loudly. He stared over at the man. "Fred?" he called out in a loud voice. "Officer Davis, you write Missus Collins up one of those tickets for dumping refuse without a permit. Pay a fifty-buck fine. And you call sanitation and tell them to come pick up this trash." He pointed at the body at his feet.

"Hey," said the man.

"That's right. Give her a ticket for shooting this piece of crap and dumping him out here."

"Hey," the man said again.

"Tell Missus Collins she dumps any more trash bodies in her front yard, it's gonna cost her fifty bucks every time."

He aimed his index finger at the dead man's brother. "Like this one here. Tell her she's got my permission to blow this sorry asshole's head off. But it's gonna cost her another fifty."

"You can't do that," the man said. His arms had dropped to his sides.

"You don't think so?" Brown said. He walked back to the man and shouted in his face. "You don't think so?"

"Hey, Tanny!" cried one of the uniformed officers. "I got fifty I can lend her."

There was a burst of laughter from some of the other policemen.

"Sure," came another voice. "Hell, we can take up a collection. Cover her until she blows away all the assholes."

"Put me in for ten," said one policeman, rubbing his shin.

"Hey," said the man.

"Hey, what?" Tanny Brown demanded.

"You can't."

"Watch what I can do," the lieutenant said quietly. "Arrest this man."

"Hey!" the man said again as one of the officers slapped handcuffs around his wrists.

"Criminal trespass. Obstruction. Battery on a police officer. Harassment. And let's see, how about conspiracy to commit murder? That's for giving his damn dumb drunk brother a gun."

"You can't," the man said again. His voice had lost its rage.

"Those are all felonies, asshole. I'll bet you don't have a damn permit for that gun, either. And let's add driving under the influence."

"Hey, I ain't drunk."

Tanny Brown stared at the man. "Take a good look," he said quietly. "You ever see this face again, and it's gonna be real trouble. Got that?"

"You can't do this."

"Take him in," Brown said to the uniformed officers. "Show him a bit of county hospitality."

"A pleasure," murmured the man who had been kicked. He jerked the handcuffed man around savagely.

"Take it easy," Brown said. The uniformed officer stared at the lieutenant. "Okay," Brown added, smiling. "Not too damn easy." He whispered one more command. "And make sure the bastard gets put in a cell with the biggest, meanest, rasty-ass black folks we've got in stir. Maybe they can teach him not to call people names."

Two of the officers burst into brief laughter.

Tanny Brown turned his back on the protesting man being dragged toward a squad car, walked back to the trailer, and spoke quietly to the woman cowering inside.

"Missus Collins, we got to go to the police station. We're gonna read you your rights down there. Then I want you to call up that attorney, have him come help you out. You got that?"

She nodded. "I need to call my kids."

"There'll be time for that."

He turned to the uniformed officer. "You get one of the female officers out here quick to transport her. See that she gets something to eat on the way."

"What charge?" the policeman asked.

Tanny Brown turned, staring out at the sprawled lump that remained in the yard. "How about discharging a firearm within town limits? That'll hold things until I talk to the state attorney."

He went back outside and stood next to the body.

Stupid, he thought. So stupid.

He glanced down at his watch. A lot of dying tonight, he thought.

He looked at the dead man's eyes. The face faded, pushed out of the way by his memory of his first look at Joanie Shriver's body stretched out in the center of an embarrassed, angry group of searchers. They were standing at the edge of the swamp, beads of dirty-brown water and strands of green muck clinging to their boots and waders. He remembered wanting to touch her, to cover her, and forcing himself not to, steeling himself to the sturdy, official processing of violence.

He swallowed back the vision. It was all my fault, he thought. I will set it right. I will not lose that one.

Tanny Brown, struggling with visions of death, moved off slowly toward his squad car, believing nothing had ended that night. Not even the life demanded by the state.

It was hurrying toward dawn when Bruce Wilcox called. The first insinuations of light were cheating the darkness out of the trees and sky, giving the world edges and shapes.

Brown had spent the remainder of the night in taking a confession from Mrs. Collins; two hours of quiet, bitter history of sexual abuse and beatings, which had been, more or less, what he'd anticipated. The stories are always the same, he'd thought, only the victims change. He had then argued with a gruff assistant state attorney, irritated at being awakened, and negotiated with a divorce lawyer suddenly in over his head. Self-defense, he had insisted to the prosecutor, who had wanted her charged with second-degree murder. They had finally compromised on manslaughter, with the understanding that if there had been a crime committed that night, it paled in comparison to the crimes inflicted upon the woman.

Exhaustion curled around him, like his fingers gripping the

pen as he signed the last of his reports, when the phone on his desk buzzed.

"Yes?"

"Tanny? It's Bruce. Scratch one mass murderer. He went through with it."

"I'll be damned. What happened?"

"He basically told everyone to go fuck themselves and sat in the chair."

"Jesus." Brown realized his fatigue had dissipated.

"Yeah. Old Sully was one evil motherfucker right to the end. But that wasn't what was so damn interesting."

Tanny Brown could hear the excitement in his partner's voice, a childish enthusiasm that flew in the face of the hour and the awfulness of everything that had happened.

"Okay," he asked. "What's so interesting?"

"Our boy Cowart. Man, he spent all day squirreled away with that creep, all alone, listening to the bastard confess to maybe forty murders. All over Florida, Louisiana, and Alabama. A regular one-man crime wave. Anyway, our boy Cowart comes out of this little tea-and-sympathy session all shaky pale. He just about lost it when his fellow vultures turned the heat on him. They were whaling on him with questions something fierce. It reminded me of wrestling matches, you know, where you know you're outclassed, and you keep trying one move after another, and the opponent has got all the answers, counters everything, until you know you got no chance and you're just in it until the whistle blows. Hurting more and more."

"That is interesting."

"Yeah. And after he got tired of letting his buddies in the press chew him over and spit him out, he took off like the devil was nipping at his heels."

"Where'd he go?"

"Back to Miami. At least, that's what he said he was gonna do. Hell, I don't know for sure. He's supposed to meet those detectives from Monroe County later today. They weren't none too pleased with our boy Cowart, either. He knows something about those deaths down there that he ain't saying."

"How do you know that?"

"Well, hell, Tanny. I'm just guessing. But the man looked like he was pretty seasick with all he'd heard. And I don't think he told the half of it."

Brown sat back, listening to the excited tones in his partner's voice. It was easy for him to picture the reporter squirming

under the pressure of information. Sometimes, he thought, there
are things we don't want to learn. His mind calculated rapidly,
like doing sums.

"Bruce, you know what I think?"

"Bet it's the same thing I'm thinking."

"I bet Cowart got told something he didn't want to hear.
Something that screwed around with the way he had it all figured
out."

"Life ain't quite so neat and tidy, sometimes, is it, boss?"

"Not at all."

"Well, it wouldn't have fazed that cold-hearted bastard to
listen to someone tell him about any bunch of murders, no matter how many. I mean, just about everybody had Sully figured
for more than he'd owned up to, so that weren't no great surprise . . ." Wilcox began, only to be interrupted, the thought
finished by Brown.

"There's only one murder that means anything to him."

"That's for damn sure."

And only one murder that means anything to me, Tanny
Brown thought.

He drove through the weak dawn light slowly, his mind
churning with questions. He spotted the paper boy on his bicycle
zigzagging up the street, and he pulled in behind him. The boy
turned at the sound of the car, recognized the detective and
waved before rising up on his pedals and racing ahead. Brown
watched him maneuver amidst the wan morning shadows that
blurred the edges of the neighborhood, making it appear like a
photograph slightly out of focus. He pulled into his driveway
and looked about for an instant. The detective saw modern security: measured rows of clean stucco and cinder-block houses
painted in shiny white or quiet pastels, all marked with well-
trimmed shrubs and bushes, green lawns, and late-model cars
parked in the driveways. A simple, middle-class existence. Every
house within a ten-block neighborhood planned by a single contracting company, designed to create a community both unique
and uniform at the same time. No Old South here. Some doctors, some lawyers, and what was once the working class, policemen, like himself. Black and white. Just modern America
moving forward. He looked down at his hands. Soft, he thought.
A desk man's hands. Not like my father's. He glanced at his
thickening middle. Christ, he thought, I belong here.

Inside the house, he hung his shoulder holster on a hook next to two book bags stuffed with notebooks and loose-leaf papers. He removed the pistol and, as was his habit, first checked the chambers. It was a .357 magnum with a short barrel, loaded with wadcutters. He hefted the pistol in his hand and reminded himself to book some time at the department's shooting range. He realized it had been months since his last practice session. He opened a drawer and found a trigger lock, which he slid around the firing mechanism. He put the gun in the drawer and reached down to remove his backup pistol from his ankle holster.

He could smell bacon frying in the kitchen and he walked that way, past Danish furniture and framed prints. He stood for a moment in the doorway to the kitchen watching his father, who was bent over the stove, cracking eggs into a skillet.

"Hello, old man," he said quietly.

His father didn't move but cursed once as some bacon grease splattered onto his hand.

"I said, good morning, old man."

His father turned slowly. "I didn't hear you come in," he said, smiling.

Tanny Brown grinned a greeting. His father didn't hear much anymore. He went over and put an arm around the man's wide shoulders. He could feel the old man's bones beneath the thin cotton of his faded work shirt. He gave his father a small squeeze, thinking how skinny he'd become, how fragile he felt, as if he would break under the pressure of his son's hug. He felt a shadow of sadness inside, remembering a time when he'd thought there was nothing those arms couldn't lift and hold, now realizing there was little they could. All that strength robbed by disease. He thought, You grow up angry and pushing for that day when you're stronger and tougher than your father, but when it comes it makes you embarrassed and uncomfortable.

"You're up early," the son said as he released his grip.

His father shrugged. He hardly slept anymore, Brown knew. A combination of pain and stubbornness.

"And what you calling me 'old man' for? I ain't so damn old. Still whup you if I had to."

"You probably could," Brown replied, smiling. This was a lie both enjoyed.

"Sure could," insisted his father.

"The girls up yet?"

"Nah. I heard some shifting about. Maybe the bacon smell will wake 'em. But they're soft and young and don't like getting up none. If your mama was still with us, she'd see they got up right and smart first cock crow, yessir. It'd be them in here fryin' this bacon. Making biscuits, maybe.''

Brown shook his head. "If their mama was still here, she'd tell them to sleep in and get their beauty rest. She'd let them miss the school bus and take them herself.''

Both men laughed and nodded their heads in agreement. Brown recognized that his father's complaints were mainly fiction; the old man doted on his granddaughters shamelessly.

His father turned back to the stove. "I'll fix you some eggs. Musta been a tough night?''

"Wife shot her ex-husband when he came looking for her with a handgun, Dad. It wasn't anything unique or special. Just mighty sad and bloody.''

"Sit down. You're probably beat. Why can't you work regular hours?''

"Death doesn't work regular hours, so neither do I.''

"I suppose that's your excuse for missing services this past Sunday. And the Sunday before that, too.''

"Well . . . ,'' he started.

"Your momma would whip you good if she were alive today. Hell, son, then she'd whip me good for letting you miss services. It ain't right, you know.''

"No. I'll be there Sunday. I'll try.''

His father scrambled the eggs in a bowl. "I hate all this new stuff you got in here. Like this damn electric stove thing. Nuclear food cooker, whatever the hell it is.''

"Microwave.''

"Well, it don't work.''

"No, you don't know how to work it. There's a difference.''

His father was grinning. Brown knew the old man felt a contradictory superiority, having grown up in a world of icehouses and outhouses, well water and wood stoves, having made his life out of an old, familiar world, and finally, been taken in his old age into a home that seemed to him closer to a rocket ship than a house. All the gadgets of middle class amused his father, who saw most of them as useless.

"Well, I don't see what the hell good it's for anyway, 'cept maybe for thawing stuff out.''

He thought his father correct on that score.

He watched as the old man's gnarled hands swiftly dished the omelet into the skillet and tossed the eggs, folding them expertly. It was remarkable, the son thought. Arthritis had stolen so much of his mobility; old age, much of his sight and hearing; a bout with heart disease had sapped most of his strength, leaving him gaunt with skin that used to burst with muscles now sagging from his arms. But the old tanner's dexterity had never left him. He could still take a knife and slice an apple into equal pieces, take a pencil and draw a perfectly straight line. Only now it hurt him to do so.

"Here you go. Should taste good."

"Aren't you gonna join me?"

"Nah. I'll just make enough for the girls. Me, just a bit of coffee and some bread." The old man looked down at his chest. "It doesn't take a lot to keep me going. Couple a sticks on the fire, that's all."

The old man slid slowly, in obvious discomfort, into a chair. The son pretended not to notice.

"Damn old bones."

"What?"

"Nothing."

They sat in silence for a moment.

"Theodore," his father said quietly, "how come you never think of finding a new wife?"

The son shook his head. "Never find another like Lizzie," he said.

"How you know if you don't look?"

"When Mama died, you never hunted out a new wife."

"I was already old. You're still young."

Brown shook his head. "I've got all I need. I've still got you and the girls and my job and this house. I'm okay."

The old man snorted but said nothing. When his son finished, he reached out for the plate and carried it stiffly over to the sink.

"I'll go wake the girls," Brown said. His father only grunted. The son paused, watching the father. We're quite a pair, he thought. Widowed young and widowed old, raising two girls as best we can. His father started to hum to himself as he scrubbed away at the plates. Brown stifled a sudden, affectionate laugh. The old man still refused to use the dishwashing machine and wouldn't allow any of the others to use it either. He'd insisted that there was only one way to tell if something were truly clean, and that was to clean it yourself. He thought that proper, in its own way. When the girls had complained, shortly after his father had moved in, he'd explained only that his father was set in his ways. The explanation had sat unquietly in the household for a few days, until the weekend, when Tanny Brown had loaded both girls into his unmarked squad car and driven north fifty miles, just over the Alabama border to Bay Minette. They drove through the dusty, small town with its stolid brick buildings that seemed to glow in the noontime heat, and out past a long, cool line of hanging willows, into the farm country, to an old homestead.

He'd taken the girls across a wide field, down to a little valley where the heat seemed to hang in the air, sucking the breath from his lungs. He'd pointed to a group of small shacks, empty now, staggered by the passing of time, faded reds and browns, splintered with age, and told them that was where their grandfather had been born and raised. Then he'd taken them back toward Pachoula, pointing out the segregated school where his father had learned his letters, showing them the site of the farm where he'd worked hard to rise to be caretaker, and where he'd learned the tanning business. He showed them the house their grandfather had purchased in what had once been known as Blacktown, and where their grandmother had built up her seamstress business, gaining enough of a reputation that her talents cut across racial boundaries, the first in that community. He'd shown them the small white frame church where his father had been deacon and his mother had sung in the choir. Then he'd taken them home and there had been no more talk of the dishwasher.

I forget, too, he thought. *We all do.*

The hallway outside the girls' room was hung with dozens of family pictures. He spotted one of himself, in his fullback's outfit, cradling a football. He could see where the slick, shiny material of the jersey was frayed up near the shoulder pads. The red-and-gray uniforms at his school had been the used outfits from a neighboring white district. *The girls don't understand that,* he thought. *They don't understand what it was like to know that every uniform, every book in the library, every desk in the classrooms, had once been used in the white high school, and then discarded.* He recalled picking up his secondhand helmet for the first time and seeing a dark sweat line on the inside. He had touched the padding, trying to see if it felt different. Then he'd raised his fingers to his nose to check the smell. He shook his head at the memory. *The war changed that for me,* he thought. He smiled. Nineteen-sixty-nine. The march on Washington had been six years before. The Civil Rights Bill would pass the year after. The Voting Rights Bill in 1965. The whole South was convulsed with change. He'd returned from the ser-

vice and gone to college on the GI Bill and then, coming home
to Pachoula, had learned that the all-black school where he'd
carried the ball was no longer. A large, ugly, stolid cinder-block
regional high school was under construction. There were weeds
growing on the playing fields he'd known. The red-and-brown
dirt that had streaked his uniform was covered by a tangled
growth of crabgrass and stinkweed. He remembered cheers, and
thought there had been too few victories in his life.

He shook his head again. Mustn't forget, he thought. He remembered the epithet that had burst from the dead man's brother's lips a few hours earlier. None of it has changed.

He knocked on his eldest daughter's door. "Come on, Lisa!
Rise and shine. Let's go!" He turned quickly and banged away
on the younger girl's door. "Samantha! Up and at 'em. Hit the
deck running. Schooltime!"

The groans amused him, turning his thoughts momentarily
away from Pachoula, the murdered girl, and the two men who'd
occupied space on Death Row.

Tanny Brown spent the next half hour in suburban-father
school-day routine, prodding, cajoling, demanding, and finally
accomplishing the desired result: Both girls out the door, with
homework intact, lunches made, in time to catch the school bus.
With the two girls gone, his father had retreated to his bedroom
to try to take a nap, and he was left alone with the growing
morning. Sunlight flooded the room, making him feel as if everything was twisted about. He felt like some odd nocturnal
beast trapped by the daylight, lurching from shadow to shadow,
searching for the familiarity and safety of night.

He looked across the room and his eyes focused on an empty
flower vase that stood on a shelf. It was tall, with a graceful
hourglass shape, and a single painted flower climbing up the
ceramic side. It made him smile. He remembered his wife buying the vase when he took her on a vacation to Mexico, and
hand-carrying it all the way back to Pachoula, afraid to trust it
to doormen, luggage handlers, or porters. When they returned
home, she put it in the center of the dining-room table and
always kept it filled with flowers. She was like that. If there was
something she wanted, there was no end to what she would do
to accomplish it. Even if it meant carrying a silly vase by hand.

No flowers anymore, he thought, except for the girls.

He remembered how hard they'd tried to save her at the emergency room, how, when he'd arrived, they were still working,

crowded around, running adrenaline and plasma lines, massaging her heart, trying to coax some life into her body. He'd known with a single look that it was useless. It had been something left over from the war, a way of understanding when some invisible line had been crossed and when, even with all of science gathered, connected, and being utilized, death still beckoned inexorably. They'd worked hard, passionately. She had been there herself, some twenty minutes earlier, working alongside all of them. Twenty minutes to get her raincoat, maybe make some small, end-of-the-workday joke, say good night to the rest of the emergency-room crew, walk to her car, drive five blocks and be rammed broadside by a drunk driver in a pickup truck. Even after she was dead, when they knew there was no hope, they kept working. They knew she would have done the same for them.

He stared at the ceiling but couldn't sleep, regardless of how exhausted he was. He realized that he no longer wondered when he would get over missing her, having come to understand that he would never get over her death. He had reached an accommodation with it, which was sufficient to get him from day to day.

He rose and walked into his youngest daughter's room, moved over to her bureau and started to push aside some of the girlish things collected there, a case overflowing with beads and rings and ribbons, a toy bear with a torn ear, an old loose-leaf binder stuffed with a different year's schoolwork, a tangle of combs and brushes. It did not take long to find what he was searching for: a small silver frame with a photo inside. He held it up in front of him. The frame gleamed when it caught the sunlight.

It was a picture of two little girls, one black, one white, one raven-haired, one blonde, arm-in-arm, giggling, braces and wildly mussed makeup, feather boas and dress-up clothes.

He looked at the two faces in the photograph.

Friends, he thought. Anyone would look at that picture and realize that nothing else counted, that they just liked each other, shared secrets and passions, tears and jokes. They had been nine and mugging shamelessly for his camera. It had been Halloween, and they had dressed up in colorful, cacophonous outfits, outdoing each other with wild, outrageous appearance, all laughter and unfettered childish glee.

He was almost overcome with fury. All he could see was Blair Sullivan, mocking him. I hope it hurt, he thought. I hope it ripped your soul from your body with all the pain in the world.

Sullivan's face disappeared, and he thought of Ferguson.

You think you're free. You think you're going to get away with it. Not a chance.

He looked down at the picture in his hand. He especially liked the way the girls had their arms around each others' shoulders. His daughter's black arm hung down around the front of Joanie Shriver's body, and Joanie's arm hung around his daughter's, so the two girls were hugging close, framing each other.

Her first and best friend, he thought.

He stared at Joanie's eyes. They were a vibrant blue. The same color as the Florida sky on the morning of his wife's funeral. He had stood apart from the rest of the mourners, clutching his two daughters beneath his arms, listening to the drone of the preacher's voice, words about faith and devotion and love and being called home to the valley, and hearing little of it. He had felt crippled, unsure whether he would be able to summon the energy to take another step. He had pinned his daughters to his sides, aware only that each of them was convulsed with tears. He had wanted to be enraged but knew that would have been too simple, that he was instead going to be cursed with a dull constant agony blended with the terror that with their mother gone, he would somehow lose his daughters. That with their center ripped away, they couldn't hold together. He had lost his tongue, didn't know what to say to them, didn't know what to do for them, especially Samantha, the younger, who had sobbed uncontrollably since the accident.

The other mourners had kept their distance, but Joanie Shriver had pulled away from the comforting grasp of her own father, serious beyond her years, wearing her best dress and, eyes filled with tears, had walked past the lines of people, right up to him and said, "Don't you worry about Samantha. She's my friend and I will take care of her." And in that moment, she'd reached out and taken hold of his daughter's hand and stood there holding it as well. And she'd been true to her word. She'd always been there, whenever Samantha needed to turn to someone. Weekends. Lonely holidays. After school days. Helping him to restore a routine and solidity to life. Nine years old and wiser by far than any adult.

So, he thought, she was more than just her friend. She was my friend, too. Saved our lives.

Self-hatred filled him. All the authority and power in the world, and I couldn't protect her.

He remembered the war. Medic! they called, and I went. Did

I save any of them? He remembered a white boy, one week in the platoon, a cowboy from Wyoming who'd taken a round in the chest, a sucking chest wound. It'd whistled, taunting him as he struggled to save the soldier. He'd had his eyes locked onto Tanny Brown, watching through the haze of hurt and shock for a sign that would tell him he was going to live or die. He'd still been looking when the last breath wheezed through his chest. It was the same look that George and Betty Shriver had worn when he came to their door carrying the worst news.

Brown shook his head. How long have I known George Shriver? Since the day I went to work in his father's store and he took a mop and worked next to me.

His hand twitched. I've buried too many. He looked at the picture a final time before setting it back on top of the bureau. It's not over, he insisted. I owe you too much.

He walked from his daughter's room into his bedroom. He no longer thought of exhaustion or rest. Propelled by outrage and debt, he began collecting a change of clothes and stuffing them into an overnight bag, wondering when the next commuter flight down to Miami left the airport.

THIRTEEN
A HOLE IN THE STORY

H‍e had no plan.

Matthew Cowart faced the day after the execution of Blair Sullivan with all the enthusiasm of a man who'd been told he was next. He drove his rental car rapidly through the night, down more than half the length of the state, jumping on Interstate 95 south of Saint Augustine. He cruised the three-hundred-plus miles at an erratic pace, often accelerating to ninety miles per hour, oddly surprised he was not stopped once by a trooper, though he passed several heading in the opposite direction. He soared through the darkness, fueled by all the furious contradictions ricocheting back and forth in his head. The first morning sunshine began to rise as he pushed past the Palm Beaches, shedding no light on his troubles. It was well after dawn when he finally deposited the car with a surly Hertz agent at Miami International Airport, who had difficulty understanding why Cowart had not returned the vehicle to its North Florida origin. A Cuban taxi-cab driver, jabbering about baseball and politics without making a distinction between the two and using an energetic mixture of languages, muscled his way through the city's morning rush-hour traffic to Cowart's apartment, leaving the reporter standing alone at the curbside, staring up into the wavy, pale blue heat of the sky.

He paced about his apartment uncomfortably, wondering what to do. He told himself he should go in to the newspaper but was unable immediately to summon the necessary energy. The newspaper suddenly no longer seemed a place of sanctuary, but instead a swamp or a minefield. He stared down at his hands, turning them over, counting the lines and veins, thinking how ironic it was that so few hours earlier he'd been desperate to be alone and now that he was, he was incapable of deciding what to do.

He plumbed his memory for others trapped in the same type of circumstances, as if others' mistakes would help diminish his own. He recalled William F. Buckley's efforts to free Edgar Smith from Death Row in New Jersey in the early sixties and Norman Mailer's assistance to Jack Abbott. He remembered the columnist standing in front of a bank of microphones, angrily admitting to being duped by the killer. He could picture the novelist fighting through the glare of camera lights, refusing to talk about his murderous charge. I'm not the first reporter to make an error, he thought. It's a high-risk profession. The stakes are always tough. No reporter is immune from a carefully executed deception.

But that only made him feel worse.

He sat up in his seat, as if talking to someone in a chair opposite him and said, "What could I have done?"

He rose and started pacing about the room. "Dammit, there was no evidence. It made sense. It made perfect sense. Dammit. Dammit."

Rage suddenly overcame him, and he reached out and swept a stack of newspapers and magazines from a countertop. Before they had settled, he picked up a table and overturned it, crashing it into a sofa. The thud of the furniture smashing together was intoxicating. He started to mutter obscenities, picking up pace, assaulting the room. He seized some dishes and threw them to the floor. He swept clear a shelf filled with books. He knocked over chairs, punched the walls, finally throwing himself down next to a couch.

"How could I have known?" he shouted. The silence in the room was his only answer. A different exhaustion filled him, and he leaned his head back and stared at the ceiling. Abruptly, he laughed. "Boy," he said, affecting a lugubrious Hollywood-Southern accent, "you done fucked up good. Fucked up righteous. Done fucked up in a unique and special way." He drew out the words, letting them roll around the disheveled apartment.

He sat up quickly. "All right. What are we going to do?"

Silence. "That's right," he laughed again. "We just don't know, do we?"

He rose and walked through the mess to his desk and tore open a bottom drawer. He shuffled through a stack of papers until he found a year-old copy of the Sunday paper with his first story. It had already started to yellow slightly. The newsprint felt brittle to his touch. The headline jumped at him and he started reading through the story.

"Questions raised about Panhandle murder case," he abbreviated the words of the opening paragraph out loud. "No shit."

He continued to read as far as he could, past the lead and through the opening page to the jump and the double-truck inside. He wouldn't look at the picture of Joanie Shriver but stared angrily at the photos of Sullivan and Ferguson.

He was about to crumple the paper and throw it into the wastebasket when he stopped and looked at it again. Grabbing a yellow highlight pen, he started marking the occasional word or phrase. After he finished the entire story a second time, he laughed. In all the words written, there was nothing wrong. There was nothing really untrue. Nothing inaccurate.

Except everything.

He looked at what he'd written again: All the "questions" had been correct. Robert Earl Ferguson's conviction had been based on the flimsiest evidence concocted in a prejudicial atmosphere. Was the confession beaten out of Ferguson? His stories had only cited what the prisoner had contended and the policemen denied. It was Tanny Brown, Cowart thought, who had been unable to explain the length of time Ferguson had been held in custody before "confession." It had deserved to be set aside. The jury that had convicted him had been steamrollered into their decision by passions. A savagely murdered little white girl and an angry black man accused of the crime and represented by an incompetent old attorney. A perfect formula for prejudice. His own words—illegally obtained—putting him on the Row. There was no question about all that, about the injustice that had beset Ferguson in the days after Joanie Shriver's body had been discovered.

Except for one isolated detail. He had killed the little girl. At least, according to a mass murderer.

His head spun.

Cowart continued to scan through his story. Blair Sullivan had been in Escambia County at the time of the murder. That had been confirmed and double-confirmed. There was no question Sullivan had been in the midst of a murderous spree. He should have been a suspect—if the police had bothered to look past the obvious.

The only outright lie—if it was one—that he could detect belonged to Ferguson, when he had accused Sullivan of confessing to the crime. But that was Ferguson talking—carefully attributed and quoted, not himself.

And yet, everything was a lie, the explosive coupling of the two men completely obscuring whatever truth lay about.

He thought, I am in hell. The simple, terrible reality was, for all the right reasons, all the wrong things had happened.

The first two times the telephone rang, he ignored it. The third time, he stirred himself and, despite knowing there was no one he wanted to talk to, plucked the phone from its cradle and held it to his ear.

"Yes?"

"Christ, Matt?"

It was Will Martin from the editorial department.

"Will?"

"Jesus, fella, where the hell have you been? Everyone's going slightly bananas trying to find you."

"I drove back. Just got in."

"From Starke? That's an eight-hour trip."

"Less than six, actually. I was going pretty fast."

"Well, boy, I hope you can write as fast as you can drive. The city desk is screaming for your copy and we got a couple hours before first-edition deadline. You got to get your rear in gear, in here, pronto." The editor's singsong voice was filled with excitement.

"Sure. Sure . . ." Cowart listened to his own voice as if it were someone else talking on the telephone. "Hey, Will, what're the wires moving?"

"Wild stuff. They're still doing new leads on that little press conference of yours. Just what the hell happened up there, anyway? Nobody's talking about anything else and nobody knows a damn thing. You ought to see your phone messages. The networks, the *Times* and *Post*, and the newsweeklies, just for starters. The three local affiliates have the front door staked out, so we got to figure a way of getting you in here without too much fuss. There's a half-dozen calls already from homicide cops working cold cases that just happen to be on the route that Sullivan took. Everybody wants to know what that killer told you before taking his evening juice, if you'll pardon the pun."

"Sullivan confessed to a bunch of crimes."

"I know that. The wires have run that already. That's what you told everybody up there. But we've got to get the inside story right now, son. Chapter and verse. Names, dates, and details. Right now. You got it on tape? We got to get that to a typist, hell, a half-dozen typists, if need be, get some transcripts made. C'mon, Matty, I know you're probably exhausted, buddy, but you got to rally. Pop some No Doz, gulp some coffee. Just get on in here. Pump out those words. You got to move, Matty, move, before this place gets crazy. Hell, you can sleep later. Anyway, sleep's overrated. Better to have a big story anytime. Trust me."

"Okay," Cowart said helplessly. Any thought of trying to explain what had happened had dissipated in the waves of enthusiasm Will poured over the phone line. Cowart realized if Martin was this way—a man dedicated to a slow, thoughtful, editorial-page-consideration pace of events—the city desk was probably frantic with excitement. A big story has a universal impact on the staff of a newspaper. It catches hold of everyone, sucks them in, makes them feel as if they're a part of the events. He took a deep breath. "I'm on my way," he said quietly. "But how do I get past the camera crews?"

"No problem. You know where the downtown Marriott Hotel sorta hides behind the Omni Mall? On that little back street by the bay?"

"Sure."

"Well, a home-delivery truck will pick you up, right on the corner, in twenty minutes. Just jump in and come in the freight entrance."

"Cloak and dagger, huh?" Cowart was forced to smile.

"These are dangerous times, my son, demanding unique efforts. It was the best we could come up with on short notice. Now, I suppose the CIA or the KGB could think of something better, but who's got the time? And anyway, outwitting a bunch of television reporters shouldn't be the hardest damn thing in the world."

"I'm on my way." Then suddenly, he thought of the tapes in his briefcase containing the confession and the truth about Joanie Shriver's murder. He couldn't let anyone hear those words. Not until things had settled, and he'd sorted out what he was going to do. He scrambled. "Look, I need to shower first. Hold the pickup for, say, forty-five minutes. Maybe an hour."

"Not a chance. You don't need to be clean to write."

"I've got to collect my thoughts."

"You want me to tell the city editor you're *thinking*?"

"No, no, just say I'm on my way, I'm just getting my notes together. Thirty minutes, Will. Half an hour. Promise."

"No more. Got to move, son. Got to move." Will Martin made slapping sounds to punctuate the urgency of the moment. "A half hour. No more."

"Okay. I'll tell the city editor. Man he's gonna have a heart attack and it's only ten A.M. The truck will be waiting for you. Just hurry. Keep the poor guy alive another day, huh?" Martin laughed at his joke and hung up.

Cowart's head spun. He knew he was running out of choices, that the detectives would arrive at his office momentarily. Things were moving too rapidly for him to contain. He had to go in and write something. Things were expected of him.

But instead of grabbing his jacket, he seized his briefcase and pulled out the tapes. It only took him a second to locate the last tape; he'd been careful to number them as each was completed. For a moment he held the tape in his hand and considered destroying it, but instead, he took it over to his own stereo system and plugged it into the tape deck. He wound the tape through to the end, then backtracked it a few feet and punched the Play button. Blair Sullivan's gravel voice burst through the speakers, filling the small apartment with its acid message. Cowart waited until he heard the words: ". . . Now I will tell you the truth about little Joanie Shriver."

He stopped the tape and rewound it a few feet, to where Blair Sullivan said, "That's all thirty-nine. Some story, huh?" And he'd responded, "Mr. Sullivan, there's not much time." The killer had shouted then, "Haven't you paid any attention, boy?" before continuing with, "Now it's time for one more story . . ."

He rewound the tape again, backing it up to "Some story, huh?"

He went to his record and tape collection and found a cassette he'd recorded some years back of Miles Davis's "Sketches of Spain." It was an older tape, frequently played, with a faded label. He knew that there were a few feet of blank tape on the end of that recording. He put the tape in the player and found the end of the music. Then he removed the tape and placed it in his portable machine, put the small portable directly in front of his stereo speakers, and replaced Blair Sullivan's confession in the larger unit. He punched the Play button on the Sullivan recording and the Record button on the Miles Davis.

Cowart listened to the words boil around him, trying to blank them from his imagination.

When the tape was finished, he shut both machines off. He played the Sullivan section on the end of the Miles Davis tape. The clarity of the voice speaking was diminished—but still brutally audible. Then he took the tape and replaced it on the shelf with the rest of his records and tapes.

For a moment he stared at the original Sullivan tape. Then he rewound it to the spot he'd duplicated on the Davis, punched the Record button and obliterated Sullivan's words with a breathless silence.

It would seem an abrupt ending, but it would have to do. He didn't know if the tape would stand up to any professional scrutiny by a police lab, but it would buy him some time.

Cowart looked up briefly from the computer screen and saw the two detectives moving through the newsroom. They maneuvered between the desks, zigzagging toward him, ignoring the dozens of other reporters in the room, whose heads rose and whose eyes followed their path, so that by the time they arrived at his desk, everyone was watching them.

"All right, Mr. Cowart," Andrea Shaeffer said briskly. "Our turn."

The words on the screen in front of him seemed to shimmer. "I'll be finished in a second," he replied, keeping his eyes on the computer.

"You're finished now," Michael Weiss interjected.

Cowart ignored the detectives. In a moment, the city editor had rushed up and positioned himself between the two policemen and the reporter.

"We want to take a full statement, right now. We've been trying to do that for days and we're getting tired of the runaround," Shaeffer explained.

The city editor nodded. "When he finishes."

"That's what you guys said the other day, after he found the bodies. Then he had to talk to Sullivan. Then because of what Sullivan says to him, he has to be alone. Now he's got to write it all up. Hell, we don't need a statement, all we have to do is buy a damn subscription to your paper." Exasperation filled her voice.

"He'll be right there," said the city editor, shielding Cowart from the two detectives, trying to steer them away from his desk.

"Now," she repeated stubbornly.

"When he finishes," the editor repeated.

"Do you want to get arrested for obstruction?" Weiss said. "I'm really getting tired of waiting for you jerks to finish your job so that we can do ours."

"I'll call that bluff," the city editor replied. "We'll get a nice picture of you two handcuffing me to run on the front page tomorrow. I'm sure the sheriff in Monroe County will love seeing that." He held out his hands angrily.

"Look." Shaeffer stepped in. "He has information pertinent to a murder investigation. How goddamn unreasonable is it to ask him for a little cooperation?"

"It's not unreasonable," the city editor answered, glaring at her. "He also has a first-edition deadline staring him in the face. First things first."

"That's right," Weiss said angrily. "First things first. We've just got a problem with what you guys think comes first. Like selling papers instead of solving murders."

"Matt, how much longer?" the city editor asked. Neither side had moved much.

"A few minutes," Cowart replied.

"Where are the tapes?" Shaeffer asked.

"Being transcribed. Almost finished." The city editor seemed to think for an instant. "Look, how about you read what Sullivan told our man while you're waiting?"

The detectives nodded. The editor guided them away from Cowart's desk, giving the reporter a single "get going" glance as he led the detectives into a conference room where three typists wearing headsets were working hard on the tapes.

Cowart breathed in deeply. He had worked his way through a description of the execution and maneuvered through the substance of Sullivan's confession. He'd listed out all the crimes that Sullivan had confessed to.

The only remaining element was the deaths that concerned the two Keys detectives. Cowart felt stymied. It was a crucial part of the story, items that would occupy a prominence in the first few paragraphs. But it was the element that threatened him the most. He couldn't tell the police—or write in the newspaper—that Ferguson had been involved with the crimes without opening up the question why. And the only answer to why those killings had taken place went back to the murder of Joanie Shriver and the agreement the dead man claimed had been struck between the two men on Death Row.

Matthew Cowart sat frozen at his computer screen. The only

way he could protect himself, his reputation, and his career, was to conceal Ferguson's role.

He thought, Hide a killer?

His imagination echoed with Sullivan's words. *"Have I killed you?"*

For a single instant, he considered simply telling the truth about everything, but, in the same instant,. he wondered, What was the truth? Everything pivoted on the words of the executed man. A lover of lies, right to his death.

He looked up and saw the city editor watching him. The man spread his arms and made a circling gesture with both hands. Wind it up, the movement said. Cowart looked back at the story he was writing, knowing that it would parade into the paper untouched.

As he wavered, he heard a voice over his shoulder.

"I don't buy it."

It was Edna McGee. Her blond hair flounced about her face as she shook her head from side to side. She was staring down at some pages of typed paper. Sullivan's confession.

"What?" Cowart spun in his seat, facing his friend.

She frowned and grimaced as her eyes ate words. "Hey, Matt, I think there's a problem here."

"What?" he asked again.

"Well, I'm just going through these quick, you know, and sure, well, I know he's telling you straight about some of these crimes. Got to be, I mean, with the details and everything. But, well, look here, he told you he killed this kid who was working in a combination convenience store and Indian souvenir stand on the Tamiami Trail a couple of years back. He says he stopped for a Coke or something and shot the kid in the back and took the register contents before heading down to Miami. Well, shit, I remember that crime. I covered it. Remember, I started out doing a piece about all the businesses that have sprung up around the Miccosukkee Reservation, and I did a sidebar on some of the crime that has plagued the folks out there in the 'Glades? Remember?"

He gripped the desk.

"Matt, you okay?"

"I remember the stories," Cowart replied slowly.

Edna looked at him closely. "Well, they were mostly about people getting mugged on their way to the bingo games, and how the Indians have established an additional security patrol because of all these cash businesses they've got."

"I remember."

"Well, I did a bit of research on that shooting. I mean, it happened pretty much the way Sullivan says it did. And it sounds like he was inside that store at some point. And sure, the kid got shot in the back. That was in all the papers. . . ." She waved the sheaf of typed conversation in the air. "I mean, he's got it all right, in a sort of superficial way. But, he didn't do it. No way. They busted three teenagers from South Dade for the crime. Forensics matched up the weapon with the bullet in the kid's back and everything. Got a confession from one and testimony against the shooter by the wheelman. Open and shut, as they say. Two of those kids are doing a mandatory twenty-five for first-degree. The other got a deal. But there ain't no doubt who did the crime."

"Sullivan . . ."

"Well, hell, I don't know. He was in South Florida then. No doubt. I mean, I got to check the dates and everything, but sure. He probably passed right by, right about the time that crime hit the front page of the paper. The murdered kid was the nephew of one of the Indian elders, so it made a splash all over the local pages. TV was all over it, too. Remember?"

He did, vaguely, and wondered why he hadn't when Sullivan was talking to him. He nodded.

Edna shook the pile of papers in her hand. "Hell, Matt, I'm sure he was probably telling the truth about most of these crimes. But all of them? Who knows? There's one that doesn't wash. How many others?"

Cowart felt sick to his stomach. The words, "probably telling the truth" punished him. What does it mean if he lied once? Twice? A dozen times? Who did he kill? Who didn't he kill? When was he telling the truth and when wasn't he?

Maybe it was all a lie and Ferguson was telling the truth. His image of Ferguson suddenly flip-flopped from a twisted, murderous gargoyle back to the angry man trapped by injustice. Sullivan's lies, half-truths, and misinformation all rolled together in an impossible mess.

Innocent? Cowart thought.

He stared at the computer screen but remembered Sullivan's words.

Guilty?

He did.

He didn't.

Edna flapped the sheaf of papers in her hand. "There's a

couple of others here that may not wash. I'm just guessing, though. I mean, why? Huh? Why would he claim some murders that he didn't do?''

She paused and answered her own question. ''. . . Because he was one weird guy, right up to the end. And all those mass murderers seem to get off on being the biggest or the toughest or the worst. You remember that guy Henley in Texas? Helped do twenty-eight with that other guy. So, there he is, sitting in prison, when word comes out that John Gacy in Chicago has done thirty-three. So Henley calls up a detective in Houston and tells him, 'I can get the record back . . .' I mean, weird doesn't really describe it, does it?''

''No,'' replied Cowart, his insides collapsing in a turmoil of doubt.

Edna leaned over to look at the lead to his article. ''At least thirty-nine crimes. Well, that's what he said. But you better qualify it.''

''I will.''

''Good. Did he give you any real details about the killings in the Keys?''

''No,'' Cowart answered quickly. ''He just said he'd managed to arrange for them to be done.''

''Well, he had to tell you something . . .''

Cowart scrambled. ''He talked about some informal prison grapevine that even gets to Death Row. He said anything could be arranged for a price. But he didn't say what he paid.''

''Well, I wonder. I mean, you've got to write what he said. But sorting it all out. Well, hell.''

She looked up and across the newsroom toward where the two detectives were reading transcripts. ''You suppose they've got any real evidence? I think they're just hoping you'll wrap the whole thing up for them nice and easy.'' The cynicism in her voice was evident.

He looked up at her. ''Edna,'' he started.

''You want some help checking these suckers out, right?'' Edna's voice immediately filled with enthusiasm. She slapped her hand against the sheaf of papers. ''Got to know what's a definite, what's a maybe, and what's a no way, right?''

''Yes. Please. Can you do it?''

''Love to. Take a few days, but I'll get to work on it right away. I'll tell the higher-ups. You sure you don't mind sharing the story?''

''No. No problem.''

Edna gestured at the computer screen. "Better be careful not to be too explicit about old Sully's confession. It may have some more little problems. Don't dig any hole in the story you can't jump out of."

Cowart wanted to laugh or be sick, he was uncertain which.

"You know, you got to appreciate old Sully. Never wanted to make anything easy on nobody," she said, turning away.

He watched Edna McGee saunter across the newsroom to the city editor and start talking animatedly with him. He watched as they both stared down at the sheet of transcribed statements. He saw the man shake his head and then hurry over to where he was working.

"This right?" the city editor demanded.

"That's what she says. I don't know."

"We're gonna have to check every bit of all this out."

"Right."

"Christ! How're you writing the story?"

"Just as the dying man's words. Allegations unproven. No idea where the truth lies. Questions abound. All that sort of stuff."

"Go heavy with the description and be careful with details. We need some time."

"Edna said she'd help."

"Good. Good. She's going to start making calls now. When do you think you'll be able to get on it?"

"I need some rest."

"Okay. And those detectives . . ."

"I'll be right there."

Cowart looked back at the page. He plucked Sullivan's words from his notebook and closed the piece with: "Some story, huh?"

He punched a few buttons on the keyboard, shutting the screen down in front of him and electronically transporting his article over to the city desk so it could be measured, assessed, edited, and dummied on the front page. He no longer knew whether what he'd done compounded truth or lies. He realized that for the first time in his years as a journalist, he had no idea which was which, they had become so tangled in his head.

Adrift in a sea of ambiguity, he went in to see the detectives.

Shaeffer and Weiss were livid.

"Where is it?" the woman demanded as he walked through the door into the conference room. The three typists were stapling pages together at a large meeting table where the afternoon news conferences were held. When they heard the anger in the detectives' voices, they hurried, leaving a stack of paper behind as they left the room. Cowart didn't reply. His eyes swept away to a large picture window. Sunlight reflecting off the bay streamed into the room. He could see a cruise liner getting up steam, heading out Governor's Cut toward the open ocean.

"Where is it!" Shaeffer demanded a second time. "Where's his explanation of the deaths of his mother and stepfather?"

She shook a typed transcript in his face. "Not a word in here," she almost shouted.

Weiss stood up and pointed a finger right at him. "Start explaining, right now. I'm tired of all this runaround, Cowart. We could arrest you as a material witness and chuck you in jail."

"That'd be fine," he replied, trying to summon up an indignation to match that of the two detectives. "I could use some sleep."

"You know, I'm getting damn tired of you two threatening my man here," came a voice from behind Cowart. It was the city editor. "Why don't you two detectives do some work on your own? All you guys seem to want is for him to provide you with all the answers."

"Because I think he's got all the goddamn answers," Shaeffer replied slowly, softly, her voice filled with menace.

For a moment, the room remained frozen with her words. The city editor finally gestured at chairs to try and slice through some of the tension that sat heavily in the room. "Everybody sit down," he said sternly. "We'll try to get this sorted out."

Cowart saw Shaeffer take a deep breath and struggle to control herself. "All right," she said quietly. "Just a full statement, right now. Then we'll get out of your way. How's that?"

Cowart nodded. The city editor interjected. "If he agrees, fine. But any more threats and this interview is ended."

Weiss sat down heavily and removed a small notepad. Shaeffer asked the first question.

"Please explain what you told me in Starke at the prison."

She was watching him steadily, her eyes marking every movement he made.

Cowart fixed his eyes back hard onto hers. It's how she looks at suspects, he thought.

"Sullivan claimed he'd arranged for the killings."

"You said that. How? Who? What were his exact words? And why the hell isn't it on the tape?"

"He made me turn the tape machine off. I don't know why."

"Okay," she said slowly. "Continue."

"It was a brief element to the entire conversation . . ."

"Sure. Go ahead."

"Okay. You understand how he sent me down to Islamorada. Gave me the address and all. Told me to interview the people I found there. He didn't say they'd be dead. He didn't give any indication of anything, just insisted I go . . ."

"And you didn't demand some explanation before heading down there?"

"Why? He wouldn't give me one. He was adamant. He was scheduled to die. So I went. Without asking any questions. It's not so damn unreasonable."

"Sure. Go ahead."

"When I first got back to his cell, he wanted me to describe the deaths. He wanted me to tell him all the details, like how they were sitting, and how they'd been killed and everything I noticed about the scene. He was particularly interested in learning whether they had suffered. After I finished telling him everything I remembered about the two dead bodies, he seemed satisfied. Downright pleased."

"Go ahead."

"I asked him why and he said, 'Because I killed them.' And I asked how he'd managed that and he replied, 'You can get anything you want, even on Death Row, if you're willing to pay the price.' I asked him what he'd paid, but he refused to say. Said that was for me to find out. Said he was going to go to his grave without shooting his mouth off. I tried to ask him about how he'd arranged it, but he refused to answer. Then he said, 'Ain't you interested in my legacy at all?' He told me then to turn on the tape recorder. And he started confessing to all these other crimes."

Lies tripped readily from his mouth. He was surprised at how easily.

"Do you think there was a connection between the subsequent confession and the murders in Monroe County?"

That was the question, Cowart thought. He shrugged. "It was hard to tell."

"But you think he was telling you the truth?"

"Yes, sometimes. I mean, obviously he sent me down there to that house knowing something was going to happen. So he had to know they were going to be murdered. I think he got what he wanted. But how he paid the bill . . ." Cowart let his voice drain away.

Shaeffer rose abruptly, staring at Cowart. "Okay," she said. "Thanks. Can you remember anything else?"

"If I do, I'll let you know."

"We'd like the original tapes."

"We'll see," the city editor interjected. "Probably."

"They may be evidence," she said acidly.

"Well, we still need to make copies. Maybe by this afternoon, late. In the meantime, if you want, you can take a transcript."

"Okay," she said. Cowart glanced over at the city editor. The detective suddenly seemed extremely accommodating.

"If I need to get hold of you?" she asked him.

"I'll be around."

"Not planning on going anywhere?"

"Just home to bed."

"Uh-huh. Okay. We'll be in touch for the tapes."

"With me," said the city editor.

She nodded. Weiss snapped shut his notepad.

For an instant, she fixed Cowart with a glare. "You know, Mr. Cowart, there's one thing that bothers me. In your press conference after the execution, you said that Blair Sullivan talked to you about the killing of that little girl up in Pachoula."

Cowart felt his insides tumble. "Yeah . . ." he said.

"But none of that's on this transcript, either."

"He made me shut the machine off. I told you."

She smiled, a look of satisfaction. "That's right. That's what I figured happened. . . ." She paused, letting a little silence heat up the room. ". . . Except, then we'd hear Sullivan's voice saying something like: 'Turn off that tape machine,' wouldn't we?"

Cowart, fighting panic, shrugged nonchalantly. "No," he replied slowly. "He spoke of that crime at the same time he talked about the Monroe killings."

Shaeffer nodded. Her eyes squeezed hard on Cowart's face. "Ah, of course. But you didn't say that earlier, did you? Odd, though, huh? Every other crime goes on the tapes except those two, right? The one that first brought you to him and the one he ended with. Kinda unusual, that, what d'you think?"

"I don't know, Detective. He was an unusual man."

"I think you are, too, Mr. Cowart," she said. Then she pivoted and led her partner from the conference room. He watched as she marched through the newsroom and out between the exit doors. He could see the knotted muscles of her calves. She must be a runner, he thought. She has that lean, unhappy look, driven and pained. He wanted to try to persuade himself that she'd believed his story but knew that was foolish.

The city editor also let his eyes follow the detectives through the room. Then he breathed deeply and stated the obvious. "Matty," he said quietly, "that gal doesn't believe a word you said. Is that what happened with Sullivan?"

"Yes, kinda."

"This is all very shaky, isn't it?"

"Yes."

"Matty, is something going on here?"

"It's just Blair Sullivan," Cowart replied quickly. "Mind games. He ran them on me. He ran them on everyone. It was what he did with himself when he wasn't killing folks."

"But what about what that detective was implying?"

Cowart tried for a reply that would make some sense. "It was kinda like Sullivan made a distinction between some crimes. The ones that were important, the two that aren't on tape, were, I don't know, different for him. All these others were just run-of-the-mill. Stuff for his legend. I'm not a shrink. I can't explain what was going on in his mind."

The city editor nodded. "Is that what's going into the paper?"

"Yes, more or less."

"Let's make sure what we put in the paper errs on the side of caution, okay? If you have doubts about something, leave it out. Or make certain it's covered. We can always come back to it."

Cowart tried to smile. "I'm trying."

"Try hard," the city editor said. "You know, it raises more questions than it answers. I mean, who was Sullivan trying to protect? You're gonna find out, right? While Edna checks out the rest of the statement, you're going to work on that angle?"

"Yes."

"Helluva story. A person arranging a murder right before his own execution. What are we talking about, a corrupt prison guard? An attorney, maybe? Another inmate? Get some rest and get on it, okay? You got an idea where to start?"

"Sure," he answered. Not only where to start, but, he thought, where to finish: Robert Earl Ferguson.

* * *

Despite his fatigue, Cowart hung on in the newsroom throughout the remainder of the day, into the early evening. He ignored the news crews staked out in front of the building waiting for him for as long as he could. But when the news directors at each station started calling the managing editor, he was forced to go outside and made a short, unsatisfactory statement. This, of course, angered them more than placated them. They didn't leave after he ended the interview. He took no calls from other reporters trying to interview him. He simply waited for the cover of darkness. After the first edition came up, he read the words he'd written slowly, as if afraid they could hurt him physically. He made a change or two for the late edition, adding more doubt about Sullivan's confession, underscoring the essential mystery of the executed man's actions. He spoke briefly with Edna McGee and the city editor one last time, a false coordination of work. He rode the freight elevator down through the bowels of the newspaper, past the computer makeup rooms, the classified advertising sections, the cafeteria, and the assembly docks. The building hummed and quivered with the noise of the presses as they pumped out tens of thousands of issues of the newspaper. He could feel the vibration from the machines right through the soles of his feet.

A delivery truck gave him a lift for a few blocks, dropping him a short way from his apartment. He tucked a single issue of the next day's paper beneath his arm and walked through the growing city night, suddenly relieved by the anonymous sound his shoes made pacing against the pavement.

He eyed the front of his apartment building from a short distance, scanning the area for other members of the press. He saw none, and then checked for signs of the Monroe detectives. It would not be crazy to suspect they were following him. But the street appeared empty and he quickly cut through the shadows on the edges of the streetlamps, and into his lobby. For the first time since he'd moved in, he regretted the lack of security in the modest building. He hesitated for an instant in front of the elevator, then burst through an emergency door and raced up the fire stairs, his breath coming in short bursts, his feet pounding against the linoleum risers.

He opened the door to his apartment and entered the shambles. For an instant he stood in the center, waiting for his heart to settle, then went to the window and stared out across the dark bay waters. A few reflected city lights sliced through the wavy black ink, only to be devoured by the expanse of ocean.

He felt himself completely alone, but he was wrong. He did not understand that a number of people, though miles distant, were actually in the room with him, like ghosts, waiting for his next move.

Some, of course, were less far. Such as Andrea Shaeffer, who'd parked an entire block distant, but who'd intently watched his erratic course down the street through a pair of night-vision binoculars, as the reporter ducked in and out of the fringe darkness. So precise had her concentration been, that she had failed to notice Tanny Brown. He stood in a shadow of an adjacent building, letting the night surround and conceal him. He stared up at the lights of Cowart's apartment until they were extinguished. Then he waited until the unmarked patrol car carrying the woman detective slowly headed off into the city night before moving, alley-cat-like, for Cowart's apartment.

FOURTEEN
CONFESSION

Tanny Brown listened outside the door to Cowart's apartment. He could hear distant city-night sounds of traffic penetrating the still darkness, blending with the frustrated buzzing of a bottle-green bug that seemed suicidally intent upon assaulting the light fixture in the hallway. He started when he heard a pair of voices from an adjacent apartment rise in sudden laughter, then fade away. For an instant he wondered what the joke was. He listened again at the door, but no sound emanated from Cowart's apartment. He put his hand on the door handle gently, just twisting it slightly until he met resistance. Locked. He peered at the dead bolt above it and saw that the bolt was thrown.

He clenched a fist in disappointment. He hated the idea of asking Cowart for admittance. He had wanted to slip into the apartment with the stealth of a burglar, to rouse Cowart abruptly from sleep, perched like a wraith on the edge of the reporter's dream, demanding the truth.

He heard a whirring, metallic noise behind him and turned swiftly, in the same motion trying to back into a shadow. A hand went automatically to his shoulder holster. It was the elevator, rising to another floor. He watched as a small shaft of light slid through the closed entrance door, passing upward. He lowered his hand, wondering why he felt so jumpy. Fatigue and doubt. He looked back at the door in front of him, realizing that if someone spotted him standing there, they would in all likelihood summon the police, taking him for some intruder with evil intentions.

Which, he thought with a twitch of humor, was exactly what he was.

Brown breathed in deeply, clearing his head of exhaustion, concentrating on what had brought him to Cowart's door. He felt the warm breath of anger on his forehead and he rapped sharply on the thick wooden panels.

Cowart sat cross-legged on the floor amidst the ruins of his apartment, assessing his next step. When the four pistol-like cracks sounded on his door, his first thought was to remain still, frozen like a deer in headlights; his second was to take cover and hide. But instead he rose and walked unsteadily toward the sound.

He took a deep breath and asked, "Who's there?"

Trouble, thought Brown to himself, but out loud, said, "Lieutenant Tanny Brown. I want to talk to you." There was a moment of silence. "Open up!"

Cowart wanted to laugh out loud. He opened the door and peered around its edge. "Everyone wants to talk to me today. I thought you'd be some more of those damn television guys."

"No, just me," replied Brown.

"Same questions, though, I bet," Cowart said. "So, how'd you find me? I'm not in the book and the city desk won't give out my home address."

"Not hard," the detective replied, still standing in front of the door. "You gave me your home phone number back when you were getting Bobby Earl out of prison. Just a matter of calling the telephone company and telling them it was a police matter."

The two men's eyes met and the reporter shook his head. "I should have known you would show up. Everything else seems to be going wrong today."

Brown gestured with his hand. "Do I have to stand out here or may I come in?"

The reporter seemed to think this was funny, smiling and shaking his head. "All right. Why not? I was going to come see you, anyway."

He held open the door. The room behind him was black.

"How about lights?"

Cowart went to a wall and flicked a switch. The detective

stared around in surprise at the mess illuminated by the overhead light.

"Christ, Cowart. What happened here? You have a break-in?"

The reporter smiled again. "No, just a temper tantrum. And I didn't feel much like cleaning it up yet. It fits my mood."

He walked into the center of the living room and found an overturned armchair. He lifted it up and set it on its legs, then stepped back and waved the detective toward it. He swept some papers from the seat of a couch onto the floor and slumped down in the space he'd made.

"Tired," Cowart said. "Not much sleep." He rubbed his hands across his face.

"I haven't been sleeping much, either," Brown replied. "Too many questions. Not enough answers."

"That will keep one awake."

The two weary men stared at each other. Cowart smiled and shook his head in response to the silence between them.

"So, ask me a question," he said to the detective.

"What's going on?"

Cowart shrugged. "Too broad. I can't answer that."

"Wilcox told me that whatever Blair Sullivan told you before he went to the chair, it fucked you up pretty good. Why don't you tell me?"

Cowart grinned. "Is that what he said? Sounds like him. He's a pretty cold-blooded fellow. Didn't bat an eyelash when they turned on the juice."

"Why would he? You can't tell me you shed a tear over Sullivan's exit."

"No, can't say I did. Still . . ."

Brown interrupted. "Bruce Wilcox just sees things differently from you."

"Ah, well, perhaps," the reporter replied, nodding. "What would I know? So, you want to know what fucked me up, huh? Wouldn't listening to a man confess to multiple homicides shake your complacency a bit?"

"It would. It has."

"That's right. Death is your line of business. Just as much as it was Sully's."

"I guess you could say that, though I don't like to think of it that way." Brown tried to obscure the sensation that the reporter had pinned him with his first move. He sat watching the disheveled man in his disrupted apartment. He wondered how long he could keep from grabbing the reporter and shaking answers from him.

Cowart leaned back, as if picking up an interrupted story.

". . . Well, there was old Sully, talking my ear off. Old men, old women, young folks, middle-aged people, girls, boys. Gas-station attendants and tourists. Convenience-store clerks and the occasional passersby. Zip, zap. Just chewed up and tossed aside by a single wrong man. Knives, guns, strangled 'em with his hands, beat 'em with bats, chopped and shot and drowned. A variety of bad deaths. Inventive stuff, huh? Not nice, not nice at all. Makes one wonder what the world's coming to, why anyone should go on in the face of all that evil. Isn't that enough to listen to for a few hours? Wouldn't that account for my—what? Inde-cisiveness? Is that a good word?—at the prison.''

"It might.''

"But you don't think so?''

"No.''

"You think something else is bothering me, and you came all the way down here to ask me what. I'm touched by your concern.''

"It wasn't concern for you.''

"No, I suspect not.'' Cowart laughed ruefully. "I like this,'' he said. "You want a drink of something, Lieutenant? While we fence around?''

Brown considered. He shrugged, a single, why-the-hell-not motion and leaned back in his chair. He watched as Cowart rose, walked into the kitchen and returned after a moment, car-rying a bottle and a pair of glasses and cradling a six-pack of beer under an arm. He held it up.

"Cheap whiskey. And beer, if you want it. This is what the pressmen used to drink at my old man's paper. Pour a beer, drink a couple of inches off the top, and in goes a shot. Boiler-maker. Does a good job of cutting the day's tension real fast. Makes you forget you're working a tough job for long hours and little pay and not much future.''

Cowart fixed each of them a drink. "Perfect drink for the two of us. Cheers,'' he said. He swallowed half in a series of fast gulps.

The liquor burned Tanny Brown's throat and warmed his stomach. He grimaced. "It tastes terrible. Ruins both the whis-key and the beer,'' he said.

"Yeah,'' Cowart grinned again. "That's the beauty of it. You take two perfectly reasonable substances that work fine independently, throw them together, and get something horrible. Which you then drink. Just like you and me.''

The detective gulped again. ''But if you keep drinking, it improves.''

''Hah. That's where it's different than life.'' He refilled their glasses, then sat back in his chair, swirling a finger around the lip of his glass, listening to the squeaking sound it made.

''Why should I tell you anything?'' he said slowly. ''When I first came to you with my questions about Ferguson, you sicced your dog on me. Wilcox. You didn't make it real easy on me, did you? When we found that knife, were you interested in the truth? Or maybe in keeping your case together? You tell me. Why should I help you?''

''Only one reason. Because I can help you.''

Cowart shook his head. ''I don't think so. And I don't think that's a good reason.''

Brown stirred in his seat, eyeing the reporter. ''How about this for a reason,'' he said after a momentary hesitation. ''We're in something together. Have been from the start. It's not finished, is it?''

''No,'' Cowart conceded.

''The problem, from my point of view, is that I'm in something, but I don't know what it is. Why don't you enlighten me?''

Cowart leaned back in his seat and stared at the ceiling, trying to determine what he could say to the detective, and what he should not.

''It's always pretty much like this, isn't it?'' he said.

''What?''

''Cops and reporters.''

Brown nodded his head. ''Uneasy accomplices. At best.''

''I had a friend once,'' Cowart said. ''He was a homicide detective like you. He used to tell me that we were both interested in the same thing, only for different purposes. For a long time neither of us could ever really understand the other's motives. He thought I just wanted to write stories, and I thought he just wanted to clear cases and make his way up the bureaucratic ladder. What he would tell me helped me write the stories. The publicity his cases got helped him in the department. We sort of fed each other. So there we were, wanting to know the same things, needing the same information, using a few of the same techniques, more alike than we'd ever acknowledge, and distrusting the hell out of each other. Working the same territory from different sides of the street and never crossing over. It was a long time before we began to see our sameness instead of our differences.''

Brown refilled his drink, feeling the liquor work on his frayed feelings. He swallowed long and stared over at Cowart. ''It's in the nature of detectives to distrust anything they can't control. Especially information.''

Cowart grinned again. ''That's what makes this so interesting, Lieutenant. I know something you want to learn. It's a unique position for me. Usually I'm trying to get people like you to tell me things.''

Brown also smiled, but not because he thought it amusing. It was a smile that made Cowart grasp his glass a bit tighter and shift about in his seat.

''We've only had one thing to talk about, from the very start. I haven't had enough to drink to forget that one thing, have I, Mr. Cowart? I don't think there's enough liquor in your apartment to make me forget. Maybe not in the whole world.''

The reporter grew silent, then he leaned forward. ''Tell you what, Detective. You want to know. I want to know. Let's make a trade.''

The detective set his glass down slowly. ''Trade what?''

''The confession. It starts there, right?''

''That's right.''

''Then you tell me the truth about that confession, and I'll tell you the truth about Ferguson.''

Brown held his back straight, as if memory thrust rigidity into his body and his words.

''Mr. Cowart,'' he replied slowly. ''Do you know what happens when you grow up and live your life in one little place? You get so's you can sense what's right and wrong in the breeze, maybe in the smell of the day, the way the heat builds up around noon and starts to slip away at dusk. It's like knowing the notes of a piece of music so that when the band plays them, in your head you've already heard them. I'm not saying everything's always small-town perfect and there ain't terrible things happening. Pachoula isn't big like Miami, but it doesn't mean we don't have husbands who beat their wives, kids that do drugs, whores, loan sharks, extortion, killings. All the same. Just not quite so obvious.''

''And Bobby Earl?''

''Wrong from the start. I knew he was waiting to kill somebody. Maybe from the way he walked or talked or that little laugh he would make when I would pull his car over. He came from mean stock, Mr. Cowart, no different from a dog that's been bred for fighting. And it got all tarnished and banged-up worse living in the city. He was filled with hate. Hated me. Hated you. Hated everything. Walking around, waiting for that hate to take over completely. All that time, he knew I was watching him. Knew I was waiting. Knew I knew he was waiting, too.''

Cowart looked over at the narrow eyes of the detective and thought, Ferguson wasn't the only one filled with hate. ''Give me details.''

''None to give. A girl complains he followed her home. Another tells us he tried to talk her into his car. Offered her a ride, he said. Just trying to be friendly. But then a neighborhood crime watch patrol spots him cruising their streets at midnight with his headlights off. Somebody's committing rapes and assaults in the next couple of counties, but forensics can't match him up. A patrol car rousts him from outside the junior high one week before the abduction and murder, right before the end of school, and he's got no explanation for why he's there. Hell, I even ran his name through the national computer and I called the Jersey state police, see if they had anything up there in Newark. No instant winners, though.''

''Except Joanie Shriver turns up dead one day.''

Brown sighed. The liquor slopped over some of his anger. ''That's correct. One day Joanie Shriver turns up dead.''

Cowart stared at the police lieutenant. ''You're not telling me something.''

Brown nodded. ''She was my daughter's best friend. My friend, too.''

The reporter nodded. ''And?''

Brown spoke quietly. ''Her father. Owned those hardware stores. Got 'em from his father. Gave me a job after hours in high school sweeping out the place. He was just one of those people who put color way down on his list, especially at a time when everybody else had it at the top of theirs. You remember what it was like in Florida in the early sixties? There were marches and sit-ins and cross burnings. And in the midst of all that, he gave me a job. Helped me when I went away to college. And when I came back from Vietnam, he pointed me to the police force. Made some calls. Pulled some strings. Called in a favor or two. You think those little things don't amount to much? And his son was my friend. He worked in the store next to me.

We shared jokes, troubles, futures. That sort of thing didn't happen a lot back then, though you probably didn't know that. That means something, too, Mr. Cowart, in this equation. And our children played together. And if you had any idea what that meant, well, you'd understand why I don't sleep much now at night. So I had a couple of debts. Still do."

"Go on."

"Do you have any idea how much you can hate yourself for letting something happen that you could no more have prevented than you can prevent the sun from rising, or the tide from flowing in?"

Cowart looked hard, straight ahead. "Perhaps."

"Do you know what it's like to know, to know absolutely, positively, with complete certainty, that something wrong is going to happen and yet be powerless to stop it? And then, when it does happen, it steals someone you love right from beneath your arms? Crushes the heart of a real friend? And I couldn't do a thing. Not a damn thing!"

The force of Brown's words had driven him to his feet. He clenched a fist in the air between them, as if grasping all the fury that echoed within him. "So, get it now, Mr. Cowart? You beginning to see?"

"I think so."

"So, there the bastard was. Smirking away in a chair. Taunting me. He *knew,* you see. He thought he couldn't be touched. Bruce looked at me, and I nodded. I left the room, and he let the bastard have it. You think we beat that confession out of Robert Earl Ferguson? Well, you're absolutely right. We did."

Brown slapped one hand sharply against the other, making a sound like a shot. "Wham! Used the phone book, just like the bastard said."

The detective's eyes pierced Cowart. "Choked him, hit him, you name it. But the bastard hung in there. Just spat at us and kept laughing. He's tough, did you know that? And he's a lot stronger than he appears." Brown took a deep breath. "I only wished we'd killed him, right there and then, instead."

The detective clenched his fist and thrust it at the reporter. "So, if physical violence won't work, what's next? A little bit of psychological twisting will do the trick. You see, I realized he wasn't afraid of us. No matter how hard we hit him. But what was he afraid of?"

Brown rose. He pulled up his pants leg. "There's the damn gun. Just like he said. Ankle holster."

"And that's what finally made him confess?"

"No," Brown said with cool ferocity. "Fear made him confess."

The detective reached down abruptly and with a single, sudden movement, freed the weapon. It leapt into his hand and he thrust it forward, pointing straight at Cowart's forehead. He thumbed back the hammer, which made a small, evil click. "Like this," he said.

Cowart felt sudden heat flood his face.

"Fear, Mr. Cowart. Fear and uncertainty about just how crazy anger can make a man."

The small pistol was dwarfed by the hulking figure of the detective, rigid with emotion. He leaned forward, pushing the gun directly against Cowart's skull, where it remained for a few seconds, like an icicle.

"I want to know," the detective said. "I do not want to wait." He pulled the gun back so that the weapon hovered a few inches from Cowart's face.

The reporter remained frozen in his seat. He had to struggle to force his eyes away from the black barrel hole and up at the policeman. "You gonna shoot me?"

"Should I, Mr. Cowart? Don't you think I hate you enough to shoot you for coming up to Pachoula with all your damn questions?"

"If it hadn't been me, it would have been somebody else." Cowart's voice cracked with tension.

"I would have hated anyone enough to kill them."

The reporter felt a wild panic within him. His eyes locked on the detective's finger, tightening on the trigger. He thought he could see it move.

Ohmigod, Cowart thought. He's going to do it. For an instant, he thought he would pass out.

"Tell me," Brown said icily. "Tell me what I want to know."

Cowart could feel the blood draining from his face. His hands twitched on his lap. All control raced away.

"I'll tell you. Just put the gun away."

The detective stared at him.

"You were right, you were right all along! Isn't that what you want to hear?"

Brown nodded. "You see," he said softly, evenly, "it's not hard to get someone to talk."

Cowart looked at the policeman. He said, "It's not me you want to kill."

Tanny Brown held stiff for an instant. Then he lowered the gun. "That's right. It isn't. Or maybe it is, but it isn't the right time yet."

He sat back down and placed the revolver on the arm of the chair, picking up his drink again. He let the liquor squeeze the anger, and he breathed out slowly. "Close, Cowart. Close."

The reporter leaned back in his seat. "Everything seems to be cut close for me."

They were both silent for a moment before the detective spoke again. "Isn't that what you guys always complain about? People always hate the press for bringing them the bad news, right? Killing the messenger, huh?"

"Yeah. Except we don't mean it so damn literally." Cowart exhaled swiftly and burst into a high-pitched laugh of relief. He thought for an instant. "So that must have been how it happened, right? Point that thing in someone's face and one's inhibitions against self-incrimination just naturally flow away fast."

"It's not in the approved police training textbooks," Brown replied. "But you're right. And you were right about that all along. Ferguson told you the truth. That's how we got that confession. Only one small problem, though."

"I know the problem."

The two men stared at each other.

Cowart finished the statement hanging in the air between them. "The confession was the truth, too."

The reporter paused, then added, "So you say. So you believe."

Brown leaned back hard in his seat. "Right," he said. He took a deep breath, shaking his head back and forth. "I should never have allowed it. I had too much experience. I knew too much. Knew what could happen when it got into the system. But I let all sorts of wrong things get in the way. It's like hitting a patch of slick mud in your car. One minute you're in control but speeding along, the next out of control, spinning around, fishtailing down the road."

Brown picked up his drink. "But, you see, I thought we might get away with it. Bobby Earl turned out to be his own worst witness. His old attorney didn't know what the hell he was doing. We waltzed that bastard right onto the Row, where he belonged, with just a minimum of lies and misstatements. So I was thinking maybe it would all work out, you know. Maybe I

wouldn't be having any more nightmares about little Joanie
Shriver. . . ."

"I know about nightmares."

"And you came along, asking all the damn right questions.
Picking away at all the little failures, the little lies. Seeing right
through that conviction just as if it weren't there. Damn. The
more you were right, the more I hated you. Had to be, can't you
see?" He pulled hard at the glass, then set it down and poured
himself another.

"Why did you admit that Ferguson was slapped, when I came
up to interview you? I mean, it opened the door . . ."

The detective shrugged. "No, what opened the door was
Bruce exploding. When you saw that frustration and anger, I
knew you'd believe he'd beaten Ferguson, just like the bastard
said. So, by telling a small truth—that he slapped him—I thought
I could hide the big truth. It was a gamble. Didn't work. Came
close, though."

Cowart nodded. "Like an iceberg," he said.

"Right," Brown replied. "All you see is the pretty white ice
up on top. Can't see the dangerous stuff below."

Cowart laughed out loud, though the laughter had no humor
attached to it, only a burst of nervous relief and energy. "Only
one other little detail."

The detective smiled as well, speaking quickly, cutting across
the reporter's words. "You see, I know what Blair Sullivan told
you. I mean, I don't know. But I sure as hell can guess. And
that's the little detail, ain't it?"

The reporter nodded. "What was it you say you knew Bobby
Earl was?"

"A killer."

"Well, I think you may be right. Of course, you may be
wrong, too. I don't know. You like music, Detective?"

"Sure."

"What sort?"

"Pop, mostly. A little bit of sixties soul and rock to remind
me of when I was young. Makes my kids laugh at me. They call
me ancient."

"Ever listen to Miles Davis?"

"Sure."

"This is a favorite of mine."

Cowart rose and approached the stereo system. He put the
tape into the player and turned to the detective. "You don't mind
if we just listen to the end, huh?"

He punched a button and plaintive jazz filled the room.

Brown stared at the reporter. "Cowart, what're you doing? I'm not here to listen to music."

Cowart slumped back into his seat. " 'Sketches of Spain.' Very famous. Ask any expert and they'll tell you it's a seminal piece of American musicianship. It just slides its rhythms right through you, gentle and harsh all at the same time. You probably think this piece ends nice and easy-like. But you're wrong."

The mingled horns paled slowly and were abruptly replaced by Blair Sullivan's acrid voice. Brown pitched forward in his seat at the murderer's first words. He craned his neck toward the stereo speakers, his back rigid, his attention totally on what he was hearing.

". . . Now I will tell you the truth about little Joanie Shriver . . . Perfect little Joanie . . ." The executed man's voice was mocking, clear and resonant.

". . . Number forty," Cowart said on the tape.

And the dead man's laugh pierced the air.

The reporter and the police detective sat still, letting Sullivan's voice envelop them. When the tape hissed to its end and clicked off, the two men sat quietly, staring at each other.

"Damn," said Brown. "I knew it. Son of a bitch."

"Right," replied Cowart.

Brown rose and pounded one hand into another. He felt his insides spark with energy, as if the killer's words had electrified the air. He clenched his teeth and said, "I've got you, you bastard. I've got you."

Cowart remained slumped in his seat, watching the policeman. "Nobody's got anybody," he said quietly, sadly.

"What do you mean?" The detective looked at the tape machine. "Who else knows about this?"

"You and me."

"You didn't tell those detectives working the Monroe murders?"

"Not yet."

"You understand that you're withholding important evidence in a murder investigation. You understand that's a crime?"

"What evidence? A lying, twisted killer tells me a story. Blames another man for all sorts of things. What does that amount to? Reporters hear stuff all the time. We listen, process, discard. You tell me: evidence of what?"

"His goddamn confession. His description of the deaths of

his mother and stepfather. How he worked it all out. Dying declaration, just as he said, is admissible in a court of law.''

''He lied. He lied right, left, up, and down. I don't think, at the end, he understood what was truth and what was fiction.''

''Bullshit. That story sounds pretty goddamn real to me.''

''That's because you want it to be real. Look at it another way. Suppose I told you that in the rest of the interview, he made up things. Claimed murders he couldn't possibly have committed. Misstated all sorts of stuff. He was grandiose, egotistical, wanted to be remembered for his achievements. Hell, he almost claimed being a part of the Kennedy assassination and to know where Hoffa's body lies. Now, hearing all that stuff mixed together, wouldn't that make you wonder if he was telling you the truth about this little murder or two?''

Brown hesitated. ''No.''

Cowart stared at the detective.

''All right. Maybe.''

''And what about him and Bobby Earl? Just where does the betrayal start? Maybe he figured this was his way back at Bobby Earl. I mean, what meant what? And now he's dead. Can't ask him, unless you want to take a trip to hell.''

''I'm willing.''

''So am I.''

The detective glared over at Cowart, but then his frown dissipated and he nodded his head. ''I think I see now.''

''See what?''

''Why it's so damn important for you to believe Bobby Earl's still innocent. I see why you tore up your own place here. Tore up your nice little life a bit when you heard what Sullivan told you, huh?''

Cowart gestured, as if to say the detective was stating the obvious.

''Prize. Reputation. Future. Pretty big stakes. Maybe you'd prefer it just all go away, huh, Mr. Cowart?''

''It won't,'' he replied softly.

''No, it won't, will it? Maybe you can close your eyes to a lot, but you're still gonna see that little girl all dripping dead in the swamp, aren't you? No matter how hard you shut your eyes.''

''Correct.''

''And so you've got a debt, too, huh, Mr. Cowart?''

''It seems that way.''

''Need to make things right? Put the world back in order?''

Cowart didn't need to answer. He smiled sadly and took another long drink. He gestured Brown back to his seat. The detective slumped down but remained on the front rim of the chair, wound tight, as if ready to jump up.

"Okay," said the reporter. "You're the detective. What would you do first? Go see Bobby Earl?"

Brown considered carefully. "Maybe. Maybe not. Fox'll walk through the trap unless it's set just right and proper."

"If there's a trap to set. If he is a fox."

"Well," Brown said slowly, "Sullivan said a few things that can be checked out up in Pachoula. Maybe another talk with that old grandmother, and a look around her place. Sullivan said we missed something. Let's go see if he was telling the truth about that. Maybe we can start there, figure out what's the truth and what's not."

Cowart shook his head slowly. "That's right. Except we go back there and walk through the front door and there's eight-by-ten glossy photographs of Ferguson committing that murder sitting on the mantlepiece and it doesn't help a damn thing. . . ." He pointed his finger at Tanny Brown. "He can't be touched, not legally. You know that you won't ever make a case against him. Not ever. Not with that confession and with all the other stuff that's muddying up all this. It'll never happen in any court of law."

Cowart breathed in hard. ". . . And another thing. When we show up there, that old grandmother of his will know that something's changed. And as soon as she knows, he'll know."

Brown nodded but said harshly, "I still want the answer."

"So do I," Cowart said, before continuing. "But the Monroe case. Well, if he did it—and I'm only saying if—if he did it, you could make him on that." He paused, then corrected himself. "We could make him on that. You and me."

"And that might put things right? Put him back on Death Row, clear the slate? That what you're thinking?"

"Maybe. I hope so."

"Hope," said the detective, "is something I have never placed much faith in. Like luck and prayer. And anyway," he continued, shaking his head, "same problem. One lying man says a deal's been made. But the only corroboration of that deal is dead in Monroe County. So, you think maybe we can find some weapon on Bobby Earl? Maybe he used a credit card to buy a plane ticket and rent a car, so we can place him down there on the day of the murder? You think he let someone see him? Or maybe he shot his mouth off to some other folks? You think he was so stupid that he left prints or hair or any damn bit of forensic evidence which your dear friends in the Monroe sheriff's department will generously hand over to you with no questions asked? You don't think he learned enough the first time around, so that he did this clean?''

"I don't know. I don't know that he did it."

"If he didn't do it, then who the hell did? You think Blair Sullivan struck some other deals in prison?''

"I only know one thing. Making deals, running head games, manipulation, it was what he lived for.''

"And died for."

"That's right. Maybe that was his last deal.''

Brown relaxed in his seat. He picked up his pistol and twirled it around, stroking a finger across the blue metal. ''You stick to that, Mr. Cowart. You stick to that *objectivity*. No matter how goddamn stupid it makes you look.''

Cowart felt a sudden rush of anger. ''Not as goddamn stupid as someone beating a confession out of a murder suspect so the man gets a free ride.''

There was a brief quiet between the two men before the detective said, ''And there's that one other thing on the tape, right? Where Sullivan says 'Someone just like me . . .' '' He looked hard at the reporter. ''Didn't that make your skin crawl just a bit, Mr. Cowart? What do you suppose that means?'' The detective spoke through tightly clenched teeth. ''Don't you think that's a question we ought to answer?''

"Yes," Cowart replied, bitterness streaking the word. Silence gripped the two men again.

"All right," Cowart said. ''You're right. Let's start.'' He looked over at the policeman. ''Do we have an agreement?''

"What sort of agreement?''

"I don't know.''

Brown nodded. ''In that case, then, I suspect so,'' replied the policeman.

Both men looked at each other. Neither believed the other for an instant. Both men knew they needed to find out the truth of what happened. The problem, each realized silently to himself, was that each man needed a different truth.

"What about the Monroe detectives?'' Cowart asked.

"Let them do their job. At least for now. I need to see what happened down there for myself.''

"They'll be back. I think I'm the only thing they've got to go on.''

"Then we'll see. But I think they'll head back to the prison. That's what I'd do if I were them." He pointed to the tape. ". . . And if I didn't know about that."

The reporter nodded. "A few minutes back you were accusing me of breaking the law."

Brown rose and fixed the reporter with a single, fierce glance. Cowart glared back.

"There's likely to be a few more laws broken before we get through with all this," the policeman said quietly.

FIFTEEN
———STANDING OUT

A BURST of heat seemed to bridge the territory between the pale blues of the ocean and the sky. It wrapped them in a sticky embrace, squeezing the breath from their lungs. The two uneasy men walked slowly together, keeping their thoughts to themselves, their feet kicking up puffs of gray-white dust, crunching against the odd shells and pieces of coral that made up Tarpon Drive. Neither man thought the other an ally; only that they were both engaged in a process that required the two of them, and that it was safest together. Cowart had parked his car adjacent to the house where he'd found the bodies. Then they'd begun walking door-to-door, armed with a photograph of Ferguson appropriated from the *Journal*'s photo library.

By the third house, they'd established a routine: Tanny Brown flashed his badge, Matthew Cowart identified himself. Then they'd thrust the photo toward the inhabitants, with the single question, "Have you seen this man before?"

A young mother in a thin yellow shift, her hair drooping in blond curls around her sweat-damp forehead, had shushed her crying child, hitched the baby over to her hip, and shaken her head. A pair of teenage boys working on a dismantled outboard engine in the front of another yard had studied the picture with a devotion unseen in any schoolroom and then been equally negative. A huge, beer-gutted man, wearing oil-streaked jeans and a denim jacket with cut-off sleeves and a Harley Davidson Motorcycles patch above the breast had refused to speak with them, saying, "I ain't talking to no cops. And I ain't talking to no reporters. And I ain't seen nothing worth the telling." Then he'd slammed the door in their faces, the thin aluminum of the frame rattling in the heat.

They moved on, working the street methodically. A few folks had questions for them. "Who's this guy?" and "Why're you asking?"

Cowart realized quickly that Brown was adept at turning an inquiry into a question of his own. If someone asked him, "This got something to do with those killings down the street?" he would turn it back on the questioner, "Do you know anything about what happened?"

But this question was greeted with blank stares and shaken heads.

Brown also made a point of asking everyone if the Monroe Sheriff's Department had questioned them. They all replied that they had. They all remembered a young woman detective with a clipped, assured manner on the day the bodies were discovered. But no one had seen or heard anything unusual.

"They're all over it," Tanny Brown mumbled.

"Who?"

"Your friends from Monroe. They've done what I would've done."

Cowart nodded. He looked down at the photograph in his hand but refused to put any words to the thoughts that seemed to lurk just beyond the glare of the day.

Sweat darkened the collar of the detective's shirt. "Romantic, huh?" he grunted.

They were standing on the outside of a low, chain link fence that protected a faded aqua-colored trailer with an incongruous pink plastic flamingo attached with gray duct tape to the front door. The sun reflected harshly off the steel sides of the trailer, making the entire edifice glow. A single air-conditioning unit, hanging from a window, labored against the temperature, clanking and whirring but continuing to operate. Ten yards away, roped to a skewed pole sunk into the hard-rock ground, a mottled brown pit bull eyed the two men warily. Matthew Cowart noticed that the dog had closed its mouth tight, despite the heat which should have caused its tongue to loll out. The dog seemed alert, yet not terrifically concerned; as if it was inconceivable to the animal that anyone would question its authority over the yard or trespass within its reach.

"What do you mean?" Cowart replied.

"Police work." Brown looked over at the dog and then to the door. "Ought to shoot that animal. Ever see what one of those can do to you? Or to a kid?"

Cowart nodded. Pit bulls were a Florida mainstay. In South Florida, drug dealers used them as watchdogs. Good old boys living near Lake Okeechobee raised them in filthy, illegal farms, training them for fights. Homeowners in dozens of tract developments, terrified of break-ins, got them and then acted surprised when they tore the face off some neighbor's child. He'd written that story once, after sitting in a darkened hospital room across from a pitifully bandaged twelve-year-old whose words had been muffled by pain and the inadequate results of plastic surgery. His friend Hawkins had tried to get the dog's owner indicted for assault with a deadly weapon, but nothing had come of it.

Before they could move from the front, the door to the trailer opened and a middle-aged man stepped out, shading his eyes and staring at the two men. He wore a white T-shirt and khaki pants that hadn't seen a washing machine in months. The man was balding, with unkempt strands of hair that seemed glued to his scalp, and a pinched, florid, unshaven face. He moved toward them, ignoring the dog, which shifted about, beat its tail twice against the ground, then continued to watch.

"Y'all want somethin'?"

Tanny Brown produced his badge. "Just a question or two."

"About those old folks got their throats slit?"

"That's right."

"Other police already asked questions. Didn't know shit."

"I want to show you a picture of someone, see if you've seen him around here. Anytime in the last few weeks, or anytime at all."

The man nodded, staying a few feet back of the fence.

Cowart handed him the photograph of Ferguson. The man stared at it, then shook his head.

"Look hard. You sure?"

The man eyed Cowart with irritation. "Sure I'm sure. He some sort of suspect?"

"Just someone we're checking out," Brown said. He retrieved the picture. "Not hanging around here, or maybe driving by in a rental car?"

"No," the man said. He smiled, displaying a mouth of brown teeth and gaps. "Ain't seen nobody hanging around. Nobody casing the place. Nobody in no rental car. And for damn sure, you're the only Negro I seen around here, ever.''

The man spit, laughed sarcastically and added, "He looks like you. Negro.''

He pronounced the word *knee-grow*, elongating the two syllables into a harsh singsong, imbuing the word with mockery, turning it into an epithet.

Then the man turned, grinning, and gave a little whistle to the dog, who rose instantly, back hairs bristling, teeth bared. Cowart took a step back involuntarily, realizing that the man probably spent more time, effort, and money on maintaining the dog's mouth than his own. The reporter retreated another step before noticing that the detective hadn't budged. After a moment punctuated only by the deep-throated continual growling of the dog, the policeman stepped back and silently moved down the street. Cowart had to hurry to keep pace.

Brown headed back toward the reporter's car. "Let's go," he said.

"There are a few other houses.''

"Let's go," Brown repeated. He stopped and gestured broadly at the decrepit homes and trailers. "The bastard was right.''

"What do you mean?''

"A black man driving down this street in the middle of the day would stand out like a goddamn Fourth of July rocket. Especially a young black man. If Ferguson had been here, he'd have had to sneak in under cover of midnight. He might have done that, maybe. But that's a big risk, you know.''

"Where's the risk at night? Nobody'd see him.''

The policeman leaned up against the side of the car. "Come on, Cowart, think about it. You've got an address and a job. A killing job. What you've got to do is come to some place you've never been. Find a house you've never seen before. Break in and kill two people you don't know, and then get out, without leaving any evidence behind and without attracting any attention. Big risk. Take a lot of luck. No, you want to do some homework first. Got to see where you're going, what you're up against. And how's he gonna do that without being seen? None of these folks go anywhere. Hell, half of them are retirees sitting outside no matter how damn hot the sun gets, and the other half never held a job more'n maybe five or ten minutes. They got nothing much to do except watch.''

Cowart shook his head. "Happens all the time," he replied. "What do you mean?''

"I mean, it happens. Suppose Sullivan gave him the layout. All the information he needed."

Brown paused. "Maybe," he said. "But I'd think that after spending three years on the Row, Ferguson might be wary of doing something that might put him back there, if he wasn't real careful."

That made sense to the reporter. Still, he was reluctant to give up on the idea. "Why does he have to come last week? Maybe he came last year. First thing, after getting out of prison. Soon as the hubbub dies down and his face has been out of the newspapers and television for a couple of weeks. Comes down, innocent as all get-out, walks all around the place. He knows they're an old couple. Not going to change a damn thing. Gets a feel for the location, what he's going to have to do. Maybe knocks on the door, tries to sell them some encyclopedias or a magazine subscription. Gets himself inside just long enough to get a good look around before they kick him out. Then walks away. It makes no difference who sees him because he knows they're gonna forget by the time he comes back."

Brown nodded his head, eyeing Cowart. "Not bad, for a reporter," he said. "Maybe. It's something to think about." He allowed a small grin to rub the edges of his lips before adding, "But, of course, that isn't what you want to know, is it? You want to know how he couldn't do it. Not how he could, right?"

Cowart opened his mouth to reply but then stopped.

"And, here's another little idea, Cowart," Brown continued. "You'll like this one 'cause it makes your man seem innocent. Suppose, just for a minute, that Blair Sullivan did arrange, like he said, for these killings to happen—but not with Bobby Earl. Somebody totally different. And what he wanted to guarantee is that nobody would look under the right stone for the slime that he made those arrangements with. How better could he guarantee that than by telling you that Mr. Innocent was the killer? He knew that sooner or later someone would be walking up and down this street with a picture of Bobby Earl in hand. And if Bobby Earl's name gets into the paper again, that'd give just about anybody time enough to hide what they did. A little bit of extra confusion."

The detective paused. "You know how important it is to make a murder case fast, Cowart? Before time just worries away at facts and evidence until there's nothing left?"

"I know it's important to move rapidly. That's what you did in Pachoula and look what the hell happened."

Brown scowled.

Cowart felt the sweat under his arms run down, tickling his ribs. "Anything's possible," he replied.

"That's right."

Brown straightened up and rubbed a hand across his forehead, as if trying to shift about the thoughts that were contained within. He sighed deeply. "I want to see the murder site," he said. He started down the street, striding swiftly, as if by moving about quickly he could somehow elude the heat that had gathered about them.

When they reached the street outside number thirteen, the policeman hesitated, turning again to Cowart. "Well, at least he had that going for him."

"What?"

"Look at the house, Cowart. It's a real good place to kill somebody."

He swept his arm about. "Set back from the street. No real close neighbors. See the way the house is angled? At night there's no way anybody'd see anything going on inside unless they just happened to be standing right out front. And close, too. You think that Mister Rotten Teeth down there walks that pit bull around at night? No way. I'd bet a week's pay that once the sun goes down, and everybody's had a chance to have a drink or two, the TV sets are on and the only people out on this street are those teenagers. Everybody else is either drunk, watching reruns of *Dallas*, or busy praying for the day of judgment. I guess they didn't know it was closer than they thought."

Cowart let his eyes flow about the exterior of the house. He envisioned the place at night and thought Brown correct. There would be an occasional outburst as some couple fought. That might mingle with the sounds of television sets playing too loudly. Broken bottle, drunk arguments, maybe a dog barking. And, even if someone did hear a car leaving fast, they'd probably assume it was some kids fighting the ubiquitous boredom with recklessness.

"A real good killing place," Brown said.

There was a yellow police tape surrounding the house. The detective slipped underneath it. Cowart followed him around the back.

"In there," Brown said, pointing at the broken rear door.

"It's sealed."

"Screw it." He tugged the door open with a single pull, breaking the yellow tape.

Cowart hesitated, then stepped inside the house behind him.

The death smell lingered in the kitchen, mingling with the heat, giving the room a tomblike oppressiveness. There were signs of police processing throughout the small space; fingerprint dust streaked the table and chairs. Chalk notes and arrows showed locations. Each of the blood splotches remained on the floor, though samples had clearly been scraped from them. Cowart watched as Brown absorbed and assessed each sign.

Tanny Brown went through an internal checklist. In his mind's eye, first he saw the forensic teams steadily working the scene, the busywork of death. He knelt down next to one of the swatches of blood that had turned almost black against the light linoleum of the floor. He reached out and rubbed a finger against it, feeling the slick, brittle consistency of dried blood. When he rose, he pictured the old man and woman, gagged and bound, awaiting death. For an instant he wondered how many times they had sat in the same chairs and shared breakfast or dinner, or discussed the Bible, or did whatever they did that was routine. It was one of the awful things about homicide work; that the banal, humdrum world in which most folks lived was suddenly rendered evil. That the places people thought safe were abruptly made deadly. In the war, of all the wounds he'd tended, he'd hated those caused by mines the most: toe-poppers, Bouncing Bettys, and worse. It was not so much the savagery of the damage the mines did as the manner in which they did it. You put your shoe down on the ground, took a single step, and were betrayed. If you were lucky, you only lost a foot. Did these people know they were living on a minefield? he wondered. He turned toward Cowart.

At least he understands that, he thought. Even the ground is unsafe. Brown left the kitchen, leaving Cowart standing next to the dying spot.

He walked quickly through the small house, inventorying the lives that had festered there. Barren, he thought, clinging to Jesus and waiting for Mr. Death to come calling. They probably thought they were being stalked by old age, when it was something altogether different. He stopped in front of a small closet in the bedroom, marveling at the row of shoes and slippers that were lined up across the floor, like a regiment on parade. His father would do the same; the elderly like everything in its place. A pile of knitting, balls of yarn, and long silver needles were gathered in a basket in the corner. That surprised him: What would you knit down here? A sweater? Ridiculous. He saw a pair of small plaster figurines on the bureau, two bluebirds, throats wide open as if singing. *You saw*, he mentally spoke to the birds. *Who came here?* Then he shook his head at the mockery of it all. His eyes kept sweeping the room. A room of little comfort, he thought. *Who killed you?* he asked himself. Then he moved back into the kitchen, where he found Cowart standing, staring at the bloodstained floor. He turned.

"Learn anything?" Cowart asked.

"Yes."

"What's that?" Cowart asked, surprised yet eager.

"I learned that I'd like to die someplace lonely and private, so's folks don't come and inspect all my things," Tanny Brown replied.

Cowart glanced down at a chalk notation on the floor. It said *Nightclothes*.

"What's that?" Brown asked.

"The old woman was naked. Her clothes were folded up nice and neat, just as if she was planning to put them away in a drawer instead of getting killed."

Brown straightened up abruptly. "Folded carefully?"

Cowart nodded.

The policeman eyed the reporter. "You remember where we found Joanie Shriver?"

"Yes." Cowart pictured the clearing at the edge of the swamp. He realized he was being asked a question but wasn't certain what it was. He walked around the clearing in his mind; remembering the splotch of blood where the little girl had been killed, the way the shafts of sun had torn through the canopy of trees and vines. He walked to the edge of the black, still swamp water and stared down beneath the tangled roots to where Joanie Shriver's body was submerged, then he followed it back to where the searchers had taken her, until finally he remembered what they'd found at the edge of the killing place: her clothes.

Folded carefully.

It had been the sort of detail that had occupied a prominent spot in his original story, a small, little irony that had made the moment more real in newspaper prose; the implication being that the little girl's killer had an odd neat streak within him, and that rendered him somehow more terrifying and more tangible all at once.

He turned toward the detective. "That says something."

Brown, filled with a sudden fury, allowed rage to reverberate within him for a moment before clamping down hard on it and shutting it away. "It might," he struggled to say. "I'd like it to say something."

Cowart gestured toward the house. "Is there anything else that suggests that . . ."

"No. Nothing. Maybe something that says who got killed but nothing that says who did the killing. Excepting that little detail."

He looked over at Cowart before continuing. "Although you probably still want to think of it as a coincidence."

Then he stepped over the bloodstains on the floor and headed out, without looking back, aware that the sunshine outside the small house illuminated nothing he thought important.

The two men walked quietly away from the murder scene, back to their car.

"Do you have a professional opinion?" Cowart asked.

"Yes."

"You feel like sharing it?"

The policeman hesitated before replying. "You know, Cowart, you go to some crime scenes and you can still feel all the emotions, right there in the room. Anger, hatred, panic, fear, whatever, but they're all hanging around, like smells. But in there, what was there? Just someone doing a job, like you or me or the postman that was here when you found the damn bodies. Whoever went in there and killed those old folks knew about one thing, for sure. Killing. He wasn't scared. And he wasn't greedy. All he was concerned about was one thing. And that's what happened, isn't it?"

Cowart nodded.

Brown returned to the driver's side of the car and opened the door. But before sliding behind the wheel, he looked across the roof toward Cowart.

"But did I see anything in there that told me for sure that Ferguson did that crime?" He shook his head. ". . . Except whoever did that crime took time to fold some clothes neatly and then sure seemed mighty comfortable and familiar with a knife. And I know one man who likes knives, don't I?"

They drove out of the Upper Keys, leaving Monroe County and reentering Dade, which gave Cowart a sense of being on familiar ground. They passed a huge sign that directed tourists toward Shark Valley and the Everglades National Park, continuing toward Miami, until Brown suggested they stop for something to eat. The detective lieutenant vetoed several fast-food outlets, until they reached the Perrine–Homestead area. Then he turned the car off the highway and headed down a series of meager streets strewn with bumps and potholes. Cowart looked at the houses they swept past: small, square, single-story cinder-block homes with open jalousie windows like razor slashes in front and flat red-tile roofs adorned with large television antennas. The front lawns were all brown dirt streaked with an occasional swatch of green crabgrass. More than a few had cars up on blocks and auto parts strewn about behind chain link fences. The few children he saw playing outdoors were black.

"You ever been in this part of your county, Cowart?"

"Sure," the reporter replied.

"Covering crimes?"

"That's right."

"You wouldn't come out here to cover stories about kids who get college scholarships or parents that work two jobs and raise their children right."

"We'd come out for those stories."

"But not often, I'll bet."

"No, that's true."

The policeman's eyes covered the community rapidly. "You know, there are a hundred places like this in Florida. Maybe a thousand."

"Like what?"

"Places that scratch at the edges both of poverty and stability. Not even lucky enough to be categorized as lower middle class. Black communities which haven't been allowed to flourish or fail, just allowed to exist. All the houses are two-income, you know, only both incomes are pretty small. The guy who works in the county refuse center and his wife who's an in-home nurse. This is where they come to get started on the American dream, you see. Home ownership. Local schools. They feel comfortable here. It's not like they're willing to blaze any trails. They just want to get along and go along and maybe make things a bit better. Got a black mayor. Got a black city council. Police chief's probably black and so's the dozen guys he's got working for him."

"How do you know?"

"I get offers, you see. Career cop. Head of homicide for the Major Crimes Unit of a county force. In law enforcement in the state I may not be well known, but at least I'm known, if you follow. So I get around the state a bit. Especially to little places like Perrine."

They continued to drive through the residential district for several blocks. Cowart thought the land seemed harsh and unfertile. Almost everything grows in South Florida. Leave a spot of ground untended and the next thing you know it's covered with vines and ferns and greenery. But not here. There was a dustiness to the earth that seemed to belong in some other location, Arizona or New Mexico or some place in the Southwest. Some place closer to the desert than the swamp. Brown steered the car onto a wide boulevard and eventually pulled the car to a stop. They were in front of a small strip shopping center. At one end was a huge warehouse food chain, and at the other a cavernous discount toy store. In between were two dozen smaller businesses, including a single restaurant.

"There we go," the policeman said. "At least the food'll be fresh and not cooked according to some formula devised in some corporate headquarters."

"So, you've been here before?"

"No, I've just been in dozens of places like it. After a while, you get so you can recognize the type." He smiled. "That's what being a cop is all about, remember?"

Cowart stared down at the toy store at the end of the shopping mall.

"I was here once. A man kidnapped a woman and child coming out of the store. Just snatched them at random as they walked through the door. Drove them around for half the day, periodically stopping to molest the woman. A state trooper heading home after the day shift finally stopped the car when he thought something was suspicious. Saved her life. And the kid's. Shot the guy when he pulled a knife. One shot. Right through the heart. Lucky shot."

Brown paused and followed Cowart's eyes toward the toy store.

"They were buying party favors for the kid's second birthday," the reporter said. "Red and blue balloons and little conical white hats with clowns on them. They still had the bag when they were rescued."

He remembered seeing the bag clutched tightly in the woman's free hand. The other held her child, as they were gently deposited in the back of an ambulance. A blanket had been draped around them, though it had been May and the heat was oppressive. A crime like that has a frost all its own.

"Why'd the trooper stop them?" Brown asked.

"He said because the driver was acting suspiciously. Weaving. Trying to avoid being looked at."

"What page did your story go on?"

Cowart hesitated, then replied, "Front page. Below the fold."

The detective nodded. "I know why the trooper stopped the car." He spoke quietly. "White woman. Black man. Right?"

Cowart knew the answer, but was slow to say yes. "Why do you want to know?"

"Come on, Cowart. You were once quick with the statistics to me, remember? Wanted to know if I knew the FBI stats on black-on-white crime. Well, I do know them. And I know how rare that sort of crime is. And I also know that's what gets your goddamn story on the front page instead of being cut to six paragraphs in the middle of the B-section roundup. Because if it had been black-on-black crime, that's where it would have landed, right?"

He wanted to disagree, but could not. "Probably."

The policeman snorted. " 'Probably' is a real safe answer, Cowart." Brown gestured widely with his arm. "You think the city editor would have sent one of the stars from downtown all the way out here if he wasn't damn sure it was a front-page story? Nah, he'd have let some stringer or some suburban reporter file those six paragraphs."

Brown turned toward the restaurant door, speaking as he started to cross the parking lot. "You want to know something, Cowart? You want to know why this is a tough place to live? It's because everyone knows how close they are to the ghetto. I don't mean in miles. What's Liberty City, maybe thirty, forty miles away from here, right? No, it's the closeness of fear. They know they don't get the same dollars, the same programs, the same schools, the same any damn thing. So they have to cling to that dream of lower-middle-class status just like it was some life preserver leaking air. They all know what it's like in the ghetto, it's like it sucks away at them, trying to pull them back all the time. All those get-up-early-and-be-on-time-every-morning jobs, all those paychecks that get cashed as soon as they get cut, those little hot houses, are all that keeps it away."

"What about in North Florida? Pachoula?"

"Pretty much the same. Only up there, the fear is that the Old South—you know, the backwoods, no plumbing, tar paper shack poverty—will reach out and snag you once again."

"Isn't that what Ferguson came from? From both?"

The detective nodded. "But he rose up and made it out."

"Like you."

Brown stopped and turned toward Cowart. "Like me," he said with a low edge of anger in his voice. "But I don't welcome that comparison, Mr. Cowart."

The two entered the restaurant.

It was well past the lunch hour and before the evening rush, so they had the place to themselves. They sat in a booth alongside a window overlooking the parking lot. A waitress in a tight white outfit that exaggerated her ample bosom, and a gum-chewing scowl that indicated that any suggestive remarks would be greeted with little enthusiasm, took their order and passed it through a window to a solitary cook in the back. Within seconds they could hear the sizzle of hamburgers frying, and seconds later the scent hit them.

They ate in silence. When they'd finished, Brown ordered a slice of key lime pie with his coffee. He took one bite, then speared another, this time gesturing with the fork toward Cowart.

"Hey, homemade, Cowart. You ought to try a piece. Can't get this up in Pachoula. At least, not like this."

The reporter shook his head.

"Hell, Cowart, I bet you're the type that likes to stop at salad bars for lunch. Keep that lean, ascetic look by munching on rabbit food."

Cowart shrugged in admission.

"Probably drink that shitty bottled water from France, too."

As the detective was speaking, Cowart watched as the waitress moved behind him, into another booth. She had a razor-scraper in her hand, and she bent over to remove something from the window. There was a momentary scratching sound as she cleaned tape from glass. Then she straightened up, putting a small poster under her arm. Cowart caught a glimpse of a young face. The waitress was about to turn away when, for no reason that he could immediately discern, he gestured for her.

She approached the table. "Y'all gonna try that pie, too?" she asked.

"No," he answered. "I was just curious about that poster." He pointed at the paper she'd folded under her arm.

"This?" she said. She handed it over to him, and he spread it out on the table in front of him.

In the center of the poster was a picture of a young black girl, smiling, wearing pigtails. Underneath the picture, in large block letters, was the word MISSING. This was followed by a message in smaller lettering: DAWN PERRY, AGE 12, FIVE FEET TWO INCHES, 105 POUNDS, DISAPPEARED THE AFTERNOON 8/12/90, LAST SEEN WEARING BLUE SHORTS, WHITE T-SHIRT AND SNEAKERS, CARRYING BOOK BAG. ANYONE WITH ANY KNOWLEDGE OF HER WHEREABOUTS CALL 555-1212 AND ASK FOR DETECTIVE HOWARD. This message was completed with a large print: REWARD.

Cowart looked up at the waitress. "What happened?"

The waitress shrugged as if to say that giving information wasn't part of her job. "I don't know. Little girl. One day's she's there. The next, she's not."

"Why are you taking the sign down?"

"Been a long time, mister. Months and months. Ain't nobody found that girl by now, I don't suspect this sign's gonna make any difference. And anyway, my boss asked me to yesterday, and I forgot until just now."

Cowart saw that Brown had started examining the poster. He looked up. "Police ever come up with anything?"

"Not that I'd know. Y'all want something else?"

"Just a check," Brown replied. He smiled, creased the flyer and slid it onto the table between them. "I'll take care of this for you," he said.

The waitress walked away to make their change.

"Makes you wonder, doesn't it?" Brown said. "You get into the right frame of mind, Cowart, and all sorts of terrible things just pop right in, don't they?"

He didn't reply, so the detective continued. "I mean, you hang close to death enough and unusual things just jump up, like they were so normal and routine you'd ignore them if you weren't thinking so hard about how and when people kill each other."

Cowart nodded.

Brown leaned back after stabbing at the last few crumbs of pie on his plate. "I told you the food would be fresh," he said. Then he pushed forward abruptly, closing the distance between them.

"Steals your appetite away, doesn't it, Cowart? A little coincidence for dessert, huh?"

He tapped the folded flyer. "I mean, it probably doesn't amount to anything, right? Just another little girl that disappeared one day. And it probably doesn't fit in, time and opportunity and all that. But it is interesting, isn't it? That a little girl disappears not too far from the highway leading down to the Keys. I wonder if it was from in front of a school.''

Cowart interrupted. "Fifty miles from Tarpon Drive.''

The detective nodded.

"And absolutely nothing that indicates anything about the cases that happen to concern us.''

"So," Brown said slowly. "Why'd you want to see it, when the waitress was pulling it down?''

The policeman crumpled up the flyer into a ball and stuck it into his pocket as he pushed back in his seat and rose to leave the restaurant.

The two men stopped on the sidewalk outside. Cowart looked down toward the toy store at the end of the mall and saw that a blue-shirted man was sitting outside the door, carrying a truncheon at his side. Security, he realized. He wondered why he hadn't noticed the man before. He guessed that he'd been added after the kidnapping, as if the guard's presence would prevent another lightning strike from occurring in the same spot. He remembered that even with the police gathered outside, people had continued to walk into the store, and that a steady stream of adults and children, all carrying large plastic bags filled with various toys, had continued to emerge, ignoring the savagery that had started on the sidewalk.

He turned toward Brown. "So, what now? We've been to the Keys and all we've got are more questions. Where now? Why don't we go see Ferguson?''

The detective shook his head. "No, first let's go back to Pachoula.''

"Why?''

"Well, it would be nice to know that Sullivan was telling you the truth about one thing at least, right?''

The two men separated warily shortly after returning to Miami and thick black night had encased them. The day's heat seemed to linger in the air, giving the dark a weight and substance. Cowart dropped Brown outside the downtown Holiday Inn, where he'd obtained a room. The hotel was across from the county criminal courts building, about halfway between the Orange Bowl and the start of Liberty City, in a sort of urban no-man's-land defined by hospitals, office buildings, jails, and the slums' ubiquitous creep into their midst.

Once inside his room, Brown tore off his jacket and kicked

off his shoes. Then he sat on the edge of the bed and dialed a telephone number.

"Dade County Sheriff. South Station."

"I want to speak with Detective Howard."

He heard the line being transferred and a moment or two later a clipped, official-sounding man's voice came over the line. "This is Detective Howard. Can I help you?"

"Maybe. This is Detective Lieutenant Brown, Escambia County . . ."

"How yah doing, Lieutenant? What can I do for you?" The man's voice instantly lost its military tone, replaced with a simple jocularity.

"Ahh," Brown said, sliding instantly into the same tones, "probably nothing more than a wild goose chase. And it sounds pretty crazy, but I'd appreciate a little information about this young kid, a Dawn Perry, disappeared a few months back . . ."

"Yeah, heading home from the civic center. Christ, what a damn mess . . ."

"What exactly happened?"

"You got some sort of line on her?" the detective asked abruptly.

"No," Brown replied. "To be honest, I just saw the flyer and something in it reminded me of a case I once worked. Just thought, you know, I'd check it out."

"Hell," the detective answered. "Too bad. For a minute I got hopeful. You know how it is."

"So, can you fill me in a bit?"

"Sure. Not that much to tell. Little girl, not an enemy in the whole wide world, goes off to her swim class at the civic center one afternoon. School's out, you know, so they run all sorts of programs down there for the kids. Last seen by a couple of her friends walking toward her home."

"Anyone see what happened?"

"No. One old lady, lives about midway down the street—you know, it's all old houses with air conditioners blasting away in every window, makes a damn racket. Anyway, this one old gal can't afford to run the electrics, you know, not so much, so's she sitting in her kitchen next to a fan, and she hears a little scream and then a car pulling away real fast, but by the time she can get out there, the car's already two blocks away. White car. American make. That's all. No plate, no description. Book bag with her swimsuit left on the street. Old lady was pretty sharp, give her that. Calls in what she sees. But by the time a patrol car finds her house, listens to her story, and gets out a BOLO, well, things are pretty much history. You know how many white cars there are in Dade County?''

"A lot."

"That's right. Anyway, we work the case best we can with what we got. Hell, we could only get one of the television stations to run the girl's picture that night. Maybe she wasn't cute enough, I don't know . . .''

". . . Or the wrong color."

"Well, you said it. I don't know how those bastards make up their minds what's news anyway. After we got the flyers out, we took a couple of dozen calls saying she'd been spotted here, there, all over. But none were good, you know. We checked out her family real good, wondered if maybe she'd been snatched by someone she knew, but, hell, the Perrys were good folks. He's a clerk for DMV, she works in an elementary school cafeteria. No problems at home. Three other kids. What the hell could we do? I got a hundred other files on my desk. Assaults. B and E. Armed robbery. I even got a couple of cases I can make. Got to spend time valuably, you know. Probably the same for you. So, it just turned into one of those cases where you gotta wait for someone to find her body, and then Homicide will take it over. But that maybe never happens. We're so damn close to the edge of the Everglades down here. You can get rid of someone pretty damn fast. Usually it's drug dealers. Like to just drive down some old deserted access road, dump some body out in the 'Glades. Let that old swamp water take care of hiding their work. Easy as one-two-three. But same technique works for just about anybody, if you catch my drift.''

"Anybody."

"Anybody who likes little girls. And doesn't want them to tell anybody what happened to 'em." The detective paused. "Actually, I'm kinda surprised we don't work a hundred cases like this one. If you get that kid in your car without being made, well, hell, ain't nothing you can't get away with."

"But you didn't . . .''

"Nah, we didn't have any others like this. I checked with Monroe and Broward, but they didn't have anything, either. I ran a sex offender profile through the computer and got a couple of names. We even went and rousted a couple of the creeps, but both were either out of town or at work when Dawn disappeared. By that time it was already a couple of days old, you know . . .''

"And?"

"And nothing. Nada. Zilch. No evidence of anything, except a little girl is long gone. So, tell me about your case. Ring any bells?"

Brown thought hard, considering what to respond. "Not really. Ours was a white girl coming out of school. Old case. Had a suspect, but couldn't make him. Almost."

"Ahh, too bad. Thought maybe you had something that might help us."

Brown thanked the detective and hung up the telephone. His thoughts drove him to his feet. He walked to the window and stared out into the darkness. From his room, he could see up onto the major east-west highway that cut into the center of Miami, and then led away, toward the thick interior of the state, past the suburban developments, the airport, the manufacturing plants and malls, past the fringe communities that hung on the backside of the city, toward the state's swampy core. The Everglades gives way to Big Cypress. There's Loxahatchee and Corkscrew Swamp and the Withlacoochee River and the Ocala, Osceola and Apalachicola state forests. In Florida, no one is ever far from some nowhere, hidden, dark place. For a few moments he watched the traffic flee through his line of sight, headlights like tracer rounds in the darkness. He placed a hand to his forehead, reaching as if to hide his vision for an instant, then stopped. He told himself, it's just another little girl that disappeared. This one happened in the big city and it got swallowed up amidst all the other routine terrors. One instant she's there, the next she's not, just like she never existed at all, except in the minds of a few grieving folks left with nightmares forever. He shook his head, insisting to himself that he was becoming paranoid. Another little girl. Joanie Shriver. There have been others since. Dawn Perry. There was probably one yesterday. Probably one tomorrow. Gone, just like that. An elementary school. A civic center. The lights beyond his window continued to soar through the night.

There was only one other person in *The Miami Journal* library when Cowart arrived there. She was a young woman, an assistant with a shy, diffident manner that made it difficult to speak to her directly, since she kept her head down, as if the words she spoke in reply were somehow embarrassing. She quietly helped Cowart get set up on one of the computer terminals and left him alone when he punched in *Dawn Perry*.

The word *Searching* appeared in a corner of the screen, followed rapidly by the words *Two Entries.*

He called them up. The first was only four paragraphs long and had run in a police blotter roundup well inside a zoned insert section that went to homes in the southern part of the county. No story had appeared in the main paper. The headline was: POLICE REPORT GIRL, 12, MISSING. The story merely informed him that Dawn Perry had failed to return home after a swimming class at a local civic center. The second library entry was: PO-LICE SAY NO LEADS IN MISSING GIRL CASE. It was a little longer than the first, repeating all the details that had previously run. The headline summed up all the new information in the story.

Cowart ordered the computer to print out both entries, which only took a few moments. He didn't know what to think. He had learned little more than what the waitress had told him.

He stood up. Tanny Brown was right, he told himself. You are going crazy.

He stared around the room. A number of reporters were working at various terminals, all concentrating hard on the green glowing computer screens. He had managed to slip back into the library without being seen by anyone on the night city desk, for which he was grateful. He didn't want to have to explain to anyone what he was doing. For a moment, he watched the reporters at work. It was the time of night when people wanted to head home, and the words that would fill the next day's paper got shorter, punchier, driven at least in part by fatigue. He could feel the same exhaustion starting to pour over him. He looked down at the two sheets of paper in his hand, the printout of the two entries documenting the disappearance of one Dawn Perry. Age twelve. Sets off one hot August afternoon for a swim at the local pool. Never comes home. Probably dead for months, he told himself. Old news.

He took a step away from the computer terminal, then thought of one other thing, a wild shot. He went back to the computer and punched in the name *Robert Earl Ferguson.*

The computer blipped and within a moment returned with the words *Twenty-four Entries.* Cowart sat back down at his seat and typed in: *Directory.* Again, the library computer came up with a list. Each entry was dated, and its approximate length given. Cowart scanned the roster of stories, recognizing each one. There was the original story and the follow-up pieces, the sidebars, and then the stories following the release, and finally the most recent, the stories he'd written after Blair Sullivan's

execution. He scanned the list a second time, and this time
noticed an entry from the previous August. He looked at the
date and recognized it as the time he'd taken his own daughter
to Disney World on vacation. It was a month after Ferguson had
been released, in the time before his case had been thrown out
of court. It was also four days before Dawn Perry had stepped
out of the world. It was measured in the listing: *2.3 inches. A
brief.* He called it up on the screen.

The entry was from a Religion page roundup. This was the
weekly listing of sermons and speeches given at churches
throughout Dade County the following day. In the midst of the
group was the item: FORMER DEATH ROW INMATE TO SPEAK.

Cowart read:

. . . Robert Earl Ferguson, recently released Florida Death
Row inmate unjustly accused of an Escambia County murder,
will speak on his experiences and how his religious devotion
has sustained him through the criminal justice system at the
New Hope Baptist Church, Sunday, 11 A.M.

The church was in Perrine.

SIXTEEN
THE YOUNG
==============DETECTIVE

DETECTIVE Andrea Shaeffer greeted the dawn from her desk.

She had tried sleep, only to find it elusive, then fitful. Rising in the compressed black of the early morning, she had discarded an awful dream of blood and torn throats, dressed, then driven to the Monroe County Sheriff's Department homicide substation in Key Largo. From where she sat in the second-floor offices, she could stare through a window and see a pinkish ridge of light painted on the edge of the night. She imagined the slow disintegration of the darkness out on the Gulf Stream, where the razor-sharpness of morning seemed to carve shapes onto the tossing waves and finally, with a great slash, cut the horizon free from the ocean.

For a moment she wished she were out on her stepfather's fishing boat, rigging hooks in the near-black, her legs spread against the bounce and shock of the swells, her hands, slippery from handling bait, rapidly twisting wire leaders and tying knots in monofilament. The fishing would be good today. There would be big thunderheads lurking far out over the water and the heat would stir up narrow waterspouts that would show even blacker and more terrifying against the sky. But the fish would rise toward the surface, hungry, anticipating the storm, eager to feed. Dance around on the edges of the gathering winds and keep the baits moving, she thought. Fast baits, for kings and wahoos and especially billfish. Something that scratches and slaps at the

waves, furrowing through the dark Gulf Stream waters, irresist-
ible to the big fish searching for sustenance.

That was what I always liked about fishing, she thought: not
the fight against the hook and line, no matter how spectacular;
nor the last impetuous panic at boatside; nor the back-slapping
accomplishment or the beery congratulations. What I liked was
the hunt. Her eyes stared through the homicide office window
while her mind churned over what she knew and what she didn't
know. When the light finally seemed to have succeeded in its
daily battle, she turned away, back to the spread of papers that
were strewn about her desk.

She glanced at the summary report she'd prepared after questioning the neighbors on Tarpon Drive. No one had seen or
heard anything of note. Then she fingered the report from the
medical examiner's office. Proximate cause of death in both subjects was the same: abrupt severing of the right carotid artery
leading to sudden massive loss of blood. *He was left-handed,*
she thought. *Stood behind them and drew the blade across their
throats.* Skin around the wounds was only mildly frayed. *A
straightedge razor, maybe a carbon steel hunting knife. Something real sharp.* Neither victim showed any signs of significant
postmortem injury. *He killed them and left.* Premortem injuries
included bruising around each victim's arms, which was to be
expected. The killer had tied them savagely, the rope cutting
into the skin. A strip of duct tape had gagged them. The male
victim had a contusion on his forehead, a split lip, and a fractured pair of ribs. The knuckles on his right hand were skinned
with trace residue of paint, and the chair legs had scratched the
linoleum kitchen floor. *At least he fought, if only for an instant.
He must have been second, jamming his hands against the frame
of his chair as he struggled, fighting to get free until he was
slammed across the chest and in the head.* There was no sign of
sexual trauma to the woman, although she had been found naked. *Humiliation.* Shaeffer remembered seeing the old woman's
nightclothes folded neatly in the kitchen corner. Folded carefully. By whom? Victim or killer? Fingernail scrapings were
negative. Both victims had been body-printed at the morgue,
but without success.

Shaeffer tossed the papers onto the desktop. No help, she
thought. At least no obvious help.

She picked up the crime-scene preliminaries, struck with the
language of the documents she was reading. Death reduced to
the most clipped, unevocative terms. Things measured, weighed,

photographed, and assessed. The rope that had been used to bind the elderly couple was quarter-inch nylon clothesline, available in any hardware store or supermarket. Two pieces, one measuring forty-one inches, the other thirty-nine and one-half, had been cut from a twelve-foot length discovered by the back door. The killer had made a slipknot, looped that over his victims' wrists, then doubled and tripled it, ending with a simple square knot to hold it all together.

An ordinary, nondistinctive knot, temporary, improvised at the scene. Strong enough for the moment of killing but one that, given time, could have been worked loose. That suggested something to her: not a local, someone from somewhere else. Keys folks for the most part knew their knots; they'd have tied something sturdier, nautical.

She nodded. Middle of the night. He broke in. Subdued them, tied them, gagged them. They thought they were going to be robbed and acquiescence would save their lives. No chance. He simply killed them. Maximum terror. Quick. Efficient. No extra time. A silent knife. No gunshot to arouse nosy neighbors. No robbery. No rape. No slamming door, race-away panic.

A killer who arrives, murders, and exits, pausing only to open a Bible on the table between his victims, unseen, unheard by everyone except his victims. She thought, All murders leave a message. The drug dealer's body found decomposing in the mangroves with a single gunshot wound to the back of his head, gold watch and diamond jewelry still dangling from his wrists, sends one sort of message. The young woman who thinks it's okay just this once to hitchhike home from the restaurant where she waits on tables and ends up three counties away, naked, dead, and violated, sends another. The old man in the trailer who finally tires of tending his wife's degenerative cancer and shoots her and then himself and dies clutching a fifty-five-year-old wedding album is telling a different story.

She looked down at the crime-scene photos. The glossy eight-by-ten pictures summoned up her memory of the oppressive heat in the death room and the nauseating smell of the bodies. It always made it worse when nature had had time to work on a murder scene; any residual dignity left over from their lives had dissipated swiftly in the soaring temperatures. It also played havoc with the investigative process. She had been taught that every minute that passed after a homicide made a successful resolution less likely. Old, cold cases that get solved get headlines. But for every one that results in an indictment, a hundred remain behind, each a tangled knot of suppositions.

Two old people who helped bring into the world and deform a mass murderer are themselves murdered. What the hell sort of crime is that?

Revenge. Maybe justice. Possibly a perverse combination of the two.

She continued looking through the crime-scene reports. There were two partial footprints outlined in blood, lifted from the linoleum floor. The chain tread of the soles had been identified as coming from a pair of hightop Reebok basketball shoes, sized between nine and eleven. The soles were of a style manufactured within the past six months. Some cloth fibers had been uncovered sticking to the swatch of blood that had littered the old man's chest. They were of a cotton-polyester blend commonly associated with sweat clothes. Entry to the house had been accomplished through the rear door. Old, rotting wood had torn apart at the first touch of a steel screwdriver or chisel. She shook her head. This was commonplace in the Keys. The sun, wind, and salt air destroyed door frames, a fact with which every two-bit burglar frequenting the hundred and sixty miles between Miami and Key West was well familiar.

But no two-bit burglar had performed this crime.

She grabbed a pen and made some notes to herself: Canvas the hardware stores, see if anyone purchased a knife, rope, and screwdriver or small crowbar. Talk to all the neighbors again, see if anyone saw a strange car. Check the local hotels. Did he bring the Bible with him? Check the bookstores.

She did not hold out much hope for any of this.

She continued: Check the crime lab with samples of the skin where the throats were sliced. Perhaps a spectrographic examination would show some metal fragments that might tell her something about the murder weapon. This was important. She ordered her thoughts with a military precision: If a killer leaves nothing of evidentiary value, no part of himself, like semen or fingerprints or hair, then to place him in that room, one must find what he took with him—the murder weapon, blood residue on his shoes or clothes, some item from the house. Something.

Shaeffer rubbed her eyes for an instant, letting her thoughts turn toward Cowart. What is he hiding? she asked herself. Some piece of the crime that means something to him. But what?

She drew a portrait of the reporter in her head, sketching in the look in his eyes, the tone of his voice. She did not know much about reporters, but she knew that they generally wanted to appear to know more than they did, to create the illusion that they were sharing information rather than simply seducing it. Cowart did not fit this profile. After their initial confrontation at the crime scene, he had not asked her a single question about the murders on Tarpon Drive. Instead, he had done his worldly best to avoid being questioned.

What does that tell you? That he already has the answers.

But why would he hide them from her? To protect someone. Blair Sullivan? Impossible.

He needs to protect himself.

But that still didn't get her anywhere. She doodled on the empty pad in front of her, drawing concentric circles that grew darker and darker as she filled in the space with ink.

She remembered a lecture from her police academy days: Four out of five killers know their victims.

All right, she told herself. Blair Sullivan tells Matthew Cowart that he arranged the killing. How can he do this from Death Row?

Her heart sank. Prisons are worlds unto themselves. Anything can be obtained, if one is willing to pay the price, even a death. And everyone inside knows the mechanics of prison barter and exchange. But for an outsider to penetrate the machinations of those worlds was difficult, sometimes impossible. The ordinary leverages of life that a policeman so depended on—the fear of social or legal sanctions, of being held accountable—didn't exist within a prison.

She envisioned her next step with distaste: questioning all the prison people who had come in contact with Sullivan. One of them should be the pipeline, she thought. But what does he pay with? He didn't have any money. Or did he? He didn't have any status. He was a loner who went to the chair. Or was he?

How does he pay that debt?

And why does he tell Matthew Cowart?

A thought jumped into her head suddenly: Perhaps he'd already paid.

She took a deep breath.

Blair Sullivan contracts for a killing and we assume that payment is due upon completion of the contract. That is natural. But—turn it around. Shaeffer warmed suddenly, feeling her imagination trip like so many switches. She remembered the explosive excitement she felt when her eyes picked out the broad, dark shape of the billfish rising through the green-black waters to strike at the bait. A single moment, electric, exhilarating, before the battle was joined. The best moment, she thought.

She picked up the telephone and dialed a number. It rang three times before a groan slid over the line.

"Yeah?"

"Mike? It's Andy."

"Christ. Don't you even want to sleep?"

"Sorry. No."

"Give me a second."

She waited, hearing a muffled explanation to his wife. She made out the words "It's her first big case . . ." before the conversation was obscured by the sound of running water. Then silence, and finally the voice of her partner, laughing.

"You know, dammit, I'm the senior detective and you're the rookie. I say sleep, you're supposed to sleep."

"Sorry," she apologized again.

"Hah," he replied. "No sincerity. Okay, what's on your mind?"

"Matthew Cowart." When she spoke his name, she made up her mind: Don't play your hand quite yet.

"Mister I'm-Not-Telling-You-Everything Reporter?"

"The same." She smiled.

"Boy, that sonuvabitch has me frosted."

It was easy for her to envision her partner sitting at the side of his bed. His wife would have grabbed his pillow and jammed it over her head to drown out the noise of conversation. Unlike many detective partnerships, her relationship with Michael Weiss was businesslike and impersonal. They had not been together long—long enough to share an infrequent laugh, but not long enough to care what the joke was. He was a sturdy man, unimaginative and hotheaded. Better at showing pictures to witnesses and thumbing through insurance company records. That he'd acquired ten years of experience to her few months was a thought she dismissed rapidly. Leaving him behind was easy for her.

"Me, too."

"So what do you have in mind?"

"I think I ought to work him a bit. Just keep showing up. At his office. His apartment. When he goes jogging. When he takes a bath, whenever."

Weiss laughed. "And?"

"Let him know we're going to sit on him until we learn what he really has to tell us. Like who committed that crime."

"Makes sense to me."

"But someone's got to start working the prison. See if some-one there knows something, like maybe that guard sergeant. And I think somebody'd better go through all Sullivan's posses-sions. Maybe he left something that'll tell us something."

"Andy, couldn't this conversation have waited until, say, eight A.M.?" Exhaustion mingled with wry humor in Weiss's voice. "I mean, hell, don't you want to sleep a bit?"

"Sorry, Mike. I guess not."

"I hate it when you remind me of myself. I remember my first big case. I was breathing fire, too. Couldn't wait to get on it. Trust me. Take it slow."

"Mike . . ."

"Okay. Okay. So you'd rather muscle the reporter than start interviewing cons and guards, right?"

"Yes."

"See," Weiss laughed, "that's the sort of intuitiveness that will get you ahead in this department. All right. You go bother Cowart, I'll go back to Starke. But I want to talk. Every day. Maybe twice a day, got it?"

"Absolutely."

She had no idea if she intended to comply. She hung up the telephone and started to straighten her desk, sliding documents into files, organizing reports into neat stacks, clipping her own notes and observations onto the folders, placing pens and pen-cils into a cup. When she was satisfied with the order imposed on her working surface, she allowed herself a small surge of anticipation.

It's all mine, she thought.

She headed back to Miami beneath a midday sun that burned off the hood of the car, humming to herself, snatches of Jimmy Buffett tunes about living in the Florida Keys, daydreaming as she drove fast.

She was new to homicide work, only nine months out of a patrol car and three months from working burglaries, elevated by ability and an equal opportunity suit brought on behalf of all the women and minorities in the department. She was consumed by ambition, filled with energy and the belief that she could defuse her lack of experience with hard work. That had been her solution to almost all problems, since she had been a lonely child growing up in the Upper Keys. Her father had been a Chicago police detective, killed in the line of duty. She had often reflected upon the phrase "the line of duty," thinking how impoverished a concept it truly was. It pretended to give some sort of military importance to what she had come to understand was a moment of extraordinary mistake and bad luck. It was as if something necessary had been achieved by his dying, when she knew that to be a lie. Her father had worked bunco, usually dealing with cheapskate scam artists and confidence men, trying to stem the never-ending tide of retirees and immigrants who thought they could get rich by investing in one bizarre idea after another. He and his partners had raided a boiler-room operation one morning. Twenty women and men at desks working the telephones, calling folks up with a gold-investment scheme. Neither the scheme nor the raid was anything unusual, just part of daily business for both the criminals and the police. What had been unforeseen was that one of the men working the phones was a hotheaded kid with a concealed gun, who'd never taken a fall before and so never learned that the criminal justice system was going to let him go with nary a whimper. A single shot had been fired. It'd penetrated a partition made out of cheap wallboard and struck her father in the chest on the other side, where he'd been writing down the phony names of the people being arrested.

Useless, she thought. Just useless.

He'd died with a pencil in his hand.

She had been ten, and her memories were of a burly man who'd roughhoused with her incessantly, treating her boyishly when she was young, then taking her on trips to Comiskey Park to see the White Sox as she grew older. He'd taught her to throw and catch, and to appreciate physical strength. Life had seemed extraordinarily ordinary. They'd lived in a modest brick house. She'd gone to the neighborhood parish schools, as had her older brothers. The short-barreled pistol her father wore to work had seemed somehow less important than the jackets and loud ties that he affected. She had kept only one picture of the two of them, taken outdoors after a snowstorm, standing next to a snowman they'd constructed together. They had flung their arms around the snowman as if he was their friend. It had been early April, when the Midwest was trying to shake the long winter, only to be rewarded with a final blast of cold. The snowman had had a baseball hat, and rocks for eyes, broken branches for arms. They'd tied a scarf around its neck and sculpted a goofy smile on its face. It had been a terrific snowman, almost alive.

It had melted, of course. The weather had turned rapidly and within a week it was gone.

They had come to the Keys a year after his death.

Miami had actually been the target; there were relatives there. But they had slid south when her mother had gotten a job managing a restaurant next to a sportfishing dock. That was where her stepfather had come from.

She liked him enough, she thought. Distant yet willing to teach her what he knew about the business of hunting fish. When she thought of him, she thought of the deep, reddish brown the sun had turned his arms and the precancerous white specks that cluttered his skin. She had always wanted to touch them but had never done so. He still ran his fishing charters out of Whale Harbor and called his forty-two-foot Bertram sportfisher "The Last Chance," which his clients all thought referred to fishing, rather than the tenuous existence of the charter-boat skipper.

Her mother had never told her so, but she believed she had been a child of accident, born just as her parents entered middle age, more than a decade younger than her brothers. They had left the Keys as quickly as age and education would allow, one to practice corporate law in Atlanta, the other to a modestly successful import-export business in Miami. The family joke was that he was the only legal importer in that city, and consequently the poorest. For some time she had thought that she would follow first the one brother, then the other, while she treaded water at the University of Florida, keeping her grade-point average high enough for graduate school.

She had decided to join the police after being raped.

The memory seemed to blister her imagination. It had been the end of the semester in Gainesville, almost summer, hot and humid. She had not intended to attend the frat-house party, but an abnormal psychology final had left her drained and lethargic, and when her roommates pressed her to join them, she had readily agreed.

She recalled the loudness of everything. Voices, music, too many people jammed into too small a space. The old wooden-frame building had shaken with the crowd. She'd gulped beer fast against the heat, rapidly losing her edge, dizzying into a casual acceptance of the night.

Well after midnight, hopelessly separated from her roommates, she'd started home alone, having rejected a thousand efforts at imposed companionship. She was just drunk enough to feel a liquid connectivity with the night, unsteadily maneuvering beneath the stars. She was not so soused that she couldn't find her way home, she remembered, just enough so that she was taking her time about it.

An easy mark, she thought bitterly.

She had been unaware of the two men coming out of the shadows behind her until they were right upon her, grabbing at her, tossing a jacket over her head, and pummeling her with fists. No time for screaming, no time to fight her way free and try to outrun them. She hated this part of the memory more than any other.

I could have done it. She felt her calf muscles tighten. High school district one-mile champion. Two letters on the women's track team. *If I could have just gotten free for one second, they would never have caught me. I'd have run them into the ground.*

She remembered the pressure of the two men, crushing her with their weight. The pain had seemed intense, then oddly distant. She had been afraid of being suffocated or choked. She had struggled until one had punched her, an explosion of fist against her chin that had sent her head reeling far beyond any dizziness created by liquor. She had passed out, almost welcoming the darkness of unconsciousness, preferring it to the awfulness and pain of what was happening.

She drove hard toward Miami, picking up speed as she plunged through the memory. *Nothing happened,* she thought. *Wake up raped in a hospital. Get swabbed and prodded and invaded again. Give a statement to a campus cop. Then to a city detective. Can you describe the assailants, miss? It was dark. They held me down. But what did they look like? They were strong. One held a jacket over my head. Were they white? Black? Hispanic? Short? Tall? Thickset? Skinny? They were on top of me. Did they say anything? No. They just did it.* She had called home, hearing her mother dissolve into useless tears and her stepfather sputter with rage, almost as if he were angry with her for what had happened. She spoke finally to a rape-counseling social worker who had nodded and listened. Shaeffer had looked across at the woman and realized that her compassion was part of her job, like the people hired at Disney World to wave in friendly fashion and false spontaneity at the tourists. She walked out and returned to her home and waited for something to happen. It didn't. No suspects. No arrests. Just one bad night when something went wrong on a college campus. Frat-house hijinks. Swallow the memory and get on with life.

Her bruises healed and disappeared.

She fingered a small white scar that curled around the corner of her eye. That remained.

There had been no talk in her family of what had happened. She returned to the Keys and found that everything was the same. They still lived in a cinder-block house with a second-story view of the ocean, and paddle fans in each room that shifted the stalled humid air about. Her mother still went to the restaurant to make certain the key lime pie was fresh and the conch fritters were deep fried and that everything was in place for the daily arrival of tourists and fishing mates, who rubbed shoulders at the bar. A routine gradually cut from life by the passing of years stayed the same. She went back to work on her stepfather's boat, just as if nothing had changed within her. She remembered she would look up at him stolidly riding the flying bridge, staring out from behind dark sunglasses across the green waters for signs of life, while she labored below in the cockpit, fetching clients' beers, laughing at their off-color jokes, baiting hooks and waiting for action.

She adjusted her own sunglasses against the highway glare.

But I had changed, she thought.

She had taken to writing her mother letters, pouring all the hurts and emotions of what had happened to her onto pages of slightly scented lilac-colored notepaper purchased at the local pharmacy, words and tears staining the thin, fragile sheets. After a while, she no longer wrote about the violation she felt, the hole she thought those two faceless men had torn at the center of her core, but instead about the world, the weather, her future, her past. The day she went for her preliminary police exam, she had written: *I can't bring Dad back . . .* but it made her feel better to give this silent voice to the feeling within her, no matter how predictable she thought it was.

Of course, she never mailed any of those letters or showed them to anyone. She kept them collected in a fake leather binder she'd purchased at a crafts show in suburban Miami. Lately, she had taken to writing synopses of her cases in the letters, giving words to all her suppositions and guesses, keeping these dangerous ideas out of official notes and reports. She wondered sometimes whether her mother, if she'd actually read any of those letters ostensibly addressed to her, would be more shocked by what had happened to her daughter or by what her daughter saw happening to others.

She pictured the old couple on Tarpon Drive. They had no chance, she thought. They knew what they'd produced. Did they think they could bring Blair Sullivan into the world and not have to pay a price? Everyone pays.

Shaeffer thought of the first time she'd raised the heavy .357 magnum Colt revolver that was the standard sidearm of the Monroe deputies. Its heft had been reassuring: a solidity in her grasp that whispered into her ear that she would never be a victim again.

She touched the gas pedal and felt the unmarked cruiser shoot forward, climbing through the seventies and eighties, surging through the midday heat.

She had put one of six into the target the first day. Two of six the next. By the time she'd finished the six-week training, all six of six, gathered tightly in the center. She'd continued practicing at least once a week, every week, after that. She'd branched out as well, gaining a proficiency with a smaller automatic and learning how to handle the riot pump that was locked into each car. Lately, she had started taking time on the range with a military-issue M-16 and had adopted a NATO-style nine-millimeter for her own use.

She pulled her foot from the pedal and let the car slow back to the speed limit. She stared up into her rearview mirror and watched another car ride up hard behind her, then swing out into the lane next to her. It was a state policeman in an unmarked Ford, hunting for speeders. She'd obviously sailed through his radar, bringing him out of hiding, only to have him make her car.

He peered across at her from behind dark aviator shades.

She smiled and gave an exaggerated shrug, seeing the man's face break into a grin. He raised one hand as if to say, No big deal, then accelerated past her. She picked up her radio and switched to the state police frequency.

"This is Monroe homicide one-four. Come back."

"Monroe homicide, this is Trooper Willis. I clocked you doing ninety-five. Where's the fire?"

"Sorry, Troop. It was a nice day, I'm working a good case, and I decided to air it out a bit. I'll keep it down."

"No problem, one-four. Uh, you got time to have a bite to eat?"

She laughed. A high-speed pickup. "Uh, negative right now. But try me in a couple of days at the Largo substation."

"Will do."

She saw him raise his hand and peel to the side of the road. He will have hopes for a few days, she thought, and wanted to apologize in advance. He will be disappointed. She had one rule: She never slept with anyone who knew she was a police officer. She never slept with anyone she would ever have to see a second time.

She touched the scar by her eye a second time.

Two scars, she thought. One outside, one inside.

She continued north toward Miami.

A receptionist outside the newsroom of *The Miami Journal* informed her that Matthew Cowart was not in the office. Surprise flooded her, followed swiftly by a quickening of excitement. *He's looking for something,* she thought. *He's after somebody.* She asked to see the city editor, while she sorted through her suspicions. The receptionist spoke briefly on the telephone, then motioned her toward a couch, where she waited nervously. Twenty minutes passed before the city editor emerged from between the double doors to see her.

"I'm sorry to have kept you waiting," he said quickly. "We were in the news conference and I couldn't get out."

"I would like to talk with Cowart again," she said, trying to remove all the surprise and anticipation from her voice.

"I thought you got a statement the other day."

"Not completely."

"No?" He shrugged as if to say he had no sympathy for lost opportunities.

"A few things perhaps he can straighten out."

"I'm sorry, but he's not here," the city editor said. He frowned widely. "Perhaps I can help you?"

She recognized how insincere this offer was. "Well," she said with mildly false enthusiasm, "I just can't get it straight in my head how Sullivan made his contacts and set up his arrangements . . ." She waved a hand to cut off a question from the city editor. ". . . I know, I mean, I'm not sure what Mr. Cowart can add, but I still just don't have a feel for all this and was hoping he could help."

She thought this sounded safe enough. She suspected a softening in the city editor's tones.

"Well, hell," he said, "I think everyone's trying to understand the same damn thing."

She laughed. "It's quite a situation, isn't it?"

He nodded, smiling but still wary. "I think he's filled you in as best as he can. But . . ."

"Well," she replied slowly, "perhaps now that he's had some time to reflect on what he heard, he can remember something else. You'd be surprised what folks can remember after they've had some time to think about it."

The city editor smiled. "I wouldn't be surprised at all. What people remember about things is our trade, too." He shuffled his feet a bit and ran a hand through his thinning hair. "He's off on a story."

"So, where's he gone?"

The city editor hesitated before replying. "North Florida."

He looked for an instant as if the act of actually giving out a piece of information would make him ill.

Shaeffer smiled. "Big place, North Florida."

The city editor shrugged. "This story has only happened in two places. You know that. At the prison in Starke and a little town called Pachoula. I shouldn't have to spell that out for you. Now, I'm sorry, Detective Shaeffer, but I have to get back to work."

"Can you tell Cowart I need to talk with him?"

"I'll tell him. Can't promise anything. Where will you be?"

"Looking for him," she said.

She got up as if to leave, then thought of one other thing. "Can I take a look at Cowart's original stories?"

The city editor paused, thinking, then gestured toward the newspaper library. "They'll help you there," he said. "If there's any problem, have them contact me."

She stood at a desk, flipping through a huge bound volume of copies of *The Miami Journal*. For an instant, she was struck by the wealth of disaster the newspaper documented, then she came upon the Sunday edition with Matthew Cowart's initial story about the murder of Joanie Shriver. She read through it carefully, making notations, taking down names and dates.

As she rode the elevator down to the main entrance, she tried to settle all the thoughts that swept about within her. The elevator oozed to a halt on the ground floor, and she started to walk from the building, only to stop abruptly in the center of the lobby.

This story has only happened in two places, the editor had said. She thought about the box that Cowart was in. What brings him to Blair Sullivan? she thought.

The murder of a little girl in Pachoula.

What's at the core of that crime?

Robert Earl Ferguson.

Who links Sullivan to Cowart?

Robert Earl Ferguson.

What props up his prize?

Robert Earl Ferguson.

She turned on her heel and walked back into the corner of the *Journal* lobby, where there was a bank of pay telephones. She checked her notes and dialed directory information in Pensacola. Then she dialed the number that the electronic voice had given her.

After dealing with a secretary, she heard the attorney's voice come on the line.

"Roy Black here. How can I help you, miss?"

"Mr. Black," she said, "this is Andrea Shaeffer. I'm at *The Miami Journal.* . . ." She smiled, enjoying her minor deception. "We need to get ahold of Mr. Cowart, and he's gone up to Pachoula, to see your client. It's important to run him down, and no one seems to have a number here. I wonder if you could help me on that. Really sorry to bother you . . ."

"No problem at all, miss. But Bobby Earl's left Pachoula. He's back up in Newark, New Jersey. I don't know why Mr. Cowart would go back to Pachoula."

"Oh," she said, layering her voice with disingenuous surprise and false helplessness. "He's working on a follow-up after Blair Sullivan's execution. Do you think Mr. Cowart will go up there instead? He was very vague about his itinerary and it's important we track him down. Do you have an address? I hate to bother you, but no one can find Mr. Cowart's Rolodex."

"I don't like giving out addresses," the attorney said reluctantly.

"Oh," she continued breezily, "that's right. I guess not. Oh, boy, how'm I gonna find him now? My boss is gonna have my head for sure. Do you know how I could trace him up north?"

The attorney hesitated. "Ahh, hell," he said finally. "I'll get it for you. Just got to promise you won't give it out to any other news outlets or anybody else. Mr. Ferguson is trying to put all this behind him, you know. Get on with things."

"Boy, would you? I promise. I can see that," she said with phony enthusiasm.

"Hang on," said the attorney. "I'm looking it up."

She waited patiently, eagerly. The meager falsehoods and playacting had come easily to her. She wondered whether she could catch the next flight north. She was not precisely sure what she would do with Ferguson when she found him, but she was certain of one thing: The answers to all her questions were hovering about somewhere very close to that man. She envisioned his eyes as they had stared out at her from the pages of the newspaper. The innocent man.

SEVENTEEN
=NEWARK

THE plane dipped down beneath a thin cover of clouds on its final approach into the airport, and she could see the city, rising in the distance like so many children's blocks tossed into a pile. A flaccid early-spring sun illuminated the jumble of tall, rectangular office buildings. Staring through the window, she felt a damp April chill and had a momentary longing for the unequivocal heat of the Keys. Then she thrust everything from her mind except how to approach Ferguson.

Carefully, she decided. Play him like a strong fish on light tackle; a sudden move or too much pressure will break the line and set him loose. It's only the barest of threads. Nothing tied Ferguson to the murders on Tarpon Drive except the presence of a single reporter. No witnesses, fingerprints, or bloodwork. Not even a modus operandi, the sexual assault-murder of a little girl having little in common with the terror slaughtering of an elderly couple. And according to Cowart and his newspaper, he wasn't even guilty of the first half of that equation.

As the plane twisted through the airspace, she could see the broad ribbon of the New Jersey Turnpike snaking below her as it sliced north and south. She was struck with a sudden depression that she'd allowed herself to head off on some crazy tangent and would be better served by simply grabbing the first flight back to Florida and working at Weiss's side. Everything had seemed clear standing in the lobby of *The Miami Journal*. The murky, gray skies of New Jersey seemed to mock the uncertainty that filled her.

She wondered if Ferguson had learned anything the first time around. Probably. Her impression of him, gleaned from Cowart's words, was that he was clever, educated, and not at all like most convicts. That was too bad. One of the contradictory truisms of police work was that the prisonwise suspect was *not* harder to trip up. In fact, the opposite was true. But Ferguson, she suspected, was a different case.

Still . . . she remembered a moment on her stepfather's boat a half-dozen years earlier. They'd been fishing in the early evening, catching the outgoing tide as it ran fast between the pylons of one of the Keys' innumerable bridges. The client had hooked a big tarpon, well over a hundred and twenty pounds. It had jumped twice, gills shaking, rattling its head back and forth, then sounded, its sleek silver shape slicing through the darkening waters. It had run with the current, using the force of the water to help it fight against the pressure of the line. The client had hung on, stubbornly, grunting, legs spread, back bent, fighting against the strength of the fish for nearly an hour. The big fish had pulled on, dragging line from the reel, heading toward the bridge pylons.

Smart fish, she thought. Strong fish. It had known that if it could get in there, it could sever the line on a barnacle. All it had to do was run that taut, thin length of monofilament against a pylon. The fish had been hooked before. It knew the pain of the barb in its jaw, the force of the line pulling it toward the surface. Familiarity gave it strength. There was no panic in its fight. Just a steady, intelligent savagery as it made for the bridge and safety.

What she'd done had seemed crazy. She had jumped to the man's side and in a single, impulsive motion, twisted the drag on the reel down all the way, virtually locking it. Then she'd shouted, "Toss it over! Toss it over!" The man had looked wildly at her, and she'd seized the rod from his hands and thrown it over the side of the boat. It had made a small wake as it was towed rapidly away. "What the hell . . ." the man had started angrily, only to be interrupted when her stepfather pivoted the boat in the channel and roared underneath the bridge, throttling down on the far side.

She could see her stepfather standing on the flying bridge, peering through the growing darkness until he finally pointed. They all turned and saw the rod, its cork handle bobbing at the surface twenty yards away. They came alongside and she bent over and grasped it from the water, loosening the drag in almost the same moment. "Now," she had said to the fisherman, "land him." The man had pulled back on the rod, breaking into a grin when he felt the weight on the other end. The still-hooked tarpon exploded from the surface in shock and surprise when it felt the point of the hook drive hard once again into its jaw. It had jumped fast, soaring through the air, black water streaming from its sides. But she'd known it was the big fish's last run; she could sense the defeat in each shake of its head and twist of its body. Another ten minutes and they had the tarpon to the side of the boat. She'd lip-gaffed the fish and brought it out of the water. There had been a flurry of photos, and then they'd returned the fish to the channel waves. She'd leaned over the side, holding the fish, reviving it gently. But before setting it loose, she'd seized one of its silver scales, the size of a half-dollar, and broken it off. She'd put the scale in her shirt pocket as she watched the fish swim off slowly, its scythelike tail slicing through the warm water.

Smart fish. Strong fish.

But I was smarter and that made me stronger.

She pictured Ferguson again. Hooked before, she thought.

The airplane droned and bumped to a halt. She gathered her things together and headed for the exit.

The liaison captain at the Newark Police Department arranged for a pair of uniformed officers to accompany her to Ferguson's apartment. After a few brief introductions and modest small talk, the pair drove her through the city toward the address she'd given them.

Shaeffer stared out at streets she thought cut from a subdivision of hell. The buildings were all dirty brick and dark concrete, rimmed with grime and helplessness. Even the sunlight that caught the street seemed gray. There was a never-ceasing procession of small businesses, clothing stores, bodegas, cut-rate loan offices, appliance centers, and furniture rental showrooms, each clinging with decrepit energy to the edges of the littered sidewalks. There were black steel bars everywhere; inner-urban necessities. A different cluster of idle men, teenage gangs, or gaudy hookers seemed to occupy each corner. Even the fast-food outlets, with their uniform codes of cleanliness and order, seemed frayed and tattered, a far cry from their suburban counterparts. The city was like a has-been fighter, hanging on in the latter rounds of one too many fights, staggering but still inexplicably standing on its feet because it was too old or stupid or stubborn to fall.

"You said this dude is in school, Detective? No way. Not down here," said one of the officers, a taciturn black man with gray hair touching his temples.

"That's what his attorney told me," she replied.

"There's only one school down here. Where you learn whoring and pimping and dealing and how to do a B and E. I don't know what you'd call that school."

"Well, maybe," said his partner driving the car, a younger man with sandy blond hair and a drooping mustache. "That's not altogether true. There's plenty of decent folks down here . . ."

"Yeah," interrupted the older policeman. "Hiding behind steel grates and bars."

"Don't pay any attention to him," the partner said. "He's a burnt-out case. He's also not mentioning the fact that he started out down here and worked his way through night school. So it ain't impossible. Maybe your man's riding the commuter train out to New Brunswick and attending classes at Rutgers. Or grabbing evening classes at St. Pete's."

"Don't make any sense. Why live in this rathole unless you have to?" the older policeman answered. "If he's got some money, he could live out there. Only reason to live down here is if you ain't got a chance of being someplace else."

"I can think of another reason," said the younger cop.

"What's that?" Shaeffer asked.

The policeman gestured with his arm. "You want to hide. You want maybe to get swallowed up a bit. Best place in the world."

He pointed at an abandoned building, pivoted in his seat and looked back at her. "Parts of these cities, they're like the jungle or a swamp. We pass a building like that, been hit by fire, abandoned, whatever, there's no way to know what's really inside. People live in there without electricity, heat, water. Gangs hang out, hide weapons. Hell, there could be a hundred dead bodies in one of those buildings and we'd never find 'em. Never even know they were there."

He paused for a moment. "Perfect place to get lost. Who the hell'd ever come down here looking for someone unless they really needed 'em?" he asked.

"I guess I would," she said quietly.

"What d'you need this man for?" asked the driver.

"He may have some information about a double homicide I'm working."

"You think he's gonna give us some trouble? Maybe we ought to have some backup. This drug-related?"

"No. More like a contract killing."

"You promise us? I mean, I don't want to go walking in on some beady-eyed guy holding a Uzi and a pound of crack."

"No. Not at all."

"Is he a suspect?"

She hesitated. What was he? "Not exactly. Just someone we need to talk to. Could go either way."

"Okay. We're gonna take your word for it," said the younger man. "But I'm not wild about it. What you got on this guy, anyway?"

"Not much."

"So you're just hoping he'll say something that you can take to the bank, right?"

"That's the idea."

"Fishing expedition, huh?"

She smiled at the irony. "Right."

She could see him look over at his partner for an instant. The officers humphed and drove on. They swept past a cluster of men hanging in front of a small grocery store. She could see the eyes of the inhabitants of the inner-city world following them. No doubts about who we are, she thought. They made us in a microsecond. She tried to focus on the faces on the street, but they blurred together.

"Down here," said the policeman driving. "Middle of the block."

He steered the car into an empty space between a four-year-old cherry-red Cadillac with balloon whitewalls and velour upholstery, and a wreck, stripped of anything worthwhile. A small boy was sitting on the curb next to the Caddy.

"Home sweet home," said the younger officer. "How're you gonna play this, Detective?"

"Nice and easy," she replied. "Talk to the super first, if there is one. Maybe a neighbor. Then just knock on his door."

The older policeman shrugged. "Okay. We'll just stay a step behind you. But when you get inside, you're pretty much on your own."

Ferguson's building was tired red brick, a half-dozen stories high. Shaeffer took a step toward it, then turned and faced the boy sitting on the curb. He was wearing a glistening white, expensive pair of hightop basketball shoes beneath tattered sweatpants.

"How you doing?" she asked.

The boy shrugged. "Okay."

"What're you up to?"

The boy gestured. "I watch the wheels. You police?"

"You got it."

"Not from 'round here."

"No. You know a man named Robert Earl Ferguson?"

"Florida man. You looking for him?"

"Yes. He inside?"

"Don't know. No one sees him much."

"Why not?"

The boy turned away. "Guess he's got something going."

Shaeffer nodded and walked up the steps to the entranceway, trailed by the two uniformed officers. She checked a bank of mailboxes, finding Ferguson's name scratched on one. She took down the names of some neighbors as well and found a name with the abbreviation "Supt." written after it. She rang that buzzer and stood next to an intercom. There was no reply.

"It don't work," said the older officer.

"Nothing like that works down here," added the younger.

She reached out and pushed on the apartment-house door. It swung open. She felt a momentary embarrassment.

"I guess things like locks and buzzers still work down in Florida," said the older policeman.

The interior of the apartment house was cavelike and dark. The hallways were narrow, scratched with graffiti and smelling vaguely of refuse tinged with urine. The younger policeman must have seen her nose wrinkle in distaste, because he said, "Hey, this one's a helluva lot better than most." He gestured. "You don't see any drunks living in the hallway, do you? That's a big deal, right there."

She found the super's apartment beneath the stairwell, knocked hard three times and after a moment heard noises from inside. Then a voice. "Whatcha want?"

She held her badge up to the peephole. "Police, sir," she replied.

There was a sound of clicking as three or four different locks were unfastened. Finally the door swung open, revealing a thin, middle-aged black man, barefoot beneath work clothes.

"You Mr. Washington? The superintendent?"

He nodded. "Whatcha want?" he repeated.

"I want to come in out of the hallway," she said briskly.

He opened the door and let the three of them inside. "I ain't done nothing."

Shaeffer glanced about at the threadbare furniture and tattered carpets, then turned toward the super and asked, "Robert Earl Ferguson. Is he upstairs?"

The man shrugged. "Maybe. I guess so. I don't pay much attention to comings and goings, you know."

"Who does?"

"My wife does," he said, pointing.

She turned and saw a short black woman, as wide as her husband was thin, standing quietly beneath an archway, steadying herself with an aluminum walker.

"Mrs. Washington?"

"That's right."

"Is Robert Earl Ferguson upstairs?"

"He should be. Ain't gone out today."

"How would you know?"

The woman struggled forward a step, carefully placing the walker in front of her. Her breath came in rapid, sharp, wheezing gasps.

"I don't move so good. I spends my days over there . . ." She pointed toward a front window. "Watching what's going on in this world before I leaves it behind, doing a little knitting, and the such. I get to know pretty much when people come and goes."

"And Ferguson, does he have a schedule? Is he regular?"

She nodded. Shaeffer took out a notepad and made some notations. "Where's he go?"

"Well, I don't know for sure, but he's usually carrying some of those college books in a bag. Like a knapsack kinda bag. Put it on your back like you're gonna be in the army or take a hike or something. He goes out in the afternoons. Don't see him come back till late at night. Sometimes he goes off with a little suitcase. Don't come back for a couple of days. I guess he travels some."

"You're still there, late? Watching?"

"Don't sleep too good, neither. Don't walk too good. Don't breathe too good. Don't do nothing too good now."

Andrea Shaeffer felt excitement quickening. "How's your memory?" she asked.

"Memory ain't limping around, that what you mean. Memory's fine. Whatcha need to know?"

"A week to ten days ago. Did Ferguson go out of town? Did you see him with that suitcase? Was he gone for a day or two? Anything unusual. Anything out of the routine?"

The woman thought hard. Shaeffer watched her mentally sorting through all the comings and goings she'd witnessed. The woman's eyes narrowed, then widened slightly, as if an image or memory crossed rapidly through her head. She opened her mouth as if to say something, her hand fluttering away from the grip on the aluminum walker. But before the words came out, Shaeffer saw the woman reconsider, as if a second thought had tripped the first. The woman's eyes narrowed, hesitating on the notepad that hovered in the detective's hands. Finally, she shook her head.

"Don't think so. But I'll consider it some more. Can't be absolutely sure without thinking on it for a piece. You know how it is."

The detective watched the woman shift about. She remembers something, she thought. She just won't say it. "You sure?"

"No," the woman said warily. "I might remember something after I set my mind on it a spell. A week to ten days ago, that what you say?"

"That's right."

"I'll do some thinking."

"All right. You do that. Is there anyone else who might know?"

"No, ma'am. He keeps to himself. Just heads out in the afternoons. Comes back at night. Sometimes early. Sometimes a bit later. That boy never makes noise, never causes a ruckus, just quiet. He don't even have a girlfriend. What you need to know all this for? What sort of police trouble he in?"

"You know anything about what he's been doing the past few years? Down in Florida?"

Mr. Washington interrupted. "We heard he did some time down there. But that's all."

"Doing time ain't much of a crime around here, ma'am. Just about everybody's done some time," interjected the wife. She looked over at her husband. "And Lord knows, those that ain't done any time are probably gonna end up doing some before too long. That's the way down here. Yes, ma'am."

"How's he pay his rent?" Shaeffer asked.

"In cash. First of the month. No problem."

She made a note of that.

"But it ain't that much, you know. This place ain't fancy, in case you haven't noticed."

"Did you ever see him with a knife? Like a hunting knife? Ever see one in his apartment?"

"No, ma'am."

"A gun?"

"No, I don't think so. But I expect most folks down here's got one hid somewhere."

"Anything at all you remember about him. Anything out of the ordinary?"

"Well, it ain't ordinary down here to spend your time with those books."

Shaeffer nodded. She handed both husband and wife her business card, embossed with the shield of the Monroe County sheriff's office. "You think of something, you can call me. Collect. I'll be at this number here for a couple of days." She wrote down the exchange of the motel near the airport where she'd parked her bag.

They both stared dutifully at the cards as she let herself out. In the hallway, the older policeman looked at her. "Learn anything? It didn't sound all that exciting to me. 'Cept maybe that old gal was lying to you when she said she didn't remember a week ago."

"She sure as hell remembered something," said the younger officer.

"You guys saw it, too?"

"Couldn't hardly miss it. But hell, I don't know what it means. More'n likely nothing. What do you think, Detective?"

"We're getting there," she replied. "Time to see if the man's home."

EIGHTEEN
THE CONVENIENT
=====MAN

SHE took a slow, deep breath to try to control her surging heart, and knocked on the door. The apartment house hallway was dark, despite a window at the end that allowed some weak light to slide past a layer of gray grime. She had little idea what to expect. An unmade killer, she thought. What is he? One side of a triangle. A man who studies but sometimes packs a suitcase and goes someplace for several days. She knocked again and after a moment came the expected answer. "Who's there?"

"Police."

The word hung in the air in front of her, echoing in the small space. A few seconds passed.

"What do you want?"

"To ask you some questions. Open the door."

"What sort of questions?"

She could sense the man's presence just inches away, hidden by the slab of brown wood. "Open the door."

The two officers stiffened behind her, and each stepped back slightly, out of the direct line. She rapped again on the door.

"Police," she repeated. She did not know what she would do if he refused to open.

"All right."

She had no time to feel relief. She thought she heard a catch in his voice, a small hesitation, like the reluctance of a child caught doing something improper. Perhaps, she thought, he'd turned away just before speaking, letting his eyes quickly survey his apartment, trying to guess what it was that she might see. Evidence? Evidence of what?

There was a sound of dead bolts being thrown and chain locks being removed, and then the door swung open slightly. Andrea Shaeffer stared at Robert Earl Ferguson. He was wearing jeans and sneakers and a baggy, faded maroon sweatshirt that draped around his shoulders, several sizes too large, obscuring his true shape. His hair was cropped close, he was clean-shaven. She almost stepped back in surprise; the force of the man's anger struck her like a blow. His eyes were fierce, penetrating. They severed the space between them.

"What do you want?" he asked. "I haven't done anything."

"I want to speak with you."

"You got a badge?" he demanded.

She held up her shield for him to inspect.

"Monroe County? Florida?"

"That's right. My name's Shaeffer. I work homicide."

For a moment she thought she saw uncertainty course through Ferguson's face, as if he were trying hard to remember something elusive.

"That's down below Dade, right? Below the edge of the 'Glades?"

"Right."

"What do you need me for?"

"May I step inside?"

"Not until you tell me why you're here."

Ferguson seemed to look her over in the silence that swept over them. She realized they were almost the same height and that his slight build seemed hardly more substantial than her own. But he was also the sort of man to whom size and strength were irrelevant.

"You're a long ways from home," he said.

He turned and glared at the two officers hanging just behind her shoulder. "What about them?"

"They're local."

"Scared to come down here alone?" His eyes narrowed unpleasantly. The two backup officers stepped forward, closing the gap between them. Ferguson remained in the doorway, folding his arms in front of his chest.

"No," she replied immediately, but the word only prompted a small grin that raced away rapidly.

"I haven't done anything," he repeated, but with a flat tonality, like a lawyer saying something for a transcript.

"I didn't say you had."

Ferguson smiled. "But you wouldn't come all the way from Monroe County, all the way up here to this delightful place just to see me if you didn't have a good reason, right?" He stepped back. "All right. You can come in. Ask your questions. Got nothing to hide."

This last sentence was spoken loudly and directed at the two New Jersey policemen.

She stepped forward into the apartment. As soon as she was past him, Ferguson moved between her and the two backup officers, blocking their route.

"I didn't invite you two goons," he said abruptly. "Just her. Unless you got a warrant."

Shaeffer turned in surprise. She saw both Newark policemen bristle instantly. Like all cops, they were unaccustomed to getting orders from civilians.

"Move out of the way," the older policeman said.

"Forget it. She has a question. She can come in and ask it."

The younger officer moved to put his hand on Ferguson's chest, as if to thrust him aside, then seemed to think better of it. Shaeffer blurted out, "It's all right. I can handle this."

The two policemen wavered.

"It's not procedure," the older one said to her. He turned to Ferguson. "You want to push me, punk?"

Ferguson didn't move.

Shaeffer made a small, sweeping gesture with her hand. There was a momentary pause, then the two backup officers stepped back into the hallway.

"All right," the older one said. "We'll wait here." He turned toward Ferguson. "I've got a good memory for faces, asshole," he whispered. "And yours just made my list."

Ferguson sneered at the man. "And you've made mine," he said.

He started to close the door, only to have the younger officer shoot an arm out, stiff-arm like a football player, and say, "This stays open, huh? No trouble that way."

Ferguson's hand dropped away from the door. "If that's the way you like it." He turned and led Shaeffer into the apartment. As he walked, he said, "I've seen them before. Just like half the COs on Death Row. Think they got to be tough. Don't know what tough really is."

"What is tough, Mr. Ferguson?"

"Tough is knowing a time and date. Knowing you're per-

fectly healthy but society has delivered to you a terminal illness.
Tough is knowing every breath draws you one breath closer to
the last one."

He stopped in the center of a small living room. "But what
about you, Detective? You think you're tough, too?"

"When I have to be," she replied.

He didn't laugh but stared at her with a mixture of distrust
and mockery. "Have a seat," he said. Ferguson slid onto the
corner of a well-worn couch.

"Thanks," she replied. But she didn't sit. Instead, she started
to walk slowly around the room, inspecting, at the same time
keeping an eye on him. It was something she'd been taught.
Keep to her feet while the subject sits. It will make almost anyone nervous and makes the questioner seem more powerful. His
eyes trailed her closely.

"Looking for something?"

"No."

"Then tell me what you want."

She went to a window and glanced out. She could see the
pimp's red car and up and down the block, which was empty of
life.

"Not much to look at," she said. "Why would anyone live
here? Especially if they didn't have to."

He did not answer her question.

"Whores on the corner. A crack house half a block away.
What else? Thieves. Street gangs. Addicts . . ." She looked
hard at him. "Killers. And you."

"That's right."

"What are you, Mr. Ferguson?"

"I'm a student."

"Any others down here?"

"None that I've met."

"So why do you live here?"

"It suits me."

"You fit in?"

"I didn't say that."

"Then why?"

"It's safe." He laughed slightly. "Safest place on earth."

"That's not an answer."

He shrugged. "You live within yourself. Not in that world.
Inside. That's the first lesson you learn on Death Row. First of
many. You think you forget what you learn there just because
you're out? Now, tell me what you want."

Instead of answering, she continued to move through the small apartment. She looked in at a bedroom. There was a narrow single bed and a solitary scarred brown wooden chest of drawers. She could see some clothes hung in a meager closet recessed into a black wall. The kitchen had a small refrigerator, stove, and a sink. A stack of chipped, utilitarian plates and cups drained next to the sink.

Back in the living room, she noticed a small table in the corner with a portable typewriter sitting on it and papers strewn about. Next to the table was a bookcase made from cinder blocks and cheap unpainted pine boards. She approached the desk and inspected the books on the shelves, immediately recognizing several of the titles: a book on forensic medicine by a former New York City medical examiner, one on FBI identification techniques put out by the government, a third book on media and crime, written by a professor at Columbia University. She had read them in her own course work at the police academy. There were many others, all relating to crime and detection, all well worn, clearly purchased secondhand. She pulled one from a shelf and flipped it open. Certain passages were highlighted in yellow marker.

"These your markings?"

"No. Tell me what you want."

She put the book down and let her eyes sweep over the papers on the desk. She noticed on one sheet a series of addresses, including Matthew Cowart's. There were several listings from Pachoula, and a lawyer in Tampa that she didn't recognize. She picked it up and gestured toward him.

"Who are these people?" she asked.

He seemed to hesitate, then replied, "I owe letters. People who supported me in my fight to get out of prison."

She put the paper down. Next to the desk was a stack of newspapers. She bent down and flipped through them. There were local sections and front pages. Some of the newspapers were from New Jersey, others from Florida. She saw issues of *The Miami Journal*, *The Tampa Tribune*, *The St. Petersburg Times*, and others. She took out an issue of *The Newark Star-Ledger* and saw a headline that read: FAMILY OFFERS REWARD IN MISSING DAUGHTER CASE.

"This sort of thing interest you?" she asked.

"Same as it does you," Ferguson answered. "Isn't that true, Detective? When you pick up a newspaper, what's the first story you read?"

She did not reply but glanced down at the newspapers again. She noticed there was a crime story on each page. Other headlines leapt out at her: POLICE PROBE EVIDENCE IN ASSAULT and NO LEAD IN ABDUCTION, POLICE SAY.

"Where'd you get these papers?"

He glared at her. "I go back to Florida with some frequency. Give speeches at churches, to civic groups." His eyes locked onto her own. "Black churches, black civic groups. The sort of people who understand how an innocent man gets sent to Death Row. The sort of people who don't think it's so damn unusual for a black man to get harassed by the cops. Who wouldn't think it so damn strange that every cheap homicide cop in the state who can't get anywhere on some damn case would roust an innocent black man."

He continued to stare at her, and she dropped the newspaper she was holding back onto the pile.

"I study criminology. 'Media and Crime.' Wednesdays, five-thirty P.M. to seven-thirty P.M. It's an elective. Criminology 307. Professor Morin. That's why I collect newspapers."

She let her eyes sweep over the desk again.

"I'm getting an A," he added. He restored the mocking tone to his voice. "Now, tell me what you want," he insisted.

"All right," she said. The force of his gaze was making her uncomfortable. She stepped away from his desk and returned to face him directly.

"When were you last in the Florida Keys? Upper Keys. Islamorada. Marathon. Key Largo. When did you go down there to talk to some civic group?" She made no attempt to conceal her sarcasm.

"I've never been in the Keys," he replied.

"No?"

"Never."

"Of course, if I had someone telling me the contrary, that would say something, wouldn't it?" She lied easily, but the implicit threat seemed to wash off him.

"It would say someone was feeding you false information."

"You know a street called Tarpon Drive?"

"No."

"A house. Number thirteen. Ever been there?"

"No."

"Your friend Cowart's been there."

He didn't reply.

"You know what he found there?"

"No."

"Two dead bodies."

"Is that why you're here?"

"No," she lied. "I'm here because I don't understand something."

A cold rigidity rode his voice. "What don't you understand, Detective?"

"You, Blair Sullivan, and Matthew Cowart."

There was a momentary silence in the room.

"I can't help you," he said.

"No?" Ferguson had the ability to make someone uncomfortable simply by remaining still, she thought. "All right. Tell me what you were doing in the days before your old buddy Blair Sullivan got juiced."

For an instant, a look of surprise sliced across his face. Then Ferguson answered, "I was here. Studying. Going to classes. My course list is on the wall there."

"Right before Sullivan went to the chair. Did you take one of your little trips?"

"No."

He pointed at the wall. She turned and saw a list taped to the faded paint. She went over and wrote down the times and places and professors' names. Professor Morin and 'Media and Crime' were on the list.

"Can you prove it?"

"Do I have to?"

"Maybe."

"Then maybe I can."

Shaeffer heard a siren sweep by in the distance, its sound penetrating into the small room.

". . . And he was never my buddy," Ferguson said. "In fact, he hated me. I hated him."

"Is that right?"

"Yes."

"What do you know about the murders of his stepfather and mother?"

"Is that your case?"

"Answer the question."

"Nothing." He smiled at her, then added, "No. I know what I read and saw on television. I know they were killed a few days before his execution and that he told Mr. Cowart that he managed to arrange the deaths. That was in the papers. Even made *The New York Times*, Detective. But that's all." Ferguson seemed to relax. His voice abruptly took on the tone of someone who enjoyed verbal fencing.

"Tell me how he could arrange those killings," she asked. "You're the Death Row expert."

"That's right, I am." Ferguson paused, thinking. "There are a couple of different ways. . . ." He grinned at her unpleasantly. "First thing I'd do is pull the visitor lists. They log every visitor onto the Row. Every lawyer, reporter, friend, and family member. I'd go back to the day Sullivan arrived on the Row and I'd check every single person who came to see him. There were quite a bunch, you know. Shrinks and producers and FBI specialists. And of course, eventually, Mr. Cowart . . ." Ferguson's voice had a slightly animated edge to it. ". . . And then I'd talk to the guards. You know what it takes to be a guard on Death Row? You've got to have a bit of the killer in you, you know, because you're always aware that one day it could be you strapping some poor sucker into the chair. You've got to want to be that man." He held up his hand. "Oh, hell, they'll tell you that it's just a job and nothing personal and nothing different from any other part of the prison, but that ain't true. You got to volunteer for Q, R, and S wings. And you got to like what you're doing. And like what you might have to do."

He looked up at her, eyes alert. ". . . And I don't suppose if you don't think it's such a damn hard thing to strap somebody into a chair and fry their ass it'd be such a damn hard thing to go tie somebody in a chair and cut their throat."

"I didn't say they had their throats cut."

"It was in all the papers."

"Who?" she asked. "Give me a name or two."

"You're asking me to help you?"

"Names. Who on the Row would you talk to?"

He shook his head. "I don't know. But they were there. You could tell, you know. The Row is a society of killers. It didn't take too long to figure out that some of the jailers belonged on the other side."

He continued to grin at her. "Go and see for yourself," he said. "Shouldn't take a sharp detective like yourself too long to figure out who's bent and who's not."

"A society of killers," she said. "Where did you fit in, Mr. Ferguson?"

"I didn't. I was on the fringe."

"How much would you have to pay?"

He shrugged. "I don't know. A lot? A little? Currency is a

hard thing to estimate, Detective, because the right person will do the wrong thing for a lot of different reasons.''

"What do you mean?"

"Well, Blair Sullivan, for example. He'd likely kill you for no reason at all. With no other payment than the sheer pleasure of it all, huh, Detective? You ever meet anybody like that? I don't bet so. You look a bit young and inexperienced for that.''

His eyes followed her as she shifted position. "And you know, Detective, there's some men on the Row hate the police so bad, they'd kill a cop for free. And enjoy every second of it. Especially if they could, you know, draw it out. Make it last.''

He mocked her with lilting tones. "And they'd take a special pleasure in killing a lady cop, don't you think, Detective? A special, unique, and very terrible pleasure.''

She didn't reply, simply letting the harsh words flow over her like cold water.

". . . Or Mr. Cowart. Seems to me he'd do just about anything for a good story. What do you think, Detective?''

She felt a surge within her. "What about you, Mr. Ferguson? What payment would you ask to kill somebody?''

His smile slid away. "Never killed anybody. Never will.''

"That's not the question, Mr. Ferguson. What payment would you ask for?''

"It would depend,'' he replied, with ice quiet riding his voice.

"Depend on what?'' she demanded.

"Depend on who it was I was going to kill.'' He stared across the room at her. "Isn't that true for everybody, Detective? There are some killings that would require big money, right? Other's you'd do for nothing.''

"What would you do for nothing, Mr. Ferguson?''

He smiled again. "Can't really say. Never thought about it.''

"Really? That's not what you told those two Escambia detectives. Not what a jury found.''

Barely contained rage creased the complacency of his face, and he replied in bitter, low tones, "That was beat out of me. You know that perfectly well. Judge threw it out. I never did anything to that little girl. Sullivan did, he killed her.''

"And the price?''

"In that case,'' Ferguson said coldly, "the price was paid in pleasure.''

"What about Sullivan and his family? What do you think he'd have paid for those deaths?''

"Blair Sullivan? I suspect he'd have paid with his soul to take them with him."

Ferguson leaned forward, lowering his voice. "You know what he told me, before I figured out he was the person who killed the little girl that had put me on the Row? He used to talk about cancer, you know. Like some damn doctor, he knew so much about the disease. He would simply start in talking about deformed cells and molecular structures and DNA breakdowns and how just this little, tiny, microscopic wrong was working away within you, wreaking evil right through your whole body and working hard so that it would get in your lungs and colon and pancreas and brain and whatever, just make you rot away from within. And when he'd finish his lecture, he'd lean back and say why he was just the same damn thing, no different at all. What do you think of that, Detective?"

Ferguson leaned back, as if relaxing, but Shaeffer could see the muscles beneath his sweatshirt twitch. She didn't reply but started to move about the apartment again. The floor seemed to sway slightly beneath her feet.

"He talked to you about death?"

Ferguson leaned forward. "On Death Row, it's a frequent subject."

"And what did you learn?"

"I learned that it's about the most common thing around, ain't it, Detective? Why, it's just everywhere you turn. People think dying is something special, but it isn't, is it?"

"Some deaths are special."

"Those must be the ones you're interested in."

"That's right."

She saw him lean forward slightly, as if anticipating her next question.

"You like sneakers?" she asked abruptly. For an instant, she thought it was someone else speaking in the small room.

He looked slightly surprised. "Sure. Wear them all the time. Everybody here does."

"How about that pair. What sort are they?"

"These are Nikes."

"They look new."

"Just last week."

"Got another pair in the closet?"

"Sure."

She strode across in front of him, heading toward the back

bedroom. "Just sit still," she said. She could sense his eyes tracking her, burning into her back.

In the closet there was a pair of hightop basketball shoes. She picked them up. Damn! she thought abruptly. They were Converse and old and worn enough to have ripped near the toe. Still, she turned them over and inspected the soles. Near the ball of the foot the rubber had been rubbed smooth. She shook her head. That would have shown up. And the sole tread configuration was different from the Reeboks that the killer had worn when he visited number thirteen Tarpon Drive. She replaced the shoes and returned to face Ferguson.

He looked at her. "So, you've got a shoeprint from the murder scene, right?"

She remained silent.

". . . And you just all of a sudden thought you'd better check my closet." He stared at her. "What else have you got?" After a moment, he answered his own question. "Not much, right? But what brings you here?"

"I told you. Matthew Cowart. Blair Sullivan. And you."

He didn't respond at first. She could see his mind working rapidly. Finally he spoke in a flat, angry voice. "So, this is how it's gonna be? From now on? Is that right? Some tired-ass Florida cop needs to make somebody on a killing and I'm going to be the convenient one, right? Convicted once, so I'm a likely candidate for just about anything you can't make right away."

"I didn't say you were a suspect."

"But you wanted to see my sneakers."

"Routine, Mr. Ferguson. I'm checking everyone's sneakers. Even Mr. Cowart's."

Ferguson snorted a half laugh. "Sure you are. What sort does Cowart wear?"

She continued the lie rapidly. "Reeboks."

"Sure. They must be new, too, because last time I saw him he was wearing Converse just like my old ones."

She didn't reply.

"So, you're checking everyone's sneakers. But I'm the easy one, right? Wouldn't it be something to connect me to that killing, huh, Detective? That'd get you some headlines. Maybe get you a promotion, too. Ain't nobody going to question your motives."

She turned it back on him. "Are you? Why are you so easy?"

"Always have been, always will be. If not me, then someone like me: young and black. Makes me automatically a suspect."

She shook her head.

He half-rose from his seat in sudden anger. "No? When they needed someone fast in Pachoula who'd they come to see? And you? You figure that just because I knew Blair Sullivan, that made me someone you'd better talk to fast. But I didn't, damn you! That man almost cost me my life. I spent three years on Death Row for something I didn't do because of cops like you. I thought I was a dead man just because I was convenient for the system. So, screw you, Detective. I ain't gonna be convenient for nobody no more. I may be black, but I'm no killer. And just because I am black, doesn't make me one."

Ferguson slid back into his seat. "You wanted to know why I chose to live here? Because here people understand what it is like to be black and always be a suspect or a victim. That's what everyone here is. One or the other. And I've been both, so that's why I fit. That's why I like it, even though I don't have to be here. You understand that, Detective? I doubt it. Because you're white, and you'll never know."

He rose again, and stared out the window. "You'll never understand how someone can think this is home." He turned to her. "Got any more questions, Detective?"

The wealth of his fury had overcome her. She shook her head.

"Good," he said quietly. "Then get the hell out."

He pointed toward the door. She stepped toward it.

"I may have more questions," she said.

He shook his head. "No, I don't think so, Detective. Not again. Last time I was polite to a couple of detectives it cost me three years of my life and nearly killed me. So, you've had your chance. And now it's finished."

She was in the doorway. She hesitated, as if reluctant to leave but feeling at the same instant an immense relief at getting out of the small space. She turned toward him, but he was already closing the door on her. She had a quick glimpse of his eyes, narrowed in anger, before the door slammed shut. The clicking sound of the locks being thrown echoed in the hallway.

NINETEEN
PLUMBING

FOR most of the ride, the three men were silent.

Finally, as they turned off the highway, the police cruiser bumping against the hard-packed dirt of the secondary road, Bruce Wilcox said, "She's not gonna tell us a thing. She'll grab that old shotgun of hers and kick us off her place fast as a hungry mosquito can bite your naked ass. We're wasting our time."

He was driving. Next to him in the front seat, Tanny Brown stared through the windshield without replying. When a shaft of light slipped through the canopy of trees and struck him, it made his dark skin glisten, almost as if wet. At Wilcox's words, he raised a hand and made a small dismissive gesture, then dropped back into thought.

Wilcox humphed and drove on for a moment or two. "I still think we're wasting our time."

"We aren't," Brown growled as the car skidded and swayed on the rough road.

"Well, why not?" the detective asked. "And I wish you two'd fill me in on all this."

He twitched his head toward Cowart, sitting in the center of the rear seat, feeling more or less like one of the prisoners who generally occupied that location.

Brown spoke slowly. "Before Sullivan went to the chair, he implied to Cowart that there was evidence that we missed out at the Ferguson homestead. That it's still there. That's what we're doing now."

Wilcox shook his head. "Tanny, you ain't telling me the half of it. You know, he was just jerking Slick's chain." He spoke as if Cowart wasn't in the car. "I supervised that search myself. We took the place apart. Tapped every wall for a hollow spot. Pulled up the floorboards. Sifted through all the coals in that old stove to see if he'd burned anything. Crawled under the damn house with a metal detector. Hell, I even bought that damn tracking dog in, scented him, and led him through the place myself. If the creep had hid something, I'da found it."

"Sullivan said you missed something," Cowart insisted.

"Sullivan told the pencil pusher back there a lot of things," Wilcox said to his partner. "Why are we paying any damn attention to it?"

"Hey," Cowart said. "Give it a rest, will ya?"

"Where'd he tell you to look?"

"He didn't. Just said you missed something. Made an obscene joke about having eyes in my backside."

Wilcox shook his head. "And anyway, it won't do no good to find something." He glanced over at Brown. "You know that, boss, well as I. Ferguson's history. Gotta move on."

"No," Tanny Brown answered slowly. "He's not."

"So we find something? What's the point? Fruit of the poisonous tree. We can't use anything against Ferguson that stems from an illegal act. You gotta go back to that confession. If he'd a told us where everything was, exactly how he killed little Joanie, the whole shooting match, and then the judge tosses out that confession? Well, everything that follows goes, too."

"But that's not what happened," Cowart said.

Brown interrupted. "Right. Not exactly. It might give some lawyers something to argue over." He hesitated before continuing. ". . . But I'm not expecting to win this case in court." He did not amplify.

After a second's silence, Wilcox started in again. "I don't even think Ferguson's grandmother'll let us look around unless we've got a warrant. Hell, I don't think she'd even tell us if the sun was up without an order from a judge. Waste of time."

"She'll let Cowart look."

"When we drive him up? No way."

"She will."

"She probably hates the press worse'n I do. After all, they helped put her little darling on the Row in the first place."

"Then got him out."

"I don't think that's the way she thinks. She's an old Baptist

Bible-thumper. She probably believes that Jesus Hisself came down and opened the prison gate for her darling little boy, because she bombarded Him with prayers every Sunday at the meeting house. Anyway, even if she does let him in and let him poke around, which she won't, he doesn't even know what to look for. Or even how to look for it.''

"Yes, he does."

"Okay, then suppose, just suppose, for the sake of fuckall, that he finds something. What does that do for us?"

"One thing," Brown replied. He rolled down his window, letting some of the day's heat slip into the police cruiser, where it quickly overcame the stale cold of the air conditioner. He spoke softly, his voice barely cresting the wind noise from the window. "Then we'll know that about this, at least, Sullivan was telling the truth."

"So what?" Wilcox snapped. "What the hell does that do for us?"

The question drew more silence from the police lieutenant.

"Then we'll know what we're dealing with," Cowart finally interjected.

"Hah!" Wilcox snorted.

He drove on, gripping the steering wheel tightly, frustrated by the sense that his friend and partner and his adversary had shared some information to which he was not privy. It gave him an angry, hateful feeling within. He drove hard, raising a cloud of brown dust behind, half-wishing some mangy old dog or squirrel would run out in front of the car. He punched the accelerator, feeling the rear fishtail slightly on the dirt, scrabbling for thrust.

Cowart watched a tree line on the edge of a distant forest. "Where does that go?" he asked, pointing.

"Eventually to where we found Joanie. Edge of the same swamp. Runs back a half dozen miles or so before spreading out and curling toward town. Quicksand that'll kill ya and mud so thick you step in, it's like you put your foot in glue. Mile after mile of dead trees, weeds, and water. All dark and looks kinda the same. Get lost back in there, take a month to find your way out. If ever. Bugs, snakes, and gators and all sorts of slimy, crawling things. But good bass fishing, some real hawgs hanging underneath the dead wood. You just gotta be careful," Wilcox answered. "Not that you'd care."

As the police cruiser careened down the back road, jerking and swaying with the bumps and ruts, Cowart thought of the folded sheets of computer paper that contained the stories he'd printed out in the *Journal*'s library. They were inside his suit coat pocket, rubbing uncomfortably against his shirt, as if they had some radioactive quality that made them glow with heat. He had not shared the information with Tanny Brown.

It could just be coincidence, he insisted to himself. The man gave a speech in a church. Four days later a little girl disappears. That doesn't add up to anything. You don't know if he was still around or what he did after going to that church service, where he was, what he was doing. Four days. He could have been all the way back in Pachoula. Or Newark. Or Mars, for all you know.

His memory abruptly filled with the photograph of Joanie Shriver hanging on the wall at the elementary school. He saw the eyes of Dawn Perry staring out with little girl's insouciance and enthusiasm from the page of the police flyer. White and black. His throat felt suddenly dry.

"Getting close," Wilcox announced.

His partner's words cracked through Tanny Brown's thoughts. When he had arrived home in Pachoula, he had quickly been inundated in the routine of his life. One of his daughters had failed to get the lead in the class play; the other had discovered that her date curfew was an hour earlier than any of her friends'. These were problems of considerable dimension, items that needed his immediate attention. There were certain duties that his father simply would not perform; making the rules was one of them. "Your house. I'm just a visitor here," the old man had said. He'd been quite content, however, to listen to the younger complain about not getting the acting role. Tanny Brown wondered if the old man's occasional deafness was not an advantage in those situations.

He had lied to them about where he'd been, lied, as well, about what he was doing. And, he realized, he would have lied if anyone had asked him what he was afraid of. He had been relieved that both girls were caught up in their own lives, with that uniquely obsessive way children have. He had looked at the two of them, only half-listening to their complaints, and seen the picture of Dawn Perry that he still kept in his coat pocket. Why are they any different? he wondered.

He had castigated himself: You cannot be a policeman and survive if you allow yourself to see events as anything other than cases with file numbers. He had forced himself to cling to what he knew, what he could testify to. He kept denying his instincts, because his instincts insisted there was something out there that was far more terrible than he'd ever considered.

"There we go," Wilcox said.

They approached the shack rapidly, rattling loose stones against the undercarriage. Wilcox slammed the car to a halt and stared out, up at the tired wooden-frame house before saying, "Okay, Cowart, let's see you talk your way inside." He turned and glared at him.

"Give it a rest, Bruce," Brown grumbled.

Cowart did not reply but stepped out of the car and moved quickly across the dust of the front yard. He glanced back once, seeing the two detectives leaning side by side against the cruiser, watching his progress. He turned his back on them and climbed up the steps to the front porch. He called out, "Missus Ferguson? You home, ma'am?"

He shaded his eyes, blinded as he stepped from the bright sunlight of the front yard into the dark shade of the porch. He tried to make out some movement inside but couldn't at first.

"Missus Ferguson? It's Matthew Cowart. From the *Journal*."

There was still no reply.

He knocked hard on the doorframe, feeling it rattle beneath his knuckles. The whitewashed boards were peeling.

"Missus Ferguson, ma'am? Please."

Then, finally, a scratching sound came from the darkness within. A moment passed before a disembodied voice floated through the shadows within the shack toward him. The voice had lost none of its crackling edge and angry tone. "I know who you are. Whatcha ya'll want this time?"

"I need to talk to you again about Bobby Earl."

"We done talked and talked, Mr. Reporter. I ain't hardly got no words left. Ain't you heard enough now?"

"No. Not nearly. Can I come in?"

"What? Y'all only got inside questions?"

"Missus Ferguson, please. It's important."

"Important for who, Mr. Reporter?"

"Important for me. And for your grandson."

"I don't believe that," she replied.

There was another silence. Cowart's eyes slowly adjusted to the shade, and he began to make out shapes through the screen door. He could see an old table with a flowered water pitcher on top and a shotgun and a cane standing in a corner. After a moment, he heard footsteps approaching the door and finally the wispy old black woman hovered into view, her skin blending with the darkness of the interior, but her silver hair catching the light and shining at him. She was moving slowly and scowling as if the arthritis in her hips and back had penetrated her heart as well.

"I done talked with you enough already. What more you need to know?"

"The truth," he responded abruptly.

The old woman's scowl creased into a laugh. "You think you can find some truths in here, white boy? What, you think I keep the truth in a little jar by the door or somethin'? Pull it out when I needs it?"

"More or less," he replied.

She cackled unpleasantly. He watched her eyes sweep past him out toward the yard where the two detectives waited. She fixed her eyes on the two policemen, staring hard, then, after a long pause, shifting back to Cowart. "You ain't coming alone, this time."

He shook his head.

"You on their side now, Mister White Reporter?"

"No." He forced the lie out rapidly.

"Whose side you on, then?"

"Nobody's side."

"Last time you came here, you was on my grandson's side. Something different now?"

He searched hard for the right words. "Missus Ferguson, when I was at the prison, talking with the man who everybody thinks killed that little girl, he told me a story. A story all filled with killing, lies, half-truths, and half-lies. But one thing he said was that if I came here and looked, I would find some evidence."

"What sort of evidence?"

"Evidence that Bobby Earl committed a crime."

"How would this man know that?"

"He said Bobby Earl told him."

The old woman shook her head and laughed, a dry, brittle sound that broke off in the hot air between them.

"Why should I let you poke around and find something that's just gonna do my boy some harm? Cain't y'all leave him alone? Let him make hisself into something? Things is finished and over. Let the dead rest and let the living get on."

"That's not the way it works," he said. "You know that."

"All I know is you come 'round here looking to stir up a new patch of trouble for my boy. He don't need it."

Cowart took a deep breath. "Here's the reason. Missus Ferguson, you let me in and I look around, I don't find anything and that's it. The story becomes another lie that man told me, and that's all there is to it. Life goes on. Bobby Earl'll never have to look back. Those two detectives will walk out of your life and out of his life. But if I don't look, then they're never gonna be satisfied. Neither will I. And it'll never end. There will always be some questions. They won't ever go away. It'll stick with him all his days. See what I'm saying?"

The old woman hung a hand on the door handle, thinking.

"I see that point," she said finally, easing her words out carefully. "But suppose I let you in and you find this awful somethin' that that man told you about. What then?"

"Then Bobby Earl will be in trouble again."

She paused again before replying. "I don't truly see how my boy wins much if'n I let you in."

Cowart stared at the old woman hard and let loose his final weapon. "If you don't let me in, Missus Ferguson, then I'm going to assume you're hiding the truth from me. That there is some evidence hidden inside. That's what I'm going to tell those two detectives out there, and then a couple of things will happen. We'll come back with a warrant and search the place anyway. And no one's going to sleep until they make a case against your grandson, Missus Ferguson. I promise you that. And when they make it, I'll be right there, with my newspaper, and all the other papers and television stations, and you know what'll happen, don't you? So it seems to me you've only got one choice. Understand?"

The old woman's eyes immediately blistered hate.

"I understands perfect," she snarled. "I understands that white men in suits always get what they want. You want to get in, all right. You gonna get in, no matter what I say."

"All right, then."

"Come back with a paper from some judge, huh? They been here with one of those and it ain't done them no good at finding something. You think things different now?" She snorted in disgust.

Finally she unlatched the screen door with a click and held it open perhaps six inches.

"That man in prison, he tells you where to be looking?"

"No. Not precisely."

The old woman grinned unpleasantly. "Good luck, then."

He stepped into the house, like stepping out of one world and into another. He was accustomed—as much as anyone could become accustomed—to urban inner-city squalor. He had trailed his friend Vernon Hawkins to enough ghetto crime scenes so that he was no longer shocked or surprised by city poverty, rats, and peeling paint. But this house was different and unsettling.

Cowart saw a rigid, barren poverty, a place that made no concession to comfort or aspiration, only stiff lives, hard-lived, ruled by desperate anger. A crucifix hung on the wall over a threadbare sofa. An old wood rocker with a single yellowed lace doily on its seat stood in the corner. There were a few other chairs, mostly hand-hewn wood. On a mantelpiece above a fireplace was a portrait of Martin Luther King Junior and an old photograph of a lithe black man in an austere black suit. He guessed it was her late husband. There were a few other photographs of family members, including one of Robert Earl. The walls were dark brown wood, giving the house the semblance of a cave. Only random shafts of sunlight penetrated the windows, losing their fight against the shadows inside. He could see down a hallway to a kitchen where an old-fashioned wood stove dominated the center of the room. But everything was immaculate. Frayed age was everywhere, but not a particle of dust. Mrs. Ferguson probably treated a speck of dirt the same way she treated visitors.

"It ain't much, but it's mine," she said grimly. "No bank man come by saying he owns this place. It be all mine. Paying it off killed my husband and like to kill me, too, but I been happy here, even if it ain't so high and mighty a place."

She hobbled over to the window and stared out.

"I know that Tanny Brown," she said bitterly. "I knows his momma, she dead, and his daddy. They worked hard for Mister White Man and rose up thinking they be better than us. Ain't no truth in that. I remembers when he was little, stealing oranges off'n trees in the white men's groves. Now he's all grown up into a big policeman and thinks he's mighty fine. He ain't no better'n my grandson, hear?"

She turned away from the window. "So, go on, Mister White Reporter. Whatcha gonna look for? Ain't nothing here for you, boy. Cain't you see that?" She waved her arms around her, gesturing. "Ain't nothin' here for nobody."

He did see that.

Cowart glanced around and felt that Wilcox had been right. He had no idea what he was searching for or where to search. He had a sudden image of Blair Sullivan laughing at him.

"No," he said. "Where's Bobby Earl's room?"

The old woman pointed. "Down on the right. Go ahead."

Cowart moved slowly down the corridor in the center of the shack. He glanced in at the old woman's bedroom. He saw a Bible open in the center of an old double bed covered with a single white knit coverlet. Austere and icy. Comfort only in those words read, and precious little comfort at that. He walked past a small bathroom, no bigger than a closet, with a single basin and toilet. The fixtures shone with a polished newness. Then he turned into Ferguson's room.

It, too, was barren, a monk's quarters. A single window high on the wall let in a little light. There was an iron bed, a hand-hewn wooden table, a small chest of drawers, and a chair. An old plank had been nailed to one wall to hold a modest collection of paperback books. *Manchild in the Promised Land* and *The Invisible Man* butted up against some science-fiction novels. A pair of fishing rods were stacked in the corner, along with a scratched cheap plastic tackle box.

Cowart sat on the edge of the bed, feeling the soft mushiness of the springs. He let his eyes roam over the meager items in the room, searching for some sign. What should a killer's room look like?

He didn't know. He looked about, remembering how Ferguson had insisted to him that coming to Pachoula after Newark, New Jersey, was like stepping into a summer camp, that it was warm and special, some sort of Huck Finn-like adventureland. *Where the hell is that?* Cowart thought, staring around himself at the blank walls, the passionless items of furniture.

Where to start? He couldn't imagine that something as potent as evidence of a murder would be obvious, so he started in on the drawers of the bureau, feeling foolish, certain that he was simply going over well-searched territory. He rifled through a few changes of clothing without finding anything that he imagined could help him. He ran his hands down behind the bureau drawers, to see if something was concealed there. You're some detective, he thought. He climbed down on his knees and did the same with the bed. He felt the mattress. Then he tapped the walls, looking for a hollow spot.

To conceal what? he kept asking himself.

He was on his hands and knees, tapping at the floor when Ferguson's grandmother hovered in the doorway.

"They done that," she said. "Way back when. Now, ain't ya satisfied yet?"

He stood up slowly, close to embarrassment. "I don't know."

She laughed at him. "You finished now."

He straightened his clothes. "Let me talk to the detectives."

She cackled again and trailed him back through the house and onto the front porch as he walked across the dirt yard to the two detectives.

Tanny Brown spoke first, but his eyes reached past Cowart, up at the old woman, before returning to settle on the reporter. "Well?"

"Nothing that seemed like evidence of anything except being poor."

"Told you so," Wilcox said. He looked over at Cowart, his voice softening somewhat. "You go into Ferguson's room?"

"Yeah."

"Not much there, right?"

"A couple of books. Fishing pole. Tackle box. Few clothes in the drawers, that's it."

Wilcox nodded. "That's how I remember it. That's what bugged me so damn much. You know, you walk into most anybody's room, no matter how rich or poor they are, and there's something in there that says something about who they are. But not in there. Not in that whole house."

Brown rubbed his forehead. "Damn," he said. "I feel stupid and I am stupid."

Cowart broke into his thoughts. "The trouble is, I don't know what you did when you were there before, and what's different now. I could be picking something up that might mean something to you, but not to me."

Wilcox seemed to have let some of his antagonism slide away in the growing heat of the day. "That's what I thought would happen. Here, maybe this will help."

He walked around to the trunk of the vehicle and opened it. Several accordion paper folders were stacked inside, next to a riot shotgun, a pair of flak jackets, and a large crowbar. He rifled swiftly through the files, finally seizing several stapled sheets of paper. He handed them to Cowart.

"Here's the inventory from the search back then. See if that helps."

The papers started with a list of items seized from the house and their disposition. There were several articles of clothing. These were noted as "Returned after analysis. Negative findings." Some knives had been taken from the kitchen as well. These, too, were marked "Returned."

The inventory also listed what items had been taken from what part of the house. There were brief descriptions of the methods used to search each room and the locations searched. Cowart saw that Ferguson's room had been exhaustively processed, with negative results.

"You see anything inside we missed?" Wilcox asked.

Cowart shook his head.

"Tanny, we're wasting our time."

Cowart looked up from the papers to see that the police lieutenant had stepped aside while he was reading, fixing his eyes on the old woman. She stayed on the edge of her porch, glaring back at him, their eyes locked onto each other.

"Tanny?" Wilcox asked.

The policeman didn't reply.

Cowart watched the detective and the old woman try to stare each other down. He was aware of the sweat streaking down beneath his shirt and the clammy damp that matted his hair to his forehead.

Brown spoke after a moment, without removing his eyes from the old woman. "Look again," he said. "I think we're missing something obvious."

"Christ, Tanny . . ." Wilcox started again, only to be cut off by the police lieutenant.

"Look at her. She knows something and knows we don't have a clue. Damn. Keep looking."

Wilcox shrugged, muttering something under his breath which dissipated in the midday heat. Cowart dropped his eyes to the sheets of paper, trying to process them as carefully as the policeman had once processed the house. He went over the sheets, room by room, talking out loud toward Wilcox as he did. "Front room: fingerprinting, all items inspected, none seized, floorboards loosened, walls tapped, metal detector used; grandmother's room: searched and examined for hidden items, none found; storeroom: cutting shears seized, cleaning rags seized, towel seized, floorboards removed; Ferguson's room: clothing seized, walls and floors examined, vacuumed for hair samples; kitchen: cutlery inspected and seized, stove ashes examined, sent to lab, crawl space inspected . . ." He looked up. "It seems pretty complete . . ."

"Hell, we spent hours in that place, checking every damn loose nail," Wilcox said.

Brown continued to stare up at the old woman.

"It seems to be the same today," Cowart said, "except I guess she turned the storeroom into a toilet. Little room between hers and Ferguson's?" he asked.

"Yeah. More like a closet than a storeroom, really," Wilcox said.

Cowart nodded. "Toilet and basin now."

Wilcox added, "I heard Ferguson put that in. Used some of the money he got from some Hollywood producer who wanted to tell his life story. Progress reaches the sticks."

In that moment, it seemed that the sunlight pouring down on top of them redoubled, a sudden explosion of heat that sucked all the air out of the yard.

"So before, where did they . . ."

"Old outhouse way 'round the back."

"And?"

"And what?"

"It's not on the list here," Cowart said slowly. He could feel a sudden pounding in his temples.

Brown spun away from Mrs. Ferguson, eyes burrowing into his partner. "You searched it, right?"

Wilcox nodded, hesitantly. "Ahh, yeah. Sort of. The warrant was for the house, so I wasn't sure if it was covered, exactly. But one of the technicians went inside, sure. Nothing."

Brown stared hard at his partner.

"C'mon, Tanny. All it was was smells and shits. The tech went in, poked about and got the hell out of there. It was in the search report." He pointed down to a sentence in the midst of the sheets of paper. "See," he said hesitantly.

Cowart stumbled away from the car. He remembered Blair Sullivan's words: "If you got eyes in your ass."

"Goddammit," he said. "Goddammit." He turned toward Brown. "Sullivan said . . ."

The policeman frowned. "I recall what he said."

Cowart turned abruptly and started walking around the side of the shack, toward the back. He heard Ferguson's grandmother's voice driven across the heat toward him, penetrating like an arrow. "Where you heading, boy?"

"Out back," Cowart said brusquely.

"Ain't nothing there for you," she shouted shrilly. "You can't go back there."

"I want to see. Goddammit, I want to see."

Brown caught up with him quickly, the crowbar from the trunk of the car in his hand. The two men strode around the corner of the house as the woman's protests slid away in the blistering sunlight. They saw the outhouse in a corner, near some trees, back away from everything. The wooden walls had faded to a dull gray. Cowart walked up to it. Cobwebs covered the door. He seized the handle and pulled hard, tugging, as it opened reluctantly, making a screeching sound of protest, old wood scraping against old wood. The door jammed, partway open.

"Watch out for snakes," Brown said, grabbing at the edge of the door and pulling hard. With a final tug that shook the entire structure, the door swung wide.

"Bruce! Get a goddamn flashlight!" Brown yelled. He took the end of the crowbar and swept more spiderwebs aside. A scuttling, scratching sound made Cowart jump back as some small beast fled from the sudden light pouring through the open door.

The two men stood, shoulder to shoulder, staring at the wooden toilet seat, carved from a board, polished by use. The stench in the small space was dull and thick. It was an old smell that clogged their breathing, a smell closer to death or age than waste.

"Under there," Cowart said.

Brown nodded in agreement.

"Way down."

Wilcox, slightly out of breath from running, joined them, thrusting the black flashlight toward his partner.

"Bruce," Brown asked quietly, "the crime-scene guy. Did he pull the seat? Did he check through the stink?"

Wilcox shook his head. "It was nailed down tight. The nails were old, I remember, because he made me come in and double-check. There was no sign that anything had been pulled up and then replaced. You know, like hammer marks or scrapes or anything . . ."

"No obvious sign," said Brown.

"That's right. Nothing jumped out when we looked at it." His eyes flashed angrily.

"But . . ." Brown said.

"That's right. But," Wilcox replied, "I can't guarantee he

didn't have some way of getting down into the shit hole that we didn't see. The tech went in, checked with a light, and then came out, like I told you. I stuck my head in, looked around, and that was it. I mean, one of us would've seen anything shoved down that hole . . .''

"If you wanted to hide something, and you didn't think you had much time and you wanted to be sure it'd be the last place searched in the most perfunctory fashion . . .'' Brown's voice hovered between lecture and anger.

"Why not take it out into the woods and bury it?''

"Can't be certain it won't be found, especially when we bring the damn dogs in. Can't be certain you won't be seen. But one thing's for sure. Nobody's gonna go down there into a shit hole that don't have to.''

Wilcox nodded. His voice curled up softly in despair. "You're right. Dammit. D'you think . . .''

His thought was interrupted by a sudden, shrill cry from behind them.

"Get away from there!''

The three men turned and saw the old woman standing on a back stoop, holding an old double-barreled shotgun at her hip.

"I will blow you straight to hell if'n you don't move away from there! Now!''

Cowart froze in position, but the two detectives instantly started to move slowly apart, one right, one left, spreading the distance between the three men.

"Mrs. Ferguson,'' Brown started.

"You shut up!'' she said, swinging the gun toward him.

"Come on, Mrs. Ferguson . . .'' Wilcox pleaded quietly, lifting both his hands up in a gesture more of supplication than surrender.

"You, too!'' the old woman cried, swinging the barrels toward him. "And both you men stop moving.''

Cowart saw a quick glance go between the partners. He didn't know what it meant.

The old woman turned back toward him. "I tole you to get away from there.''

He lifted his arms but shook his head. "No.''

"What you mean, no? Boy, don't you see this shotgun? I'll use it, too.''

Cowart felt a sudden rush of blood to his head. He saw all the fury masking the fear in the old woman's eyes and knew then she knew what she was hiding. *It's there,* he thought. *Whatever*

it is, it's there. It was as if all the frustration and exhaustion he'd
felt for the past days coalesced in that second, and outrage overcame whatever reason he had left. He shook his head.

"No," he said again, louder. "No, ma'am. I'm going to look
in there, even if you have to kill me. I'm just too damn tired of
being lied to. I'm too damn tired of being used. I'm too damn
tired of feeling like some goddamn fool all the time. You got it,
old woman? I'm too damn tired!"

With each repetition of the phrase, he'd stepped toward her,
covering half the distance between them.

"You stay away!" the old woman shouted.

"You gonna kill me?" he shouted back. "That'll do a helluva
lot of good. You just shoot me right in front of these two detectives. Go ahead. Goddammit, come on!"

He began to stride toward her. He saw the shotgun waver in
her arms.

"I means to!" she screamed.

"Then go ahead!" he screamed back.

His rage was complete. It overcame the delusion he'd clung
to of Ferguson's innocence, so that it all poured out of him. "Go
ahead! Go ahead! Just like your grandson killed that little girl in
cold blood! Go ahead! You gonna give me the same chance he
gave her? You a killer too, old woman? This where he learned
how to do it? Did you teach him how to slice up a little defense-
less girl?"

"He didn't do nothing!"

"The hell he didn't!"

"Stand back!"

"Or what? You maybe just taught him how to lie? Is that it?"

"Stay away from me!"

"Did you, goddammit? Did you?"

"He didn't do no such thing. Now get back or I'll blow your
head off!"

"He did it. You know it, goddammit, he did it, he did it, he
did it!"

And the shotgun exploded.

The blast shredded the air above Cowart's head, singeing him
and knocking him, stunned, to the ground. There was a rattle
of bird shot against the walls of the outhouse behind him; shouts
from the two detectives, who simultaneously went for their own
weapons, screaming, "Freeze! Drop the gun!"

The sky spun above him and his nose filled with the smell of
cordite. He could hear a thumping sound deep beyond the ring-

ing from the shotgun's explosion, which confused him, until he realized it was the echo of his own heart in his ears.

Cowart sat up and felt his head, then stared at his hand, which came away damp from sweat, not blood. He stared up at the old woman. The detectives both continued to shout commands, which seemed lost in the heat and sun.

The old woman looked down at him. Her voice was shrill. "I told you, Mr. Reporter Man, I told you once before, I'd spit in the eye of the devil hisself if'n it'd help my grandson."

Cowart continued to stare at her.

"You dead?" she asked.

"No," he replied quietly.

"I couldn't do it," she said bitterly. "Like to blow your head clean off. Damn."

Her skin had turned an ashen gray. She dropped the weapon to her side.

"Only got one shell," she said.

She looked over toward the two detectives, who were approaching her, weapons drawn, crouched and ready to fire. She fixed her eyes on Brown.

"Should have saved it for you," she said.

"Drop the weapon."

"You gonna kill me now, Tanny Brown?"

"Drop the weapon!"

The old woman humphed at him. Slowly, she took the shotgun and carefully set it against the door behind her. Then she stood and faced him, folding her arms.

"You gonna kill me now?" she asked again.

Wilcox bent toward Cowart. "You okay, Cowart?"

"I'm okay," the reporter replied.

He helped pull Cowart back to his feet. "Christ, Cowart, that was something. You really lost it."

Cowart felt suddenly elated. "No shit," he laughed.

Wilcox turned toward Brown. "You want me to cuff her and read her her rights?"

The detective shook his head, reached over, and grasped the shotgun, cracking it open to check the double chambers. He pulled out the spent shell and flipped it to Cowart. "Here. A souvenir."

Then he turned back to Ferguson's grandmother. "You got any other weapons lying around?"

She shook her head at him.

"You gonna talk to me now, old woman?"

She shook her head again and spat on the ground, still defiant.

"Okay then, you can watch. Bruce?"

"Boss?"

"Find a shovel in the storeroom."

The police lieutenant holstered his revolver and handed the emptied shotgun back to the old woman, who scowled at him. He walked back to the outhouse and gestured to Cowart. "Here," he said, handing the reporter the crowbar. "Seems like you earned first swipe at this thing."

The old wood protested slowly at the assault first with the crowbar, then with the shovel Wilcox discovered by the side of the shack. But when it finally cracked and gave way, it tore apart rapidly, exposing a fetid hole in the earth. Quicklime had been used for sanitation. White streaks covered the gray-brown mass of waste.

"In there somewhere," Cowart said.

"I hope you got all your shots," Wilcox muttered. "Anybody got any open cuts or sores? Better be careful."

He grabbed the shovel out of Brown's hands.

"It was my search fucked up three years ago. Mine, now," he whispered grimly. He took off his coat jacket and found a handkerchief in a pocket. This he tied around his face, over his nose and mouth. "Damn," he said, his words muffled by the makeshift mask. "You know this ain't a legal search," he said to Brown, who nodded. "Damn," Wilcox said again.

Then he stepped down into the ooze and muck.

He groaned once, muttering a series of expletives, then he set to uncovering each layer of refuse, scraping away with the shovel.

"You keep your eyes on the shovel," he said, breathing through his mouth, hard. "Don't let me miss something."

Brown and Cowart didn't reply. They just watched Wilcox's progress. He kept at it steadily, carefully, slowly working his way through the pile. He slipped once, catching himself before sliding down into the hole, but coming up with waste streaking his arms and hands. Wilcox simply swore hard and continued working with the shovel.

Five minutes passed, then ten. The detective continued to dig, pausing only to cough away some of the stench.

Another half dozen swipes with the shovel and he muttered, "Got to be down a couple of years, now. I mean, how much shit can that old lady produce in a year?" He laughed unhappily.

"There!" Cowart said.

"Where?" Wilcox asked.

"Right there," said Tanny Brown, pointing. "What's that?"

The corner of some solid object had been uncovered by a swipe with the shovel.

Wilcox grimaced and reached down gingerly, seizing the object. It came free with a sucking sound. It was a rectangular piece of thick synthetic material.

Brown crouched down, staring, took the material by the corner and held it up.

"You know what this is, Bruce?"

The detective nodded. "You bet."

"What?" Cowart asked.

"One slice of car carpet. You remember, in Ferguson's car, on the passenger side, there was a big piece of carpeting cut out. There it is."

"You see anything else?" Brown asked.

Wilcox turned back and poked with the shovel in the same location. "No," he said. "Wait, unh-hunh, well, what have we here?"

He plucked what appeared to be a solid mass of refuse from the muck, and handed it to Brown. "There it is."

The police lieutenant turned toward Cowart. "See," he said.

Cowart stared hard and finally did see.

The lump was a pair of jeans, a shirt, and sneakers and socks all rolled tightly together, tied with a shoelace. The years of being under the refuse, covered with lime, had worn them away to tatters, but they were still unmistakable.

"I'll bet the farm," Wilcox said, "that there's blood residue on those clothes somewhere."

"Anything else down there?"

The detective struggled for another moment with the shovel. "I don't think so."

"Come on out, then."

"With pleasure." He scrambled from the pit.

The three men wordlessly walked back into the yard. They spread the items out carefully in the sun. "Can they be processed?" Cowart asked after a moment had passed.

Brown shrugged. "I suspect so." He looked at the items quietly. "Don't really need to."

"That's right," said Cowart.

Wilcox was trying to clean himself up as best as possible. He looked up from the task of shaking the clods of waste from his clothes over toward his partner.

"Tanny," he said softly. "I'm sorry, buddy. I should have been more careful. I should have figured."

Brown shook his head. "You know more now than you did then. It's okay. I should have double-checked the search report." He continued to look down at the items. "Damn," he said, finally. "Dammit to hell." He looked up at Cowart. "But now we know, don't we?"

Cowart nodded.

The three men picked up the clothing and particle of carpet gingerly and turned back toward the house. They saw the old woman standing alone, watching them from her perch on the back stoop. She stared at them helplessly. Cowart could see her hands quivering at her sides.

"It don't mean nothing!" she yelled, searching for defiance. One arm rose slowly from her side and she shook a fist at them. "Throw all sorts of old stuff away! It don't mean nothing at all!"

The two detectives and the reporter walked past her, but she continued to shout after them, the words soaring across the yard, up into the pale blue sky. "It don't mean nothing! Can't you hear? Damn your eyes, Tanny Brown! It don't mean nothing at all!"

TWENTY

TRAPS

Tanny Brown drove the police cruiser aimlessly down the streets of the town where he'd grown up, Cowart next to him, waiting for the detective to say something. Wilcox had been dropped at the crime lab with the items seized from the outhouse. The reporter had thought that they would return immediately to the police offices to map out their next step, but instead found himself moving slowly through the town.

"And so?" he finally asked. "What's next?"

"You know," Brown said slowly, "it's not really much of a town. Always played second fiddle to Pensacola and Mobile. Still, it was all I knew. All I ever really wanted. Even when I went away in the service and then to Tallahassee for college, always knew I wanted to come back here. What about you, Cowart? Where's home for you?"

Cowart pictured the small brick house where he'd grown up. It had been set back from the street, with a large oak tree in the front yard. It had had a front porch with a creaky, swinging love seat in the corner that was never used, and had grown rusty with the passing of winters. But almost immediately the picture of the house faded and what he saw was his father's newspaper, twenty years earlier, through a child's eyes, before computers and electronic layout machines. It was as if his understanding of the world had been channeled through the battered, steel-gray desks and wan fluorescent lights, past the cacophony of constantly ringing telephones, the voices raised in newsroom give-and-take, the whooshing sound of the vacuum tubes that linked the newsroom with composing, the machine gun rat-a-tat-tat of fingers slamming the keys of the old manual typewriters that banged out the history of the day's events. He'd grown up wanting nothing more than to get away, but away had always been interpreted to mean something the same, only bigger, better. Finally, Miami. One of the nation's finest newspapers. A life defined by words.

Maybe, he thought, a death defined by them, as well.

"No home," he replied. "Just a career."

"Aren't they the same?"

"I suppose. It's hard to make distinctions."

The detective nodded.

"So what are we going to do?" Cowart asked again.

The detective had no easy response. "Well," he said slowly, "we know who really killed Joanie Shriver."

Both men felt a palpable, physical depression with those words. Brown thought, *I knew. All along, I knew.* But he still couldn't shake the sensation that something had changed.

"You can't touch him, right?"

"Not in a court of law. Bad confession. Illegal search. We've been all over that."

"And I can't touch him, either," Cowart said, bitterness streaking his voice.

"Why? What happens if you write a story?"

"You don't want to know."

Brown suddenly steered the car to the curb, jamming on the brakes. He slammed the car out of gear and pivoted toward the reporter in a single motion.

"What happens?" he asked furiously. "Tell me, dammit! What happens?"

Cowart's face reddened. "I'll tell you what happens: I write the story and the whole world jumps on our backs. You think the press was tough on you before? You have no idea what they're like when they smell blood in the water. Everyone's going to want a piece of this mess. More microphones and notepads and camera lights than you've ever seen. Stupid cop and stupid reporter screw up their jobs and let a killer go free. There isn't a front page, a prime-time news show in this country that won't scream for that story."

"What happens to Ferguson?"

Cowart scowled. "It's easiest for him. He simply denies it. Smiles at the cameras and says, 'No, sir. I didn't do anything.

They must have planted that evidence there.' A setup, he'll say, a cheap trick by a frustrated cop. He'll say you planted the evidence there after finding it someplace else—someplace where Blair Sullivan told me to find it, just like the knife. Got me to go along, or tricked me into going along, makes no difference. I'm the conduit for covering your mistakes. And you know what? A lot of people will believe it. You beat a confession out of him once. Why not try some other scheme?''

Brown opened his mouth, but Cowart wasn't done. ''Then, suppose he files a defamation suit? Remember *Fatal Vision?* He filed a crazy suit and right away everyone seemed to forget that he was convicted of slaughtering his wife and kids when they got so damned concerned over what that writer did or didn't do. Who do you think is going to be slicker on the air? More persuasive? What are you going to do when Barbara Walters or fucking Mike Wallace leans across the table, cameras rolling, lights making you sweat, and asks you, 'Well, now, you really did order your man to beat Mr. Ferguson, right? Even though you knew it was against the law? Even though you knew if anyone found out, he would go free?' And what good is it going to do for you to say anything? How're you going to answer those questions, Detective? How're you going to make it seem like you wouldn't go and plant evidence at Ferguson's home? Tell me, Detective, because I'd surely like to know.''

Brown glared at Cowart. ''And what about you?''

''Oh, they'll be just as tough on me, Detective. America is used to killers, familiar with the species. But failures? Ahh, failures get special, unique attention. Screwups and mistakes aren't the American way. We tolerate murder, but not defeat. I can just see it: 'Now, Mr. Cowart, you won a Pulitzer Prize for saying this man was innocent. What do you expect to win by saying he's not?' And then it'll get tougher. 'Guilty? Innocent? What do you want, Mr. Cowart? Can't have it both ways. Why didn't you tell us this before? Why did you wait? What were you trying to cover up? What other mistakes have you made? Do you know the difference between the truth and a lie, Mr. Cowart?' ''

He took a deep breath. ''You got to understand one thing, Detective.''

''What's that?''

''There's only going to be two people anyone thinks is guilty here. You and me.''

''And Ferguson?''

"He walks. Inconvenienced but free. Maybe even a hero in the right places, with the right people. Even more of a hero than he currently is."

"To do . . ."

"To do whatever he likes . . ."

Cowart opened the car door and stepped out of the vehicle. He stood on the sidewalk, letting the breeze dry his emotions. His eyes swept down the street, stopping at an old-fashioned barber shop that still had the traditional revolving pole, and watched the tri-colors swirl in an endless route, always moving but never arriving. He was only peripherally aware that Brown had gotten out of the car and was standing a few feet behind him.

"Suppose," the detective said coldly to Cowart's back, "suppose he's already doing whatever he likes."

Another little girl. A Dawn Perry. Disappeared one day. *"May I go to the pool for a swim? Be back before dinner . . ."*

"Now we know what he likes, don't we, Cowart?"

"Yes."

"And there's nothing stopping him from taking up where he left off, before his little vacation on Death Row, right?"

"No. Nothing. So what do you suggest we do, Detective?"

"A trap," said Brown flatly. "We set a trap. We sting him. If we can't get him on something old, we should get him on something new."

Cowart knew, without turning, that the man's face was set in granite anger. "Yes," he said. "Go on."

"Something unequivocal, that makes it clear who he is. Clear so that when I arrest him and you write the story, no one has any doubts whatsoever. None, got it? No doubts. Can you write that story, Cowart? Write it so that he has no way out?"

Matthew Cowart had a sudden memory of watching a Maine fisherman bait lobster traps with pieces of dead fish before slinging them over the side of his boat into the ice-black coastal waters. It had been a summer vacation, when he was young. He remembered how fascinated he had been with the simple, deadly design of the lobster traps. A box made of a few pieces of wood and chicken wire. The beasts would crawl in one end, unable to resist the allure of the rotting carcass, then, after feeding, be unable to maneuver about and retreat through the narrow entrance. Captured by a combination of greed, need, and physical limitations.

"I can write that story," he replied. He looked over at the

detective and added, "But traps take time. Have we got time, Detective? How much?"

Brown shook his head. "All we can do is try."

Brown left Cowart alone in his office while he went off saying he needed to check on whether Wilcox had returned with preliminary laboratory results on the clothing and the piece of auto carpet. The reporter looked around for a moment at the various citations and photographs that he'd previously inspected, then he picked up the telephone and called *The Miami Journal*. A switchboard operator connected him with Edna McGee. Cowart wondered how many people had been fooled by the breeziness of her tones, not knowing that beneath them lay a steely mind that thrived on detail.

"Edna?"

"Matty, Matty, where have you been? I've been leaving messages all over for you."

"I'm back up in Pachoula. With the cops."

"Why them? I thought you were going to Starke to try and work the prison angle."

"Uh, that's next."

"Well, I would get there. *The St. Pete Times* reported today that Blair Sullivan left several file boxes filled with documents, diaries, descriptions, I don't know what else. Maybe something that described how he set up those murders. The paper said that Monroe detectives are going through the stuff now, looking for leads. They've also been interviewing everyone who worked on Death Row during Sullivan's stay. And they've got lists of visitors as well. I made some calls and filed a bit of a catch-up story. But the city desk is wondering where the hell you are. And especially wondering why the hell you didn't file that story before that son of a bitch from St. Pete did. Not pleased, Matty, they're not pleased. Where have you been?"

"Back in the Keys. Here."

"Got anything?"

"Nothing for the paper, yet. Got a lead or two . . ."

"Like what?"

"Edna, give me a break."

"Well, Matty, I'd get cracking and think of filing something spectacular pretty soon. Like, right away. Otherwise the wolves will be at the door, howling for their dinner. If you get what I mean."

"You make it clear. And appetizing."

Edna laughed. "No one wants to go from being caviar to dog food."

"Thanks, Edna. You're really reassuring."

"Just a warning."

"It's been heard. So, what have you come up with?"

"Following the trail of your Mr. Sullivan has been quite an education in the creative use of lying."

"What do you mean?"

"Well, of the forty or so killings he owned up to, I right now say he did about half. Maybe a little less."

"Only twenty . . ."

He heard himself speak those words and realized how silly they sounded. *Only twenty.* As if it made him only half as evil as someone who killed forty people.

"Right. For sure. At least, twenty that sound persuasive."

"What about the others?"

"Well, some he clearly didn't do because other people are serving time, or even sitting on Death Row, for the crimes. He just sort of stitched the stories into the fabric of his own story, see? Like I told you about the crime on the Miccosukkee Reservation, for one example. He also told you at one point that he killed a woman up outside of Tampa. A woman he met in a bar, promised her a good time, ended up killing her, you remember that one?"

"Ahh, sure, I remember he didn't say a lot about it, except to sort of delight in the fun of killing her."

"Right. That's the one. Well, he had all the details right, except for one thing. The guy who did that crime also did two other women in that area and occupies a cell about thirty feet away from Blair Sullivan's old home on Death Row. He just slid that story right in amidst two others that check out. Wasn't until I started checking up there that it rang a bell. See what he did? Just grabbed that other guy's crime—and there ain't no doubt the other guy was the killer—and just added it into his grand total. Did that a couple of other times, with other crimes that guys are on the Row for. Sort of like a quarterback throwing a lot of short passes in the final quarter of a game that's already won. He was, like, inflating his stats." Edna laughed.

"But why?"

Cowart could sense Edna's shrug through the telephone line. "Who knows? Maybe that's why all those FBI folks were so damn interested in talking to Sully before he checked out."

"But . . ."

"Well, let me give you one theory. Call it McGee's Postulate, or something nice and scientific like that. But I asked around a bit, you know, and guess what? They always figured Ted Bundy for some thirty-eight killings. Could have been more, but that's the figure that we got, and that's what he ended up talking about before heading off to hell, himself. My guess is that old Sully wanted to do him a couple better. They found at least three different books about Bundy amongst Sully's personal effects, you know. Nice detail, that, huh? The next best killer, if you want to call it that, waiting on Death Row is that guy Okrent, the Polish guy from Lauderdale, remember him? He had the little problem with prostitutes. Like, he killed them. He's only around eleven officially, but unofficially, he's at about seventeen or eighteen. He was on the same wing as Sully, too. You beginning to see my thinking here, Matty? Old Sully wanted to be famous. Not only for what he was doing, but for what he did. So, he took a few liberties."

"I see what you're driving at. Can you get someone to say it, and put it in the paper?"

"No sweat. Those FBI guys will say whatever I want them to. And there are those two sociologists up in Boston who study mass murderers. I spoke with them earlier. They *love* McGee's Postulate. So, all in all, it should run tomorrow, if I work late. Or the next day, which is a lot more likely."

"That's great," Cowart said.

"But, Matty, it would go a lot better if you had something to run alongside it. Like a story saying who killed those old folks down in the Keys."

"I'm working on it."

"Work hard. That's the only question still out there, Matty. That's what everyone wants to know."

"I hear you."

"They're getting a bit frantic over at the city desk. They want to put our world-famous, crack, ace, and only occasionally incompetent investigative team on it. Lobbying hard, so I hear."

"Those guys couldn't figure out . . ."

"I know that, Matty, but there are people saying you're overwhelmed."

"I'm not."

"Just warning you. Thought you'd want to know all the politicking going on behind your back. And that story in *The St. Pete Times* didn't help your cause any. It doesn't help either that no one knows where the hell you are ninety-nine percent of the time. Jeez, the city editor had to lie to that Monroe detective the other morning when she came in here looking for you."

"Shaeffer?"

"The pretty one with the eyes that look like she'd rather be roasting you on an open spit than talking with you."

"That's her."

"Well, she was here, and she got the semi-runaround and that's a marker they hold on you now."

"All right. I hear you."

"Hey, break that case. Figure out who zapped the old couple. Maybe win another big one, huh?"

"No, I don't think so."

"Well, nothing wrong with fantasizing, right?"

"I guess not."

He hung up the phone, muttering obscenities to himself, but precisely whom or what he was cursing, he didn't know. He started to dial the number for the city editor, then stopped. What could he tell him? Just then he heard a noise at the door and looked up to see Bruce Wilcox. The detective seemed pale.

"Where's Tanny?" he asked.

"Around. He left me here to wait for him. I thought he was looking for you. What did you find out?"

Wilcox shook his head. "I can't believe I screwed up," he answered.

"Did the lab find anything?"

"I just can't believe I didn't check the goddamn shithouse back then." Wilcox tossed a couple of sheets of paper onto the desk. "You don't have to read them," he said. "What they found was material resembling blood residue on a shirt, jeans, and the rug. Resembling, for Christ's sake. And that was looking through a microscope. All had deteriorated almost to the point of invisibility. Three years of shit, lime, dirt, and time. There wasn't a hell of a lot left. I watched that lab tech spread out the shirt and it, like, almost fell apart when he started to poke at it with tweezers. Anyway, not a damn thing that's conclusive. They're gonna send it all off to a fancier lab down in Tallahassee, but who knows what they'll come up with. The technician wasn't real optimistic."

Wilcox paused, taking a slow, long breath. "Of course, you and I know why those things were there. But getting up and saying they were evidence of anything, well, we're a long ways from being able to say that. Damn! If I found them three years ago, when everything was fresh, you know, they just dissolve that shit and stuff right off and there's the blood." He looked up at Cowart. "Joanie Shriver's blood. But now, they're just a couple of pieces of tired old clothes. Damn."

The detective paced the office. "I can't believe how I screwed up," he said again. "Screwed up. Screwed up. Screwed up. My first goddamn big case."

He was clenching his fists tightly, then releasing them before tightening them once again into a ball. In, out. In, out. Cowart could see the detective's muscles shifting about beneath his shirt. The high-school wrestler before a match.

Tanny Brown sat in a recently emptied office at a vacant desk making telephone calls. The door was shut behind him, and in front of him was a yellow legal pad for notes and his personal address book. He had to leave messages at the first three numbers he tried. He dialed a fourth number and waited for the phone to be picked up.

"Eatonville Police."

"Captain Lucious Harris, please. This is Detective Lieutenant Theodore Brown."

He waited patiently before a huge voice boomed over the receiver. "Tanny? That you?"

"Hello, Luke."

"Well, well, well. Long time, no hear. How's it goin'?"

"Ups and downs. And you?"

"Well, hell. Life ain't perfect by no means. But it ain't terrible, neither, so I guess I got no complaints."

Brown pictured the immense man on the other end of the line. He would be in a uniform that would be too tight in the places where his three hundred pounds made no pretense toward muscle, and around his neck, so that his head seemed to rest on the starched white collar with its gold insignia. Lucious Harris had a big man's hesitancy to anger and a constant, bubbling outlook that made his entire life seem a feast on which he was continually dining. He'd always enjoyed calling the big man because no matter how evil the world had seemed, his response was always energetic and undefeated. Tanny Brown realized he no longer made those calls.

"How're things in Eatonville?" he asked.

"Ha! You know, we're actually becoming something of a tourist trap, Tanny. Folks coming to visit because of all the attention we got because of the late Miz Hurston. Ain't gonna compete with Disney World or Key West, I guess, but it's kinda nice to see new faces around town.''

Brown tried to picture Eatonville. His friend had grown up there, its rhythms were in the locutions of his voice. It was a small town, with a singular sense of order about it. Almost everybody who lived there was black. It had gained some notoriety in the writings of Zora Neale Hurston, its most prominent resident. When she had been discovered first by the academicians and then the film people, Eatonville had been discovered as well. But mostly, what it was, was a small town for black people, run by black people.

There was a small pause before Lucious Harris asked, ''So. You don't ever call me no more. Hard to tell we are friends. Then, of course, I see you got yourself a bunch of publicity, but it ain't the sort that folks naturally go out of their way to acquire, right?''

''That's true.''

''And now, some more time passes, and you're on the phone, but it ain't to talk about how come you ain't called. And it ain't to talk about anything other than something special, am I right?''

''Just taking a wild shot, Luke. Thought you might be able to help.''

''Well, let me hear it.''

Tanny Brown breathed in deeply and asked, ''Unsolved disappearances. Homicides. In the last year. Children, teenagers, girls. And black. Anything like that in your town?''

The policeman was quiet. Brown could feel a sense of constriction coming over the line.

''Tanny, why you asking me this now?''

''I just got . . .''

''Tanny, you tell me the straight truth. Why you calling me with this now?''

''Luke, I'm just shooting in the dark. I got a bad feeling about something, and I'm just poking around.''

''You poked something solid here, my man.''

Brown felt instantly frozen inside. ''Tell me,'' he asked softly. He noticed that the booming voice on the other end of the line had tightened, narrowed, as if the words suddenly carried more freight.

''Wild child,'' Harris said slowly. ''Girl named Alexandra Jones. Thirteen. Part of her still be eight, part of her eighteen. You know the type. One minute she be all sweetness and polite, come baby-sit for Missus Harris and me, the next minute I sees her smoking a cigarette outside the convenience store, acting all grown-up and tough.''

"Sounds like my own daughters," Brown said inadvertently.

"No, your gals got a hold of something, and this little gal didn't. Anyway, she got some confusion and this makes her wild, you know. She starts to think this little town be too small for her. Run away once, her daddy go find her couple miles down the road, dragging along a little suitcase. Daddy be one of my patrolmen, so we all knows about it. Run away twice, and this time we find her all the way in Lauderdale, just outside, on Alligator Alley, thumbing rides from the semi drivers that passes that way. Trooper spots her, and they brings her home. Third time she run is three months back. Her momma and daddy driving every road they can to find her, figure this time she's heading north to Georgia where they got relatives and the gal's got a cousin she sweet on. Put out a BOLO. I talks to departments all over the state. Flyers out, you know the drill. Only she never shows in Georgia. Or Lauderdale or Miami or Orlando or any damn place. Where she shows is in Big Cypress swamp, where some hunters find her three weeks ago. Find what's left of her, which is just some bones. Picked clean by the sun and little animals and birds. Not a pretty sight. Gotta make ID through dental records. Cause of death? Multiple stab wounds, the M.E. figures, but only 'cause there are nicks and cuts in some of the bones. Not even that be conclusive. And not even any clothes laying about. Whoever done her stashed the clothes someplace else. I mean, it ain't too damn a mystery what happened to her, now, is it? But figuring out who did it be a different matter for sure.''

Brown said nothing. He heard Harris take a deep breath.

". . . Ain't never gonna make this case, no sir. You know how many interviews we've logged on this one, Tanny? More'n three hundred. And that's been me and my chief of detectives, Henry Lincoln, you know him. A couple of major-crimes guys from the county put in some time, too. Don't mean shit. No witnesses, 'cause nobody saw her get picked up on the road. No forensics, 'cause there ain't hardly nothing left of her. No suspects, even though we ran profiles and rousted all the usual likely folks. No nothing. When you get right down to it, all we really gonna do is just help her folks try and understand and maybe go down to the church an extra time myself, see if a little prayer or two won't help. You know what I pray for, Tanny?''

"No," he replied hoarsely.

"Tanny, I don't pray we make this guy. No, 'cause I don't even think the Almighty gonna be able to make this case. I just prays that whoever did it just come by Eatonville this one time, and that he heads on off to someplace new and some other town, someplace where someone sees 'im and they got mobile forensic teams and all that new scientific stuff, and where maybe he makes a mistake and gets hisself busted bad. That's what I prays for."

The police captain was quiet, as if thinking. " 'Cause I figures that gal goes terrible, you know. Pain and fear, Tanny. Pain, fear, and terror something special, and no one wants to know about it."

He paused again. "And then you calls me with this question come out of the blue, and I'm wondering what you got that makes you ask this question of me."

Silence gathered on the line.

"You know the man that came off the Row?" Brown said.

"Sure. Robert Earl Ferguson."

"He ever been in Eatonville?"

Lucious Harris stopped. Brown could hear a sharp intake of breath on the other end of the line before the big man said, "I thought he was innocent. That's what the papers and TV says."

"Has he ever been in Eatonville? Around the time that gal disappeared?"

"He was here," Harris responded slowly.

Brown felt a half-grunt, half-groan escape between his lips. He realized his teeth were shut tight. "When?"

"Not close time. Maybe three, four months back before little Alexandra disappeared. Gave a speech in a church. Hell, I went to see him myself. He was right interesting. Talked about Jesus standing by your side and giving you the light of day no matter how dark the world seems."

"What about . . ."

"Stayed a couple of days. Maybe a Saturday, then a Sunday, then drove off. Back to some school, I heard. I don't think he was here when Alexandra Jones takes off. I'll check hotels and motels, but I don't know. Sure, he coulda come back. But what makes you think . . ."

Brown leaned forward at the desk, a throbbing behind his temples. "Check for me, Luke. See if you can't put him in the area when the gal disappears."

"I'll try. Ain't gonna do no good, I don't suspect. You saying he's not innocent?"

"I'm not saying nothing. Just check, will ya?"

"No problem, Tanny. I'll check. Then maybe we'll have a talk 'cause I don't like what I'm hearing in your voice, my friend."

"I don't like it either," Brown replied. He hung up the telephone.

He remembered Pachoula in the moments after Joanie Shriver disappeared. He could hear the sirens picking up, see the knots of people forming on the street corners, talking, then setting off in search. The first camera crews were there that night, not long after the first telephone calls from the newspapers had started to flood into the switchboard. A little white girl disappears while trying to walk home from school. It's a nightmare that strikes a vulnerability within everyone. Blond hair. Smile. Wasn't four hours before that face was on the television. Every minute that passed made it worse.

What did he learn? Brown thought. He learned that the same event would be ignored, no cameras and microphones, no Boy Scouts and National Guardsmen searching the swamp, if he changed one single aspect of the equation: Turn white into black.

Fighting to maintain composure, Brown rose and went to find Cowart. A large map of the state of Florida hung in the offices of Major Crimes and he paused next to it. His eyes went first to Eatonville, then down to Perrine. Dozens, he thought. There are dozens of small, black enclaves throughout the state. The leftover South. Pushed by history and economics into little pockets of varying success or poverty, but all with one single thing in common: None were anyone's idea of a mainstream. All handled by undermanned, sometimes ill-trained police forces, with half the resources available to white communities and twice the problems with drugs and alcohol and robbery, frustration and despair.

Hunting grounds.

TWENTY-ONE
CONJUNCTION

ANDREA Shaeffer returned late to her motel room. She double-locked the door behind her, then checked the bathroom, the small closet, beneath the bed, behind the drapes, and finally the window, determining that it was still closed tight. She fought off the urge to open her pocketbook and remove the nine-millimeter pistol concealed within. A sense of misshapen fear had dogged her since leaving Ferguson's apartment. As the weak daylight had dissipated around her, she had felt a tightness, as if she were wearing clothes several sizes too small.

Who was he? she asked herself.

She reached into her small suitcase and rummaged around until she found some of the lavender-scented notepaper that she used to write unmailed letters to her mother. Then she switched on the small lamp at a tiny table in the corner of the room, pulled up a chair and started writing.

Dear Mom, she wrote. *Something happened.* She stared at the words at the top of the page. *What did he say?* she asked herself. *He said he was safe.* From what?

She leaned back in her chair, chewing on the end of her pen like a student searching for the answer on a test. She remembered being taken into a lineup room, despite her protests that she would be unable to recognize the two men who'd attacked her. The lights had been dimmed and she was flanked by a pair of detectives whose names she could no longer recall. She had watched intently as two sets of men were brought in and lined up against the wall. On command, they had turned first to the right, then the left, giving her a view of their profiles. She remembered the whispered admonitions from the detectives: *Take your time*, and *Is there anyone who seems familiar?* But she had been unable to make any identification. She had shaken her head at the detectives, and they'd shrugged. She recalled the look that had passed over their faces, and remembered then that she had decided that she wouldn't be helpless. That she wouldn't let anyone get away free ever again after delivering so much hurt.

She looked down at the unmailable letter and then wrote: *I met a man filled with death.*

That's it, she thought. She examined all that Ferguson had shown her: anger, mockery, arrogance. Fear, but only in short supply—only when he was uncertain why I was there. But once he learned, it evaporated. *Why?* Because he had nothing to fear. *Why?* Because I was there for the wrong reason.

She put the pen down beside the paper and stood up.

What's the right reason? she demanded.

Shaeffer rose and walked over to the double bed. She sat down and drew her knees up beneath her chin, wrapping her arms around her legs to hold them steady while she balanced precariously on the edge of the bed. For a moment or two she rocked back and forth, trying to determine what her course of action should be. Finally she imposed a discipline on her thoughts, unfolded and reached for the telephone.

It took her a few tries to track Michael Weiss down, finally reaching him through the superintendent's office at the state prison in Starke.

"Andy? That you? Where have you been?"

"Mike. I'm up in Newark, New Jersey."

"New Jersey. Jesus. What's in New Jersey? You were supposed to be sitting on Cowart in Miami. Is he in New Jersey?"

"No, but . . ."

"Well, where the hell is he?"

"North Florida. Pachoula, but . . ."

"Why aren't you there?"

"Mike, give me a moment and I'll explain."

"It'd better be good. And another thing. You were supposed to be checking in, like, all the time. I'm in charge of this investigation, you do remember, don't you?"

"Mike, just give me a minute, huh? I came up here to see Robert Earl Ferguson."

"The guy Cowart got off Death Row?"

"Right. The guy who was in the cell next to Sullivan."

"Up to the moment he tried to reach through the bars and strangle him?"

"Yeah."

"So?"

"It was . . ." She hesitated. "Well, unusual."

There was a momentary pause before the senior policeman asked, "How so?"

"I'm still trying to put my finger on it."

She heard him sigh. "What's this got to do with our case?"

"Well, I got to thinking, Mike. You know, Sullivan and Cowart were like two sides of a triangle. Ferguson was the other leg, the connection that brought them together. Without Ferguson, Cowart never sees Sullivan. I just figured I better go check him out. See if he had an alibi for the time the killings took place. See if he knew anything. Just get a look at the guy."

Weiss hesitated before saying, "Well, okay. That doesn't exactly not make sense. I don't know what it adds, but it's not crazy. You're thinking there's some link between the three of them? Maybe something that contributed to the murders?"

"Sort of."

"Well, if there was, why wouldn't that bastard Cowart have put that into his story in the paper?"

"I don't know. Maybe because he was afraid it would make him look bad?"

"Look bad? Jesus, Andy, he's a whore. All reporters are whores. They don't care about yesterday's trick, only today's. If he had something, he'd have put it into the paper lickety split. I can see the headlines: DEATH ROW CONNECTION UNCOVERED. I don't know if they got type big enough for that story. They'd go crazy. Probably win him another damn prize."

"Maybe."

Weiss snorted. "Yeah, maybe. Anyway, you got anything independent that gets this guy Ferguson to Tarpon Drive?"

"No."

"Like anybody make him, down in Islamorada? Any of those folks you questioned on Tarpon Drive mention a black man?"

"No."

"How about a hotel receipt or plane ticket or something? What about bloodwork or prints or a murder weapon?"

"No."

"So you went all the way up there, just because somehow he was connected to the other two players here?"

"Right," she said slowly. "It was sort of a hunch."

"Please, Andy. They have hunches on Perry fucking Mason, not in real life. Don't talk to me about hunches. Just talk to me about what you learned from the creep."

"He denied any direct knowledge of the crime. But he had some interesting insights into the way things work on Death Row. Said that most of the guards there are only a step away from being killers themselves. Suggested we focus on them."

"That makes sense," Weiss replied. "It's also precisely what I'm doing right now and you should be doing, too. The guy had an alibi, right?"

"Said he was in class. He's studying criminology."

"Really? Now that's interesting."

"Yeah. He had a bookcase filled with textbooks on forensics and detection. Said he used them in class."

"Okay. Can you check that out and then, when it turns out to be true, get back down here?"

"Uh, sure. Yeah."

There was a momentary quiet on the line before Weiss said, "Andy, why do I detect a note of hesitation in your voice?"

She paused before replying. "Mike, you ever have the sensation that you just talked with the right guy, but for the wrong reason? I mean, this guy made me sweat. I don't know how else to put it. He was wrong. I'm sure of it. All wrong. But why, I can't say. Just spooked me good."

"Another hunch?"

"A feeling. Christ, Mike, I'm not crazy."

Weiss waited an instant before asking, "How spooked?"

"Up in the ninety-ninth percentile." She could sense the older detective thinking hard.

"You know what I'm supposed to say, right?"

She nodded as she answered. "That I'm to take a cold shower, or a hot shower, whatever, and then forget it. Let the creep do whatever he's doing and make his mistake somewhere and let those cops take care of it and get my tail back down to the Sunshine State."

He laughed. "Christ," he said. "You even sound like me."

"So?"

"Okay," he said slowly. "Take the right shower. Then poke around as much as you want to for a day or so. I can carry on here without much trouble. But when it's all said and done and you don't have anything, I want you to write up a report with all your guesses and feelings and whatever the hell else you think is appropriate, and we'll send it off to a guy I know with the New Jersey State Police. He'll just laugh it off, but, hey, at least you won't think you're crazy. And your ass will be covered.''

"Thanks, Mike," she said, oddly relieved and frightened in the same moment.

"Oh," he said, "a couple other things. You haven't even asked what the hell I've found out down here."

"What?"

"Well, Sullivan left about three boxes filled with personal things. Mostly books, radio, little television, Bible, that sort of shit, but there were a couple of real intriguing documents. One was his whole appeal, all mapped out, ready to file with the court, *pro se*. All he had to do was hand it to an official and bingo, automatic stay of execution. And you know something? The sucker made a pretty convincing argument for prejudicial statements to the jury by the prosecutor that nailed him. I mean, he might have stretched that one out for years.''

"But he never filed it.''

"Nope. But that's not all. How about a letter from a producer named Maynard out in LaLa Land. The same guy who bought the rights to your friend Ferguson's life story after Cowart made him into a star. Made the same offer to Sullivan. Ten grand. Actually, not quite ten grand. Ninety-nine hundred. For exclusive rights to his life story.''

"But Sullivan's life was in the public record, why would he pay . . .''

"I spoke with him earlier today. The slick said it was standard operating procedure before making a movie. Tie up all the rights. And, he said Sullivan promised him he was going to file the appeal. So the guy had to make a move to get the rights, otherwise Sullivan could have messed him up as long as he was appealing his case. Surprised the hell out of the guy when Sullivan went to the chair.''

"Keep going.''

"Well, so there's ninety-nine hundred bucks floating about somewhere and I'm thinking, we find out what happened to that money and we find out how Sullivan paid for those two killings.''

"But we've got a Son of Sam law. Victims' rights. Sullivan couldn't collect the money. It was supposed to go to the victims of his crimes.''

"Right. Supposed to. The producer deposited the money in a Miami bank account according to instructions Sullivan gave him as part of the deal. Producer then writes a letter to the Victims' Rights Commission in Tallahassee, informing them of the payment, just as he's required to by law. Of course it takes the bureaucrats months and months to figure anything out. In the meantime . . .''

''I can guess.''

''Right. The money exits, stage left. It's not in that account anymore. The victims' rights people don't have it and Sullivan sure doesn't need it, wherever he is.''

''So . . .''

''So, I'm guessing we trace that account, maybe we can find the sucker who opened it up and emptied it out. Then we'll have a reasonable suspect for a pair of homicides.''

''Ten thousand dollars.''

''Ninety-nine hundred. Real interesting number, that. Gets around the problem with the federal law requiring documentation of money transactions above ten grand . . .''

''But ninety-nine hundred isn't . . .''

''Hell, up there they'd kill you for a pack of smokes. What do you suppose somebody'd do for almost ten grand? And remember, some of those prison guards aren't making much more than three, four hundred a week. Ten big ones probably sound like a whole helluva lot of money to them.''

''What about setting up the account?''

''In Miami? Got a phony driver's license and a fake social security number? I mean it's not exactly like they spend a lot of time in Miami regulating what goes on at the banks. They're all so damn busy laundering heavy bucks for drug dealers, they probably never even noticed this little transaction. Christ, Andy, you can probably close out the damn account at an automatic teller, not even have to look a real person in the eyes.''

''Does the producer know who opened it?''

''That idiot? No way. Sullivan just provided the number and the instructions. All he knows is that Sullivan screwed him by telling his life tale to Cowart, so it all went splat into the paper when this guy thought it was going to be his exclusively. Then double-screwed him by jumping into the electric chair. He ain't too pleased by circumstances.''

Shaeffer was quiet. She felt caught between two different whirlpools.

Weiss spoke quickly. ''One other little detail. Real intriguing.''

''What's that?''

"Sullivan left a handwritten will."

"A will?"

"That's right. Quite an interesting piece of paper. It was written right over a couple of pages of the Bible. Actually, the Twenty-third Psalm. You know, Valley of Death and Fearing No Evil. He just wrote it in a black felt-tip pen right over the text, then stuck a marker between the pages. Then he wrote a note, which he stuck on top of the box, saying, 'Please read the marked passage . . .' "

"What's it say?"

"He says he wants all his stuff left to a prison guard. A Sergeant Rogers. Remember him? He's the guy who wouldn't let us see Sully before the execution. The one that ushered Cowart into the prison."

"Is he . . ."

"Here's what Sullivan wrote: 'I leave all my earthly possessions to Sergeant Rogers, who . . . ,' get this, '. . . came to my aid and comfort at such a critical moment, and whom I could never repay for the difficult services he's performed. Although I've tried. . . .' " Weiss paused. "How do you like that?"

Shaeffer nodded, although her partner couldn't see her head move. "Makes for an interesting combination of events."

"Yeah, well guess what?"

"Tell me."

"The good sergeant had two days off three days before Cowart found those bodies. And you know what else he's got?"

"What?"

"A brother who lives in Key Largo."

"Well, damn."

"Better than that. A brother with a record. Two convictions for breaking and entering. Did eleven months in county lockup on an assault charge—that was some barroom beef—and arrested once for illegal discharge of a weapon, to wit, a three-fifty-seven magnum pistol. Charge dropped. And it gets a little better. Remember your crime-scene analysis? The brother's left-handed, and both of the old folks' throats were cut slicing right to left. Interesting, huh?"

"Have you spoken with him?"

"Not yet. Thought I'd wait for you to get here."

"Thanks," she said. "I appreciate it. But one question."

"What's that?"

"Well, how come he didn't get rid of Sullivan's stuff after the execution? I mean, he had to figure if Sullivan was going to double-cross him, that would be where he would leave the message, right?''

"I thought of that, too. Doesn't exactly make sense for him to leave those boxes laying about. But maybe he's not that smart. Or maybe he didn't figure Sully for quite the character he is. Or maybe it just slipped his mind. But it sure was a big slip.''

"All right," she said. "I'll get there."

"He's a real good suspect, Andy. Real good. I'd like to see if we can put him down in the Keys. Or check phone records, see if he wasn't spending a lot of time talking to that brother of his. Then maybe we go talk to the state attorney with what we've got." The detective paused before saying, "There's only one thing that bothers me, you know . . .''

"What's that?"

"Well, hell, Andy, that's a pretty damn big arrow pointing right at that sergeant that Sully left. And I hate trusting Sullivan, even if he's dead. You know the best way to screw up a murder investigation is to make somebody look like they did something. Even if we can eliminate other suspects, you know, some defense attorney is going to trot those suspects out at trial and mess up some jury's mind. I think Sully knew that, too.''

Again, she nodded vigorously. Weiss added, "But, hey, that's just my own paranoia talking. Look, we make this guy, Andy, it's gonna be commendations and raises for the two of us. It'll be like giving your career a jump start. Trust me. Come on back here and get a piece. I'll keep interviewing people until you get here, then we'll head back down to the Keys.''

"All right," she said slowly.

"I still hear a 'but' in your voice."

She was torn. Her partner's enthusiasm, coupled with his success and the sudden thought that she was missing out on the biggest case to which she'd ever been connected seemed to flood over all the fears she felt. She picked her head up and looked about the room. It seemed as if the shadows within her had diminished. For a moment, she wavered. "Maybe I should just bag it and head home.''

"Well, do what you think is right. That'd be okay with me. A lot warmer down here, anyway. Aren't you cold up there?''

"It's cold. And wet.''

"Well, there you have it. But what about this guy Ferguson?''

"A bad guy, Mike," she found herself saying again. "A bad guy.''

"Well, look, hell. Go check out his schedule, poke about,

make sure that alibi is as good as he says it is, then do what I said and forget it. It's not wasted time if it'll put the locals on to him. Maybe there's something floating about up there, you know. And anyway, all I've got in line for the next day or so are interviews with everybody who worked on the Row. Our sergeant is just one of the big pile. You know—routine questions, nothing to get him excited or nervous, make him think he's lost in the woodwork. Then zap. I'll wait until you get here. I'd like to see you work him over. Meanwhile, satisfy your curiosity. Then get down here.''

He paused, then added, "See what a reasonable boss I am? No yelling. No swearing. Who would complain?''

She hung up the telephone wondering what she should do. It made her think of that moment when her mother had packed her and as many possessions as would fit into their old station wagon and left Chicago. It had been late on a gray, windy day, the breeze kicking up whitecaps on Lake Michigan: Adventure coupled with loss. She remembered closing the car door with a bang, slicing off the chill, and thinking that that was the moment when she'd realized her father was truly dead and would never return to her side. Not when she'd come down the stairs at her house to find a priest and two uniformed police captains standing in the vestibule, holding their hands in front of them, unable to meet her eyes. Not the funeral, even when the single piper had started playing his heartbreaking dirge. Not the times when her classmates had stared at her with that uniquely cruel children's curiosity about loss. That afternoon.

There are such junctures in childhood, she realized, and later, when things get pressed together beneath a clear, hard shell. Decisions made. Steps taken. An irrevocability to life. It was time to make such a decision now.

She recalled Ferguson. She could see him grinning at her, sitting on the threadbare couch, laughing at the homicide detective.

Why? she asked herself again.

The answer jumped instantly at her.

Because she was asking about the wrong homicide.

She lay back on the bed. She decided she was not ready to leave Robert Earl Ferguson quite yet.

The light rain and gloom persisted into the following morning, carrying with it a penetrating damp cold. The gray sky seemed to blend with the murky brown of the Raritan River as it flowed by the edge of the brick and ivy campus at Rutgers. She made her way across a parking lot, tugging the inadequate comfort of her trench coat tight around her, feeling like some odd sort of refugee.

It did not take her long to get swept up in the stolid pace of the university bureaucracy. After arriving at the Criminology Department and explaining to a secretary why she was there, she'd been rerouted to an administration building. There she'd received a lecture on student confidentiality from an assistant dean who, despite a tendency to drone on, had finally provided her with permission to speak with the three professors she was searching for. Finding the three men had proven equally difficult. Office hours were erratic. Home telephone numbers weren't available. She'd tried waving her badge about, only to realize that it had little impact.

It was noontime when she found her first professor, eating lunch at the faculty union. He taught a course on forensic procedure. He was wiry-haired, slight of build, wore a sportcoat and khaki slacks, and had an irritating habit of looking off into the air next to her as he spoke. She had only one concrete area of questioning, the time surrounding the murders in the Keys, and felt a bit foolish chasing it, especially knowing what she did about the prison guard. Still, it was a place to start.

"I don't know what sort of help I can be," the professor replied between bites of tired green salad. "Mr. Ferguson is an upper-echelon student. Not the best, but quite good. B-plus, perhaps. Not an A, I doubt that, but solid. Definitely solid. But then, that's to be expected. He has a bit more practical experience than many of the students. Little joke, I guess, right there. Real aptitude for procedure. Quite interested in forensic sciences. Steady. No complaints."

"And attendance?"

"Always take attendance."

"And the days in question?"

"Class met twice that week. Only twenty-seven students. Can't hide, you know. Can't send your roommate in to pick up the assignments. Tuesdays and Thursdays."

"And?"

"Right here. In my notebook."

The professor ran thin fingers down a column of names. "Ahh. Perfect."

"He was there?"

"Never missed a class. Not this month. A few other absences, earlier in the year. But I showed those as excused absences.''

''Excused?''

''Means he came to me with a good reason. Got the assignments himself. Did the makeup work. That sort of thing. That's dedication, especially in these days.''

The professor snapped his notebook shut and returned to his plate of greens and dried fruit.

Shaeffer found the second professor outside a lecture hall in a corridor swamped with students hurrying to classes. This man taught the history of crime in America, a large survey course designed to accommodate a hundred students. He carried a briefcase and an armful of books and couldn't remember whether Ferguson was present on specific dates, but he did show the detective a sign-in sheet, where Ferguson's signature appeared prominently.

It was creaking toward afternoon, a gray, rancid light filling the hallways of the university, and Shaeffer felt angry and disappointed. She had not held much hope that she would discover his absence from the university at the time of the murders; still, she was frustrated by the sense that she was wasting time. She thought she knew little more about the man than she had when she'd started out in the morning. Surrounded by the constant press of students, even Ferguson had begun to diminish in her mind. She started asking herself, What the hell am I doing?

She decided to head back to her motel, then, at the last moment, changed her mind again and decided to knock on the door of the third professor. If there was no answer, she told herself, she'd go straight back to Florida.

She found his cubicle after several wrong turns and rapped sharply on the door, then stepped back as it swung open to reveal a stocky man, wearing 1960s-style granny glasses beneath an uncombed mop of straggly sand-colored hair. The professor wore a loose-fitting tweed sportcoat with a dozen pens stuck in the breast pocket, one of which seemed to have leaked. His tie was loose around his collar and a substantial paunch tugged at the belt of his corduroy trousers. He had the appearance of someone awakened from a nap taken in his clothes, but his eyes moved swiftly to take in the detective standing in front of him.

''Professor Morin?''

''Are you a student?''

She produced her badge, which he inspected. ''Florida, huh?''

"Can I ask you a few questions?"

"Sure." He gestured for her to enter his office. "I was expecting you."

"Expecting?"

"You want to know about Mr. Ferguson, right?"

"That's correct," she said as she stepped into the cubicle. It was a small space, with a single dirty window that overlooked a quadrangle. One wall was devoted to books. A small desk and computer were tightly jammed against the other wall. There were copies of newspapers taped to the few remaining empty spots. There were also three bright watercolors of flowers hung about, contradicting the grimy appearance of the office. "How did you know?"

"He called me. Said you'd be checking on him."

"And?"

"Well," the professor said, speaking with the bubbly enthusiasm of someone who has been shut in too long, "Mr. Ferguson has a fine attendance record. Just perfect. Especially for the time period he said you were interested in."

He sat down hard in a desk chair that bounced with his weight. "I hope that clears up any misunderstandings you might have." The professor smiled, displaying perfectly white, even teeth, which seemed to contradict his disheveled appearance.

"He's quite a good student, you see. Quite intense, you know, which puts people off. Very much a loner, but I guess Death Row has something to do with that. Yes, intense, dedicated, wound tight. Don't see that in too many students. A little scary, but ultimately refreshing. Like danger, I suppose."

Professor Morin burbled on. "Even the policemen and women we get in here trying to advance their careers, they just see this as part of a process of collecting credits and getting ahead. Mr. Ferguson is more of a scholar."

There was a single hardbacked chair in a corner, scarred and worn with hard use, which she slid into. It was obviously designed to keep visiting students and their concerns totally uncomfortable, and thereby in the office as briefly as possible.

"You know Mr. Ferguson well?" she asked.

The professor shrugged. "As well as any. Actually, yes. He's an interesting man."

"How so?"

"Well, I teach 'Media and Crime,' and he has a good deal of natural expertise in that area."

"And so?"

"Well, he's been called upon on numerous occasions to give his opinions. They are always, how shall I say it? Intriguing. I mean, it's not every day that you teach a course to someone who has firsthand experience in the field. And who might have gone to the electric chair had it not been for the media."

"Cowart."

"That's correct. Matthew Cowart of *The Miami Journal*. A Pulitzer Prize and well deserved, I might add. Quite a job of reporting and writing."

"And what are Ferguson's opinions, Professor?"

"Well, I would say he is extremely sensitive to issues of race and reporting. He wrote a paper examining the case of Wayne Williams in Atlanta. He raised the issue of the double standard, you know, one set of rules reporting on crime in the white community and another for reporting on crimes in the black community. It's a distinction I happen to subscribe to as well, Detective."

She nodded.

Professor Morin swiveled in his desk chair, ebbing back and forth as he spoke, clearly enamored of his own voice.

". . . Yes, he made the point that the lack of media attention in black-community crimes invariably leads to a diminishment of resources for the police, lessening of activity by the prosecutorial bodies and makes crime seem a commonplace fabric of the society. Not unsophisticated, this view. The routinization of crime, I suppose. Helps explain why fairly a quarter of the young black male population in this nation is or has been behind bars."

"And he was in class?"

"Except when he had an excuse."

"What sort of excuses?"

"He gives occasional lectures and speeches, often to church groups down in Florida. Up here, of course, no one really has any idea of his past. Half the students in the class hadn't even heard of his case at the beginning of the semester. Can you believe that, Detective? What a commentary on the quality of students today."

"He goes back to Florida?"

"On occasion."

"You happen to have those dates?"

"Yes. But I thought he told me you were only interested in the week that . . ."

"No, I'm interested in the other times as well."

Professor Morin hesitated, then shrugged. "I don't suppose

it will hurt anything.'' He turned to a notebook, flipped rapidly through some pages and finally came to an attendance sheet. He handed this over to her, and she quickly copied down the dates Ferguson had been absent from class.

''Is that all, Detective?''

''I think so.''

''See. It's all quite routine and ordinary. I mean, he blends in here. Has a future as well, I suspect. Certainly has the capability of getting his degree.''

''Blends in?''

''Of course. We're a large, urban university, Detective. He fits in.''

''Anonymous.''

''Like any student.''

''Do you know where he lives, Professor?''

''No.''

''Anything else about him?''

''No.''

''And he doesn't make your skin shrivel a bit when you speak with him?''

''He has an intensity, like I said—but I don't see how that should make him into a suspect for a homicide. I suppose he wonders whether he'll ever be free from the interest of the police in Florida. And I think that's a legitimate question, Detective, don't you?''

''An innocent man has nothing to fear,'' she answered.

''No,'' the professor shook his head. ''I think in our society it's often the guilty who are safe.''

She looked over at the professor, who was gathering himself as if to launch into some quasi-radical, leftover sixties tirade. She decided to decline this particular lecture.

She stood and left the room. She wasn't sure what she'd heard, but she'd heard something. *Anonymous.* She walked partway down the corridor until struck with the thought she was being watched. She turned suddenly and saw the professor closing the door to his office. The sound reverberated in the hallway. Her eyes swept about, searching for the students who'd flooded the area earlier, and who now seemed to have been absorbed by the offices, classrooms, and lecture halls.

Alone.

She forced a shrug onto her shoulders. It's daytime, she told herself. This is a crowded, public place. She started walking rapidly. She could hear her shoes making a slapping sound

against the polished linoleum of the floor, which echoed slightly
about her ears. She began to hurry, picking up her pace, increasing the solitary sound around her. She found a stairwell and
pushed ahead, moving quickly. The stairwell was empty as well.
She took the stairs swiftly, almost jumping down the half-flights.
She stopped abruptly when she heard a doorway behind her
open and close and realized, suddenly, that someone else's footsteps were moving fast on the stairs behind her. She stopped,
shoving herself against the wall, reaching into her pocketbook
for her weapon as the sound increased and approached. She
squeezed herself tight into a corner, feeling the reassuring grip
of her pistol beneath her fingers. She looked up and saw the eyes
of a young student, loaded with notebooks and texts, untied
basketball shoes flapping in his hurry. The student barely looked
at her as he swept past, obviously late. She closed her eyes.
What's happening to me? she asked herself. She released her
grip on the pistol. *What did I hear?* She headed through the
stairwell exit, spying the doors to the building in front of her.
The late afternoon sky beyond the glass entranceway seemed
gray and funereal but beckoning.

She pushed herself quickly toward it.

She did not see Ferguson, only heard him.

"Learn what you wanted, Detective?"

The hiss of his question made her jump.

She pivoted toward the sound, jerking her hand into her pocketbook, stepping back, almost as if struck with a blow. Her eyes
locked onto Ferguson's, and she saw the same, unsettling grin
crease his face.

"Satisfied?" he asked.

She squared her shoulders toward him.

"Did I frighten you, Detective?"

She shook her head, still unable to respond. She could feel
her hand around the pistol grip, but she did not remove it from
the bag.

"Are you going to shoot me, Detective?" he asked harshly.
"Is that what you're looking for?"

Ferguson stepped forward, out of the shadowed spot against
the wall that had concealed him. He wore an olive-drab army
surplus jacket and had a New York Giants cap on his head. A
satchel, which she presumed was filled with books, was slung
over his shoulder. He looked like almost every other student that
she'd seen in that corridor that day. She controlled her racing
heart and slowly removed her hand from the pocketbook.

"What do you carry, Detective? A thirty-eight, police issue? Maybe a twenty-five-caliber auto? Something small but efficient?"

He stared at her. "No, I bet something larger. Got to prove something to the world. A three-fifty-seven with a magnum load. Or a nine-millimeter. Something that helps you think you're tough, right, Detective? Strong and in charge."

She did not reply.

He laughed. "Won't share that information, huh?"

Ferguson unslung his book bag, setting it on the floor. Then he spread his arms in mock surrender, almost supplication, palms out. "But you see, I'm unarmed, aren't I? So what have you got to fear?"

She breathed in and out sharply, trying to clear the surprise of seeing him from her head, so that she could come up with some appropriate response of her own.

"So, did you find out what you wanted, Detective?"

She exhaled slowly. "I found out some things, yes."

"Discovered I was in class?"

"That's right."

"So, there wasn't any way I could be down in Florida and do that old couple, right? You figured that out yet?"

"It doesn't seem so. I'm still checking."

"Got the wrong guy, Detective." Ferguson grinned. "You Florida cops always seem to get the wrong guy."

She met his eyes coldly. "No. I don't know that, Mr. Ferguson. I think you're the right guy. But I just haven't figured out what for yet."

Ferguson's eyes flashed toward her. "You're all alone, aren't you, Detective?"

"No," she lied. "I have a partner."

"Where is he?"

"Working."

Ferguson stepped past her, glancing out the double glass doors toward the walkways and parking lots. Rain streaked the air, tumbling down with a depressing ferocity.

"Gal got beaten and raped right out there the other evening. Little late coming out of class. Just after night fell. Some guy just grabbed her, dragged her down behind that little lip at the edge of the parking lot. Did her right there. Knocked her out and did her. Didn't kill her, though. Broke her jaw. Broke her arm. Took his pleasure."

Ferguson continued to look through the doors. He raised his

arm and pointed. "Right out there. That where you're parked, Detective?"

She clamped her mouth shut.

He turned toward her. "They got no suspects yet. Gal's still in the hospital. Ain't that something, Detective? Just think about it. You can't even be safe walking across a campus. Finding your car. Not even in a motel room, neither, I guess. Doesn't that make you a bit nervous? Even with that big old gun stuck down there in that pocketbook where you can't reach it in near enough time."

Ferguson stepped away from the doors. He turned and looked past Shaeffer, and she became aware of the sound of voices approaching them. She kept her eyes on Ferguson, however, eyeing him as he watched a gaggle of students approach. Their voices suddenly swarmed about her. She saw Ferguson nod at one of the men in the group and heard a young woman say, "God! Look at that rain!" The bunch gathered coats and umbrellas and surged past the detective, out into the damp air. She felt a cold burst as the door swung open and then swept shut.

"So, Detective. Did you finish? Did you learn what you came up here for?"

"I know enough," she replied.

He smiled. "Don't like to give folks a straight answer," he said. "You know, that's such an old technique. I probably have a description of it in some textbook right here with me now."

"You're a good student, Mr. Ferguson."

"Yes, I am," he said. "Knowledge is important. Sets you free."

"Where did you learn that?" she asked.

"On the Row, Detective. Learned a lot right there. But mostly, I learned that I have to educate myself. Wouldn't have no future at all if I didn't. End up just like all those other poor folk waiting for the Death Squad to come shave their skulls and slap 'em down in that chair."

"So you came to school."

"Life's a school, ain't it, Detective?"

She nodded.

"So, now you going to leave me alone?" he demanded.

"Why should I?"

" 'Cause I ain't done nothing."

"Well, I don't know if I think so, Mr. Ferguson. I don't know that yet at all."

His eyes narrowed. He spoke evenly and slowly. "That's a

dangerous approach, detective.'' She didn't answer, so he continued. ''Especially if you're alone.''

He looked at her, then smiled, and gestured toward the door. ''I suspect you'll want to be leaving now, right? Before it gets real dark. Not much light left out there. I'd guess maybe fifteen, twenty minutes, no more. Wouldn't want to get lost looking for that rental car, now would you? What color was it, Detective? A silver-gray? Hard to find on a dark, wet night. Don't get lost, Detective. There are some bad folks out there. Even on a college campus.''

She stiffened. He had hit the right color for the rental car she was driving. A guess, she thought. A lucky guess.

Ferguson stepped back, away from the door, giving her an open path to the rain and gloom.

''You be careful now, Detective,'' he said mockingly.

Then he turned and walked back into the classroom building, disappearing down a side corridor. She listened for a moment, trying to hear the retreat of his footsteps but couldn't. She turned and looked again at the rain pelting down against the trees and sidewalks. She tightened her raincoat and pulled up the collar. It required a stiffening of will to force her feet to move.

The cold soaked into her immediately. She felt rain sliding down her neck. She started to move quickly, damning the awkward shoes that kept sliding on the footpath. Her head swiveled about, searching behind her, in front of her, making certain that she didn't spot Ferguson following her. When she reached the rental car, she checked the backseat before tossing her things in and throwing herself behind the wheel. She punched down the door locks immediately. Her hand shook slightly as she thrust the key into the ignition, and then slapped the car into gear. As the car started to move, she felt better. As she steered out of the parking lot, relief started to fill her. She picked up speed and pulled onto a two-way street. Out of the corner of one eye she thought, for just an instant, that she saw a hunched-over figure in an olive-drab coat, but when she tried to turn and look carefully, the figure had disappeared, lost in a group of students standing at a bus stop. She fought off a surge of fear and drove on. The heater on the little car started to whir with effort and hot air that seemed as if it had come from a can poured over her, warming her face but not her thoughts.

What did he learn on Death Row? she asked herself.

He learned to be a student.

Of what?

Of crime.

Why?

Because everyone else on Death Row had failed some test. They were all men who'd committed crime after crime, sometimes killing after killing, and finally ended up trapped and caught and awaiting the chair, because they'd screwed up. Even Sullivan screwed up. She remembered a quotation from one of Matthew Cowart's stories: "I'd of killed more if I hadn't been caught." But Ferguson, she thought, got a second chance. And he's determined not to blow it this time.

Why?

Because he wants to keep doing whatever he's doing for as long as he wants.

Her head struggled with dizziness. She spoke to herself in the third person, trying to settle herself with familiar tones.

"Ohmigod, Andy girl, what have you stumbled on?"

She tried to blank her mind and drove on into the night, searching for her motel. She let the road flow by outside the car, concentrating on nothing except finding a safe spot to order her thoughts. She stared up once into the rearview mirror, struck with the sudden panic that a car was tailing her, but she saw the headlights turn away. She gritted her teeth and drove through the rain steadily. When she saw the lights of the motel loom up in front of her, she felt a momentary relief, but she could find no parking spot near the front of the lot and was forced to swing her vehicle into a space some fifty yards and innumerable shadows from the lighted entrance. She shut off the engine and took a single deep breath, eyeing the distance she would have to travel. She had a sudden thought: It was easier in a uniform, driving a squad car. Always in touch with the dispatcher. Never really alone. Always part of a team of officers cruising the highways in regular fashion. She reached over and removed the nine-millimeter from her pocketbook. Then she got out of the car and walked directly to the front of the motel, eyes sweeping the area in front of her, ears sharpened for any sound behind her. Not until she was within a dozen feet of the doorway did she return the pistol to her pocketbook. An elderly couple bundled in overcoats, exiting the motel as she entered, must have seen the flash of dark metal with its unmistakable shape. She caught a snatch of their frightened conversation as she stepped past them. "Did you see that? She had a gun . . ."

"No, dear, it must have been something else . . ."

And that was all.

A young man in a blue blazer was working behind the desk. She asked for her key and he handed it over, saying as he did, idly, "Oh, there was a fellow looking for you earlier, Detective."

"A fellow?"

"Yes. Didn't want to leave a message. Just asked for you."

"Did you see the person?"

"No. It was the guy who had the desk before me."

She could feel something within her trying to break loose. "Did he say anything else? Like a description?"

"Ahh, yes. He said the gentleman was black. That's what he said. Some black fellow was asking about you, but didn't want to leave a message. Said he'd get in touch. That's all. Sorry, that's all I can remember."

"Thank you," she said.

She forced herself to walk slowly to the elevator.

How did he find me? she asked herself.

The elevator swooshed her upward and she padded down the corridor to her room. As before, she checked all the empty spots in the room after double-locking the doors. Then she sat heavily on the bed, trying to deal with the mundane, which was what she was going to do about getting supper, though she didn't feel particularly hungry, and the complicated, which was what she was going to do next about Robert Earl Ferguson.

When she pictured him, she tried to see him without the smirking look on his face but couldn't.

The knock at the door crashed through her fears.

It made her snatch her breath and rise in a single motion. She found herself frozen, staring at the door.

There was another sharp rap on it. Then a third.

She reached down once again, freeing the pistol from her handbag, cocked it, and approached the door, holding her finger on the outside of the trigger guard, as she had been taught to do when uncertain what she was facing. There was a convex peephole on the door. She leaned toward it to see what was on the other side, but just as she did, another crash came against the door, and she jumped back.

She forced toughness onto her anxiety, reached for the door handle and in a single, swift motion, threw the dead bolts and tugged the door open. In the same moment, she raised her pistol to eye level, sighting down the barrel.

The door swung open and she saw Matthew Cowart.

He was standing in the hallway, hand half-raised to knock

again. She saw his face freeze when he spied the weapon in her hand. Silence like a knife filled the space between them. He raised his hands slowly and then she saw that he was accompanied by two other men. She lowered the weapon.

"Cowart," she said.

He nodded. "That's quite a greeting," he managed to croak out. "Everyone seems to want to point guns at me lately."

Her eyes slid to the other two men.

"I know you," she said. "You were at the prison."

"Wilcox," the detective replied. "Escambia County. This is my boss, Lieutenant Brown."

She turned and stared at the hulking figure of Tanny Brown. He seemed to bristle with intensity, and she saw his eyes take her in, pausing for a moment on the pistol in her hand.

"I see," he said slowly, "that you've been to see Bobby Earl."

TWENTY-TWO
═══════TAKING NOTES

$\mathbf{T}$HE three detectives and the solitary newspaperman took up uncomfortable positions in the motel room. Wilcox stood, back up against the wall, close to the windows, occasionally glancing out through the darkness at the headlights that trailed by, keeping his thoughts to himself. Shaeffer and Brown occupied the only chairs in the room, on either side of a small table, like poker players waiting for the final card to be dealt. Cowart perched uneasily on the edge of the bed, slightly apart. Someone in an adjacent room was playing a television loudly; voices from a news show filtered through the motel walls. Some tragedy, he thought, reduced to fifteen seconds, thirty if it is truly terrible, delivered with a practiced look of concern.

He glanced at Andrea Shaeffer. Although clearly surprised when she had opened the door on the three men, she had let them enter without comment. Introductions had been brief, small talk nonexistent. They were all aware of what had brought them together in a small room in an alien city. She shuffled a few notes and papers together, then turned to the three men and asked, "How did you find me?"

"The local police liaison office told us," Brown said. "We checked in there when we arrived. They said they'd accompanied you to see Ferguson."

Shaeffer nodded.

"Why did you do that?" Brown asked.

She started to answer, stopped, stared over at Cowart and then shook her head. "Why are you here?" she demanded.

The reporter didn't want to answer that question, but Tanny Brown, speaking in measured, officious tones, replied, "We're here to see Ferguson, too."

Shaeffer looked at the police lieutenant.

"Why? I thought you were finished with him. And you, too," she gestured at Cowart.

"No. Not yet."

"Why?"

Again, Brown was the one to answer. "We're here because we have reason to believe that there were errors made in the original prosecution of Ferguson. We think there may have been mistakes made in Mr. Cowart's stories. We're here to investigate both aspects."

Shaeffer looked both angry and surprised. "Mistakes? Errors?" She turned to the reporter. "What sort of mistakes?"

Cowart realized he would have to answer her this time. "He lied to me."

"About what?"

"About the murder of the little girl."

Shaeffer shifted about in her seat. "And now you're here for what?"

"To set the record straight."

The cliché prompted a cynical smile. "I'm sure that's real important," she said. She glanced over at Brown and Wilcox. "But it doesn't explain why you're traveling with this company."

"We want the record straight as well," Brown said. As soon as he spoke the words, he recognized he'd made an error of his own. He realized that the young woman across from him was measuring him and that, so far, he'd failed.

Shaeffer thought for a moment. "You're not here to arrest Ferguson?"

"No. Can't do that."

"You're here to talk to him?"

"Yes."

She shook her head. "You guys are lying," she said. She sat back hard, crossing her arms in front of her.

"We . . ." Brown began.

"Lying," she interrupted.

"Because . . ." Cowart said.

"Lying," Shaeffer said a third time.

The reporter and the police lieutenant stared at her, and after a small quiet, just enough time to let the word fester in their imaginations, she continued. "What record?" she said. "There is no record. There's only one very wrong man. Mistakes and errors. So what? If Cowart made some mistake, he'd be here alone. If you, Detective Brown, made some mistake, you'd be here alone. But together, that means something altogether different. Right?"

Tanny Brown nodded.

"Is this a guessing game?" she asked.

"No. Tell me what brought you here, then I'll fill you in."

Shaeffer considered this offer, then agreed. "I came to see Ferguson because he was connected to both Sullivan and Cowart and I thought he might have specific information about the killings in the Keys."

Brown looked hard at her. "And did he?"

She shook her head. "No. Denied any knowledge."

"Well, what would you expect?" Cowart said under his breath.

She turned to him. "Well, he was a damn sight more cooperative than you've been." This was untrue, of course, but she thought it would quiet the reporter, which it did.

"So, if he had no information and he denied any connection," said Brown, "why are you still here, Detective?"

"I wanted to check out his alibi for the time period that the murders took place."

"And?"

"It did."

"It did?" Cowart blurted. She glared at him.

"Ferguson was in class that week. Didn't miss any. It would've been damn hard for him to get down to the Keys, kill the old couple, and get back, without being late for something. Probably impossible."

"But, goddammit, that's not what Sullivan . . ."

Cowart stopped short, and Shaeffer pivoted toward him. "Sullivan what?"

"Nothing."

"Sullivan what, dammit!"

Cowart felt suddenly sick. "That's not what Sullivan told me."

Tanny Brown tried to step in, but a single glance from Shaeffer cut him off before he could speak a word. Unbridled rage filled her; for a moment the world turned red-tinged. She could feel an explosion within her, and her hands shook with the effort to contain it. *Lies,* she thought, staring at the reporter. *Lies and omissions.* She took a deep breath. *I knew it.*

"Sullivan told you when?" she asked slowly.

"Before going to the chair."

"What did he tell you?"

"That Ferguson committed those crimes. But it's not that . . ."

"You son of a bitch," she muttered.

"No, look, you've got to understand . . ."

"You son of a bitch. What did he tell you, exactly?"

"That he'd arranged with Ferguson to switch crimes. Took Ferguson's crime in return for Ferguson committing this one for him."

She absorbed this and in an instant saw the crevasse the reporter was in. She had no sympathy. "And you didn't think this was *relevant* for the people investigating the murders?"

"It's not that simple. He lied. I was trying to . . ."

"And so you thought you could lie, too?"

"No, dammit, you've got to understand . . ." Cowart turned toward Tanny Brown.

"I ought to arrest you right now," she said bitterly. "Could you write that one up from your own cell, Mr. Cowart? REPORTER CHARGED WITH COVER-UP IN SENSATIONAL MURDER CASE. Isn't that how the headline would read? Would they run that on the front page with your goddamn picture? Would it be the truth for once?"

They glared at each other until something occurred to Cowart. "Yeah. Truth. Except it wasn't the truth, was it, Detective?"

"What?"

"Just what I said. Sullivan told me Ferguson did that old couple, but I didn't know whether to believe him or not. He told me lots of things, some of them lies. So I could have told you, and at the same time I would have had to put it in the paper— *had to,* Detective. But now, you're telling me that Ferguson had an alibi, so it would have been all wrong. He didn't do that old couple, no matter what Sullivan said. Right?"

Shaeffer hesitated.

"Come on, godammit, Detective! Right?"

She could think of no way to disagree. She nodded her head. "It doesn't seem that way. The alibi checks out. I went out to Rutgers and spoke with three different professors. In class each day that week. Perfect attendance. Also, my partner has come up with other information as well.''

''What other information?''

''Forget it.''

There was another pause in the room while each person sorted out what they'd heard. Tanny Brown spoke slowly.

''But,'' he said carefully, ''something else. Right? If Ferguson isn't your suspect, and he has no information to help your investigation, you should be on an airplane heading south. You wouldn't be sitting around here, you'd be down with your partner. You could have checked out Ferguson's class schedule by telephone, but instead you went and saw some people in person. Why is that, Detective? And when you open your door you've got a nine-millimeter in your hand and your bags aren't packed. So why?''

She shook her head.

''I'll tell you why,'' Brown said quietly. ''Because you know something's wrong, and you can't say what.''

Shaeffer looked across at him and nodded.

''Well,'' Brown said, ''that's why we're here, too.''

Dawn light streaked the street outside Ferguson's apartment, barely illuminating the wedge of gray clouds that hovered over the city, poised for more rain. Shaeffer and Wilcox pulled one car to the curb at the north end of the street, while Brown stopped at the southern end. Cowart checked his tape recorder and his notebook, patted his jacket pocket to make certain that his pens were still there, and turned toward the policeman.

Back in the motel room, Shaeffer had turned brusquely to them and said, ''So. What's the plan?''

''The plan,'' Cowart had said softly, ''is to give him something to worry about, maybe flush him out of his cover, do something that we can follow up on. We want to make him think that things aren't as safe as he supposes. Give him something to worry about,'' he repeated, smiling wanly. ''And that's me.''

Now, out in the car, he tried to make a joke. ''In the movies, they'd have me wear a wire. We'd have a code word I could say that would signal I needed help.''

''Would you wear one?''

''No.''

''I didn't think so. So we don't need a code word.''

Cowart smiled, but only because he could think of nothing else to do.

"Nervous?" Brown asked.

"Do I act it?" Cowart replied. "Don't answer that."

"He won't do anything."

"Sure."

"He can't."

Cowart smiled again. "I kinda feel like an old lion tamer who happens to be taking a stroll through the jungle, and he runs across some former charge that he maybe used a whip and chair on a bit too much. And he looks down at that old lion and realizes that they're not in his circus cage anymore, but on the lion's turf. Get the picture?"

Brown smiled. "All he's going to do is growl."

"Bark is worse than his bite, huh?"

"I guess, but that's dogs, not lions."

Cowart opened the car door. "Too many mixed metaphors here," he said. "I'll see you in a few minutes."

The cool damp air curling above the dirty sidewalk slapped him in the face. He walked swiftly down the block, passing a pair of men asleep in an abandoned doorway, a huddled mass of gray-brown tattered clothing, grown together to ward off the cold night. The men stirred as he walked near them, then slipped back into early-morning oblivion. Cowart could hear a few street noises a block or two away, the deep grumble-whine of diesel bus engines, the start of morning traffic.

He turned and faced the apartment building. For a moment, he wavered on the stoop, then he stepped within the dark entranceway and rapidly climbed the stairs to the front of Ferguson's apartment. He'll be asleep, the reporter told himself, and he'll awaken to confusion and doubt. That was the design behind the early-morning visit. These hours, between night and day, were the most unsettling, the transition time when people were weakest.

He took a deep breath and pounded hard on the door. Then he waited. He could hear no sound from within, so he pounded hard again. Another few seconds passed, then he heard footsteps hurrying toward the door. He bashed his fist against the door a third and fourth time.

Dead bolt locks started to click. A chain was loosened. The door swung open.

Ferguson stared out at him. "Mr. Cowart."

Killer, Cowart thought, but instead, he said, "Hello, Bobby Earl."

Ferguson rubbed a hand across his face, then smiled. "I should have figured you would show up."

"I'm here now."

"What do you want?"

"Same thing as always. Got questions that need answers."

Ferguson held the door wide for him and he stepped inside the apartment. They moved into the small living room, where Cowart rapidly peered about, trying to take it all in.

"You want coffee, Mr. Cowart? I have some made," Ferguson said. He gestured toward a seat on the couch. "I have some coffee cake. You want a slice?"

"No."

"Well, you don't mind if I help myself, do you?"

"Go ahead."

Ferguson disappeared into the small kitchen, then returned, carrying a steaming coffee cup and a tin plate with a coffee cake on it. Cowart had already set up his tape recorder on a small table. Ferguson put the coffee cake next to it, then carved a piece off the end. Cowart saw that he used a gleaming steel hunting knife to cut the cake. It had a six-inch blade with a serrated edge on one side and a grip handle. Ferguson put the knife down and popped the cake into his mouth.

"Not exactly kitchen equipment," Cowart said.

Ferguson shrugged. "I keep this handy. Had some break-ins. You know, addicts looking for an easy score. This isn't the best neighborhood. Or maybe you didn't notice."

"I noticed."

"Need a little extra protection."

"Ever use that knife for something else?"

Ferguson smiled. Cowart had the impression that he was being teased the way a younger child will tease an older sibling mercilessly, knowing that the parents will side with him. "Now, what else could I use this for, save cutting an occasional piece of bread and slicing off some peace of mind?" he replied.

Ferguson took a sip of coffee. "So. Early-morning visit. Got questions. Come alone?" He stood up, went to the window, and peered up and down the street.

"I'm alone."

Ferguson hesitated, staring hard for an instant or two in the direction where Brown had parked his car, then turned back to the reporter.

"Sure."

He sat back down. "All right, Mr. Cowart. What brings you here?"

"Have you spoken with your grandmother?"

"Haven't spoken to anyone from Pachoula in months. She doesn't have a telephone. Neither do I."

Cowart glanced around but couldn't see a phone. "I went to see her."

"Well, that was nice of you."

"I went to see her because Blair Sullivan told me to go look for something there."

"Told you when?"

"Right before he died."

"Mr. Cowart, you're driving at something and I surely have no idea what."

"In the outhouse."

"Not a nice place. Old. Ain't been used for a year."

"That's right."

"I put some plumbing in. A thousand bucks, cash."

"Why'd you do it?"

"What? Put plumbing in? Because it's cold to walk outside and do your business in the wintertime."

Cowart shook his head. "No. That's not what I mean. Why did you kill Joanie Shriver?"

Ferguson stared hard at Cowart and then leaned back in his chair. "Haven't killed nobody. Especially that little gal. Thought you knew that by now."

"You're lying."

Ferguson glared at him. "No."

"You raped her, then you killed her, left her body in the swamp, and stuck the knife under the culvert. Then you returned home and saw that there was blood on your clothes and on a piece of the rug in your car, so you cut that out, and you took it and wrapped up the clothes and buried them under all this shit and muck in that outhouse, because you knew that no one in their right mind would ever look there for them."

Ferguson shook his head.

"You denying it?" Cowart asked.

"Of course."

"I found the clothing and the rug."

Ferguson looked surprised for an instant, then shrugged. "Came all this way to tell me that?"

"Why did you kill her?"

"I didn't. I told you."

"Liar. You've been lying from the start."

Cowart thought the statement should anger Ferguson, but it did not, at least outwardly. Instead he smiled, reached forward, slowly cut himself another slice of cake, lingering with the knife in his hand for just a moment, then took another sip of coffee.

"The lies are all Sullivan's. What else did he tell you?"

"That you killed his folks down in the Keys."

Ferguson shook his head. "Didn't do that crime, neither. Helps explain what that pretty detective was doing poking about up here, though."

"Why'd you kill Joanie Shriver?" Cowart asked again.

Ferguson started to rise, anger finally creasing the edge of his voice. "I didn't do that crime! Goddammit, how many times I got to say that?"

"Then how did that stuff get in your outhouse?"

"We used to throw all sorts of things away down there. Clothes, auto parts that didn't work, trash. You name it. Those clothes you thinking of, I threw them out 'cause they got covered with pig's blood, 'cause I helped a neighbor slaughter an old sow. And I was walking home through the woods and got surprised by an old skunk and got nailed good with its damn stink. And hell, I had a little extra money, so I wrapped up those clothes and just threw 'em out, they was almost worn out anyways. Went and bought a new pair of jeans downtown."

"And the rug?"

"The rug got cut up by accident. Got torn when I put a chainsaw on the floor of the car. I cut out the square 'cause I was going to replace it with a new piece of rug. Got arrested first, though. Just chucked it down there, same as everything else."

Ferguson looked over at Cowart warily. "You got lab results that say differently?"

Cowart started to shake his head, but then stopped. He didn't know whether Ferguson had spotted the slight movement.

"You think I'm so damn stupid that after I got out of prison, if that stuff were evidence of some damn crime, especially a first-degree murder, I wouldn't go get it and make sure it was disappeared for good? What do you think, Mr. Cowart? You think I didn't learn anything on Death Row? You think I didn't learn anything taking all those criminology courses? You think I'm stupid, Mr. Cowart?"

"No," said Cowart. "I don't think you're stupid." His eyes locked onto Ferguson's. "And I think you've learned a great deal."

The two men were quiet for an instant.

"How did Sullivan know about that outhouse?"

Ferguson shrugged. "He told me once, before we had our little disagreement, said he once strangled a woman with her pantyhose, then flushed the stockings down the toilet. Said once they got into that septic system, weren't no one gonna find them. Asked me what I had at my house, and I told him we had that old outhouse and we used to throw all sorts of stuff in there. I guess he just put two and two together and made up a story for you, Mr. Cowart. So when you looked hard enough and thought hard enough and expected to find something, you sure as hell did. Isn't that the way things work? When you go looking for sure for something, you're likely to find it. Even if it ain't what you really are looking for."

"That's a convenient story."

Again, Ferguson bristled briefly, then relaxed. "Can't make it any prettier. But if you listen, seems to me that you'll hear a bit of Blair Sullivan in it. Man was able to twist about anything into something useful for him, wasn't he, Mr. Cowart?"

"That's true," he replied.

Ferguson gestured toward the tape recorder and the notepad that Cowart held in his hand.

"You here looking for some sort of story, Mr. Cowart?"

"That's right."

"Well, this is all old news."

"I don't know about that."

"Old story. Same old story. You been talking to Tanny Brown. That man is never gonna give up, is he?"

Cowart smiled. "No," he answered. "He's never going to give up."

"Damn him," Ferguson said bitterly. But then his voice lost the touch of fury that had accompanied the epithet and he added, "But he can't touch me now."

Cowart could feel a helplessness sinking within him. He tried to imagine what Tanny Brown would ask, what question could break through the hard shell of innocence that covered Ferguson. For the first time, he began to understand why Brown had loosened his partner's fists to obtain the confession to murder.

"When you go south to talk to some church group, Bobby Earl, or when you go to some civic center, do you give the same speech every time, or do you make it a bit different for different audiences?"

"I change it about a bit. It depends on whom I'm speaking to. But mostly it's the same message."

"But the thrust of it?"

"That remains the same."

"Tell me what you say."

"I tell folks how Jesus came and brought light right into the darkness of that cell on Death Row, Mr. Cowart. I tell them how faith will abide you through the most dangerous of times. How even the worst sinner can be touched by that special light and find comfort in the words of God. I tell them how truth will always rise up and cut through evil like a great shining sword and show the path to freedom. And they say Amen to that, Mr. Cowart, because that is a message that comforts the heart and soul, don't you think?"

"I think it does. And are you a regular churchgoer up here in Newark?"

"No. Here I'm a student."

Cowart nodded. "So, how many times have you given this speech?"

"Eight or nine."

"You got the names of the churches, community centers, whatever?"

"This for a story?"

"Give me the names."

Ferguson stared hard at Cowart, then shrugged, as if unconcerned. Rapid-fire he raced through a short list of churches, Baptist, Pentecostal, and Unitarian, adding the names of a few civic centers. The names of the towns they were in followed just as swiftly. Cowart struggled to get the information into his notebook. His pen made a scratching sound against the page, and he saw his handwriting flying about between the blue-ruled lines. Ferguson finished and waited for Cowart to say something. The reporter counted. Perrine was on the list.

"That's only seven."

"Maybe I forgot one or two."

Cowart stood up, driven to his feet by the turbulence he felt within him. He moved away from Ferguson, toward the bookcase. His eyes scanned the titles, just as Shaeffer had done when she visited the apartment.

"You must be an expert, after reading all these," he said.

Ferguson watched the reporter carefully. "Assigned readings."

Cowart turned back. "Dawn Perry," he said quietly. He

moved behind Ferguson's desk, as if that would afford him momentary protection if Ferguson came after him.

"The name is unfamiliar," Ferguson replied.

"Little girl. Black. Just twelve years old. On her way home from a swimming club one day last August, just a couple of days after you gave that speech down there."

"No. Can't say I place her. Should I know her?"

"I think so. Perrine, Florida. Swim club's about three, four blocks from the First Baptist Church of Perrine. Did you tell the congregation about Jesus's light that came and visited you? I guess they didn't know what else that light might mean."

"You asking a question, Mr. Cowart?"

"Yes. Why'd you kill her?"

"Little girl's dead?"

"Disappeared."

"I didn't kill her."

"No? You were there. She disappears."

"*That* a question, Mr. Cowart?"

"Tell me how you did it."

"I didn't do anything to that little girl." Ferguson's voice remained cold and even. "I didn't do anything to any little girls."

"I don't believe you."

"Belief, Mr. Cowart, is in great supply. People will believe almost anything. They'll believe that UFOs visit little towns in Ohio and that Elvis was spotted buying Twinkies in a convenience store. They'll believe that the CIA is poisoning their water and that a secret organization actually runs the United States. But proving something, Mr. Cowart, is much more difficult."

He looked at the reporter. "Like murder."

Cowart remained stock still, listening to Ferguson's voice as it swirled around him.

"You need motive, you need opportunity, and you need physical evidence. Something scientific and certain that some expert can get up in a court of law and say without dispute happened, like a fingerprint or blood residue. Or even maybe this new DNA testing, Mr. Cowart. You know about that? I do. You need a witness, and lacking that, maybe an accomplice to testify. And if you don't have any of those, you damn well better have a confession. The killer's own words, nice and clear and indisputable, but we know all about that, don't we? And you got to have all these things, all sewn together into a nice fabric, because otherwise, you've got nothing except awful feelings and guesses. And just because some little girl got snatched away, right out there on the outskirts of that big old evil city, Mr. Cowart, and I happened to be in that town some two days earlier, well, that isn't proof of anything, is it? How many killers you think there are in Miami at any given moment? How many men wouldn't think twice about grabbing some little girl who was walking home, just like you said? You think the cops down there haven't run profiles and questioned all the creeps? They have, Mr. Cowart. I'm certain of it. But you know what? I'm not on anybody's list. Not anymore. Because I am an innocent man, Mr. Cowart. You helped me become one. And I intend to stay that way.''

"How many?" Cowart asked, almost whispering. "Six? Seven? Every time you give a speech, does somebody die?"

Ferguson narrowed his eyes, but his voice remained steady. "White man's crime, Mr. Cowart. Don't you know that?''

"What?''

"White man's crime. Come on, think of all the killers you've read about. All the Specks, Bundys, Coronas, Gacys, Henleys, Lucases, and our old buddy Blair Sullivan. White men. Jack the Ripper and Bluebeard. White men. Caligula and Vlad the Impaler. White men, Mr. Cowart. They're all white men. You take a tour of any prison and they're gonna point at Charlie Manson or David Berkowitz and you're gonna see white men, because they're the people who give in and get those strange urges. This is not to say that there ain't an occasional exception that maybe proves the rule, you know. Like Wayne Williams down in Atlanta; but there are so many questions about him, aren't there? Hell, there was even a movie on television questioning whether he was the one that did all those young men down there in that fair city. Remember that, Mr. Cowart? No, snatching little girls off the street and leaving 'em dead someplace dark and forgotten ain't typical of black men. What we do is crimes of violence. Sudden, uncontrollable bursts with knives or guns and noise. City crime, Mr. Cowart, with witnesses and crime scenes fairly dripping with evidence, so that when the cops get around to putting us in jail there ain't no questions left around. Raping joggers and shooting rival crack dealers and strong-arming convenience store clerks and assaulting each other, Mr. Cowart, ain't that right? Typical stuff that makes white folks buy fancy alarms for their suburban homes and feeds the criminal justice system with its daily quota of black men—but not serial killing. And you know what else, Mr. Cowart?''

"What?"

"That's the way the system likes it. The system isn't comfortable with things that don't quite match up into statistics and categories."

Ferguson looked over at him. "How you gonna write that story up, Mr. Cowart? The one that doesn't fit into some nice, safe, expected niche? Tell me, are newspapers real good at telling people things that strange? That unexpected? Or do you go about your business of reporting over and over again all the same old stuff, just with different faces and words?"

He didn't reply.

"And you think you're gonna write something like that without any proof?"

"Joanie Shriver," Cowart said.

"Goodbye to her, Mr. Cowart. She's long gone. Best you understood that. Maybe make your friend Tanny Brown understand that, too."

Cowart remained standing next to Ferguson's desk. He leaned across it, gripping the edges for balance. "I will write the story, you know that, don't you?"

Ferguson didn't reply.

"I'll put it all in the paper. All the falsehoods, all the lies, every bit of it. You can deny it and deny it, and you know what, don't you?"

"What?"

"It'll work. I'll go down. Maybe Tanny Brown'll go down. But you know what will happen to you, Bobby Earl?"

"Tell me," he said coldly.

"You won't go to jail. Nope. You're right about that. Not enough evidence. And a whole lot of people will believe you when you say it is all a setup. They'll still believe you when you say you're innocent. Most folks'll want to blame me, and the cops, and they'll rally around you, Bobby Earl. I promise."

Ferguson continued to stare at Cowart.

"But you know what you're gonna lose? Anonymity."

Ferguson shrugged, and Cowart continued. "Come on, Bobby Earl. You know what you do when you've got an old house cat that likes to hunt? Likes to kill birds and mice and then drag them into your nice clean suburban house? You put a bell around that cat's neck, so that no matter how clever and quiet and stealthy that old hunting cat is, it can't ever get close enough to some poor little starling to get its claws around it."

Ferguson's eyes narrowed.

"You think those fine churches still gonna ask you to come give that nice speech if there's just a little bit of a question remaining? You think they might be able to find some other speaker for that Sunday? One that they are damn certain isn't going to hang around or come back some other time and pluck some little girl off the street?"

Cowart saw Ferguson stiffen with anger.

"And the police, Bobby Earl. Think of the police. They're always going to wonder, aren't they? And when something happens, and it will happen, won't it, Bobby Earl? When something happens they'll be looking at you first. How many times you think you can do it, Bobby Earl, without making some little mistake? Forget something. Maybe get seen once. That's going to be all it takes, isn't it? Because you just make that one little mistake and the whole world's going to come down square on your head, and you won't be able to look up again until you're right back where you were when we had our first conversation. And this time there won't be any *Miami Journal* writer looking to help you get out, will there?"

Cowart watched as Ferguson coiled himself on the seat, rage spreading like a gasoline fire across his face. He saw the man's hand edge toward the hunting knife and felt himself freeze with instant fear.

I'm dead, he thought.

He wanted to search around, try to find something to protect himself with, but he could not remove his eyes from Ferguson. For an instant, he remembered: I needed a word. A word that would summon Tanny Brown. But he had none.

Ferguson half rose from his seat, then stopped. Cowart felt his hand close on a sheaf of papers. Then Ferguson sat back down slowly.

"No," he said. "I don't think you'll write that story."

"Why?"

Ferguson looked down on the table in front of him, where Cowart had placed his tape recorder. For a moment, Ferguson seemed to watch as the tape absorbed silence. Then he said, in a firm, distinct voice, leaning toward the machine, "Because not a word of it would be true." After another second or two passed, he reached over and punched off the Record button.

"You know why you won't write that story? I'll tell you why. There are a lot of good reasons, but first off, because you know what you don't have? You don't have any facts. You don't have any evidence. All you have is a crazy combination of events and lies, and I know some editor'll look at all that and think it has no place in the paper. And you know what else you don't have, Mr. Cowart? All newspaper stories are all made up of 'according to's' and 'police said's' and 'spokesmen confirmed's' and all sorts of other folks contributing documents and reports, and that's where you get the bones for your story. The rest of the flesh is just the detail that you've seen and the detail that you've heard, and you haven't seen or heard anything important enough to build a story.

"And that's one reason why you don't scare me, Mr. Cowart. Tell me," he said. "Do I scare you?"

Cowart nodded.

"Well, that's good. Do you suppose I scare your friend Tanny Brown, as well?"

"Yes and no."

"Now that's a strange answer for a man who aspires toward precision. What do you mean?"

"I think he fears what you're doing. But I don't think he's scared of you."

Ferguson shook his head. "Tell me something, will you? Why is it that people always fear something happening to them? Personal fear. Like you right now. Scared that maybe I'll pick up this hunting knife and come over there and cut your heart out. Isn't that right? Just walk right over there and slice you from balls to throat and take out what I want. What do you think? You think I'm such an expert killer that I could do that? Then maybe just stick your bloody remains someplace special, make it look like you stumbled around down here, got caught up with some of the locals, you know. Some of the folks down here aren't too partial to white people wandering around. Think I could make it seem like some gang maybe had a little fun carving up a white reporter who got lost looking for an address? Think I could pull that off, Mr. Cowart?"

"No."

"You don't think so? Why not, if I'm such an expert?"

"I don't . . ."

"Why not!" Ferguson demanded sharply. His hand closed on the knife handle.

"Blood," Cowart answered rapidly. "The bloodstains. You couldn't hope to get them sufficiently cleaned up."

"Good. Keep going."

"Maybe somebody saw me come in. A witness."

"That's good, Mr. Cowart. There's an old landlady here who

keeps a watch on such things. She might have seen you come in. Maybe one of the derelicts outside would remember seeing you. That's possible as well, but they'd make a poor witness. Keep going.''

"Maybe I told somebody where I was going."

"No," Ferguson grinned. "That wouldn't amount to anything. No proof you ever got here."

"Prints. I've left prints in here."

"Didn't take the cup of coffee you were offered. That might have left prints and saliva. What else you touched? The desk. The papers there. I could clean those.''

"You couldn't be sure."

Ferguson smiled again. "That's right."

"Other things. Hair. Skin. I might fight back. Cut you. That'd put some of your blood on me. They'd find it."

"Maybe. At least now you're thinking, Mr. Cowart."

Ferguson leaned back. He gestured at the hunting knife. "Too many variables. You're right about that. Too many angles to cover. Any student of criminology would know that." Ferguson continued to stare at him. "But I still don't think you'll write that story, Mr. Cowart."

"I'll write the story," Cowart insisted softly.

"You know something? You know there are other ways of cutting out somebody's heart? Don't always have to use a big hunting knife . . .''

Ferguson reached over and grasped the blade. He held it up, twisting it in his hand so that it caught a small bit of gray light that forced its way through the window.

". . . No, sir. Not at all. I mean, you'd think this was the easiest way to cut out your heart, Mr. Cowart, but it really isn't.''

Ferguson continued to hold the knife up in front of him. "Who lives at 1215 Wildflower Drive, Mr. Cowart?''

Cowart felt a surge of dizzying heat.

"In that nice Tampa suburb. Rides that yellow school bus every day. Plays down in the park a couple of blocks distant. Likes to help her mother in with the groceries and watch her new baby brother. Of course, you wouldn't care much about that little baby now, would you? And I don't know how much you'd care about the mother, either. Divorce sometimes makes people just fill up with hate and so I can't really tell your feelings about her one way or the other. But that little girl? Now, that's a whole different matter."

"How do you know about . . ."

"They were in the newspaper. After you won that prize." Ferguson smiled at him. "And I like to do a bit of research every now and then. Finding out about them wasn't too hard."

Cowart's fear was complete. Ferguson continued to eye the reporter. "No, Mr. Cowart. I don't think you're going to write that story. I don't think you've got the *facts*. I don't think you've got the *evidence*. Isn't that right, Mr. Cowart?"

"I'll kill you," Cowart croaked.

"Kill me? Whatever for?"

"You go near . . ."

"And what?"

"I'm saying I'll kill you."

"That'd do you a lot of good, wouldn't it, Mr. Cowart? After the fact? Ain't nothing matter much after something's done, does it? You see, you'd still have that memory, wouldn't you? It'd be there first thing in the morning, last thing at night. It'd be in every dream you had while you slept. Every thought you had while awake. It'd never leave you alone, would it, Mr. Cowart?"

"I'll kill you," he repeated.

Ferguson shook his head. "I don't know. I don't know if you know enough about death and dying to do something like that. But I'll say this for you now, Mr. Cowart."

"What?"

"Now you're beginning to know a bit of what it's like living on Death Row."

Ferguson rose, leaned over and opened the cassette door on the recorder. He removed the cassette and slipped it in his pocket. Then he picked up the tape recorder from the table. With a single, abrupt motion, he threw it at the reporter, who caught it before it smashed to the floor.

"This interview," Ferguson said coldly. "It never happened."

He pointed toward the door. "Those words? They never got spoke." Ferguson eyed the reporter, whispering, "What story you got to write, Mr. Cowart?"

Cowart shook his head.

"What story, Mr. Cowart?"

"No story," he replied, his voice cracked and brittle.

"I didn't think so," Ferguson replied.

Cowart, head reeling, stumbled into the hallway. He was only vaguely aware of the door closing behind him, of the sound of the locks being thrown. Stale, damp air trapped him in the dark space, and he clawed at his collar, trying to loosen it so he could breathe. He fought his way down the stairs, tore at the front door, slamming it open and battling his way to the street. The rain had started up; droplets scarred his coat and face. He did not look back up toward the apartment, but instead started to run, as if the wind in his face could eradicate the fear and nausea he felt within. He saw Tanny Brown exit from the driver's side door of their rental car, staring at him expectantly. Breathing hard, Cowart waved at him, trying to get him to return to the vehicle. Then he seized the car door handle and jerked it, leaping into the car, jamming himself into the warm, moist interior.

''Get me out of here,'' he whispered.

''What happened?'' Brown asked.

''Get me the hell out of here!'' Cowart shouted. He reached across and grabbed the ignition, grinding it. The engine fired up. ''Go, goddammit! Go!''

Tanny Brown, eyes wide in surprise, but face marked with a sense of understanding, shifted the car in gear. He pulled out into the street, stopping only at the north end, pulling across from where Wilcox and Shaeffer had parked. He rolled down his window.

''Bruce, you two stay here. Watch Ferguson's place.''

''How long?''

''Just watch it.''

''Where are you . . .''

''Just don't let Ferguson get out of your sight.''

Wilcox nodded.

Cowart pounded on the dashboard. ''Go! Goddammit! Get me out of here!''

Tanny Brown punched the gas, and they pulled away, leaving the two other detectives behind in some confusion.

TWENTY-THREE

DETECTIVE SHAEFFER'S ———*NEGLIGENCE*

T HE two detectives spent most of the day parked a half block from the doorway to Ferguson's apartment house. Their surveillance had no subtlety; within the first hour after Brown and Cowart's departure, everyone living within a two-city-block radius, not merely those criminal in nature or inclination, was aware of their presence. For the most part, they were ignored.

A minor-league crack dealer, accustomed to using an alleyway adjacent to their position, cursed them loudly as he bustled about, searching for a suitable replacement location; two members of a local street gang, wearing embossed jackets and headbands, sporting the preferred expensive hightop basketball shoes favored in the inner city, paused next to their rental car and mocked them with obscene gestures. When Wilcox rolled down the window and shouted at them to leave, they merely laughed in his face, imitating his southern accent with rancorous delight and only mildly concealed menace. Two prostitutes, wearing red high heels and sequined hot pants beneath slick black raincoats, flaunted their business at the detectives, as if sensing they would not budge for the likes of them. At least a half dozen homeless, decrepit folk, pushing the ubiquitous shopping carts filled with urban flotsam and jetsam, or merely staggering through the wet day, knocked on their windows, requesting money. A couple went away with whatever spare change the two detectives could muster. Others simply marched past, oblivious to anything save the demands of whatever unseen individual it was with whom they conversed so steadily.

The steady drizzle that kept the street-life parade down to a damp minimum kept most of the other residents of the block indoors, behind their barred windows and triple-locked doors. The rain and gray skies darkened the day, driving the gloom deeper.

More than once, each detective had asked, "What the hell happened to Cowart?" But in the isolation of their car, they could not reach an answer. Wilcox had walked to a corner pay phone and tried reaching the two absent men at the motel, but without success. Lacking any information, knowing only what Brown had ordered as he drove off, they remained on the street, letting the hours pass in stultifying frustration.

They ate fast food purchased from a take-out joint, drank coffee that had grown cold from Styrofoam cups, wiped humid moisture from the windshield endlessly so they could see ahead. Twice, each had walked two blocks to an oil-stained gas station to use bathrooms that stank with a pungent mixture of disinfectant battling excrement. Their conversation had been limited, a few halfhearted attempts at finding some commonality, lapsing into long silences. They had spoken a bit of technique, of the difference in crimes between the Panhandle and the Keys, knowing that differences were merely superficial. Shaeffer had asked questions about Brown and Cowart, but discovered that Wilcox merely idolized the first and despised the latter, though he was unable to say precisely why he felt either emotion. They had speculated about Ferguson, Wilcox filling the other detective in on his experiences with the onetime convicted man. She had asked him about the confession, and he'd replied that every time he'd hit Ferguson, he'd felt as if he was shaking loose another piece of the truth, the way someone would shake fruit from a tree. He said it without regret or guilt, but with an underlying anger that surprised her. Wilcox was a volatile man, she thought, far more explosive than the immense lieutenant he was partnered to. His rage would be sudden and dramatic. Tanny Brown's would be colder, more processed. No wonder he couldn't forgive himself for indulging in the luxury of having his partner beat a confession out of the man. It must have been an aberration, a window on a part of him that he must hate.

They saw no signs of Ferguson, though they expected he knew they were there.

"How long are we going to stay?" Shaeffer asked. Streetlights did little to slice the evening darkness. "He hasn't shown all day, unless there's a backdoor exit. Which there probably is, and he's probably off somewhere laughing at us."

"Little longer," Wilcox replied. "Long enough."

"What are we doing?" Shaeffer continued. "I mean, what's the point?"

"The point is to let him know someone's thinking about him. The point is, Tanny told us to watch Ferguson."

"Right," she replied. She wanted to add, But not forever. Time seemed to slip away from her. She knew that Michael Weiss at the state prison would be wondering where she was. Knew, as well, that she had to come up with a good reason for still being there. A good, solid, official-sounding reason.

Shaeffer stretched her arms wide and pushed her legs against the fire wall of the car, feeling the muscles ache with the stiffness of inactivity.

"I hate this," she said.

"What? Watching?"

"Right. Just waiting. Not my style."

"What is your style?"

She didn't reply. "It'll be dark in another ten minutes. Too dark."

"It's dark now."

Wilcox motioned up at the apartment entrance, but did not connect a comment to the gesture.

Shaeffer glanced about the outside of the car. She thought the street had the same appearance as the raincoats that the two prostitutes who'd accosted them earlier had; a sort of slick, glistening, synthetic sense. It was almost like being caught on a Hollywood set, real and unreal all at the same moment. She felt a sudden shiver run down her spine.

"Something wrong?" Wilcox asked. He'd caught the movement out of the corner of his eye.

"No," she replied hastily. "Just a little bit of the creeps, you know. This place is awful enough in the daylight."

He let his eyes sweep up and down the street.

"Sure ain't like anything at home," he said. "Makes you feel like you're living in a cave."

"Or a cell," she added.

Her pocketbook was on the floor, between her feet. It was a large, loose leather bag, almost a knapsack. She nudged it with her toe, just pulling open the top, revealing the contents and reassuring herself that all the essentials it contained were still in place: notebook, tape recorder, spare tapes, wallet, badge, a small makeup case, nine-millimeter semiautomatic pistol with two extra clips, loaded with soft-nosed wadcutters.

Wilcox caught the motion as well. "Me," he smiled, "I still like a three-fifty-seven short-nose. Fits up under the jacket nice. Put in a magnum load, bring down a bear."

He glanced around at the darkness crawling over their car. "Plenty of bear around here, too," he added. He patted his coat, on top of his left side.

In the distance a siren started up, like some cat in heat. It grew louder, closer, then just as swiftly faded away. They never saw the lights of whatever it was.

Wilcox put his hand up and rubbed his eyes for an instant. "What do you think they've been doing?" he asked.

"I don't know," she replied quickly. "Why don't we get the hell out of here and find out? Place is starting to make me nervous."

"Starting?"

"You know what I mean." Unsettled anger marched briskly in her voice. "Jesus, look at this place. I feel like it could eat us up. Just gulp and swallow. Those two city cops that brought me down here the other day weren't none too pleased to be here, either, and it was daytime. And one of them was black."

Wilcox grunted in assent.

It was clear to both of them, though unsaid throughout the day, that their position was precarious: a pair of white southern cops, out of their jurisdiction, out of their element, in an unfamiliar world.

"Okay," Wilcox drawled slowly. His eyes swept up the street again. "You know what gets to me?" he asked.

"No. What?"

"Everything looks so damn old. Old and used up." He pointed through the windshield, down the street toward nothing. "Dying," he said. "It's like it's all dying."

He did not amplify the statement. He remained rigid in his seat, staring out at the world surrounding them.

"I don't know how, but I think he's got all this figured out somehow. I think he's just a step or two ahead of us. Had us made from the start." His voice was whispered, angry.

"I don't know what you're saying," Shaeffer replied. "Made what? Figured what?"

"I'd like to get just one more shot at him," he went on,

ignoring her questions. "One more bite at the apple. I wouldn't let him screw with me this time."

"I still don't know what you're driving at," she said, alarmed at the coldness in his voice.

"I'd like to get my face in his one more time. Like to get us alone again in some small room, see if he walks away this time."

"You're crazy."

"That's right. Crazy mad. You got it."

She shrank back in her seat again. "Lieutenant Brown had orders."

"Sure. And we've followed them."

"So, let's get out of here. Find out what he wants to do next."

Wilcox shook his head. "Not until I see the bastard. Not until he knows it's me out here."

Shaeffer put her hand up and waved it back and forth rapidly. "That's not how to play him," she said swiftly. "You don't want him to take off."

"You haven't got this figured out yet, have you?" Wilcox replied, his teeth set. "Have you lost one yet? How long you been doing homicides? Not damn long enough. You ain't had somebody do a job on you like Ferguson."

"No," she said. "And I don't mean to."

"Easy for you to say."

"Yeah, but I still know enough not to make one mistake into two."

Wilcox started to reply angrily, but then nodded. "That's right," he said. He took a deep breath. "That's right."

He settled back in his seat, as if the wave of anger and memory that had beat on his shore was slowly receding. "Right, right, right," he said slowly. "Don't want to play the hand before we see all the cards."

Shaeffer expected him to reach out and start the car. She saw Wilcox's hand lift toward the ignition. But as his fingers closed on the protruding key, he stopped, suddenly rigid, eyes burning straight ahead.

"Son of a bitch," he said softly.

She looked up wildly.

"There he is," Wilcox whispered.

For an instant her view was obscured by the moisture on the windshield, but then, like a camera coming into focus, she, too, spotted Ferguson. He had hesitated just for an instant on the top landing, pausing as almost everyone does before forcing themselves to step into the damp, dark, cold night air. She saw he was wearing jeans and a long blue coat, carrying a satchel over his shoulder. Hunched against the drizzle, he rapidly stepped down from the apartment building, and without even glancing in their direction, headed off swiftly away from them.

"Damn!" Wilcox said. His hand had dropped away from the ignition. He seized the car door. "I'm gonna follow him."

Before she could protest, wild impulse filled him. He thrust himself out the door, feet hitting like shots against the pavement. Slamming the door behind him, he started up the street.

Shaeffer reached across the front seat, grabbing first at Wilcox's coattails, then at car keys. She saw him moving away and tried to extricate herself from the car. Her door was locked; the first pull on the handle produced nothing. Her handbag caught on the seat adjustment lever between her feet. It seemed leaden with weight. The seat belt grabbed at her clothes. Her shoes slipped on the slick pavement. When she finally got herself out, she saw she would have to run to catch up with Wilcox, who was already twenty yards down the street and moving fast.

She cursed and ran, holding her bag in one hand, the car keys in the other. It took her another ten yards to reach him.

"What the hell are you doing?" she demanded, seizing his arm.

He pulled away. "I'm just gonna follow the bastard a bit! Let go!"

He continued his quick march after Ferguson.

She stopped, stealing a breath of air, and watched as he kept going. Again she put her head down and ran to catch up. She pulled alongside him, struggling to keep pace. She could see Ferguson a half block distant and moving swiftly himself, not looking back, just plowing through the darkness, apparently oblivious to their presence.

She grasped Wilcox's arm a second time.

"Let go, goddammit!" he said, angrily snatching his arm from her hold. "I'll lose him."

"We're not supposed . . ."

He turned, briefly, furiously. "Get the damn car! Keep up! Come with me! Just don't get in my goddamn way!"

"But he . . ."

"I don't care if he knows I'm back here! Now get out of my goddamn way!"

"What the hell are you doing?" she half shouted.

He waved furiously in her direction as if dismissing the question contemptuously. He spun away from her and, half running, tried to close the distance between Ferguson and himself.

Shaeffer hesitated, unsure. She saw Wilcox's back, pushing through the night, looked farther and saw Ferguson disappear around a corner. Wilcox increased his pace at the same moment.

She mumbled expletives to herself, turned, and ran fast back to the car. Two ancient street people, both women bundled in thick wads of coats with knit wool caps jammed on top of their heads, had materialized out of the gloom, blocking her path. One was pushing a shopping cart, cackling, while the other was gesturing wildly. They screeched at her as she pushed toward them. One of the old women reached out and tried to grab her as she went past, and for an instant they collided. The old woman spun and fell to the sidewalk, her voice wailing with anger and shock. Shaeffer stumbled, righted herself and, tossing an apology to the woman, ran to the car. The woman's shrieks followed after her. Two men had come out onto a front stoop despite the rain, and one of them called at her, "Hey! Whatcha doin' lady? Big rush, hey?'' She ignored them and threw herself into the driver's seat.

She ground the ignition and stalled the car.

Swearing continuously in a torrent of expletives, caught up in half panic and confusion, completely uncertain what Wilcox was doing, she stabbed at the engine again, pumping her foot on the gas pedal and twisting the ignition key. The engine caught and she slammed the car into gear, pulling out into the street without even glancing backward. The tires spun on the wet pavement and the car fishtailed sickeningly for an instant before shooting ahead.

Accelerating hard down the block, she rammed the car around the corner. She spotted Wilcox halfway down the block, catching sight of him as he swept into the weak light of a streetlight. She strained her eyes but could not see Ferguson.

Again she punched the car, and the engine responded sluggishly, complaining. She cursed the underpowered rental vehicle and felt a momentary longing for her own squad car back in the Keys. She came abreast of Wilcox just before the end of the block. He was turning down a one-way street, heading against the traffic. She rolled down her window as fast as she could, feeling the drizzle on her forehead.

"Keep going!" Wilcox gestured swiftly. "Head him off.''

The detective plowed after his quarry, picking up his pace,

breaking into a jog. Shaeffer shouted some quick word of agreement and spun the car down the rain-slicked street.

She had to go an extra block before she could turn. She ran a red light, sweeping around a corner, causing a pair of teenagers on the curb to leap back, angrily shouting obscenities after her. The street was narrow, lined with dark, decrepit buildings that seemed to block her sight. A pair of cars were double-parked in midblock. She blared the horn hard as she crawled past, leaving an inch or less on either side of her car.

At the next corner, she jerked the car back to the right, heading back toward the spot where she figured to catch up with Wilcox and Ferguson. Her mind raced with words; what to say, how to act. She realized that something was happening that was out of any control she might once have had. She concentrated on the road, fighting the night, trying to spot the two men as they maneuvered through the city streets.

They were not there.

She slowed the car, peering ahead, peering sideways down the veinlike alleyways and rubble-strewn clots of abandoned space. Shadows seemed to build into solid darkness. The street was abruptly empty of any people.

She stopped the car in the center of the street and jumped out, standing in the open doorway, looking both ways for any sign of the two men. Seeing none, she cursed loudly and slid back behind the wheel.

Dammit, she told herself. They must have turned down another street or cut through a vacant lot. He might have ducked down an alleyway.

She accelerated hard again, trying to guess and gauge, trying to catch up with the two men. She raced around another corner, only to feel a plummeting despair.

Still no sign of them.

She slapped the car into reverse, backing into the street from which she'd turned, and then jammed the car into forward. She sliced through the blackness sharply, still searching. She drove another block fast, then stabbed the brakes.

No one.

She felt a tightness winding within her. She had no idea what to do. Battling panic, she pitched the car quickly to the curb and jumped out. Walking fast, she headed in the direction in which she thought they should have been moving, still trying to think logically. Retrace their steps, she insisted to herself. Head them off. They can't be far. She strained her eyes against the shadows,

her eyes searched for the sound of a raised voice. Then she
picked up her pace and started to run. Her shoes made a solitary
slapping sound against the sidewalk pavement. The sound increased, like a drumroll gaining momentum, until finally, flat
out, she sprinted toward the empty night.

Bruce Wilcox had turned once, just long enough to catch a
glimpse of the rental car's taillights disappearing down the street,
before he centered all his concentration on keeping up with
Ferguson.

He increased his pace, surprised that he couldn't narrow the
distance between him and his quarry. Ferguson had a subtle
quickness to him; without breaking into a run, he was moving
swiftly, working his way around the spots of light that littered
the street, blending with the surroundings.

He thought his legs seemed heavy, slow, and he furiously
demanded more of them. Ahead, he saw Ferguson turn again,
at another street corner, and he pushed himself hard to catch
up.

A pair of bedraggled prostitutes were working the corner,
using the sodium-vapor streetlight to advertise their presence.
They ducked back as he approached, shrinking against a storefront.

"Where'd he go?" Wilcox demanded.

"Who, man?"

"Ain't seen nobody."

He swore at them, and they both laughed, mocking him as
he pushed past. The side street down which Ferguson had headed
seemed cavernous, yawing back and forth like a ship in heavy
weather. He caught a glimpse of Ferguson forty yards ahead,
really just a shape that had more substance than the remaining
shadows in the street, and he ran hard after it.

His mind raced alongside him.

He had no grasp of what he was going to say, what he was
going to do, driven merely by the need to catch up with the
chased man. Images jumped rapidly in and out of his head: It
seemed as if the world he was cutting through was mixing crazily with his memory. A derelict lying semistuporously in an
abandoned doorway sang out as he cruised past, but the voice
reminded him of Tanny Brown's. A dog barked hard, throwing
itself against a chain, and he remembered the search for Joanie
Shriver's body. Dirt-streaked aluminum garbage cans reflected
weak streetlamp light, and he thought of the sucking, oozing

sensation between his hands as he pulled free the useless evidence from the outhouse refuse pit. This last memory drove him harder in pursuit.

He looked ahead and saw Ferguson reach the end of the block. He seemed to pause, and Wilcox saw the man turn. For one microscopic moment, their eyes met across the night.

Wilcox couldn't contain himself. "Stop! Police!" he shouted.

Ferguson didn't hesitate. Running now, he fled.

Wilcox yelled a single, "Hey!" then tucked his chin down and ran hard. All pretense of surveillance or tailing Ferguson was lost now in a single-minded, headstrong chase. He sucked in wind and started pumping his arms, feeling his feet lighten against the rain-slicked pavement, no more plodding, determined pursuit, but now a sprint.

His burst of speed pushed him a bit closer, but Ferguson, too, rapidly settled into a hard run. They seemed evenly matched, feet hitting the pavement in unison, the distance between them maintaining a frustrating constancy.

The world around him turned vaporous, indistinct. He could feel the effects of his sprint. His wind was shortened, his heart beating fast. He tore air from the night to fill screaming lungs.

Another city block passed. He saw Ferguson turn again, still driving forward, seemingly unaffected by the run. Wilcox pushed on, sliding as he tried to cut the corner closely, his feet scrabbling on the pavement. For a sickening instant, he felt a dizziness, a stab of vertigo, and then he lost his balance. The cement came up fast, like a wave at the beach, striking him solidly. Breath exploded from him. A shock of red pain swept across his eyes. He heard some article of clothing tearing and felt a gritty taste in his mouth. He slid, partly stunned, finally coming to rest against a streetlight. Instinct fought against shock and hurt, and he forced himself back to his feet, rising, struggling to regain his rhythm. He had a sudden memory of a high-school wrestling championship when he'd been thrown through the air, and as he tumbled toward the mat, his mind had razored off a decision as to what move to employ so that when his opponent's arms sought to encircle him, he was already rolling free. He blinked hard and found himself running again, racing forward, trying to grasp where he was and what he was doing, but finding the blow from the street had scrambled his senses, and he was being driven merely by wild fury and impatient desire.

As he ran, he saw Ferguson abruptly slice across the street, heading toward a dark, empty lot. Headlights from an approaching car trapped him for an instant. There was a loud screeching sound, followed instantly by the blare of a horn.

For an instant, he thought it was Detective Shaeffer, and he cheered, "That's it! Cut the bastard off!"

Then he saw that it wasn't. A sudden shot of anger pierced him: Where the hell is she? He pushed on, dodging the same car, leaving the driver shouting imprecations at the two wraith-like shapes that had disappeared as swiftly as they had materialized.

He scrambled over rubble and debris, which grabbed at his ankles like tendrils in a swamp. He caught a glimpse of Ferguson up ahead, maneuvering with identical difficulty through the abandoned junk of the inner city. For an instant, Ferguson rose up on top of a pile of boxes and an old refrigerator, outlined by a distant streetlamp. Their eyes met for a second time and Wilcox impulsively yelled, "Stop. Police!" again. He thought he saw a flash of recognition and disbelief in Ferguson's eyes. Then the quarry vanished, leaping down out of the meager light. Wilcox muttered obscenities and struggled on.

He leapt up over a pile of bricks, but his foot caught the top, and he could feel the mass crumbling beneath his sudden weight. He felt himself pitched forward, and he threw out his hands to try to break his fall. He succeeded in preventing a broken-neck tumble—but his right hand slammed down on a jagged piece of rusty metal. One edge sliced through his palm, three fingers were jammed back fiercely, and his wrist almost buckled from the blow. He screamed in agony, struggling again to balance himself, grabbing his mangled hand with his left. He could feel the skin parted and swelling with sticky damp blood. His fingers and wrist were instantaneously on fire; broken, he thought, cursing himself, goddammit, goddammit, goddammit. He squeezed the hand into a tight balled fist, clutched it close to his chest, and battled on, picking another pile of debris to climb, to try and spot the pursued man.

He bent over at his waist to catch his breath, denying the pain in his hand and wrist. Standing carefully to keep his balance on this new pile of trash, he saw Ferguson vaulting a jagged and twisted chain link fence at the back of the vacant lot. He watched as Ferguson sprinted across an alleyway, hesitated for an instant, then ducked up some stairs and into a deserted building.

All right, he said to himself. You're tired, too, you bastard. Catch your breath in there. But you're not going to get away.

Ignoring the throbbing in his torn and broken hand, he pushed himself across the last few yards of the lot and scrambled over the chain link fence. He jogged to the abandoned building's door and stared at it, breathing hard with exertion.

All right, he said again. He gingerly reached into his jacket pocket and found a handkerchief, which he used to bind up his wound as best as possible. It was difficult to see in the darkness, but he suspected he would need stitches to close the cut. He shook his head. Probably a tetanus shot as well. With the hand-kerchief swiftly soaking up the blood that continued to pulse through his palm, he tried to flex his fingers and wrist, only to receive a sharp needle of pain racing up his arm. He touched the skin carefully, trying to feel for broken bones. It was already swelling rapidly, and for a moment he wondered if the Escambia County employee's insurance policy would take care of the whole thing. Line of duty, he thought. Got to be. He gritted his teeth against the shooting sensation that raced up his arm and hoped that some doctor would simply put a cast on the damn thing and that he wouldn't need an operation.

He looked up and down the alleyway. Damp, rain-slicked debris littered the narrow space. He peered up, trying to see if anyone was in any of the buildings, but no one was visible. It seemed an area of abandoned apartments, perhaps warehouses; it was hard to tell; the light was limited, diffuse, emanating from streetlights thirty yards away.

For a moment, he paused. If he could spot Detective Shaeffer, he thought, but then he didn't complete the mental equation. It would be nice to have a backup.

He shrugged doubt away, replacing it with the headstrong bluster with which he was more familiar. I don't need any help to grab that squirrelly son of a bitch, he told himself. Even with one hand, I can handle him.

He believed this completely. He stepped up to the front door.

Ferguson's headlong passage had jammed it open, in mis-taken invitation. The doorway opening was like a stripe of deeper black against the velour fabric of the night. He put his back to the door and stopped, listening.

As he hesitated, he freed his revolver from his shoulder hol-ster. The weight of the gun in his damaged hand was impossible; like grabbing a red-hot coal from a fire. He squeezed his eyes shut for an instant, gently shifting the weapon into his left hand. He opened his eyes and stared down at the gun. Can you hit something left-handed? he asked himself. Something close, maybe. If you have to. He spoke to himself in the third person. Are you sure? Suppose he's armed? You'll be okay. Just collar the bastard. Arrest him and sort it out later. Even if you just have to let him go. Put some fear into him. Let him know he's got big trouble and you're it.

He sorted through the sounds, defining, compartmentalizing, analyzing. He put a label to each small noise, giving it a shape and identity so that he would know it was nothing to fear. A dripping noise was rain in a gutter, leaking through the roof. A swishing sound was traffic, blocks distant. A rasping sound was his own breathing. Then, from deep within the building, a small sound of boards creaking.

There he is, Wilcox thought. He's close. He's inside and he's close.

Taking a single deep breath, he crouched low and stepped into the abandoned building.

It seemed at first as if he'd been enveloped by a blanket. The weak alleyway light disappeared. He cursed himself for not bringing a flashlight, not recognizing that his own was all the way back in Florida. He wished he smoked; then he would have matches or better, a lighter, in his pocket. He tried to remember if Ferguson smoked and thought he did. He hunkered down, still pushing his ears to locate his quarry, letting his eyes adjust to the dark. He thought, Can't see much. But just enough.

He moved carefully into the building. There were stairs leading up to his left, a stairway down to his right. An old apartment house, he thought. Why would anyone have ever lived here? He took a step and heard his own weight creak against the decrepit floor. A new worry flooded him. Christ! There could be a hole or something. Suppose those stairs give way? He used his gun hand as best he could for balance, holding it out perpendicular to his body, maintaining contact with the wall, all the time clutching his damaged hand close to his chest.

He went to the right, the stairway down. He had a sudden thought, He's a rat, Ferguson. An earth animal. He'll go down, deeper. That's where he'll feel safe.

He stopped to listen again.

Nothing.

Means nothing, he told himself. He's here.

He continued, slowly, feeling his way as best as possible. He damned the sounds he made. His own breathing seemed to scratch the darkness like fingernails on a blackboard. Each step he took thundered. His steady progress into the core of the building seemed to crash and rattle with noise.

He fought against the urge to say something, wanting to wait until he was very close before he demanded surrender. The stairs seemed solid beneath his feet, but he did not trust them. He put each foot forward slowly, testing it with a portion of his weight, like some reluctant bather facing cold water. He counted each rise; at twenty-two he reached the basement. A clammy damp sensation, cooler than the already chilled air, reached up from beneath to greet him. He stepped down. He could sense the cement under his feet and thought, Good. That will be quieter. He took a single step and squished into a puddle of water, which instantly soaked through his shoes. Damn! he said to himself.

He crouched, listening again. He was unsure whether the breathing he heard was his own or Ferguson's. He's close, the detective said to himself. He took a deep breath and held it, to try and locate the sound.

Close. Very close.

He breathed in again and caught a smell that seemed thick and awful, covering him with evil. It was a familiar smell, but one he couldn't immediately place. The little hairs on his neck rose; his arms grew prickly hot despite the cold air: Something died in here, he shouted to himself. Something's dead close by.

His head pivoted about, trying to see anything in the solid black space, but he was blind.

Electric fear and excitement hurtled through him. He lifted up and took three small steps farther into the basement, still maintaining contact with the wall with his gun hand. It was wet and soft to his touch. He thought about rats and spiders and the man he was pursuing.

He could stand it no longer. "Ferguson, boy, come on out. You're fucking under arrest. You know who this is. Put your fucking hands up and come on out."

The words seemed to echo briefly in the small room, dying swiftly as silence swept over them.

He waited. There was no reply.

"Goddammit, c'mon, Bobby Earl. Cut this shit. It ain't worth the trouble."

He took another step forward.

"I know you're here, Bobby Earl. Goddammit, don't make this so damn hard."

Doubt abruptly creased his heart. Where is the son of a bitch?, he shouted to himself. He stiffened with tension, fear, and anger.

"Bobby Earl, I'm gonna shoot your fucking eyes out unless you come out right now!"

There was a scratching noise to his right. He tried to turn fast in that direction, pulling his gun from the wall toward the sound. His mind could not process what was happening, only that it was pitch black, and he was not alone.

For a microsecond, he was aware of the shape swooshing through the air toward him, aware that someone, grunting with exertion, had risen up out of the darkness beside him. He tried to command himself to duck back, and he raised his broken hand to try and ward off the blow. He fired once in panic, haphazardly, aiming at nothing except fear; the explosion crashed through the darkness. Then a length of metal pipe smashed against his shoulder and ear. Bruce Wilcox saw a sudden immense burst of white light in his eyes, then it disintegrated into a whirlpool blackness far deeper than he'd ever imagined. He staggered back, aware that he could not let himself slip into unconsciousness. He felt damp cement against his cheek, and he realized he'd fallen to the floor.

He raised his hand to deflect a second blow, which arrived with a similar hissing sound as the lead pipe sliced the cold basement air. It thudded into his already broken arm, sending red streaks of pain across the darkness in his eyes.

He did not know where or how he'd lost his revolver, but it was no longer in his hand. But he reached out savagely with his left arm, and his fingers found substance. He tugged hard, heard a ripping noise, then felt a body slam down on top of his.

The two men became entwined in the darkness, struggling, their breath mingling. Wilcox simply fought against the shape of the man he grasped, trying to find his throat, his genitals, his eyes, some critical organ that he could attack. They rolled together, thudding against the walls, smashing through the wet puddles on the floor. Neither man spoke, other than grunts of pain and outrage which burst unbidden from their lips.

They wrestled in the pitch black, pinned together by pain.

Bruce Wilcox felt his fingers encircle his attacker's neck, and he squeezed hard, trying to choke the life from the man. His useless right hand rose and joined his left, completing a ring around his opponent's life. Wilcox grunted with exertion.

He thought, I've got you, you bastard.

Then pain spiked his heart.

He did not know what it was that was killing him, did not know even who was killing him, only that something had ripped through his stomach and was rising toward his heart. He felt panic surge past the instant agony; his hands dropped away from the killer's neck, tumbling down to his midsection, where they closed around the handle of the knife that had ruined his fight. He felt a single insignificant groan escape from his lips, and he crumpled back to the wet floor.

He did not know it, knew nothing anymore, but it would be almost ninety seconds before he rattled out his last breath and died.

TWENTY-FOUR
————PANDORA'S BOX

HER solitude was complete.

Andrea Shaeffer peered down the empty streets, eyes penetrating the gloom and mist, searching for some sign of her companion. She retraced her route for what seemed to be the tenth time, trying to impose reason on the disappearance, only to find that each footstep drove her deeper into despair. She refused to speculate, instead allowing herself to fill up with complaining expletives and anger, as if her inability to find the man were mere inconvenience rather than disaster.

She paused beneath a streetlight and steadied herself by leaning against it.

She would even have welcomed the sight of a Newark patrol car, but none came into view. The streets remained empty. This is crazy, she thought. It's not late. It's barely night. Where is everybody? The rain continued to thicken, hammering down on her. When she finally spotted a single woman, working a street corner in desultory fashion, she was almost pleased, just to see another human being. The woman was slouched against a building, trying to shield herself from the elements, her enthusiasm for another assignation on a cold, wet night, clearly limited. Andrea Shaeffer approached her carefully, producing her badge from about ten feet away.

"Miss. Police. I want a word."

The woman took a single look and started to move away.

"Hey, I just want to ask a question."

The woman kept moving, picking up her pace. Shaeffer followed suit.

"Dammit, stop! Police!"

The woman slowed and turned. She eyed Shaeffer with apprehension. "You talking to me? Watcha want? I ain't doing nothing."

"Just a question. You see two men come running through here, fifteen, twenty, maybe thirty minutes ago? A white guy, a cop. A black guy in a dark raincoat. One chasing the other. You see them come by here?"

"No. I ain't seen nothing like that. That it?"

The woman stepped back, trying to increase the distance between the detective and herself.

"You're not listening," Shaeffer said. "Two men. One white, one black. Running hard."

"No, I ain't seen nothing, like I told you."

Andrea felt anger creaking about inside her, pushing at the edge of its container. "Don't bullshit me, lady. I'll make some real goddamn trouble for you. Now, did you see anything like that? Tell me the damn truth or I'll run you in right now."

"I ain't seen no men chasing. I ain't seen no men at all tonight."

"You had to see them," Andrea insisted. "They had to come by here."

"Nobody's come by here. Now leave me alone." The woman stepped back, shaking her head.

Shaeffer started to follow, only to be surprised by a voice behind her.

"Whatcha bothering people for, lady?"

She turned nervously. The question had come from a large man wearing a long black leather coat and a New York Yankees baseball cap. Rain droplets had formed at the edge of the brim. He was a dozen feet away, striding toward her steadily, his voice, his body, all uttering menace.

"Police," she said. "Stand back."

"I don't care who you are. Come down here, bothering my lady here. Whatcha doing that for?"

Andrea Shaeffer seized hold of her pistol and brought it out, leveling it at the approaching man.

"Just stay there," she said coldly.

The man stopped. "You gonna shoot me, lady? I don't think so."

He spread his hands a bit, his face grinning. "I think you

ain't where you should be, lady policeman. I think you ain't got any backup and you're all alone and I think you got some trouble here, maybe.''

He stepped forward.

She clicked back the action, chambering a round, readying the pistol. ''I'm searching for my partner,'' she said between clenched teeth. ''He was chasing a suspect. Now, did you see a white cop chasing a black man down here, thirty minutes ago? Answer that, and I won't shoot your balls off.''

She dropped the angle of the gun, so that it was pointing toward the man's crotch.

That made him hesitate. ''No,'' he said, after pausing. ''Nobody come down here.''

''You sure?''

''I'm sure.''

''All right,'' she said. She started to maneuver past the man. ''Then I'm leaving. Got that? Nice and easy.''

She slid by him, walking backward up the street. He turned slowly, watching her. ''You got to get out of here, miss policewoman. Before something bad happens to you.''

That was both a threat and a promise. As she moved away, she watched the man drop his raised hands and heard him mutter an expletive, drawing it out so that it trailed after her. She kept her weapon in her hand and turned and walked away, heading back to where she had left the car, now completely at a loss and totally frightened.

Her hand trembled slightly when she started the ignition. With the car running and the doors locked, she felt a momentary security, which allowed her anger to renew itself. ''That damn stupid sonuvabitch. Where the hell is he?''

Her voice seemed cracked and whining, and she regretted using it. She shook her head hard and stared out the window, for a single moment allowing herself the reassuring fantasy that Bruce Wilcox would come walking out of some shadow any second, out of breath, sweating, wet, and uncomfortable.

She let her eyes wander up and down the street, but she could not see him.

''Damn,'' she said out loud again.

She was reluctant to put the car in gear, to move, thinking that sure enough, one minute after she pulled away from the curb he would emerge, and that she would have to apologize later for abandoning him.

"But I haven't, goddammit," she argued with herself. "He left me."

She had little idea what to do. Night had taken a firm grip on the inner city, the rain had redoubled in intensity, steady sheets of gray sweeping down the street. If the cocoon of the car was warm and safe, it only added to her sense of isolation. Putting her hand on the shift lever and switching the car into gear took a painful, exaggerated effort. Driving a single block seemed exhausting.

She traveled slowly, painstakingly searching the area, back to Ferguson's apartment. She paused, staring up at the building but could see no lights. She pulled to the curb and waited for five minutes. Then another five. With no sign of anything, she drove back to where she had last seen Wilcox. Then she drove up and down the adjacent streets. She tried to tell herself, He caught a cab. He flagged down a patrol car. He's waiting back at the motel with Cowart and Tanny Brown. He's down at the precinct house taking a statement from Ferguson, wondering where the hell I am. That's probably it. He probably got him to talk and he's locked in some little room with Ferguson and a stenographer, getting a statement, and he doesn't want to break the momentum by sending someone out to look for me. He figures I'll know what the hell to do, anyway.

She steered the car onto a wide boulevard leading away from the inner city. In a moment, she found the entrance to the turnpike and a few moments later was heading back to the motel. She felt like a child, young and terribly inexperienced. She had failed to follow procedure, to follow routine; failed to adhere to her own judgment and had managed to screw up badly.

She fully expected Bruce Wilcox to scream at her for losing sight of him and failing to back him up. She swore to herself, Christ! That's the first thing they teach you in the academy.

Her sense of independence wavering, she drove into the parking lot of the motel and swiftly collected her things, pushing herself across the rainswept lot toward the room where she thought the three men would be waiting impatiently for her.

Cowart thought death was stalking him. He had fled from Ferguson's apartment in fear and anxiety, trying to restrain his emotions with little success. Tanny Brown had first pressed him for details of the conversation the two men had had, then had let Cowart slip into silence when the reporter refused to answer. There was little doubt in the policeman's mind that something had happened, that Cowart was genuinely frightened, and he supposed he would have taken some cynical pleasure in that discomfort had the source been any different.

They had ended up driving to New Brunswick and Rutgers, with no real reason other than to see where Ferguson was attending classes. After walking through the rain, hunched against the damp cold, dodging students, Cowart had finally described the conversation. He had raced through Ferguson's denials and interpretations, used dialogue and detail, filled in the policeman as fully as possible, until he had reached the point where Ferguson had threatened him and his daughter. That he had kept to himself. He could see the detective's eyes hard on his own face, awaiting something. But he would not say it.

"What else?"

"Nothing."

"Come on, Cowart. You were freaked. What did he say?"

"Nothing. The whole thing freaked me."

Now you're beginning to know a bit of what it's like living on Death Row . . .

Tanny Brown wanted to hear the tape.

"Can't," Cowart replied. "He took it."

The detective asked to see Cowart's notes, but the reporter realized that after the first page or so, his note-taking had evaporated into useless scrawls. The two men each felt ensnared. But they didn't share this, either.

It was early evening when they returned to the motel, stymied by rush-hour traffic and their mutual lack of cooperation. Brown left Cowart in his room and went off on his own to make telephone calls, after promising to return with some take-out food. The policeman knew that more had happened than he'd been told about, but also understood that information would eventually come his way. He did not think that Cowart would be able to maintain his fear and silence for too long. Few people could. After receiving a scare like that, it was only a matter of time before he'd need to share it.

He had little idea what their next step would be, but assumed it would be in reaction to something Ferguson did. He pondered the sense in simply arresting Ferguson again and charging him with Joanie Shriver's murder. He knew it would be legally hopeless, but it would at least get Ferguson back to Florida. The alternative was to continue doing what he had done when he had spoken to his friend in Eatonville: start working all the empty cases in the state until he found something that could get him back into court.

He sighed. It would take weeks, months, maybe longer. *Do you have the patience?* he asked himself. For a moment he tried to picture the little girl in Eatonville who had disappeared. Like my own daughters, he thought. How many others will die while you're doing the mule work of a homicide policeman?

But he had no choice. He started making calls, following up on some of the messages to various police departments in the state of Florida that he'd managed a few days earlier. Work the pattern, he insisted to himself. Research every little town and backwater village that Ferguson has visited in the past year. Find the missing girl in each one, then find the piece of evidence that will lock him to it. There will be some case, somewhere, where the evidence hasn't been tainted or destroyed. It was slow, painstaking work, and he realized that every hour that it took put some child, somewhere unknown, closer to death. He hated every second that slipped past him.

Cowart sat in his small room, trying to make a decision, any decision. He looked down and examined his notes, the shaky handwriting mocking him. He could just make out the list of visits Ferguson had made to Florida since being released from Death Row and returning to Newark for school. Seven trips. Have seven little girls died? he wondered.

Did someone die on each trip?

Or did he wait and return some other time?

Joanie Shriver. Dawn Perry. There had to be others. His head filled with a steady parade of little girls, all walking abroad in the world, girls in shorts and T-shirts or jeans and wearing ponytails, all alone and innocent, all prey. In his mind's eye he could see Ferguson creeping up toward them, arms open, face smiling, full of assurance and bluff and measured death. He shook his head as if to free himself of the image, and it filled instead with Blair Sullivan's words. He remembered the condemned man speaking on the ease with which he took life.

Are you a killer, Cowart?

Am I? he wondered.

He looked down at the list of Florida visits and felt a tremor race down his arms into his fingertips, where it remained like some wayward electric current, humming and buzzing.

There are some people dead who wouldn't be, if not for you. Little girls.

Sullivan had found safety in the randomness of his deaths. He'd killed people he didn't know, who merely by accident had had the misfortune to cross his path. By minimizing the context of murder, he had hamstrung the abilities of the police investigating each case. Cowart suspected that Ferguson was doing the same. After all, he'd learned at the side of an expert. Sullivan had taught Ferguson one crucial thing: to become a student of his loathsome desires.

He remembered his trip to the *Journal*'s library and pictured the headline on the small story: POLICE SAY NO LEADS IN MISSING GIRL CASE. Of course not, he thought. There are no leads. There is no real evidence. At least, none that you know of. Just one innocent man taking his time to pluck children out of this world.

Cowart took a deep breath and let all the accumulated elements of fact, supposition, and imaginary crime cascade through his head, torrents of evil swept together into a single turbulent theme, all rushing toward an image of his own daughter, waiting at the end. It seemed to him that up until that moment he had been living in some moral twilight, all the deaths that circumscribed his relationship with Blair Sullivan and Robert Earl Ferguson out of his control. That was no longer the case.

Cowart let his head sink into his hands and thought, Is he killing someone now? Today? Tonight? When? Next week? He raised it again and looked up into the mirror hanging above the dresser.

"And you, you goddamn fool, you were worried about your reputation?"

He shook his head, watching his own reflection admonish him. Not going to have a reputation now, unless you do something and do it quickly, he told himself.

What can you do?

He was reminded of a story his friend Edna McGee had once written for the *Journal*. She had learned that the police in one Miami suburb were investigating a half dozen rape-assaults that had occurred along a single stretch of highway. When she had confronted the detectives handling the investigation, they had insisted she not write a word. They complained that a story in the paper would alert the serial rapist to the fact that they were on to him, and he would change his routine, alter his distinctive style, move to a different location, and slip through the decoys and stakeouts they had planned. Edna McGee had considered this request, then ignored it, believing it wiser to warn the other, unsuspecting women who were nightly traveling the rapist's route.

The stories had run, front page, Sunday edition, above the fold, along with a police composite of the suspect that stared out in malevolent black and white from the hundreds of thousands of newspapers that hit the streets. The detectives working the case were, predictably, furious, thinking that their quarry would be scared off.

But that wasn't what had happened. The rapist hadn't committed any half dozen rapes. The number had actually been in excess of forty. Almost four dozen women had been assaulted, but most, in pain and humiliation, had refused to go to the police. Instead, they had gone home after being victimized, thanking their lucky stars they were still alive, trying to mend their ripped bodies and torn self-esteem. One by one, they had all called Edna, Cowart remembered. Tears and hesitancy, sobbing voices, barely able to wring through their misery the horror that had befallen them, but anxious to tell this reporter, if perhaps she could save another woman, somewhere, from falling prey to this man. Within a few days of the story running, they had all called. Anonymous and terrified, but they had called. Each one thought they had been alone, a solitary, single victim. By the end of the week, Edna had the full license plate number of the rapist's car, a much improved description of the vehicle and the assailant, and dozens of other small details that had led the police to the man's door one night, a fortnight after the stories ran, just as he was readying himself to head out.

Cowart leaned back remembering. He weighed Ferguson's threat in his hands to see if it had substance.

Do it, he told himself.

Take it all, all the lies, the mistakes, the illegally obtained evidence, everything, and put it into a story and run it in the paper. Do it right away, before he has a chance to move. Smash into him with words and then run and take your daughter and hide her.

It's the only weapon you have.

"Of course," he said out loud, "your buddies in the business are going to tear you limb from limb for writing that story. Then you're going to be drawn and quartered, keelhauled, and your head placed on a stake. After that, things are gonna get real rough, because your wife is going to hate you and her husband is going to hate you and your daughter isn't going to understand, but maybe, if you're lucky, she won't hate you." But it was the only way.

He sat back on the bed and thought, You're going to bring the whole world down on your head and his head. And then, maybe everyone will get what they deserve. Even Ferguson.

Inch-high headlines, full-color pictures. Make certain the wires pick it up, and the newsweeklies. Hit the talk shows. Keep shouting out the truth about Ferguson until it's a din that deafens him and overcomes all his denials. Then no one will ignore anything. Surround him, wherever he goes, with notepads, flashbulbs, and camera lights. Paint him with attention so that wherever he tries to hide, he glows with suspicion. Don't let him slide into the background, where he can continue to do what he does.

Steal his invisibility. That will kill him, Cowart thought.

Are you a killer, Cowart?

I can be.

He reached over to the telephone to call Will Martin, when there was a sharp rap at the motel door. Probably Tanny Brown, he thought.

He got up, his head filling with the words of the story he was preparing to write as he opened the door and saw Andrea Shaeffer standing in the corridor.

"Is he here?"

Her hair was damp and bedraggled. Rain streaked her tan coat, making dark slashes. Her eyes pitched past Cowart immediately, searching the space behind him desperately. Before he could speak, she asked again, "Is Wilcox here? We got separated."

He started to shake his head, but she pushed past him, glanced around the room, turned, and said, "I thought he'd be here. Where's Lieutenant Brown?"

"He'll be back in a moment. Did something happen?"

"No!" she snapped, then, modulating her voice, "We just lost sight of each other. We were trying to tail Ferguson. He was on foot and I was in the car. I thought he'd have called by now."

"No. No calls. You left him?"

"He left me! When's Lieutenant Brown gonna be here?"

"Any minute."

She strode into the small room and stripped off her damp raincoat. He saw her shiver once. "I'm frozen," she said. "I need some coffee. I need to change."

He reached into the small bathroom, grabbed a white bath towel and tossed it to her. "Here. Dry off."

She rubbed the towel over her head, then over her eyes. He saw that she lingered with the towel as it crossed her face, hiding for just a moment or two behind the fluffy, white cotton. She was breathing heavily when she dropped the towel away.

Cowart was about to continue asking her questions, when there was another rapping at the door.

"Maybe that's Wilcox," she said.

It was Tanny Brown. He carried a pair of brown paper bags in his hands, pushing them toward Cowart as he came through the door. "They only had mayonnaise," he said. His eyes took in the sight of Shaeffer, standing rigidly in the middle of the room. "Where's Bruce?" he asked.

"We got separated," she said.

Brown's eyebrows curved upward in surprise. At the same moment, he felt a solid shaft of fear drop through his stomach. He blanked his mind instantly to everything save the problem at hand and moved slowly into the room, as if by exaggerating the deliberate quality of his pace, he could temper the thoughts that instantly threatened to fill his imagination. "Separated? Where? How?"

Shaeffer looked up nervously. "He spotted Ferguson coming out of his apartment and set off on foot after him. I tried to get ahead of them both in the car. They were moving quickly, and I must have misjudged. Anyway, we got separated. I looked for him throughout a five-, six-block area. I went back and tried to find him at Ferguson's apartment. He wasn't either place. I figured he either made his way back here or flagged down a patrol car. Or a cab."

"Let me get this straight. He went after Ferguson . . ."

"They were moving fast."

"Had Ferguson made him?"

"I don't think so."

"But why would he?"

"I don't know," Shaeffer replied, half in despair, half in fury. "He just saw Ferguson and exploded out of the car. It was like he needed to face him down. I don't know what he was going to do after that."

"Did you hear anything? See anything?"

"No. It was like one minute they were there, Wilcox maybe fifty yards or less behind Ferguson, the next, no sign of anything."

"What did you do?"

"I got out, walked the streets, questioned people. Nothing."

"Well," Tanny Brown asked, with irritation, "what do you *think* happened?"

Shaeffer looked over at the big detective and shrugged. "I don't know. I thought he'd be back here. Or at least have called in."

Brown looked over at Cowart briefly. "Any phone messages?"

"No."

"Did you try calling whatever the hell precinct house is in that district?"

"No," Shaeffer said. "I just got here a couple of minutes ago."

"All right," Brown said. "Let's do that, at least. Use the phone in your own room, so, in case he calls, this line won't be tied up."

"I need to change," Shaeffer said. "Let me just . . ."

"Make the calls," Brown said coldly.

She hesitated, then nodded. She extricated her room key from a pocket, nodded once toward the two men, started to say something to Tanny Brown, obviously thought better of it, and left.

The two men watched her exit.

"What do you think?" Cowart asked.

Brown turned and snapped at him, "I don't think anything. Don't you think anything either."

Cowart opened his mouth to reply, then stopped. He merely nodded, recognizing that the detective's demand was impossible. The absence of information was inflammatory. They both sat, eating cold sandwiches, wordlessly waiting for the phone to ring.

It was nearly half an hour before Shaeffer returned.

"I got through to the desk sergeants at precincts twelve, seventeen, and twenty," she said. "No sign of him. At least, he hasn't checked in there. None of them had any unusual calls, either, they said. One had a team working a shooting, but that was gang-related. They all said the weather was keeping things quiet. I called a couple of emergency rooms, as well, just on the off chance, you know. And the central dispatch for fire/rescue. Nothing."

Brown looked at the two of them. "We're wasting time," he said abruptly. "Let's go. We're going to go find him. Now."

Cowart looked down at his notebook. "You know, Ferguson

has a late class tonight. Forensic procedures. Eight to ten thirty. Maybe he tailed him all the way out to New Brunswick.''

Brown nodded and then shook his head. ''That's possible. But we can't wait.''

''What good will it do to race out of here? Suppose he's on his way back?''

''Suppose he isn't?''

''Well, he's your partner. What do you think he's doing?''

Shaeffer breathed out slowly. That's it, she thought to herself. Got to be. He probably chased the bastard right onto some connecting bus and then to a train and hasn't had the chance to call in. And now he's tailing him back and it'll be midnight before he gets in. A small wave of relief washed over her. It was warm, comforting. It distanced her from the steel feelings of helplessness that had trapped her when she'd lost sight of Wilcox. She became aware, suddenly, of the lights in the room, the plastic, uniform decorations and furnishings, the quiet familiarity of the setting. It was, in that instant, as if she'd returned to the brightly lit surface from a mine shaft sunk deep into the earth's core.

The safety of this reverie was smashed by the harsh sound of Brown's voice. ''No. I'm going out now.'' He pointed at Shaeffer. ''I want you to show me where everything happened. Let's go.''

Cowart reached for his coat, and the three headed back out into the night.

As Shaeffer drove, Tanny Brown hunched in his seat in the car, in agony.

He would have called, Brown knew.

There was no doubt in his mind that Wilcox was impetuous, sometimes to the point of danger. He was ruled too much by impulse and arrogant confidence in his abilities. These were the qualities that Tanny Brown secretly enjoyed the most in his partner; he felt sometimes that his own life had been so rigid, so clearly defined. Every moment of his entire being had been dedicated to some carefully constructed responsibility: as a child sitting at Sunday dinner after church, listening to his father say, ''We will rise up!'' and taking those words as a command; carrying the ball for the football team; bringing help to the wounded in war; becoming the highest-ranking black on the Escambia force. He thought, There is no spontaneity in my life. Hasn't been for years. He realized that his choice of partners had been made with that in mind; that Bruce Wilcox, who saw the world in terms of simple rights and wrongs, goods and evils, and who never thought hard about any decision, was the perfect balance for him.

I'm almost jealous, Brown thought.

Memory made him feel worse.

He knew, instinctively, that something had happened, yet was incapable of reacting to this phantom disaster. When he searched the inventory of his partnership, he could find dozens of times that Wilcox had gone off slightly half-cocked, only to return to the fold contrite and chastened, red-faced and ready to listen to the coal-raking he would receive from Tanny Brown. The problem was, all these instances had taken place back within the secure confines of their home county, where they had both grown up and where they felt a safety and security, not to speak of power.

Tanny Brown found himself staring out the window at the rigid black night.

Not here, he thought. We should never have come here.

He turned away angrily toward Cowart.

I should have let the bastard sink alone, he thought.

Cowart, too, stared out at the night. The streets still glistened with rain, reflecting weak lights from streetlamps and the neon signs from bar windows. Mist rose above the pavement, mingling with an occasional shaft of steam that burst from grates, as if some subterranean deities were angry with the course of the night.

As Shaeffer drove, Tanny Brown's eyes swept up and down the area, probing, searching. Cowart watched the two of them.

He did not know when he had come to the realization that this search would be futile. Perhaps it was when they had dropped down off the expressway and started winding their way through the middle of the city, that the heartlessness of the situation had struck him. He was careful not to speak his feelings; he could see, with each passing second, that Brown was moving closer to some kind of edge. He could see as well, in the erratic manner that Shaeffer steered the car, that she, too, was staggered by Wilcox's disappearance. Of the three, he thought, he was the least affected. He did not like Wilcox, did not trust him, but still felt a coldness inside at the thought that he might have been swallowed up by the darkness.

Shaeffer caught a movement out of the corner of her eye and swerved the car to the curb. "What's that?" she said.

They all turned and saw a pair of men, crusted, abandoned,

homeless, fighting over a bottle. As they watched, one man kicked the other savagely, knocking his antagonist to the sidewalk. He kicked again, swinging his leg like a pendulum, smashing it into the side and ribs of the fallen man. Finally, he stopped, reached down, seized a bottle, and clutched it close. He started to leave, seemed to think better of it, walked back and slammed his foot into the head of the beaten man. Then the assailant slithered away, moving from shadow to shadow, until disappearing.

Tanny Brown thought, I've seen poverty, prejudice, hatred, and evil and hopelessness. His eyes traveled the length of the street. Not like this. The inner city looked like the bombed-out remnants of a different nation that had just lost some terrible war. He wanted desperately to be back in Escambia County. Things there may be wrong or evil, he told himself, but at least they're familiar.

"Jesus," Cowart said, interrupting the policeman's thoughts. "That guy may be dead."

But as soon as the words left his lips, they all saw the beaten man stir, rise, and limp off into a different darkness.

Shaeffer, wishing she could be anywhere else, put the car back in gear and for the third time drove them past the spot where she had lost sight of Wilcox.

"Nothing," she said.

"All right," Brown said abruptly, "we're wasting our time. Let's go to Ferguson's apartment."

The entire building was dark when they pulled in front, the sidewalks devoid of life. The car had barely ceased moving when Brown was out the door, moving swiftly up the stairs to the entrance. Cowart pushed himself to keep pace. Shaeffer brought up the rear, but called ahead, "Second floor, first door."

"What are we doing?" Cowart asked.

He got no reply.

The big detective's shoes resounded against the stairs, a machine-gun sound of urgency. He paused momentarily in front of Ferguson's apartment, reaching beneath his coat and producing a large handgun. Standing just to one side, he made a fist and crashed it down hard a half dozen times on the steel reinforced door.

"Police! Open up!"

He pounded again, making the whole wall shake with insistence. "Ferguson! Open up!"

Silence battered them. Cowart was aware that Shaeffer was

close to him, her own weapon out and held forward, her breathing raspy-fast. He pushed his back against the wall, the solidity affording him no protection.

Brown assaulted the door again. The blows echoed down the hallway. "Dammit, police! Open up!"

Then nothing.

He turned toward Shaeffer. "You're sure . . ."

"That's the right one," she said, teeth clenched.

"Where the hell . . ."

All three heard a scraping noise from behind them. Cowart felt his insides constrict with fear. Shaeffer wheeled, bringing her weapon to bear on the sound, crying out, "Freeze! Police!"

Brown pushed forward.

"I ain't done nothing," said a voice.

Cowart saw a stout black woman in a frayed pale blue housecoat and pink slippers at the base of the apartment stairs. She was leaning on an aluminum walker, bobbing her head back and forth. She wore an opaque shower curtain cap, and brightly colored curlers were stuck in her hair. There was a ridiculousness in her appearance that pricked the tension building within him, deflating his fear. He instantly felt as if the three of them, guns drawn, faces set, were the ludicrous ones.

"Whatcha making all the noise for? You come in, like to raise the dead with all that pounding and shouting and racket like I never heard before. This ain't no crack house full of junkies. People live here got jobs. Got work and got to get their sleep at night. You, mister policeman, what you doing, making like some sledgehammer pounding?"

Tanny Brown stared down at the woman. Andrea Shaeffer slid past him. "Mrs. Washington? You remember me from the other day. Detective Shaeffer. From Florida. We're looking for Ferguson again. This is Lieutenant Brown and Mister Cowart. Have you seen him?"

"He left earlier."

"I know, shortly after six, I saw him leave."

"No. He come back. Left again, 'bout ten. I saw him from my window."

"Where was he going?" Tanny Brown demanded.

The woman scowled at him. "How'm I s'posed to know? Had a couple of bags. Just left. There you go. Didn't stop to say no hellos or goodbyes. Just went walking out. Be back, mebbe. I don't know. I didn't ask no questions. Just heard him bustling 'bout up here. Then out the door, no looking back."

She stepped back. "Now, maybe you let some of the folks get some sleep."

"No," Tanny Brown said immediately. "I want in." He gestured with his revolver toward the apartment.

"Can't do that," said the woman.

"I want in," he repeated.

"You got a warrant?" she asked slyly.

"I don't need a goddamn warrant," he said. His eyes burned toward the woman.

She paused, considering. "I don't want no trouble," she said.

"You don't get the key and open that door, and you'll see more trouble than you've ever known," Brown said.

The woman hesitated again, then turned and nodded.

Her husband, who'd been out of sight, hove into view. He carried a jangling key ring. He was wearing an old pajama top over a pair of faded and tattered khaki trousers. His feet were stuck into untied boots. He moved his stringy legs rapidly up the stairs.

"Shouldn't be doing this," he said, glaring at Brown. He pushed past and faced the apartment door. "Shouldn't be doing this," he repeated.

He started feeding keys into the lock. It took three before the door swung open.

"Oughta have a warrant," he said. Tanny Brown immediately pushed past him, ignoring his words. He found a light switch on the wall and quickly walked through the apartment, gun out, checking the bathroom and bedroom, making certain they were alone.

"Empty," he said. The words echoed the sensation that tore within him. Empty and cold and like a tomb. He stared around the silent space, knowing what had happened yet refusing to allow himself to think what was loose in the world. He walked through the center of the small apartment, over to the desk where Ferguson had once sat. The student, he thought. An assortment of papers had fallen in disarray to the floor. He kicked at them and looked up and saw Matthew Cowart staring about at the room.

"Gone," Cowart said. His voice was shocked and quiet.

The reporter took a deep breath. He had expected Ferguson to be there, mocking them all, thinking himself forever just beyond their reach. There's no time now, he realized. He could feel the story he had been planning to write slipping through his fingers. No time. He's out there and he will do whatever he wants. The reporter's mind raced through scene after scene. He had no idea what Ferguson intended, whether his child was at risk or not. Or some other child. Nothing was safe. He looked over at Tanny Brown and realized the detective was thinking precisely the same thing.

The night closed rapidly toward dawn but promised no relief from the darkness that had descended upon each of them.

TWENTY-FIVE
━━━━━━━━━━━*LOST TIME*

THEY lost hours to fatigue and bureaucracy.

Tanny Brown felt trapped between procedure and fear. After discovering Ferguson's apartment empty, he had felt compelled to report Wilcox's disappearance to the local police, while at the same time believing that every instant passing distanced him from his quarry. He and Shaeffer had spent the remainder of the night with a pair of Newark gold shields, neither of whom fully understood why they had each arrived from a different part of the state of Florida to question a man suspected of no current crime. The two gold shields had listened blankly to her account of the stakeout with Wilcox and acted surprised when she described how he'd taken off into the gloom and darkness after Ferguson. Their approach seemed to express a certain acceptance that whatever Wilcox had got, he'd deserved; it made no sense to them that a man, out of his jurisdiction, far from any familiar territory, driven by anger, would pursue a man deep into a country they clearly thought was not a part of the United States, but some alien nation with its own rules, laws, and codes of behavior. Tanny Brown bristled at their attitudes, thinking them racist, if logistically correct. Shaeffer marveled at their callousness. More than once, she promised herself that no matter how terrible things might become for her as a policewoman, she would never succumb to what she heard in their voices.

More time was spent by her taking them to the spot where she'd last seen Wilcox and showing them the route that she'd followed in her search. They had returned to Ferguson's apartment, but there was still no sign of him. The two gold shields clearly didn't believe that he had left the city, however.

Shortly before dawn, they told Brown they would put out a BOLO for Wilcox and would assign a team to canvas the streets asking for him. But they insisted Brown contact his own office, as if they actually believed that Wilcox would show up in Escambia County.

Cowart spent the night waiting in his motel room for the two detectives. He had no idea how great the threat might be to him or his daughter, only knew that as each minute slid past, his position worsened and his only weapon, the news story, grew more remote. No story would have an impact unless he knew where Ferguson was. Ferguson had to be trapped by the story, he had to be immediately surrounded with questions, mired in denials. It was the only way Cowart could buy time to protect himself. Ferguson abroad in the world was a constant, invisible danger. Cowart knew that before a word appeared in the paper, he had to find Ferguson once again.

He stared at his wristwatch, seeing the second hand race through each minute, reminded of the clock on Death Row.

Now you're beginning to know a bit . . .

He realized he could delay no further. Ignoring the sure-to-be terrifying impact of the middle-of-the-night call, he picked up the telephone and dialed his ex-wife's number.

It rang twice before he heard her new husband's voice groan an acknowledgement.

"Tom? It's Matt Cowart. Sorry to disturb you, but I've got a problem and . . ."

"Matt? Jesus. Do you know what time it is? Christ, I've got to be in court in the morning. What the hell is going on?" Then he heard his ex-wife's voice stumbling through the darkness. He couldn't hear what she said but heard her new husband's response. "It's your ex. He's got some sort of emergency, I guess."

There was a pause, then he heard both voices on the phone.

"Okay, Matty? What the hell is it?"

The lawyer's tones had taken over, irritated, imperious. Before he could answer, the man added, "Oh, Christ, there's the baby waking up. Shit."

Matthew Cowart wished he'd rehearsed a speech. "I think Becky's in danger," he said.

The phone line was quiet for a moment, then both people responded.

"What danger? Matty, what are you talking about?" It was his ex-wife.

"The man I wrote about. The one on Death Row. He threatened Becky. He knows where you live."

Another pause before Tom responded, "But why? You wrote he didn't kill anyone . . ."

"I might have been wrong."

"But why Becky?"

"He doesn't want me to write anything different."

"Now look, Matt, what did this man say, exactly? Let's get this straight. What sort of threat?"

"I don't know. Look, it's not that, I don't know, it's all . . ." He realized the impossibility of what he was saying.

"Matt, Christ. You call in the middle of the damn night and . . ."

The lawyer was interrupted by his wife. "Matty, is this serious? Is this for real?"

"Sandy, I wish I could tell you what was real and what isn't. All I know is this man is dangerous and I no longer know where he is and so I had to do something, and I called you."

"But Matt," the lawyer interjected. "We need to know some details. I need to have some appreciation of what the hell this all means."

Matthew Cowart felt a sudden rage slide within him. "No, you goddamn don't. You don't need to know a goddamn thing except Becky may be in danger. That there's one goddamn dangerous man out there and that he knows where you live and he wants to be able to strike at me through Becky. Got that? Got it good? That's all you need to know. Now, Sandy, pack a damn bag and take Becky someplace. Someplace neutral. Like up to Michigan to see your aunt. Do it right away. First flight in the morning. Just go until I get this straightened out. I will get it straightened out, I promise you. But I can't do that unless I know Becky's safe and out of danger and someplace where this man can't get to her. Just go now. Do you understand? It's not worth the risk."

There was another momentary pause, then his ex-wife replied, "All right."

Her husband immediately interjected. "Sandy! Jesus, we don't know . . ."

"We'll know soon enough," she said. "Matty, will you call me? Will you please call Tom and explain this? As soon as you can?"

"I will."

"Jesus," said the new husband. Then he added, "Matty, I hope this isn't some crazy . . ." He stopped, hesitated, then said, "Actually, I hope it is. I hope it is all crazy. And when you call me with your goddamn explanation, it's a good one. I don't understand why I just don't call the police, or maybe hire a private investigator . . ."

"Because the damn police can't do anything about a threat! They can't do anything until something happens! She won't be safe, even if you hire the goddamn National Guard to watch over her. You've just got to get her someplace where this guy can't reach her."

"What about Becky?" his ex-wife said. "This is going to scare the hell out of her."

"I know," Cowart replied. Despair and impotence seemed to curl about him like smoke. "But the alternatives are a whole lot worse."

"This man . . ." the lawyer started.

"The man is a killer," Cowart said between clenched teeth.

The lawyer paused, then sighed. "Okay. They'll take the first flight out. All right? I'm gonna stay here. The guy didn't threaten me, did he?"

"No."

"Well. Good."

Another silence crept onto the line, before Cowart added, "Sandy?"

"Yes, Matt?"

"Don't hang up the telephone and think all of a sudden that this is silly and you don't have to do anything," he said, his voice steady, low, and even. "Leave right away. Keep Becky safe. I can't do anything unless I know she's safe. You promise me?"

"I understand."

"Promise?"

"Yes."

"Thank you," he said. He felt relief and tension battling within him. "I'll call you with details when I have them." Sandy's new husband grunted in assent. Cowart put the telephone down gingerly, as if it were fragile, and leaned back on the motel bed. He felt better and awful at the same time.

When Brown and Shaeffer returned to the motel room, discouragement seemed to ride their shoulders, perched on top of exhaustion.

Cowart asked, "Did you get anywhere?"

Shaeffer answered for them both. "The local cops seem to think we're crazy. And, if not crazy, then incompetent. But mostly, I think, they don't really want to be bothered. Might have been different if they could see something in it for them. But they don't."

Cowart nodded. "Where does that leave us?"

Brown replied softly, "Chasing a man guilty of something, suspected of everything, with evidence of nothing." He laughed softly. "Jesus, listen to me. Should have been a writer like you, Cowart."

Shaeffer rubbed her hands across her face slowly, finally pushing her hair back tightly from her forehead, pulling the skin taut as she did so, as if this would clear her vision.

"How many?" she asked, turning toward the two men. "There's the first one, the one you wrote about . . ."

Both men were silent, guarding their fears.

"How many?" she demanded again. "What is it? You think something bad will happen if you share information? What could be worse than what we've got?"

"Joanie Shriver," Cowart replied. "She's the first. First we know about. Then there's a twelve-year-old girl down in Perrine who disappeared . . ."

"Perrine?" Shaeffer said. "No wonder he . . ."

"No wonder what?" Cowart demanded.

"It was his first question for me. When I went to see him. He wanted to be certain that it was a Monroe County case I was investigating. He was quite concerned over where the border between Dade and Monroe counties is. And once he was certain, he relaxed."

"Damn," Cowart whispered.

"We don't know anything for certain about her," Brown interjected. "It's really speculation . . ."

Cowart rose, shaking his head. He went over to his suit coat and extricated the computer printouts that he had been ferrying about. He handed them to Brown, who swiftly read them.

"What are those?" Shaeffer asked.

"Nothing," Brown replied, frustration creeping into his voice. He crumpled the pages together, then handed them back. "So he was there?"

"He was there."

"But there's still nothing against him."

"No body, you mean. Though, judging from what she said, I suspect that girl's body is somewhere in the Everglades, close to the county line."

"Right." Cowart turned to Shaeffer. "See, that's two. Two so far . . ."

"Three," Brown added quietly. "A little girl in Eatonville. Disappeared a few months back."

Cowart stared hard at the policeman. "You didn't . . ." he started.

Brown shrugged.

Cowart, hands quivering with anger, picked up his notepad. "He was in Eatonville about six months ago. At the Christ Our Savior Presbyterian Church. Gave his speech about Jesus. Is that when . . ."

"No, sometime later."

"Damn," Cowart said again.

"He went back. He must have gone back when he knew no one would be looking."

"Sure he did. But how do you prove it?"

"I'll prove it."

"Great. Why didn't you tell me?" Cowart's voice cracked with rage.

Brown replied with equal fury. "Tell you? So you can do what? So you can put it in the damn paper before I've got a chance to get somewhere on the case? Before I've had a chance to check every small black town in Florida? You want me to tell you so you can tell the world and save your reputation?"

"Get somewhere! How many people are going to die while you put together a case? If you can put together a case!"

"And what the hell will be accomplished by putting it in the newspaper?"

"It'd work! It'd smoke him out!"

"More like it would just warn him so he'd start being even more careful."

"No. Everybody else would be warned . . ."

"Yeah, so he'd change his pattern and there's not a courtroom in the world I'd ever get him into."

Both men had moved to their feet, eyes locked, poised as if about to come to blows. Shaeffer held up her hand, cutting the two men off. "Are you both crazy?" she asked loudly. "Are you out of your minds? Haven't you shared any information? What's the point of secrets?"

Cowart looked at her and shook his head. "The point is, no one ever tells everything. Especially the truth."

"How many people are dead because . . ." she started, then cut herself off. She realized that she herself possessed information that she was reluctant to share. Cowart caught it, though.

"What are you hiding, Detective? What do you know you don't want to talk about?"

She realized she had no choice.

"Sullivan's parents," she said. "Ferguson was right. He didn't do it."

"What?"

She described everything Michael Weiss had told her: the Bible, the guard, the brother.

Cowart looked surprised, and then shook his head. "Rogers," he said. "Who'd have thought it?" It wasn't nonsense, though. Rogers seemed to be into everything at Starke. Nothing would have been easier for him, but yet . . . "One thing I don't understand," said Cowart. "If it was really Rogers, then why did Sullivan spend all that time implicating Ferguson in the murder to me, while at the same time writing Rogers' name in that Bible?"

Brown shrugged. "Best way to guarantee *someone* gets away with murder. Multiple suspects. Tell you one thing. Point some other evidence another direction. Wait until some defense attorney gets ahold of that. But mostly, I think he did it because he was a sick man, Cowart. Sick and full of mischief. It was just his way of dragging down everybody into the same hell that awaited him: you, Ferguson, Rogers . . . and three cops he didn't even know."

Everyone was silent for a moment. "So maybe Rogers did it, and maybe he didn't," Cowart said. "Right now, old Sully must be down there laughing his damned head off." He shook his head again. "So what does it mean?"

"It means," Shaeffer spoke up, "that we can forget about Sullivan. Forget his mind games. Let's worry about Ferguson and his victims. Three, you think?"

"He made seven trips south. Seven we know about."

"Seven?"

Cowart lifted his arms in surrender. "We don't know when it was for research, when he went for action. What we do know is—Christ!—what we *suspect* is—three little girls. One white. Two black. And Bruce Wilcox."

"Four," she said quietly.

"Four," Tanny Brown said heavily. He stood, as if insisting that fatigue was something wrong, and began pacing about the small room like a prisoner in a cell. "Can't you see what he's doing?" he said abruptly.

"What?"

Brown's voice carried an urgency that seemed to quiver in the small room. He looked at the young detective. "What is it we do? A crime occurs and our first assumption is that, while unique, it will still fit directly into a clear-cut, recognizable category. Ultimately, we figure it will be typical of a hundred others, just like it. That's what we're taught, what we expect. So we go out and look for the usual suspects. The same suspects that ninety-nine times turn out to be the right ones. We process everything at the crime scene, hoping that some bit of hair or blood spatter or fiber sample will point right at one of the people on the short list. We do this because the alternative is so terrifying: that someone unconnected to anything except murder has walked onto the scene. Someone you don't know, that nobody knows, that may not be within a hundred or a thousand miles of the crime anymore. And did it for some reason so warped that you can't even contemplate it, much less understand it. Because if that's the case, you've got a chance in a million of making a case and maybe not even that. That's why we went to Ferguson in the first go-round, when little Joanie was killed. Because we had a crime and he was on the short list . . .''

Brown looked at Shaeffer and then toward Cowart. "But now, you see, he's figured that out."

The detective hunched forward, slapping a fist into a palm to accentuate his words. "He's figured out that distance helps keep him safe, that when he arrives in some little town to kill, no one should know him. No one will pay any attention to him. And no one will make him when he grabs his victim. And who does he grab? He learned what happens when he snatched a little white girl. So now he goes to places where the police aren't quite as sophisticated and the press isn't as aware, and grabs a little black girl, because that ain't hardly going to get anyone's attention, not the same way Joanie Shriver did. So he goes and does these things, then he comes back up here and returns to school and there ain't nobody looking for him. Nobody."

Brown paused before adding, "Nobody now, except us three."

"And Wilcox?" Cowart asked.

Brown took a deep breath. "He's dead," he replied flatly.

"We don't know that," Shaeffer said. The idea seemed impossible to her. She knew it to be true yet couldn't stand to hear it said.

"Dead," Brown continued, voice picking up momentum. "Somewhere close to here. And that's the reason Ferguson's running. That's his first rule. Kill safe. Kill anonymously. Use distance. It's such a damn easy formula."

He stared at the young detective. "He was dead as soon as you lost sight of him."

"You shouldn't have left him," Cowart said.

She turned, bristling. "I didn't leave him! He left me. I tried to stop him. Dammit, I don't have to listen to this! I don't even have to be here!"

"Yes, you do," Cowart said. "Don't you get it, Detective? There's a real bad guy out there. Because of accidents, bad judgment, mistakes, bad luck, whatever. And when you add it all up, he let him go . . ." Cowart pointed sharply at Tanny Brown, ". . . and I let him go . . ." He punched an index finger against his own chest, then turned it, like a pistol, toward her. ". . . And now, you've let him go, too. Just like that."

He took a deep breath. "In effect, there's only one of us that actually caught up with him. Wilcox. And now . . ."

"He's dead," Brown said again. He stood in the center of the room, clenching his hands into fists, then releasing them slowly. "And we're the only people really looking for him." He, too, punched a finger at her. "Now you owe, too."

She felt a sudden dizziness, as if the floor of the motel room were pitching beneath her like her stepfather's fishing boat. But she knew what they said was true. They had created the problem. Now it was up to them to find a solution.

Wilcox and some little girls, she told herself.

These two have no idea, she thought. They don't know what it's like to feel yourself pinned down and attacked, to know that you might be about to die and can do nothing to stop it. She envisioned the last minutes the little girls must have experienced in a rush of horror that robbed her of her breath and rekindled her determination.

"Got to be found, first, though," she said. "Who's got a suggestion?"

"Florida," Cowart said slowly. "I think he's gone back to Florida. That's what he knows. That will be where he thinks he's safest. He has two worries, it seems to me. He's worried about me and he's worried about Detective Brown. I don't think he has you connected in all this. Did he see you with Wilcox?"

"I don't think so."

"Well, maybe that's an advantage."

Cowart turned to Brown. His head was filled with something Blair Sullivan had told him: *Got to be a free man to be a good killer, Cowart.* He knows that, the reporter realized. So he said it.

"But you and I, well, that's different. He needs to know he's free of us. Then he can get on with what he's been doing, without worrying and always looking over his back."

"How does he do that?"

The reporter took a deep breath. "The other day. When I saw him. He threatened my daughter. He knows where she lives with her mother, in Tampa."

Tanny Brown started to say something, then stopped.

"That's why . . ."

"Tell me about the threat," the detective demanded.

"He just said he knew where she lived. He didn't say what he would do. Only that he knew who she was and that would prevent me from writing anything about him. Especially unproven allegations connecting him to other crimes."

"And will it?"

"Well, what would you do?" the reporter replied angrily.

"You think that's where he's gone now? To Tampa. To . . ."

"Cut out my heart. Those are his words."

"Is that what you think?"

Cowart shook his head. "No. I think he believes he has me wrapped up. That he doesn't have to do anything to keep me quiet."

Tanny Brown stared hard at him. "I have daughters, too," he said. "Did he threaten them?"

Cowart felt a slight queasiness. "No. He never mentioned them."

"He knows where they live, too, Cowart. Everyone in Pachoula knows where I live."

"He never said anything."

"Did he know I was outside, when he was busy threatening you? Did he know I was there, close by?"

"I don't know."

"Why didn't he mention them, Cowart? Wouldn't the same threat work against me as well?"

Cowart shook his head. "No. He knows you wouldn't back off."

Brown nodded. "At least you got that right. So, Mister Reporter, how does he deal with me? If I'm his remaining problem, how does he get rid of me?"

Cowart thought hard. Only one possibility came to mind, so he spoke it quickly. "He probably wants to do the same to you that he did to Wilcox. Lead you into a trap somewhere, and . . ."

He paused. "Maybe I'm wrong. Maybe he's figured he should just run. Boston, Chicago, L.A., any city with a large urban inner city. He could disappear, and, if he's got the patience, after a while start in doing what he wants, once again."

"You think he's got that patience?" Shaeffer asked.

Cowart shook his head. "No. I don't know that he thinks he even needs to be patient. He's won at every step. He's arrogant and on a roll and he doesn't think we can catch him. And even if we do, what can we do to him? He beat us before. Probably thinks he can do it again."

"Which means there's only one place he can be going," Tanny Brown said abruptly. He looked around at them. "Only one place. Back where it started."

"Pachoula," Cowart said.

"Pachoula," the detective agreed. "Home for him. Home for me. Place he thinks is safe. Even if everybody there hates him, it's still where he's safe and comfortable. Good place to start things, or finish them. And that's where I think he's going."

Cowart nodded and gestured toward the telephone. "So, call. Get his grandmother's house staked out. Get him picked up."

Brown hesitated, then walked to the telephone. He punched numbers on the dial rapidly, then waited while the line was connecting. After a moment, he said, "Dispatch? This is Lieutenant Brown. Connect me with the day-command duty officer."

He paused again before continuing. "Randy? It's Tanny Brown. Look, something has come up. Something important. I don't want to go into details now, but I want you to do something for me. I want you to assign a pair of squad cars to spend the day in front of the high school. And I want another car in front of my house. And tell whoever you send to tell my old man I'll be back as soon as possible and he'll get his explanation then, okay?"

The detective paused, listening. "No. No. Just do what I ask, all right? I appreciate it. No, don't worry about my old man. He can handle himself. It's my daughters I'm worried about . . ." He paused, listening, then added, "No, nothing that specific. And I'll take care of all the paperwork when I get back. Today, if possible. Tomorrow, for sure. What are they looking for? Anyone who doesn't fit. Got that? Anyone." He hung up the telephone.

"You didn't tell them about Ferguson," Cowart said with surprise. "You didn't tell them anything."

"I told them enough. He hasn't got that much of a lead on us. If we hurry, we can catch up with him before he's ready for us."

"But what if . . . ?"

"No ifs, Cowart. The squad cars will keep him away until we get there. And then he's mine." He glared at them. "No one else's. *I* finish this. Understand?"

They were quiet a moment, and then Cowart went to his bureau and found an airline schedule stuck in a corner of his small suitcase.

"There's a noon flight to Atlanta. Nothing down to Mobile until late afternoon. But we can fly to Birmingham and drive from there. Should get to Pachoula by day's end."

Tanny Brown nodded. He glanced over at Shaeffer, who mumbled an approval.

"Day's end," the policeman said quietly.

TWENTY-SIX
═══THE BRIAR PATCH

THEY crossed the Alabama border into Escambia County, moving fast as the Gulf evening crowded them toward night. The southern sky had lost its eggshell-blue vibrancy, replaced by a dirty gray-brown threat of bad weather streaking the horizon. An unsettled hot wind gusted about them, sucking and pulling with occasional bursts at the car windows, stripping away the residual cold and damp they felt from the Northeast. They cut past dust-streaked farms and stands of tall pine trees, whose towering, erect bearing reminded Cowart of spectators rising in a stadium at the moment of tension. Their speed underwrote the doubts they all felt. They all felt an urgency, a need to rush ahead, uncertainty shadowing their path. The countryside hurtled past them; there hardly seemed enough space to breathe on the narrow roadway. Cowart grabbed at the armrest when they bore down on an ancient school bus, painted a gleaming snow white, bouncing and jiggling slowly down the one-lane road. Tanny Brown had to push hard on the brake to keep from slamming into the back end. Cowart looked up and saw, hand-lettered on the back of the bus over the emergency-exit door, in a flowing, joyously enthusiastic bright red script, the words: STILL TIME TO WELCOME YOUR SAVIOR!

And, below that, in slightly smaller but equally florid writing: NEW REDEMPTION BAPTIST CHURCH, PACHOULA, FLA.

And finally, on the bumper, an exhortation in large, bubbling letters: FOLLOW ME TO JESUS!

Cowart rolled down his window and could just make out the thunderous voices of the church choir bursting beyond the heat, above the grinding and groaning of the bus engine. He strained his hearing but couldn't make out the words of the hymn they were singing, though elusive strands of music poked at him.

Tanny Brown jabbed the steering wheel of the rental car, punching the gas pedal simultaneously. With a quick thrust, they maneuvered past the bus. Cowart stared up and saw dozens of black people, swaying and clapping to both the rocky ride and the energy of the singing. The sound of their voices was swept away by speed and distance.

They continued through the growing darkness. The weakening light seemed to blur the straight edges of the houses and barns, made the twisting road they traveled less distinct, almost infirm.

"Jesus works overtime in this county," Brown said. "Gathering in the souls."

Brown had driven silently, unable to shake a memory that had crashed unbidden into his thoughts. A wartime moment, horrible yet ordinary: He'd been in country seven months, and his platoon had been crossing an open area; it was near the end of the day, they were close to camp, they were hot, filthy, tired, and probably thinking more of what was waiting for them, which was food, rest, and another uncomfortable, breathless night, than paying attention, which made them immensely vulnerable. So, in retrospect, it shouldn't have come as a great surprise when the air had been sliced by the single sound of a sniper's weapon, and one of the men, the man walking the point, had dropped with a suddenness that Brown thought was as if some irritated god had reached down and tripped the unsuspecting man capriciously.

The man had called out, high-pitched with fear and pain, *Help me! Please.*

Tanny Brown hadn't moved. He had known the sniper was waiting in concealment for someone to go to the wounded man. He had known what would happen if he went. So he had remained frozen, hugging the earth, thinking, *I want to live, too.* He had stayed that way until the platoon leader had called in an artillery strike on the line of trees where the sniper hid. Then, after the forest had been smashed and splintered with a dozen high-explosive rounds, he'd gone to the wounded man.

He was a white boy from California and had been in the

platoon only a week. Brown had hovered above him, staring at the man's ravaged, hopeless chest, trying to remember his name.

He had been his last wounded man. And he had died.

A week later, Brown had rotated home, his tour of duty cut short as it was for many medics. Back to Florida State University, the criminal justice training program, and finally a spot on the force. He hadn't been the first black to join the Escambia County Sheriff's Office, but it had been tacitly understood that he would be the first to amount to anything. He'd had much going for him: Local boy. Football star. War hero. State-college diploma. Old attitudes eroding like rocks turned to sand by the constant pounding of the surf.

He felt a tinge of guilt. He realized he'd often heard the memory cries of wounded men, but they had always been the cries of men he'd saved. They were easy voices to recall, he thought. They remind you that you were doing something right in the midst of all that wrong. This was the first time he'd thought of that last man's cry.

Did Bruce Wilcox cry for help? he wondered. I left him, too.

He realized that he would have to tell Wilcox's family. Luckily, there was no wife, no steady girlfriend. He remembered a sister, married to a career naval officer stationed in San Diego. Wilcox's mother was dead, he knew, and his father lived alone in a retirement home. There were dozens of old-age homes in Escambia County; it was a veritable growth industry. He recalled his few meetings with Wilcox's father: a rigid, harsh old man. He hates the world already. This will simply add to it. Abrupt fury creased his thoughts: *What do I say? That I lost him? That I put him on a stakeout with an inexperienced detective from Monroe County and he vanished? Presumed dead? Missing in action? It's not like he was swallowed up by some jungle.*

But he realized it was.

He flicked on the car's headlights. They immediately caught the small, red pinprick eyes of an opossum, poised by the side of the road, seemingly intent on challenging the car's wheels. He held the wheel steady, watching the animal, which, at the last moment, twitched and dove back into a ditch and safety.

In that moment he wished that he, too, could dive for cover.

No chance, he told himself.

Not long after, he pulled the car into the parking lot of the Admiral Benbow Inn on the outskirts of Pachoula and deposited

Cowart and Shaeffer on the sidewalk, where their faces were lit by a gleaming white sign bright enough to catch the attention of drivers heading up the interstate. "I'll be back," he said cryptically.

"What're you going to do?"

"Arrange backup. You don't think we should go get him alone, do you?"

Cowart thought about what Brown had said up in Newark. It had not occurred to him that they might seek assistance. "I guess not."

Shaeffer interrupted. "What time?"

"Early. I'll pick you up before dawn. Say, five-fifteen."

"And then?"

"We'll go out to his grandmother's place. I think that's where he'll be. Maybe we'll catch him asleep. Get lucky."

"If not?" she asked. "Suppose he's not there. Then what?"

"Then we start looking harder. But I think that's exactly where he'll be."

She nodded. It seemed simple and impossible at the same time.

"Where're you going now?" Cowart asked again.

"I told you. Arrange backup. Maybe file some reports. I definitely want to check on my family. I'll see you here just before the sun comes up."

Then he put the car in gear and accelerated swiftly away, leaving the reporter and the young detective standing on the sidewalk like a pair of tourists adrift in a strange country. For a moment, he glanced in the rearview mirror, watching the two before they moved into the motel lobby. They seemed small, hesitant. He turned the car, and they dropped away from his sight. He felt an unraveling starting within him, as if something wound tight was beginning to work loose. He could feel bitterness welling inside him as well, taste it on his tongue. The night swept around him, and for the first time in days he felt quiet. He let the reporter and the detective fall from his thoughts, not completely, but just enough to allow his own anger freer rein. He drove hard, rapidly, hurrying but heading nowhere specific. He had absolutely no intention of filing any reports or arranging for any backup officers. He told himself, The accountancy of death can wait.

Cowart and Shaeffer checked into the motel and headed into the restaurant to get something to eat. Neither felt particularly hungry but it was the proper hour, so it seemed the natural thing to do. They ordered from a waitress who seemed uncomfortable in a starched blue-and-white outfit perhaps a size too small for her that pulled tightly across her ample chest, and who seemed only mildly interested in taking their order. As they waited, Cowart looked across at Shaeffer and realized that he knew almost nothing about her. He realized as well that it had been a long time since he'd sat across from a young woman. The detective was actually attractive behind the razor-blade personality she projected. He thought, If this were Hollywood, we would have found some intense common emotion in everything that had happened and fall into each other's arms. He wanted to smile. Instead, he thought, I'll be satisfied if she simply converses with me. He wasn't even sure she would do that.

"Not much like the Keys, huh?" he said.

"No."

"Did you grow up down there?"

"Yes. More or less. Born in Chicago but went down there when I was young."

"What made you become a police officer?"

"This an interview? You going to put this in a story?"

Cowart waved a hand at her dismissively but realized she was probably right. He probably would put every small detail he could into the story, when he got around to describing all that had happened.

"No. Just trying to be civil. You don't have to answer. We could sit here in silence and that would be fine with me."

"My father was a policeman. A Chicago detective until he got shot. After his death we moved to the Keys. Like refugees, I guess. I thought I might like police work, so I signed up after college. In the blood, I suppose you might say. There you have it."

"How long have you . . ."

"Two years in patrol cars. Six months working robbery-burglary. Three months in major crimes. There. That's the history."

"Were the Tarpon Drive killings your first important case?"

She shook her head. "No. And all homicides are important."

She wasn't sure whether he'd absorbed this company lie or spotted it, for he dropped his head to his salad, a chunk of iceberg lettuce with a single quarter of tomato glued to the side with Thousand Island dressing. He speared the tomato with a fork and held it up. "New Jersey Number Six," he said.

"What?"

"Jersey tomatoes. Actually, it's probably too early for them, but this one feels like it could be a year old, at least. You know what they do? Harvest them green, long before they're ripe. That way they're real firm, hard as a damn rock. When you slice them, they stay together. No seeds and oozing tomato flesh falling out, which is how the restaurants want them. Of course, nobody'd eat a green tomato, so they inject them with a red dye to make them look like the real thing. Sell them by the billions to fast-food places."

She stared across the table at him. He's babbling, she thought. Well, who could blame him? His life is in tatters. She looked at her hand. Maybe we have that in common.

They both sat silently for a few moments. The taciturn waitress brought their dinners and tossed the plates down in front of them. When she could stand it no longer, Andrea Shaeffer finally asked, "Just tell me what the hell you think is about to happen."

Her voice was low, almost conspiratorial, but filled with a rough-edged insistence. Cowart pushed slightly back from the table and stared at her for an instant before replying. "I think we're going to find Robert Earl Ferguson at his grandmother's house."

"And?"

"And I think Lieutenant Brown will arrest him for the murder of Joanie Shriver, again, even if it is useless. Or obstruction of justice. Or lying under oath. Or maybe as a material witness in Wilcox's disappearance. Something. And then you and he are going to take everything we know and everything we don't know and start to question him. And I'm going to write a story and then wait for the explosion."

Cowart paused, looking at her. "At least he will be in hand and not out there doing whatever it is he's doing. So he'll be stopped."

"And it's going to be that easy, is it?"

Cowart shook his head. "No," he replied. "Everything's dangerous. Everything's a risk."

"I know that," she said calmly. "I just wanted to be certain you knew it as well."

Silence crept over them again, imposing itself on their thoughts for a few awkward moments before Cowart said, "This has happened quickly, hasn't it?"

"What do you mean?"

"It seems like a long time since Blair Sullivan went to the chair. But it's only been days."

"Would you rather it be longer?" she asked.

"No. I want it to end."

Andrea Shaeffer started to say one thing, changed her mind, and asked another. "And what happens when it ends?"

Cowart didn't hesitate. "I get the chance to go back to doing what I was doing, before all this started. Just a chance."

He did not say what he thought was a more accurate answer: *I get the chance to be safe.*

He laughed sarcastically. "Of course, I'm probably going to get chewed up pretty bad in the process. So will Tanny Brown. Maybe you, too. But . . ." He shrugged, as if to say it no longer mattered, which was a lie, of course.

Shaeffer digested this. She thought people who wanted things to return to the way they were before were almost always hopelessly naive. And never happy with the results. Then she asked, "Do you trust Lieutenant Brown?"

Cowart hesitated. "I think he's dangerous, if that's what you mean. I think he's close to the edge. I also think he's going to do what he says."

Cowart thought of adding to his statement, *I think he's filled with unmitigated fury and a hatred of his own.* "But he didn't get to where he is now by breaking rules. He got there by playing the game. Toeing the line. Behaving precisely the way people expected him to behave. He violated that once, when he let Wilcox beat that confession out of Ferguson. He won't fall into that trap again."

Shaeffer agreed. "I think he's close to an edge, too. But he seems steady." She wasn't sure whether she believed this or not. She knew the same thing could be said of Cowart, and of herself as well.

"Makes no difference," Cowart said abruptly.

"Why?"

"Because we're all going to see this through to the end."

The waitress came and removed their plates, inquiring whether they cared for dessert. Both refused and refused coffee as well. The waitress, remaining sullen, seemed to have anticipated their responses; she had already totaled their check and dropped it unceremoniously on the table between them. Shaeffer insisted on paying her half. They walked to their rooms without further conversation. They did not say good night to each other.

* * *

Andrea Shaeffer closed the door behind her and went straight to the bureau dresser in the small motel room. Images from the past few days, snatches of conversations, raced through her head, ratcheting about in a confusing, unsettling manner. But she steeled herself and started to act slowly, steadily. She placed her pocketbook down deliberately on the top and removed her nine-millimeter semiautomatic pistol. She released the clip of bullets from the handle, checking to make certain that it was fully loaded. She pulled back the action on the pistol as well, sighting down the barrel, making sure that all the moving parts were in working order. She reloaded the weapon and placed it down in front of her. Then she rummaged through the pocketbook, searching for her backup clip of bullets. She found this, checked it, then put it next to the gun.

For a few moments she stared down at the weapon.

She thought of hours spent practicing with the nine-millimeter. The Monroe County Sheriff's Department had set up a combat practice range on a deserted spot just below Marathon. It was a simple procedure; while she walked through a series of deserted buildings, little more than the cinder-block shells of homes bleached white by the constancy of sun, a range control officer electronically operated a series of targets. She'd been good at the procedure, scoring consistently in the nineties. But what she'd enjoyed the most was the electricity of the practice sessions, the demand to see a target, recognize it as friend or foe, and fire or hold fire accordingly. There was a sense of being totally involved, unconcerned by anything save the sun, the weight of the handgun in her hand, and the targets that appeared. In a killing zone. Comfortable, alone with the single task of proceeding through the course.

She looked down at the weapon again.

I've never fired except at a target, she thought.

She remembered the mist and cold of the streets in Newark.

It wasn't like what she had expected. She had not even known that she was in combat in those moments. The people on the sidewalk, the threatening looks and motions, the hopeless pursuit through the streets. It was the first time it had been for real, for her. She gritted her teeth. She promised herself not to fail that test again.

She set the weapon down on the bed and reached for the telephone. She found Michael Weiss on her third try.

"Andy, hey!" he said quickly. "Jesus, am I glad to hear from you. What's been happening? What about your bad guy?"

This question almost made her laugh.

"I was right," she said. "This guy's real wrong. I have to help this Escambia cop with an arrest, then I'll be there."

She could sense Weiss absorbing this cryptic statement. Before he could say anything, she added, "I'm back in Florida. I can get to Starke tomorrow, okay? I'll fill you in then."

"Okay," he said slowly. "But don't waste any more time. Guess what I came up with?"

"Murder weapon?"

"No such luck. But guess who made a dozen phone calls to his brother in the Keys in the month before the murder? And guess whose brand-new pickup truck got a speeding ticket on I-95 right outside Miami twenty-four hours before Mister Reporter finds those bodies?"

"The good sergeant?"

"You got it. I'm going over to the truck dealer tomorrow. Gonna find out just exactly how he purchased that new four-by-four. Red. With fat tires and a light bar. A redneck Ferrari." Weiss laughed. "Come on, Andy, I've done all the legwork. Now I need your famous cold-hearted questioning technique to close the door on this guy. He's the one. I can feel it."

"I'll get there," she said. "Tomorrow."

She hung up the telephone. Her eyes landed on the pistol resting beside her. She cleared her mind and picked up her handgun, and, cradling it in her arms, lay back on the bed, kicking off her shoes but remaining fully clothed. She told herself to get some sleep and closed her eyes, still holding the gun tight, slightly irritated with Matthew Cowart for perceiving the truth: That she was in this to the end.

Cowart locked the door behind him and sat on the side of the bed. For a few seconds he looked down at the telephone, half as if he expected it to ring. Finally he reached down and seized the receiver. He pushed button number eight to receive a long-distance line, then started to punch in his ex-wife and daughter's number in Tampa. He touched nine of the eleven digits, then stopped.

He could think of nothing to say. He had nothing to add to what he'd told them in the early morning hours. He did not want to learn that they had not taken his advice and were still exposed and vulnerable, sitting in their fancy subdivision home. It was safer to imagine his daughter resting safely up in Michigan.

He disconnected the line, pushed number eight again, and

dialed the number for the main switchboard at *The Miami Journal*. Talk to Will or Edna, he thought. The city editor or the managing editor or some copyboy. Just talk to someone at the paper.

"*Miami Journal*," said a woman's voice.

He didn't reply.

"*Miami Journal*," she said again, irritated. "Hello?"

The operator hung up abruptly, leaving him holding a silent telephone in his hands.

He thought of Vernon Hawkins and wondered for a moment how to dial heaven. Or maybe hell, he thought, trying to make a joke with himself. What would Hawkins say? He'd tell me to make it right, and then get on with life. The old detective had no time for fools.

Cowart looked at the telephone again. Shaking his head, as if refusing some order that had not been given, he held it back to his ear and dialed the number for the motel's front desk.

"This is Mr. Cowart in room one-oh-one. I'd like to have a wake-up call at five A.M."

"Yes, sir. Rising early?"

"That's right."

"Room one-oh-one at five A.M. Yes, sir."

He hung up the phone and sat back on the bed. He felt a sickening amusement at the thought that in the entire world, the only person he could think of to talk with was the night clerk at a sterile motel. He put his head down and waited for the appointed hour to arrive.

The night draped itself around him like an ill-fitting suit. A cashmere heat and humidity filled the black air. Occasional streaks of lightning burst through the distant sky, as a big thunderstorm worked out in the Gulf, miles away, beyond the Pensacola shoreline. Tanny Brown thought it seemed as if some distant battles were taking place. Pachoula, however, remained silent, as if unaware of the immense forces that warred so close by. He turned his attention back to the quiet street he was riding down. He could see the school on his right, low-slung and unprepossessing in the darkness, waiting for the infusion of children that would bring it to life. He listened to the crunching sound the car tires made as he drove slowly past, and paused for an instant beneath the willow tree, looking back over his shoulder toward the school.

This is where it all started. It was right here she got into the car. Why did she do that? Why couldn't she have seen the danger and run hard, back to safety? Or called out for help?

It was the age, he realized, the same for his own daughter. Old enough to be vulnerable to all the terrors of the world, but still young enough not to know about them. He thought of all the times he'd sat across from his daughter and Joanie Shriver and considered telling them the truth about what lurked out in the world, only to bite back the horrors that echoed in his head, preferring to give them another day, another hour, another minute or two of innocence and the freedom it brought.

You lose something when you know, he thought.

He remembered the first time someone had spat the word "nigger" at him, and the lesson that had gone with it. He'd been five years old and he'd gone home in tears. He'd been comforted by his mother, who'd made him feel better, but she hadn't been able to tell him that it would never happen again. He had known something was lost for him, from that moment on. You learn about evil slowly but surely, he thought. Prejudice. Hatred. Compulsion. Murder. Each lesson tears away a bit of the hopefulness of youth.

He put the car in gear and drove the few blocks to the Shriver house. There were lights on in the kitchen and living room and for an instant, he considered walking up to the front door and going inside. He would be welcomed, he knew. They would offer him coffee, perhaps something to eat. Once we were friends, but no longer. Now I am nothing to them except a reminder of terrible things. They would show him to a seat in the living room, then they would politely wait for him to tell them why he had come by, and he would be forced to concoct something vaguely official-sounding. He would be unable to tell them anything real about what had taken place because he was unsure himself what the reality was.

And finally, he realized, they would get to talking about their daughter, and they would say that they missed seeing his own child come around, and this would be too hard to hear. It would all be too hard to hear.

But he waited outside, simply watching the house until the lights blinked off and whatever fitful sleep the Shrivers found late at night arrived.

He felt an odd invisibility, a liquid connectivity moving slowly through the black air. For a moment he considered the awful thought that Robert Earl Ferguson felt the same, moving through the darkness, letting it hide him from sight. Is that the way it is?

he asked himself. He couldn't answer his own question. He drove down streets he'd known since his childhood, streets that whispered of age and continuity, before bumping into the newer, suburban subdivisions that shouted of change and the future. He felt the texture of the town, almost like a farmer rubbing soil between his fingers. He found himself on his own street; he spotted a marked police cruiser parked halfway down the block and crunched to a stop behind it.

The uniformed officer jumped instantly from behind the wheel, hand on his weapon, the other wielding a flashlight which he shone in Tanny's direction.

He got out of his car. "It's me, Lieutenant Brown," he said quietly.

The young officer approached him. "Jesus, Lieutenant, you scared the hell out of me."

"Sorry. Just checking."

"You heading inside, sir? Want me to take off?"

"No. Stay. I have some other business to attend to."

"No problem."

"See anything unusual?"

"No, sir. Well, yes, sir, one thing, but probably nothing. Late-model dark Ford. Out-of-state plates. Rolled by twice about an hour ago. Slow-like, as if he was watching me. Shoulda got the plate numbers, but missed them. Thought I'd go after him, but he didn't come by again. That's all. No big deal."

"You see the driver?"

"No, sir. First time, I didn't really notice. Just paid attention, like, the second time he rolled on by. That's what got my attention. Probably nothing to it. Somebody down visiting relatives got lost, more'n likely."

Tanny Brown looked at the young policeman and nodded. He felt no fear, just a cold understanding that maybe death had slowly cruised past.

"Yes. More than likely. But you stay alert, all right?"

"Yes, sir. I'm gonna be relieved in a half hour or so. I'll make sure whoever shows gets the word about the Ford."

Tanny Brown lifted his hand to his forehead, as if in salute, and returned to his own car. He looked once toward his house. The lights were off. School night, he thought. A wave of domestic responsibilities burst over him. He realized much of his life had been obscured by the pursuit of Robert Earl Ferguson. He did not feel guilty about this; it was in the nature of police work to reach an agreement with obsession, shutting off the normalcy of life. He felt a surge of comfort. Good for you, Dad. Make them get their homework done early, shut off the damn television before they can complain too hard, and get them into bed.

For an instant, he wanted to go inside and peer down at the sleeping faces of his daughters, perhaps look in on the old man, who was probably snoring in a lounge chair, a whiskey dream in his head. The old man often took a glass or two after the girls were asleep; it helped fog the pain of arthritis. On occasion, Tanny Brown joined his father in a glass; his own pains sometimes needing similar blocking. He found a smile on his own face, a satisfaction of domesticity. For an instant he imagined his dead wife beside him in the car, and he had half a mind to talk to her.

What would I say? he asked himself.

That I haven't done all that badly, he thought. But now I need to put things right. Put the broken things back together as best as I can.

Make it all safe again.

He nodded and steered the car away from the curb. He drove away, passing through familiar routes, past remembered places. He could sense Ferguson's presence like some bad smell lingering over the town. He felt better moving about, as if by staying alert he served as some sort of shield. He did not even consider sleep; instead he traveled up and down through the roads of his memory, waiting for enough of the night to end so he would be able to see clearly enough to do whatever he had to do.

TWENTY-SEVEN
TWO EMPTY
CHAMBERS

AT first the dawn light seemed reluctant to force its way into the shadows. It gave doubt to shapes, turning the world into a quiet, suspect place. It had still been dark when Tanny Brown picked up Cowart and Shaeffer from the motel. They had driven through empty streets, past lamps and neon signs, weak illumination that only heightened the inevitable sense of loneliness that accompanies the early morning. They passed few other cars, only an occasional pickup truck. Cowart saw no one on the sidewalks. He spotted a few people sitting along a counter inside a doughnut shop; that was the only sign that they were not alone.

Brown drove swiftly, cruising through stop signs and two red lights, and within a few minutes they had passed through the town and were heading into the surrounding countryside. Pachoula seemed to stumble and fall behind them; the earth appeared to reach out and entangle them, dragging them inside the variegated maze of drooping willow trees, huge, twisted bramble bushes, and stands of pine. Light and dark, muted greens, browns and grays, all seemed to blend together fluidly, making it seem as if they were heading into a shifting sea of forest.

The police lieutenant turned off the main road, and the car shuddered and bumped as it hit the hard-packed dirt that cut beneath the canopy of trees toward Ferguson's grandmother's shack. Cowart felt a fearful surge of familiarity, as if there was something awful and yet reassuring in the idea that he'd been down the road before.

He tried to anticipate what would happen but found only an unsettling excitement. He had a quick memory of the letter he'd received so many months ago: . . . *a crime that I DID NOT COMMIT.* Gripping the armrest, he stared straight ahead.

From the backseat, Andrea Shaeffer's voice penetrated the thick air. "I thought you said you'd arrange for backup. I don't see anybody. What's going on?"

Brown answered abruptly, with a clipped tone designed to preclude further questions, "We can get help if we need it."

"What about some uniforms? Don't we need some uniforms?"

"We'll be okay."

"Where's the backup?"

He gritted his teeth and answered bitterly, "It's waiting."

"Where?"

"Close."

"Can you show me?"

"Sure," he replied coolly. He reached inside his jacket and removed his service revolver from his shoulder holster. "There. Satisfied?"

This word crushed the conversation and filled Shaeffer with an empty fury. It did not surprise her that they were proceeding alone. In fact, she realized she preferred it. She allowed herself to envision Ferguson's face when she arrived at his grandmother's shack. *He thought he'd scared me off. Thought he had me running,* she told herself. *Well, here I am. And I'm not some little twelve-year-old that can't fight back.* She reached down and put her hand on her own pistol. She looked over at Cowart but saw the reporter's eyes staring ahead, oblivious to what had just been said.

In that moment, she thought that she would never, ever again get as close to the core of being a policeman as that moment and the next moments to come. The clarity of their pursuit seemed to have gone past such worldly considerations as rights and evidence, and entered into some completely different realm. She wondered if closeness to death always made people crazy, and then answered her own question: Of course.

"Okay," she said after a moment's pause, adrenaline starting to pump and not completely trusting her own voice. "What's the plan?"

The car lurched as it hit a bump.

"Jesus," she said, as she grabbed her seat. "This guy really lives out in the sticks."

"It's all swamp, right over there," Cowart answered. "Poor farmland off the other direction." He remembered that it had been Wilcox who'd pointed this out to him before. "What is the plan?" he asked Tanny Brown.

The police lieutenant slowly steered the car to the side of the road and stopped. He rolled down his window and damp, humid air filled the interior. He gestured down, through the gray-black blend of light and dark. "Ferguson's grandmother's shack is about a quarter mile that way," he said. "We're going to walk the rest of the way. That way we won't wake anyone unnecessarily. Then it's simple. Detective Shaeffer, you go around the back. Keep your weapon ready. Watch the back door. Just make certain he doesn't hightail it out that way. If he does, just stop him. Got that? Stop him. . . ."

"Are you saying . . ."

"I'm saying stop him. I'm damn certain the procedures are the same in Monroe County as they are up here in Escambia. The bastard's a suspect in a homicide. Several homicides, including the disappearance of a police officer. That's all the probable cause we'll need. He's also a convicted felon. At least he was once . . ." Brown glanced over at Cowart, who said nothing. "So, you know what the guidelines are on use of deadly force. You figure out what to do."

Shaeffer paled slightly, her skin turning wan like the air around them. But she nodded. "Got it," she replied, imposing a rigid firmness on her voice. "You think he's armed? And maybe waiting for us?"

Brown shrugged. "I think he's probably armed. But I don't think he'll necessarily be alert and waiting. We moved fast to get here, probably just as damn fast as he did. I don't think he'll be quite ready. Not yet. But remember one thing: This is his ground."

She grunted in assent.

Tanny Brown took a deep breath. At first his voice had been cold, even. But he then dropped the menacing tones, substituting a weariness that seemed to indicate he thought things were heading to an end.

"You understand?" he asked. "I just don't want him running out the back door and heading into that swamp. He gets in there, I don't know how the hell we'll find him. He grew up in there, and . . ."

"I'll stop him," she said. She did not add the words *this time*, though they were in each of the three's heads.

"Good," Brown continued. "Cowart and I will go to the front. I don't have a warrant, so I'm kinda making things up as I go along. What I figure is, I'm going to knock, announce, and then I'm going to go in. Can't think of any other way to do it. The hell with some procedures."

"What about me?" Cowart asked.

"You're not a police officer. So I have no control over what you do. You want to tag along? Ask your questions? Do whatever you want, that's fine. I just don't want some lawyer coming in later and saying I violated Ferguson's rights—again—because *I* took you with me. So you're on your own. Stand back. Come in. Do whatever. Got it?"

"Got it."

"That fair? You understand?"

"It's fine." Cowart nodded his head. Separate but the same. One man knocks on the door with a gun, the other with a question. Both seeking the same answers.

"Are you going to arrest him?" Shaeffer asked. "On what charge?"

"Well, first I'm going to suggest he come in for questioning. See if he'll come along voluntarily. But he's coming in. If I have to, I'll re-arrest him for Joanie Shriver's death. What'd I say yesterday? Obstruction of justice and lying under oath. But he's coming with us, one way or the other. Once he's in custody, then we're going to sort out what's happened."

"You're going to *ask* him . . . ?"

"I'm going to be polite," Brown said. A small, sad smile worked the corners of his mouth for a moment. "With my gun drawn, cocked, finger on the trigger, and pointed right at the bastard's head."

She nodded.

"He doesn't walk away," Brown said quietly. "He killed Bruce. He killed Joanie. I don't know how many others. But there are others. It stops here."

The statement filled the air with quiet.

Cowart looked away from the two detectives. He thought, There comes a point where the proofs required in a court of law don't seem to make much difference. A few strands of light had surreptitiously passed through the branches of the trees, just enough to give shape to the road before them.

"What about you?" the police lieutenant asked Cowart suddenly. His voice cracked the silence. "Have you got all this straight?"

"Straight enough."

Brown put his hand on the door handle, jerked it hard, and thrust the car door open. "Sure," he said, unable to keep a small mockery from his voice. "Then let's go."

And he was out of the car, striding up the narrow black dirt roadway, his broad back hunched forward slightly, as if he was heading into the strong winds of a storm. For an instant, Cowart watched the policeman's sturdy progress, and he thought to himself, *How could I have ever presumed to understand what is truly inside him? Or Robert Earl Ferguson?* In that moment, both men seemed equally mysterious. Then he shed the thought as rapidly as possible and quickly fell in pace with him. Shaeffer took up position on the other side, so the three marched in unison, their footsteps muffled by the morning fog that coiled like gray smoke snakes around their feet.

Cowart spotted the shack first, wedged back in a clearing where the road ended. The damp swamp mists had gathered around the front, giving it a spectral, eerie appearance. There was no light inside; his first glance saw no movement at all, though he expected they had arrived just on the near side of waking. The old woman probably rises to beat the cock's crow, he thought, and then complains to the old bird that it's not doing its job. Cowart slowed his pace along with the others, lurking on the edge of the shadows, inspecting the house.

"He's here," Brown said quietly.

Cowart turned to him. "How can you tell?"

The police lieutenant pointed toward the far side of the shack. Cowart followed the trail with his eyes and saw the rear end of the car protruding past the edge of the porch. He looked carefully and could just make out the dirty blue-and-yellow colors of the license plate: New Jersey.

"That's his kinda car, too," Brown said softly, gesturing. "A couple of years old. American make. I'll bet it doesn't have anything special to it at all. Nondescript. A blend-right-in kinda car. Just like he used to have."

He turned toward Shaeffer. He put his hand on her shoulder, gripping it firmly. Cowart thought it was the first familiar gesture he'd seen the big detective make toward the young woman.

"There's only the two doors," he said, continuing to keep his voice low, almost inaudible, but not the same way that a whisper disappears, hissing. His voice had a firmness to it. "One in front, that's where I'll be. And the one in back, where you're going to be. Now, best as I can recollect, there's windows on the left side, there . . ." He pointed, sweeping his hand in the direction of the side of the house that butted up close to the surrounding woods. "That's where the bedrooms are. Any windows on the right I'll be able to cover, either from inside, in the front living room, or the porch. So watch that back door, but keep in mind he might try to go out the window. Just be ready. Stay on your toes. Okay?"

"Okay," she replied. She thought the word wavered coming out of her mouth.

"I want you to stay there, in position, until I call you. Okay? Call you by name. Keep quiet. Keep down. You're the safety valve."

"Okay," she said again.

"Ever done anything like this before?" Tanny Brown asked abruptly. Then he smiled. "I suppose I should have asked that question some time earlier . . ."

She shook her head. "Lots of arrests. Drunk drivers and two-bit burglars. And a rapist or two. Nobody like Ferguson."

"There aren't many like Ferguson to practice on," Cowart said under his breath.

"Don't worry," Brown said, continuing to smile. "He's a coward. Plenty brave with little girls and scared teenagers, but he ain't got it in him to handle folks like you and me. . . ." Brown spoke this softly, reassuringly. Cowart wanted to blurt out Bruce Wilcox's name, but stopped himself. ". . . Keep that in mind. There ain't gonna be anything to this. . . ."

He let his voice roll with its Southern inflection, giving a contradictory ease to what he was saying. ". . . Now, let's move before it gets lighter out and folks start waking up."

Shaeffer nodded, took a step forward, and stopped. "Dog?" she whispered hurriedly, nervously.

"None." Brown paused. "As soon as you get to the corner, there, then I'm heading toward the front. You keep working your way around the back. You'll know when I get to the door, 'cause I ain't gonna be quiet when I get there."

Shaeffer closed her eyes for one second, took a deep breath, and forced bravado into her heart. She told herself, No mistakes this time. She looked at the small house and thought it a small place, with no room for errors. "Let's do it," she said. She stepped across the open space quickly, slightly crouched over, a half-jog that cut through the mist and wet air.

Cowart saw that she had her pistol in her hands and was holding it down but ready, as she maneuvered toward the corner of the house.

"You paying attention, Cowart?" Brown asked. His voice seemed to fill some hollow spot within the reporter. "You getting all this?"

"I'm getting it," he replied, clenching his teeth.

"Where's your notebook?"

Cowart held up his hand. He clutched a thin reporter's notebook and waved it about. Brown grinned. "Glad to see you're armed and dangerous," he said.

Cowart stared at him.

"It's a joke, Cowart. Relax."

Cowart nodded. He watched the policeman as his eyes fixed on Shaeffer, who'd paused at the corner of the shack. Brown was smiling, but only barely. He straightened up and shook his shoulders once, like some large animal shaking sleep from its body. Cowart realized then that Brown was like some sort of warrior whose fears and apprehensions about the upcoming battle dropped away when the enemy hove into view. The policeman was not precisely happy, but he was at ease with whatever danger or uncertainty rested inside the shack, beyond the fragile morning light and curling gray mists. The reporter looked down at his own hands, as if they were a window to his own feelings. They looked pale but steady. He thought, Made it this far. See it through. "Actually," he replied, "that's not a bad joke at all. Given the circumstances."

Both men smiled, but not at any real humor.

"All right," said Tanny Brown. "Wake-up call."

He turned toward the shack and remembered the first time he'd driven up to the house searching for Ferguson. He hadn't understood the storm of prejudice and hatred he was unleashing with his arrival. All the feelings that Pachoula wanted to forget had come out when Robert Earl Ferguson had been taken downtown for questioning in the murder of little Joanie Shriver. He was determined not to live through that again.

Brown set off swiftly, pacing directly across the hard-packed dirt of the shack's front yard, not looking back once to see if Cowart was following him. The reporter took a single deep breath, wondered for a moment why the air seemed suddenly dry to his taste, realized it wasn't the air that was dry at all, and moved quickly to keep stride with the police lieutenant.

Brown paused at the foot of the steps to the front door. He turned to Cowart and hissed, "If things go to hell fast, make sure you stay out of my line of fire."

Cowart nodded quickly. He could feel excitement surging through his body, chasing the fears that reverberated within him.

"Here we go," said the policeman.

He took the stairs two at a time, in a pair of great leaps. Cowart scrambled behind him. Their feet made a clattering noise against the whitewashed old wooden boards, which added creaks and complaints to the sudden sounds that pierced the morning silence. Brown gathered himself to the side of the door, just off-angle, motioning Cowart to the other side. He swung open a screen door and grasped the doorknob. He twisted it carefully, but it refused to move.

"Locked?" whispered Cowart.

"No. Just jammed, I think," Brown replied.

He twisted the knob again. He shook his head at Cowart. Then he took his empty hand, balled it into a fist and slammed it three times hard against the blistered wooden frame, shaking the entire house with urgency.

"Ferguson! Police! Open up!"

Before the echoes of his booming voice died away, he'd grabbed the screen door frame and wrenched it aside. Then he stepped back and raised his foot, kicking savagely at the door. The frame cracked with a sound like a shot, and Cowart jumped involuntarily. Brown gathered himself a second time, aiming carefully, and kicked again.

The door buckled and opened partway.

"Police!" he cried again.

Then the huge detective threw his entire bulk, shoulder first, against the door like some crazed fullback smashing toward the goal with the game on the line.

The door gave way with a torn, splintering sound.

Tanny Brown pushed it viciously away and jumped into the front parlor, half-crouched, weapon raised and swinging from side to side. He yelled again, "Police! Ferguson, come out!"

Cowart hesitated for a moment, then, swallowing hard, stepped in behind him, his thoughts jumbled, the noise from the assault on the door ringing in his ears. It was like stepping off a cliff's edge, he thought. It seemed as if wind was rushing by his ears, screaming velocity.

"Dammit!" Brown called out, as if starting another command, then he stopped short, his words sliced, as if by a razor.

Robert Earl Ferguson stepped out of a side room.

For an instant, his dark skin seemed to blend with the gray morning shadows that crept about the interior of the shack. Then he moved slowly forward, toward the hunched-over police lieutenant. The killer wore a loose-fitting navy T-shirt and faded jeans, hastily tugged on. His feet were bare and made small slapping sounds against the polished hardwood floor. His arms were raised languidly, almost insouciantly, as if in a surrender of irony. He stepped forward into the living room and faced Tanny Brown, who straightened slowly, cautiously, keeping a static distance between himself and the killer. A false grin worked the sides of Ferguson's face, and his eyes swept around quickly. He fixed for a moment on the burst door, then on Matthew Cowart. Then he stared directly at Brown.

"You gonna pay for that door?" he asked. "It wasn't locked. Just a bit stiff. No need to break it down. Country folk don't need to lock their doors. You know that. Now, what you want with me, Detective?"

There was no urgency or panic in the killer's voice. Simply an infuriating calm, as if he'd been waiting for their arrival.

"You know what I want with you," Brown said. His teeth remained clenched tightly and he trained his weapon on Ferguson's chest.

But the two men kept distant, looking across the small room toward each other, warily.

"I know what you want. You want someone to blame. Always the same thing," Ferguson said coldly.

He eyed the pistol pointing at him carefully. Then he looked directly at the policeman, narrowing his gaze so that it seemed as harsh as his voice.

"I ain't armed," he said. He held both hands out, palms forward. "And I ain't done nothing. You don't need that gun." When Tanny Brown didn't move the pistol barrel, Cowart saw a single moment of nervousness and doubt flit through Ferguson's eyes. But it disappeared as rapidly as it arrived. Ferguson sounded like a man standing just beyond range. Cowart glanced over at Brown and realized, He can't touch him.

The killer turned toward Cowart, ignoring the policeman. He

turned the corners of his mouth up into a smile that sent a chill right through the reporter.

"That what you're here for, too, Mr. Cowart? I been expecting the detective to show, but I figured you'd come to your senses. Or you got some other reason?"

"No. Just still looking for answers," Cowart replied hoarsely.

"I thought our little talk the other day filled you up with answers. I can't hardly imagine you got any questions left, Mr. Cowart. I thought things were pretty clear."

These last words were spoken in a soft, slow, harsh voice.

"Nothing is ever clear," Cowart replied.

"Well," Ferguson said carefully, gesturing at Brown, "there's one answer you got already. You see what this man does. Kicks in a door. Threatens folks with a gun. Probably getting ready to beat my ass again."

Ferguson spun toward Brown. "What you want to kick out of me this time?"

Tanny Brown didn't reply.

Cowart shook his head. "Not this time," he said.

Ferguson scowled angrily. The muscles on his arms tightened into knots and the veins in his neck stood out.

"I can't tell you nothing," Ferguson replied, anger soaring through his words. He took a single step toward the reporter, but then stopped himself. Cowart saw him fight for some internal control, win, and relax. He leaned up against a sidewall. "I don't know nothing. And say, where's your partner, Lieutenant? You gonna beat me again? I miss Detective Wilcox. You gonna need his help, huh?"

"You tell me where he is. . . ." Tanny Brown said. His voice was steel-edged, words like swords cut the space between the two men. "You were the last person to see him."

"Now really?" Ferguson seemed like a man who'd lain awake preparing his replies, as if he'd known what was going to happen that morning. His voice picked up pace. "Might I lower my hands here, before we talk?"

"No. What happened to Wilcox?"

Ferguson smiled again. He lowered his hands anyway. "Shit if I know. He gone someplace? I hope he's gone to hell." The smile widened into a mocking grin.

"Newark," said Tanny Brown.

"Same thing as hell," Ferguson replied.

Brown's eyes narrowed slightly. After a moment's pause, Ferguson started speaking. "I never saw him there. Damn, just got back to Pachoula last night, myself. It's a long drive from there down here. You say Wilcox was in Newark?''

"He saw you. He chased you."

"Well, don't know nothing about that. There was one crazy white man chased me the other night, but I didn't see who it was. He never got that close. Anyway, I lost him on some back street. It was raining hard. Don't know what happened to him. You know, the part of that city where I live, lots of folks get chased all the time. It ain't that unusual to have to put your feet down fast. And I sure wouldn't want to be some white guy walking alone down there after dark, if you catch my drift. Unhealthy place. People there'd cut your heart out if they thought they could sell it for another hit of crack cocaine.''

He looked over at Cowart. "Isn't that right, Mr. Cowart? Cut your heart right out.''

Matthew Cowart felt a dizzying burst of anger sweep through his head. He stared across at the killer and felt things slipping within him. Rage and frustration overpowered reason, and he stepped forward, past Tanny Brown, punching a pencil at Ferguson. "You lied. You lied to me before and you're lying now. You killed him, didn't you? And you killed Joanie. You killed them all. How many? How many, goddammit?''

Ferguson straightened. "You're talking crazy, Mr. Cowart,'' he replied, coldly calm. "This man . . .'' He gestured toward Tanny Brown, ". . . has filled you with some sort of crazy. I ain't killed nobody. I told you that the other day. I'm telling you that now.''

He looked over to the policeman. "Got nothing to threaten me on, Tanny Brown. Got nothing that's gonna last a minute in court, that some lawyer won't just rip and shred. Got nothing.''

"No,'' Cowart said. "I've got it all.''

Ferguson's eyes sent a surge of anger toward Cowart. The reporter could feel a sudden heat on his face.

"You think you got some special line on the truth, Mr. Cowart? You don't.''

Ferguson's hands balled tightly into fists.

Brown stepped forward, shouldering Cowart aside.

"Screw this. Screw you, Bobby Earl. I want you to come downtown with me. Let's go . . .''

"You arresting me?''

"Yeah. For the murder of Joanie Shriver. Again. For obstruction of justice. For hiding those clothes in the outhouse. For lying under oath at your trial. And as a material witness in Bruce Wilcox's disappearance. That'll give us plenty to sort through.''

Tanny Brown's face seemed set in iron. His free hand went into a jacket pocket and emerged with handcuffs. He held his weapon toward Ferguson's face. "You know the drill. Face the wall and spread.''

"You arresting me?" the killer said, taking a step back, his voice rising a pitch, moving closer to anger again. "I already walked on that crime. The rest is bullshit. You can't do that!''

Tanny Brown raised the service revolver. "Watch me,'' he said slowly. His eyes burned toward Ferguson. "You should never have let me find you, Bobby Earl, because it's all over for you. Right now. It's all ended.''

"You haven't got nothing on me.'' Ferguson laughed coldly in response. "If you had, you'd be here with some fucking army. Not just one damn reporter with a bunch of damn fool questions that don't amount to nothing.''

He spat the words out like obscenities.

"I'm going to walk free, Tanny Brown, and you know it.'' He laughed. "Walk free.''

But Ferguson's words contradicted a nervous shift in his body. His shoulders crunched forward, his feet moved wide, as if poised to receive a blow in a prize fight.

Tanny Brown saw the movement. "Just give me the chance,'' he said. "You know I'd love it.''

"I'm not going with you,'' Ferguson said. "You got a warrant?''

"You're coming with me,'' Brown insisted. His voice was even, furious. "I'm going to see you back on Death Row. Hear? Where you belong. It's all over.''

"It's never over,'' the killer responded, stepping back.

"Ain't nobody going nowhere,'' cracked a brisk voice.

All three men pivoted toward the sound.

Cowart saw the twin barrels of the shotgun before the small, wiry body of Ferguson's grandmother came into view. The gun was leveled at Tanny Brown.

"Nobody going nowhere,'' the old woman repeated. "Least of all Death Row.''

Brown instantly moved his pistol, bringing it to bear on the woman's chest, crouching as he did so. She was wearing a ghostly white nightgown that fluttered around her figure when she moved. Her hair was pinned up, her feet bare. It was as if she'd stepped from the comfort of her bed into a nightmare. She cradled the shotgun under her arm, pointing it at the policeman, just as she had when she'd fired at Cowart.

"Miz Ferguson," Tanny Brown said quietly, while holding himself in firing position. "You got to put that weapon down."

"You ain't taking this boy," she said fiercely.

"Miz Ferguson, you got to show some sense . . ."

"I don't know nothing about showing sense. I know you ain't taking my boy."

"Miz Ferguson, don't make things harder than they are."

"Hard makes no difference to me. Life's been hard. Maybe dying's gone be easy."

"Miz Ferguson, don't talk that way. Let me do my job. It will all come right, you'll see."

"Don't you sweet-talk me, Tanny Brown. You ain't brought nothing but trouble into this home."

"No," Brown said softly, "it hasn't been me that brung the trouble. It's been your boy here." He had slid immediately into rhythmic southernisms, as if trying to speak the same language to a confused foreigner.

"You and that damn reporter. I shoulda killed you before." She turned toward Cowart and spat her words. "You ain't brought nothing but hate and death with you."

Cowart didn't reply. He thought there was some truth in what she said.

"No ma'am," Brown continued, soothing. "It ain't been me. And it ain't been him. You know who it's been that brought the trouble."

Ferguson stepped to the side, as if measuring the shotgun blast's spread. His voice had a cruel, clear edge to it. "Go ahead, Granmaw. Kill him. Kill 'em both."

The old woman's face filled with a sudden surprise.

"Kill 'em. Go ahead. Do it now," Ferguson continued, moving back toward the old woman.

Tanny Brown took a step forward, still ready to fire.

"Miz Ferguson," he said, "I've known you a long time. You knew my folks and cousins and we went to church together once. Don't make me . . ."

She interrupted angrily. "Y'all left me behind some years ago, Tanny Brown!"

"Kill 'em," whispered the grandson, stepping next to her.

Brown's eyes switched toward Ferguson. "You freeze! You son of a bitch! And shut up."

"Kill them," Ferguson said again.

"It's not loaded," Cowart said abruptly.

He remained rooted in his spot, wanting desperately to dive for cover but incapable of ordering his body to respond to his fear. He thought, It's a guess. Try it.

"She used up her last shot on me the other day. It's not loaded," he said.

The old woman turned toward him. "You're a fool if'n you think that." She stared coldly at the reporter. "You gone bet your life I didn't have no fresh shells?"

Tanny Brown kept his pistol aimed at the woman. "I don't want to shoot," he said.

"Maybe I do," she replied. "One thing's I know. You ain't taking my grandson again. Gone have to kill me first."

"Miz Ferguson, you know what he's done . . ."

"I don't care what he's done. He's all I got left and I ain't gone let you take him away again."

"Did you ever see what he did to that little girl?" Cowart asked suddenly.

"I don't care," she replied. "No business of mine."

"That wasn't the only one," Cowart said slowly. "There have been others. In Perrine and Eatonville. Little black children, Miz Ferguson. He's killed them, too."

"Don't know nothin' about no children," she answered, her voice quavering slightly.

"He killed my partner, too," Tanny Brown said quietly, as if speaking the words loudly would cause whatever restraint he still had to shatter and break.

"I don't care. I don't care about none of that."

Ferguson stepped behind his grandmother. "Hold them there, Granmaw," he said. He ducked away, down the house's central corridor.

"I'm not going to let him get away," Brown said.

"Then either I'm gonna shoot you, or you're gonna shoot me," the old woman replied.

Cowart could see Brown's finger tighten on the trigger. He could also see the gunpoint waver slightly.

Silence like weak morning light filled the room. Neither the old woman nor Tanny Brown moved.

He won't do it, Cowart thought. If he was going to shoot her, he already would have. In the first moment, when he first saw the shotgun. He won't do it now.

Cowart looked over at the policeman and saw tidal surges pulling at the man's emotions.

Tanny Brown felt his insides squeeze together. Acid ill taste ruined his tongue. He stared across at the old woman and saw her wispy aged fragility and steel will simultaneously.

Kill her! he told himself.

Then: How can you?

It was all in balance in his head, weights furiously sliding back and forth.

Robert Earl Ferguson stepped back into the room. He was dressed now, a gray sweatshirt thrown over his head, hightop sneakers on his feet. He carried a small duffel bag in his hand.

He tried one last time. "Kill 'em, Granmaw," he said. But his voice lacked the conviction that he thought she might do what he demanded.

"You go," she said icily. "You go and don't ever come back."

"Granmaw," he said. He spoke her name not with affection or sadness but a frustrated inconvenience.

"Not to Pachoula. Not to my house. Never again. Y'all too filled with some evil I can't understand. You go do it someplace different. I tried," she said bitterly. "I may not have been much good, but I tried my best. It'd been better if you'd a died young, not to bring all this wrong down here. So you take it and never bring it back. That's all I can give you now. You go now. Whatever happens now, after you leave my door, that's your business, no more mine. Understand?"

"Granmaw . . ."

"Ain't no more blood, no more, after this," she said with finality.

Ferguson laughed. He dropped all inflection from his voice and replied, "Okay. That's the way you want it, it's fine with me."

The killer turned toward Cowart and Brown. He smiled and said, "I thought we'd get this finished today. Guess not. Some other time, I suppose."

"He's not going," Brown said.

"Yes, he is," said the old woman. "You want him, then you gone have to find him someplace other than this my home. My home, Tanny Brown. It ain't much, but it's mine. And you gone have to take all this evil business someplace else, same as I told him. Same goes for you. I won't have no more of it here. This is a house where Jesus dwells, and I want it to stay that way."

And Tanny Brown nodded. He straightened up, a movement that spoke of acquiescence. He did not drop the pistol but kept it trained on the grandmother, while the killer slid past him, a few feet apart, moving steadily but warily toward the front door. Brown's eyes followed him, the barrel of his pistol wavering slightly as if trying to follow the killer's path.

"Just go," said the old woman. Some deep sadness creased her voice and her old eyes seemed rimmed with red grief tears. Cowart thought suddenly, He's killed her, too.

Ferguson stepped into the doorway, moving gingerly around the splintered door. He looked back once.

Brown, furious defeat riding his words, said, "It makes no difference. I'll find you again."

And Ferguson replied, "And if you do, it still won't mean a damn thing, because I'll walk away clean again. I always will, Tanny Brown. Always."

Whether or not this was a false boast was irrelevant. The word's possibility reverberated in the space between the two men.

Cowart thought the world had been turned upside down. The killer was walking free, the policeman rooted in spot. He told himself, Do something! but was unable to move. All he could see was a constancy of fear and threat like some awful nightmare vision before him. It's up to me, he thought. He started to blurt this out, stopped, and then saw the killer's face widen abruptly with surprise. Then he heard the shout.

"Everyone freeze!"

High-pitched and nerve-edged, the words shattered the glassine air.

Andrea Shaeffer, crouched over into a shooter's stance, arms extended, nine-millimeter pistol cocked and ready, was ten feet behind Ferguson's grandmother, down the hallway leading toward the rear kitchen door, which she'd slipped past without being seen or heard.

"Drop that shotgun!" she yelled, trying to cover anxiety with noise.

But the old woman did not. Instead, turning as if in some sepia-toned, herky-jerky antique film, she spun toward the sound of the detective's voice, swinging the shotgun barrel in front of her as if readying to fire.

"Stop!" screamed Shaeffer. She could see the twin barrels like predator's eyes pointing directly at her chest. She knew only that death often walked with hesitation and this time she could not let it slip through her grasp.

Cowart's mouth opened in a single, incomprehensible shout.

Brown called, "No!" but the word was swallowed by the deep
burst of the detective's pistol as Shaeffer fired.

The huge handgun bucked violently in her hands and she
fought to control it, suddenly alive with evil intent. Three shots
burst through the morning still, exploding in the small, dark
house, deafening, echoing through the rooms.

The first shot picked up the elderly woman and threw her
back as if she weighed no more than a breath of wind. The
second shot crashed into the wall, sending wood and plaster
fragments into the air. The third bullet shattered a window and
disappeared into the morning. Ferguson's grandmother's arms
flung out, and the shotgun clattered from her grasp. She tumbled
backward, smashing into the wall, and then slumping down,
arms outstretched, as if in supplication.

"Jesus, no!" Tanny Brown cried again.

The policeman stepped toward the woman, then hesitated.

He tore his eyes away from the fast-growing splotch of crimson blood that stained Ferguson's grandmother's nightgown. He
fixed first on Cowart, who was standing, frozen, in spot, mouth
slightly agape. The reporter blinked, as if awakening from a bad
dream, said, "Jesus Christ," himself, then suddenly turned toward the front door.

Ferguson had disappeared.

Cowart pointed and shouted, not words but simply surprise
and anger. Tanny Brown jumped toward the empty space.

Andrea Shaeffer entered the room, her hands shaking, her
eyes locked onto the dying woman.

Brown tore through the front door, out onto the porch. Sudden quiet shocked him; the world seemed a wavy, infirm sight
of mists and shafts of dawn light. There was no sound. No sign
of life. His eyes swept the yard, then he turned toward the side,
instantly seeing Ferguson moving rapidly for the car parked by
the side of the shack.

"Stop!" he shouted.

Ferguson paused, but not in response to the command. Instead he squared himself to the policeman and raised his right
hand. There was a short-barreled revolver in it. He fired twice,
wildly, the shots slashing the air around the detective. Brown
was pierced with a sudden familiar memory: The deep booming
sounds were like those of his partner's gun. Fury, like a storm,
burst within him. He shouted out "Stop!" again, and ran in-
sanely forward on the porch, rapidly returning fire.

His shots missed the killer but struck the car. A window

exploded glass. The demon sound of metal scoring metal and
ricocheting off into the morning filled the air.

Ferguson fired again, then turned away from the car and ran
toward the line of trees on the far side of the clearing. Tanny
Brown anchored himself on the edge of the porch and screamed
to himself to take careful aim. He took a deep breath, his eyesight glowing red with fury and anger and saw the killer's back
dancing onto the small pistol sight. He thought, Now!

And pulled the trigger.

The gun jumped in his hand and he saw his shot fly astray,
splintering into the trunk of a tree.

Ferguson spun once, facing Tanny Brown, fired another wild
shot and disappeared into the darkness of the forest, running
hard.

As Brown went through the front door, Shaeffer walked
quickly over to Ferguson's grandmother. She knelt down, her
pistol still in her hand, reached out with her free hand and gently
touched the woman's chest, like a child touching something to
see if it is real. She drew back fingertips smeared with blood.
The old woman tried to breathe in one final time; it made a
sucking, rattling sound. Then she wheezed out in death. Shaeffer stared at the figure in front of her and then turned toward
Cowart.

"I didn't have a choice. . . ." she said.

The words seemed to force action back into the reporter's
limbs. He stepped across the room and seized the shotgun from
the floor. He swiftly cracked it open and stared at the two empty
chambers, one for each barrel.

"Empty," he said.

"No," Shaeffer replied.

He held the weapon up to her.

"No," she said again, quietly. "Damn."

She looked toward the reporter, as if seeking reassurance.
She seemed suddenly terribly young.

"I didn't have a choice," she repeated.

From outside, they heard the crash of shots.

Matthew Cowart ducked involuntarily. It seemed to him that
the silence between the gun reports was somehow deeper, thicker,
and he felt like a swimmer treading water in the ocean. He took
a shallow breath and jumped toward the front door. Andrea Shaeffer moved in swiftly behind him.

He saw Tanny Brown's back at the edge of the porch and

realized the policeman was feverishly emptying spent casings from his revolver. The shells clattered against the wooden boards at his feet, and he started to jam fresh bullets into the gun's cylinders.

"Where is he?" Cowart asked.

Brown spun toward him. "The old woman?"

"She's dead," Shaeffer replied. "I didn't know . . ."

He interrupted, "You couldn't help it."

"The shotgun was empty," Cowart said.

Tanny Brown stared at him but had no response, save a single, sad shrug of his shoulders. Then, in the same instant, he straightened up and pointed toward the forest.

"I'm going after him."

Shaeffer nodded, feeling that she was being tugged along by some current she could not see, only feel. Matthew Cowart nodded as well.

Tanny Brown pushed past the two of them, leaped off the porch, and moved rapidly across the clearing toward the edge of shadows some thirty yards distant. He picked up his pace as he crossed the open space so that by the time he reached the small cut in the darkness that had swallowed up Ferguson, he was loping in an easy run, not pushed into a sprint, but making up for each moment that the killer had stolen.

He was aware of the harsh breathing of the two others a few feet behind him, but he paid them no mind. Instead, he leaned forward into the cool green half-light of the forest, eyes dead ahead on a small trail, searching for Robert Earl Ferguson, knowing that it would not be long before the chased creature turned in ambush to fight. He told himself, This is my country, too. I grew up here, too. It's as familiar to me as it is to him.

He reassured himself with lies and pushed on.

Heat fractured the morning, rising about them with sticky insistence, sucking at their strength as they penetrated the tangled branches and vines in pursuit. They clung to the small path, Shaeffer and Cowart following the swath cut by Tanny Brown's single-minded search. He forced himself ahead steadily, trying to anticipate what Ferguson would do.

There were occasional signs that Ferguson, too, was following the path. Tanny Brown spotted a footprint in the wet earth. Cowart noticed a small swatch of gray material stuck on the end of a thorn, pulled from the killer's sweatshirt.

Sweat and fear clogged their eyes.

Brown remembered the war, thought, I've been here before, felt a joint apprehension and excitement within him and continued. Shaeffer plodded on, seeing only the old woman's body tossed by death into a corner of the shack. The vision blended with a distant memory of the sight of Bruce Wilcox disappearing into the gloom of the inner-city night. She thought death seemed to be mocking her; whenever she tried to do what was right it tripped her, sent her sprawling into wrong. She had so much to correct and had no idea how to do it.

Cowart thought each step was pushing him further into a nightmare. He'd lost his notebook and pen. A ridge of brambles had stolen them from his hand and sliced open a line of blood that pulsated and stung infuriatingly. For an instant he wondered what he was doing there. Then he told himself, Writing the last paragraph.

He jogged to keep up.

The ground beneath their feet began to ooze and grasp at their shoes. A thick, damp heat surrounded them. The forest seemed to grow more snarled and knotted together as it gave way to swamp, almost as if the two elements of nature were struggling over possession of the earth beneath their feet. They were streaked with grime and dirt, their clothes ripped. Cowart thought that somewhere there was morning, with clarity and warmth, but not there, not beneath the mat of overhanging tree branches that shut out the sky. He was no longer aware how long they had been pursuing Ferguson. Five minutes. An hour. It seemed to him that they'd all been pursuing Ferguson all their lives.

Tanny Brown stopped abruptly, kneeling down and signaling the two others to crouch. They huddled up close to him and followed his gaze.

"Do you know where we are?" whispered Shaeffer

The police lieutenant nodded. "He knows," Brown replied softly, gesturing toward Cowart.

The reporter breathed in hard. "Not far from where the little girl's body was found," he said.

Brown nodded.

"Can you see anything?" Shaeffer asked.

"Not yet."

They stopped and listened. Cowart heard a bird rise through the branches of a nearby bush. There was a small noise from adjacent underbrush. A snake, he thought, taking cover. He shivered despite the warmth. A breeze moved across the tree-tops, seeming very distant.

"He's out there," Brown said.

He gestured toward a break in the thick mire of swamp and forest. Shafts of sunlight measured a small open space in the path before them. The clearing couldn't have been more than ten yards across, surrounded by the maze of greenery. They could see where the path they were following sidled between two trees on the far side, like a slice of darkness.

"We have to cross that open space," he said quietly. "Then it's not too far down to the water. The water runs back, miles. Goes all the way to the next county. He's got a couple of options: Keep going, but that's tough country to cross, and when he gets out on the other side, assuming he can without getting lost or bit by a snake or chewed on by an alligator or whatever, he'll be cold and wet and knows maybe I'll be waiting. What he'll really want to do is double back, get past us and back out the easy way. Get back to his car, get over the Alabama border and start to make things happen for himself that way."

"How's he going to do that?" Cowart asked.

"Lead us on. String us out. Then make a move." Brown paused before adding, "Precisely what he has been doing."

"And the clearing?" Cowart asked. His voice was slow with fatigue.

"A good place to do it."

Shaeffer stared directly ahead. She spoke with a sullen, awful finality. "He means to kill us."

None of them wanted to debate that observation.

"What are we going to do?"

Brown shrugged. "Not let him."

Cowart stared at the opening in the forest and said quietly, "That's what it always comes down to, right? Eventually you always have to step out into the open."

Tanny Brown, half rising, nodded. He glanced back toward the small space and thought it a good spot to turn and fight. It would be the spot he would select. There's no way around it. No way to avoid it. We have to cross through it. He thought it suddenly unfair that the edge of the swamp seemed to be conspiring with Ferguson to help him escape. Every tree branch, every obstacle, hindered them, hid him. He scanned the tree line, searching for any sign of color or shape that didn't fit. Make a move, he said to himself. Just a single little twitch that I can see. He cursed to himself when he saw none.

He saw no option, except going ahead. "Watch carefully," he whispered.

He stepped out into the clearing, pistol in his hand, muscles tense, listening. Shaeffer was only two feet behind him. She kept both hands on her pistol, thinking, *This is where it will end.* She was overcome by the desire to do a single thing right before she died. Cowart picked himself up and followed behind her another couple of feet. He wondered whether the others were as frightened as he was, then wondered why that made any difference.

The silence shrouded them.

Tanny Brown wanted to scream out. The sensation that he was walking into a gunsight was like pressure on his chest. He thought he could not breathe.

Cowart could feel only the heat and an awful vulnerability. He thought himself blinded.

But it was he that saw the small movement before anyone else. A quiver of leaves and shake of bushes, and a gray-black gun barrel that pointed toward them. So he shouted, "Watch out!" as he dove down, oddly surprised in the wave of dread that swept over him that he was able to process anything at all.

Tanny Brown, too, had thrown himself forward at the first syllable of panic that came from Cowart. He rolled, trying to bring his weapon up into a firing position, not really having any idea where to shoot.

Shaeffer, however, did not duck. Screaming harshly, she had turned toward the movement, firing her weapon once without taking aim at anything. Her shot spun crazily into the sky. But the deep roar of the nine-millimeter was bracketed by three resonant blasts from Ferguson's pistol.

Brown gasped as a bullet exploded in the dirt by his head. Cowart tried to force himself into the wet earth.

Shaeffer screamed again, this time in sudden pain.

She spun down to the ground like a bird with a broken wing, clutching at her mangled elbow. She writhed about, her voice pitched high with hurt. Cowart reached out and dragged her toward him as Brown rose, taking aim but seeing nothing. His finger tightened but he did not fire. As he paused, he heard an explosion of trees and bushes as Ferguson ran.

Cowart saw the detective's pistol hanging limply from her hand, blood pulsing down her wrist and staining the polished steel of the weapon. He seized the gun and raised himself up, tracking the sounds of the escaping man.

He was not aware that he'd stepped over some line.

He fired.

Wildly, letting the racket from the gun obliterate any thoughts of what he was doing, he tugged on the trigger, sending the remaining eight shots in the clip whining into the thick trees and underbrush.

He kept pulling after the magazine was emptied, standing in the center of the clearing listening to the echoes from the weapon.

He let the pistol drop to his side, as if exhausted.

All three seemed frozen for a moment, before Shaeffer moaned in pain at the reporter's feet and he bent down toward her. The sound picked up Tanny Brown, switching him back into action. He scrambled across the wet earth and hastily inspected the wound to the detective's arm. He could see smashed white bone protruding through the skin. Deep arterial blood pulsed through the ripped flesh. He glanced up at the forest as if searching for some guidance, then back down. Working as rapidly as he could, he tore a strip of cloth from his own jacket, then twisted it into a makeshift tourniquet. He broke a green branch from an adjacent tree limb and used that to tighten the bandage. His hands worked skillfully; old lessons never forgotten. As he twisted the wrapping tight, he could see the blood flow diminish. He looked up at Cowart, who had risen and gone to the edge of the clearing, eyes staring into the dark forest.

The reporter still gripped the pistol in his hand.

Brown saw Cowart lean forward into the black hole in the clearing, then step back, looking down at his hand.

"I think I got him," the reporter said. He turned toward Brown and held out his palm.

It was smeared with blood.

Brown rose, nodding. "Stay with her," he said.

Cowart shook his head. "No, I'm coming with you."

Shaeffer groaned.

"Stay with her," Brown repeated.

Cowart opened his mouth, but the policeman cut him off. "Now it's mine," he said.

The reporter breathed out hard and harsh. Emotions smashed into him. He thought of everything he'd set in motion and thought, It can't stop for me here.

Shaeffer moaned again.

And he realized he had no choice.

He nodded.

Matthew Cowart waited with the wounded detective, but felt more alone than ever before.

The police lieutenant turned and plunged ahead, angling through the net of brambles and branches that reached out and grabbed at his clothes, scratching like wildcats at his skin and eyes. He moved hard and fast, thinking, If he's wounded, he will run straight. He thought he had to make up lost seconds spent fixing the detective's arm.

He saw the blood splotch that Cowart had found as he passed out of the clearing, then another some fifteen yards into the swamp. A third marked the trail a dozen feet after that. They were small, a few crimson droplets of blood standing out against the green shadows.

He raced on, sensing the black water that lay ahead.

The forest crashed around him. He thrust apart all the tendrils and ferns that blocked his path. His pursuit now was all speed and power, a tidal force of fury. He smashed aside anything that hindered his way.

He did not see Ferguson until he was almost on top of him.

The killer had turned, leaning up against a gnarled mangrove tree at the edge of the expanse of swamp water that ran inkily behind him. A line of dark blood had raced down from his thigh to his ankle, standing out against the faded blue of his jeans. He was pointing his weapon directly at Tanny Brown as the policeman burst ahead, running directly into the line of fire.

He had one thought only: I'm dead.

Glacial fear covered everything within him, freezing memories of family, of friends, into a winter death tableau. He thought the world suddenly stopped. He wanted to dive for cover, throw himself backward, hide somehow, but he was moving in slow motion and all he could do was fling a hand up across his face, as if that might deflect the bullet he was certain was about to fly his way.

It was as if his hearing was suddenly sharpened; his sight piercing. He could see the hammer on the pistol creeping backward, then slamming forward.

He opened his mouth in a silent scream.

But all he heard were two empty clicks as the hammer of the killer's pistol twice hit empty chambers. The noise seemed to echo in the small space.

A wild look of surprise crossed Ferguson's face. He looked down at the pistol as if it were a priest caught in a lie.

Tanny Brown realized he had fallen to the ground. Damp dirt clung to him. He shifted to his knees, his own revolver pointing straight ahead.

Ferguson grimaced. Then he seemed to shrug. He held his hands wide in surrender.

Tanny Brown took a deep breath, heard a hundred voices within his head screaming contradictory commands: Voices of duty or responsibility shouting disagreement with voices of revenge. He looked up at the killer and remembered what Ferguson had said: *I'll walk away clean again.* The words joined the tumult and turbulence within him, reverberating like distant thunder. The sudden cacophony deafened him so that he hardly heard the report from his own weapon, was aware only that he'd fired by the pulse in his fist as the gun seized life.

The shots crushed into Robert Earl Ferguson, forcing him back into the embrace of the thorny branches. For an instant his body contorted with confusion and pain. Disbelief rode his eyes. He seemed to shake his head, but the movement was lost as surprise turned to death in his face.

Minutes stretched around him.

He remained on his knees, facing the killer's body, trying to collect himself. He fought a dizzying surge of vertigo, followed by a wave of nausea. This passed, and he waited for his racing heart to slow. After a moment, he sucked in the first gasp of air he was aware of breathing since the pursuit had begun.

He looked at Ferguson's sightless eyes.

"There," he said bitterly. "You were wrong."

Thoughts crowded his imagination and he stared over at the killer's body. He spotted the short-barreled revolver lying in the dirt where Ferguson had flung it in death. The gun was as familiar to him as his partner's voice and laugh. He knew there was only one way Ferguson could have obtained the weapon, and a sheet of pain and sadness curved through him. He looked back at Ferguson and said out loud, "You wanted to kill me with my partner's gun, you sonuvabitch, but it wouldn't do it for you, would it?" His eyes slid to the streaks of blood marking the spot where Cowart's wild shot had ripped into the flesh of Ferguson's leg. He couldn't have made it much farther with a wound like that. Certainly not to freedom. A single, lucky shot that had killed him as much as the twin blasts from Brown's own weapon.

Brown put his hand to his forehead, feeling the cool metal of his pistol like holding an ice cube to a headache. His imagination worked hard, and he looked over at Ferguson and asked, "Who were you?" as if the killed man could answer. Then he turned and started moving back down the trail toward where he'd left Cowart and Shaeffer. He looked back once, over his shoulder, just to make certain that Ferguson hadn't moved, that he'd remained pinioned by death in the briars. It was as if he didn't trust death to be final.

He walked slowly, aware for the first time that the day had taken over the forest. Shafts of light burned through the ceiling of branches, illuminating his path. It made him feel slightly uncomfortable. He had a sudden, odd preference for shadows.

It took him a few minutes to reach the small clearing where Cowart remained with Shaeffer.

The reporter looked up. He had taken off his jacket and wrapped it around the detective, who had paled and was shivering despite the growing heat. Blood from her mangled elbow had seeped through the makeshift bandage. She was conscious but fighting shock.

"I heard shots," Cowart said. "What happened?"

Brown sucked in harshly. "He got away," he replied.

"He what!" blurted Cowart.

"Get him," moaned Shaeffer. She twisted about in pain and anger, on the verge of unconsciousness.

"He was heading across the water," Brown replied. "I tried from a distance, but . . ."

"He got away?" Cowart asked, disbelievingly.

"Disappeared. Headed deep into the swamp. I told you what'd happen if he got in there. Never find him."

"But I hit him," Cowart complained. "I'm sure I did."

The policeman didn't reply.

"I hit him," the reporter insisted.

"Yes. You hit him," Brown answered softly.

"Why, what, what're . . ." Cowart started to blurt. Then he stopped and stared at the policeman.

Tanny Brown shifted uncomfortably beneath the reporter's gaze, as if he was being slapped with difficult questions. He took hold of himself and insisted, "You've got to take her back. Get her help. She's not hurt too bad, but she needs help now."

"What about you?"

"I'm going to go back. Take one more look. Then I'll follow you."

"But . . ."

''When we get back to Pachoula, we'll put out an APB. File formal charges. Put him on the national computer wire. Get the FBI involved. You go write your story.''

Cowart continued to stare at Brown, trying to see past the policeman's words.

''He got away,'' Brown repeated coldly.

And then Cowart did see. Shock and fury fought for space within him. He glared at the policeman. ''You killed him,'' Cowart said. ''I heard the shots.''

Tanny Brown said nothing.

''You killed him,'' he said again.

Brown shook his head, but said, ''You understand something, Cowart. If he dies out there, then no one ever knows. Not about Bruce Wilcox. Not about any of the others. It just stops, right there. And no one will give a damn about Ferguson. They'll just care about you and me. A policeman with a personal vendetta and a reporter trying to save his career. No one will want to hear about suspicions and theories and tainted evidence. They'll just want to know why we came out here and killed a man. An innocent man. Remember? An innocent man. But if he gets away . . .''

Cowart looked hard at the policeman and thought, It ended. But it never ends. He breathed in deeply. ''The guilty man runs,'' he finished the policeman's sentence.

''That's right.''

''Then it keeps going. People keep hunting. Answers . . .''

''People keep looking for answers. You make them. I make them.''

Cowart breathed in air like steam that scorched within him. ''He's dead. You killed him . . .''

Brown looked at Cowart.

''. . . I killed him,'' the reporter continued.

He hesitated, then added the obvious. ''. . . We killed him.'' The reporter took another deep breath.

A whirlwind of thoughts tore through his head. He could feel the morning heat rising around him. He saw Ferguson, remembered Blair Sullivan's laughing *Have I killed you, too, Cowart?*; answered *No* to this vision, hoping he was right; remembered in a torrent of memory his family, his own child, the murdered child, the children that had disappeared and all that had happened. He thought, It's a nightmare. Tell the truth and be punished. Tell a lie and it will all come right. He could feel himself sliding, as if he'd lost his grasp on the face of a sheer cliff. But it was one he'd elected to climb himself. Summoning a burst of energy, he imagined slamming an ice pick into the granite and arresting his fall. He told himself, You can live with it, alone. He looked over at Tanny Brown, who was bent over, checking Andrea Shaeffer's bloody wrap, and realized he was mistaken. The nightmare would be shared. He glanced at Shaeffer. At least, he thought, her wound will scar over and heal.

"No," he said, after a moment's pause. "He got away."

Tanny Brown said nothing.

"Just like you said. Into the swamp. Get back there, no one could find him. Could go anywhere. Atlanta. Chicago. Detroit. Dallas. Anywhere."

He bent down and lifted the wounded policeman from the earth, working his shoulder under her arm.

"Write the story," Tanny Brown said.

"I'll write the story," Cowart replied.

"Make them believe," the policeman said.

"They'll believe," Cowart answered.

He said it without anger.

Brown nodded.

Matthew Cowart started to steer Andrea Shaeffer back down the path toward civilization. She leaned against him. He could sense her teeth gritting against pain, but she did not complain. His mind began to churn beneath the weight of the wounded detective. Write it so that she gets a commendation for bravery. Tell everyone how she stood up to a sadistic killer and took a bullet for her trouble. Heroine cop. The television boys will eat it up. So will the tabs. It'll give her a chance, he thought. Words began to pump into him, strengthening him. He could see columns of newsprint, headlines racing from high-speed presses. He threw an arm around Shaeffer's waist. He'd managed perhaps ten feet when he turned and looked at the police lieutenant, still standing on the edge of the clearing.

"Is this right?" the reporter asked. The question burst from him, unbidden.

Brown shrugged. "There's never been any right in this. Not from the start. Never been any choice, either."

Cowart nodded. It was the only truth he felt comfortable with. He didn't smile, but said, "Seems like an odd time to start trusting each other."

Then he turned and continued to help the wounded young woman toward safety. She moaned slightly and leaned against him. It was a small thing he was doing, he told himself. But at least he was saving one person. He took solace in the thought he might have saved others as well.

Tanny Brown watched Cowart help Shaeffer. He saw the two disappear into the tangle of lights and shadows. Then he headed back through the brush to the edge of the swamp. It only took him a few minutes to locate Ferguson's body.

The dead weight pulled against him as he extricated Ferguson from the trap of brambles. The swamp water was cold against his body as he slid into it. He put his foot down and felt the sucking ooze beneath him. Then he pushed away, dragging the body through the water, away from the land, toward a maze of trees, laden with hanging ferns and vines, some fifty yards away, deeper into the swamp. He half-dragged, half-pushed the killer's body through the water, puffing with exertion, struggling with the bulk, until he came to the spot. He gathered his last strength and pushed hard on Ferguson's body, submerging it, forcing it underneath and between the roots, until it was snared beneath the surface of the water. He had no idea if it would stay there forever or not. Ferguson had wondered the same thing once, he realized. He pushed himself back and then looked from a few feet away and saw that he could see no sign of the body. The roots held all. The water covered all.

Light penetrated the trees and hit the black water surface, making it gleam for an instant. He turned away from the dead spot and swam easily toward the home shore.

Coming in May 1995 to bookstores everywhere.

Published in hardcover by Ballantine Books.

THE SHADOW MAN

by John Katzenbach

Read on for a spellbinding sneak preview of
THE SHADOW MAN . . .

he asked himself. He couldn't answer his own question. He

Just Cause   485.

normalcy of life. He fell   of comfort. Good for you, Dad

FEAR like a halo of light seemed to illuminate the elderly woman standing outside. Her face was rigid, pale, drawn tight like a knot, and she looked up at Simon Winter with such helplessness that for a moment he stepped back, as if struck by a sudden strong gust of wind, and it took an instant for him to recognize his neighbor of almost ten years.

"Mrs. Millstein, what is the matter?"

The woman reached out her hand, grasping at Simon Winter's arm, shaking her head as if to say that she could not force words past fright.

"Are you all right?"

"Mr. Winter," the woman said slowly, the words creaking past lips squeezed together, "thank goodness you were home. I'm so alone and I didn't know what to do. . . ."

"Come inside, come inside. Please, what is the matter?"

Sophie Millstein stepped forward shakily. Her fingernails sliced into the flesh of Simon Winter's arm, her grip like a climber threatened with a fall down some sheer precipice.

"I didn't believe, Mr. Winter," Sophie Millstein started softly. But then her words picked up speed, following in a torrent of anxiety. "I don't think any of us really believed. It seemed so distant. So impossible. How could he be here? Here? No, it just seemed too crazy, so none of us believed. Not the rabbi or Mr. Silver or Frieda Kroner. But we were wrong, Mr. Winter. He is here. I saw him today. Tonight. Right outside the ice-cream store on the Lincoln Road Mall. I stepped out, and there he was. He just looked at me, Mr. Winter, and I knew right then. He has eyes like razors, Mr. Winter. I didn't know what to do. Leo would have known. He would have said, 'Sophie. We must call someone,' and he would have had the number right there, ready. But Leo's gone and I'm all alone and he's here.''

She looked helplessly at Simon Winter.

''He will kill me, too,'' she said, gasping.

Simon Winter steered Sophie Millstein into his living room, depositing her on the sagging couch.

''No one's going to kill anyone, Mrs. Millstein. Now, let me get you a drink of something cold and then you can explain what has you so frightened.''

She looked wildly at him. ''I must warn the others!''

''Yes, yes. I'll help you, but please, have a drink and then tell me what is the matter.''

She opened her mouth to reply, but then seemed to lose her grip on the words, so no sound came out. She put a hand to her forehead as if taking her temperature and said, ''Yes. Yes, please, iced tea if you have it. It's so hot. Sometimes, in the summer, it seems as if the air is just burning up.''

Simon Winter swept up his suicide letter and pistol from the coffee table in front of Sophie Millstein and hurried into the kitchen. He found a clean glass into which he poured water, ice cubes, and instant tea mix. He left his letter on the counter, but before taking the glass back to Sophie Millstein, he paused and reloaded his weapon with the five bullets in his pocket. He looked up and saw the old woman staring blankly in front of her as if watching some memory. He felt an odd excitement, coupled with a sense of urgency. Sophie Millstein's fear seemed thick and choking, filling the room like smoke. He breathed hard and hurried to her side.

''Now, drink this,'' he said in the same tones one would use to a fevered child. ''And then take your time and explain what has happened.''

Sophie Millstein nodded, seizing the glass with both hands, gulping at the frothy brown liquid. She swallowed hard, then put the glass to her forehead. Simon Winter saw her eyes fill with tears.

''He will kill me,'' she said again. ''I don't want to die.''

''Mrs. Millstein, please,'' Simon Winter said. ''Who?''

Sophie Millstein shuddered and whispered in German: *"Der Schattenmann."*

"Who? Is that someone's name?"

She looked wildly at him.

"No one knew his name, Mr. Winter. At least, no one who lived."

"But who . . ."

"He was a ghost."

"I don't understand. . . ."

"A devil."

"Who?"

"He was evil, Mr. Winter. More evil than anyone could think. And now he's here. We didn't believe, Mr. Winter, but we were wrong. Mr. Stein warned us, but we didn't know him, so how could we believe?"

Sophie Millstein shuddered hard.

"I'm old," she whispered. "I'm old, but I don't want to die."

Simon Winter held up his hand. "Please, Mrs. Millstein, you must explain yourself. Take your time and tell me who this person is and why you're so frightened."

She took another long pull at the iced tea and set the glass down in front of her. She nodded slowly, trying to regain some composure. She lifted her hand to her forehead, her fingers stroking her eyebrows gently, as if trying to loosen a hard memory, and then she wiped away the tears that were gathering in her eyes. She took a deep breath and looked up at him. He saw her hand drop to her throat where, for just an instant, she fingered the necklace she wore. It was distinctive, a thin gold chain that held a stamped replica of her first name. But what separated this necklace from the type worn by teenagers seemingly everywhere was the presence of a pair of small diamonds at either end of the *S* in *Sophie*. Simon Winter knew her late husband had dipped into his modest pension fund and given her the necklace on the birthday before his heart failed, and, like the wedding ring on her finger, she did not remove it.

"It is such a difficult story, Mr. Winter. It happened so long ago, sometimes now it seems like a dream. But it was no dream, Mr. Winter. More a nightmare. Fifty years ago."

"Go on, Mrs. Millstein."

"In 1943, Mr. Winter, my family—Mama, Papa, my brother Hansi—we were still in Berlin. Hiding out . . ."

"Go on."

"It was such a terrible life, Mr. Winter. There was never a

moment, not one second, not even the time between heartbeats, Mr. Winter, when we thought we were safe. There wasn't much to eat, and we were always cold, and we thought every morning when we awakened that that would be our last night together. Every second, it seemed, the risk grew. A neighbor might grow curious. A policeman might demand your papers. Would you step on the trolley car and spot someone who recognized you from before the war, before the yellow stars? Maybe you would say something, any little thing, Mr. Winter. A gesture, a tone, some slight nervousness, something that would betray you. There are no more suspicious people in the world than the Germans, Mr. Winter. I should know. I was one of them once. That would be all it took, just a tiny hesitation, maybe a frightened look, anything that indicated you were out of place. And then it would be over. By 1943 we knew, Mr. Winter. I mean, perhaps we didn't know it all, but we knew. Capture was death. It was that simple. Sometimes at night, I used to lie in bed, unable to sleep, praying that some British bomber would drop their load short, Mr. Winter, right on top of all of us, and so we could all go together and end all the fear. I would be shivering, praying for death, and my brother Hansi would come over and hold my hand until I fell asleep. He was so strong. And resourceful, Mr. Winter. When we had nothing to eat, he could find some potatoes. When we had no place to stay, he would find us a new flat, or a basement somewhere, where there weren't any questions and we could spend a week, or maybe more, still together, still surviving.''

"What happened to? . . ."

"He died. They all died."

Sophie Millstein took a deep breath.

"I told you. He killed them. He found us and they died."

Simon Winter started to interject another question, but she held up a quivering hand.

"Let me just finish this, Mr. Winter, while I still have the strength. There were so many things to be frightened of, but I suppose the worst were the catchers."

"The catchers?"

"Jews like us, Mr. Winter. Jews that worked for the Gestapo. There was a building on Iranishestrasse. One of those awful gray stone buildings the Germans love so much. The Jewish Bureau of Investigation was what they called it. That was where he worked, where all of them worked. Their own freedom depended on their hunting us down."

"And this man you think you saw today . . ."

"Some were famous, Mr. Winter. Rolf Isaaksohn, he was young and arrogant, and the beautiful Stella Kubler. She was blond and pretty and looked like one of their Nordic maidens. She turned in her own husband. There were others, too. They took off their stars and moved about the city, just looking, like birds of prey."

"The man today . . ."

"*Der Schattenmann*. He was in all our nightmares. It was said that he could pick you from a crowd of people, just as if he alone could see some glow to your skin, some look in your eyes. Maybe it was the way you walked or some smell you had. We didn't know. All we knew was if he found you, death would come knocking at your door. People said that he would be there in the darkness when they came for you, and he would be there when they shipped you out in the morning gloom on the transport train for Auschwitz. But you wouldn't know, you see, because no one saw his face and no one knew his name. If you saw his face, they said, you would be taken to the basement at the Alexanderplatz prison, where it was always night, and everyone knew that no one came out of the basement, not ever, Mr. Winter. And he would be there to see you die, so that the last eyes you saw on this earth would be his, Mr. Winter. He was the worst. The worst by far, because it was said that he enjoyed what he was doing, and because he was so good at it. . . ."

"And today?"

"Here. Here on Miami Beach. I truly believe I saw him today."

Take a journey inside the criminal
mind with these novels of suspense
by bestselling author
JOHN KATZENBACH

DAY OF RECKONING

Meet Megan and Duncan Richards. You might know them. He's a banker, she's in real estate. They have two teenage daughters and a young son. They live in a lovely home. Everything about them suggests they've come a long way from 1968 and their activist past. After all, anyone who was young in 1968 has an activist past. But Megan and Duncan are a little different. They got in a little over their heads, involved with a beautiful woman who called herself Tanya and led a radical group called the Phoenix Brigade. They took part in a robbery that Tanya insisted would run smoothly and bloodlessly. It didn't. That was eighteen years ago.

While the Richards family is enjoying its domestic tranquility, Tanya is just finishing a prison term. More precisely, she's spent eighteen years planning revenge against the two people she blames for what happened that day. It will be sweet. It will be torturous. She will start with their son.

IN THE HEAT OF THE SUMMER

Crack reporter Malcolm Anderson is trapped by his hottest story—trapped between his editors who want him to keep the story alive, by the cops who want him to help catch a killer, by his girl-friend who wants their lives safe again, and by his own fascination with the tortured murderer looking to get even for the sins of Vietnam.

In Miami, they call July the "mean season," and this summer, a clever, elusive killer is terrorizing the entire city. His frequent phone calls to Anderson feed the reporter his biggest front-page stories, stories that make Anderson a national celebrity. And they could make him the killer's next victim.

THE TRAVELER

Miami. New Orleans. Kansas City. Omaha. Chicago. Cleveland. A man, a woman, a car, and a camera on a sentimental journey through the past. He kills, he photographs, she writes about it—or she dies, too. He reviews her notes and makes sure she gets it right.

Detective Mercedes Barren has reason to give chase: her niece was a victim. So does psychiatrist Martin Jeffers, a specialist in sex offenders and more than a passing acquaintance for the killer. An odyssey. A trek. A nightmare that lasts well into the following day . . . and into the night again.